"Guy Gavriel Kay's exquisite Asian-inspired epic
fantasy offers a fresh twist on intrigue and adventure....
Here you'll find all the scheming and skulduggery that give
Game of Thrones its zest, refined to the subtlest of arts."
—LAURA MILLER, SALON.COM

"Kay has the uncanny ability to depict the grand sweep
of historical events through the eyes of those living through
them....What's even more amazing is how through his
careful rendering of character and environments
we are drawn into this history."
—SEATTLEPI.COM

"Exquisitely rendered alternate
historical fantasy....Readers will savor a
flawed, complex culture, meticulously researched
and re-created in powerful prose."
—PUBLISHERS WEEKLY

"Mirroring the glittering, doomed
Song Dynasty of China, it portrays a world of
changing traditions, casual cruelty, and strict codes
of honor and respect...a powerful and complex
tale told with simplicity and elegance."
—LIBRARY JOURNAL
(STARRED REVIEW)

Praise for the Novels
of Guy Gavriel Kay

River of Stars

"With *River of Stars*, Kay transports readers to a dazzling court and the ravages of war, with language almost impossibly multilayered in its nuance and tone, offering a series of insights that exquisitely build on each other. Even more than in previous books, each sentence seems shaped to further enhance the book's themes, recalling the craftsmanship of the man-made peony blossom that is a recurring image throughout. Here, too, emotional intensity is amped up more than ever, the shattering catharsis even more complete."   —The Huffington Post

"[*River of Stars*] may be the finest work of a major novelist—and a pretty thrilling adventure tale to boot. . . . Kay is precise and judicious in his selection of scenes to dramatize, in his skill at finding the key moments that define a character or a culture, and in his carefully restrained yet crucial deployment of fantastic elements. . . . This is no innocent Middle Earth threatened by Mordor, but a highly problematical society in which such honor is hard to locate. It's one of Kay's recurring themes, and it's never been handled with such complexity, scope, and insight as it is in *River of Stars*."   —Gary K. Wolfe, *Locus*

"This is stunning stuff from one of fantasy fiction's finest. From one of fiction's finest, frankly."   —Tor.com

"The master of the historical fantasy has found a canvas large enough for his ambitions. Guy Gavriel Kay's second novel based on the Chinese past is his finest work so far, a vision of tremendous scope, achieved through precise, intimate observation of a brilliant culture in the throes of disintegration and rebirth . . . a book [that] you don't want to be over."   —Cecelia Holland, *Locus*

"Endlessly graceful, perfectly attuned to time and place and character and mood, never a line out of place, the prose in *River of Stars* is beautifully crafted at the sentence level: lyrical, but in a muted fashion, beautiful but not clamoring for attention, and often bearing the burden of sorrow. . . . *River of Stars* is a beautifully crafted, moving novel, and one I can't recommend highly enough."   —Fantasy Literature

"I don't think it's a stretch to say that Kay is the greatest fantasist of our generation. . . . It's hard for me to quantify how much I enjoyed *River of Stars*, but I'll be thinking about this book for a long time."   —Fantasy Book Critic

continued . . .

"I wrote in my review of *Under Heaven* that I was actually reluctant to read *River of Stars*, since it was all but unimaginable that an author could manage to capture such lyrical magic twice in a row, but Kay has done just that."   —Beauty in Ruins

"Every two or three years, Guy Gavriel Kay releases a new novel [that] never fails to amaze me. . . . Spanning decades, *River of Stars* is a novel about destiny and how individuals and their actions can shape the course of history. Beautifully crafted and complex, populated with well-drawn men and women, it should stand on its own as one of Guy Gavriel Kay's signature works. . . . I'm aware that it's still early in the year. But as things stand, *River of Stars* is now in pole position and will be the speculative fiction title to beat in 2013."   —Pat's Fantasy Hotlist

Under Heaven

"Guy Gavriel Kay's *Under Heaven* isn't quite historical fiction, nor is it quite fantasy. It's set in a slightly reimagined Tang dynasty China, sometimes seems reminiscent of films like *Crouching Tiger, Hidden Dragon*, and depicts the unimaginable consequences of a single generous gift. Most important of all, it is the novel you'll want for your summer vacation."   —*The Washington Post*

"Guy Gavriel Kay is peerless in plucking elements from history and using them to weave a wholly fantastical tale that feels like a translation of some freshly unearthed scroll from a time we have yet to discover."
—*The Miami Herald*

"Completely transporting . . . combines the best of historical and fantasy novels to create a great read where you don't know what could happen next."   —Laura Miller, book reviewer for Salon.com

"I loved, loved, loved *Under Heaven*. It had everything in it that made me such a fan of Guy Kay in the first place. I thought the new one was perfect."   —Nancy Pearl, book commentator for NPR's *Morning Edition*

"*Under Heaven* is virtually everything a reader could want in a book: a thrilling adventure, a love story, a coming-of-age tale, a military chronicle, a court-intrigue drama, a tragedy, and on and on. It is a sumptuous feast of storytelling, a beautifully written tale with a beating, breaking heart at its core that will have readers in tears by its final pages."
—*The Globe and Mail* (Canada)

"Guy Gavriel Kay, hunting in the twilight zone between fact and dream, has written a shimmering novel, a fantasia on Tang China, the epitome of Chinese civilization, as beautiful and as alien as the rings of Saturn . . . a beautiful, compulsive read."   —*Locus*

RIVER
OF STARS

GUY GAVRIEL
KAY

 NEW AMERICAN LIBRARY

New American Library
Published by the Penguin Group
Penguin Group (USA) LLC, 375 Hudson Street,
New York, New York 10014

USA | Canada | UK | Ireland | Australia | New Zealand | India | South Africa | China
penguin.com
A Penguin Random House Company

Published by New American Library, a division of Penguin Group (USA) LLC. Previously
published in Roc hardcover and Viking Canada editions.

First New American Library Trade Paperback Printing, April 2014

 REGISTERED TRADEMARK—MARCA REGISTRADA

New American Library Trade Paperback ISBN: 978-0-451-41609-4

The Library of Congress has cataloged the hardcover edition of this title as follows:

Kay, Guy Gavriel.
River of stars/Guy Gavriel Kay.
p. cm
ISBN 978-0-451-46497-2
1. Fathers and daughters—Fiction. I. Title.
PR9199.3.K39R58 2013
813'.54—dc23   2013002317

Printed in the United States of America
1   3   5   7   9   10   8   6   4   2

for Leonard and Alice Cohen

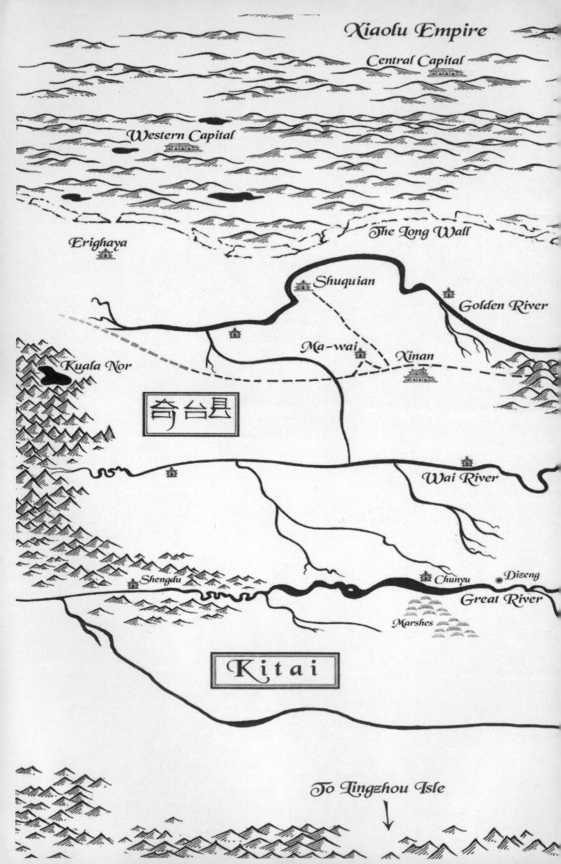

PRINCIPAL CHARACTERS

❧

(A partial list, characters generally identified by their role when first appearing)

Associated with the court
Emperor Wenzong of Kitai
Chizu, his son and heir
Zhizeng ("Prince Jen"), his ninth son

Hang Dejin, prime minister of Kitai
Hang Hsien, his son

Kai Zhen, deputy prime minister of Kitai
Yu-lan, his wife
Tan Ming, one of his concubines
Wu Tong, a eunuch, Kai Zhen's ally, a military commander
Sun Shiwei, an assassin

Elsewhere in Kitai
Ren Yuan, a clerk in the western village of Shengdu
Ren Daiyan, his younger son

Wang Fuyin, sub-prefect in Shengdu
Tuan Lung ("Teacher Tuan"), founder of an academy in Shengdu

Zhao Ziji, a military officer

Lin Kuo, a court gentleman
Lin Shan, his daughter and only child
Qi Wai, husband to Shan

Xi Wengao ("Master Xi"), formerly prime minister, a historian

Lu Chen, friend to Xi Wengao, a poet, exiled
Lu Chao, Chen's brother, also exiled
Lu Mah, Chen's son

Shao Bian, a young woman in the Great River town of Chunyu
Shao Pan, her younger brother

Sima Peng, a woman in Gongzhu, a hamlet near the Great River
Zhi-li, her daughter

Ming Dun, a soldier
Kang Junwen, a soldier, escapee from occupied lands

Shenwei Huang, a military commander

On the steppe

Emperor Te-kuan of the Xiaolu
Yao-kan, his cousin and principal adviser

Yan'po, kaghan of the Altai tribe
Wan'yen, war-leader of the Altai
Bai'ji, Wan'yen's brother

Paiya, kaghan of the Khashin tribe

O-Pang, kaghan of the Jeni tribe
O-Yan, his youngest brother

PART ONE

CHAPTER I

Late autumn, early morning. It is cold, mist rising from the forest floor, sheathing the green bamboo trees in the grove, muffling sounds, hiding the Twelve Peaks to the east. The maple leaves on the way here are red and yellow on the ground, and falling. The temple bells from the edge of town seem distant when they ring, as if from another world.

There are tigers in the forests, but they hunt at night, will not be hungry now, and this is a small grove. The villagers of Shengdu, though they fear them and the older ones make offerings to a tiger god at altars, still go into the woods by day when they need to, for firewood or to hunt, unless a man-eater is known to be about. At such times a primitive terror claims them all, and fields will go untilled, tea plants unharvested, until the beast is killed, which can take a great effort, and sometimes there are deaths.

The boy was alone in the bamboo grove on a morning swaddled in fog, a wan, weak hint of sun pushing between leaves: light trying to declare itself, not quite there. He was swinging a bamboo sword he'd made, and he was angry.

He'd been unhappy and aggrieved for two weeks now, having reasons entirely sufficient in his own mind, such as his life lying in ruins like a city sacked by barbarians.

At the moment, however, because he was inclined towards thinking in certain ways, he was attempting to decide whether anger made him better or worse with the bamboo sword. And would it be different with his bow?

The exercise he pursued here, one he'd invented for himself, was a test, training, discipline, not a child's diversion (he wasn't a child any more).

As best he could tell, no one knew he came to this grove. His brother certainly didn't, or he'd have followed to mock—and probably break the bamboo swords.

The challenge he'd set himself involved spinning and wheeling at speed, swinging the too-long (and also too-light) bamboo weapon as hard as he could, downstrokes and thrusts—without touching any of the trees surrounding him in the mist.

He'd been doing this for two years now, wearing out—or breaking—an uncountable number of wooden swords. They lay scattered around him. He left them on the uneven ground to increase the challenge. Terrain for any real combat would have such obstacles.

The boy was big for his age, possibly too confident, and grimly, unshakably determined to be one of the great men of his time, restoring glory with his virtue to a diminished world.

He was also the second son of a records clerk in the sub-prefecture town of Shengdu, at the western margin of the Kitan empire in its Twelfth Dynasty—which pretty much eliminated the possibility of such ambition coming to fulfillment in the world as they knew it.

To this truth was now added the blunt, significant fact that the only teacher in their sub-prefecture had closed his private school, the Yingtan Mountain Academy, and left two weeks ago. He had set off east (there was nowhere to go, west) to find what might be his fortune, or at least a way to feed himself.

He'd told a handful of his pupils that he might become a ritual master, using arcane rites of the Sacred Path to deal with ghosts and spirits. He'd said that there were doctrines for this, that it was even a suggested life for those who'd taken the examinations but not achieved *jinshi* status. Teacher Tuan had looked defensive, bitter, telling them this. He'd been drinking steadily those last weeks.

The boy hadn't known what to make of any of that. He knew there were ghosts and spirits, of course, hadn't realized his teacher knew anything about them. He wasn't sure if Tuan Lung really did, if he'd been joking with them, or just angry.

What he did know was that there was no way to pursue his own education any more, and without lessons and a good teacher (and a great deal more) you could never qualify for the prefecture civil service tests, let alone pass them. And without passing those first tests the never-spoken ambition of going to the capital for the *jinshi* examinations wasn't even worth a waking night.

As for these exercises in the wood, his fierce, bright dream of military prowess, of regaining honor and glory for Kitai ... well, dreams were what happened when you slept. There was no path he could see that would now guide him to learning how to fight, lead men, live, or even die for the glory of Kitai.

It was a bad time all around. There had been a tail-star in the spring sky and a summer drought had followed in the north. News came slowly to Szechen province, up the Great River or down through the mountains. A drought, added to war in the northwest, made for a hard year.

It had remained dry all winter. Usually Szechen was notorious for rain. In summertime the land steamed in the humidity, the leaves dripped rainwater endlessly, clothing and bedding never dried. The rain would ease in autumn and winter, but didn't ever cease—in a normal year.

This hadn't been such a year. The spring tea harvest had been dismal, desperate, and the fields for rice and vegetables were far too dry. This autumn's crops had been frighteningly sparse. There hadn't been any tax relief, either. The emperor needed money, there was a war. Teacher Tuan had had things to say about that, too, sometimes reckless things.

Teacher Tuan had always urged them to learn the record of history but not be enslaved by it. He said that histories were written by those with motives for offering their account of events.

He'd told them that Xinan, the capital of glorious dynasties, had held two million people once, and that only a hundred thousand or so lived there now, scattered among rubble. He'd said that Tagur, to the west, across the passes, had been a rival empire long ago, fierce and dangerous, with magnificent horses, and that it was now only a cluster of scrabbling provinces and fortified religious retreats.

After school was done some days, sitting with his older students, he'd drink wine they poured respectfully for him and sing. He'd sing, *"Kingdoms have come, kingdoms have gone / Kitai endures forever ..."*

The boy had asked his father about these matters once or twice, but his father was a cautious, thoughtful man and kept his counsel.

People were going to starve this winter, with nothing from the tea harvest to trade at the government offices for salt, rice, or grain from downriver. The state was supposed to keep granaries full, dole out measures in times of hardship, sometimes forgive taxes owed, but it was never enough, or done soon enough—not when the crops failed.

So this autumn there were no strings of cash, or illicit tea leaves kept back from the government monopoly to sell in the mountain passes to pay for a son's education, however clever and quick he was, however his father valued learning.

Reading skills and the brush strokes of calligraphy, poetry, memorizing the classics of the Cho Master and his disciples ... however virtuous such things were, they did tend to be abandoned when starvation became a concern.

And this, in turn, meant no chance of a life for the scholar-teacher who had actually qualified for the examinations in the capital. Tuan Lung had taken the *jinshi* examinations twice in Hanjin, before giving up and coming home to the west (two or three months' journey, however you travelled) to found his own academy for boys looking to become clerks, with perhaps a legitimate *jinshi* candidate among the really exceptional.

With an academy here it was at least possible that someone might try the provincial test and perhaps, if he passed, the same imperial examination Lung had taken—perhaps even to succeed there and "enter the current," joining the great world of court and office— which he hadn't done, since he was back here in Szechen, wasn't he?

Or had been, until two weeks ago.

That departure was the source of the boy's anger and despair, from the day he bade his teacher farewell, watching him ride away from Shengdu on a black donkey with white feet, taking the dusty road towards the world.

The boy's name was Ren Daiyan. He'd been called Little Dai most of his life, was trying to make people stop using that name. His brother refused, laughing. Older brothers were like that, such was Daiyan's understanding of things.

It had begun raining this week, much too late, though if it continued there might be some faint promise for spring, for those who survived the winter that was coming.

Girl-children were being drowned at birth in the countryside, they'd learned in whispers. It was called *bathing the infant*. It was illegal (hadn't always been, Teacher Tuan had told them), but it happened, was one of the surest signs of what was in store.

Daiyan's father had told him that you knew it was truly bad when boys were also put into the river at birth. And at the very worst, he'd said, in times when there was no other food at all ... he'd gestured with his hands, not finishing the thought.

Daiyan believed he knew what his father meant, but didn't ask. He didn't like thinking about it.

In fog and ground-mist, the early-morning air cool and damp, the breeze from the east, the boy slashed, spun, thrust in a bamboo wood. He imagined his brother receiving his blows, then barbarian Kislik with their shaved scalps and long, unbound fringe hair, in the war to the north.

His judgment as to the matter of what anger did to his blade skills was that it made him faster but less precise.

There were gains and losses in most things. Speed against control represented a difference to be adjusted for. It would be different with his bow, he decided. Precision was imperative there, though speed would also matter for an archer facing many foes. He was exceptionally good with a bow, though the sword had been by far the more honoured weapon in Kitai in the days (gone now) when fighting skills were respected. Barbarians like the Kislik or Xiaolu killed from horseback with arrows, then raced away like the cowards they were.

His brother didn't know he had a bow or he'd have claimed it for himself as Eldest Son. He would then, almost certainly, have broken it, or let it be ruined, since bows needed caring for, and Ren Tzu wasn't the caring-for sort.

It had been his teacher who had given the bow to Daiyan.

Tuan Lung had presented it to him one summer afternoon a little more than a year ago, alone, after classes were done for the day, unwrapping it from an undyed hemp cloth.

He'd also handed Daiyan a book that explained how to string it properly, care for it, make arrow shafts and arrowheads. It marked a change in the world, in their Twelfth Dynasty, having books here. Teacher Tuan had said that many times: with block printing, even a sub-prefecture as remote as theirs could have information, printed poems, the works of the Master, if one could read.

It was what made a school such as his own possible.

It had been a private gift: the bow, a dozen iron arrowheads, the book. Daiyan knew enough to hide the bow, and then the arrows he began to make after reading the book. In the world of the Twelfth Dynasty, no honourable family would let a son become a soldier. He knew it; he knew it every moment he drew breath.

The very thought would bring shame. The Kitan army was made up of peasant farmers who had no choice. Three men in a farming household? One went to the army. There might be a million soldiers, even more (since the empire was at war again), but ever since savage lessons learned more than three hundred years ago it was understood (*clearly* understood) that the court controlled the army, and a family's rise to any kind of status emerged only through the *jinshi* examinations and the civil service. To join the army, to even think (or dream) of being a fighting man, if you had any sort of family pride, was to disgrace your ancestors.

That was, and had been for some time, the way of things in Kitai.

A military rebellion that had led to forty million dead, the destruction of their most glittering dynasty, the loss of large and lucrative parts of the empire ... That could cause a shift in viewpoint.

Xinan, once the dazzling glory of the world, was a sad and diminished ruin. Teacher Tuan had told them about broken walls, broken-up streets, blocked and evil-smelling canals, fire-gutted houses, mansions never rebuilt, overgrown gardens and market squares, parks with weeds and wolves.

The imperial tombs near the city had been looted long ago.

Tuan Lung had been there. One visit was enough, he'd told them. There were angry ghosts in Xinan, the charred evidence of old burning, rubble and rubbish, animals in the streets. People living huddled in a city that had held the shining court of all the world.

So much of their own dynasty's nature, Teacher Tuan told them, flowed like a river from that rebellion long ago. Some moments could define not only their own age but what followed. The Silk Roads through the deserts were lost, cut off by barbarians.

No western treasures flowed to Kitai now, to the trading cities or the court in Hanjin. No legendary green-eyed, yellow-haired dancing girls bringing seductive music. No jade and ivory or exotic fruits, no wealth of silver coins brought by merchants to buy longed-for Kitan silk and carry it back west on camels through the sands.

This Twelfth Dynasty of Kitai under their radiant and glorious emperor did not rule and define the known world. Not any more.

Tuan Lung had taught this to that same handful of them (never in class). In Hanjin, at the court, they still claimed to rule the world, he said, and examination questions expected answers that said as much. *How does a wise minister use barbarians to control barbarians?*

Even when they carried wars to the Kislik, they never seemed to win them. Recruited farmers made for a large army but not a trained one, and there were never enough horses.

And if the twice-yearly tribute paid to the much more dangerous Xiaolu in the north was declared to be a *gift*, that didn't change what it really was, their teacher said, over his end-of-day wine. It was silver and silk spent to buy peace by an empire still rich, but also shrunken—in spirit as well as size.

Dangerous words. His students poured wine for him. "*We have lost our rivers and mountains,*" he sang.

Ren Daiyan, fifteen years old, dreamed at night of glory, swung a bamboo sword in a wood at dawn, imagined himself the commander sent to win their lost lands back. The sort of thing that could only happen in a young man's imagining.

No one, Teacher Tuan said, played polo, perfecting their horsemanship, in the palace or parks of Hanjin the way they had once in Xinan's walled palace park or city meadows. Red- or vermillion-belted civil servants didn't pride themselves on their riding skills, or train with swords or bows, vying to best each other. They grew the nails on the little fingers of their left hands to show the world how they disdained such things, and they kept the army commanders firmly under their thumbs. They chose military leaders from their own cultured ranks.

It was when he'd first heard these things, the boy Daiyan remembered, that he'd begun coming to this grove when tasks and rain allowed, and cutting himself swords. He'd sworn a boy's oath that if he passed the examinations and arrived at court he'd never grow his little fingernail.

He read poetry, memorized the classics, discussed these with his father, who was gentle and wise and careful and had never been able even to dream of taking the examinations.

The boy understood that Teacher Tuan was a bitter man. He had seen it from the beginning of his time in the academy, a clerk's clever younger son being taught to write properly, learn the teachings of the Masters. Clever, diligent, a good brush stroke already. Perhaps a genuine candidate for the examinations. His father's dream for him. His mother's. So much pride, if a family had a son do that. It could set them on a road to fortune.

Daiyan understood this. He'd been an observant child. He still was, at the edge of leaving childhood behind. Later this same day, in fact, it would end.

After three or four cups of rice wine, their honourable teacher had sometimes begun reciting poems or singing sad songs about the Xiaolu's conquest of the Fourteen Prefectures two hundred years ago—*the Lost Fourteen*—the lands below the ruins of the Long Wall in the north. The wall was a meaningless thing now, he told his pupils, wolves running through it, sheep grazing back and forth. The songs he sang distilled a heart-torn longing. For there, in those lost lands, lay the surrendered soul of Kitai.

So the songs went, though they were dangerous.

ᘒᘓ

Wang Fuyin, sub-prefect in that same town of Shengdu, Honglin prefecture, Szechen province, in the twenty-seventh year of the reign of Emperor Wenzong of the Twelfth Dynasty, was rendered more unhappy, later that morning, than he could express.

He was not diffident about expressing himself (unless he was reporting to the prefect, who was from a very good family and intimidated him). But the information that had just arrived was so unwelcome, and so unambiguous in what it demanded of him, that he was left speechless. There was no one around to abuse, in any case—which was, in fact, the essence of the problem.

When someone came to any *yamen* in Kitai from any village bringing an allegation of murder, the sequence of actions to be followed by the civil administration at that *yamen* was as detailed as anything could be in a famously rigid bureaucracy.

The sub-prefecture sheriff would leave for the village in question with five bowmen to protect him and keep order in what might turn out to be an unruly location. He would investigate and report. He was obliged to set out the same day if word reached the *yamen* before midday, or at dawn the next morning if otherwise. Bodies decomposed rapidly, suspects fled, evidence could disappear.

If the sheriff should be elsewhere engaged when such a message arrived (he was, today), the judicial magistrate was to go himself to investigate, with the five bowmen and within the same time constraints.

If the magistrate, for whatever reason, was also absent or indisposed (he was), the sub-prefect was tasked with the immediate journey and inquiry, including any inquest required.

That, alas, meant Wang Fuyin.

No lack of clarity in the regulations. Failure to comply could mean strokes with the heavy rod, demotion in rank, even dismissal from civil office if your superiors disliked you and were looking for an excuse.

Civil office was what you dreamed of after passing the *jinshi* examinations. Being given a sub-prefect's position, even in a far western wilderness, was a step, an important step, on a road that might lead back to Hanjin, and power.

You didn't want to fail in something like this, or in anything. It was so easy to fail. You might pick the wrong faction to align with, or have the wrong friends at a viciously divided court. Sub-prefect Wang Fuyin had no friends at court yet, of course.

There were three clerks at the *yamen* this morning, filing, reading correspondence, adding up tax ledgers. Local men, all of them. And all of them would have seen a miserable, frightened peasant arrive on his donkey, muddy and wet, *before* midday, then heard him speak of a man slain in Guan Family Village—most of a day's long, awkward, dangerous ride east towards the Twelve Peaks.

Probably more than a day, Wang Fuyin thought: which meant staying overnight along the way in some sodden, flea-and-rat-infested hovel without a floor, animals kept inside, a handful of bad rice for his meal, rancid wine or no wine, thin tea, while tigers and bandits roared in the cold night.

Well, bandits were unlikely to roar, Fuyin corrected himself (a fussy, precise man), but even so ...

He looked at the pale, emerging sun. It had rained lightly overnight, third night in a row, thank the gods, but it was turning into a mild autumn day. It was also, undeniably, still morning, and the clerks would know the protocols.

The sheriff had gone north two days ago to deal with taxation arrears towards the hill passes. Sometimes a chancy exercise. He had taken eight bowmen. He was supposed to have five, but he was a cowardly man (in Wang Fuyin's view), and though he'd claim he was training the newer ones, he was just increasing his own protection. In addition to farmers unhappy about taxes, bandits in the west country were endemic. Bandits were everywhere in Kitai, really, and there were always more in times of hardship. There existed texts on how to deal with outlaws (Fuyin had read some on the long journey west), but since arriving, he'd decided the texts were useless. You needed soldiers and horses and good information. None of these were ever present.

Neither was the judicial magistrate, Wang Fuyin sometimes felt.

Having taken his own escort of five bowmen, their honourable magistrate was on his monthly three-day "retreat" at the nearby Five Thunder Abbey of the Sacred Path, seeking spiritual enlightenment.

It seemed that he had negotiated this privilege from the prefect (Wang Fuyin had no idea how) years before. What Fuyin knew, having arranged to know it, was that the magistrate's path to enlightenment consisted mainly of time spent among the women (or one particular woman) at the convent adjacent to the abbey.

Fuyin was extremely jealous. His wife, from a better family than his own and not shy about reminding him, had been deeply unhappy to be posted here. She'd made him aware of that on the journey, and on a daily basis since they'd arrived a year ago, her words like the tedious dripping of rainwater from the eaves of their small house.

The one singing-girl place in Shengdu was dismally unpalatable for a man who had known the best houses in the pleasure district of the capital. Wang Fuyin didn't make nearly enough money to afford a concubine, and had yet to figure out how to arrange his own spiritual retreats to the convent by the Five Thunder Abbey.

It was a hard life he lived.

The village messenger, he saw, had led his donkey to the water trough in the space in front of the *yamen* and was letting it drink. He was also drinking himself, head down beside the donkey's. Wang Fuyin kept his face impassive, fastidiously adjusted the sleeves and collar of his robe, and strode into the *yamen*.

"How many bowmen are still here?" he asked the senior clerk.

Ren Yuan stood up (his manners were very good) and bowed before replying. Local clerks were not "in the current," not true civil servants. As recently as twenty years ago, before the reforms, they'd been unpaid, reporting to a *yamen* for two-year terms, drafted from among the two highest ranks of local farmers and villagers.

That had changed with the "New Policies" of Prime Minister Hang Dejin—over considerable opposition. And that had been just one part of a conflict at court that was still destroying and exiling people. In some respects, the subversive thought occasionally came to Wang Fuyin, it wasn't so bad to be out of the way in the west just now. One could drown in the current in Hanjin these days.

"Three bowmen are with us at the moment, honourable sir," his senior clerk said.

"Well, I need five," said the sub-prefect coldly.

"You are permitted to go with four. It is in the regulation. When necessity requires and so on. You just file a report."

That was his junior taxation clerk. He didn't stand up. Fuyin didn't like him.

"I know that," he said (he'd forgotten, actually). "But we only have three, so that doesn't help very much, does it, Lo Fong?"

The three clerks just looked at him. Pale sunlight came into the *yamen* through the open windows and doors. It had become a lovely autumn morning. Wang Fuyin felt like beating someone with a rod.

An idea came to him.

It was born of irritation and circumstance and the fact that Ren Yuan was standing directly in front of him at his desk, hands clasped, head diffidently lowered, showing his grey hair, threadbare black cap, and simple hat pins.

"Ren Yuan," he said. "Where is your son?"

His clerk looked up, then quickly down again, but not before Sub-prefect Wang saw, pleasingly, apprehension. "Ren Tzu has accompanied Sheriff Lao, honourable sir."

"I know this." The clerk's older son was being trained as a guardsman. You needed strong young men with you to deal with collecting taxes. It was Fuyin himself who would have the final say as to whether Tzu was hired. The young man wasn't especially intelligent, but you didn't have to be for some tasks. The salaries paid to clerks, even under the New Policies, were small. One benefit attached, however, was the chance to have sons follow into the *yamen*. That was how things were done now.

"No," said Fuyin, musingly. "I mean your younger son. I can make use of him. What is his name ... ?"

"Daiyan? He is only fifteen years old, honourable sub-prefect. He is still a student."

"Not any more," said Fuyin sourly.

The local teacher, Tuan Lung, would be missed. He hadn't become a friend, but his presence in Shengdu had been ... a benefit. Even Fuyin's wife had approved of him. Lung was educated, well mannered (if a little quick with irony). He knew history and poetry, had experience of Hanjin, obviously, and needed to be pleasingly deferential to the sub-prefect, since he'd failed the examinations twice and Fuyin had passed them, first attempt.

"Master Wang," said his chief clerk, bowing again, "it is my hope that my unworthy younger son be made a runner, and perhaps even a clerk in the *yamen* one day, yes. But I would not have dared to ask you until he is older ... perhaps two years, or even three."

The other clerks were listening avidly. Events had certainly broken the tedium of a morning. A murder in Guan Family Village, and now this.

They employed four, sometimes five runners at the *yamen*—two were outside the door now, ready to sprint with messages through town. Ren Yuan's aspirations for his son were reasonable, and so was the timing he'd proposed. (He was a reasonable man.)

But that wasn't where the sub-prefect was going this unhappy morning, facing the prospect of a dismal ride and a bad night, with a dead body at the end of it.

"Yes, all that might happen," said Fuyin in his most judicious tone, "but right now I need him for something else. Can the boy stay on a horse?"

Ren Yuan blinked. He had a lined, long, anxious face. "A horse?" he repeated.

The sub-prefect shook his head wearily. "Yes. Send a runner for the boy. I want him immediately, with whatever he needs for the road. And his bow," he added crisply. "He is to bring his bow."

"His bow?" said the hapless father.

But his voice revealed two things. One, he knew exactly what the sub-prefect had in mind now. And two, he knew about the bow.

Wang Fuyin was aware of it because it was his duty to know such things. Information mattered. The father would have his own means of having learned what the boy doubtless thought was a secret.

If the sub-prefect had had a more effective half-smile, one that conveyed amusement and superiority, he'd have used it then. But his wife had told him that when he essayed such an expression he looked as if he were suffering from stomach distress. He contented himself with another small headshake.

"He's been trying to make himself capable with the bow. I have no doubt you know it." A thought struck him. "Indeed, I imagine Teacher Tuan will have informed you at the time of his desire to present the boy with such a gift."

Another shrewd guess, confirmed by the father's expression. The distress of the day was not altered, but small pleasures could be extracted, including his clerk's apprehension. Well, really! If Ren Yuan thought the journey unsafe for his son, what did that suggest it might be for his superior? One could grow indignant!

Wang Fuyin decided to be indulgent. "Come, come," he said. "It will be a useful experience for him, and I *do* need a fourth bowman." He turned to the third clerk. "Send a runner for the boy. What is his name again?"

"Daiyan," said the father, quietly.

"Find Ren Daiyan, wherever he might be. Tell him he's needed at the *yamen*, and to bring the bow Teacher Tuan gave him." The sub-prefect allowed himself a half-smile, after all. "And arrows, of course."

∽

His heart had begun pounding the moment the runner from the *yamen* found him coming back across the fields from the bamboo grove.

It wasn't fear of the journey. At fifteen you didn't *fear* an opportunity like this: riding out of town, a temporary bowman guarding the honourable sub-prefect, keeping order for the emperor. How could you be afraid of that?

No, his fear had been a boy's: that his parents would disapprove of what he'd been doing, be angered by his having kept a secret— the times with the bow, firing at targets, making arrows, mornings with bamboo swords.

Turned out, they'd known all along.

It seemed that Teacher Tuan had spoken to them before-hand about the gift. He had explained it as a way of channelling Daiyan's independence and energy, guiding his spirit to balance, building confidence ... that these things might matter as he pursued his studies towards the examinations, maybe Hanjin, the court.

His mother had told him this at home when he came hurrying back with the runner, who waited outside. She spoke so quickly Daiyan barely had time to absorb it all. Both his parents knew about his morning forest rituals? Well, you needed to go off and be alone somewhere to think about that. Such information could change the world, your sense of it.

And it seemed the sub-prefect knew about this, too. And had summoned Daiyan—by name!—to guard him on a journey to one of the villages. To deal with a murder!

Could the Queen Mother of the West be turning her face towards him, after all? Could he be worthy of such good fortune?

His mother had been as efficient as ever. She masked feelings with brisk motions. She packed him a satchel of food and cold tea and a change of clothing (his father's, in fact, they were of a size now) lest he embarrass them among strangers and the sub-prefect. Her expression did not change—not in front of the waiting runner—when Daiyan came back from fetching his bow and quiver from their hiding place in the shed. He took the satchel from her hands. He bowed twice. She bowed back, briskly. He said goodbye.

"Bring honour to your family," she said, as she always did.

He hesitated, looking at her. She reached up then and did something she used to do when he was younger: tugged at his hair, not hard enough to hurt or dislodge the hairpins, but touching him. He went out. He looked back and saw her in their doorway as he went off with the runner.

His father, at the *yamen* when they arrived, looked afraid.

Daiyan wasn't sure why, it wasn't so far they were going, only to Guan Village. They would be there before sundown almost certainly. But Daiyan's father was a man who could look pleased or concerned at times when people around him showed entirely different moods. It was puzzling to a boy, always had been.

The sub-prefect was not happy. He was visibly angry, in fact. Wang Fuyin was plump, a lazy man (everyone knew that), and would be displeased because he was forced to make this trip himself, instead of sending the sheriff or magistrate and waiting in comfort for their report.

It wasn't a reason for his father to look so distressed, or be working to try to hide it. Ren Yuan wasn't good at concealing his emotions or his thoughts. His gentleness wasn't always an asset, either, his younger son had long ago decided.

He loved him for it, though.

MID-AFTERNOON, hint of a colder wind. They were riding into it, east out of Shengdu towards the world. The river was out of sight on their right, though they could sense it beyond the forest, a presence in changed birdsong, different birds flying. There was a steady shrieking of gibbons from the steep slopes north of the road.

There were nightingales in these woods. Daiyan's brother had come here hunting them. In Hanjin, at the court, they wanted nightingales for some enormous garden the emperor was building. Officials paid considerable sums for them. It was folly, of course. How could a caged bird survive the journey from Szechen? They'd have to go downriver through the gorges, then by imperial courier north. If the couriers rode fast ... the very idea of a birdcage bouncing by a saddle was sad and amusing, both. Daiyan liked nightingales. Some complained they kept you awake at night, but he didn't mind that.

In the distance ahead, with the mist gone and the day bright, the Twelve Peaks loomed. There were only eleven, of course. Daiyan had long ago given up counting the explanations for this. The peaks were holy in both the teachings of the Cho Master and those of the Sacred Path. Daiyan had never been this close to them. He'd never been this far from Shengdu—and wasn't that a sad thought, that someone at fifteen had never been more than a few hours' ride from his town? He'd never ridden a horse this far. That was an adventure in itself.

Their pace was faster than he'd expected it to be. The sub-prefect clearly hated his mount. Hated all horses, most likely, but even though he'd selected a mare with a placid gait and a wide back, he'd grown even more obviously unhappy from the moment they'd left the town behind. A man who preferred city streets to a country path, as the saying went.

Wang Fuyin was constantly looking around, left and right, behind them. He startled at the gibbons when they grew loud, though the cries were almost constant and should have been unsurprising by now. They were sad, eerie sounds. Daiyan had to admit that. Gibbons could warn you of a tiger, though. They were important that way. They were also meat in a famine, but hard to catch.

The sub-prefect insisted on stops to allow him to step down and stretch. Then, standing on the road, he'd seem to become aware that they were alone in wilderness, himself and only four guards, with the Guan Village farmer somewhere behind them on his donkey. Wang Fuyin would order one of them to help him back on his horse (he was not agile) and they'd set off again.

He made his feelings clear: he didn't like being out here listening to wild animals shrieking and he didn't want to remain out here any longer than necessary. Their pace was quick. Guan Family Village wasn't going to offer much of anything, but it had to be better than a lonely autumn path between cliff and forest with the day soon waning.

The farmer had dropped far behind. Didn't matter. They did know where the village was, and it wasn't as if a sub-prefect could be expected to wait for a villager on a donkey. There was a dead man ahead of them—and who knew what lay between where they were and that body?

Then, rounding a curve in the path, the sun behind them, they saw, all of them saw, one thing—or several—that lay between. Stood between, more accurately.

Four men stepped out of the forest on the right side of the road. There was no obvious way in or out, they were just suddenly there, on the path ahead of them. Blocking it.

Three of them held drawn swords, Daiyan saw. One carried a staff, thick as a fist. They were roughly dressed in drawstring trousers and tunics, one was barefoot. Two were extremely big men. All looked capable of handling themselves in a fight—or anything else out here. They were absolutely silent.

And there was no doubt as to what they were.

His heart was steady, which was interesting. Daiyan felt strangely calm. He heard the gibbons above them. They seemed louder, as if agitated. Maybe they were. The birds were quiet.

The sub-prefect exclaimed in anger and fear, threw up a hand to halt their progress. They stopped about twenty paces from the outlaws blocking their way. They were outlaws, of course they were. And reckless, to be accosting a party of five, mounted. On that thought, Daiyan turned around.

Three more in the road behind them. Same distance away. All with swords there.

They could try to break through, he thought. These men were on foot. They could gallop right at the outlaws in front, and perhaps ...

That wasn't going to happen. Not with Sub-prefect Wang Fuyin as one of the riders. He would be the man the bandits had come for, Daiyan thought: a sub-prefect could fetch a considerable ransom. Daiyan and the other guards were unimportant.

Which meant they weren't worth leaving alive.

As best he was able to reconstruct the moments that followed, thinking back, it was on that thought that he moved. It wasn't a worked-out, deliberate thing; he couldn't say any planning or calculation went into what happened. It was a little frightening, in truth.

He had drawn his bow, slotted an arrow, and killed the first man in front of them before he could really say he was aware of what he was doing. His first death, first man sent through the tall doors into night. First ghost.

The second arrow was loosed, a second man died before anyone had reacted to the first. At that point one of the outlaws cried out. Daiyan's third arrow was already flying, also aimed ahead of them.

(Speed mattered for archers. He remembered thinking that in the woods this morning, a lifetime ago.)

One man was left standing in front of them after that arrow struck. Later, Daiyan would shape (and teach) ideas about how you dealt with a divided set of enemies, whether a handful or an army, but he was doing it properly that morning by instinct.

There came another shout—behind him. But he killed the fourth man in front before turning his horse with his knees, drawing another arrow, and shooting the foremost of those who had decided to charge towards them. Take down the nearest first, he would later teach.

That man died about ten paces away, sword still in hand for a moment, then falling to the path. The arrow was in his chest. They didn't have much in the way of armour, these outlaws. Daiyan didn't remember *noting* that, but he probably had. Otherwise he might have aimed for their faces.

The other two bandits faltered, seeing they were suddenly in a bad circumstance. Faltering wasn't the best course of action. Daiyan shot the sixth man just as he broke stride and was starting to turn away to the woods. Not as precise an arrow; it caught the outlaw in the thigh. He went down screaming, high, oddly shrill.

The last one was running back to the forest. He died at the edge of the trees.

The whole thing lasted only moments. A blur and a flash, gibbons shrieking all through. The extreme strangeness of how time could be so slow that he could see (and would remember) individual gestures, expressions, and yet also be so impossibly fast.

Daiyan assumed he had been breathing through it all—breathing was important in archery—but couldn't say that he had been. Nor had he been aware of movement, anything at all, from the sub-prefect or the other guards. Not after Wang Fuyin's first outraged, frightened cry. He'd put arrows in seven men, himself. But that was too easy a way to say it. Men had been living and were dead. He'd killed them. You could divide your own life with something like that, Ren Daiyan thought.

You'd never killed anyone. Then you had.

It is well known, inevitable, that legends take shape around the early lives of those who become celebrated or notorious. The stories can grow fanciful, gather luridly exaggerated details: that is what a legend is. A hundred men killed single-handedly. An enemy city, walls three times a man's height, scaled by night, alone. An immortal poem written by a supernaturally gifted child with his father's ink and brush. An imperial princess seduced in a courtyard of the palace beside a fountain, then pining away for love.

In the matter of Ren Daiyan and his first encounter with outlaws on a path east of Shengdu one autumn day—the day he left home and changed his life—the tale retained considerable accuracy.

That was because Sub-prefect Wang Fuyin, later to become a figure of note himself, recorded the incident in an official dispatch while reporting also his own successful investigation, arrest, and execution of a murderer in a nearby village.

Sub-prefect Wang went into some detail as to how he had conducted this investigation. It was ingenious, and he was commended for it. That successful inquiry, in fact, would set Wang Fuyin on his own altered path. He became, by his own account, a changed man from that day, with new purpose and direction.

He retold the story of the outlaws and Ren Daiyan in his late-in-life memoirs, drawing upon his early writings (copies carefully kept) from those days when he'd just begun his career, in remote Szechen.

He was as particular and precise in old age as he had been when young, and he prided himself all his life on his strong prose (and calligraphy). The number of outlaws in his memoir remained seven. Ren Daiyan was always fifteen years of age (not twelve, as in some versions). Wang Fuyin even wrote that one of the bandits was only wounded by Daiyan. Another of their bowmen had leaped—

dramatically—from his horse to dispatch that seventh man where he lay on the ground.

Fuyin, white-haired at the time of this writing, allowed himself a hint of irony in describing that last "courageous" action. He was well known by then for wit, for clear exposition, for his books on judicial investigation (which had become texts for all magistrates in Kitai), and for being a survivor of the chaos of their time.

There were not many such survivors among those who had been at or near the centre of power in those days. It had taken skill, tact, an ability to choose friends well, and a great deal of luck.

Luck was always part of it, one way or another.

DAIYAN WAS AWARE, immediately, that his life had just changed. What followed on that lonely path between forest and cliffs felt destined, necessary, not truly a matter of choosing. It was more as if the choice had been made for him, he was only the agency of its working.

He got down from his horse. He walked over and took his arrows from the bodies of the slain men. The sun was west, shining along the path, under-lighting clouds. A wind was blowing. He remembered feeling chilled, and thinking that might be a reaction to what had just happened.

You'd never killed anyone. Then you had.

He took the arrows from the men behind them first. One of them right next to the trees. Then he went and pulled out four from the outlaws on the road ahead, the ones they'd seen first. Without giving it a great deal of thought, he turned over the body of the largest man and he took the two crossed swords and their leather scabbards from that man's back.

The swords felt very heavy. He'd been working with bamboo, after all. Earlier today. This same morning. A boy in a grove. He placed the twinned scabbards on his back, removing his quiver to do so then putting the quiver back on and adjusting it and the bow, finding positions for them, balancing himself with the new weight of the swords. It was going to take time to get used to this, he thought, standing in the roadway in the wind, the sun beginning to go down.

Looking back, he realized that he'd already understood, by then, what had happened to him in that place, in those moments.

It had something to do with how easy it had been. How effortless, intuitive: the decision made, then the sequence of movements. Understanding exactly where to shoot first, and next, and next. They were alive, and menacing, those men. They were dead. And how brief the time elapsed. That felt strange. How sharp a rent a handful of moments made in the fabric of a life. This—this world of bow and swords—this was meant to be his element, these moments had shown him that, and he needed to enter a place where he could pursue mastery. You had your dreams. A boy's dreams, and then ...

Birdsong was resuming. The gibbons had never stopped.

He looked back once, he remembered, towards Shengdu, to where his parents were, and then he left his life behind, walking into the woods, entering among the dark trees (darker than his own bamboo grove) exactly where the outlaws had emerged in front of them, so little time ago.

CHAPTER II

There were a great many men in the army of Kitai, but they were not good soldiers and they were not well led. Most of them were farmers, sons of farmers, desperately unhappy to be so far from home—and fighting in northern lands.

They knew millet and wheat, or two-crop rice, vegetable plots, orchard fruits, silk farms, growing and harvesting tea. A number of them worked the salt flats or the salt mines, and for these the army was a better life than the near-slavery and early death they'd known and expected.

Next to none of them had any idea why they were fighting Kislik barbarians, marching through a yellow wind and blowing sand that stung and cut whenever the wind grew strong. Tents and tent pegs blew away in that wind. The Kislik had horses, and they knew these lands, knew the terrain and the weather, could attack and retreat, kill you and be gone.

As far as most of the two hundred thousand men in the Imperial Pacification Army of the Northwest were concerned, the barbarians could keep this bitter place.

But their own sage and illustrious emperor, ruling in Hanjin with the mandate of heaven, had judged the Kislik to be presumptuous and arrogant, needing to be taught a stern lesson. His advisers had seen opportunities here: fame and power, rising within the court hierarchy. For some of them this war was also a test, a preparation for the true enemy, which was the even more presumptuous Xiaolu empire north of Kitai.

There was a treaty with the Xiaolu, had been for two hundred years (broken at intervals, never irreparably). By its terms the steppe people still held the Fourteen Prefectures they had taken, below the Long Wall of Kitai.

The glorious emperor's father and grandfather had not been able to win them back, by diplomacy or threat of arms, though they had tried both. Not even an offered princess had sufficed. The Xiaolu knew what they had: by holding those hilly lands with their narrow passes they ensured that all the northern cities of Kitai were open to horsemen racing down a wide plain. They *held* what was left of the Long Wall. It meant nothing now, was only a ruined marker of what Kitai had once been.

To give this back for a princess?

There were seeds in all of this, if one looked closely, and thought about it, for what was coming. Not just in the larger sweep and tumble of time but, very specifically, for the soldiers in the northwest who were to march doggedly through blowing, shifting sands north towards Erighaya, capital city of the Kislik, on the far side of the desert that lay west of the Golden River's bend.

Those troops would carry orders to besiege and destroy Erighaya, and bring Kislik leaders in chains to Hanjin. They were to claim steppe wives and daughters to service and assuage the army, and be slaves, and so humble the barbarians of the northwest before the gathered and glorious might of Kitai and its emperor.

They forgot something, though, heading north. They really did forget something.

❧

In a springtime before that northern march took place, a girl was walking beside her father amid chaos and excitement in a very crowded city.

You could declare it madness, a collective fever, the way in which Yenling, second city of the empire, was transformed during the Peony Festival.

Every spring, for the two weeks when the king of flowers bloomed, it became nearly impossible to move along Yenling streets and lanes, or find a room at an inn.

Houses great and small were filled with returning family and guests from out of town. People offered space, three or four to a bed or a pallet on the floor, to strangers for considerable sums. A place to sleep for a delirious spring interlude, before normal life resumed.

There was nothing resembling normal life during the festival.

Long Life Temple Road all the way down to the principal western gate, and both sides of Moon Dike Road, were crowded with hastily erected tents and pavilions selling peonies.

Yao Yellows (affectionately called "The Palace Lady") and Wei Reds cost thousands of cash for a single perfect blossom. Those were the most glorious graftings, the celebrated ones, and only the wealthiest could claim them.

But there were less extravagant varieties. Zuo Purple and Hidden Stream Scarlet, Sash Maroon, the Nine Petal Pearl, the exquisite, tiny petals of the Shuoun. Ninety different kinds of peony could be found in Yenling as the sun returned in spring, their blooming an occasion for joy, whatever else might be happening in the empire, on its borders, in the world.

When the first blossoms appeared a postal express began, racing east each morning along the reserved middle lane of the imperial road. There were six stations between Yenling and Hanjin. A fast relay of riders and horses could do it in a day and a night, carrying flowers, so that the Son of Heaven might share in the glorious splendour.

Yenling had been celebrated for its peonies for more than four hundred years, and the peony had been the imperial flower for longer than that.

It was derided by ascetic philosophers, declared to be artificial—peonies were grafted, constructed by man, not natural. It was disdained as gaudy and sensuous, too seductively *feminine* to justify exaltation, especially compared to the austere, masculine bamboo or flowering plum.

These views were known but they didn't matter, not even at court. The peony obsession had become a supreme case of popular wisdom (or madness) overriding the reflections of sages.

Everyone who could came to Yenling at festival time.

People walked the streets with flowers pinned to their hats. Aristocrats were carried in their chairs, and so were high-ranking members of the civil service in their long robes. Simple tradesmen crowded the lanes, and farmers pushed into the city to see the flowers and the entertainment.

The more important gardens made a great deal of money for their owners as peonies were sold outside their gates or along the streets.

The Wei family, those artisans of the flower, charged ten cash just to enter their walled garden and take the small boat across to the island in the pond where their best peonies were grown. The family hired guards; you were beaten if you touched a blossom.

There was immense skill to the grafting of the flawless, redolent blossoms. People paid to walk along winding paths to see and smell the profligate profusion. They would line up for hours, then come back to see the changes from one day to the next.

Even women were among them, bright blossoms in their hair. This was a time of year, and a place—Yenling during the Peony Festival—when the increasing restrictions on women's movements were superseded, simply because they could not be enforced.

It was springtime. There were loud, excited crowds and the heady scent of extravagantly coloured blossoms. There was flute music, singing, dancers in the streets, jugglers, storytellers, men with trained animals. Wine and food were sold in booths, throngs given over to merriment—and to undeniably immoral behaviour in courtyards and lanes and bedchambers (not only in the pleasure district) as twilight descended each day.

Another reason for philosophers to lament the folly and the flower.

WALKING BESIDE HER FATHER, Shan is dizzy with excitement and trying not to show it. That would be undignified, childlike.

She is concentrating on *seeing* everything, taking it in, registering details. Songs succeed (or fail) in the details, she believes. They are more than the pairing of words and music. It is the acuteness of observation that sets a work apart, makes it worth ... worth anything, really.

She is seventeen years old this spring. Will be married by this same season next year. A distant thought still, mostly, but not a displeasing one.

But right now she's in Yenling with her father amid the morning crowds of the festival. Sight, sound, smell (flowers everywhere and a heavy crush of bodies; the glory and the assault, she thinks). She is hardly the only woman here, but she's aware of people looking at her as she and her father make their way back up Long Life Temple Road from the city wall.

People had begun looking at her about two years ago. One would have to be in love or a poet to name her beautiful, but there seems to be something about the way she walks or stands, the way her gaze moves and then settles on objects or on people, that draws the attention of others back to her. She has wide-set eyes, a long nose, long fingers. She is tall for a woman. She gets the height from her father.

Lin Kuo is an extremely long-limbed man, but so self-effacing he has stood with a slight stoop for as long as his daughter can remember—as if denying any proud assertion of height, or endlessly ready to bow respectfully.

He had passed the *jinshi* examinations on his third attempt (perfectly honourable) but has never received a posting, even to the provinces. There are many men like that, graduates without a position. He wears the robes and belt of a civil servant and carries the title of court gentleman, which just means he is without office. He claims the monthly salary attached to that title. He writes with perfectly acceptable calligraphy, and has just completed (and had printed) a small book on gardens in Yenling, which is why they are here.

He has no obvious enemies—important these days—and seems to be unaware that he's considered a figure of amusement by some. His daughter, more observant perhaps, has registered this, however.

He is instinctively kind, a little afraid of the world. His only expression of adventurousness lies in the fact that he has educated his one living child as if she were a boy. Not a trivial decision, not without consequence, if one thinks of individual lives as important.

Shan has read the classics and the poets, major and minor, back to the beginnings of writing in Kitai. She has a very good running hand and an even better formal one. She sings, of course, can play a *pipa*—most women from good families can do that—but she also writes songs, the new *ci* form emerging in this Twelfth Dynasty, words grafted (like peonies! she suddenly thinks) to well-known melodies of the countryside or the pleasure districts.

Her father has even had bows made for each of them, with a supply of arrows. They've taken lessons together from a retired archer he found, another quiet reaction against the customs of the day, where all well-bred men (let alone their daughters!) loftily disdain all military traditions.

It is not proper for a girl to do any of this, of course. In music they are to pluck a *pipa* fetchingly, and sing the words men write. The women doing such singing tend to be entertainers and courtesans. It has always been so.

Lin Kuo has betrothed his daughter this past winter, taking care and thought, to a man he believes will accept what she is, and be happy in that. It is more than any daughter can expect.

Shan loves her father without reserve or condition, though also without illusions as to his limitations.

She loves the world, too, this morning, equally without illusions—or so she proudly believes. She is very young.

She is wearing a crimson peony in her hair, carrying a yellow one, as they walk towards the home of the man her father has come to visit. They do have an invitation: Lin Kuo would not be going there without one.

Two and a half years have passed, on this bright morning, since the boy, Ren Daiyan, also young but without a similar belief that he understood the world (yet), walked into a forest east of his village, carrying a bow and bloodied arrows, and two swords from a man he'd killed.

THERE WAS NO FIGURE more respected in Kitai than Xi Wengao of Yenling. Craggy-faced and white-haired now (what was left of his hair), he knew his stature, was not above taking pride in it. You lived your life as honourably as you could, were rewarded, in some instances, with recognition in your lifetime.

He was a civil servant and a scholar, the official historian of the dynasty, a poet. He had even written songs when younger, had made the *ci* form almost acceptable among serious writers. (Others of his circle had followed, pushing the form even further.) He was renowned for his calligraphy, for advancing the careers of disciples at court. He was a celebrated lover of beauty (including the beauty of women) and had held just about every important office there was through the years, including prime minister to the last emperor and then, briefly, to the son who reigned now.

That "briefly" told its tale, of course.

In his garden, awaiting guests, he sipped Szechen tea from a green celadon cup—that gorgeous green, in honour of the season. One of those visiting this morning was a source of great sorrow, another promised to be a diversion. In late-morning light he thought about emperors and court factions and the arc of a man's life. You could live too long, he thought, as well as not long enough.

Some lives didn't actually have an arc, not in the eyes of the world. Yes, everyone could pass from tottering child to vigorous man and then become someone for whom a change in the weather or a walk as far as the gazebo in his garden brought an ache in knees and back, but that wasn't a career arc. A farmer didn't arc, he passed through good or bad years, depending on the weather, on locusts, on whether a son was drafted into the army and marched away to war at sowing time.

But a civil servant in Kitai could rise and fall—and rise and fall again, depending on the mood at court, on whether a battle had been lost in the west or a comet seen in the sky, frightening an emperor. He could even be exiled—a greater fall, like a celestial object hurtling to the earth.

That kind of fall could kill you if you were sent all the way south to the lands of sickness and decay.

He had friends down there now. If they were still alive. Letters came infrequently from towards the pearl divers' sea. It was a grief. These were men he had loved. The world was a hard place. One needed to learn that.

He was exiled himself, of course, but only this far, only to Yenling, his family home. A distance from court, from influence, but not a hardship.

He was too well known, too widely admired for even Hang Dejin and his followers to ask the emperor to do more. Even a prime minister set on changing the ways of a thousand years knew better than to push too hard on that.

In fairness, it was unlikely that Prime Minister Hang wanted him dead. They had exchanged letters and even a poetry sequence once. Years ago, but still. They had debated policies with courtesy before the last emperor, though not in front of the son, the current one. Times changed. Arcs. His old rival Hang was ... old now, too. It was said his eyesight was failing. There were others, younger, colder, near the throne now.

Still, he had only been ordered *away* from Hanjin, from palace and office. He was allowed his own house and garden, books and brush, ink stone and paper. He hadn't been driven ten thousand *li* south to a place from which men did not return.

They didn't execute out-of-favour civil servants in the Twelfth Dynasty of Kitai under the Emperor Wenzong. That, he thought wryly, would have been barbaric, and theirs was an emperor of exquisite cultivation. They just sent members of the disgraced faction away, sometimes so far that their ghosts couldn't even return to threaten anyone.

One of the two men coming to him today was on his way to a savage exile: across the Great River and the rice-rich lands, over two mountain ranges, through thick, wet forests, all the way to the low-lying, poisonous island that was only nominally part of the empire.

Lingzhou was where the very worst political offenders were sent. They were expected to write their last letters or poems in the steaming heat and die.

He'd been a pupil once, the one going there now, a follower, though he'd moved far beyond that. Another man he loved. Perhaps (probably?) the one he'd loved most of all of them. It would be important today, Master Xi told himself sternly, to preserve equanimity. He would break a willow twig in farewell, the old custom, but he must not shame himself or weaken the other with an old man's tears.

It was a reason he'd invited the second visitor. To change the tone and mood. Impose the restraint that preserved dignity, the illusion that this was not a final meeting. He was old, his friend was banished. Truth was, they were never going to climb again to a high place on the Ninth of Ninth Festival and celebrate friendship with too much wine.

It was important not to think about that.

Old men wept too easily.

He saw one of his woman servants, the young one, coming from the house and through the garden. He preferred messages to be brought by the women, not his steward. It was unusual, but he was in his own home, could devise his own protocols, and he so much enjoyed the sight of this one—in blue silk today, her hair elegantly pinned (both things also unusual, she *was* only a servant)—as she approached along the curved pathway to the gazebo where he sat. He had curved all the paths when he designed his small garden, just as they were curved or angled at court. Demons could only travel a straight line.

She bowed twice, announced his first visitor. The amusing one, as it turned out. He wasn't really in a mood for that, but he didn't want to be desperately sad when the other one came. There were too many memories, called back by a springtime morning.

Then he saw that Lin Kuo had someone with him, and his mood did change a little. It was a source of immediate inward wryness. He had always been able to laugh at himself. A saving feature in a powerful man. But how was it that even today, at his age, the sight of a very young girl, fresh-faced to face the world, graceful and awkward at the same time (she was tall for a woman, he saw), poised on the threshold of life, could still enchant him so much?

Once, a long time ago—another memory, a different kind— his enemies had tried to drive him from power by claiming he'd incestuously seduced a young cousin. There had been a trial. The accusation had been a lie and they had failed, but they'd been clever with it, and there was an interval when his friends had feared for him. This had been in the years when the faction ugliness at court had begun to claim lives.

His accusers had presented a song at the trial, purporting to be something he'd written to her. It was even a good song. You needed to respect your foes at this court. But the real cleverness had been that they'd chosen to attack him this way, given his well-known love of women.

All his life. His too-long life.

That sweet, shy cousin had died years ago, a wife and mother. His own wives had died, both of them. He'd liked the second one better. Two concubines were gone, and mourned. He hadn't taken another. Two sons were dead. Three emperors he'd known. Too many friends (too many enemies) to name or number.

And still the girl approaching beside the long, eager figure of Lin Kuo caused him to set down his green cup and rise (despite his knees) to greet the two of them on his feet. It was a *good* thing, he told himself. You could be dead while alive, lose all taste for life, and he didn't want to do that.

He had strong opinions on where Hang Dejin and his followers were leading the emperor with their New Policies, and he was vain enough to believe his views might matter, even now. He loathed the long, foolish war against the Kislik, for one thing.

Lin Kuo bowed three times, stopping and advancing, which was flattering but excessive from another *jinshi* scholar and an invited guest. His daughter stayed a proper two steps behind and performed a proper two bows. Then, after hesitating, she offered a third.

Xi Wengao stroked his narrow beard and kept a smile from his face: she was matching her father's manners, out of respect, to be in step with him, but clearly she had been inclined to stop after the proper level of salutation.

Not a word spoken, already an interesting girl. Not formally beautiful, he noted, but an alert, curious face. He saw her glance at his celadon teacup and the lacquered tray, take in details of the gazebo. He'd had the upper panels painted by San Tsai in the style of Chang Shao of the Seventh Dynasty.

Tsai was also dead. Last year. Another friend gone.

"Councillor, it is a very great honour to see you again," said Lin Kuo. He had a light, pleasant voice. Wengao wasn't an imperial councillor any more, but he didn't mind being called one.

"The honour is surely mine," he said formally, "that you grace a sad exile's home with your esteemed presence. And bringing ... ?"

"My daughter, councillor. Her name is Shan. I have long wished to show her the Peony Festival, and have presumed to bring her with me to meet your excellence."

"No presumption at all. You are welcome, child." He smiled this time.

She didn't smile back; a watchful face. "It is a privilege for me, sir, to be in the presence of the man instrumental in elevating the status of written songs in our time. I have read your essay on the *ci* form, with profit and illumination."

Xi Wengao blinked. *This is a good thing*, he told himself again. Something to be cherished. That life could still surprise you.

Even from a man, the words would have been assured, a supremely confident thing to say as a first remark. This was, of course, a girl. A young woman, obviously unmarried, a peony in her hair, another in her hand, and she stood in his garden, specifying that among all he'd done ...

He sat down, motioned Lin Kuo to a chair. The tall man sat with another bow. The daughter remained standing, moving a little behind him. Wengao looked at her. "I will confess that essay is not what I normally expect to be saluted for."

Lin Kuo laughed, indulgently. "She writes *ci* herself, councillor. I suspect she has wanted to say this to you for some time."

The daughter flushed. Parents could create awkwardness for their children, but Kuo had spoken with a vivid, appealing pride. And

Xi Wengao, for many reasons, had never subscribed to the more extreme limitations proposed by Cho teachers on the freedom allowed women in their time.

He knew too much about the past, for one thing. He loved women too much, for another. The ripple of voices, dance of eyes, their hands, their scent. The way some of them could read a gathering in an instant, and then guide it. He had known women like that. He had loved some of them.

"I shall enjoy reading or hearing her own *ci*, then," he said, looking from daughter to seated father. Then he offered a gift, a kindness: "But come, come, let me see it! You wrote of having completed your book. Is it true, Master Lin?"

The father's turn to flush. "Hardly a book! A mere essay, an exercise in a style, commentaries on a few gardens here. Including, of course, your own serene refuge."

"Serene? This ill-tended space? You can hardly even call it a proper garden. I have no peonies, for one thing." He meant it as a jest.

"Why not, sir, if I may ask?"

The girl had wide-set eyes and that direct gaze. She held a yellow peony in her left hand. She had slipped it into and out of the sleeve of her robe when she'd bowed with arms folded. He was a man who noticed things like that. She was dressed in green for spring, a shade very like that of his teacups.

He said, "I would dishonour them, Miss Lin. I lack the skill and patience to grow and graft the king of flowers, and have no gardener with those gifts. It seemed to me wise for an aged scholar to plan a garden around reserve, simplicity. Peonies are too passionate for me now."

"Your writings are your flowers," said Lin Kuo, which was certainly graceful enough. One could, Wengao thought, underestimate the fellow. For one thing, for a man to bring up a daughter able to speak as she just had suggested complexity.

Complexity. Xi Wengao had lived a life torn between the seductive lure of that and a hunger for simplicity. The palace, deadly battles there, and then solitude where he could take up his brush and write.

Had he chosen to be here it would have been one thing. But he had not, and Hang Dejin was still prime minister, implementing his New Policies with an increasingly vicious group of younger associates.

Kitai was at war under their guidance—foolish, futile war—and the government of a distracted emperor was vulgarly engaged in trade and commerce, even in loans to farmers (whether they wanted them or not). And now came word of a revision of the *jinshi* examination system that he, Wengao, had put in place himself.

So he wasn't happy to be exiled just now, no.

He heard a sound from towards the house, quickly turned. Saw Lu Chen—the familiar, dearly loved face. He had come.

His protégé, his friend, was smiling—as always, it seemed—as he walked up behind the girl in blue. He was on his way, escorted by guards, to what was meant to be his death.

A lesson here, a bitter poem: you could enjoy the unexpected arrival of a young girl on a spring morning, but you couldn't hide from heartbreak behind her slender form.

Chen had lost weight, he saw. Not surprising, in his present circumstances. A brown hemp traveller's robe hung loosely upon him. His manner, though, as he approached the gazebo and bowed, was as it always was: genial, open, pleased by the world, ready to be engaged or amused by it. You would never know by looking at the man that he was as profound a thinker as the world had today, the acknowledged master poet of their age. Celebrated as belonging with the giants of the Third and Ninth.

He also shared, Wengao knew, some of those earlier poets' legendary appreciation for good wine (or less-than-good wine, when occasion required).

Wengao stood up again, so did Lin Kuo, very quickly. For his own mild amusement, he had not alerted the court gentleman that there was another guest arriving, and obviously not who it was.

But every man with a connection to the literary or the political world knew Lu Chen—and his current fate. He wondered for a moment if the daughter would, then he saw the expression on her face.

He felt a flicker of envy, like a long tongue from an old fire. She hadn't looked at him that way. But he was old, really old. Could barely stand from a chair without wincing. Chen wasn't a young man—his hair under the black felt hat and his narrow, neat beard were both greying—but he didn't have knees that made walking an ambitious exercise. He was straight-backed, still a handsome man, if thinner-faced than he ought to be, and seeming tired now, if you knew him and looked closely.

And he was the man who had written "Lines On the Cold Food Festival" and the "Red Cliff" poems, among others.

Wengao was properly (if judiciously) proud of his own poetry over the years, but he was also a good reader and a sound judge, and he knew whose lines deserved to be remembered. Who deserved the look a young girl offered now.

"You are drinking tea, my dear friend?" Chen exclaimed, in mock dismay. "I was relying on your spiced wine!"

"It will be brought for you," Wengao replied gravely. "My doctors have advised that tea will serve me better at this hour of the day. I sometimes pretend to heed them." He glanced briefly at his girl. She nodded, and headed back towards the house.

"Probably serve me better too." Chen laughed. He turned. "I believe this is Court Gentleman Lin Kuo? Your late wife was a distant kinswoman of mine."

"She was, honourable sir. You are gracious to recall it and to know me."

"Hardly so!" Chen laughed again. "They were the better family in Szechen. We were the poor-but-earnest scholars in training."

Not true about his family, Wengao knew, but typical of Chen. He made the other introduction himself.

"And here is Miss Lin Shan, daughter of Master Lin and his late wife. He has brought her to see the peonies."

"As well he should," said Chen. "The splendour of the flowers needs no further adornment, but we cannot have too much of beauty."

The father looked amusingly happy. The daughter ...

"You are too kind, Master Lu. It counts as a poet's lie to suggest I have any beauty to add to Yenling in springtime."

Chen's smile became radiant, his delight manifestly unfeigned. "So you think poets are liars, Miss Lin?"

"I believe we have to be. Life and history must be adapted to the needs of our verses and songs. A poem is not a chronicle like a historian's." She looked at Xi Wengao with that last, and allowed herself—for the first time—a shy smile.

We. Our.

Wengao looked at her. He was wishing, again, that he was younger. He could *remember* being younger. His knees ached. So did his back, standing. He moved to sit again, carefully.

Lu Chen strode to the chair and helped the older man. He made it seem a gesture of respect, courtesy to a mentor, not a response to need. Wengao smiled up at him and gestured for the other two men to sit. There were only three chairs, he hadn't known the girl was coming.

The girl was astonishing.

He asked, because he couldn't help himself, though it was too quick, "Old friend, how much time do we have with you?"

Chen didn't let his smile fade at all. "Ah! That depends on how good the wine proves to be when it arrives."

Wengao shook his head. "Tell me."

There were no secrets here. The two Lins would know—everyone knew—that Chen had been banished to Lingzhou Isle. It was said that the deputy prime minister, Kai Zhen—a man Wengao despised—was in charge of these matters now, as the prime minister aged.

Wengao had heard it said there were a dozen kinds of spiders and snakes on Lingzhou that could kill you, and that the evening wind carried disease. There were tigers.

Chen said quietly, "I imagine I can stay one or two nights. There are four guards accompanying me, but as long as I mostly keep moving south, and offer them food and wine, I believe I'll be permitted some stops to visit friends."

"And your brother?"

The younger brother, also a *jinshi* scholar, had also been exiled (families seldom escaped), but not so far, not to where he'd be expected to die.

"Chao's with his family at the farm by the Great River. I'll go that way. My wife is with them, and will stay. We have land, he can farm it. They may eat chestnuts some winters but ..."

He left the thought unfinished. Lu Chao, the younger brother, had a wife and six children. He had passed the examinations startlingly young, ranked third in the year his older brother was first. Had received the honours that came with that, held very high office, served twice as an emissary to the Xiaolu in the north.

He had also remonstrated steadily, speaking out at court and in written memoranda against the New Policies of Hang Dejin, arguing carefully and well, with passion.

You paid a price for that. Dissent and opposition were no longer acceptable. But the younger brother wasn't the poet and thinker who had shaped the intellectual climate of their day. So he had been exiled, yes, but would be permitted to try to survive. Like Wengao himself, here in his own garden in his own city. Undoubtedly, Kai Zhen would congratulate himself on being a compassionate man, a judicious servant of the emperor, attentive to the teachings of the Masters.

Sometimes it was difficult to escape bitterness. They were living, Wengao thought, schooling his features, in a terrible time.

His guest said, changing the mood, turning to the girl, "As to poets and lies, you may be right, Miss Lin, but would you not agree that even if we alter details we may aspire to deeper truth, not only offer falsehoods?"

She flushed again, so directly addressed. She held her head high, though. She was the only one standing, again behind her father's chair. She said, "Some poets, perhaps. But tell me, what man has written verses about courtesans or palace women happy in themselves, *not* wasting away or shedding tears on balconies in sorrow for vanished lovers? Does anyone think this is the only truth for their lives?"

Lu Chen thought about it, giving her his full attention. "Does that mean it is not a truth at all? If someone writes of a particular woman, must he intend her to stand for every single one?"

His voice in debate was as remembered, crisp and emphatic. Delighted to be engaged, even by a girl. Thrust and counter-thrust, as with a sword. No one at court knew how to use a sword any more. Kitai had changed; men had changed. This was a woman debating with Chen, however. You had to remind yourself it was a girl, listening to her.

She said, "But if only the one tale is told, over and over, no others at all, what will readers decide is true?" She hesitated, and Wengao caught what must—*really?*—be mischief in her eyes. "If a great poet tells us he is at the Red Cliff of a legendary battle, and he is, in fact, fifty or a hundred *li* upriver, what will travellers in a later day think when they come to that place?"

She lowered her gaze and clasped her hands demurely.

Wengao burst out laughing. He clapped in approval, rocking back and forth. It was well known that Lu Chen had indeed mistaken where he was, boating on the Great River with friends on a full moon night. He'd decided he and his companions had drifted under the cliffs of the famous Third Dynasty battle ... and he'd been wrong.

Chen was grinning at the girl. He was a man who could be moved to passionate fury, but not by a conversation such as this. Here, playing with words and thoughts, he was in his element, and joyous. You could almost forget where he was going.

One or two nights he'd said he could stay.

Chen turned to the father, who was also smiling, though cautiously. Lin Kuo would be ready to beat a retreat. But Chen bowed to him, and said, "I honour the father of such a daughter. You will be careful in how she is wed, Court Gentleman?"

"I have been, I believe," the other man said. "She is betrothed to Qi Wai, the son of Qi Lao. They will be wed after the New Year."

"The Qi family? The imperial clan? What degree of relationship?"

"Sixth degree. So it is all right," said the father.

Within five degrees of kinship to the emperor, imperial clan members could marry only with permission of the court office in charge of them. Outside that degree, they led a more normal life, though could never hold office, or take the examinations, and they were all required to live in the clan compound in Hanjin beside the palace.

Imperial kin had always been a problem for emperors, especially those not entirely secure on the Dragon Throne. Once, the nearer males in line might have been killed (many times they had been, in wide, bloody reapings), but Twelfth Dynasty Kitai prided itself on being civilized.

Of course it did, Wengao thought, looking at his friend. These days the clan was simply locked away from the world, each of them given a monthly stipend, dowries for the women, the cost of burial rites—all of which was a serious budgetary concern, because there were so many of them now.

"Qi Wai?" he said. "I don't know him. I believe I have met the father. The son is an intelligent man, may I hope?"

"He is a young historian, a collector of antiquities."

It was the girl, speaking up for herself, for her husband-to-be. This was inappropriate, of course. Xi Wengao had already decided he didn't care. He was a little in love. He *wanted* her to speak.

"That sounds promising," said Chen.

"I would not inflict my unruly daughter on a man I felt incapable of accepting her nature," the father said. "I beg forgiveness for her impertinence." Again, despite the words, you could hear pride.

"As well you should!" cried Lu Chen. "She has just reminded me of one of my most grievous errors in verse!"

A short silence, as the father tried to decide if Chen was truly offended.

"The poems are wonderful," the girl said, eyes downcast again. "I have them committed to memory."

Chen grinned at her. "And thus, so easily, I am assuaged. Men," he added, "are too readily placated by a clever woman."

"Women," she murmured, "have too little choice but to placate."

They heard a sound. None of them had seen the servant approaching again in her blue silk. Xi Wengao knew this girl very well (she spent some nights warming him). She wasn't happy just now. That, too, was predictable, if unacceptable.

The wine would be good. His people knew which wines to offer guests, and Lu Chen was known to be his favourite.

Wengao and the girl (of course) had tea. Lin Kuo joined Chen in drinking the spiced wine, doing it as a courtesy to the poet, Wengao decided. Food was brought. They lingered in morning light, listening to birdsong in his garden, in a gazebo decorated with paintings by San Tsai, done in a style of long ago.

SHE IS AWARE that the servant girl from the garden this morning doesn't like her, though a servant (even a favoured one) ought not to let that show.

The girl probably thinks she isn't revealing it, Shan decides. But there are ways for a servant to stand, or respond just a little slowly to requests or orders. There are even ways of unpacking a guest's belongings in the chamber offered her for the night, and messages can be read in such things.

She is used to this. For some time it has been true of almost every woman she meets, of whatever rank or status. Men tend to be made uneasy, or sometimes amused, by Shan. Women dislike her.

It is not at all certain, to this point in her life, if her father has really given her a gift with how he's chosen to educate her.

Some gifts are complex, she has long ago decided. *Small things can change a life*, a poet had written, and that is true, but the equally obvious truth is that large things can do the same. Her brother's death had been a large thing, in their family if not in the world.

In the years that followed it, the only other child, the thin, clever daughter, had received, slowly at first, as an experiment—the way an Arcane Path alchemist might gradually heat liquid in a flask— and then more decisively, the education a boy was offered if he intended to try for the *jinshi* examinations and a civil servant's robe.

She wasn't, of course, going to write any examinations, or wear robes with the belt of any rank at all, but her father had given her the learning to do so. And he had made her perfect her writing skills and the brush strokes of her calligraphy.

The songs, the *ci*, she had discovered on her own.

By now, her brush strokes are more confident than his. If it is true, as some said and wrote, that the innermost nature of a person shows in their calligraphy, then her father's caution and diffidence are there to be seen in his neat, straight, formal hand. Only when he'd travelled and written letters home in a running hand (no one but Shan and her mother had ever seen that hand) did his passion for life show through. From the world Lin Kuo hides this, in his writing, in his lanky, agreeable, slightly stooped form.

Her own hand, in both formal and running scripts, is bolder, stronger. Too much so for a woman, she knows. Everything about her life is like that.

The servant has withdrawn at her command, again just a little too slowly. And she's left the door not quite fully closed on the dark corridor. Shan thinks of calling her back, but doesn't.

The room is at the back of the house, nearest the garden. Master Xi's home is too deliberately modest to have a separate wing for women, let alone a building, but the men are at the front. She isn't sure if their host and the poet have gone to bed. Her father has. Father and daughter had withdrawn from the dining room together, to leave the two old friends time alone by lamplight, with wine. It wasn't an action that needed to be discussed. So much sadness here, Shan thinks, however much Xi Wengao has tried to hide it.

There are noises in the garden at night. A flap of wings, cry of an owl, crickets, wind in leaves, wind chimes, faintly. Shan sees that their host has left two books for her in the room. A lamp with a long wick is lit to read by if she wants. One text is a scroll, the other a printed book, beautifully stitched binding. There is a desk, a single chair. The bed is large, curtained, a curved blue ceramic pillow with a painting of white plum blossoms.

Master Xi is old enough to simply enjoy what she is, not be disturbed by it. He appears to find her learning amusing. Not necessarily the response she wants. But she is seventeen, and a girl. What response did one expect?

Perhaps, inwardly—not for speaking aloud—what she really wants is for the songs, the *ci* she labours to craft, to be read or heard, and considered for their merits—or lack of them. She isn't vain, she knows how much she doesn't know yet.

Lu Chen had said at dinner that he'd like to hear them sung.

He is, in many ways, the master of all men of their day, the poets and thinkers, at any rate. Yet he smiled easily, laughed with abandonment, jesting through the meal, pulling the three of them in that direction, scattering toasts (even to her!) from a steadily refilled wine cup. Forcing the mood towards lightness. Towards it, but not really arriving there.

He is going to Lingzhou Isle. The expectation is that he will die. That is what happens there. There is a weight of pain, almost of panic inside Shan when she thinks about it. And something else she can't identify. Bereavement? The bitter wine of loss-to-come? She feels a strangeness, almost wants to weep.

Men broke willow twigs when parting from friends, a gesture of farewell, entreating heaven for a return. But could you break a twig for someone going where Lu Chen was going? With so many rivers and mountains between?

She had been too bold in those first moments this morning. She knows it, knew it as she spoke. She'd felt awed by his arrival, overwhelmed—but fiercely determined not to yield to that or show it. Sometimes, Shan is aware, she feels so strong a need to be seen and heard that she forces an encounter, declaring her presence.

Look at me! she can hear herself crying. And no one wants to be ordered to do that.

In a way, she is too much the opposite of her father, who stands among others as if ready to take a step backwards, saying with his posture, his clasped hands, *I am not even here if you don't wish me to be.*

She loves him, honours him, wants to protect him, wants *him* to be properly seen as well, even if he is happier withdrawing towards shadows. There are only the two of them in the world. Until she weds and leaves the house.

It is too easy to dismiss Lin Kuo, his daughter thinks for the hundredth time or more. Even his small book on the gardens here, presented to Master Xi today. Of course it isn't an important work, but it is carefully, wittily done, offers observations that might last: a portrait in words of Yenling, a part of it, in these years of the dynasty under Emperor Wenzong, may he reign a thousand years upon the Dragon Throne.

It is called the Dragon Throne again. She must be tired, or over-tired, her thoughts are drifting. Shan knows why it has that name once more. She has learned such things because of her father. They are there for her, in her mind. Can you *unlearn*? Go back to being something else? A girl like all the others?

At their dynasty's founding, the court sages and philosophers had decreed that one reason for the fall of the glorious Ninth had been their deviation from right behaviour—an overindulgence in the ways and symbols of women. And foremost of these had been renaming the imperial throne the Phoenix Throne.

The phoenix is the female principle, the dragon is male.

Empress Hao of the early Ninth made that change while ruling as regent for her young son, and then ruling in spite of him when he grew older and wanted—in vain—to govern in his own name.

He died, instead. It is generally believed he was poisoned. The title and decoration of the Ninth Dynasty throne was not changed back after Empress Hao herself passed to the gods. And then, at the height of that dynasty's glory, came General An Li, accursed in Kitai and in heaven, bringing terrible rebellion.

Even after peace was finally restored, glory was never the same. Everything changed. Even the poetry. You couldn't write or think the same way after eight years of death and savagery and all they'd lost.

The lion in the wild, wolves in the cities.

And then, years later, that diminished dynasty finally crumbled away, so that still more chaos and war came to blood-soaked Kitai, through a hundred years of brief, failed dynasties and fragmented kingdoms.

Until the Twelfth rose, their own, a new glory.

A more limited glory, mind you, with the Long Wall lost and crumbling, barbarians south of it, the Silk Roads no longer Kitai's, the Fourteen Prefectures lost.

But they called the throne the Dragon Throne again, and told cautionary tales about ceding too much influence to women. In the palace, in the home. Women are to remain in their inner quarters, to offer no opinions on matters of ... on anything, really. They dress more soberly now. No long, wide sleeves, no bright colours, low-cut gowns, intoxicating scents at court or in a garden.

Shan lives these realities, and she knows their origins: the theories and writings, disputes and interpretations. She knows the great names and their works and deeds. She's steeped in poetry, has memorized verses from the Third and Seventh, the Ninth, before and after the rebellion.

Some lines were remembered through everything that happened.

But who knew what words or deeds would last? Who made these decisions? Was surviving down the years a matter of accident as much as excellence?

She stands by the desk and lamp, suddenly weary, without even the energy to cross the room and close the door the servant has left ajar. It has been an intense day.

She is seventeen, and will be wed next year. She doesn't think (though she might be wrong) that either of the men here fully grasped her father's careful choice of a husband for her from the imperial clan.

A daughter-in-law in Kitai is the servant of her husband's parents. She leaves her home and becomes a lesser figure in theirs. The parents can even send her back (and keep her dowry) if she is judged insufficiently respectful. Her father has spared her that, knowing what she is (what he has caused her to be).

The imperial clan have all the servants any of them will ever need, paid for by the court office that administers the clan. They have doctors assigned, and entertainers and alchemists and cooks.

Astrologers, though only by daylight and with permission. They have sedan chairs, single or double, at their disposal when they wish to (again with permission) leave the compound by the palace, where they are expected to live forever.

There are funds for formal clothing and adornments for banquets or ceremonies when their presence is required. They are creatures to be displayed, symbols of the dynasty. They are buried in the clan graveyard—which is here in Yenling. There isn't enough room in Hanjin. From one graveyard to another, someone had once said.

A woman marrying into the clan lives a different life. And it can be a *good* life, depending on the woman, on her husband, on the will of heaven.

She will have a husband, less than a year from now. She has met him. That, too, is unusual, though not forbidden—and such matters are conducted differently within the imperial clan. Her father's *jinshi* degree, his status as a court gentleman, had given more than enough stature for him to address, through intermediaries, a family in the clan. Marrying into the imperial ranks isn't universally desired. It is such a sequestered life, shaped by ceremony and regulation, so many living so closely together as their numbers grow.

But for Shan it offers a promise of sorts. Among these people, already marked apart, her own differences might blend, silk threads weaving with each other. It is possible.

And Wai—Qi Wai—is a student himself, her father had determined. A little different, too, it seems. A man (a boy, still, really) who has already travelled (with permission) to search out ancient steles and bronzes in the countryside, and brought them home to catalogue.

This wasn't your usual son of the indolent imperial clan, pursuing wine and pleasure in the entertainment districts of Hanjin because there was no ambition possible for him. Sometimes, perhaps out of boredom as much as anything, some of them drifted into intrigues against the throne. They were executed for that.

Qi Wai had been stiff but courteous, sitting with his mother and her aunt on the one occasion they were together, taking tea, after the first negotiations had proceeded satisfactorily. Her father had made it clear to her (and to them, she believed): in his view the marriage turned on the two young people finding or anticipating an affinity.

Shan thought they had, at least potentially, that day.

He'd looked younger than her (was a year older). He was plump, had the wispy beginnings of a scholar's chin beard. The attempt at dignity that implied was amusing at first, then endearing. He had small, smooth hands. His voice was low but clear. He'd be feeling shy, too, she remembers thinking.

She had taken pains with her appearance, which she didn't always do, but her father had worked hard and carefully to arrange this meeting, and he deserved that much of her. Besides, it was all interesting. She'd worn blue *liao* silk in a sober cut, gold-and-lapis-lazuli hairpins. Her lapis earrings, too. They had been her mother's.

She allowed Wai to see her mind working as they talked. He'd know about her eccentric education by now, but she didn't push forward her manner of thinking the way she sometimes did, to provoke a response.

He spoke—this man, Qi Wai, who would, apparently, be her husband—of a rare Fifth Dynasty stele he'd found north of the capital, close to the border with the Xiaolu. She wondered if he had been trying to impress her with his bravery going up there, then decided he didn't think that way. There was a long-established peace, trade, a treaty. He'd gone to where he'd heard there were antiquities to be found. The border hadn't entered his mind.

He became animated talking about this funerary stele, the writing on it. The record of some long-dead civil servant's life and deeds. She had to see it, he urged. Perhaps tomorrow?

Even at that first meeting it had occurred to Shan that she might have to become the practical one in this marriage.

She could manage that, she'd thought. Wai hadn't recognized a quote from a poem she'd offered without emphasis, but it wasn't a well-known line, and he'd seemed at ease discussing with a woman how objects from the past excited him. She'd decided there were worse passions to share with a husband.

The idea of *sharing* wasn't usually a part of marriage. (Nor was passion, really.)

Her father had offered her another gift here, it seemed. If the boy was still a boy, a little eccentric and intense, he would grow (she would grow). The mother hadn't seemed overwhelming, though the usual disapproval of Shan's education was there. It was always there.

She'd bowed to her father, after, and told him she would be honoured to marry Qi Wai if the Qi family approved of her, and that she hoped to bring grandchildren one day for him to teach as he'd taught her. She holds to that. She can picture it.

This evening, however, listening to crickets in the night, she finds herself sad and restless, both. Part of this will be the adventure of where they are. Travel has not been a great part of her life. Yenling at festival time can make anyone overexcited. Not to mention the men she's met today: the one in whose home they are sleeping, and the other one.

She ought never to have said what she'd said about his "Red Cliff" poems. What had she been thinking? He'd have decided, right then, in the gazebo, that she was a vain, presumptuous girl, evidence of the error of educating women. He had laughed, smiled, engaged in conversation with her, but men could do that and think very different thoughts.

She *had* told him she'd memorized the two poems. She hopes he'll remember that, accept it for the apology it was (partly) meant to be.

It is dark outside the silk-paper windows. No moon tonight, the crickets continuing, wind, the birds quiet now. She glances at the bed. She isn't sleepy any more. She is gazing at the books on the desk when she hears a footfall in the corridor.

She is not afraid. She has time to wonder at herself, that she seems to have not closed her door after all, when he steps inside.

"I saw the light," he says, quietly.

Half a truth. His chamber is at the front, other side of the dining chamber. He had to have come this way in order to see her light. Her mind works like this. Her heart is racing, she notes. She is truly not fearful, though. Words are important. You don't think or write *afraid* when it is the wrong word.

She is still wearing the blue jacket with gold buttons from dinner, there are phoenixes on it. Her hair is still pinned, though without the flower now, which is in a vase by the bed.

She bows to him. You can start with a bow.

He says, not smiling, "I shouldn't be here."

Of course he shouldn't, Shan thinks. It is an offence against courtesy—to her, to her father, to their host.

She does not say that. She says, "I should not have left the door open."

He looks at her. His eyes are grave above a long nose and the neat, grey-and-black chin beard. His own hair is also pinned, no hat, the men had removed their hats at dinner, a gesture meant to indicate freedom from restraint. There are lines at the corners of his eyes. She wonders how much he's had to drink, how it affects him. The stories, widely shared, say it doesn't, very much.

He says, "I'd have seen a light under the door. I could have knocked."

"I would have opened it for you," she says.

She hears herself say that and is amazed. But not afraid.

He is still beside the door, has not come farther in.

"Why?" he asks, still quietly. He has been cheerful all day, for the three of them. Not now. "Why would you have opened it? Because I am being sent away?"

She finds herself nodding. "That is also the reason you are here, isn't it?"

She watches him consider it. Is pleased he hasn't offered the too-easy, quick denial, flattering her. "One reason," he murmurs.

"One reason for me, then, too," she says, from where she stands by the desk, by the bed, near the lamp and two flowers.

Something shrieks from the garden, sudden and loud. Shan startles, catches herself. She is too much on edge, not that it is surprising. Something has just died outside.

"A cat hunting," he says. "Perhaps a fox. Even amid beauty and order, that happens."

"And when there is no beauty, no order?"

She regrets that, even as she says it. She's pushing again.

But he smiles. First time since entering. He says, "I am not going to the island intending to die, Miss Lin."

She can't think of what to say to that. *Say nothing, for once*, she tells herself. He is looking at her from across the room. She can't read that gaze. She has brought only ordinary hairpins to travel, but wears her mother's earrings.

He says, "People live on Lingzhou Isle, you know that. I just said the same thing to Wengao."

People who have grown up there, she thinks. Who grow accustomed to (if they survive childhood) the diseases and the endless, steaming rainfall and the heat.

She says, "There are ... there are spiders."

He grins at that. She has meant for him to do so, wonders if he knows. "Enormous spiders, yes. The size of houses, they tell me."

"And they eat men?"

"Poets, I am told. Twice a year a number of spiders come from the forests into the square of the one town and they must be fed a poet or they will not leave. There is a ceremony."

She allows herself a brief smile. "A reason not to write poetry?"

"I am told they make prisoners at the *yamen* compose a verse in order to receive their meals."

"How cruel. And that qualifies them as poets?"

"The spiders are not critical, I understand."

He will be another kind of prisoner there. Not in a jail, but watched, forbidden to leave. This folly is not as amusing as he wants it to be, Shan thinks.

He seems to come to the same conclusion. "I asked if you would offer me one or two of your songs, if you remember?"

Remember? Men can say the strangest things. But she shakes her head. "Not now. Not like this."

"Poetry suits a bedchamber. Songs even more."

Stubbornly she shakes her head again, looking down.

"Why?" he asks gently.

She hasn't expected gentleness. She meets his gaze across the room. "Because that is not why you came," she says.

His turn to fall silent. Mostly silence outside now, as well, after that death in the garden. Wind in the plum trees. Spring night. And now, Shan realizes, she is afraid, after all.

It is not easy, she thinks, to make your way in the world while insisting on a new path. She has never been touched by a man. She is to be married early next year.

And this man is past her father's age, has a son older than her, a first wife dead, a second living with his brother's family, for Lu Chen will not bring her to the island with him—whatever he might say about not going south to die. He has had concubines, written poems for them and for pleasure-district courtesans. It is said that if he named a red-lantern girl in a poem, she could triple her rates. She doesn't know if he is taking a woman south with him.

She doesn't think he is. His son will be coming, to be a companion. And perhaps to bury his father one day, or bring the body north for burial, if that is allowed.

Lu Chen says, "I am not so vain, or unmannerly, to have imagined anything beyond talking here tonight."

She draws a breath, and with it (with his words) her fear seems to have gone, as quickly as it had flowered within. She can even smile, carefully, looking down.

"Not even imagined?" she asks.

Hears him laugh, her reward. "I deserve that," the poet says. "But, Miss Lin ..." His tone has changed, she looks up. "We may imagine much, but not always allow these visions to enter the world. We all live this way."

"Must we?" she asks.

"I think so. The world falls apart, otherwise. There are men I have imagined killing, for example."

She can guess who one or two of those might be. She draws a breath, finding courage. "I think ... I think you meant to honour me, coming here. Sharing these thoughts. I know how wide the space is between us, because of my sex, my age, my inexperience. I want only to tell you that I am not ... that you need not ..."

She is short of breath. Shakes her head impatiently. Pushes forwards. Says, "You need not assume I would be offended if you came into the room now, Master Chen."

There. Said. And the world has not broken asunder. No other animal has screamed outside. Burning suns are not falling, shot down by arrows of legend.

And she will not, she *will* not live defined or controlled by what others think or say. Because this is the life, the path, hard and lonely, her father has put her on—never realizing it would be so, never intending this when he began to teach her and they discovered, together, that she was quicker and brighter and perhaps even deeper than almost any man they knew.

But not more so than this one. He is looking at her with a different expression now. But has not stepped forward, and whatever she is, however bold she might force herself to be, she cannot cross to him. It is beyond her.

He says, unexpectedly, "You might make me weep, Miss Lin. Thinking of your life."

She blinks at that. "Not what I want to do."

"I know that." A faint smile. "The world is not going to allow you to be what you might be. You understand?"

She lifts her head. "It hasn't allowed you to be. Why should it let—"

"Not the same. You know it."

She does. Lowers her head.

"Nor need you challenge it with every breath, every encounter. You will break yourself, as if on rocks."

"You did. You challenged. You've never held back from saying when you thought ministers or even the emperor were—"

"Again, not the same. I have been allowed to find my view of the world, and give voice to it. There are risks to doing so, changing times make for changing fortunes, but it is still not the same as what lies ahead of you."

She feels chastened, and yet oddly reassured, sustained. He *sees* her. She makes herself meet his gaze. "Is this how you always respond when a woman offers you—"

A third time he stops her, a lifted hand this time. Not smiling. She is silent, waits.

He gives her (she will always remember it that way) a gift. "No woman, or man, has ever offered quite what you just have. I would destroy the gift by accepting it. It is necessary, for both of us, that I leave you now. Please believe I am honoured beyond words or deserving, and that I will be equally honoured to read your writing when you choose to send it to me."

Shan swallows hard. Hears him say, "You are now another reason why I intend to survive Lingzhou and return. I would like to watch you live your life."

"I don't ..." She is finding it difficult to speak. "I don't think I will be so much worth watching."

His smile, celebrated, harnessed to the intransigence of courage. "I think you will," says Lu Chen.

He bows to her. Does it twice. Walks from the room.

Closes the door quietly behind him.

She stands where she has been standing. She is aware of her breathing, the beating of her heart, is conscious of her body in a new way. She sees the lamp, the books, flowers, the bed.

One difficult breath. Her mouth a thin line of determination. She *will* not live the life others choose for her.

She crosses the room, opens the door.

The hallway is dark but the light from her room spills into it. He turns at the sound, a figure in the corridor, halfway along. She steps into the hallway. She looks at his dark shape in the shadows the world offers her (offers all of them). But there is light. Behind her in the room, and sometimes there may even be light ahead. He has stopped. She can see he has turned to look at her. There will be light for him to see her, where she stands.

"*Please?*" she says.

And extends a hand, holding it out towards the shape of a good man, in the darkness of a house that is not hers, and a world that is.

CHAPTER III

Military Officer Zhao Ziji, attached to a garrison in Hsiang Prefecture in the central rice lands south of the Great River, was sweating in hidden leather armour as his party walked through midsummer heat.

He wore a wide-brimmed merchant's hat and a rope-belted hemp tunic over loose trousers as a disguise. His throat was dry as a desert bone, and he was ferociously angry with the lazy incompetents he was shepherding north like so many lambs through dangerous country towards the river. He was unable, in fact, to think of many occasions when he had been less happy.

Perhaps as a boy, when his sisters had seen him urinating once and had begun making jokes about the size of his private parts. He had beaten them both for it, which was his right, but that never stopped mockery once it started, did it?

You had to go off when you were old enough and do something reckless: join the army in a district far from home, to get entirely away from such laughter and the nicknames based on it. Even then you could lie in your cot in a barracks and imagine someone from home arriving in the morning, joining your company, and greeting you with a cheerful "Hai, Ziji Shortcock!" thereby afflicting your life here, too.

It wasn't even *true*, for one thing. Not one singing girl had ever commented! Nor had any soldier, pissing beside him in a field or a latrine, raised an eyebrow, in any of the companies he'd served with or led. It had been utterly unfair for the girls to say such things about an eleven-year-old.

One of his sisters was dead, he'd wish or think no ill of her, for fear of rousing a ghost. The other was married to a man Ziji understood to be harsh with her when he drank, and had a mother-in-law with a sour disposition. He ought to feel sympathy. He didn't. You said certain things, damaged someone's life, and your own fate might take a different course because of it. Ziji believed that.

He also believed—indeed, he knew with certainty—that the hilly country through which they were now passing, carrying their prefect's birthday gift for Deputy Prime Minister Kai Zhen, and three nightingales in cages for the emperor's garden, was a place that just about *bred* outlaws.

The cages had been difficult to hide. They were in sacks, tied on the donkeys. He hoped the nightingales wouldn't die. It would be bad for him if they did.

He never stopped looking around as they went. He kept imagining bandits springing up, armed and wild, from the brown grass by the path, from behind hummocks, surging from copses of trees or the darker woods they passed.

He had twelve men, seven of them soldiers. They had disguised themselves and the treasure they carried. They were on foot, carrying travellers' packs, only six donkeys for the whole party's gear. They looked like lesser merchants who had banded together heading for the river, not affluent enough to be riding, not obviously worth robbing—but enough of them to dissuade bandits from doing something foolish. Outlaws liked easy targets, not real fighting.

On the other hand, Ziji wasn't certain his men would fight, if it came to that. He had begun, days ago, to regret having pushed himself forward as the man to lead the prefect's party this year. Of course it was an honour; of course if they got to Hanjin and were well received (or received at all) it would redound to the prefect's name—and Zhao Ziji's. This was how you rose in rank, wasn't it? Earned enough eventually to take a wife, have sons of your own.

Or, instead, how you got yourself killed in bandit country in a baked-out summer. Or endured angry muttering from those you were commanding (soldiers and civil servants, both) and were pushing through broiling heat towards the safety of a boat. Once on the water they could go downriver to the Grand Canal. Once on a canal flatboat they were, essentially, safe and in the capital.

But you had to get to the river first, and they were, Military Officer Zhao judged, still two nights away. This evening they should be able to reach a village he knew. Tomorrow was likely to require camping out, a fire, rotating guards. He was driving his party hard, but if he didn't it was going to be three nights, not two. Not a good idea.

In both the last two years, the deputy prime minister's birthday gifts from Hsiang Prefecture, where Kai Zhen had been posted for many years, had not reached illustrious Minister Kai, the honoured patron of the honourable prefect of Hsiang.

Ziji had been frightening his party with threats of tigers and bandits and a rumour of ghosts and fox-spirits lurking on this trail after dark. (He was afraid of fox-spirits himself.)

But some of their group were bureaucrats, not pleased about having been instructed by the prefect that they were to accept the command of a soldier all the way to Hanjin. Once there, the magistrate in the party would take control, but not until they were inside Hanjin's walls. There had been no ambiguity in the orders when they'd departed. Ziji had made it a condition of his volunteering for the task. (No one else had wanted it, not after the last two years.)

All of his party were wilting like spring flowers in summer drought. Well, he was suffering, too, Ziji thought. He wasn't urging them along in this harsh white sunlight for his pleasure. He'd have happily travelled by night, but the danger was overwhelming.

The moaning was constant. You'd have thought they'd be smart enough to save their energy. He had promised a midday rest, and it wasn't midday yet. On the other hand, he thought, smelling his own sweat, feeling how it had soaked his armour under the tunic, it was getting close to it, and there were all those tales of party leaders murdered by their men. After which the story was always given out by the ones who survived that the leader had been drunk, incompetent, disrespectful of his prefect or even the emperor. One or two or all of those things.

He'd heard those stories. He'd actually believed some of them in the past. He didn't any more.

"Rest stop on that rise ahead!" he suddenly called out.

His voice was a cracked croak. He cleared his throat and said it again. "There should be shade, and we can see both ways up there. We'll go double-quick when we start up again, though, to make the village for tonight. I am telling you all now!"

They were too exhausted to cheer. Or too angry with him. As of yesterday the magistrate had insisted on riding one of the donkeys. He was older, it didn't ruin their disguise, but he was the one the others kept approaching for low-voiced exchanges, with sidelong glances at Ziji. Did they think he couldn't see those looks?

On the whole, a rest was probably wise. It wouldn't do his career any good if he was murdered by his own party. Ho, he thought. A joke! His ghost could torment them, but that wouldn't help him much in the matter of a promotion and a wife one day.

He'd remembered rightly from three trips to the river: there was a level spot at the top of this rise. The upward slope was long, but the promise of rest carried them there.

From up here he could indeed see the dusty road both ways, north and south. There was a dense wood to the east and a smaller stand of oak trees on the west side of the roadway. Ziji sank down beneath one of those oaks, after guiding the donkeys into the shade. He liked animals, and he knew they were suffering.

He'd heard a wandering holy man, one of those from the high plateaus of Tagur (which had once been an empire, some said), preaching back home to a ragged crowd that if a man behaved badly in life he would return as an animal of some kind, to make amends for his errors. Young Ziji didn't exactly believe it, but he did recall the simple piety of that man in his dark-red robe, and he treated his animals as well as he could to this day. *They* didn't mumble and plot against you, he thought.

He remembered something. With an effort and a curse, he made himself get up and pull back the cloth from the three birdcages. The cages were made of beaten gold, studded with gems, far too valuable to be exposed, but there was no one up here to see, and the birds were at risk of dying under covers in this heat. They weren't going to sing, not in cages at midday.

Before going back to his tree past sprawled, exhausted men (some were already asleep, he saw) Ziji stepped into the road again, in the brutal sun, and looked both ways.

He swore viciously. The magistrate glared at him, in mid-swig from a water flask. The very refined magistrate of Hsiang Prefecture didn't like soldiers' language. *Well, fuck you with a shovel,* Zhao Ziji thought. *You don't like the way soldiers talk, you try getting yourself to the river without them!*

And without dealing with the imminent arrival of another party from along the road behind them. They hadn't been able to see them while on level ground. Up here they could. That was why a fucking *soldier* had waited until they'd reached this point to stop.

He rasped an order for one of his men to cover the cages. Those coming up to the long slope, openly, on a midday road, were almost certainly another party of merchants, but merchants could whisper of gilded, gem-covered nightingale cages as readily as anyone.

The other party showed a natural anxiety as they reached the point on the upward slant of the road where a dozen or so men could be seen sitting or lying among trees by the path.

Ziji had gone back to sitting against an oak. His short sword was hidden beneath his long, loose tunic. He was aware that the other soldiers in their party, unhappy as they were, were also disinclined to be killed, and would be alert. But then the magistrate stood up, officious and foolish, and sketched a bow that proclaimed, for anyone who knew enough to recognize it, that he was no humble merchant on the road.

"Greetings to your company. Have you any wine with you?" he asked.

Ziji winced, barely restrained himself from swearing.

"*None!*" exclaimed the leader of the other party. "None at all! We have nothing you might wish to steal! You would not kill men for water!"

"It has happened." The magistrate chuckled, thinking himself witty.

"There's a stream not far ahead!" cried one of the other party. "It hasn't dried up! You need not—"

"We mean you no harm," Ziji said from where he sat.

The other party, six men, country folk, were carrying their goods on their backs, not even a single donkey with them. Ziji added, "Take the other side of the road. There is shade enough for everyone. We'll be on our way soon."

"Going to the river?" the other leader asked, less anxious now. He was neatly shaven, older than Ziji, spoke roughly but not rudely. Ziji hesitated. He didn't want companions—it would be too easy for their deception to be revealed, and any talk of who they were or what they carried was dangerous.

"We are," said the magistrate officiously. He was irritated, clearly, that Ziji was the one addressed. "I believe it is two or three days from here," he added.

The other group had begun crossing to the far side of the road, into the shade there. Their leader lingered a moment, sweating, as they all were, his tunic blotchy. He spoke to Ziji again, not the magistrate. "We're not going so far. We've hemp clothing for the village up a bit and the silk farm by it."

Peasant clothes. They wouldn't get much for them, but in hard times you did what you could.

"*Those who spin silk wear hemp*," Ziji quoted.

The other man spat in the roadway. "Truth there," he said.

He crossed to join his own party. Ziji saw his soldiers watching them closely. He was pleased with that. Fear of death could make a man sharper, even when he was dulled by heat and weariness.

A little later, as Ziji was beginning to think of rousing his party and carrying on, they saw the next figure approaching along the slope.

This one was alone. A young man under a rice farmer's straw hat, shirtless in the burning sun, carrying two large, covered buckets, one at each end of a pole across the back of his exposed neck. Despite the weight he strode steadily uphill with the vigour of youth.

Being alone, he was an obvious target. On the other hand, he clearly had nothing worth taking, and bandits tended not to disrupt the peasants, lest the villagers turn against them and help the militia. For the most part, officers of the law were more hated in these days of taxes and conscription for the war in the northwest than those who preyed on merchants and travellers.

Ziji didn't stand up. He realized, however, that his mouth had begun to water at the sight of those buckets.

"You have wine to sell?" cried one of his own soldiers, rashly.

"Not to us he doesn't!" Ziji rasped.

There were old tricks on the road, and he knew enough of them.

"I do not," said the young man loudly as he crested the hill. "These are for the silk farm. I do this every day, they pay us five cash for each bucket."

"We will save you the walk, however far it is. We'll give you ten cash right here," said the magistrate eagerly. He was on his feet.

"We will not!" said Zhao Ziji.

He also stood up. It was difficult, what he was doing. He could almost taste that wine, the sweetness of it.

"Never matters what you will or what you won't," the shirtless peasant said stubbornly. "They are expecting me at Risheng's and they pay me. I give these to you I lose their business and my father beats me for it."

Ziji nodded his head. "Understood. Carry on, lad. Good fortune to you."

"Wait!"

It was the other party's leader, emerging from the trees across the road. "We will give you fifteen cash for one bucket. You carry the other to the silk farm and give it to them for free. You come out ahead, they get a bucket of wine for nothing. Everyone is happy!"

"We aren't!" cried the magistrate loudly. Ziji's men were muttering.

The boy with the wine hesitated as the leader of the other merchants came up to him. Fifteen cash was a great deal to pay for a bucket of country wine, and his load would be lightened for the rest of a very hot day. Ziji saw him wrestle with this.

"I don't have a ladle," the boy said.

The merchant laughed. "We have ladles, that's no matter. Come, take my money, pour us wine. Divide what's left in the two buckets and ease your walk. It's going to be hotter this afternoon."

That was true. And the right thing to say, Ziji thought. He was dying for a drink, but he didn't want to die drinking it, and he knew too many stories.

"We'll give you twenty cash!" the magistrate cried.

"*We will not!*" Ziji snapped. This was overriding his authority and he couldn't allow it. "We aren't buying." Broke his heart, almost, to say the words.

"These offered first, anyhow," the young man said (he wasn't a merchant, clearly). He turned to the others. "Right, then. Fifteen cash in my palm and you get one bucket."

It was done quickly. The other merchants came out from the trees as their leader counted coins for the wine seller. Ziji was aware of two things. Extreme thirst, and hatred coming at him like a second blast of heat from his own party.

The other merchants unhooked a bucket from the pole, removed the lid right in the road, which was foolish, Ziji thought. They began taking turns with a long-handled ladle. With the bucket's cover off, you could smell the sweet, pale wine. Or maybe that was his imagination.

With six men drinking quickly (too quickly, Ziji thought, on a hot day) it was finished in no time. The last man raised the bucket with two hands and tilted it to his face. Ziji saw wine dribble down his chin. They didn't even pour an offering for the spirits of this place.

Ziji wasn't happy with any of this. Being a leader wasn't always as pleasurable as it was thought to be, he decided.

Then, as the wine seller carefully counted again the coins he'd been given, Ziji saw one of the men from the other merchant party slip behind the seller and, laughing, remove the top of the second bucket. "Five cash for five scoops!" he cried, and dipped the ladle.

"*No!*" the boy cried. "That isn't what we said!"

The laughing merchant picked up the heavy, now-open bucket and ran awkwardly with it towards the woods. Some wine sloshed out, Ziji saw wistfully. "Give him ten coins!" the man yelled over his shoulder. "More than he deserves!"

"No!" the wine seller shouted again. "You are cheating me! I'll have my family watch for you on the way back!"

That was a real threat, Ziji thought. Who knew how many were in his family, how many friends they'd have, and these merchants would have to head home this way. Indeed, they were going to the same silk farm the wine seller was. The man running with the bucket had made a mistake.

"Bring it back!" their leader cried, obviously coming to the same conclusion. "We won't cheat him."

We won't risk cheating him, was more like it, Ziji thought sourly. He noticed the running-away fellow take a quick drink from the second bucket. Now he reluctantly brought it back from the shade of the woods—where they should have been drinking, slowly and out of the sun, all along.

"Just one more scoop!" he said, dipping his ladle again.

"No!" cried the boy again, rushing up and slapping the ladle from the man's hand. It fell into the wine; he pulled it out and threw it angrily away.

"Leave him alone," said the leader. "We are honest men, and I don't want a party lying in wait when we come home tomorrow!"

There was a short silence.

"Twenty-five cash for what's left of that bucket!" Ziji's magistrate cried suddenly. "I have it in my hand!"

The boy turned to him. It was a ridiculous sum. It marked them as carrying more money than was safe, if they could be this extravagant.

But Ziji was really very thirsty now and he had noticed something. It had been possible the second bucket was poisoned, the first one being a ruse, kept clean. But a man had just drunk from it and was standing in front of them, laughing, pleased with himself.

"Yes, we'll give you that," Ziji said, making a decision.

He didn't want his own men killing him, and he really wanted a scoop or two of wine. He added, "And tomorrow you can carry two buckets to the silk farm and offer them for nothing instead of ten cash. They'll forgive you, and you know it. And you get to turn back right now and go home."

The boy stared at him. Then he nodded. "All right. For twenty-five. Cash first."

Ziji's men let out a cheer. First happy sound all day, he thought. The magistrate hastily reached inside his robe and counted out coins (showing too heavy a purse in the process). The others all stood up and were watching as he dropped the money into the wine seller's palm.

"Bucket's yours," the boy said. "Well, the wine is. I need the bucket."

One of Ziji's soldiers picked it up and, showing more good sense than the other merchants had, carried it to their shade. Another rushed for two ladles from the gear on one of the donkeys. They crowded around the bucket.

With a leader's almost inhuman restraint, Ziji stayed where he was. "Save me two scoops at the end," he called. He wondered if that would earn him any goodwill.

He wondered if they'd save him the two scoops.

The other party retreated across the roadway, chattering loudly and laughing—there had been an adventure here, and they'd drunk wine very fast. They would probably sleep now, Ziji thought.

The wine seller moved away from both groups and found some shade, waiting for his bucket. His day had just been made easy. He could turn around and go home.

Ziji watched his men around the wine, drinking too quickly. The magistrate, predictably, had just taken a third scoop. No one was going to gainsay him. Except Ziji, perhaps. Reluctantly, he stood up. He'd have been happier if they'd done it properly and carried the bucket over to their leader with the two last scoops.

He sighed. Things were seldom done properly these days. It was a sad world in which they lived. He glanced across the road to the woods on the other side.

All six merchants were walking into the roadway. Three carried swords. Two held their walking staffs as weapons now. The wine seller rose to his feet. He crossed towards the other merchants, not hurrying. One of them handed him a short bow and a quiver of arrows. The man was smiling.

Ziji opened his mouth and shouted a warning.

In that same moment the magistrate toppled heavily into the grass. An instant later another of Ziji's men did the same. Then a third.

In an alarmingly short interval they were all sprawled on the ground, as if drugged. Of course drugged, Zhao Ziji thought. He was facing seven men alone.

"This isn't worth dying for," said the young wine seller gently.

He seemed to have taken the lead here, improbably. His bow was trained on Ziji. He added, "Although, if you insist, or feel there is no reason to go on living, I will kill you."

"How ... ?" Ziji stammered.

"With an arrow!" The clean-shaven man who had appeared to lead the merchants laughed.

"No, Fang. He means how was it done. He is a thinking soldier. Some of them are." The shirtless wine seller's manner had changed. He didn't seem so young any more.

Ziji looked at them. He'd had none of the wine but felt light-headed, dizzy with fear and dismay.

The young one said, "Two ladles. Shanbao powder in the second one when Lao brought the bucket back and dipped it but I didn't let him drink. Remember?"

Ziji remembered.

He said, "How ... how did you know?"

The wine seller—who wasn't really a wine seller—shook his head impatiently.

"Really? There's a party from Hsiang on this road every summer, heading for the capital. Kai Zhen's gifts. You don't think country people are smart enough to realize that? That they might let us know when you set out, how many, how you are dressed? For a small share of what we take? And to get at the minister who created the Flowers and Rocks program that is killing people and destroying the countryside to build a garden in Hanjin?"

So much for disguises, Ziji thought. He tried to think of a threat that would mean anything to these men. He took a moment, but nothing came to him.

"You might as well kill me," he said.

The men in the road grew quiet. They hadn't expected that. "Truly?" said the wine seller.

Ziji nodded towards the magistrate. "I assume they are drugged, not dying? That one will blame me when he wakes up. The prefect will believe him. He's a ranking civil servant. I'm just—"

"A soldier," said the young man. He looked thoughtful now. "He doesn't have to wake up."

He swung his bow over and trained an arrow on the magistrate in the grass.

Ziji shook his head. "Don't. He did nothing wrong. This was my error. We don't drink that wine, you wouldn't have attacked twelve with seven."

"Yes, we would," the man with the bow said. "Half of you dead with arrows before we'd fight, and that half would all be soldiers. The others are useless and you know it. Tell me, do you want him dead?"

Ziji shook his head. "It does nothing for me, and he's only greedy, not evil."

"They're all evil," said one of the outlaws. He spat. The wine seller said nothing.

"Besides," Ziji added, "any of them will tell the same story, and it was my job to stop them from drinking that wine."

"We can kill them all." Not the wine seller, one of the others.

"No," said Ziji. "Just me. My price to pay. I might be executed if I go back, anyhow. May I have a moment to pray?"

The wine seller had an odd expression on his face. He looked young again. He *was* young. "We don't need to kill you," he said. "Join us."

Ziji stared.

"Think about it," the young one went on. "If you are right, you have no future in that prefecture, or in the army, and you may be executed. There's at least a life with us."

"I don't like it," said one of the others.

"Why?" said the young one, his eyes still on Ziji. "This is how I joined you, back when. And how did you come to be one of the Marsh Outlaws, Kui? Wandering through villages asking for honest work?"

There was laughter.

At least he knew who these were now, Ziji thought. The Outlaws of the Marsh were the largest bandit group in Kitai south of the Great River. Every year there were urgent requests to Hanjin to send an army to deal with them. Every year these were ignored. There was a war being fought: the southern prefectures were expected to deal with local bandits themselves.

It was all true, Ziji thought: he had no life left at the barracks. Either because he'd be executed, or beaten and jailed by an enraged prefect, or simply because he'd never be promoted now. He'd probably be sent to the war.

He said that. "I could go fight the Kislik."

The other man nodded. "They'll likely send you there. They need soldiers. You did hear about the disaster?"

Everyone had heard. It wasn't a new story. A deep thrust ordered north through the desert, aimed at Erighaya, horses and foot soldiers, far into enemy lands, then halted outside the walled Kislik city because—amazingly—they hadn't brought siege engines. They'd forgotten them. No one had checked. It was madness, an utterly improbable tale, and it was true.

What sort of army could do that? Ziji had wondered when the

news reached their barracks. Kitai had ruled and subjugated the whole world once. Rulers from all over had sent them gifts, horses, women, slaves.

Their northwestern army's supply lines had been severed behind them. Over half their soldiers had died on the retreat from Erighaya. Almost seventy thousand men, Ziji had heard. A terrifying number. They had killed their commanders on the way south, it was reported. Eaten them, some said. Starving men in a desert, far from home.

And Deputy Prime Minister Kai Zhen, in overall command of that campaign, was receiving birthday gifts from all over Kitai, timed to arrive at court this autumn.

"Don't go back," said the young man with the bow. "We can use good men. The emperor needs to be made aware his servants and policies are evil and incompetent."

Zhao Ziji looked at him. A life, he thought, could change quickly. It could turn like a water wheel on some isolated hilltop in summer heat.

"That's what you are doing?" he said, perhaps too wryly for someone facing an arrow. "Sending memoranda to the emperor?"

"Some go into the woods for money. Food. Some for a life of freedom. Some like to kill. I'm ... some of us are also trying to say something, yes. Enough voices, we might be heard."

Ziji looked at him.

"What is your name?" He wasn't sure why he asked.

"Ren Daiyan," said the other, promptly. "They call me Little Dai."

"You aren't so little."

The other man grinned. "I was young when I started, west of here. And besides, I have a small cock."

The others burst into laughter. Ziji blinked. A strange sensation came over him.

"Is that so?" he said.

"Of course not!" one of the outlaws cried. Someone made a loud, crude jest, the kind Ziji knew from soldiers in barracks too long without women.

Something altered inside him, as if a key had turned in a lock. "I'm Zhao Ziji," he said. And, for the first time in his life, added, "They call me Ziji Shortcock."

"Truly? Ho! We were born to be companions then!" cried the man named Ren Daiyan. "*To seek women and wine and live forever!*" Words from a very old song.

In the laughter that followed, Zhao Ziji stepped into the roadway and became an outlaw.

He felt, astonishingly, as if he were coming home. He looked at the young man—Ren Daiyan was surely ten years younger than him—and knew, in that same moment, that he would follow this man all his life, until one or the other or both of them died.

CHAPTER IV

She has made herself wait before trying again, striving for inner harmony, sitting very still at her writing desk. The first three attempts at the letter have been unsatisfactory. She is aware that tension, fear, the importance of what she is writing are affecting her brush.

That must not be permitted. She breathes deeply, eyes on a lotus tree she's always liked in the courtyard. It is very early morning, autumn. Outside her window the compound is quiet, even with the extreme crowding in the space assigned the imperial family members.

She is alone in their house. Her husband is away, north, in search of steles to buy or transcribe, bronzes, artifacts for their collection. It is a collection now; they are becoming known for it.

Qi Wai is travelling near the border again, towards the lands possessed (for a long time now) by the Xiaolu. It ought to be all right. They are at peace—a peace they buy each year. Her husband's father has told them that most of their silver comes back in trade at the authorized border trading towns. He approves of the payments, though if he did not he wouldn't say so. Members of the imperial family live watched, careful lives.

In dealings with the Xiaolu, the Kitan emperor is still the "uncle," the emperor of the Xiaolu is his "nephew." The uncle kindly gives "gifts" to the nephew. It is a fiction, a courtly lie, but lies can be important in the world, Lin Shan has come to understand.

The world is a terrible place.

She chides herself, inwardly. Bitter thoughts will not bring calm. She ruined her first attempt at the letter not only with an anxious brush but with a tear that fell on the page, making the strokes for the word *councillor* blur and run.

On the desk are the Four Treasures of the Room of Literature: ink stone, ink stick, paper, brushes. Her husband brought her back a red ink stone, offered it as a gift at the New Year's Festival. It is beautiful, old, Fourth Dynasty, he thinks.

For this letter, though, she is using her own first ink stone, from childhood. The one her father gave her. There might be, she thinks, some magic residing in it, a spiritual power to make the ink it grinds more persuasive.

She needs it to be, or her heart will break.

She takes up her stick again, pours water from the beaker into the ink stone's hollow. Gestures she has performed all her life, rituals by now. She grinds the black ink stick into the stone, using her left hand as she has been taught (by her father).

She knows exactly what she wants to say in this letter, how many characters, how much ink she needs. You always grind a little more than you need, she has been taught (by her father). If you are forced to grind again, in order to finish, the texture at the end of your writing will be different from the beginning, a flaw.

She sets the ink stick down. Lifts the brush in her right hand. Dips it in the ink. She is using the rabbit's-hair brush for this letter: it makes the most precise characters. Sheep's hair is more bold, but though she needs the letter to seem confident of its virtue, it is still a plea.

She sits as she must sit. She adopts the Pillowed-Wrist Position, left hand under right wrist, supporting it. Her characters are to be small, exact, not large and assertive (for which she'd have used Raised-Wrist Position). The letter will be in formal hand. Of course it will.

A writer's brush is a warrior's bow, the letters it shapes are arrows that must hit the mark on the page. The calligrapher is an archer, or a general on a battlefield. Someone wrote that long ago. She feels that way this morning. She is at war.

Her brush is directly above the paper, vertical. Each finger plays a part. Her grip is firm; the strength of arm and wrist must be controlled and sure.

Controlled and sure. It is imperative that she not weep. She looks out the window again. A single servant has appeared, is sweeping the courtyard in morning light. Another brush, a broom.

She begins.

ιℓℵσ

His eyesight had become the important difficulty. He didn't sleep easily these nights, and he didn't walk as he used to, but what old man did? Too much wine gave him headaches, beginning while he drank, not even waiting politely for morning. Such sad things were part of what time did to men when the hair turned white and the sword arm failed, as a poet had written.

The prime minister of Kitai had never had a sword arm. The very idea was, briefly, amusing. And senior court officials didn't walk very much (or at all) within the palace or outside it. He had a cushioned, covered, ornately gilded chair and bearers to carry him where he needed to go.

And he could destroy people without touching a blade.

No, the infirmity that mattered was his sight. It was reading letters, tax records, prefectural documents, memoranda, reports from informants that had become a challenge. There was a cloudiness at the edge of each eye now, creeping inwards like mist over water, approaching the land. You could make that image a symbol for a poem, but only if you wanted to let others know this was happening, and he didn't. It wasn't safe.

His son helped him. Hsien seldom left his side, and they had tricks to conceal his trouble. It was important at this court not to be seen as so aged and frail one couldn't even read the morning's civil service documents.

He half believed that some of those who'd be happier if he was gone had taken to using deliberately small calligraphy, to show up his difficulty. It would be clever if they were doing that, the sort of thing he might have done himself once. He lived under few illusions. Emperors were capricious, unstable. Power was not a dependable condition.

Hang Dejin, still prime minister to the sage and illustrious Emperor Wenzong, often thought of retiring.

He had asked the emperor for permission to do so many times over the years, but those had been ploys, a public stand in the face of opposition at court. *If the emperor in his wisdom thinks his servant is misguided, I beg leave to withdraw in shame.*

He'd have been shocked if any of those requests had been accepted.

Lately, he had begun to wonder what would happen if he offered again. Times changed, men changed. The long Kislik war was going badly. The emperor still didn't know the extent of that. If and when he learned, there could—there *would*—be consequences. That needed managing. It could be done, there were ways, but Dejin knew he wasn't the man he had been even three years ago.

If blame for the fighting fell to him—and it could—that would almost certainly mean disgrace and departure (or worse).

In that case, the deputy prime minister, Kai Zhen, would surely succeed him. And would dominate Kitai, given an emperor with a preference for painting, calligraphy (his own was widely seen as the most elegant in the world), and the extravagant garden he was building north and east of this palace.

The garden (the Genyue), and the Flowers and Rocks Network to supply it, had been Kai Zhen's idea. A brilliant one, in so many ways. Dejin had approved of it originally, and reaped the benefit of the emperor's distraction for some time. There might now be a price to be paid.

The question was, who would do the paying?

Deputy Minister Kai probably believed he was ruling now, Dejin thought wryly. After all, there was only an old, almost-blind man between him and the emperor, and though Zhen might speak of honouring his superior for initiating the reform policies, there was little doubt in Hang Dejin's mind that the younger man saw the older one as weak now, trammelled in old ways of doing things.

Old ways, such as restraint, courtesy, respect, Dejin thought, still wryly. He had grown wealthy in power, accustomed to his stature and to being feared, but he hadn't sought rank with the *intent* of acquiring wealth.

He had seen his differences with Xi Wengao and the other conservatives as a battle for what Kitai should be, needed to be, for the good of the empire and its people. It was a pious, self-indulgent thought, and he was aware of that, but it was also, Hang Dejin told himself, *true*.

He shook his head. His son glanced at him, a blurred, moving shape, then turned back to his own pile of documents. Bitterness wasn't a useful state of mind, Dejin reminded himself. You made mistakes if that was what drove you. You spoke without proper contemplation words you could be made to regret. He had often provoked such rashness in rivals. He knew how to make use of anger, passion, outrage in others.

The light was good in their working room today, here on the western side of the palace's main courtyard. Back in the Ninth Dynasty, in Xinan before it fell to ruins, the civil servants had had an entire palace building to themselves: the Purple Myrtle Court.

Here in Hanjin, splendid as it was, there simply wasn't enough space for that. Space was part of what they'd lost all through the empire, and not just in a crowded capital. They'd lost land in the north, in the northwest, lost the protection of the Long Wall, lost tribute, lost access to (control of!) the trade routes to the west and the wealth they'd brought, year over year.

Hanjin had more than a million souls living within or beside its walls—in an area only a fraction of what Xinan had enclosed three hundred years ago.

If you went to the ruins of the old capital, walked in through smashed gates, stood among weeds and grass and broken stone, heard the calling of birds or saw animals loping along the vastness of what had once been the imperial way, almost five hundred paces wide ... you could be forgiven for thinking that Hanjin's main thoroughfare, running from this palace to the southern gates was ...

Well, it was eighty paces across, to be precise.

He'd had it measured, not long after arriving at court, all those years ago. Eighty paces was a very wide street, entirely suitable for processions and festivals. But it wasn't Xinan, was it?

And Kitai wasn't what Kitai had been.

What of it? he'd thought then, and still thought, most of the time. Were they to bow their heads in shame because of what had happened centuries before any of them were born? Tear out what was left of greying hair? Surrender to the barbarians? Give their women to them? Their children as slaves?

The prime minister grunted in dismissal of such a thought. The world came to you as it came, you dealt with what you had.

He saw his son lift his head again from the papers he was

working through. Dejin made a gesture: nothing of importance, he signalled to Hsien, carry on.

There were two communications on his own desk. They had been handed to him by his son without comment. He had read them both in the good light. Excellent calligraphy in each case, one familiar (and celebrated), the other new to him.

The letters were a part of what had made him bitter and nostalgic on a bright morning in autumn. Autumn was a good season in Hanjin, summer's heat and the yellow dust receding, winter winds not yet come. The plum trees flowering late. A bright string of festivals ahead. He wasn't a man for watching street dancing or revellers carrying coloured lanterns but he liked his wine as well as the next person, and he enjoyed festival food, though he needed to be careful what he ate and drank now.

The letters were addressed to him personally, one written in the voice of long—if difficult—acquaintance, the other with extreme deference and formality. Both were supplications in the same matter. They made him angry with what they revealed, since it was new to him and should not have been.

It wasn't as if the fate of every single member of the opposing faction needed to be reviewed by the prime minister of Kitai. There were far too many of them, he had more important tasks and burdens.

He had set in motion, himself, the process of disgracing and exiling the ousted faction over twenty-five years ago, without doubting himself for a moment. There had been carved steles, copied from the new young emperor's own hand, his exquisite Slender Gold calligraphy, naming the banished. The steles had been placed in front of every prefectural *yamen* in the empire. Eighty-seven names the first time, one hundred and twenty-nine a year later. He remembered the numbers. Those names he had reviewed himself, or selected.

The empire, the court, the world under heaven had needed clarity and direction after a turbulent time. Though there might once have been merit to cacophony at court, the back and forth of factions in favour and out, Hang Dejin had been sure of his virtue and the wisdom of his policies. He'd regarded those who disagreed with him as not just wrong, but dangerous—destructive of peace and order and the changes Kitai required.

The empire needed these men silenced and gone.

Besides, they had started it! The conservatives had been in power between the last emperor's death and the coming of age of the current one, in the years when the dowager empress reigned. They had reversed everything and initiated the exiling of Hang Dejin's New Policies faction.

Dejin had spent several years writing poetry and letters from his country estate near Yenling, banned from court, power, influence. He'd remained wealthy (power brought wealth, it was a law of nature), never tasted again the hardship he'd left behind when he'd passed the *jinshi* examinations, but he'd been very far from the corridors of the palace.

Then Emperor Wenzong took the throne. Wenzong had summoned back to court the sage, Hang Dejin, who had been his tutor. Restored as prime minister, Dejin had extended to the conservatives the fate they'd imposed on him and his own people. Some of those he exiled were men he had admired, even in their battles. You couldn't let that guide you, not with so much at stake.

They were sent away. Across rivers, over mountains. Sometimes they died. Reform would always have opponents, men clinging fiercely to the old ways, whether out of genuine belief or because those old ways had made their family fortunes.

It didn't matter which. That was what he'd come to understand. When you were reshaping an empire you couldn't be looking over your shoulder for intrigue, cunning opposition, worrying if a tail-star seen one spring or summer might send a panicky emperor hurrying to perform appeasing rituals—and straight back to the old ways.

You needed a cleared field before you and no danger behind. Comets had put him out of power twice in his early years, once under the late emperor, once with Wenzong. Being unpredictable was the prerogative of those who sat the Dragon Throne. Their loyal advisers needed to limit the consequences.

That was why Kai Zhen's idea of an imperial garden had been so brilliant. Dejin had allocated considerable funds and resources to the newly created Flowers and Rocks Network. Not enough, in the event, not nearly enough. The sums grew. The Genyue had taken on a life of its own. All gardens did that, but ...

The human labour required throughout the empire and the level of taxation demanded had begun to be overwhelming. And with the emperor enraptured by the Genyue, it was too late to stop or scale back, despite rebellion stirring in the south and west and growing outlaw bands in forests and marshes.

The emperor knew what he wanted for his garden, and you couldn't tell an emperor he wasn't going to get it. He wanted Szechen nightingales, for example, hundreds of them. Boys and men went hunting there, stripping the forests of songbirds. Wenzong wanted a mountain brought, as a symbol of the Five Holy Mountains. He wanted cedarwood and sandalwood from the south, a bridge, entirely of gold, leading to an island with pavilions of marble and onyx and rosewood, set in an artificial lake. He wanted trees on the island made of silver, among the real ones.

Sometimes you set events in motion, like a river, and if it flooded, or grew engorged ...

It was possible that some of what he'd done or permitted through the years had been less than perfectly judged and implemented. What man alive (or ever living) would claim perfection?

The prime minister of Kitai adjusted his black, fur-trimmed robe. There was a breeze coming through the window and he caught a chill too easily these days.

For diversion he had tried, not long ago, to think of a good thing about growing old. He'd thought he might write (or dictate) an essay about it. The best he'd been able to come up with was that you might be less at the mercy of the desires of your body.

No one would send a woman to seduce him from his purposes now. Not any more. He read the second letter again, on that thought.

Then he summoned his bearers and went looking for the emperor.

THE EMPEROR OF KITAI was walking in his garden.

It pleased him to do this on any day that was fair, and this one was, a mild morning in autumn, approaching the Ninth of Ninth Festival. The emperor knew there were some among his court who felt he should never walk out of doors. He found them deficient in proper understanding. How could one appreciate, and amend, the paths and byways and the vistas of a garden if one did not walk them oneself?

Although, to call where he strolled a "garden" was to stretch the word almost out of recognition. The enclosed space here was so extravagant, yet so cunningly landscaped, that it was impossible, unless one went right to the walled edges, to know where it ended.

Even at the margins, trees had been densely planted to obscure where the Hanjin city wall began. The palace guard patrolled outside, where the garden's gates led into the city, or to the palace and its courtyards to the west. You couldn't see them from within the Genyue.

It was a world he was making here. Hills and lakes shaped to careful design (and then reshaped, whatever the cost, after consulting geomancers). Spiralling paths up mountains that had been raised for him, with waterfalls that could be activated at his desire. There were gazebos and pavilions hidden deep in groves for summer coolness, or situated where sunlight might fall on an autumn or spring day. Each of these was provided with the tools of painting or writing. The emperor might be moved to take up his brush at any moment.

There was also a new magnificence, a central, defining object now in the Genyue. A rock so wide and high (the height of fifteen tall soldiers!), so magnificently pitted and scarred (it had been brought up from a lake, the emperor understood, he had no idea how) that it could truly be said to constitute an image of one of the Five Holy Mountains. A young sub-prefect posted nearby had learned of it—and made his fortune by alerting the administrators of the Flowers and Rocks Network.

It had taken, apparently, a year to claim it from the depths and bring it to Hanjin, overland and then along the Great River and canal. The emperor imagined there must have been some degree of labour and expense involved with something so massive. He didn't attend to such details, of course.

He had been *very* attentive as to where the colossal mountain-rock was situated once it arrived. There had been, he understood, some unfortunate deaths in the Genyue itself during the process of moving it into the precisely proper spot. He had first wanted it to surmount and emerge from a hill (a hill they'd made), for greatest effect, but then it had to be shifted after consultation with his geomancers of the Arcane Path and learning their calculations as to auspices.

He probably ought to have consulted them before the first positioning. Ah, well. Decisions in the garden were so complex. He was trying to mirror Kitai, after all, provide a spiritual centre for his realm, ground it securely in the goodwill of heaven. That was part of an emperor's duty to his people, after all.

But now ... now it was where he needed it. He sat in one of his pavilions, this one mostly of ivory, with green jade inlays, and he looked up at his mighty rock with a glad heart.

The Emperor Wenzong was famously compassionate: word of those labourers' deaths—right here in his garden—had grieved him. He wasn't supposed to have learned about them, he knew. His advisers were zealous in protecting him from sorrows that might burden the too-generous imperial heart. The Genyue was meant to be a place of calm for him, a refuge from the cares the world brought to those burdened with responsibility.

In his famed calligraphy style, Slender Gold, the emperor had recently devised a clever way of shaping the thirteen brush strokes of the word *garden* to suggest something beyond what was ordinarily meant, when referring to his own garden.

It was a measure of imperial subtlety, one of his closest advisers had said, that the august emperor had done this, instead of devising or demanding an entirely new word for what was being built here under his wise and benevolent eye.

Kai Zhen, the deputy prime minister, was quite astute in his observations, Emperor Wenzong felt. It had been Minister Kai, of course, along with the eunuch Wu Tong (most recently commanding the Pacification Army against the Kislik in the northwest) who had devised the Flowers and Rocks Network which had allowed the shaping of this garden. The emperor was not a man to forget such loyalty.

There were even nightingales here, you heard them in the evenings. Some had, sadly, died last winter. They were going to try to keep them alive, indoors, this winter, and Minister Kai had assured him that more were on their way even now from warmer climes to grace his groves with their music of the south.

A fine phrase, the emperor had thought.

Prime Minister Hang Dejin, his childhood tutor, his father's and his own long-time adviser, was growing old. A melancholy, autumnal reflection. Another sorrow for the imperial heart. But it was also the way of life under heaven, as the Cho Master had taught them all. What man could avoid his end?

Well, there *were* ways to try. The emperor was following in another imperial tradition, taking a sequence of elixirs prepared for him each day by his occult masters of the Arcane Path. Kai Zhen had frequently and eloquently expressed his hope that these might prove efficacious.

There had also been sessions by candlelight wherein the leader of these same clerics (Kai Zhen had introduced him to the palace) invoked the spirit of Wenzong's revered father to pronounce his approval of measures being undertaken for the governance of the realm, including the Genyue and the new music being devised for the performance of imperial rites.

Tuning the ritual instruments in a manner derived from the measured lengths of the middle, ring, and little fingers of the emperor's left hand had been, the spirit of his father declared, a celestially harmonious idea.

Emperor Wenzong had taken this deeply to heart. He remembered being near to tears that night.

His own talents were not, truthfully, those of a man inclined to weigh matters of taxation and village administration, whether the army was made up of hired soldiers or a rural militia, how leaders were chosen in the countryside, or loans arranged for farmers—and repayment enforced.

He did pay attention to the examination questions for *jinshi* candidates, had even devised some of these himself. And he enjoyed presiding over the final testing days in his yellow robes of ceremony.

He'd been a painter and a calligrapher, from early in life. Noted for both, exalted for both, well before he'd taken the throne. He knew what he was, hadn't ever pretended to be otherwise. He had wanted the Dragon Throne because it was *there*, and properly his, but his passions lay in another realm.

He had certainly done his duty as emperor. He'd fathered sons (many of them) and had them taught the ways of the Path and the Cho Master. He satisfied the imperial women, one each morning, two at night, according to the sequence presented to him by the Inner Quarters Registrar, dutifully denying himself a climax except (upon being advised) with the most innocent and youthful of his women. In this way, according to his arcane advisers, the female essence of his wives and concubines would bolster his essence, not drain it away.

This, too, was a burden and responsibility. His strength was the strength of Kitai. His virtue was the virtue of an empire.

He performed all the imperial rites, faithfully.

He'd returned to his father's course of governance, after the unfortunate period when his mother ruled. Because it had been his father's dream (as explained to him), he'd initiated war against the ungrateful Kislik in the northwest—and he did ask about it now and again. But it was important for an emperor to have trustworthy and diligent advisers so the imperial spirit could be allowed to flower and flourish ... in the great garden of the world under nine heavens. Beyond all his duties, the emperor's well-being, the soaring of his spirit, affected the well-being, the spirit of all Kitai.

Kai Zhen had put it that way just a few days ago in this very pavilion, which was Wenzong's favourite now, with its view of the new rock-mountain.

The emperor intended to make Minister Kai a gift: a small painting he'd made here, a springtime landscape with flowering bamboo, an oriole, blue hills. The deputy prime minister had admired it, eloquently.

The emperor's paintings were the most desired gift in Kitai.

It was a great shame, they had agreed, looking at it together, that Prime Minister Hang would not be able to see the details clearly any more. He was suffering the afflictions of age, Kai Zhen had suggested, in much the way autumn and winter succeed a brilliant spring. A garden like the Genyue could teach lessons like that.

This garden was—everyone said it—the heart-stopping wonder of the world. It was a mirror of Kitai in miniature, which was its purpose. Just as the emperor's well-being and right behaviour were integral to preserving the mandate of heaven, so, too, it had been decided by his advisers, would an imperial garden designed to encompass the scope and balance of Kitai act to *preserve* that scope and balance.

It made so much sense.

His passion for this stupendous accomplishment wasn't an affectation, an avoiding of tasks and cares. No. His labours here, his personal instructions to landscapers and architects, were at the heart—the very heart—of his duty to his people!

So the emperor of Kitai thought, sitting in an autumn pavilion in the sunlight of morning, with a view of his new mountain. He was contemplating making a painting, at ease in heart and mind, when he heard a strange sound from along the path where a gardener had moved out of sight sweeping leaves. The emperor looked at his guards. They stared straight ahead, expressionless. He heard the sound again.

The gardener was, if the emperor was not mistaken, crying.

PRIME MINISTER HANG DEJIN found the emperor, as expected, in the pavilion before the mountain. What he saw, however, was unexpected in the extreme. He thought, at first, that his weakened eyes were failing him again, but when he stepped carefully from his chair onto the groomed path, he realized they were not.

The emperor was standing at the edge of his pavilion. He was not writing, or painting, or gazing at his rock-mountain. He was looking down at a man prostrate on the path below him.

The man on the ground was trembling with terror. Given that he was—very obviously—a simple palace gardener (his rake lay beside him) in the actual, immediate presence of the emperor of Kitai, that fear was readily understood. The imperial guards had edged close. All were motionless, hands to swords, faces like stone warriors.

The emperor's face was also cold, Dejin saw as he came near enough. It was not a customary expression for Wenzong. He could be demanding or inattentive, but seldom appeared angry. He did now.

Later, Hang Dejin would be caused to think (and even write a letter to an old friend) about how accidents of timing could have so great an impact on the way the world unfolded. You could decide this was the working of heaven, that such moments were not accidents at all, or you could see them as indicators of the limits placed by the gods on what mortal men could control, even if they were wise.

Dejin took the second view.

Had he not come looking for the emperor this morning with two letters in his robe, had the deputy prime minister been with Wenzong when the gardener was summoned into the imperial presence, significant matters would have proceeded otherwise than they did. He wrote that in his letter.

He made a formal obeisance. Emperor Wenzong had graciously stipulated that his senior councillors need not observe full court protocol when they were with him in his garden, but instinct suggested to Hang Dejin that this was a moment of importance and he offered all three prostrations. His mind was working quickly, however stiff his body was. He did not understand what had happened here and he needed to do so.

"Principal Councillor," the emperor said, "we are pleased to see you. We would have sent for you to come to us. Approach." Very formal, including the old title. There were meanings in everything, for those who knew how to find them.

"I am honoured to anticipate the emperor's desire," Dejin said, rising and coming forward. "Has something disturbed imperial tranquility?"

Of course something had, but it needed to be asked, to elicit a response—and a chance to sort this out.

"This man, this ... gardener has done so," Wenzong said.

Dejin could see the emperor's agitation, a hand moving up and down an ivory column, stroking it steadily.

"And your serene excellence permits him to live? This is yet another indication of the emperor's benevolent—"

"No. Listen to us."

The emperor had just interrupted him. It was astonishing. Hang Dejin folded his hands in his sleeves and lowered his head. And then, listening, he understood, and the prime minister of Kitai saw, as a shaft of sunlight slicing down through storm clouds, opportunity shining.

He had summoned the gardener into his presence, the emperor said, because of the distressing sound of his weeping. Inquiring directly, he had learned that the labourer's tears were for his son, who had just been reported dead. The son, it seemed, had been in the Pacification Army, among the recruits sent against the Kislik capital in the northwest.

The gardener had just told him, the emperor said, what all of Hanjin apparently knew: that half the Kitan army had been destroyed some time ago, on a retreat from Erighaya. It seemed that they had been deficiently led and supplied.

Hang Dejin privately considered it remarkable (and very wrong) that the gardener was still alive, after speaking so many words to his emperor. It was unbearably presumptuous, deserving decapitation. Where had the world come, if garden servants could behave this way? At the same time, he felt a surge of warm feelings towards the man lying face down on the ground, sweating through his tunic. Sometimes it happened that you received aid, illumination, from the most unexpected sources.

"We have just had the leader of our guards here to confirm this disturbing information," the emperor said.

Wenzong's voice was thin, cold. He really was very angry. The guards stared straight ahead, still alert to the presence of the gardener. Dejin wasn't sure which was their leader, the uniforms were identical. The faces even looked alike to his weak eyes. Wenzong preferred that in his guards, for the harmony.

It appeared that the leader—whichever one it was—had indeed echoed the story told by the gardener. It was not a new tale. The first word of disaster had reached Hanjin last year. Even servants had heard it by now.

The emperor had not.

Hang Dejin said, carefully, "My lord, it is a lamentable truth that the Pacification Army suffered terrible losses."

The emperor of Kitai stared bleakly down at him. The emperor was a tall man and was standing three steps up, in the pavilion. His writing seat and desk were behind him. The rock-mountain that had destroyed fields and killed so many men (you didn't say that) loomed beyond, sunlit, magnificent. There was a breeze.

"You knew of this, councillor?"

Opportunity, and the need for extreme care. But Hang Dejin had been in the palace for a long time, at the summit of all possible achievement. You didn't arrive there and survive without knowing how to deal with moments such as this.

"I knew, because I was able to learn it through my own sources, celestial lord. The military reports went to the deputy prime minister. He has not presented them in council or at court yet. The emperor will recall that responsibility for the Pacification Army led by the eunuch Wu Tong was given directly to General Wu's advocate and supporter, Minister Kai. This was done at Kai Zhen's own request, which I did not oppose. It was therefore not my place to diminish the honourable Kai Zhen by speaking to the emperor of this tragedy before he ... decided to do so himself."

Decided to do so was good, Hang Dejin thought. So was *diminish*.

It was all true, what he'd said. It just wasn't the heart of the truth. Of course Dejin had known what had happened as soon as word came, of course he hadn't carried it to the emperor ... but that had been a shared, tacit agreement among all who led Kitai at this court.

The disaster of Erighaya was one that could imperil them all if Wenzong took it in a certain way. They had all aligned themselves with this war, for various reasons. This nightmare could undo everything, the reforms, their own positions. It could bring back the conservatives! Xi Wengao! The Lu brothers!

Tidings of this sort could do that. A very large expeditionary army sent to take a barbarian capital city, but not securing its supply lines ... and *forgetting* the siege equipment for when it arrived before the walls?

What did that demand, for those responsible? What form of execution was adequate, even if the general of that army was the much-loved Wu Tong, who had devised the network that had created this garden?

Wu Tong himself had evidently fled south ahead of his army. He was still in the west, keeping away from court. Still alive. Sending artifacts and trees for the Genyue.

What Dejin had heard, disturbingly, was that in the retreat through the desert, harassed by barbarians all the way south, the starving, thirst-maddened soldiers of Kitai had begun killing their officers and drinking their blood.

People in the countryside ate each other (and their children) in times of extreme famine; it was a sad truth of a hard world. But for the discipline of a Kitan army to break down so utterly? That was terrifying. It brought to mind all the histories of what armies—and their generals—could do if not firmly held in check, under control.

Better, in some ways, an incompetent, preening, greedy general like Wu Tong than some brilliant leader with the love of his soldiers. *His* soldiers. Not the emperor's.

That choice between evils, thought Hang Dejin, had become part of this dynasty, and they were all involved in it here at court.

Your thoughts were your own. What he said, as the emperor gazed coldly down at him, was, "My humblest apologies, celestial lord. That the serenity of this garden should be marred by such tidings is a grief to me. Shall I have the gardener removed from the imperial presence? He must be punished, of course."

"The gardener stays," said Wenzong. Too bluntly. This remained an unbalanced moment. "His son has died. He will not be punished. He told us only truth." He paused. "We have sent for Kai Zhen."

Hearing that—just the name, without the title—it became an exercise in self-mastery for the prime minister not to smile.

For safety, he lowered his head as if in chastened acquiescence to the majesty of the imperial will. After a precisely timed pause, he murmured, "If the esteemed deputy prime minister is to be with us soon, perhaps my lord will be good enough to assist his servant by reviewing two letters I have received today. The calligraphy in both is exceptional."

He handed up the second letter first, the one in which the brush strokes would not be familiar.

He still knew how to talk to Wenzong. Of course he did. He'd tutored him as a boy.

The emperor reached down and took the letter from his hand. He glanced at it casually, then looked more closely. He sat at the dark-green marble desk, and read.

He looked up. "This is a character-filled hand. A man of conviction and integrity."

It had to be said quickly, lest the emperor feel he'd been deceived: "It is a woman writing, gracious lord. I, too, was greatly surprised."

Wenzong's expression would have been diverting at a less significant moment. The light was good and he was close enough— Dejin could still see.

The emperor's mouth opened above the thin, dark beard, as if to exclaim aloud. Then it closed again as he turned back to the letter from Lady Lin Shan, daughter of Court Gentleman Lin Kuo.

There was an interval of stillness. Dejin heard the breeze in the leaves of trees, and autumn birdsong, and the frightened breathing of the gardener, still face down on the path, still trembling.

Hang Dejin watched his emperor read, saw him savouring brush strokes, saw him smile—then look startled and dismayed. In those two expressions, the one chasing the other across the imperial features, he knew he had won. There were pleasures left in life, small ones, larger ones.

Wenzong looked up. "Her strokes are both firm and graceful. We find this unexpected."

Dejin had known that would be his first remark. Men were what they were, their passions showed through.

He nodded respectfully, saying nothing.

The emperor looked back to the letter, then at Dejin again. "And the second one? You mentioned two letters?"

"The second is from Xi Wengao, my lord. He adds his voice to her plea."

"Your old enemy writes you letters?" A faint imperial smile.

"My old adversary, celestial lord. I have too much respect for him, as I know the emperor does, to name him an enemy."

"He banished you when in power, and you exiled him in turn."

"To his home, my lord. Away from court, where his agitations were doing the empire harm. But not—"

"Not all the way south." The emperor lifted the letter. "Not to Lingzhou Isle. What did this man, Lin Kuo, do that this should be his fate?"

A gift, really. The world could hand you opportunities, and it was almost a disgrace not to pluck them like fruit.

"If we believe the daughter and Master Xi, and I will say that I do believe them, he visited Xi Wengao in Yenling to present to him a book he'd written about gardens."

"Gardens?"

Part of the gift, of course, part of the fruit hanging from the plum tree of this autumn morning.

"Yes, my lord. But it happened to be on the day Lu Chen came to Yenling to bid farewell to his mentor before going to Lingzhou, to his own banishment. It was many years ago. The order of exile for Lin Kuo has just been given, however."

"Lu Chen. Another enemy of yours."

"Another man whose views I considered wrongly judged and dangerous. My lord, I have his poetry in my bedchamber."

The emperor nodded. "And this Lin Kuo is now ordered to Lingzhou? For visiting Xi Wengao?"

"Years ago. At the wrong time. The emperor has read the letter. He was taking his young daughter to see the peonies. And bringing his garden book to present to Master Xi."

"Ah! Yes. We remember now. We know that book," said the emperor of Kitai.

Another plum, dropping into one's hand.

"I did not know this, celestial lord." (It was true.)

"He had it presented to us when it was completed. We looked through it. Pleasantly conceived, artfully bound. Not insightful about the spiritual nature of gardens, but a charming gift. I believe he mentioned Xi Wengao's garden."

"So I understand, my lord."

"And went to present the book to him?"

"Perhaps also to introduce his daughter."

Reminded, Wenzong looked again at the letter. "Extraordinary," he said. He looked up. "Of course, it isn't *proper* for a woman to write like this."

"No, my lord. Of course not. It is, as you say, extraordinary. I believe the father taught her himself, then arranged for tutors." (Xi Wengao's letter had reported as much.)

"Indeed? Does that make him a subversive man?"

Unexpected. One needed to be alert, always. There were so many dangers here.

"It might, my lord. I rather think it makes him an attentive father."

"He ought to have looked to marrying her, then."

"She is wed, my lord. To Qi Wai, of the imperial clan. Sixth degree. Xi Wengao states as much."

An alert look. Emperors were attentive when the imperial clan was mentioned. "An honourable marriage."

"Of course, my lord."

Another pause. One still heard the gardener breathing raggedly. Dejin half wished the man were gone, but he knew he would be useful, any moment now.

The emperor said, "We find this appeal filial and persuasive, with evocative brush strokes."

"Yes, celestial lord."

"Why would our adviser send a simple man like this to Lingzhou Isle?"

It was as if he were biting into a plum through taut, firm skin, so vivid and sweet was the taste.

"Again, alas, I cannot answer. I am ashamed. I knew nothing of this until these letters this morning. I permitted Minister Kai to take command of dealing with remaining conservative faction members. He petitioned for that responsibility, and I was too kind-hearted to deny him. I confess it might have been an error."

"But Lingzhou? For visiting someone whose garden he had described in a book? We are told ... we understand it is a harsh place, Lingzhou Isle."

"I also understand as much, my lord."

Even as he said this, a thought came to Dejin. And then another, more profound, in its wake.

Before he could be cautious and stop himself, he spoke the

first thought, "It might be regarded as a gesture of the celebrated imperial compassion if the poet Lu Chen were now permitted to leave the isle, august lord. He has been there some time."

Wenzong looked at him. "*That* is where he is? Lu Chen?"

It was entirely possible the emperor had forgotten.

"It is, celestial lord."

"He was a leader of that faction. With Xi Wengao. You exiled him yourself, did you not?"

He answered promptly. "I did the first time, yes. South of the Great River. But when his political poems continued to be written and circulated he was ordered farther away. He is ... a challenging man."

"Poets can be difficult," said the emperor in a musing tone. He was pleased with his own observation. Dejin could hear it.

"I did not order him to Lingzhou, my lord. Across the mountains was what I suggested. Sending him to the isle was Councillor Kai's decision. He also ordered his writings gathered and destroyed."

"And yet you have some in your bedchamber." The emperor smiled.

A careful pause. A rueful smile. "I do, my lord."

"We do, as well. Perhaps," said the emperor of Kitai, smiling even more, "we must be exiled, ourselves."

One of the imperial guards would later remember that.

Wenzong added, "We recall his lines. *Wise men fill the emperor's court, so why do things get worse? / I'd have been better off dying, as bride to the river god.* Do you know the poem?"

"I do, revered lord." Of course he knew it. It had been an attack on him.

"That was during a flood of the Golden River, wasn't it?"

"It was."

"We sent relief, did we not?"

"You did, my lord. Very generously."

The emperor nodded.

They heard a sound. Dejin found it interesting how his hearing seemed to have improved as his eyesight failed. He turned. The figure of Kai Zhen could be seen approaching, on foot along the path from the palace gate. He was able to see the man hesitate as he took in Dejin's presence and someone lying face down on the path before the emperor.

Only the briefest hesitation, however, barely a checked stride, you could miss it if you weren't watching for it. The deputy prime minister was as smooth, as polished, as green jade made by the finest craftsmen in Kitai, masters of their trade, in a tradition going back a thousand years.

AFTERWARDS, BEING CARRIED back to the palace, Prime Minister Hang would take careful thought concerning what had just taken place. In his working room again, surrounded by papers and scrolls, with many lamps lit to make it easier for him to see, he would speak with his son and make arrangements for someone to be protected, and for the gardener to be found and executed.

The man had heard far too much, lying on the ground throughout the exchanges before and after Kai Zhen arrived at the pavilion. He would be uneducated but he wasn't a mute, and the times were dangerous.

Some days later he would learn that the man had not been found. He wasn't, evidently, a fool. It had proved extremely difficult even to establish his identity. None of them there that morning had asked his name, of course, and there were, Prime Minister Hang was informed, four thousand, six hundred men employed in the emperor's garden.

Eventually they would determine, through the Genyue supervisors' records, who he was—a man from the north. Guards sent to his residence would find it empty, with signs of a hasty departure. Well, they *knew* it had been a hasty departure. The gardener was gone, his wife and a child were gone. None of the neighbours knew where. He hadn't been a talkative man. Northerners tended not to be.

There was a grown son living in a house outside the walls. He was interrogated. He did not know where his parents and young sister had gone, or so he would maintain right up until he died under questioning.

It was disappointing.

Holding high office (for so many years) meant that you had done, and would have to continue doing, unpleasant things at times. Actions inconsistent with philosophic ideals. It was necessary, at such moments, to remember that one's duty was to the empire, that weakness in power could undermine peace and order.

Difficult as it was for a virtuous man to have someone killed merely for overhearing a conversation, it was even more difficult to discover that the order, once given, had not been carried out.

He would also give thought to the imperial guards who had been standing by that morning. They were trusted favourites of the emperor, always with him, not men one could order executed. Not without consequences. He had them promoted in rank, instead.

You did what you could.

CHAPTER V

"Deputy Kai," the emperor of Kitai had said in his garden that morning, "we are displeased."

Kai Zhen, standing below him on the brushed path, inclined his head in sorrow. "My lord, I live to amend anything that causes this, any errors your servants have committed. Only tell me!"

Wenzong's face remained chilly. "We believe it is the deputy prime minister's errors that have disturbed our morning."

Even with bad eyesight, Dejin could see Zhen's eyes flicker towards him, then back to the emperor. *Dance a little,* he thought. Unworthy malice, perhaps, but he had cause.

He watched as Kai Zhen sank to his knees. Dejin envied him the ease of the movement. The deputy prime minister's beard and hair were still black, his back was straight. His eyes, undoubtedly, were keen.

Impatiently, Wenzong motioned him upright. Zhen took a careful moment then he did rise, head still lowered, hands folded submissively in sleeves. Dejin wondered if they were shaking. It was possible.

Looking down at the smoothed gravel path (and at the gardener lying on it), Zhen said, "Our fates are in the emperor's hands, always. It is a grief to me if I have erred in your service."

"Excess," said Emperor Wenzong, "can be an error as much as neglect."

Hang Dejin blinked. It was an elegant phrase. Wenzong could surprise. Although it would not do to dwell upon the emperor's own neglect of duties. For one thing, that habit had allowed Dejin to control and shape Kitai these many years.

Kai Zhen, smooth as finest silk, murmured, "Zeal in your service may indeed lead me to excessive devotion. I will admit it."

But Wenzong was in a dark, sharp mood. He shook his head at the sleek evasion. "Why is Court Gentleman Lin Kuo exiled to Lingzhou Isle?"

Dejin could almost feel Zhen's relief. He now knew what he was facing. A small matter, easy to address.

The deputy prime minister said, "The emperor is so gracious! To offer imperial guidance on minor affairs of state! It humbles his servants!" His voice was rich. He was a handsome man. No one would ever have said either about Hang Dejin, even when he was young.

"We have seen petitions on the court gentleman's behalf. We would know why our well-known benevolence has been compromised in this matter."

That placed things in a different light. Zhen could be seen absorbing this. He cleared his throat. "Celestial lord, it must surely be the task of your servants to defend you and the empire. As dangers mount around us and—"

"What danger did Court Gentleman Lin Kuo present, Deputy Kai?"

Yet another interruption. The emperor was in a dangerous mood.

A real hesitation for the first time, as Zhen registered this too.

"I ... he was allied with the conservatives, of course, my lord. That evil faction intent on destroying all peace!"

"He wrote a book on the gardens of Yenling. He sent it to us last year. We read it and approved of it."

At this point, thought Hang Dejin, happily silent, his expression composed, Deputy Minister Kai would believe he understood the gravity of the moment.

"My lord, he visited with the exiled Xi Wengao."

"Years ago! Many visit him. It is not forbidden. He presented him with a copy of his book. Master Xi's garden is described in it. We ask again, what is it Lin Kuo has done? Really. *Lingzhou Isle?*"

"The ... the banished poet was there that same day! They met with Lu Chen on his way to exile. It was ... it was an obvious moment of plotting!"

Time to speak. "Xi Wengao, whose honour we will not impeach, has written to say that the court gentleman had no idea Lu Chen would be present. Xi Wengao writes that he was grieving for his friend, and asked Lin Kuo to attend upon him the same day to brighten his own mood. Lin Kuo brought his young daughter, now married into the imperial clan. She writes the same thing. What plot did you uncover from that day?"

There was nothing so obvious as hatred in the look Zhen gave him, but it could chill you, nonetheless, if you weren't his superior, still, and used to such glances over the years. And they hadn't yet reached the heart of this morning. He knew that; Zhen did not.

Kai Zhen said, "Xi Wengao, all his life, has been loyal to his friends and followers."

"A trait," said the emperor, "we admire." He paused. "We choose to give instruction in this matter. The order of exile for Lin Kuo will be rescinded and notice conveyed to him immediately. He is to be raised two ranks in the civil service by way of redress and given the proper adjustments in salary and housing. His daughter and her husband will attend upon us in our garden. We wish to meet this woman. Her calligraphy is exceptional. From today, all names proposed and punishments decreed for those remaining in the conservative faction are to be reviewed by the prime minister. We are displeased, deputy councillor."

Naturally Kai Zhen went straight to his knees again. Quite close to the gardener, in fact. He pressed his forehead to the gravel of the path.

"My life is yours, celestial lord!" he cried.

"We know this," said Wenzong.

He could be impressive, Dejin thought, when moved to engage with his power. It rarely happened. You could sometimes regret that.

The emperor said, "Remain as you are, and advise us where General Wu Tong is, your chosen commander in the northwest. Explain why he has not been brought to court to tell us what happened in the Kislik war. We have learned this morning, for the first time, from a *gardener*, what the whole of Hanjin seems to know!"

He did not trouble (he was the emperor) to hide his anger.

And here, of course, was the true and deadly menace of the morning. Kai Zhen would be realizing it, Dejin thought. His heart would be hammering, sweat would be on his body, his bowels would probably be clenching and releasing with fear.

He would be aware that he could lose all power and rank, could even die today. Or be exiled to Lingzhou Isle.

∽

On the isle that same day—south and south away, beyond peaks and rivers, rice fields and marshes and jungles, across a white-waved, wind-chopped strait, barely even within the world of Kitai—morning prayers and thanks were once more being offered that the summer rains had ended.

The rains arrived at Lingzhou with the west wind in the third

month and lasted into autumn. The downpour, the steaming damp
and the heat, and the diseases they brought were what tended to
kill people, mostly those from the north.

Those born south of the coastal mountains, and the natives
of Lingzhou itself, were better able to deal with the illness and
enervation that came with a sodden summer in a place seen by
many as lying adjacent to the afterworld.

There were giant snakes. They were not legends. They slithered
through muddy village lanes, or stretched themselves along dripping
branches in the dark-leaved forest.

There were poisonous spiders, many different kinds. Some so
small they could hardly be seen as they killed you. You never, ever
put on boots or shoes without shaking them out first, prepared to
jump back.

There were tigers unique to the south. Their roaring could
sometimes fill the thick nights of the isle under clouds or stars. The
sound was said to paralyze a man if he heard it from too near. They
killed many people each year. Being cautious wasn't enough if the
tiger god named you.

There were ghosts, but there were ghosts everywhere.

Wondrous flowers grew enormous blossoms, brilliantly coloured,
dizzying perfumes. But it was dangerous to go walking out to see
them in meadows or by the forest's edge, and during summer
downpours it was impossible.

Even indoors, in the worst of rain and wind, life became
precarious. Lanterns would swing wildly and blow out. Candles
on altars could be knocked over. There were fires in huts while
rain slammed outside and thunder boomed the anger of gods. One
might sit in a sudden midday blackness, shaping poems in one's
head, or speaking them aloud, voice pitched above the crashing and
the drum of the rain, to the loyal son who had come to the end of
the world as a companion.

When it grew calm, and it was possible to write, Lu Chen

took brush and paper, ground his ink, and busied himself with descriptions in poems, and in letters north.

He offered in his correspondence a resolute, defiant good humour. He had no idea if the letters would reach their destinations (they were mostly to his brother Chao, some to his wife, both living on the farm south of the Great River) but there was little for him to do here but write, and it had always been the essence of his soul.

Poetry, essays, letters, memoranda to the court. A habitation built in the mind. He had some books with him, damaged by the damp after several years now. He had the Cho classics committed pretty much to memory, however, and a great deal of poetry. He had written once, long ago, that he truly believed he could find contentment anywhere. That belief was being tested. Along with his ability to laugh, or make others laugh.

Paper was hard to come by. There was one temple housing six clerics of the Path at the edge of the village, and the current elder admired Lu Chen, knew his poetry. Chen walked over there most days, watchful on the muddy path near the forest. They drank the harsh, yellow-tinted island wine and talked. He liked to talk to intelligent men. He liked to talk to anyone.

At intervals, one of the clerics would make the crossing—dangerous in the rainy season—to the mainland for news and supplies, and arrange to obtain paper for him. Thus far the administrators here (the new one was very young, very unhappy, not surprisingly) had not stopped this, though they were aware of it, of course.

They'd had, to this point, no instructions in the matter. Those might yet come. The hatreds of the faction years could reach this far. He was here, wasn't he? He was proof of hatred. He did think (though never said) that it might have been a woman who had wanted him sent here to die. No way to be sure, but the thought was there. He had decided, from the start, to be difficult about dying.

The clerics took his letters across the strait as well, entrusted them to others journeying over the mountain barrier, through narrow, crumbling passes above chasms, amid the shrieking of gibbons. That was how letters travelled back into the world from this far away.

In exchange for their kindnesses he had written a poem on a wall of their temple.

He was so well known that when word reached the mainland people might come, even to Lingzhou, to see Lu Chen's writing here. They'd make offerings at the temple. Stay a night or two, pay for that. That was how such matters tended to unfold. He had done wall poems before. His presence here might be a benefit to some.

The brush strokes of the poem, written last spring, were already disappearing in the dampness, though. They hadn't survived a single summer's rains. There was a lesson in that, he supposed, about the aspirations of men to do something that would endure. He tried to find it amusing. He was usually able to find amusement in the world.

He had written on the wall about the human spirit, resilience, friendship, red and yellow flowers at the forest's edge, and ghosts.

There was a ghost lingering by their cabin.

He had seen her twice for certain on the roof: once at sunrise as he walked out, once as he returned at twilight. It did not seem malevolent. It was not a personal ghost, he was sure of that, not one that had followed them here. It was a ghost of the village, the island, of this cottage. No one he asked knew anything about her. There was no name given him.

He'd seen her hair, unbound. It hid her face. There was a phrase, often used in poetry, about the cloud of a courtesan's hair. The ghost's was more like smoke, he thought.

He added a candle for her on their altar. They spoke the prayers and made offerings, invoking rest for her unquiet soul. It was likely she had never been buried. That could happen to a person, or to thousands on a battlefield.

He was worried about his son. Beginning this past summer, Lu Mah coughed at night when he lay down, and through the night hours. It seemed to be easing as the dry season finally came, but he was aware this might be his hope as a father, not the truth of things.

It was early morning now, not raining and not yet too hot. Time, soon, to rise from bed. He and Mah were doing exercises each morning whenever it was possible—to the amusement of the villagers, who often gathered to watch them. Twirling and stretching, they used staffs to mock-fight in front of the cottage, holding them like swords at times. "I will be a bandit yet!" he'd cry (and had written of this to his brother, mocking himself). "I will bring back the memory of young Sima Zian!"

His son laughed. That was good.

It was interesting, Lu Chen thought, how many of the references a man made reached specifically to the Ninth. It was as if they were all marked (scarred? diminished?) by glory achieved four hundred years ago, and by the rebellion and the fall.

Sima Zian, one of the master poets, had lived (mostly) before the rebellion. *A chasm in the world*, another poet had called the civil war that had ensued. The world, Lu Chen thought, exiled on Lingzhou Isle, confronted you with chasms—or jagged peaks—all the time.

He was trying to decide how to persuade Mah to leave. *He* was the one exiled. Children might have their lives undone by a father's disgrace but there were precedents for rising above that, given the passage of time and changes at court.

Problem was, he was certain the boy would not go. For one thing, he wasn't a boy any more. Lu Mah was of an age to take the *jinshi* examinations (he wouldn't be allowed to now) and certainly to make his own decisions. He would never defy a direct order from his father, but Chen wasn't ready to break his son's heart that way, instructing him to leave.

He could remember travelling to the capital with his own father (long gone, dearly missed) and his brother. He'd been twenty-three years old. Three months' journey to Hanjin, to prepare for and take the examinations. He had come first in their year; Chao, two years younger, had come third. They launched you into life like an arrow, results like that—and sometimes you landed in strange places. Arrows could go astray.

There came a time, he thought, lying in his cot-bed, when the years you had lived, your memories, stretched too much further behind than the years you could imagine in front of you.

He lay there a little longer, thinking of his dead wife and his living one, and women he had loved. There was a girl here who tended to their cottage. He did not lie with her. His son did, when Chen was with the clerics at the temple. It was better that way. His thoughts drifted to another girl, the one in Wengao's home in Yenling. His last visit there.

She had offered herself to him, a spring night during the Peony Festival, standing in the corridor outside her room in a spill of light. He had looked back (vivid memory!) at the *youngness* of her. And had realized what she was doing. An illumination, like a lamp.

He had bowed to her, and shaken his head. "My everlasting thanks," he'd said. "But I cannot accept such a gift."

She'd be married now, for years. Perhaps with children. She'd been offering him her innocence that night, in sorrow: for strength on a terrible journey, and on Lingzhou.

She had been remarkably clever, Chen remembered, for someone so young. Over and above the fact that this had been a woman, a girl. He had encountered clever women, after all.

Too great a gift she'd been offering. He was, he thought, a man easier with giving gifts than accepting them. Nor did he follow Arcane Path teachings in the matter of lovemaking. (The emperor did, everyone knew.) You did not spend a night with a woman, Lu Chen had always believed, for whatever mystical strength you might gain from her.

You did it for pleasures you could share.

He wasn't a good observer of doctrines. He would admit to that. He'd said it to the clerics here, his first visit, when they rang their one tall bell and prayed. He offered prayers with them, sincerely, but after his own fashion. His own doctrines were about compassion, the brush strokes of words, painting, conversation, enduring friendship, family. Laughter. Music. Service to the empire. Wine. The beauty of women and of rivers under stars. Even if you thought you were at the Red Cliffs of legend and you weren't.

You needed to be able to laugh at yourself, too.

Watching the light in the east, he smiled. It was a good memory, that corridor in Xi Wengao's house many springs ago. She had been generous, he had been virtuous. You could hold to such moments, hold them up to morning's light.

It was time to rise, before the heat grew stupefying. He dressed in his hemp robe, worn through, too big for him now with the weight he'd lost. He put on his hat, as always, pinned thinning hair. He didn't look at mirrors any more. He lit candles, poured out three cups of wine, prayed for his parents' souls, and his wife's, at the small altar they had made here at world's end. He prayed for the ghost-woman. That whatever had denied her rest might ease and pass, be forgiven or forgotten.

Mah had been up earlier, as always. He had rice and chestnuts on the fire in the front room, and yellow wine warmed for his father.

"I think we'll see the sun again today," Lu Chen pronounced. "I propose we rally our wild bandit company and storm the fortress of the evil district overlord."

"We did that yesterday," his son said, smiling back at him.

❧

His concubines were wailing in the women's quarters like unburied ghosts. Kai Zhen, deputy prime minister of Kitai—until this morning—could hear them across the courtyard. Their voices twined and clashed unmelodiously. He had a large house (he had several large houses) but they were making a great deal of noise in their lamenting.

He felt like wailing himself, in truth. Or killing someone. He paced his principal reception room, window, wall, window, then back again, too agitated to sit, to eat, take wine, compose letters. What letters could he write?

His world had just ended. It had exploded like one of those new devices that launched fire-arrows over the walls of cities under siege.

Wu Tong, his protégé, his ally in the Flowers and Rocks Network and a shared ascent to power, hadn't taken siege weapons north against the Kislik capital.

Sometimes the known, verified truth remained impossible to believe.

Had the eunuch and his commanders been driven mad by desert winds? Tormented to that state by some malign spirit intending their destruction? Intending Kai Zhen's even more?

How did you forget *siege weapons* on your way to take a city?

This morning's business of the court gentleman—that insignificant garden-book writer whose name he could barely recall was trivial, it was nothing! Or it should have been. What were the chances the emperor, obsessed with the ideal placement of a new Szechen rock, or aligning a row of pagoda trees, would pause to read a letter, or care about a meaningless figure's exile?

Even if he did, even if the accursed blind one brought it to him for his own black reasons, it should have been a simple matter to prostrate oneself, express bottomless contrition, and reverse the order of exile, explaining it away as a matter of zeal in the service of the emperor. He couldn't even remember what had been irritating him the day he decreed Lingzhou Isle for a nonentity. He could barely remember doing it.

How could such a man matter in the unfolding of the world? He didn't. That was the point! Even with an apparently well-crafted letter from his unnatural daughter—her life a smear on the proper conduct of a woman—Wenzong would have done no more than raise an imperial eyebrow from under his hat and suggest the exile might be made less onerous.

If it hadn't been for the army, the disastrous retreat through the desert from Erighaya's walls, the lack of siege engines, the death of seventy thousand ...

The eating of officers, drinking their blood, as they retreated south.

And even with that, if it hadn't been for some nameless, unknown, impossible-even-to-imagine *gardener* (the outrageousness threatened to choke Kai Zhen) weeping near the emperor ...

How had he even *dared*? It was unjust beyond words! Kai Zhen had been dazzlingly close, brilliantly so, to having all he needed, wanted, had ever aspired to have.

Almost all his wife needed, as well. Though she would always want more. It was embedded in her being, that wanting. They never said it aloud, but he knew she thought about an empress's headdress.

The thought made him look quickly over his shoulder. By now he had a sort of intuition when she might be in a room, though her movements were utterly quiet, no brushing of a robe along the floor, no slap of slippers, sound of breathing, of keys or fan at her waist.

His wife was a silent creature when she moved, and terrifying.

They were alone in the chamber. It was richly decorated. Bronzes from the Fifth, porcelain, south sea coral, sandalwood chairs, wall panels with ivory inlays, a rosewood writing desk, poems in his own (exceptional) calligraphy hanging on the walls.

Kai Zhen had good taste, a discerning eye. He was also a very wealthy man, his fortune growing swiftly after he and Wu Tong conceived of the Flowers and Rocks. The two of them had met through that idea and risen together with it, as if from a deep lake, to transcendent heights.

Kai Zhen had come to Hanjin and the court the way one of his magnificent rocks or trees had come.

He was closer to the emperor now than the prime minister, had been for two years, he'd judged. He did that particular assessment often. It had only required patience, as the old man's eyes failed him a little more, and then again more, and his weariness under the weight of office grew ...

It had all been coming to him.

He looked across the room at his wife. His heart quailed before the agate-black fury he read in Yu-lan's eyes. Her capacity for rage was vast. Her eyes were enormous, it seemed to him. They looked as if they could swallow the room—and him—draw all down into black oblivion there.

His concubines could wail and moan. They were still doing so in the women's quarters, shrill as gibbons. His coiled, slim wife would gather venom like a snake, in deathly anger, then strike.

She had always frightened him. From the morning they'd first met and were formally engaged. Then their wedding night, which he would remember until he died; the things she had done, shockingly, the things she'd said. From that night to this day, Yu-lan had aroused in him the most intense desire he had ever known, even as he feared her. Perhaps because he feared.

A sad thing for a man, if his passion was greater, even now, for a wife of many years than for ripe and youthful concubines or courtesans, urgently anxious to please in whatever ways imagination could devise.

She drew a breath, his wife. He watched her. She wore dark-red *liao* silk, belted in linked gold, straight fitted in the fashion for well-bred women, high at the throat. She wore golden slippers on her feet. She held herself very still.

Snakes did that, Kai Zhen thought, staring at her. It was said that some northern snakes made a rattling sound like gamblers' dice before they struck.

"Why is the prime minister not dead?" she asked.

Her voice made him think of winter sometimes. Ice, wind, bones in snow.

He saw, belatedly, that her hands were trembling. Unlike her, a measure of how far lost to rage she was. Not fear. She would not fear, his wife. She would hate, and endlessly aspire, be filled with fury she could not (it seemed) entirely control, but she would not be fearful.

He would be. He was now, remembering events in the garden this morning. Such a little time ago, yet they seemed to lie on the far side of a wide river with no ferry to carry him back across. He was seeing what lay before him on this shore, knowing it as ruin.

There had been a stele raised in his honour in the city where he'd been born. He pictured it toppled, smashed, overgrown by weeds, the inscribed words of commendation lost to time and the world's memory.

He looked at his wife, heard his women crying with undiminished fervour across the courtyard.

He said, "You want me to have killed him in the Genyue? Beside the emperor, with guards standing by?" He was smooth with sarcasm and irony, but he didn't feel at his best just now and he knew this wasn't what she'd meant.

She lifted her head. "I wanted him poisoned a year ago. I said as much."

She had. Kai Zhen was aware that of the two of them she could be called the more mannish, direct. He was inclined to subtlety, observation, indirect action. Too female, if one followed the Cho Masters. But he had always argued (and believed) that at this court, at any Kitan court, mastery usually fell to the most subtle.

Unless something like this morning happened.

"It was the army, wife. Once Wu Tong's generals failed to—"

"No, husband! Once Wu Tong failed! And *you* were the one who placed the eunuch at the head of an army. I said that was a mistake."

She had. It was distressing.

"He had won battles before! And is the most loyal ally I have. He owes me everything, will never have a family. Would you have preferred a commander who would claim all glory for himself? Come home seeking power?"

She laughed harshly. "I'd have preferred a commander who'd bring proper weapons to a siege!"

There was that.

He said, hating the note in his voice, "It was that gardener! If he hadn't been—"

"It would have been someone else. You needed to denounce Wu Tong, husband! When we first heard of this. Before someone denounced you along with him."

Which is what had just happened.

"And," she added, the icy voice, "you needed to have the old man killed."

"He was *leaving*!" Zhen exclaimed. "It was aligned. He *wants* to retire. He can hardly see! Why risk a killing when it was falling to us?"

He used *us* deliberately. He wasn't capable of battling her in this mood. She was too fierce, he was too despairing. Sometimes a clash like this excited him, and her, and they would end up disrobed and entwined on the floor, or with her mounting and sheathing his sex while he leaned back in a sandalwood chair. Not today. She wasn't going to make love to him today.

It occurred to him—blade of a thought—that he could kill himself. Perhaps leave a letter asking forgiveness and pardon for his young sons? They might yet be allowed a life in Hanjin, at court.

He didn't want to do that. He wasn't that kind of person. It crossed his mind that Yu-lan was. She could easily open her mouth right now, this moment, and tell him with her next words that he needed to die.

She did open her mouth. She said, "There may yet be time."

He felt a weakness in his legs. "What do you mean?"

"If the old man dies right now the emperor will need a prime minister immediately, one he knows, one capable of governing. He might then decide to—"

It was occasionally a pleasure, a relief, something almost sexual, to see her err so greatly, be this far off the mark with the arrow of her thought.

"There are half a dozen such men in Hanjin, wife. And one of them is Hang Dejin's son."

"Hsien? That child?"

His turn to laugh, bitterly. "He is almost my age, woman."

"He is still a child! Controlled by his father."

Kai Zhen looked past her then, out the window at the courtyard trees. He said, quietly, "We have all been controlled by his father."

He saw her hands clench into fists. "You are giving up? You are just going to go wherever they send you?"

He gestured. "It will not be harsh. I am almost certain of that. We may only be sent across the Great River, home. Men return from banishment. Hang Dejin did. Xi Wengao did for a time. We have been exiled before, wife. That is when I devised the Flowers and Rocks. You know it. Even Lu Chen has been ordered freed this morning from Lingzhou Isle."

"*What?* No! He cannot ..."

She stopped, clearly shaken. He had told her about events this morning, his banishment, but not about this. His wife hated the poet with a murderous intensity. He had never known why.

He grinned, mirthlessly. Strange, how it gave him pleasure to see her caught out. She was breathing hard. Not ice now. She was very desirable, suddenly, despite everything. It was his weakness. She was his weakness.

He could see her register, after a moment, a change in him, just as he'd seen it in her. They were a match this way, he thought. They had carried each other to the brink of ultimate power. And now ...

His wife took a step towards him. She bit her lip. She never did that inconsequentially. Alone or among others, it had a meaning.

Kai Zhen smiled, even as he felt his pulses change. "It will be all right," he said. "It might take us a little time now, but we are not finished, wife."

"Someone else is," she said. "You must allow me a death."

"Not the old man's. I told you. It is too—"

"Not the old man."

He waited.

"The girl. Her letter started this."

He was startled, again. Stared at her.

"She is a disgrace," Yu-lan went on. "An offence to decent women. She offered to teach our daughter to write poetry!"

"What? I did not know this."

"They met at a banquet. Ti-yu told her that poetry was no proper thing for a woman. The other one, this Lin Shan, laughed at her."

"I did not know this," he said again.

"And now ... now she writes a letter that sends catastrophe to us!"

That wasn't entirely true, Kai Zhen thought, but his sleek, glittering wife had taken another step. Light fell upon her now.

"Indeed," was all he managed to say.

"Leave this to me," Yu-lan murmured. Meaning, he realized, many things.

With those words she had come right up to him, not so much smaller that it was difficult for her to draw his head down with her slender hands. She bit his lip, the way she often did when they began. Often, she drew blood.

"Here, wife? In our reception chamber?"

"Here. Now. Please, my lord," whispered his wife in his ear. Her tongue touched him. Her hands became busy, with him, with his clothing.

Please, my lord. Across the courtyard, young and beautiful concubines, bodies washed and scented for him, were wailing for the fate that had overtaken all of them. The autumn light came into the room through the western windows. It had become late afternoon. It would be cold tonight in Hanjin.

KAI ZHEN WOKE. It was dark. He realized he'd fallen asleep among the scattered pillows. He tried to rouse himself. He felt languid, eased. He had scratches on one arm. He felt them on his back as well.

He heard a bird singing, a thin sound in the cold. The concubines were silent now. Yu-lan was gone. He knew what she had left him to do. She was making a mistake and he knew that, too. He just didn't feel he could *do* anything about it.

He was an immensely assured man, competent, calculating, subtle. There were only two people alive he felt he could not control.

His wife, and an old, almost-blind man.

He stood up, adjusted his clothing. The room needed lamps lit. The one bird continued to sing, as if bravely denying the cold of the world. He heard a discreet cough from a doorway.

"Yes, enter," he said. "Bring light."

Three servants came in, carrying tapers. They would have been waiting outside the chamber. They'd have stood there all evening if necessary. He was—he had been—on the cusp of being the most powerful man in Kitai.

One of the servants, he saw it was his steward, was holding a lacquered tray, standing just inside the room. Kai Zhen nodded. The sorrows of the day descended upon him again, but he would not hide from them. He opened the sealed letter on the tray, read it by the light of a lamp, lit now, on his writing desk.

He closed his eyes. Opened them.

"Where is my lady wife?" he asked.

"In her chambers, my lord," his steward said. "Shall I request her presence here?"

There was no point. He knew her. It was done by now.

Two people in the world. Yu-lan. And the old man who had written him this letter.

The day gone, the evening, the night to come. The bird outside, he thought, was not brave or gallant. It was foolish, beyond words. You couldn't deny the coldness of the world just by singing.

CHAPTER VI

He didn't know a great deal about them, they had been gone from the world for two hundred years or something like that, but Sun Shiwei often thought he'd have liked to be a Kanlin Warrior.

He'd have trained with them, wearing black, at their sanctuary on Stone Drum Mountain, now lost to Kitai, part of the surrendered Fourteen Prefectures.

He'd have done whatever rituals they did, slept with the women warriors among them (hard, lithe bodies!), been taught their secret ways of killing people.

He was good at that, killing people, but only a fool would believe there weren't ways to be better, and from what he'd always understood, legend and story, the Kanlins had been the best. They'd been couriers, emissaries, witnesses to treaties, custodians of documents and treasures, guides and guards ... many things.

The killing part was what he liked, though. A shame they were gone. A shame there were no proper records. They'd never written anything down, the Kanlins. That was part of what made something a secret. Stood to reason.

He'd have liked to be able to run right up a wall and onto a roof. Who wouldn't like that? Leap down into a courtyard and knife someone who thought they were safe in their compound because the doors and windows were barred and the walls high. Then up another wall and gone before an alarm could even be raised.

"It was Sun Shiwei!" the terrified whispers would run. "Who else could have done this? The doors were locked!"

He'd have liked that.

It was necessary to stop these drifting thoughts. He was on a mission, he had a task.

It was dark inside the compound of the imperial clan. The compound might be big, but it was also crowded. Everyone complained in here. It wasn't Sun Shiwei's task (or his inclination) to assess the living conditions of the emperor's kin, but it did help him that many people continued to mill about between individual residences and courtyards in here, even after darkfall.

They went in and out, too. None of the compound gates was closed yet. Mostly it was younger men slipping out. It was formally forbidden but generally allowed, except when there had been trouble. They went in search of wine and girls, mostly. Sometimes to dinner parties at the houses of friends in the city. Women were brought in here, and musicians. The guards at the four gates weren't especially concerned, as long as their share of whatever coins were changing hands was forthcoming.

All the better for him, of course. He'd come in with a group of giggling girls. Had even managed to feel up one or two of them. Got a saucy laugh from one. He couldn't afford those women, of course—not the kind that got invited here. For the Sun Shiweis of the world, a squeeze through silk was as good as it got with courtesans of this class.

He'd been in the imperial compound before, knew his way around. He'd escorted his employer and her daughter to women's gatherings, remained inside to take them back. He'd used the opportunities to get his bearings, in case he ever needed them. In case this evening ever came. He was skilled, even if he couldn't scale walls on the run or do some sacred, mystical spinning movement that killed four people at once. He could probably manage three if he had a wall at his back, Shiwei thought. He wouldn't have kept his job if he wasn't good. His employer was exacting. She was hard and cold, chary with anything resembling praise, and disturbingly desirable.

He'd had many nights awake, truth of it, imagining her coming to him in the dark, slipping inside, closing the door quietly behind her, her scent in his own small room ... There was fire inside her, he was sure of it. Some things a man could see.

Man could also get himself cut in half, sharing that sort of thought anywhere.

His thoughts seemed to be running away again. What happened when you had to wait in shadows for too long. He was in a covered passage between courtyards, dressed for a chilly night (part of being good at your job), and had an excuse prepared if anyone stopped to ask. They were unlikely to do that here. People came and went. The imperial clan was honoured, after a fashion, sequestered and kept track of, but ignored in almost every other way—unless they made trouble. In that case they were often killed.

Far as Shiwei was concerned, not that anyone had ever asked, they could all be drowned or used for archery practice, and Kitai would be better off. The clan cost the empire a huge amount of money every year, everyone knew it. Some of the women he'd keep, maybe. Aristocratic women had their own way of being, and he liked it, what he'd seen.

"You. What are you doing here?"

Shiwei kept his expression bland. The guard had a torch, was only doing routine rounds. He was chubby and his cloak was awry.

"Waiting for some girls. Take them back." He stayed in shadow.

"You'll wait a long time."

Shiwei offered a chuckle. "Usually do."

The torch was lifted. He saw the guard's round face. The round-faced guard saw him.

"I know you," the man said. Which was unfortunate. "You work for the deputy prime minister, not the pleasure district. Saw you with his wife here when—"

When you had to kill you did, and you needed to know when such a moment came. Couldn't leave this one alive: he'd report later, could identify Shiwei. It was unexpected, an irritation. And it changed his timing, too.

He pulled his knife from the guard's chest slowly, holding the man upright against him, shielded by the arch. He kept talking quietly, meaningless words, in case anyone passed close. He'd grabbed the torch from the dead man before he could drop it. A fallen, flaring torch would, sure as spirits flew at night, get attention. Fire was the enemy, everywhere.

Shiwei had picked his spot carefully. Edge of the courtyard where the house he wanted stood. Under cover, with a recessed space farther into the passageway where he could drag a dead man and lay him down, mostly out of sight.

Mostly was the best he was going to get. And that meant he had to move now instead of waiting for the crowd to thin and people in the compound to generally be asleep—including those in the house across the way, where he was going.

He didn't regret killing the guard. He regretted the complications it caused. They might still be awake in that house. The woman he was here to kill might be.

He knew the house, he was just about certain he knew the room. That was why he'd come early, instead of waiting until dark. He'd pretended to deliver an empty letter to their door, after getting directions from a guard other than the ones who'd watched him come through with the singing girls.

Eventually he'd seen her come into the courtyard and cross it to her home, walking with a servant, no husband in sight. She'd been out without her husband, home at twilight, brazen as you please. There were no morals left among women in the world, Sun Shiwei had often thought.

The houses were mostly similar in the compound. Variations depended on status and degree of closeness to the emperor. A few were extremely large, more than one courtyard inside their walls, but not this one.

The bedroom she'd use—or they'd use, if the absent husband ever went in to indulge himself with her—would be on the women's side, to the right at the back. Shiwei had intended to get over the wall into their courtyard then climb up to her room. He had even worked out his hand- and foot-holds for the wall, waiting here.

Couldn't do it that way now. Too many people around for a man to safely climb a wall, even at night. They might think he was just a lover, and leave it alone, or they might not. There was a moon, too, almost full. He wouldn't have picked a night with a moon, but he didn't get to do the choosing in these things, did he?

He'd been told to make this look like an assault on the woman— some vicious predator in the clan compound having his hard way with a girl, then killing her. He could deal with that part. She'd have to be dead, first, for silence and safety, but he'd done that before.

He stepped out from the archway and began crossing the courtyard, not hurrying. Timed and angled it so he wouldn't pass close to anyone, but he made sure not to seem obvious about that. He'd have liked to be wearing black. Kanlin Warriors had always worn black. It would have been pleasing to appear to victims that way: a dark apparition, a cold spirit, appearing in the night to destroy them.

But black would have been too noticeable. This wasn't the old days. He couldn't safely be distinctive. He was dressed the way an escort for musicians and singing girls would be: brown and green, tunic and trousers, a soft dark hat, no visible weapon (you didn't carry visible weapons into the clan compound unless you were an idiot). There was blood on his cloak now, but it was night and the fabric was dark.

And there wasn't anything he could *do* about it, was there?

He couldn't climb the wall and risk being seen. He wondered if a high-level Kanlin would have known how to do that, be invisible for long enough, or sense the precise moment when no one was looking. He wondered if their training taught them that. The thought made him almost sad.

But there were other ways of doing what he was here to do. He went straight for the door of her house. The doorway was recessed, under a lintel (they all were), and it was dark there. They weren't expecting guests, had no exterior torches lit. He pretended to knock, in case anyone passing looked over, but he made no sound. He wasn't a fool. He fished from his inner pocket the tool he used for doors. He tried the handle first.

It moved with a small click. There might be fools here, but they lived inside the compound, inside this house, they weren't standing in Sun Shiwei's boots tonight.

The imperial clan would all have valuable objects in their homes, but they lived in such sublime assurance of favour and protection that they didn't even lock their doors. He wondered, briefly, what kind of life could lead you to see the world that way.

He pushed the door open onto a dark hallway. Lifted a hand, as if greeting someone within. Stepped inside, closed the door silently behind him, not rushing at all. Inside, he drew a breath. It would be easy now. He was out of sight, and where he needed to be.

A thread of excitement prickled along his blood. He suppressed it. Not yet, he told himself. She needed killing first, and there would be servants down here, or even upstairs. She might even be in bed with one of them, with the husband gone. Maybe with another woman. They were said to be like that, the wives of the imperial clan.

No light on this level, no sound of movement as he listened. It was just late enough that they might be asleep after all. He moved quietly to where he knew the stairway would be, and then up, testing each stair. One creaked slightly under light pressure and he double-stepped his way over it. You learned the tricks, doing this sort of thing long enough.

He took out his knife, already bloodied. He ought to have cleaned it, but there hadn't been time. He preferred a clean knife. It felt ... well, cleaner. Top of the stairs. Hallways ran left and right, elbow-bends to corridors each way. Women's quarters would be on the right. Still no servants, no lights. They *were* asleep.

He went right, his eyes adjusting, saw calligraphy scrolls hanging on the inner wall, moved carefully around over-large tables with what looked like bronze vessels on them. He slowed down. If he banged into one of those the noise would rouse someone, bring men running from downstairs, people from outside, and everything would be marred.

He didn't bump anything. He prided himself on seeing well in the dark, a skill in his profession. He turned at the long corridor towards the back of the house. It was open on his right side here, a waist-high railing above their small courtyard. There was moonlight. He saw more bronzes below, outside, and what looked liked a funerary stele in the centre.

He had no idea what these people were doing with such things, but why would he expect to have an idea, or care? He was a weapon, they were targets. Or she was. He had been told the husband didn't matter. It was the wife who had offended. He didn't know how. It wasn't his job to know.

The corridor jogged left and then right again to where her room lay, at the back. She was on the right, over the courtyard. She'd have a balcony. He stopped and listened again. Creaks and groans of a night house. Sounds from the public spaces behind him. There was a shout back there and he stiffened, but it was an amused cry, followed by another, even more lively. Men coming back, or heading out—it wasn't too late for that. It was never too late for the pleasure districts. He might go that way himself after, he thought.

Would have to change clothing first. And he might well be satiated. The thought set his pulses going again. He was close enough for that to be all right. You worked best when you were mostly calm, but also alert, excited enough to be quicker than otherwise.

He opened the door to her room. Moonlight fell through the far window, enough for him to see the sleeping shape in the canopied bed, under coverlets. More bronzes in here. Two of them, either side of the balcony. The silk window coverings were down but let in enough light for him. There was a breeze. She was obviously not afraid of the chill of an autumn night. Or of a man coming in from her balcony.

He wasn't coming that way. He was already here. It was two long strides to the bed, and she needed to die before he enjoyed himself in the certainty of silence and night. Not that the knife wasn't another kind of enjoyment. He crossed the floor, blade in hand. He chopped downward, hard and fast. Once, twice—

A crashing, thunderous pain at the back of his head. The onset of black, then black.

THERE WERE LAMPS LIT. The light wobbled and swayed, so did the room. He was face down on the floor. His hands were bound behind his back, expertly. His boots had been removed.

He knew that last, shockingly, because he was cracked on the sole of one foot with some sort of stick. He shouted with pain.

"As I thought," came a woman's voice, behind and above him. "I told you I wouldn't kill him."

"You might have," a man said. Not angry, more an observation. "And we do need to ask our questions."

"And you will kill him after?" she asked.

"That isn't for me to say," said the man.

Sun Shiwei twisted his head but he couldn't see anyone. He had a sense there were several people in the room. The woman with the stick, at least three men. He could see the bed to his right. He had stabbed into cushions placed under coverings. One of them had fallen on the floor beside him, ripped open.

He didn't know where his knife was. He wasn't about to get it back. And if his boots were gone so was his second blade.

Through extreme pain and a pounding head an awareness emerged, took form: his coming here had been completely anticipated. He grunted, spat awkwardly, given his position. It dribbled on his chin.

He said, "I will join the army!"

Another hard blow, his other foot. He yelped again.

"Indeed?" he heard the woman say. "And why would the imperial army want an assassin?" She paused, then added, "A bad question. Why would they want an assassin with broken feet?"

"Be careful." The same man's voice again. "We need him to talk. And depending on what he says ..."

"You'd let him live? Really?"

There was no reply. The man might have nodded his head or shaken it—there was no way to tell. Sun Shiwei seized on this, though, through pain in his head and both feet.

"I will fight for Kitai!" he rasped. "I will go to the northwestern war!"

You could escape from the army, you could rise in it, you would be alive!

"Might he be castrated?" the woman asked, musingly. "That might be acceptable." She didn't sound like Lady Yu-lan, but she didn't sound the way a woman should, either.

"For others to decide, gracious lady. A magistrate is on his way. Maybe others of rank. I am not certain."

There came a sound from the corridor. Footsteps stopping at the doorway, a shadow across one lamp's light.

"There's a dead guard across the courtyard, sir. Someone found the body. Stabbed, probably a knife."

Inwardly, Sun Shiwei swore viciously. He took a ragged breath, trying to think through pain and panic. You needed to be loyal to those who paid you, but if you were dead, loyalty didn't help much on the far side, did it?

"Ah. That's why he came in so early." The woman again! How was she so assured, and how would she *know* that? She added, "That body is what will prove he isn't just an angry drunk looking to rape a woman while her husband is away."

He'd been planning to say that! No one had been killed, no one even harmed. *Put me in the army*, he'd say again. The army needed soldiers, any soldiers.

Harder now, with the dead guard out there. In fact, it became impossible.

"Mind you," the woman added thoughtfully, "we did know what he was really doing. You will allow my husband and me to thank the prime minister, later, I hope? He saved my life."

"You did much of that yourself, Lady Lin." The unseen man's voice was respectful. Shiwei still couldn't see any of them. He'd been—it was now clear—deceived and knocked unconscious by a woman.

"Only with your warning," she said. "I grieve for the guard. That will have been unintended. It forced this one to change his plans."

Exactly! thought Shiwei. *It did!*

"He'd have intended no other harm, only to kill me, then rape me after," the woman went on. She was unnaturally composed.

"After?" said the man.

"To ensure silence. The indignity to my body would have been to hide the reason for my death."

Fuck you, thought Sun Shiwei. *Fuck you and your gelded husband!*

Though that last thought brought him back to his present circumstance, and words just spoken, about castration.

"I will tell everything," he muttered, still trying to look around enough to see what he was dealing with.

"Of course you will," said the man behind him. "Everyone does under questioning."

Shiwei felt as if he was about to choke on what was suddenly lodged in his throat. His heart was pounding. His head hurt. He said, urgently, "It was the deputy prime minister! It was Kai Zhen who—"

He screamed. She'd slashed him across the back of the calves.

"A lie. You are the wife's instrument, not his," she said. "Kai Zhen is many things, but not this foolish. Not the same day he is exiled."

"You'll tell us the truth later," said another person, speaking for the first time. A colourless voice. A civil service figure? The court, someone with rank?

"I ... I can tell you right now! What do you need me to say?"

The man laughed. He *laughed*.

"You don't need to torture me! I will tell. Yes, it was the wife. Lady Yu-lan. It was. You don't need torture!"

A longer silence. The woman, for once, said nothing. It was the third person who spoke again, finally.

"Of course we do," he said gravely. "No one will believe a confession if there isn't any torture. And then you will probably die. Under interrogation, a regrettable accident, the usual way. This was all extremely foolish, as Lady Lin says. And too predictable."

He sounded almost regretful, Sun Shiwei thought. Not for the torture to come, but as if for the folly of men and women in the world.

The woman said, "If that is the case ... if he is not going to be gelded and sent to the army, may I be permitted to strike him again? I am afraid I do feel angry. It may also be foolish, but ..."

Sun Shiwei squeezed his eyes shut. The cold-voiced man spoke, judiciously. "He was here to destroy your honour and end your life. I think it can be permitted, gracious lady."

"Thank you," he heard her say.

Then she said, leaning over, speaking directly to Shiwei, close to his bleeding head, "This is for my father. For what they tried to do to him. Know that."

She straightened. He saw her shadow. Then the most appalling pain crashed over him, one foot then the other, struck full force this time, bones splintering, and he lost awareness of all things again.

CENTURIES BEFORE, the last Kanlin Warriors of Stone Drum Mountain had died on the wide, flat top of their holy mountain in the north. The Long Wall had earlier been breached in many places.

The last of them held out a considerable time, but eventually were overrun by barbarians—the emerging Xiaolu people.

The mountain sanctuary was plundered and burned.

The Kanlins on Stone Drum—about eighty of them, it was believed, at the very end—had elected to be slain there, to die fighting, rather than retreat south and surrender their sacred mountain to the steppe.

It was a complex incident in history and those who shaped and recorded the official doctrines in this Twelfth Dynasty had difficulty with it.

The black-clad Kanlins had been mystics with esoteric beliefs, and notoriously independent. They allowed women to train and fight and live freely among them. Many of their practices (not only concerning women) diverged from acceptable behaviour. They were also a military group as much as a religious one, and everyone knew what had happened in the Ninth because of military leaders. The Kanlin Warriors might have been permitted their secluded, untaxed sanctuaries back then, but this was a different era, a different world.

On the other hand, they had been honourable, loyal, and unquestionably brave, and the last ones on the summit of Stone

Drum, men and women both, had died for Kitai in one of the lost and longed-for Fourteen Prefectures.

That had to be allowed to mean something.

It had been decided that no one would be punished or criticized for making reference to that last stand on Stone Drum Mountain— for writing a song or a poem or a street theatre performance about it. But the last defence of the mountain would not become an officially sanctioned mourning ritual of any kind. It was seen as preferable that the Kanlins slip quietly from history into folk tale, peasant belief, akin to fox-women or those spirit worlds said to be hidden under oak-tree roots in forests.

Good governance, in any time, required delicate decisions of just this sort.

SHE IS FINALLY ALONE. All the men have left: the one who'd come to kill her, the guards, the soldiers, the senior official from the Ministry of Rites (a bleak, cold man). The house is hers again. She tries to decide if it is the same house.

She is waiting for tea to be brought to her. No one is asleep. She is downstairs, in the small reception room—made smaller by bronzes they've collected.

Servants are cleaning her bedchamber, discarding the knife-shredded silks and pillow. They will light incense in burners, to take away the odour of so many men in a lady's room, and the presence of so much violence.

Some of that violence had been hers. She is still not entirely certain why she'd been so insistent about that. It has to do with her father's exile, she tells herself, and that is surely true, but it might not be all the truth. She'd used her husband's second-favourite stick. It is heavy.

His favourite stick is with him now. He is away. She sits by a fire trying to decide if she is going to be able to forgive him for not being here tonight. Yes, he'd planned this journey some time ago.

They had both been preparing to go west, towards Xinan and the hills above it, the burial mounds of long-ago emperors.

Then she'd received word about her father—his shocking, unspeakable exile to Lingzhou—and of course she wasn't going anywhere at all.

Wai should not have gone either. It is hard for her to shake that thought. A husband, a son-in-law, he ought to have stayed to use whatever influence he had to help.

Problem was, he *had* no influence, and the hard truth was that if his father-in-law was named a treacherous member of an abhorred faction it was bad news for Qi Wai, and the smartest thing for him was to be as detached as possible from Lin Kuo's banishment.

It had made sense for Wai to leave Hanjin.

That didn't mean she had to forgive him for it.

She'd used his stick to strike the assassin as he strode to her bed and stabbed downwards (she might have been there, she might easily have been sleeping there). She'd been instructed not to hit him with all her strength, that he was to remain alive.

She'd hit him with all her strength.

He did remain alive. She'd thought he would, although she hadn't greatly cared in the moment. That, by itself, is disturbing. That she can kill or not kill, with indifference as to which it might be.

The tea finally comes. Her principal maidservant is agitated, trembling. The servants have not had time to deal with this. Neither has she. She is still trying to understand, and accept, the feelings of rage that rose within her tonight, looking down at the man on the floor of her bedroom, his hands bound behind his back.

It really is about her father, she decides. The assassin wasn't the one who'd ordered Lin Kuo exiled (of course he wasn't!) but he was a part of that evil, and the only part she could see, reach, strike—break bones in his feet. She had felt them break.

She'd asked if he could be castrated. She'd *wanted* that.

It is frightening, how much anger can be inside a person.

He'd be dead by night's end, the bleak man from the Ministry of Rites had told her. And the Lady Yu-lan was to be arrested in the morning. They were satisfied, he'd said before leaving, that this one had been the instrument of the lady, not her husband. The exile of her father was Kai Zhen's doing, but not this.

She watches her servant pour the tea, without the ease she usually displays, willowy as she bends. Her husband likes this servant for her grace. Qi Wai likes that in women, his wife knows. She is not especially graceful herself, not trained that way, nor soothing and assuaging in her manner. He values her intelligence (she knows it), he likes having her with him on expeditions to hunt down scrolls, bronze tripods, weapons, wine cups, artifacts of distant dynasties, but she does not ease his spirit.

She doesn't ease her own. That is not what she is. She has not yet decided what she is. She is someone who can speak of castrating an attacker, break bones in his feet.

He had come to kill her. And rape her. They had intended to send her father to Lingzhou Isle to die. The assassin's screaming hadn't distressed her. It might do so later, Shan thinks. She dismisses the servant, picks up her tea. She might hear those screams in her mind. She is afraid she will.

Her father will not be exiled now. She has a letter confirming that. It is on the desk across the room. The letter had warned that Lady Yu-lan might send someone with malevolent purpose to their house tonight. Guards would be provided. It had also informed her that the celestial emperor, in his supreme compassion, had himself rescinded the order of exile for Court Gentleman Lin Kuo. He was to be raised in rank, instead.

The serene and exalted emperor also wished to have conveyed his personal commendation to Lady Lin Shan for her well-formed brush strokes. She was commanded to attend upon him in the Genyue the following afternoon.

They are to discuss calligraphy and other matters.

Imperial guards would call for her, the letter advised. It was suggested by the writer that she might wish to bring some of her own songs, in her own hand, as gifts for the emperor.

The letter was signed by Hang Dejin, prime minister of Kitai.

The emperor wishes to see her. In his garden. She is to bring her songs. It is beyond belief. If she doesn't understand her own nature, Lin Shan thinks, how can she possibly hope to understand the world?

She begins to cry. She dislikes that, but there is no one else in the room now, and so she permits herself this. It is the middle of the night. The moon is west. She drinks hot, scented tea from Szechen in an autumn room lit by three lamps, crowded with ancient bronze, and she watches her tears fall into the cup.

There might be a song in that, she thinks. She wonders where her husband is tonight, if he has reached Xinan.

She wonders if the assassin is dead yet.

SUN SHIWEI WOULD LOSE and regain consciousness, in considerable agony, throughout that night and into the first hours of the grey, windy morning that eventually came. He did, indeed, tell them what they wished to know. They did, indeed, ensure that he died accidentally under questioning.

LATER THAT MORNING, rain beginning to fall, eight members of the Imperial Palace Army presented themselves at the gates of the city mansion of disgraced Deputy Prime Minister Kai Zhen.

Seeing them, a small crowd gathered in the street. They backed away under orders from tense, irritated guards, but did not entirely disperse. Dogs paced and barked among them, hoping for scraps. Two of the dogs began to fight each other and were separated with curses and kicks. The rain continued.

Four of the guards went inside when the gates were opened. They emerged not long after. One spoke to their commander. It was obvious, even to those watching from a distance, that the leader was both angry and afraid. He could be seen slapping nervously at his thigh.

Eventually he barked orders, his voice thin in the thin rain. The same four guards went back in through the gates. When they came out again, two were carrying what appeared to be a body wrapped in linen. The leader continued to look unhappy. They marched away, in the best order they could manage, through a muddy street.

A story began to spread. That tended to happen in Hanjin. They had come to arrest Yu-lan, the wife of the deputy prime minister. She had apparently sent an assassin into the imperial clan compound the night before. This was deeply shocking. It was unclear why she had done so. The man had been captured and questioned in the night. He had named Lady Yu-lan before dying.

She had killed herself in her own house, rather than be taken away.

An understandable decision, in the circumstances. She might have hoped to be allowed burial in the family's gravesite in the south. This was not to be. She was burned near the palace grounds and her ashes thrown into one of the canals.

The Cho teachings and those of the Sacred Path agreed that even if this created an unquiet spirit, it was not only permitted, it was necessary. Otherwise, how could the state truly punish (and deter) evildoers deserving of death? You needed to send that punishment beyond, into the spirit world. The souls of such criminals should not be granted rest.

Kai Zhen, disgraced and exiled, set forth from Hanjin two weeks later with his household (greatly reduced).

It was accepted that he'd had no part in what his wife had done, or tried to do. His exile was not unduly harsh, south of the Great River to the countryside near Shantong where he had a home among silk farms.

He lost his income and civil service rank, of course. Also, the many ways of supplementing wealth that had come with his position. But he'd had years in power, would be assured of a comfortable exile.

Journeying south, he wore mourning, left his hair unwashed and unbound, ate alone and sparingly, was seen to weep. He avoided his children, his concubines, any friends or followers who tried to see him as the family travelled into late, wet autumn and the weather began to turn colder. His grief for his wife was evident. Some declared it commendable after a long marriage; others that he was being excessive, deviating from right behaviour, proper restraint; still others that he was linking himself too closely with a murderous criminal, over and above his own errors.

LATE ONE COLD NIGHT, in a market town five days from the Great River, one of his concubines—not the youngest, but still young— takes upon herself what has to be considered a risk. She has been giving it thought for some time.

She goes from the women's quarters of the house they have occupied and crosses in darkness, shivering in the courtyard, to where the men are sleeping. She goes to the doorway of the room Kai Zhen occupies. Taking a breath, she knocks softly, but then opens the door and enters without waiting for a response.

He is alone inside. There is a fire lit. She had seen light, knew he was not asleep. She would have gone in even if he was. He is at a desk, in a lined night robe, writing by lamplight. She doesn't know what. She doesn't care. He turns, surprised.

She forces herself not to bow. Standing very straight, she says what she has rehearsed. "You are the great man of our time. We are honoured to serve you, to be near you. It is a grief to me to see you this way."

Saying *to me* is the important, dangerous, presumptuous part. She knows it. He will know it.

He stands up, setting down his brush. "Well," he says, "just now, greatness does not seem to be part of my—"

"Greatness is within you."

She interrupts him deliberately. She has a model for this. She has been in his household three years. She is skilled with flute and *pipa*. She is tall and thin and extremely clever. She has smooth skin, often commented upon.

She is also ambitious, more than she could (or would ever in her life) tell. The wife, the dead and gone wife, had often interrupted him when they were together, thinking they were unobserved.

"It is ... it is gentle of you to—"

"Gentle?" she says. And takes two small steps nearer. This, too, she has observed done by the wife. The dead wife. It was like a dance, she remembers thinking, a kind of ritual between them. Affairs of men and women often are, she has found.

He straightens his shoulders, turns fully to her, away from the desk.

"When tigers come together in the forests," she says, "is it meant to be gentle?"

"Tigers?" he says.

But his voice has changed. She knows men, knows this man.

She doesn't speak again. Only comes up to him, those small steps, as if gliding. She is wearing a scent taken from the mansion when they left. It had belonged to the wife (the dead wife). That is another risk, but risks do need to be taken, if you want anything of life.

She reaches up, both hands, draws his head down to hers.

Bites him on a corner of the lower lip. Not gently. She has never done that, has only seen it, unobserved.

Then she moves her mouth to his ear and whispers words she has been thinking about, devising, for days and days as they travelled.

She feels him respond, his breath catching, his sex hardening against her body. Her satisfaction in having been right is deeply arousing.

She services him that night on the chair by the desk, on the floor, the bed, and takes her own (real) pleasure more intensely than she ever has before, when she was only one concubine among many, terrified she might be overlooked, disappear into the wasted, empty years of a life.

Those fears are over by the time morning comes.

It is said, at the country estate where they settle, and more widely, later, that she is in some terrifying way the ghost of Yu-lan—never permitted burial—come back into the world.

He marries her in springtime. You didn't have to observe full mourning rites for someone declared a criminal. His sons are unhappy but say nothing. What are sons going to say?

She has two of the women whipped with bamboo rods that winter for whispering about her, and one pretty, too-intelligent younger concubine is branded—on the face—and dismissed.

She doesn't mind the ghost idea being cast abroad, in furtive murmurs or wine talk. It gives her another kind of power: association with a dangerous spirit. Power over him, over all of them.

Her name is Tan Ming and she *matters*. She is determined that everyone will know this before the end, whenever, however that comes. She lights a candle and prays every morning, without fail, for Yu-lan. Her husband thinks she is being virtuous.

ം

Even after all these years, even with another summer over, the heat of Lingzhou still caught him like a blow each day. It seemed impossible to have the knowledge of it prepare you for the next day, if you came from the north.

And it wasn't as if he was from the farthest north, the starting places of Kitai. He was Szechen-born. The Lu family came from humid, hot weather: rain, thunderstorms, forests of dripping leaves, fog, mist rising from the ground. They understood it. Or, he'd thought he understood, before he came to the island.

Lingzhou was a different world.

It was harder on Mah. His son had been born in Shantong, on the coast, during Chen's time as prefect there. Those had been the best years, the poet thought. A sophisticated city, between the sea and the serene wonder of West Lake. The man-made lake had been Chen's joy: pleasure boats drifting, music drifting, all day and at night, hills framing it on the inland side, singing girl houses on the shore close to the city. Elegant, well-funded religious retreats for Cho and Sacred Path dotting the northern shoreline, green roofs and yellow, the upswept curves, bells ringing the hours for prayer, the sound crossing the water.

There were fireworks on the lake at festivals, and music from pleasure boats all through the night, lanterns floating on the water ...

Not a place that would prepare you for Lingzhou Isle. Here, you needed to take any exercise in the earliest hour, before the heat battered you into torpor, lassitude, fitful daytime naps in a sweat-soaked bed.

They were doing their dawn routine, father and son, his usual frivolity that they were assailing some evil fortress, when a cleric came running up (running!) from the temple at the end of the village.

It seemed, if the man was to be believed (and understood: he was stammering with shock), that something miraculous had transpired. Honourable Lu Chen and his honourable son were entreated to come see.

The usual cluster of villagers had gathered to watch them exercise. The elder Lu, the poet, was famous and amusing, both; it was worth coming to see them. That same group trailed them west through the village, and others joined them as they went, past the *yamen* (not yet opened for the day, there was never a need for administrative haste here) and along the path—carefully, watching for snakes—to the temple.

Eventful moments, let alone loudly declared miracles, were not the daily coinage of the isle.

Red and yellow flowers, wet and heavy.
Forest's edge, the path in rain.
I remember peonies in Yenling
But this south is very different from the north.

Can an angry ghost travel this far?
Cross the strait, afflict an exile's life?
Or does Lingzhou hold only its own dead
Wherever they might have been born?

In the rainy season we lose the stars.
We do not lose friendship and loyalty,
Good talk, courtesy, the virtues of this time
As they are of any age ever in Kitai.

I think of friends far away and my heart aches.
I drink wine with new companions.
They have opened their gate to a stranger.
Kindness is a brightly feathered bird on a branch.

We listen to their bell as it rings.
We drink and they refill our wine cups.
I will count myself honoured and blessed
Whatever becomes of my last days.

He had written that in springtime on their wall, running hand, large letters, the wide brush quick. The poem emerging as if discovering itself. He was known for improvising in this way. It would seldom be one's best writing but would have a different kind of value, created right there, in the moment, as the black ink defined the wall.

They had been very happy, the clerics, entering the room after he was done, seeing his words. It would help them a great deal,

once it became known that a poem by Lu Chen was on a wall in
Lingzhou Isle.

He did this for friends, he did it for joy. He'd lived poetry all
his life: carefully revised or swiftly improvised, drunken or sober,
dark night, moonlight, morning mist, from the heart of power or
protesting against it, or exiled, finally, here.

The clerics had stared at the wall, the words. They had touched
his hands, bowing over and over. Two of them had wept. He had
suggested drinking in celebration. Said he very much wanted wine,
which was only truth. One of them had gone across the village and
come back with Lu Mah.

It had been a long evening and night of food and drink. Not the
best wine, but that wasn't always what mattered most. They had
slept there, he and his son, on cots in a guest chamber, and been
escorted home at sunrise.

That was one of the times when he'd seen the ghost on their
cottage roof.

Then, a little later, that year's rains had come, and the damp
and drip had immediately begun to cause the letters on the wall to
run and fade. The last time he'd been at the sanctuary, they'd been
almost gone.

They weren't, any more, he now saw.

The poem was back. It was strong and vivid on the temple wall,
as if he'd brushed it on yesterday. He recognized his own hand.
What man would not know his own brush? No other person had
come in and written out his poem anew. No one could do that.

His characters, which had faded towards a smeared incoherence,
were simply here again, in the running hand of the poet Lu Chen,
often proclaimed to be an equal to the giants of the Ninth.

(Others said that, not him.)

But he knew, as he stood in bewildered, humbled silence, looking
at his own words, listening to the clerics murmuring urgent prayers
and incantations, hearing the crowd behind them whispering

in awe, as he looked at his son and their eyes met, he knew that something, someone, from the spirit world had been here, was here now, and that this was—perhaps at a life's end?—a very great gift.

Honoured and blessed, he had written.

He wondered if this meant he was about to die. It could mean that.

My last days, he had written.

IT TOOK A LONG TIME, the distances and difficulty were extreme, but the message sent from Hanjin recalling him from the island, allowing him back as far as the estate where he and his brother had a farm, reached Lingzhou the next spring.

There was a date on the letter (it was an imperial document) and so they knew it had been issued the same day the Miracle of the Poem was discovered on the temple wall.

By then, travellers had begun arriving, come to see the words.

They were able to start north—Lu Chen and his son and the servant girl who asked to come with them—before the rains arrived. They waited out the wet season in the town of Fujou near the southern mountain range, amid terraced rice fields.

They crossed the mountains in autumn on high, twisting paths. Two of them reached his brother's home and his own just after the New Year's Festival, late on a mild winter's day, with a moon rising.

The girl had died one morning in Fujou.

Lu Chen had seen another ghost that afternoon—he couldn't swear it was the same one as on Lingzhou, but he thought it was, which was chilling and strange. He'd also seen a fox in the open, red-orange at twilight, staring back at him, on a walk the evening before.

He would always believe, because of these things, that her death had been meant for him. That spirits had intervened, deflected a god's arrow from him—to find her, since an immortal's loosed arrow always had to strike somewhere.

They buried her with formality and respect. Mah was grieving. Lu Chen offered prayers in her name for the rest of his days, along with those for his parents and his first wife and his dead children, and the one for the ghost, which might be hers now.

One of his most beloved late poems was about a woman's soul in the shape of a grey heron, lost on a mountainside far from home.

The other poem, the one on the wall at Lingzhou, never again faded for as long as the temple stood. It was there, drawing visitors, while the dynasty lasted, and after it ended, and after the next one ended. It survived all rains that fell, all thunderstorms, floods, calamities, until the building itself burned down one moonless winter night long afterwards, when an acolyte fell asleep tending the night fire and a wind rose up.

There was never again a spirit seen on the roof or anywhere near the cottage where Lu Chen, the celebrated Twelfth Dynasty poet, was said to have lived in the time of his exile on the island, long ago.

PART TWO

CHAPTER VII

No real poet would claim originality for an image of streams becoming rivers over distance and time: how even those that can destroy farmlands with their flooding, or thunder through gorges and over falls, begin as rivulets in the rocks of mountains, or as underground waters that find the surface and begin to flow across the land to find the sea.

Nor could the idea that rivers come together to make a single force be asserted as distinctive. The test is always in the words—and the brush strokes shaping them. There are only so many ideas, so many patterns in the world.

Rivers *do* usually begin in almost imperceptible ways. The great events and changes of the world under heaven also frequently start that way, their origins recognized only by those troubling themselves to look back.

Another idea everyone knows—historians, poets, farmers, even emperors: how much more clearly we see, looking back.

☙☙

One of the customs of the steppe—no one knew how long ago it had begun—was for kaghans of tribes offering submission to a greater one to dance for the stronger leader at the ceremonies where tribute and homage were paid.

Dancing was an act performed by women—servants, slaves, hired performers, courtesans—or by subjugated men displaying their ritual abasement for all to see.

TE-KUAN, FOURTEENTH EMPEROR of the Xiaolu, was a proud man and a dangerous one, particularly when he'd been drinking. He was equally comfortable with killing people himself or having others do it for him.

He could not read or write but he had officials who could do both, and that was the nature of an emperor, in his view, certainly on the steppe. As leader of his people, of their empire, he was required to be strong enough to control his horsemen and their commanders, subdue or neutralize neighbouring tribes and peoples, compel their tribute, and ensure that the Kitan to the south, numerous as they might be, were sufficiently fearful to make their own very large payment north in silver and silk.

Te-kuan had no problem with the Kitan naming that payment a gift. They were the people for whom words mattered, not the Xiaolu. On the steppe you had other things to think about.

Older brother, younger brother were now the Kitan terms for the two emperors. Until two years ago it had been *uncle* and *nephew*.

Te-kuan's advisers had accomplished that change. He didn't greatly care, himself, though he understood that when you dealt with the Kitan it made sense to press in ways that mattered to them, force them to bow down lower, and lower. So now he was a younger brother receiving an older one's gifts from emissaries each spring.

He knew, the whole world knew, that what he really was, was a warrior leader accepting tribute from a terrified empire. An empire whose armies couldn't even defeat the Kislik in their desert to the northwest.

The Kislik, Te-kuan thought, were nothing! He could destroy them any time he wanted, but better—his advisers had persuaded him—to let them have their harsh, bleak land and pay him tribute as well.

That had become the problem, of course. The Kislik resented paying both the Xiaolu and the Kitan for the right to survive. They'd decided to resist the one they judged weaker, if more numerous. Te-kuan had smiled, hearing of it. He'd smiled again, learning of the Kitan disaster below Erighaya.

Seventy thousand soldiers? A waste of lives so appalling it stopped the mind from thinking about it. The Xiaolu didn't *have* so many riders to lose, but theirs knew how to fight. When you could afford to lose so many of your soldiers, it meant you didn't take care of them. That was what Te-kuan thought.

The war had drained the Kislik, too, weakening both empires that bordered him. The two of them had made a peace this year, finally. They were trading again. He didn't care, so long as both kept paying the Xiaolu.

His people lived in a hard, open-to-the-heavens world. They were children of steppe and sky. Wind and drought defined them, and their herds. Here, you were judged by what you did, not by words painted with a brush. What the Kitan emperor *did* was send two hundred thousand units each of silver and silk to him every year.

Who was really the elder brother? You could laugh at their vain pretense, or grow angry at times, if you were drinking.

Te-kuan ruled over a large number of Kitan people in his own southern territories, what they still called the Fourteen Prefectures in Hanjin where his "brother" Wenzong had his court. Wenzong was said to enjoy being given his meals from the fingers of his women (sometimes chewed by them first, rumour had it!) and to need two young ones to sing him to sleep each night and remain with him in case he woke, afraid, in the dark.

The disputed lands, the Fourteen Prefectures, were still Xiaolu, in their empire, after all this time. Was it a surprise to anyone? His Kitan paid taxes, laboured, farmed fields. They were useful to him. If some were occasionally troublesome, that was what his horsemen were for. To keep order, doing whatever was necessary.

It occurred to Te-kuan, riding east in autumn for the annual ceremony with subject tribes, that he might be accused of dwelling upon words himself, if he valued being an emperor more than a kaghan.

Someone could say this. They would be wrong. It wasn't only words. It had to do with what the Xiaolu had now become.

A kaghan ruled a tribe wandering the sweep of the steppe, following their herds of cattle, sheep, goats, horses (always horses) with the seasons, battling wolves and hunger, living in yurts they carried with them, never at rest until they were left out on the grass under the sky when they died.

An empire ... an empire had cities, walls, markets for trade. There were five Xiaolu capital cities now, in each of the four directions and one in the centre. An empire had farms and granaries and taxation, and men who knew how to manage such things. That was why his Kitan subjects mattered so much. In a good year they could nearly feed the Xiaolu with their harvest. In a less good one his officials bought grain and rice from Kitai—with silver the Kitan had given them in tribute!

Empires also had subjects acknowledging their mastery. Those were the tribes that still called their leaders kaghan, Te-kuan thought.

Empires had scribes and courts and a civil service. They had builders of wooden and stone structures to set down upon the land. They knew how to divert streams, dredge canals, irrigate fields. And now there was even a Xiaolu script, a calligraphy of their own. A

Kitan had invented it for them, yes, but he was a subject of Emperor Te-kuan, served at his court.

An emperor ruled many kinds of people, not just his ancestral tribe, with their memories of wandering.

The leaders of three subject tribes were meeting him now at the gathering place by the Black River. They would pay tribute in horses, in silver and amber and furs, sometimes in gold, always in women.

Te-kuan preferred the horses and gold. He had enough women, you could never have enough horses.

He'd have preferred to send one of his sons on this journey by now. It was a long way to ride, and autumn was still hot and dry, with winds, and insects plaguing them whenever the wind died down. But he understood that it was necessary for the tribes to see him—their emperor—to acknowledge his power. Te-kuan had three thousand horsemen with him. The tribes needed to understand that he could easily be among them with an army, that there were reasons why they paid him tribute, called him lord.

Why they danced for him at night, by torchlight, after feasting.

BACK IN THE THIRD DYNASTY of Kitai, a thousand years ago, a fashion had begun of grouping things by fours. The Kitan liked order, numbering, symmetry, and they also enjoyed the debates that ensued.

So they had the Four Great Beauties (ending with Wen Jian of the Ninth, still), the Four Great Battles, the Four Deadliest Floods of the Golden River, Four Worst Betrayals, Four Greatest Calligraphers ...

In the Twelfth Dynasty, with so many clever, indolent *jinshi* graduates, grouping by fours was sometimes a source of amusement. The witty—as opposed to the wise—need to mock. They proposed the Four Loudest Belches, the Four Worst Tea Rooms in Hanjin, even silliness like the Four First Numbers. After enough wine, and in trusted company, someone might propose the Four Worst Ministers, but name only three, leaving room ...

That was a dangerous game. Wine led men into error, and trusted company was a shifting, ambiguous concept. Better to nurse one's cup and remain quiet even among those assumed to be friends. There were spies, for one thing, employed by the old prime minister and his followers—and the followers, the younger generation, were known to be worse than Minister Hang.

A small number of ironic men mocking a tradition doesn't end it. Those who jested in this way were implicitly acknowledging the power of the form. And so it was that some years after these events, one well-known list was the Four Most Calamitous Mistakes.

Among these, routinely included, was a decision made by the fourteenth emperor of the Xiaolu one autumn night, among his eastern subjects.

It was remarkable that this came to be included in a Kitan list: the Xiaolu were barbarians, and the incident in question involved their dealings with another tribe. A people the Kitan had scarcely even heard of at the time.

That obscurity underlay everything, of course. The world could change (it did change) with a swiftness beyond belief.

THE CUPS of *kumiss* remained, and the urns from which they were steadily refilled. The food and bowls had been taken away by the men assigned to serve. They were from the three tribute-giving tribes. Normally slaves would do this, or women would clear, then serve in other ways, in tents or out in the darkness on the autumn grass, but there were meanings attached to everything at these gatherings. There were no women here, other than the ones being given to the Xiaolu emperor as tribute.

There were no shamans either. Shamans were dangerous. The emperor's food was separately prepared by his own people. A eunuch tasted it. He had adopted the use of eunuchs from Kitai,

their court. Not everything they did in the south was folly. Some
of the castrates were intelligent, useful to him. Others ... tasted his
food for poison.

Men with no family to protect or advance would align themselves
with the leader they served. It made sense to Te-kuan. Family
demands, ambitious wives, could lead a man astray. The steppe was
filled from rim to rim with such stories.

Torches had been planted on poles as the sun went down and
were now burning in the space before the yurts. The labour had
been done by the three tribute-paying tribes: Khashin, Jeni, Altai.

They had arrived at the Black River before the emperor, as was
proper. They had waited for Te-kuan. They were his subjects. They
paid him tribute. They danced for him.

He would go home soon with his three thousand warriors, new
horses, a sizable tribute, and allegiances affirmed in the east. You
could find your way to a better state of mind, Te-kuan thought,
considering all of this.

The kaghan of the Khashin tribe was named Paiya. He was a big
man, but not good with *kumiss*. He was drunk already, amusingly.
A leader needed to be able to drink with his riders to keep their
respect. Paiya stood, wavered. He lifted his cup to Te-kuan, and
drank it off. He threw the cup into the fire in the centre of the circle.

Then he danced around that fire before his emperor. Sparks
leaped, torches burned black smoke, hiding the stars where the
wind carried it, then those stars could be seen again. Paiya danced
well for a man far gone in drink. Perhaps *because* he was far gone
in drink, Te-kuan thought. It would be difficult to dance like this
before another man, before your own people, if you were hard-eyed
and sober and had pride.

A thought. He watched the large, shambling leader of the
Khashin circle the fire, saw a spark land on his clothing, then
another. Te-kuan drank, held up his cup. A tall eunuch hastily
refilled it. He drank again, still thinking.

Paiya finished his dance. It had lasted long enough, no sign of resentment (though Paiya must feel it if he was half a man). He lifted a hand, palm out, in salute. The tribes of the steppe did not bow. The Xiaolu expected bowing only when Kitan emissaries came.

Under autumn stars, the kaghan of the Jeni now rose. He was new, young. The Jeni had been restive in the days of Te-kuan's father. There had been a large force sent this way, restiveness had ended. Te-kuan watched the young kaghan carefully. He saw that the man (he forgot his name, it didn't matter) was more sober than Paiya of the Khashin had been.

He danced, however. Jumping across the fire and then back, leaping high, hands outflung, heels kicking back. There was laughter and even approval. Te-kuan allowed himself to be seen smiling. Let a tribal leader find his pride and approval in dancing well for his emperor. He was a good-looking man, this one. The Jeni were a handsome people. Te-kuan wondered about the women they had brought for him, his first such thought.

Once more across the fire, a high arc, one leg before him this time, one stretched behind. Was he showing off prowess too much, asserting the force and power of the Jeni? Te-kuan stopped smiling. He drank. He looked to his left where his most trusted councillor sat (side of the heart).

Yao-kan murmured, "It is his first dance, lord of the steppe. He is presenting himself to the other two kaghans. Remember, the Altai moved on them last year, when this one's father died. There was fighting."

The Altai had taken pasturelands from the Jeni and control of a river that had marked a border, shifting tribal boundaries and access to water. It was one of the things Te-kuan was going to have to deal with in the morning. Part of why he was here.

"His name?" the emperor asked. "This one?"

"O-Pang. His father was—"

"I remember the father."

Te-kuan felt unhappy again, suddenly. His gaze went from the dancer to where the Altai sat, cross-legged on the ground, bare-chested, their hair in the style they still favoured—shaved in front and on top, long down the sides and the back, never tied. Longer than a Xiaolu woman's, Te-kuan thought sourly.

The Altai came from the northeast, towards the Koreini Peninsula, lands known to be among the worst on earth. Savage in winter: snow and ice, ice monsters prowling beyond hall fires in black nights (or so it was said). Broiling hot in summer with dried-up streams, vast clouds of mosquitoes, and biting flies that blotted the sun, killed animals, and drove men mad.

It was no wonder they sought to move south, the Altai. And west, perhaps, thought the emperor of the Xiaolu, sipping his *kumiss* again. Maybe they also wanted to move west.

There were not many of them, no large number could live in such harsh lands. That was the one good thing about the Altai, he thought. That, and their furs and amber. Their women were ugly to him, squat. Men and women had black, small, hard eyes. The men rode horses as well as anyone alive.

O-Pang of the Jeni did a last leap. Te-kuan saw him stumble a little on landing, and smiled thinly to see it. O-Pang turned and lifted a hand to his emperor. Te-kuan, all graciousness, saluted in return. He had not done that for the first kaghan. Give the young man a small gift. Keep him dancing.

He was still in his black mood. These came over him sometimes. It was possible *kumiss* had something to do with it. He looked across at the Altai again. Their long-time kaghan was named Yan'po. A scarred, barrel-chested man, older than Te-kuan. Black hair covered his arms and chest like the pelt of an animal. The Altai still worshipped animals in the old way, found totem spirits among them. Their shamans worked magic among those spirits.

There were tigers in the forests where they came from. The largest in the world, it was said. Their roaring in the night was reported to melt the strength from a man, make him unable to stand upright. Even a brave warrior would fall on the ground, meet his tiger-death blind and trembling.

It wasn't Yan'po of the Altai that the emperor was looking at in what he called his black mood. Black mood, he was thinking. Black Altai. He drained his cup. He set it on the ground beside him. He pointed. "We will have that one dance for us," he said.

He smiled, a smile none of his own people would ever confuse with amusement. "We would spare our old companion and subject, Yan'po, from dancing tonight. Let a younger man, their war-leader, outdo the kaghan of the Jeni, just as he tried to outdo him with an attack in spring."

There had been good-humoured, *kumiss*-infused talk and laughter within the circle of torches, under stars and sky. Now that stopped. There was no movement, suddenly. Even the men pouring the *kumiss* stood still. In the silence you could hear the crackle of the fire, the sound of horses in the wide night.

On the far side of the fire, the war-leader of the Altai stared straight at the emperor. He said softly, barely moving his lips, "I will not do it."

His brother, beside him on his left, also staring ahead, said, "He will kill you."

"Then he kills me. I will not do it."

"Wan'yen—"

"I will not do it. Take vengeance for me."

Someone moved on his other side. Their kaghan stood up heavily.

He said, "I have not surrendered my title, emperor of the Xiaolu people. This dance is mine to do."

"Kaghan, no!" exclaimed the war-leader beside him, quickly looking up.

"I will speak with you later," snapped the kaghan. Yan'po's thin white hair was still long, bright under the nearest torch. He had a diagonal scar down his chest from neck to hip. Two fingers of his left hand were missing.

Across the space and the flame the emperor could be seen shaking his head. "I said the war-leader, kaghan of the Altai. He led the attack on the Jeni."

"Nothing the Altai do is without my deciding it," said Yan'po. His voice was thin but clear.

"Is it so? You were by the river then, kaghan, for that battle in spring?"

Yan'po was silent. Everyone knew he hadn't been.

The emperor added, "When did the Altai tribe last go to war without their kaghan leading them? I have historians now at my court, they will wish to know. *They write things down.*" He said it viciously, like a lash.

Yan'po shifted uneasily. "I will dance," he insisted stubbornly. "It is my task and my ... my duty."

"Sit down!" said the emperor of the Xiaolu, and it was a command. "I said who I would have dance for me. Guards, if the war-leader of the Altai does not rise, shoot the three men to his left."

One of the three would be his brother.

"I am the kaghan!" cried Yan'po.

"*And I am the emperor!*" said Te-kuan.

He looked across at the Altai war-leader, beside the standing figure of his kaghan. "Do you dance, or do I kill three people and let your kaghan do it, after all? I have decided I am content either way."

The emperor's guards had drawn bows but had not fitted arrows yet. It would take no time at all to do so. These were riders of the steppe.

Wan'yen stood up.

Not a big man, but lean and muscled. His face was a mask. There came a sigh from the men gathered.

"I am honoured to spare my kaghan the need to leap about

in the dark," Wan'yen of the Altai said. Describing it, defining it that way.

Then he danced.

It was not a dance such as the others had performed, nor one that anyone had ever seen at a tribute gathering. Wan'yen danced a war. Over and around that fire, in the circle of riders assembled under stars on the grassland by the river.

He sprang over the flames as the Jeni kaghan had done, but his was not a movement meant to conjure grace or youth but a hard, fierce power. He did not kick back with his heels, or spread his legs like a slave woman hoping to attract a man and make a life out of the ruins of her capture.

He went over the fire as if over a defensive ditch in a battle. He landed on the far side (towards the emperor) with his feet spread and balanced, and one could—easily—imagine a rider's sword in his hand, or a bow. Light from behind him and light from the torches played across his body, sliding him into and out of a watcher's vision as he moved.

He circled the fire again, towards his own tribe, turning his back on the emperor. His now were the movements of a fighter in feigned retreat: the quick steps designed to draw an enemy to reckless pursuit. And then, from the far side of the fire he leaped over it again, but this time with a high head-over-heels flip, knees drawn up—the sort that the most skilled riders did from horseback to get them over a wall.

Again he came down near the Xiaolu party and their bowmen, who still held their bows. The fire sparked behind him as he landed, half a dozen paces from the emperor.

The Altai war-leader looked at Te-kuan, and in the uneven, wavering light, his gaze was not one that could be named submissive, however hard one might try.

He circled back, spinning and wheeling, crouching and springing high, his right hand extended, and one could again imagine a sword there as he approached torches and passed around them, the movements still those of a man in battle, not a dancer. He thrust, he dropped to his knees, he rolled, was up and moving.

Very calmly, Emperor Te-kuan said (his turn to look straight ahead), "He is to be killed when this stops. Tell the bowmen."

And as quietly, Yao-kan, his most trusted adviser, of his tribal group, his boyhood companion, said, "No, my lord. They have done what we asked. He is dancing."

"He is not dancing," said the emperor of the Xiaolu.

"He is! He is young, great lord, we will need his pride and skill. Remember that the Koreini in their peninsula are aggressive now. They may move west in spring. We have spoken of this. The Altai will be our first defence against them."

"Maybe the Altai. Not this one," said Te-kuan. "Look at his eyes."

"His eyes? This is night, my lord, there are torches, we have all been drinking. You have enforced their submission. We must leave the tribes a shred of pride if we are to make use of them. We want them strong."

"I want this one dead."

"Then we will have war here and no one benefits."

"I do. By his death."

"Great lord, cousin ... I entreat you."

Wan'yen was still on the far side of the flames, still moving and spinning. He was close to where the Jeni leaders sat. There had been fighting between them in spring. It was to be settled, the consequences of that, in the morning.

The emperor of the Xiaolu looked to his left, at his cousin, his companion. "This is your counsel? We are to permit this?"

"It is. When you rise to thank the tribes, look at his kaghan only. Don't even glance at this one when he sits down. Make it seem as if he was an amusement for you, a young man playing at war."

"He is not so young."

"All the better. He will fight the Koreini for you if they come!"

The emperor was silent a moment. "We are going to rule in favour of the Jeni tomorrow?"

"Of course you are," said his cousin. "And *that* will show these Altai where power lies. The limits of their defiance." The cousin smiled. "I have seen the Jeni women. I went this afternoon. I have selected two of them for you tonight, if you wish. They will ease any distress that has been caused."

The emperor looked away. He watched as the Altai's dance ended. There was no applause or laughter. The tribes were waiting. For him.

"Very well," said Emperor Te-kuan. "I will be guided by you."

Said it on the grass, autumn, under the river of stars.

He reclaimed his cup from where he had set it down. He stood, to offer his approval of the dances performed for him that night.

Watching, listening, his adviser drew a deep breath, pleased to have calmed imperial fury, avoided a confrontation that would have—surely—led to the necessity of killing the Altai kaghan and all his party, weakening an entire tribe, altering the balance here in the east.

One needed, he was thinking, to take a larger view in this game of empires and subject tribes and enemies to south and west and the far east. One needed to give wise counsel to angry, impulsive emperors who lacked, perhaps, one's own vision. A little self-pityingly, he thought of the burdens of such a role as his.

Kill the Altai war-leader? At a tribute gathering? Yao-kan shook his head, imperceptibly. *We Xiaolu*, he thought, *have a distance to go before we understand the nature of an empire.* He would do what he could, he thought, and then drank (with restraint) from his cup.

Within a brief span, a short while as such matters go, he and his cousin, the emperor, would find themselves buried to their necks in dry grass at midday, midsummer.

Sweetened blood would be poured over their heads and into their mouths, which would be forced open for that. Their arms would be trapped, embedded in the packed earth. They would be unable to do more than move their heads from side to side, and scream. There would be fire-ant mounds nearby. Screaming, of course, allowed the ants into their mouths.

Leaders of the Altai, including their war-leader and his brother, would sit in a circle, much like this one, though in sunlight, watching as the two Xiaolu were devoured, turned into skulls. It took only a little time.

Succeeding events would also unfold swiftly.

In times long after, Kitan poets and wits would name the Four Most Calamitous Mistakes.

Even the greatest rivers, crashing or spreading wide into the indifferent, encompassing sea, have small beginnings, sometimes moonlit.

CHAPTER VIII

Two things had changed Daiyan through the wind and cold of the winter now nearly over.

In their marsh they had shelter and food, though the elements could afflict them. In wooden huts and barracks behind their network of canals and the maze-like watery paths, the outlaws wintered, better off than most.

Soldiers no longer ventured into the treacherous byways of the marsh. Twice in the recent past they had done so, ordered to clean out the outlaws, and had been driven back, lost and hopeless in the intricate, changing interplay of water and wet earth, dying in numbers, many of them drowning, before the remnant retreated. After the second attempt they hadn't come again.

The outlaws of the marsh watched as the land warmed slowly towards spring along the Great River, which was very wide here. The far bank could not be seen on misty days. Songbirds returned, wild geese went north in ragged arrowheads. They saw long-limbed cranes landing, taking off. It was mating season. There were foxes. Daiyan liked the cranes but they affected his mood:

what they meant in poetry, on wine vessels, teacups, paintings. A symbol. Fidelity. He'd been taught such things once. Another life.

He observed all of this, sometimes among the others and sometimes apart, seeking space and silence under the sky, along the flat marshland. After so many years he was a leader here now, although still young for that. There was no one better with a bow. They had contests. There was no one better.

He was good with swords, too, one of the best, though not the very best. They tested that, too, in the marsh. Size made a difference with blades, if quickness was equal, and there were bigger men among them. One man had some arcane skills. He said it was a legacy of the Kanlins, who were a matter of legend.

Daiyan tried to get this one to train him, but the other was a prickly, difficult person and would not, seeing it as an advantage for himself to be the only one who could do certain things. He was probably right.

Daiyan offered to teach him archery in exchange, but the other man scorned the bow: a barbarian's weapon, he declared, a widely held view. "Kills a man you need to kill," was all Daiyan had said to him.

He had come to be known as one who needed time alone. He read books when he could get them. It was hard to keep books in the dampness of the marsh. He wrote sometimes, reflections, then destroyed these in fires or in the water.

You were allowed to be a little different if you were good in a fight and very good at devising plans and implementing them. If you brought in money and good men, dealt with the villages for food and medicine, and killed efficiently when you needed to. He was adept at making people laugh, or deflecting a quarrel, both useful among men living too close together. He grew a beard to look older, sometimes went about with a cloak and hood instead of a hat.

Thoughts assailed him, darkened his mood, drove him away into twilights, even in winter rain.

They had continued, over time, to learn the scale of the disaster in the northwestern desert: the end of the long war, aftermath of the wrecked assault on Erighaya.

Stories kept rippling, even now. The rest of the imperial army, wherever they were posted, had been gutted by the tale of that retreat. Most of the surviving leaders of the expedition had been executed. The overall commander of that army, the eunuch Wu Tong, had survived. Politics of the court, powerful friends.

Daiyan had images of killing that one himself.

He also thought: an army needed leaders, not just men to serve and fight, and the true enemy, surely (surely!) was still the Xiaolu. And the true goal, the deep longing, remained the Fourteen Prefectures. Lost, surrendered, and they still paid tribute north.

Even as a boy in the west, he had hated the tale of that surrender. He'd dreamed in a narrow bed of swinging a sword and changing everything. Nothing of that had altered for him, though so much else in life had gone differently from what he had expected— beginning with a moment on a country road.

He didn't dwell upon that memory. It was difficult. He moved his thoughts away.

He thought: Why had they been fighting the Kislik in the first place? The Kislik meant nothing that truly mattered. That he brooded upon. No one had yet explained it to him. Not that political insight was easy to come by in the world in which he moved. You couldn't just stop by a *yamen* in a market town and have a visit over spiced tea and sweet cakes with the sub-prefect.

Thinking about that, how cut off he was, would make him restless. Some mornings he'd take three or four of the newest men and go along their side of the river, hunting, gathering tidings, teaching them how to move unseen against a winter skyline. Sometimes he'd treat them to wine and a girl in wine shops at villages they knew were safe. Then they'd come back to the marsh.

This time, spring coming, the world quickening, he didn't want to be teaching. He spoke to the other leaders and left the camp one morning. He did this often enough, came home with useful information; it was accepted, even encouraged. Ren Daiyan was, everyone knew it, different.

Zhao Ziji came with him. Ziji almost always came with him.

They went east across a warming land. Saw leaves appearing, first blossoms. It rained twice, which was good. They needed spring rain here, always. They slept among trees except for a night with the ferryman who would take them across the river. The man could be trusted. He hated the tax officers and the Flowers and Rocks people, equally.

He was an old man. This had been his ferry for thirty years, he told them. His son had been meant to take it over, but he'd been claimed for the war eight years ago and died there.

He'd have carried them free of charge, they had done him a good turn or two over the years, but the outlaws, at least those under Ren Daiyan, wanted to be feared *and* trusted by those they might need. Daiyan always insisted on paying. There was pride on both sides, the man with the ferry boat, the outlaws of the marsh.

There were about six hundred of them in their marsh, one of the larger bandit companies in this part of Kitai. Daiyan was in command of a hundred.

He might be young, but it was clear what he could do. No one was shrewder at finding merchants with money and goods in this middle stretch of the river, at laying ambushes for them, or raiding the Flowers and Rocks contingents—which he did with a particular intensity. He had killed six members of a party in the autumn past, arrows, none missing.

He did let the ferryman host them for the night and offer food and wine. The man told them what he'd heard over the winter, some of it was useful, new. People went back and forth, they talked. A man at the tiller could listen.

The ferryman snored at night. Ziji kicked him and made him turn on his side when it grew loud in the small cabin by the river.

Early morning they crossed the Great River in a fine rain, listening to geese overhead, though they couldn't see them. A calm hour, the river so wide the northern bank appeared only when they were past halfway, as if out of another world or a dream.

One large town not far from the north bank, Chunyu, was a place where outlaws could come for food and tidings. It had a small barracks on its western edge, but despite the soldiers (badly trained, usually frightened), Chunyu was an uncomfortable place for government officials.

Taxes had been raised to pay for the Kislik war, and Flowers and Rocks people had simultaneously begun asserting themselves up and down the river, demanding unpaid labour. The hostility along this stretch of the river towards those reporting to the court was extreme.

It couldn't be called a lawless town, Chunyu. There were the usual appointed elders, and a militia of farmers tasked with aiding the garrison. Taxes were, in fact, collected, spring and fall. If not, the elders would be beaten, or worse. But there was no *yamen*, and the various magistrates at the sub-prefecture town to the north, formally tasked with criminal inquiries in this area, tended to let Chunyu handle its own justice.

It was far enough from the marsh, and men from their band came here rarely enough, that Daiyan wasn't worried about being recognized. There were rewards for turning in outlaws, and it was hard to blame someone whose children were starving. It was your own task, Daiyan believed, not to put yourself, or them, in a position where trouble could arise.

Which is why he later blamed himself, mostly.

Approaching the town late in the day as the skies cleared, Daiyan didn't wear his hood, it made him too distinctive. He put on a straw hat like any labourer or farmer. His bow and quiver, and both their swords, had been hidden in a wood. They'd had weapons stolen once, when hidden this way. They'd tracked the thieves and killed them.

They carried only knives. They waited until darkfall, then entered town with men coming home under stars from spring fields. They went to an inn they knew near the market square in the centre.

The proprietor had been a man of the woods himself when young. Chunyu was where he'd retired from that life. It could happen. Men did change their lives. He would know them, could be trusted.

The inn's front room was crowded. Two fires burning, lamps lit, smell of cooking and of hard-working men. End-of-day talk and laughter. A sense of life, warmth, far removed from the marsh. There were women here, serving them.

The proprietor let one of the girls take their order and bring it. Later, he walked casually past where they sat. He dropped a letter on their table. It was stained and crumpled. It was addressed to Daiyan.

He stared at it a long time, Ziji watching him.

He drained his cup and refilled it and drank again. He knew the brush strokes. Of course he did.

Dear Son,

I send this with a father's blessing in the hope that it will find you. Honourable Wang Fuyin, formerly our sub-prefect, is now chief magistrate at Jingxian. He has kindly written me that he believes you are alive and that it is possible you might at times be found at a certain town named Chunyu. I send this there, to the inn he suggests. He writes that he remains grateful to you for his life, which brings honour to our family.

*Your mother continues in good health and your brother
is now with me at the* yamen, *promoted to a guard. This
is due to the kind intervention of Sub-prefect Wang before
he left us. I am, by the grace of the gods and our ancestors,
also in health as I take up my brush.*

*I write only to tell you these things, not to offer
judgment on the choices you have made. It seems to me
that fate intervened with you and took a strong hand in
your life. This can happen.*

*I hope this letter reaches you, son. It would please me
if you were to send word of yourself, and I know it would
ease your mother's heart. I remain confident that your
upbringing and education and respect for your family's
honour will help you make proper decisions in life.*

*I wish you well, son, and will think of you during the
New Year's Festival here at home.*

> *Your father,*
> *Ren Yuan*

He hadn't really thought about it over the years, had avoided
doing so, but he supposed his hope had been that his father—the
most honourable man he knew—had simply assumed his younger
son had died, perhaps in the woods the day he saved the sub-
prefect's party.

That would have been easier in many ways.

This letter was hard.

Not to offer judgment. His father was not a man who judged, but
declining to do so carried so much courtesy and restraint. Daiyan
was sitting in an inn near the river on a spring night and he was
seeing his father in his mind. He tried not to do that, most of the
time.

A decent, virtuous man, dutiful to ancestors, family, gods,
the empire—and his son was one of the outlaws of the marsh.

Which meant robbing people, perhaps killing them. It did mean killing them.

I wish you well, son, and will think of you.

He drank a great deal that night in Chunyu as a bright moon rose. You made mistakes when you drank too much, let yourself become melancholy, wander in memories.

Ziji said it was a bad idea, but he'd insisted on leaving the inn, disdaining the girls there and going to the singing girl house. Those could be dangerous: merchants might be there, guarded, officers from the barracks, officials en route to somewhere or other across Kitai.

Daiyan had taken one of the prettiest girls to a room and had been cursory with her, an unhappy lovemaking. She had not complained: the girls were trained not to complain. And he was young, a well-made man. What felt harsh and angry to him was probably an ordinary encounter for her. He was even a somewhat important man, in his way.

Because it turned out she knew who he was.

"I'M SORRY," he muttered. "I'm a fool."

"Tonight you are," Ziji said, quietly. He was undisturbed, almost amused. It was a strength of the man, given where they were just then. "What was in that letter?"

He wasn't ready to answer, but he wasn't drunk any more, at least. Fleeing for your life in a strange town could sober a man. It was cold, middle of the night, that too-bright moon shining. They were crouched in a laneway against a stone wall, out of the moonlight. He'd left his cloak behind in the bedroom. There'd been no time to do more than throw on tunic and trousers, thrust bare feet into boots. His hair was unpinned, he had no hat.

"We need to kill that girl," he said.

"It'll be done. A word to our friend at the inn. But not yet."

It did need to be done, to send a necessary message about informing on bandits, but tonight that would mean finding her, and she was not going to be easily found right now. Not after alerting the barracks that one of the leaders of the outlaws of the marsh was in Chunyu.

The more pressing issue was not being found themselves.

He wondered what would have happened had he paid her generously in advance, been amusing and considerate. Asked her to play the flute for him, praised her music, said she was lovely enough to be in Jingxian, Shantong, Hanjin itself.

Would she still have turned him in for a reward?

There were consequences, almost always, for what you did or failed to do in life. He believed that. Fate could play a role, and chance, but your choices and decisions mattered.

Mattered to someone else, too. He might get Ziji killed tonight, not just himself. A meaningless death in a meaningless town. Before anything at all was achieved.

That angered him. From childhood, when he was still Little Dai, anger had been useful for him. He thought of his father's letter, folded in his trousers.

"How many soldiers?" he asked quietly.

They had gone out the window of the room where the girl had left him sleeping. A jump down into an alley, something done so often. You could spend time thinking about a life where this was a common activity.

Ziji had been awake earlier, still downstairs, listening to the music, drinking cautiously. He had seen the girl Daiyan had gone up with walk down the stairs and out. A little quickly, he'd thought.

He'd strolled out the door a short time later. Had been in the street beyond the lamplight when he heard the murmur and march of approaching soldiers.

"About twenty, at a guess," he said.

Daiyan swore under his breath. They weren't mystical bandits of legend, the two of them, and they had only knives. Their weapons were in a wood east of town. With his bow he could have ...

"They think it is just me," he said.

"We walked in there together. I'm not leaving, don't waste the words."

Another thing about Ziji ... he knew what Daiyan was thinking, sometimes too quickly.

"There are more than twenty," someone else said.

Both men stood up quickly, ready to run, or attack. But they'd also heard the timbre of the voice.

A child, a boy of about nine or ten, stepped into moonlight from beside a gate in the wall across the lane. He'd been in shadow, too, and surprisingly silent. These two men were extremely good at detecting people. They hadn't seen or heard him.

Daiyan stared. Small child, torn tunic, bare feet. They had killed children this young once or twice, not intentionally.

He cleared his throat. "How many more?" he asked, his voice low. Ziji checked up and down the street. The moon was much too bright, close to full. The clouds and rain of before were gone.

"Maybe two hundred," the boy said. He, too, spoke quietly.

"What?"

"There are soldiers in town tonight, my sister says. They are marching west. Stopped here on the way. I heard someone sent back to get them."

"What were you doing listening?"

The boy shrugged.

"They'll block the ways out of town," Ziji muttered.

"I think so," the boy agreed. "Will they kill you?"

A brief silence. They listened. There was a shout from somewhere to the north, then it was cut off, as if on orders.

"Yes," said Daiyan. "They will."

"Are you outlaws?"

A hesitation. "Yes," he said.

"Are you heroes?"

That he hadn't expected. Another pause.

"Not yet," he said.

Ziji made a sound. Then added, "You had best go home. They may use arrows, and arrows can miss."

"I can help you," said the boy.

The two men looked at each other.

"You can't," said Daiyan.

"You're wrong," said the boy.

Even in the circumstances, Daiyan found he had to suppress a grin. "No, I mean, we mustn't let you. It will be bad for your family if you are seen with us."

"My mother is dead and my father's at the mine and hates soldiers. He wouldn't mind my doing this. My sister might."

"Your father is at the mine now?"

"Night watchman. He's there every night."

"Where's your sister?" said Ziji, more practically.

Daiyan was fighting a sudden hilarity. They could easily be killed in this town, and a nine-year-old was offering to save them.

"Inside." The boy gestured over his shoulder.

"Why would she mind?" Ziji asked carefully.

The child made a face. "She's evil. Orders me around. Never lets me do anything."

It became a little clearer. Daiyan said, "Your father's away at night. He places her in charge?"

The boy shrugged again.

"She beats you if you go out?"

"Hah! Has to catch me first. And I know places *she* goes, and could tell Father, too."

Daiyan looked up at the moon. The world put you in strange places sometimes, he was thinking.

"You know you are supposed to be afraid of us," he said.

"Not afraid of anything," the boy said.

It was all so strange. "Ghosts?" he asked.

"Maybe ghosts," the boy admitted, after a moment.

Daiyan gazed at him. "You have a brother," he said suddenly.

The boy stared, wide-eyed. Said nothing.

"He went into the woods?"

A long pause, then a curt nod.

There was a silence.

"How do you propose to help us?" Ziji rasped.

Sounds again, nearer, front of the house behind them, beyond the wall at their back. Running footsteps. Jingle of metal. A dog barked.

"We need to get out of the lane," Daiyan said.

"Yes," agreed the boy. "Come on."

He opened the gate behind him. Neither man moved.

"Fuck," said Zhao Ziji.

"You swore!" said the boy.

Daiyan laughed silently. Couldn't help it. His mood tonight.

"Our best choice now," he said.

Ziji nodded unhappily. They crossed the lane and went through the wooden gate. A small, moonlit yard.

Unfortunately, a young woman was standing there, a slender birch rod in her hand.

"Fuck," said the boy.

Both men moved very fast.

Daiyan had the stick from her and her mouth covered hard with a hand before she could exclaim or react. He gripped her close from behind. Ziji swung the gate shut, bolted it, spun around, knife at the ready.

The woman twisted in Daiyan's grasp. Anger, not fear. He could feel her trying to free herself, struggling to bite.

"Stop it!" he said, mouth to her ear. "Listen to me. Soldiers are looking to kill us. If you want to help them, I can't release you. If you dislike the army, I can let you go."

"No!" snapped Ziji. "We need to bind her."

"Yes!" said her brother. "Tie her up! You see what she's like?" He was looking at the birch rod.

Daiyan shook his head. Later he would decide it was partly because of her hair. She had red hair. You could see that even by moonlight.

You didn't always make your decisions in life properly. You might try, but it didn't always happen.

He let her go. He said, "I doubt we know your other brother, though we might, but imagine him being the one hunted tonight."

"I'd happily see him killed," she said.

Daiyan winced. But he registered that she didn't run, or raise her voice.

"You see!" said her brother again.

"Pan, stop or I will beat you."

"They won't let you!"

"We will," said Daiyan. "Especially if you don't keep quiet."

He was listening for sounds beyond the wall.

"Inside," said the woman with red hair crisply. "We'll still have to be quiet, they can hear us out front if they are there."

She led the way into the house, which was dark except for the embers of a fire. One room, a raised platform to one side, with a curtain. Her space, most likely, with a brother and a father in here. Sometimes when a mother died life became difficult for a daughter, in many different ways.

She sat on the edge of this platform. There was one stool near the fire. She gestured. Neither man sat. Ziji went to the front of the room, towards the street. He looked out cautiously through the one window beside the door. Made a flat-hand gesture: no one there just now.

"The neighbour has a son works at the barracks. Can't let her hear us," said the girl.

"She's a sneak and a spy," agreed Pan.

"And what are you?" his sister snapped.

"He's just a boy," said Ziji, unexpectedly. "Doing what boys do."

"As if you know anything about what he does," she said.

"We are grateful," said Daiyan, "to both of you."

"And what'll that mean, exactly?" she said coldly.

"Bian!" her brother exclaimed softly, shocked.

"No, it is a proper question," Daiyan said. They were all whispering. Ziji stayed by the window, checking the street at intervals. "If we get away from here, you will not have cause to regret helping us."

"That's precise," the girl said, and laughed.

Two interesting children, Daiyan thought. Well, one was a child. The other was of an age to be married, or nearly so.

"Your hair?" Ziji asked. An inconsequential question, but her appearance was hard to ignore.

She shrugged. She looked like her brother, doing that. "My mother's ancestors came from the west. Sardia, we think. They had this hair, I'm told."

"Sardia's where the best horses used to come from," Daiyan said.

"Is that so?" she said, no interest at all. "I heard singing girls. Red hair earns a price. That's what he wanted me to be."

"Who? Your brother?" Daiyan asked. Another picture coming clearer. He was entirely sober.

She stared at him in the near-dark, surprised. Then nodded.

"Not your father?"

She shook her head.

"This is a most enjoyable conversation, but we'll all be killed if they start entering houses," Ziji said. "We need a way out."

"They'll be circling the whole town," Pan said, confidently. "I heard them say."

"Two hundred aren't enough to ring Chunyu," Daiyan said. "Not with some of them also searching houses." He thought for a moment, then explained what he wanted done ...

They opened the door a crack and Pan was out. Even knowing he was there, the boy was barely visible, a shadow in the yard, then vaulting the wooden fence (not opening the gate) and gone in the night.

"He's quick," said Ziji.

"He's impossible," said his sister.

The two men looked at each other.

"I have no wine," she said brusquely. Her posture had changed, she sat straighter, hands clasped in front of her.

Daiyan said softly, "We don't need wine. If soldiers come, we'll be out the back. You will not be linked to us. You need not fear ... in any way."

"What do you know of what I need to fear?"

No good answer to that.

"I'm sorry," he said.

"For what?"

A belated realization coming home to him. These two—both of them—were sharp, clever, not the children of a watchman. "What did ... has your father always been at the mine?"

She seemed to struggle with herself. Ziji was at the window, watching the street beyond the small front garden.

"He was a teacher," she said. "They dismissed him and branded him when my brother went to the forest."

"The soldiers?"

She nodded, a barely visible movement.

"Why did your brother go?"

"He was recruited for the Flowers and Rocks. He fought the men who came to get him, broke the arm of one, and fled."

"And they punished his father?" Ziji asked, from the window.

"Of course they did," she said. "Branded his forehead in the town square. *Father of a criminal.*"

Daiyan said, "Your ... your little brother said you like the soldiers."

She sighed. Her name was Bian, he remembered.

"He doesn't have to feed us," she said. "He's a child. I talk to some of them at the market. Sometimes we get tea or rice from one or another." She looked at Daiyan, added, "I don't do anything else for it."

He cleared his throat. He was wishing for wine now, actually. He sat down on the stool.

"I only asked because you, both of you are very ... are ..."

"We are not terrified peasants? Thank you so much," she said. He heard Ziji laugh softly.

He cleared his throat again. The silence grew uncomfortable. He said, "I've heard the horses from Sardia were the best in the world in the old days."

"So you said. How interesting. I shall make certain to tell my father when he comes home after walking twenty *li*, before he falls asleep."

"Soldiers!" said Ziji.

Daiyan stood quickly. "All right. We go out the back. Bian, you'll have to bolt the gate behind us. Thank you for trying."

"Stay where you are," she said. "They won't be searching houses in the middle of the night. Keep quiet," she added.

Then she went to the door, opened it, and stepped outside.

"What's all this?" she called out. "What's happening?"

"Shao Bian? Is that you?"

"Who else would it be, Dou Yan? What is happening?"

Daiyan and Ziji could see nothing, out of sight towards the back of the room.

"Two outlaws of the marsh!" the soldier shouted. "We're hunting them down!"

"An adventure," Bian said dryly.

"Miss Bian," another voice called, "shall we come visit with you instead?" Daiyan heard laughter.

"Of course!" she called back. "All of you, bring friends. Bring the outlaws, too!"

More laughter, a different tone.

"She can handle them," Ziji murmured.

"Dou Yan, listen," they heard her saying. "My brother is out there somewhere, chasing excitement. If you find him, beat him and send him back to me."

"Find that one? Better chase a cat in a tree," a different soldier called. Laughter again, perhaps four or five of them, then a snapped order from a distance. They heard the soldiers swear and begin moving on.

Bian stayed outside the open door. A moment later both men startled as a shadow slipped past her like a ghost.

"See?" said Pan. "She told them to beat me!"

His sister followed him in and closed the door.

"I think she gave them a reason why you might be out there," Ziji said prosaically.

"You don't understand a thing about her!" Pan sniffed.

"Talk," said Daiyan. "What did you see?"

The one-time teacher who now guarded a mine at night had raised remarkable children, he was thinking. It wasn't their concern, however. He and Ziji needed to get out of Chunyu, and then they needed to ...

And it was in that instant that he realized what else he needed to do. It was, in the strangest way, as clear and compelled as the moment he'd left a path in the far west, near home, and walked into the forest.

He would be able to name this moment, later, with precision: a night-dark springtime house in a north-of-the-river town, standing beside a clever, red-headed young woman and a quick, wild child, and Ziji.

WITH ADVANCE SCOUTING, which is what Pan had given them, it was easy enough to know where to break through. It was too easy, Daiyan kept thinking, all through the stages of that night. The army of Kitai, even those down here away from war, ought to have been better at something so straightforward as trapping outlaws inside a town.

They killed one man each, with the knives. With a need for absolute silence they had no real choice but to kill. The soldiers had been forced to spread out, as he'd guessed, fifteen paces apart, and more in places. With men diverted to searching the streets (too noisily, too easily seen in moonlight) the ring around Chunyu was inadequate to its purpose. One kill each, the bodies dragged into darkness, army clothing put on over their own, soldiers' weapons claimed.

They slipped into the line, stood on guard for a time, then simply stepped backwards, silently, away, and away, and out.

They were on the north side of town but it didn't matter, once beyond the ring. They went farther north before cutting east and finding, towards morning, the wood where they'd hidden their weapons. They kept the two extra swords. There was always a need for weapons in the marsh.

"Your names?" the girl, Bian, had asked, as they'd waited for Pan's signal it was safe to go through the yard and across the street.

"Better you don't know," Daiyan said, which was true.

"Zhao Ziji," Ziji said.

She looked at him. Ziji added, "If we survive this, we will send something to you. That is a promise. Trust the innkeeper. We ... we may be able to help Pan. A better life for him. Maybe."

"Only him?" she asked.

Daiyan would remember that.

HE DID NOT WRITE his father. He had no idea what he could say.

Once free of Chunyu, they lingered another few days on the north side of the river. They heard a story in a hamlet west of Dizeng—a major expedition planned by the Flowers and Rocks people. There was a huge rock in a lake nearby, they wanted it brought up, taken to Hanjin for the emperor's garden.

It would be a massive undertaking, according to what they heard.

Daiyan gave money to the chief elder in that small village. The marsh outlaws always did that, it went to ease tax burdens, and to secure their welcome should they need to return.

The elder confirmed something else: the new chief magistrate in Jingxian city, east along the river, was indeed Wang Fuyin, appointed a year ago. He hadn't really doubted it, after his father's letter.

It was interesting, triggered memories. Daiyan wondered what the man was like now. He had no idea what to do with this knowledge. Perhaps if he were captured near Jingxian, he'd be allowed a cleaner death?

They went back to the river and crossed with the same ferryman, this time at night—they had to wait on the north bank for a wind to die down. You needed to trust your ferryman. The stars at night, with the moon waning, were hard, bright, multitudinous.

Waiting by the riverbank they glimpsed a fox. Ziji was afraid of foxes. Something in his family history—a great-uncle destroyed by a fox-woman. Some men joked about sleeping with a *daiji*, the legendary wildness of that lovemaking. Ziji never joined in those jests. He had even been initially unsettled by the red hair of the girl in Chunyu, Daiyan knew, though he didn't tease about that. Some things a man was allowed to keep to himself, even with friends.

They returned to the marsh and the arrival of spring.

Some time in that interval, watching cranes, rabbits, more wild geese passing as winter eased its grip, hearing the first orioles, Ren Daiyan understood that if he'd reached an awareness in Chunyu it meant nothing if it wasn't acted upon. That would be harder than it had seemed in that dark house on the north shore.

He could not do anything without speaking with Ziji. Their closeness, from the time the soldier had joined them years ago, demanded as much.

He did speak, on patrol together one morning. Ziji named five others in their hundred, men he thought would be of the same mind, prepared to take the same risk. Daiyan was reluctant at first, then decided that if he was doing this he ought to be thinking in terms of other good men.

They spoke to them, one by one. All five agreed to come.

They went back across the river at the beginning of autumn. The plum blossoms had long since come and gone, then peach blossoms and peaches and summer's crabapples. They moved alertly, the autumn tax collectors were abroad. Sometimes the taxmen were adequately defended. Not always. But they weren't planning an attack. Not now.

Daiyan had told the other leaders in the marsh he was going north to get information again and that he wanted enough men to harass a particular Flowers and Rocks group, if it was still near a village he knew. He was told, routinely, to be careful.

He went away. Crossed the Great River again, same ferryman, a mild night this time, waves, different stars, leaving that part of his life behind, like a strange, flat dream of mist and marsh fires and men without women.

CHAPTER IX

Sima Peng's father has always claimed that they are descended, in some way he's never explained clearly, from a famed poet named Sima Zian.

Peng doesn't know, one way or another. It seems unlikely to her, and her husband takes the same view. Her father enjoys wine too much and is inclined to outrageous statements, and not only when drunk. People laugh at him, but he is good-natured and has never had enemies—not that any of them know about.

Both of the village's spirit mediums had asked that question, separately, when the family's troubles began.

Peng doesn't know much about her supposed ancestor. There are few books in the village, and she can't read. Poetry means little to her. She does like when people sing in their small temple of the Path, with its pretty green-tiled roof, or at festivals, or the women washing clothing in the stream. She isn't a good singer and she forgets the words too often, but she joins in on washing days. It helps the time go by.

Her older daughter had been a singer with a clear, bright voice.

Like a temple bell, it was often said by the stream. Peng remembers that. A dutiful, pleasing girl—before a demon possessed her and their lives became bad.

Now the good family from Dizeng Village that had agreed to marry her to their older son has withdrawn from the agreement. It is possible that Zhi-li *and* her younger sister might never marry now.

Sima Peng cries herself to sleep most nights, often weeps during the day when she is alone. Her husband walks the village and fields with heavy shoulders and a face like stony ground. He has beaten her for keeping him awake at night, and beaten Zhi-li, in grief and fear.

Perhaps he has been trying to drive the demon out of her.

Zhi-li laughs whenever her father strikes her. It is a terrifying sound. Sima Peng's legs lost all their strength the first time she heard it.

Neither of the village mediums had been able to drive the evil spirit from her body, or explain what might have caused a blameless girl, on the eve of a good marriage and her departure for Dizeng, to be possessed by something so dark. A spirit that made her walk abroad with hair unbound and garments shamelessly loose, and say terrible things to her mother and to villagers who asked after her health.

They had been forced to lock her up. She laughs aloud in the dead of night (neighbours hear it!) and has lost her appetite, even for river trout and fish cakes, once her favourites. Her eyes are strange and her colour bad.

Peng fears that her daughter might die, even kill herself.

She would never have declared herself a clever woman or a brave one, she is one of those of whom it is said their eyes are always downcast. But this was her daughter's life, and so when word came to their marketplace that a ritual master had arrived at Dizeng Village and had been performing rites and exorcisms there, Peng woke early the very next morning, before the sun, and set out to walk the long way east to Dizeng (most of an autumn day) to speak with him.

You brought a child into the world, fed her with your milk, clothed her and prayed for her, watched her grow in sunlight and rain. You did not turn away when a spirit from the other side set out to destroy her.

Their own rival village mediums are united in only one thing—hatred of the ritual masters—but Peng had decided in the night that she didn't care. Let them be angry, let her husband be angry when he woke and found her gone. Let her father be puzzled and silent and drink more wine. Both mediums had tried their possession ceremonies, and Zhi-li was unchanged.

She had used foul words and gestures in the presence of her little brother yesterday evening, standing right in front of the ancestral altar. Peng doesn't even understand how Zhi-li *knew* such words.

She has a little money saved from her silk-spinning, hidden in a jar beneath a floorboard in the henhouse (or it would have been turned to wine, long ago). She has brought it with her. That is dangerous, of course. Their hamlet and the road are close to the Great River and outlaws are on both banks. She relies on how desperately poor she looks to save her from these.

The outlaws tend to ally themselves with the poorer villagers. In return, they are given warnings of soldiers sent after them, word of merchants on the roads, and sometimes shelter, though that is risky.

In Sima Peng's humble view, the outlaws from the marshlands across the river and the bands on this side are less of a menace than taxation officers from the *yamen* in Dizeng, or the army claiming husbands and sons. And they are less deadly than those from the Flowers and Rocks, hounding them for brutal labour, beating those who hesitate or try to hide.

Her brother had died this past spring, still a young man, dropping dead in a meadow while helping to pull a massive boulder from their lake for the emperor's pleasure garden in far-off Hanjin.

No sorrow expressed, no compensation offered. A government official came with the body, told the family what had occurred, then turned his horse and went looking for more men (he had soldiers with him).

In the days that followed they'd claimed even more workers from their hamlet, down to small boys, until they got the accursed rock out of the lake and mounted it on logs to roll towards the river and a waiting boat. The journey to the river, too, had been a savage task, lasting through summer. Men were beaten, maimed. Five more died, and a boy. Planted fields and their crops were crushed by the passage, farms and homes flattened ahead of their progress.

For a rock. An ugly, pitted rock that destroyed lives.

Peng's husband and her father and brother had all gotten along, worked together in their shared fields. The death was a calamity.

Peng will never forget the afternoon the government rider came to tell them. She had bowed down, forehead to the beaten earth before their gate, never looking up as the official spoke from horseback above the wrapped body of her brother on the ground beside her. She'd bowed to the man as if he *honoured* the family by coming to tell her they had killed her brother.

You could grow to hate yourself, or the people who had done this and caused you to make obeisance in fear. Or you could accept that there were those born to suffer, under heaven, and you were among them. She had done that last, mostly, all her life.

Not for her daughter, though; she won't accept it for her child.

Outlaws *are* better than the Flowers and Rocks officials, Peng thinks, approaching Dizeng late in the day (farthest she's ever travelled in her life). She doesn't understand much about the world, but that much she thinks she knows.

She has been afraid she'll see the family that has broken off their engagement, but it has been a market day here and there is still a crowd. Peng walks among them in the square before the *yamen*. Stalls had been set up and are being taken down.

She has also feared she'll have to speak to some stranger, ask where the ritual master can be found, has been anxious about that all along the road. But she'd forgotten something about them, and in fact she sees the man right away. He is drinking at a table under a mulberry tree at the edge of the square, in the shade.

They always wear red hats, the ritual masters. Village mediums wear black on their heads. Peng has heard that arcane priests, the lordly ones who do rites and exorcisms for vast sums of money in big cities and at court, wear yellow hats, but she has no way of knowing if this is true, and it doesn't matter, does it?

She takes a deep breath, afraid, after all, now that she has come. She still can't believe she has done this, that she *is* doing this. She spits into the dust to get a bad taste from her mouth. She walks sturdily through the crowd in the closing-up market—smells of cooked food, animals, fruit, spilled wine—and comes to where the ritual master sits.

He is younger than she expected, a good-looking man. She thinks he might be drunk, but that may be his power, his aura, whatever lets him deal with the spirit world. She is an ignorant peasant woman, isn't she?

He is talking to someone at a table under the tree, a man from the *yamen*, a clerk, from his clothing. He turns to her as she stops in front of him. He has a stubble of beard, but his clothing is clean. Maybe he has helped someone here in Dizeng and they have cleaned his robe for him, in gratitude?

Or maybe he just paid money and had his things laundered at their stream! Why is she even thinking of such things?

She is a frightened woman from a tiny village, and too far from home. She'll have to stay overnight here, whatever happens now. Her younger daughter has been told what to say to Peng's husband, who will be very angry when he comes home from the fields to a house empty except for one crying daughter, another possessed by a demon, and a boy confused and frightened all the time because of what has happened to his sister.

Sima Peng reaches into her clothing and takes the jar from where it hangs, hidden at her waist (and has been banging her hip all the way). She kneels in the dust and extends it—everything in it—to the ritual master. When he reaches out and takes it she lowers her head and presses it to the earth before his feet. Then she brings her roughened hands forward and clasps his ankles in supplication, not speaking, not able to speak.

He is her last hope, Zhi-li's last hope.

IN THE MORNING, on the road home with an utterly unexpected escort, Peng tries to understand how the world could bring a poor woman something like this.

Two men had fallen into step with her on the far side of the market square in Dizeng as the sun was setting the day before. She had just left the ritual master all her money in a jar, with his promise to follow her in the morning back to her village. He had affairs to settle in Dizeng first, he'd told her, his voice low and kind, but he'd follow.

Stumbling away in a daze, unable to believe she'd achieved what she'd come for, Peng had been unsure what to do next. It had crossed her mind, on the way here, to leave aside a small part of her money for food and a pallet somewhere, but she'd decided that would be bad luck. If the gods were to help her, she had to give everything she had for Zhi-li.

She'd been thinking she'd try to find a stable, beg permission to bed down in straw, when two men fell in stride with her, one on each side.

She'd been terrified, trembling, her eyes on the ground. *This* was what happened to women in market towns, she knew. But it was a public place, not yet dark. If she cried out, perhaps—

"Mother Sima, will you permit us to help you?"

The voice had been calm, and he knew her name. She'd looked up cautiously, had seen a young man with a neat beard, his hair pinned under a wide straw hat. His clothing was rough and that of his older companion was the same, but his voice was educated.

She'd ducked her head again. "Hel ... help me?" she'd said.

"I would guess you gave all your money in the world to the red hat just now."

"Yes!" Peng said quickly. "I have no money at all, honourable sirs. Nothing for you to—"

"I did say help you, not rob you," he said. "We heard you talking to him." He'd seemed amused.

Peng had been desperately confused. It was so crowded here. There were so many *people* in Dizeng. She knew there were even larger villages, and great cities, but it was difficult to imagine.

The second man, on her right, had not spoken. He'd seemed alert, scanning the square.

The younger one repeated, "I offered help. Truly, we will not harm you."

"Why?" Sima Peng said. Her lips were dry. "Please? Why?"

She'd looked up again, hesitantly. His gaze was calm. You could call it a watchful face, but not a warm or friendly one.

"We are men of the woods," he said.

Men of the woods was one term for outlaws, it was what they usually called themselves. Peng was afraid again, her hands shaking.

"We often help the villagers," he said. "You know that."

They sometimes did, yes. But sometimes it was otherwise. "The ... the red hat said he would help us."

"He might," said the young man. The older one snorted with sudden amusement. She didn't understand that, either. "And so will we," said the one doing the talking. "Your village elder has assisted us at times. We don't forget."

All villages, large and small, needed to make their peace with the men of the woods. The government was worse. She had *always* thought that, even before her brother died. She wondered if she should say this.

She hadn't. She wasn't a woman accustomed to talking and that day had been so far out of the pattern of her life it was impossible to know what to do, how to act. You wove silk, you washed clothing in the stream, you fed a husband and children and your widowed father (when there was food to offer), you honoured your ancestors. You didn't have conversations with outlaws far from home.

They led her to an inn on the western edge of the village. They paid for a room and an evening meal for her. Peng had been afraid there, too. There were tales of women accosted, murdered in their beds in such inns by men who came to find them in the dark, or by ghosts.

"I will be outside your door tonight," the older outlaw had said, as if he'd heard her thoughts. The first words he'd spoken. He had a deep voice. "You need fear nothing, here, or on the road home tomorrow. You are a good woman, Mother Sima. You bring honour to your family and Kitai."

She will remember *that*. It was not the sort of thing you expected to hear a bandit—or anyone—say to you. Later, much later, she will tell people about it, all the time. By then she will be more accustomed to talking (old women seemed to be), and this will be a story she often tells.

The younger outlaw went away somewhere, the older one stayed. He even sat with her and ate with her, so she would not be alone and fearful in a large, loud dining room at an inn. She had never stayed at an inn before.

His name was Zhao Ziji, he told her. He had been in the army, but he wasn't now. He asked her questions, gently, and Peng had found herself telling him about what happened to her daughter, and then also about her brother, how the Flowers and Rocks people killed him for a rock. He told her it was a sorrow and a crime and was happening all over Kitai.

He walked her up the stairs to her room, gave her the key to lock the door from inside, and repeated that he would be outside all night, she was not to fear anything. She had never been in a house with a stairway before.

In the night, once, she had heard footsteps approaching, and then the deep voice of Zhao Ziji, speaking softly, too softly for her to make out the words, but the footsteps went quickly back the way they'd come, and then the sound of them faded away.

Peng had lain until sunrise, sleeping and waking at intervals, in a proper bed for the first time in her life, away from her village for the first time in her life, hearing dogs bark outside, dogs she didn't know, while the same moon rose that always rose.

THE RITUAL MASTER, under his favourite mulberry tree in the bright morning, was dealing with a considerable headache after a liquid last night in Dizeng. He'd have preferred a cloudy sky.

He treated his head with more wine (not spiced) and a breakfast pastry from the cookshop on the near side of the square. His friend from the *yamen* was working—he did do that sometimes—so the red hat found himself alone, contemplating departure with mild regret.

Dizeng had been a pleasant last stop at the end of summer, as it had been the year before. He'd made decent coinage here, and hadn't spent all of it in the two singing girl houses. A fair bit, yes, but not all. He had enough from his season along the river to make it worth carrying on east now to Jingxian, to deposit what he had at the large, walled Cho sanctuary south of the city.

They took a fee, of course, to guard a man's savings, but the priests were honest, and the simple truth was that you had to pay money to keep money in a hard world. He wouldn't have placed his earnings at a temple of the Path, mind you—far too much tension between ritual masters such as himself, and them. It grew tricky when yellow and red hats mixed together.

Tricky, meaning dangerous. He kept out of the larger cities, except to place his money in Jingxian and enjoy some civilized life before moving on east into autumn. He wintered in towns towards the sea, and he never did spirit work anywhere a yellow-hatted arcane priest might be. And of course the yellow hats disdained the villages where ritual masters plied the same trade.

In the villages the danger came from the local mediums, who resented (with cause, he had to admit) red hats coming through, educated, offering rites from scrolls and books, charging more than the mediums could, taking away business.

He always left money for the mediums anywhere he'd done a lot of work. They might still think violent thoughts, but they could be made less inclined to *be* murderous.

It was a delicate path he'd walked these days and years by the Great River, but it seemed to be feeding him, which was more than could be said for what he'd been doing before he discovered he had a gift for healing those afflicted from the spirit world.

An education could teach you a few things beyond classic texts and poetry and writing a decent hand.

The roads could make a man weary but the life wasn't dull or predictable. He was known now in the places he kept coming back to along the river's middle stretch, and so far no one seemed to truly hate him, or anything so dramatic. He didn't stay anywhere long enough for that to happen. You learned, among other things, how to explain failures (frequent, given the nature of the business) and to make sure your successes were sounded up and down the river—or at least this part of its long course from the western mountains to the sea.

Sitting in morning light, shifting his chair to hold the shade as the sun rose, he'd not have said he was unhappy with how his life was unfolding. Aside from the headache, of course, which was his own doing. Or perhaps the fault of a particularly affectionate girl last night. He managed a faint smile, remembering. She'd be something he'd regret leaving behind.

Someone took the chair next to him, pulled it up to the small round table, uninvited, placing a cup of tea down with a grunt.

The ritual master glanced over, bemused—there were unoccupied tables all around the square.

The stranger, a wide straw farmer's hat pulled down to shade his face, said, "Best get moving, don't you think? You've a long walk west to make it before darkfall. Or were you going to hire a donkey this morning?"

The ritual master looked at him, more sharply now.

"I'm going east this morning."

"No you aren't." The voice was quiet, but flat with certainty. "You took a woman's money yesterday and promised to go to her daughter."

He stared at this stranger with the hat brim down. "It is bad manners to listen to a private conversation." He let anger slip into his voice.

"You are right. Forgive me. What is it to steal money with a lie?"

"I don't think I need to answer to you, whoever you are. I know the officers at this *yamen* very well, by the way. If you are trying to extort—"

"Let's go talk to them. Shall we? The prefecture's chief magistrate is here in Dizeng now, as well."

The ritual master smiled thinly. "He is, indeed. I happen to know the magistrate from Jingxian."

"So do I. Met with him yesterday. I told him who did the scythe murder he's come to investigate. Also told him I was taking you west this morning, and that I'd come back here and do what he and I agreed."

A feeling of unease descended upon the ritual master.

"I think you are lying," he said. "I think you are simply an outlaw trying to lure me from my path and my hired guards."

"Your guards. Yes. Them. They left last night, in haste. They weren't good men. You'd have been at risk."

He'd wondered about that when he hired them. But this was—

"What do you mean they left? I paid them half in advance! I paid them—"

He stopped, because the other man was laughing at him.

He felt himself flushing. He said, "Listen to me, whoever you are. The money she gave me will be given to feed the poor at the Southern Cho Temple of Preserved Sanctity in Jingxian. You can come see it done. I'll even pay you to guard me there! That woman would not accept it back from me yesterday, and I cannot go west now. This is the end of my season. I need to get to Jingxian, guarded. I will even pay to have them pray for her daughter at the temple."

"I am sure many prayers have been spoken," said the other man quietly. He sipped from his tea, his face still shaded by the hat. "They don't appear to have succeeded. Are you truly able to deal with spirits, or are you completely dishonest? Should I say as much to Chief Magistrate Wang? He's a much-changed man, isn't he?"

"What does that mean?"

"Well, really, Teacher Tuan, you were the one who said—outside of class—that he was pompous and soft. Remember?"

A prickling of the skin.

"How do you know what I ... ?"

The straw hat was pushed back.

And even after many years and the changes imposed by life—on himself, on the other one—he knew who this was. He found himself uncharacteristically unable to speak at first. Then he just said the name.

The other man smiled. He had been a boy, last time seen.

LATER THAT MORNING, still not entirely sure how it had come to be, Tuan Lung, once a teacher in his own academy west of the river's gorges, now an itinerant ritual master, found himself on the road with Ren Daiyan, his one-time student in Shengdu.

His strings of cash had been left for safekeeping in the *yamen* in Dizeng Village after being counted out carefully and recorded in duplicate.

They were going west. He really hadn't intended to do that.

They had two donkeys. Daiyan said they'd need them after wasting so much of the morning at the *yamen*. He carried a bow, a quiver of arrows, and a single sword on his back. He was muscled, lean, taller, with a short beard and a thin scar above it on his left cheek.

An hour outside Dizeng, the boy Lung had used for his rituals this year stepped out from the trees. He was escorted by four men leading five donkeys.

He didn't look happy, the boy. (He hadn't been the most cheerful assistant Lung had employed, but he'd been good at what he had to do, worth what he'd been paid.)

Lung hadn't arranged for or expected the boy's appearance. He'd *expected* to be heading east this morning, had dismissed the boy, paid him off.

"You need him, don't you?" Ren Daiyan said. "Isn't that how you do what you do? Honestly or otherwise?"

He tended to speak quietly, Lung realized, but people listened. Daiyan was a little intimidating, in truth. Not exactly a big man, but he carried himself like one, and the others appeared to accept his authority.

"Are you going to explain any of this to me?" Lung demanded. "Why are you interfering with my life?"

Daiyan shook his head. "Explain? No, not now. If you save the girl, maybe on the road back. We'll all be coming back, if you save the girl."

"Ren Daiyan," he said—you couldn't call this man Little Dai— "you know I have not seen her, that the rituals are difficult and uncertain."

"I do know that," Daiyan agreed placidly. "If you had simply awakened this morning and come this way with your boy, it wouldn't have been a concern for me if you cured her or not. But now ... if you don't succeed in that village, Teacher Tuan, I might kill you. Just so you know."

Tuan Lung swallowed. "I ... I was your teacher. I taught you poetry. I gave you your first bow!"

"I thank you for all of that, honourable teacher," said the man Ren Daiyan had become. And he bowed. He said nothing more until they overtook the peasant woman trudging along with another bandit as her escort.

It was late in the day by then, not far from the accursed hamlet from which she'd come to mar his life. Daiyan spoke to her kindly, offered food and drink. She never even looked up from staring fixedly at the road. They tended to be like that, the peasants, when faced with something they didn't understand, which happened often.

Tuan Lung didn't really understand either. How could a man do his best work in something as dangerous and difficult as a demon exorcism when afraid for his own life for *other* reasons? He wanted to say that to Daiyan. And what about real gratitude to a teacher? And respect? Not just words spoken. He wanted to say that, too.

They came to the village at twilight.

It was barely a village, really, which was why he hadn't stopped here on the way east. The evening star was ahead of them, following the sun down. Lung heard a nightingale. He was surprised no one had captured it for the Flowers and Rocks Network. They were paying good money for nightingales.

Their party was observed by those still working in the fields. Well, of course they were! Eight men and a boy, most of them riding, accompanying a woman from this village? That woman on a donkey, not stumping along the road, the leader of the party striding beside her, heavily armed?

They would talk about this all fall and winter, thought Tuan Lung bitterly. He looked at Ren Daiyan, who looked back at him and grinned.

That easy smile, at sunset by a tiny village, first star shining in the west, told him, finally, how far this man had come from the boy Lung had known all those years ago. He pulled up his donkey.

"The boy and I need to stop," he said. "We'll follow you in."

He expected an argument, was prepared to insist, but Daiyan only nodded his head. "Ziji, I'll stay with these two, take the others and Mother Sima into town. We'll join you. We eat our own food tonight or pay for anything we're given."

"Of course," said another of the outlaws, the one who had been with Sima Peng when they'd overtaken them. This one led their party forward. Men from the fields were straggling in to follow them.

Lung looked at his former student. He *had* given this one his first weapon. Was he going to regret it? He said, "There are some arcane things that must be done. It is dangerous for you to—"

"You need to plant bones under a tree. I will stand watch and make sure you aren't seen. I saw an oak not far back, north of the road."

Lung had seen it too. He looked at the other man. It wasn't full dark yet.

He said, "You understand that—"

"I understand that sometimes people need to believe certain things to be healed and that sometimes they *are* healed. You are all watched more often than you know, on the roads, in the villages. Come, bury what you have to bury. No one will see you. That's my task."

Lung shook his head in wonder. Then, somehow, the humour of the situation finally struck him. He had never been, at heart, an angry man. He said, "Do you remember anything I taught you? Any poetry? Chan Du? Sima Zian?"

"I do. I buy books when I can. I'll wager they claim Master Sima as an ancestor, this family here."

"I won't take that wager," said Lung, fighting a smile.

They did what they needed to do by the tree. The boy remained unhappy, but Lung saw Daiyan give him a coin (it looked to be silver, but the light was fading) and his mood changed. On the way back to the village—which was called Gongzhu, he learned—Daiyan told him what the other outlaw, Ziji, had learned from the woman about the girl and the family. Such things mattered in the rites.

The surprise was that Daiyan knew they did.

Tuan Lung took the lead when they reached the village. He went down the one main street to the afflicted household. It was easy to find: there was a crowd by the gate. The woman, Peng, was waiting in front of the open door, beside a terrified-looking husband and an older man (her father, most likely). The two men looked befuddled and afraid. Bats were darting in twilight trees. He saw fireflies. Late in the year for them.

He greeted the family formally. He adjusted his red hat and went inside with his boy—no one else allowed, except the mother, for propriety—to see if he could save the life of a girl pushed up against the doors of death by a demon possessing her. It would be a battle, he told the family and the villagers assembled in the growing dark.

It always was.

PENG NEVER TELLS THE STORY, never does speak of what she saw that night in her own small home, in front of the ancestral altar. The night that power and ritual magic were invoked in her presence.

She had made a decision. For Zhi-li's sake, that summer's affliction needed to be forgotten. Once, she overheard her father (whom she did love and honour) talking of the ritual to another man—though he'd seen nothing, had been outside with the others. That evening she'd put an herb in his soup that gave him violent, ongoing cramps in the night.

Perhaps, she'd said to him in the morning, seeing him pale and exhausted, he had somehow offended a demon, speaking of the spirit world. Matters best not discussed by simple people such as they were, lest troubles descend again.

Over time, her memories of that evening had blurred and shifted, the way the forms of her daughter and the ritual master and the strange boy had shifted in their house after the candles were lit.

She remembers the master saying, low-voiced and intense to Zhi-li, that he *would* drive the spirit from her, she *would* be healed, but that it was almost certain she'd not be able to marry away from the village now, ever leave Gongzhu, and she would have to accept that.

Peng had begun crying then. The master said that if he or anyone were forced to try this a second time, ever, Zhi-li would almost surely die.

Then he began his invocations. The boy started to gasp and wail almost immediately, in a high voice. Peng had barely been able to look, so afraid was she.

She remembers (thinks she remembers) her daughter becoming very still even as the boy began to writhe in pain. There had been a cord attached by the master to the left wrist of each of them—she remembers that. There were three red ribbons tied along it, the same colour as his hat.

Zhi-li had been unexpectedly docile and calm from the moment she was released from the back room and brought before the master. Peng had feared she would be violent and obscene, the way she often was since her affliction began. She remembers the master instructing her to be very quiet herself and keep to a corner of the room.

As if she'd have any intention of doing anything else!

He had placed his hands over the largest candle and the colour of its flame miraculously (terrifyingly!) changed to green. The boy twisted suddenly away from that, almost pulling Zhi-li from the stool where she'd been placed before the altar.

The master continued chanting, his voice strong and deep, his hands moving in suddenly scented air. Peng didn't recognize the smell. It was sweet and heavy. Her heart had been pounding. To the end of her life she will never be certain that she didn't lose consciousness at some point in the house that night.

But she was watching and aware when Zhi-li, too, began to cry out in a strained voice (but her *own* voice!). With that, the boy fell to his knees on their dirt floor, echoing the cries harshly, as if he was feeling the same pain—or anger.

The ritual master had taken hold of the cord between the two of them with his left hand and raised his voice in a commanding shout, words Peng could not understand.

She had been covering her face with her hands then, peeking out between fingers, then looking down, so as not to see what dread darkness was being summoned into her own home.

From her own child.

The master shouted again, words she understood this time: "Demon, I invoke you! I compel you by the Fivefold Thunder! Why have you consumed this girl?"

Zhi-li had closed her eyes, her head falling back, limbs trembling so much her mother feared she'd injure herself. She wanted to go forward and clasp her child in her arms, but she stayed in her corner, as ordered, watching through the fingers of her hands before her eyes.

It was the boy who answered, a voice so deep suddenly it seemed hardly possible it came from one so young. What he said Peng could not understand, the words were contorted, broken, *angry*.

The ritual master's hair had come unpinned, she saw; it was loose down his back. He pulled sharply at the cord so that the boy toppled towards Zhi-li, on the ground beside her stool.

The master shouted again, sounding even more angry than the spirit-voice. "The *marriage*? It is over! She will not wed him! What else has brought you to harm an innocent family? Why bring evil to this village? Who are you?"

Peng saw the boy on the ground, at Zhi-li's feet, pain and rage on his features in the strange light. He cried aloud again in words she could not understand.

Then he was silent, and still.

It was suddenly very quiet in their home.

And then, "Ah!" said the ritual master softly. "I see."

The green hue of the candle's flame went away without warning. There was normal light in their home, and the strange scent was gone.

The ritual master rubbed at his face with both hands, wearily. He took a deep breath. He untied the cord that bound her daughter and his boy. The boy lay on the ground, Peng saw. His eyes were closed. He wasn't moving.

The master left him there. He gave Zhi-li a cup with a drink he had prepared. She looked up at him from the stool, wide-eyed. She took it from his hand, docile, still trembling, and drank.

The master looked over at Peng in her corner.

He was drenched in perspiration, she saw; his eyes and his long hair looked wild. The boy was still unconscious on the floor, limbs splayed. Peng looked at him. She brought down her hands. She had still been holding them to her face.

"Is he ... is he *dead*?" she remembers asking, her voice quavering.

The master shook his head tiredly. "He will sleep. So will Zhi-li soon. And after, she will be all right. It is over. The spirit identified itself to me, and will be gone when we do one needful thing."

It is over.

Sima Peng began to weep, slow tears forced from her eyes, down seamed cheeks. She clasped her hands together tightly. She looked at her daughter by candlelight, and it seemed to her that she *saw* her again. She knew that expression, those eyes. Zhi-li, too, started to cry.

"Mother?" she said.

There had never been a word she'd so longed to hear.

Peng left her corner and gathered her child in her arms. Her child who was herself again, returned to them.

SHE SPEAKS OF NONE OF THIS, not through the years of her life, not through the changes in their world.

Some things happen east of the village later that same night, and others know of them and share them, but no one knows what took place in that room with the green light and the heavy scent, and the commands and cries.

The ritual master binds up his hair and goes out her door. Many men, including her husband and father and the bandits who helped them, go with him out of town along the road in the night, bearing torches. Zhi-li sleeps, as he'd said she would. The boy remains on the floor in the house. Peng stays with both of them.

The villagers find the tree that the boy, consumed by Zhi-li's demon for the space and time of the rite, had told them to find. They dig by torchlight under stars and a half moon and there are bones lying there.

A girl cruelly murdered long ago, on the eve of her wedding, the master told them, and never found, never properly laid to rest. Her spirit had entered into Zhi-li on the eve of her own marriage and passage into womanhood.

So he explained the next morning, in sunlight, when fears recede with the arrival of day.

They buried the bones. There were only a few—wild creatures had carried off the rest, so shallow had been the grave where her murderer had hidden her. They perform the rituals, though they never knew her name, her family, where she was from, when she had died. It had to have been long ago.

Sima Peng offers candles and prayers for this unknown girl on the day of the Cold Food Festival from that time onwards.

She had taken over Zhi-li's body in pain and rage, in her own soul's unresting torment, and then left her—left her whole—when the ritual master, whose name Peng will praise until she dies, came to them and brought release in a green light.

Zhi-li will never marry, never leave their village. She goes to serve in the temple of the Sacred Path not long after that night of power, when late-season fireflies had gathered (perhaps the scent?) by their house, and torches smoked on the one long village street and then over unearthed bones along the river road. She is happy there, Zhi-li, is eventually initiated among the priestesses, is not just a servant.

Her younger sister marries well, into a village north of them. She dies bearing her first child, not long after greater troubles have begun to afflict their world. The child, a boy, survives a very little time then also dies. Peng has no grandchildren from her daughters or her son, who is called into the army at seventeen and marches away north. They never see him again after the dust of his company's going settles on the road. Her husband isn't the same man, after. She remembers that day, seeing her son recede from her. She sees it at night, in the quiet.

There is only so much a woman can do to help her children through the hard, dark, spinning sorrows of time and the world.

CHAPTER X

In summer the Jeni tribe of the steppe, in the northeast, were even farther north, near the source of the Black River, which marked the boundary of their traditional grazing lands. The river ran east from there, in hill-and-forest country, before tracking to find the sea.

The summer had been dry but not dangerously so, and the herds had found decent grazing. The Jeni's young kaghan was beginning to think about the trek south and west they would make when autumn arrived. By winter they would be a fair distance away, though never far enough to entirely avoid the knife of the north wind and the snows that came, with wolf packs starving and bold in the savage nights.

It was a hard life. It was the only life they knew.

In summer, now, the wolves remained a menace, but summer offered them ways to feed without risking encounters with men, and the wolves of these steppes were the most intelligent—and therefore dangerous—on earth. There were so many tales, including how they could, at times, cross the space between animal and human. Or how men could go the other way, becoming wolflike. Shamans bridged that divide, not always benevolently.

Goodwill, kindness, safety, tranquility, these were not the coinage of the world here, whether by daylight under the high sky of the god or at night under his stars.

Accordingly, the Jeni kept guards on watch, always. All the tribes did, across the vast swath of the steppe, running from the ridged and forested hills near here through thousands and thousands of *li* west to the deserts where no one could live and no one tried.

Which is to say there *were* guards posted on a summer night.

O-YAN, YOUNGEST AND MUCH-LOVED brother of the kaghan, was fourteen that summer, posted with other young ones on summer guard duty. Boys were eased into their responsibilities this way. Summer watch at the encampment by the river was easier than doing the same thing on a winter night when the wolves were bolder and the herds might be farther away from the body of the tribe.

There was no reason to expect more danger here than an outcast wolf or sometimes a big cat, far from its usual range, drawn by the presence of so many animals, overcoming a fear of men. It would be an outcast, too, if so.

O-Yan took his task seriously, aware that in time he would be expected to play a strong role in the tribe, helping his brother, all three of his older brothers. He was proud of his family, anxious to bring honour to them. He had spoken to the other boys on duty tonight, seven of them, about how wrong it was to be fearful, to startle at every sound from the animals.

They looked to him as their leader, and not just because of his family. O-Yan's manner, his calm, was already noted. He was reassuring by nature.

A Jeni rider, he told them (and they would be full-fledged riders soon), knew how to tell a restless horse from a threat in a dark night.

There was no moon tonight. O-Yan did admit to himself, if reluctantly, that he preferred when it was easier to see into the blackness of the steppe. But when had the world ever made things easy for men? Life was an endless series of tests. His brother, the kaghan, was fond of saying that. They didn't live in slack and indolent ease like those far to the south. The Kitan down there were soft, lazy, hardly worthy of the gift of life the sky god had given to all men.

A Kitan would die faced with the challenges of the steppe, O-Pang had told his youngest brother more than once. They'd die in a mild summer, let alone winter! And the Xiaolu, their over-lords? They were growing soft, too, steppe people building cities, living in them!

The Jeni and other tribes might acknowledge the power of the Xiaolu, offer tribute to an emperor for peace in the northeast (others did the same in the west), but they were still a proud people. Pride was coinage in the grasslands. If the price of peace in their grazing lands was an autumn tribute (and a night dance), that was a price a small tribe could agree to pay. No true leader should allow his own feelings to endanger his people.

Our tribe is our family, O-Pang would say to his brothers.

O-Yan, youngest, had listened gravely even at ten or eleven, a serious, watchful child, born into a shaman's foretelling. The old man had cast the bones of a slaughtered lamb and drunk blood in his stone bowl the night O-Yan came crying into the world. He had predicted that the boy's destiny might be as bright as any Jeni's had been since the beginnings of the tribe.

Prophecies were chancy things. You needed to survive so much—disease, famine, accidents, war—to come into your full growth as a man for any such future to unfold, or be allowed.

O-Yan, schooling himself to be relaxed and alert—a difficult conjunction—heard a sound to his right, away from the horses. It could be many things. A small animal, a snake dislodging stones.

He turned to look into the night. He took an arrow in the eye and died where he stood, brave and clever and too young. He fell with a faint clatter that might have been heard by anyone nearby listening. No one was nearby.

No one but the man who killed him knew about the small sound O-Yan had heard, which had not been an error, of course, but intended to make the boy turn, present his face and body to the arrow that claimed his life.

Well, that wasn't entirely true, that only his killer heard it. In the beliefs of the steppe, the Lord of the Sky knew all, and the Lord of Death knew when someone was coming to him. It was also possible that someone, later, spinning a tale out of the old sorrow of a young man's dying, might have added that sound to twist the hearts of listeners a little more. Storytellers do that sort of thing.

The tribe's shaman was a gifted one, a strong traveller in the spirit realm. His foretelling had not been wrong. O-Yan of the Jeni had greatness within him, largeness of soul, wisdom emerging, even young.

But the boy was killed in a moonless summer dark under stars and wisps of cloud, and certain futures ended with him, just as others opened up because he died.

This happens all the time. It is why men pray to their gods.

THE ALTAI CAME DOWN, treacherously and without warning, thundering on horseback (always on horseback) out of the dark, having forded the river and waited through the day.

The trouble with using boys as guards was that being prone to startle at sounds from their own animals could also make them more likely to miss the subtler hints (often from those same animals) of real danger.

All the young guards posted around the camp were killed by bowmen sent ahead of the Altai riders. On the steppe, archers rarely missed, even by starlight, and though the Altai themselves lived in a different landscape, nearer to and among forests, they were known—they had long been known—as the hardest fighters of all, and the best horsemen among people who could all ride.

There weren't many of them—the harsh lands towards the Koreini Peninsula could not sustain numbers. That had always been the saving, soothing factor for the tribes around them. The Altai were short, bow-legged, black-hearted, dangerously arrogant, but they weren't numerous, and that had tempered an inherent aggression.

Aggression didn't mean viciousness. No mutilations were inflicted upon the Jeni guards. The boys were simply killed. Sometimes in warfare one tribe might be savage with the men and women of another, and in the past they usually had been like that with a taken Kitan city. That was deliberate, a tactic, a tool of war to discourage resistance.

There was no message to send tonight. The Altai had no hatred of the Jeni, though their leaders bore little respect for O-Pang since his embarrassing, placating dance before the Xiaolu emperor. The Jeni were only a first, necessary step, a beginning.

This night attack was—looked at one way—the breaking of an oath sworn after that night of dancing, and the Altai had always vested pride in keeping oaths and taking revenge on those who did not.

On the other hand, as their war-leader's clever brother had explained, if they *denied* that the Xiaolu were above them, that their drunken, puffed-up emperor was the Altai's lord, the oath had no authority at all.

They had accepted the much more numerous Xiaolu for a long time. That was finished, from tonight. Their entire tribe was across the river, down from their own lands. They were all on the move, women and children and the aged, and their herds. They would not cease moving until this was over, one way or another way. It had been decided that this would be so, and sworn by firelight.

The origins of this rising dated back to dancing around another fire. They ran straight as a spear from that night to this one, when everything began to change under the sky. Not just here in a Jeni encampment by the Black River, but in the world, rippling a long way.

⚮

Daiyan and the outlaws did not linger in the village after Tuan Lung saved the girl from the demon possessing her.

In the morning, setting out to go back east, Lung had people grasping at his hands to kiss them, pleading for him to stay and heal a variety of afflictions. This happened often.

He excused himself, offering the urgency of vague, large affairs. Ren Daiyan and his men, true to Daiyan's promise, guarded him. They were undisturbed on the way back to Dizeng Village.

Daiyan rode beside him in the afternoon, through a sleep-inducing, late-season heat.

"The bones we buried and dug up?"

"Yes?"

"Why?"

Lung looked over at him. They were riding easily, in no hurry. You couldn't hurry on donkeys. The fields nearby were brown. They would need rain, or suffering would come. He knew about that. It had led him to this life. Some of the arcane priests did rain ceremonies for a fee. Sometimes they worked.

"People need help, an explanation, to understand why they fall ill, why they are healed."

"Did you drive a spirit out of her body?"

"I healed her."

"And the boy? The one who speaks in strange words and falls unconscious when you do your rite?"

"You were listening?"

Daiyan said nothing.

Lung shrugged. "I told you, people need help to understand."

"She fell ill when they arranged her marriage?"

"Yes," said Lung, "so it appears."

He looked at Daiyan and allowed himself a smile. "How much help do you need?"

After a moment the younger man smiled back. "This is enough, Teacher Tuan."

"I do good along this road," Tuan said. "We may not always understand how it happens."

They reached Dizeng in the afternoon. As the larger village came in sight, Daiyan halted his donkey and lifted a hand so the others behind would do the same.

He turned to Lung again. "You are going to Jingxian? We cannot escort you there. I will have Ziji find honest men to guard you east with your money. It will be my honour to pay for them. I hope you will allow that. You did what I asked of you, and I am grateful."

His courtesy was extreme.

"What about you? Back across the river? To the marsh?"

Daiyan smiled. "You knew I crossed from there?"

"It makes sense, when you think about it."

"Much does, when you think about it. But no, I'm not going back."

"Oh?"

Daiyan looked ahead, to where country road became dusty village street. "I am meeting with the magistrate here."

"Wang Fuyin? You spoke with him, you said."

"About his case, about you. Now ... about myself. And these others."

Tuan Lung stared at him. He opened his mouth. He said nothing, however. After a moment, they moved on, entered the village.

The next morning, heading east with the promised guards, setting out early before the heat, it occurred to him that he might have said to Ren Daiyan right there on the path, "Take me with you."

He'd have become a different man, reached a different destination with his life. He knew it even then, riding out under birdsong in morning light.

There are forks in every road, choices we make.

CHIEF MAGISTRATE WANG FUYIN, loyally serving his emperor in the important city of Jingxian, with responsibility for a number of larger and smaller towns, had been in the *yamen* of Dizeng Village towards evening, the day before.

He had stayed because he was expecting a visitor.

It surprised him, how keenly he was anticipating this meeting. But then, his life had been changed by this man, and it was a part of the Cho Master's teachings that certain persons can occur and recur in the fabric of one's life. Magistrate Wang felt at ease in thinking that the man he was waiting for was important to him.

For one thing, he had solved the case he'd travelled here to deal with—a particularly bloody killing—by virtue of information given to him by that same man, seen without warning here, years after their last moment together.

He remembered another autumn, a country path, leaves falling and fallen, in the west. Arrows from a boy, saving their lives. Then the boy was gone—into the forest, snatched from his life, claimed by the trees.

Wang Fuyin had never considered himself a poet, but images had come to him. He'd written a poem about that day. Sent it to friends in Hanjin and elsewhere, men he'd taken the examinations with. It had been unexpectedly well received, even reached the court, he was told.

In the winter and spring that had followed, Wang Fuyin had begun working very hard, not just at his tasks as sub-prefect, but learning all he could about the duties of magistrates.

He'd solved that crime in Guan Family Village, the one he'd been on his way to investigate. Had he been abducted or killed on the road a murderer might never have been apprehended. Justice had been served.

Fuyin had been young enough to feel a force asserting itself, claiming attention, pushing him forward. He really wasn't a poet—the way he thought of it changed all the time.

He wrote a small reflection that summer, a primer for magistrates identifying matters they needed to attend to when called to investigate a crime. He based it on one from the Eighth Dynasty, identified that, but added a great deal that was specific to their own time.

This, too, was well received. And this, too, reached the court. The prime minister himself, illustrious Hang Dejin, read it (or intimated that he had). He sent particular commendation, along with a gift of cash and a promotion in the emperor's name (of course) to the position of magistrate in a larger city, a *real place*, as Fuyin's suddenly much happier wife put it.

Another promotion, to the sixth rank of the civil service, had followed a year ago, bringing them to the even more real city of Jingxian. He'd teased his wife by describing it that way, reminding her of her own words. By that point she was so impressed with her startlingly ascendant husband that she'd giggled, pleasingly.

Once they were established in Jingxian, she'd taken measures and arranged for his first concubine—a lovely thing, musical, well trained in many ways, and (of course) a symbol of their rise in the world.

He'd written and had printed another small essay on the proper conduct of a magistrate when investigating crimes of violence. He was told that his writings were becoming obligatory reading for younger civil servants. An examination question this spring had apparently been based on one of them!

A posting to Hanjin seemed a reasonable thing to begin to

(cautiously) imagine, although beyond that Fuyin did not speculate. He knew his wife did. He told his concubine as much, in bed at night.

He *had* changed, and not just in his circumstances. He was clever enough to know that without those inward changes he might still be a lazy and bitter civil servant in a remote prefecture (with a bitter wife).

When word came to the *yamen* of Jingxian last fall that a young outlaw from the marshes south of the river had led a group that attacked a Flowers and Rocks party and had killed six of them himself with rapid and precise arrows, Fuyin was intrigued by a possibility.

As magistrate it was within his office to summon the surviving members of the party and he did so. They gave him a description.

Obviously, the man leading such an outlaw band would not be identical in appearance to the fifteen-year-old boy he'd last seen walking into the forest near Guan Family Village, but ...

It seemed there were tales told about this archer. One of them was that he'd come to the marsh from the far west and was notoriously the outlaws' best bowman and youngest leader.

It was enough for Fuyin to do something that was both an act of kindness and something more complex. He wrote the father, his one-time clerk.

It was known along the Great River which villages the outlaws sometimes visited. He informed the father where a letter might possibly find his son.

He'd liked Ren Yuan, a diligent, dignified man. Had appreciated him more when his own changes had begun. He'd even shown the father his first small book and been grateful for diffident (but useful) comments made before it was printed.

He didn't know if Clerk Ren would send a letter to his boy, he didn't know if anything would come of it if he did. He didn't even know for certain that the outlaw with the bow was Ren Daiyan.

Sometimes you tossed a stone into a pool.

Then one day, having come to Dizeng to deal with a murder, he did know—and all answers were affirmative, to his very great pleasure.

IT WAS ODD, in a way, but walking towards his second visit to the *yamen*, Daiyan was more apprehensive than he had been the first time. In most ways, that made no sense.

Three days ago, he'd had no idea how the magistrate he'd known as a boy would receive an outlaw leader from the marsh. Daiyan was known to have killed soldiers, civil servants, merchants. It had been entirely possible he'd be arrested, tortured, and executed—here in this village or back in Jingxian. Such a capture would be a career boost for the man who achieved it. Wang Fuyin might even have written Daiyan's father with that in mind. It was not beyond the level of intrigue for ambitious civil servants.

And yet, entering the *yamen*, he'd been as calm as he could remember. Composed, in the way he seemed to be before a raid or a fight. Combat never unsettled him. He'd learned that on a road near home.

He understood that other men—men he commanded or opposed—might be dealing with gut-roiling fear at such moments, and he'd learned to assuage or exploit this. It was part of a man's task if he wished to lead.

He did wish to lead. And to honour his father and ancestors.

That was what had led him to the *yamen* once he learned the magistrate had indeed arrived, as planned.

Someone might have thought it was an act of fate, that the chief magistrate happened to have been summoned to deal with a crime in Dizeng so soon after Ren Daiyan and his companions came across the river.

That would have been an innocent's thought.

Ziji knew the name and village of a man who'd tried to join them in the marsh two years ago. No one had trusted him. He was sent on his way, and followed. He lived alone at the edge of Dizeng Village, and it turned out he possessed a counterfeiting machine (it hadn't been hard to discover this).

The punishment for such possession was death. The man had never been arrested or even questioned. The only possible reason was that he was acting as an informer, identifying outlaws, salt and tea smugglers, tax evaders along this stretch of the river. Lives had been destroyed because of him.

Ziji and two others took him on his way home from a pleasure house on their second night. He was killed in a nearby field, dramatically—a farmer's scything hook.

The scythe was cleaned reasonably well, but not perfectly, and returned to the shed of the man they intended to have arrested for the murder.

This one had killed a woman east of here the year before. Her body had never been found (some of the lakes were very deep), but he had been identified to the outlaws, if not the law.

Justice, along the river, took diverse forms.

Daiyan had spent much of that night awake, disturbed by a question that had come to him. If they hadn't known of these two men, would he have implemented his plan with ordinary country people: killing one, implicating another, to have the magistrate summoned?

Under a summer moon he came to an answer. If you wanted to change the world, you couldn't always do pleasant things.

Sitting at the edge of a copse of trees while the others slept, looking out over silvered summer fields, he remembered old, old lines, bright as moonlight, sorrow-laden as willow twigs at parting:

> *Wolves howl. I cannot find rest*
> *Because I am powerless*
> *To amend a broken world.*

Chan Du the poet, Ninth Dynasty, had lived before and through the years of the great rebellion. He had died during the fighting and the famine. Not far from here, in fact, travelling east along the river. His last home was a place of pilgrimage. Daiyan had been there, left twigs by the memorial stele.

He wasn't like Chan Du, and he was still young. He didn't accept that the world as it came to them could not be changed. Amended.

He wasn't the boy who had fought imagined barbarians with a bamboo sword in a grove and yet, of course, he was and always would be. He went back to his cloak under the trees and slept until sunrise.

They'd waited for the body in the field to be found and word to go east, and then for the chief magistrate to come from Jingxian to deal with a murder, as was his duty.

A good leader gathered as much information as he could before moving a plan from his mind and sending it into the world. Even with that, there were many moments when you could not be sure of success, when you had to trust to ... something. The grace of the Queen Mother of the West, your alignment of stars and ancestors, the goodwill of other men. Spirits. Chance.

He didn't like such moments, which was why he was uneasy on that walk up the steps of the *yamen* again, to see the man whose life he'd saved those years ago.

FUYIN HAD GIVEN the matter of Ren Daiyan careful thought since their encounter a few days earlier.

He'd had time to do so. The murder had been swiftly solved by a device he'd used at the outset of his career, that first crime in Guan Family Village. He'd written about it, had been commended for ingenuity.

It seemed likely in the present case that the victim had been killed by a scythe (limbs hacked off, lying near the body, not a pretty sight but he'd seen it before). Chief Magistrate Wang's assistants set about gathering all the scythes in and around Dizeng. They laid them down in a meadow near hives of domestic bees. A crowd of onlookers gathered.

The bees swarmed, quickly, over the scythe with blood on it.

It was memorably dramatic.

The owner of that scythe spent more time than most did protesting his innocence, but the magistrate's men were experienced, good at all their tasks, and a confession was duly extracted that night.

The man remained alive after questioning, which was good. He would be executed here. It was salutary for neighbours (and children) to see that done, carrying a message: the emperor's justice could reach all the way to villages like Dizeng.

They also took possession of a counterfeiting device and a considerable number of false coins buried beneath the floor in the house of the victim. The chief magistrate's report would indicate that a falling-out among criminals had very likely led to the murder, and it would redound to his name that he'd dealt with two major crimes at once.

When Ren Daiyan walked into the *yamen* the second time, the evening after the murderer's confession, Fuyin insisted that they go to the best of the singing girl houses. It wasn't, in truth, so very good, but they were where they were, you made do.

He arranged for food, baths for both of them, with attendants and flute music. He'd wondered if Daiyan would be anxious, unsettled.

He saw no signs of this. The young man (he *was* still young) was both courteous and intense. He showed little lightness or humour that night (these would appear later). He was precise as to the ranks he expected for himself and his fellows as they left the outlaws of the marsh and joined the army of Kitai. He was explicit that he would never serve as a guard for a Flowers and Rocks party.

Fuyin was in a position to agree to all of this, though he did propose a modification and, after a few questions, Ren Daiyan accepted.

He and the other outlaws would not immediately be enlisted in the army. They would spend some time as the newly appointed senior guards of the chief magistrate of Jingxian. As such, Daiyan's initial rank and pay would be equivalent to a military commander of one hundred, rising to that of five hundred in the New Year's promotions in just a few months.

This would make it easier for him to be offered an even larger command when he shifted to the army itself, which was—there was no ambiguity here—his fixed intention.

He was going to fight in the north. That night he even quoted the old song to Fuyin ... *We must take back our rivers and mountains.*

Many people still seemed to think that way, Fuyin thought, all these years after the treaty that had surrendered those lands below the Long Wall.

Wang Fuyin was personally of the view that the silver and silk paid north came right back to them at the border markets. And a bought, sure peace was better than the uncertainty of war. He could (and he often did) point to the disaster of Erighaya as evidence of the damage warfare did.

Kitai in this Twelfth Dynasty was simply not, in his opinion, set up for military triumph. Once, the army had known real—and dangerous—power. Once, high-ranking civil servants could ride well, play polo on splendid horses. They could loose an arrow, handle a blade. Now bureaucrats prided themselves on avoiding such pursuits. They were plump and soft, displaying the absence of any military threat to the throne.

He kept most of this to himself that first night. "Of course, there needs to be a *war* for you to fight in the north," was all he said that evening, listening to adequate flute and *pipa* music, sipping the wine on offer in Dizeng Village.

"There will be," said Ren Daiyan.

His certainty was remarkable. Some people almost forced you to believe them, even when they spoke of the future, which no man could truly know.

They went east two days later, the two of them and Fuyin's assistants and Daiyan's six men—Chief Magistrate Wang Fuyin's newly appointed guards—to Jingxian.

ა

The last characters from the brush of Xi Wengao, scholar and historian and one-time prime minister of Kitai, had been written that same summer, in his garden in Yenling. The words were a reflection on the very different virtues of the plum blossom and the peony.

The essay was unfinished when he died but was widely printed and read (*his last words!*) throughout Kitai. Master Xi had been, by any measure, one of the ornaments of the dynasty, a figure they could propose, with pride, to sit in heaven, in the celestial garden, among the great writers and scholars of the empire's long past.

This was so, notwithstanding the fact that the last years of his life were spent exiled from power, confined to Yenling.

The battles of factions surely did not, for the wise, dictate the long-term importance of historians or poets. Not in a civilized world, and Kitai considered itself, of all things, civilized. One needed only to look north to the barbarians for a contrast.

Master Xi's last essay was about art and nature. It proposed that the blossoming of the plum in early spring was so delicately beautiful, so evocative of fragility as to render words about it or paintings of it crude, inadequate, however skilled the artist or the poet.

Men (and one or two women, the historian noted carefully) had tried to capture the plum blossom in art and words, but its *essence* eluded in exquisite simplicity.

Xi Wengao had allowed himself to explore the digressive thought that this mirrored, in certain ways, the Twelfth Dynasty itself. A smaller empire than some before it, less dramatic in its ambitions. Clothing and adornments were less provocative, porcelain and painting more subtle, too much *assertion* having become slightly embarrassing.

The peony, by contrast, was loved by many—though not all—for its drama, boldness ... assertion. For the way in which it was a created beauty, a statement by men of what they could do. Art applied to nature: grafting, designing, shaping scent and colour with the skill of the gifted, especially in Yenling.

The peony, Master Xi suggested, had been "King of Flowers" back in the Ninth and might be seen today as an echo of the power and confidence of that dynasty before the fall into chaos.

From which long period of violence and incorrect thinking this Twelfth Dynasty had emerged—as a plum blossom through winter snow!

The reflections in the essay were unfinished, alas. His conclusion was never laid on paper. The tale was that he had fallen asleep in his garden pavilion holding his brush, and had never awakened from that sleep. It was said that his soft black hat, insecurely pinned, had slipped from his head and lay beside him on the writing desk in morning light.

As a result, it was never known what the intended resolution to this essay was. Xi Wengao also eluded, even as he died.

It was reported that one of his younger woman servants died with him that day, killing herself when she discovered that his spirit had crossed through the doorways to the other world.

The rumour was that she had been more than a servant to him in the last years of his exile. It was well known how much Xi Wengao had enjoyed the presence of women throughout his life.

It had been thought that on her part this relationship was simply the old tale of a servant angling for a better life by way of slipping into the master's bed. Her death by her own hand offered a rebuke to this, for some. The more cynical pointed out that with Xi Wengao gone, her status as preferred woman in that house was lost. Rather than revert to a lowly servant's role, they suggested, she'd simply preferred to die.

Others did see in her death something benign, perhaps even the presence of love. He had been, after all, loved by many, men and women both, all his days.

In the end, as so often, no certain conclusion was possible.

Illustrious Emperor Wenzong instructed that the scholar be laid to rest with honour in Yenling, despite his exile, and that a memorial stele be raised with a record of his ranks and deeds upon it.

The woman was buried among the other servants in the cemetery at the highest point of the property. The house passed to his oldest son for a time, then changes came.

CHAPTER XI

On the ninth day of the ninth month, the Double Ninth, the Lu brothers went out alone—as they always did when the world permitted them to be together—to observe the Chrysanthemum Festival in the traditional manner.

Going off together with no one else was their own tradition, attached to the ancient one. They brought chrysanthemum wine, of course. The younger brother carried this, and the cups. The older one moved more slowly after his years on Lingzhou Isle, and carried a stick.

It was a day when people visited the graves of their dead, but their parents and ancestors were buried far to the west, and the man they were newly mourning had died in Yenling, at a writing desk.

It wasn't a particularly high place they found this time, even though that was part of the tradition. They had received word of Xi Wengao's passing just days ago and neither, gathered into sorrow, was of a mind to make an overnight journey in order to climb high.

Wengao been a mentor to both, loved by both, from the day they'd arrived in Hanjin with their father: two brothers from the west, reportedly brilliant, anecdotes and their first writings preceding them to the capital and the examinations, men pointed at the future.

Today they went to a ridge near East Slope, which was the name the older one had given their small farm. They sat on a bench under a tree and the younger one poured wine.

They looked east over the fall of the land. There was a stream, and just across it was boundary line. It was a property that could support a family if men were diligent and the weather was good.

It was not yet cold, but an awareness that autumn was upon them (always, with the coming of this day) lay within both men, along with loss.

The older brother said, "Is it possible for a man to go so far he cannot find his way back?"

The younger one, taller, thinner, looked at him. He drank before answering. He was less quick with words or brush than his brother, not really a poet, but was nearly as renowned, honoured for composure and courage and careful argument. He had been, among many things, a diplomat north to the Xiaolu.

"Of course it is possible," Lu Chao said, answering. "Are you feeling that way?"

The poet looked out at the stream. "Perhaps today."

His brother said, "Today is always hard. But you have your son here, your wife. We have each other every day now, and enough land not to starve. It is a gift, brother. You are back in Kitai."

Voicing an old thought: that Lingzhou Isle, though claimed by the empire, was a world unto itself.

Chen hadn't looked old when he was exiled, but you wouldn't name him a man in his prime now. It caused the younger one pain, thinking this, seeing it. The affection he bore his brother was the deepest of his days.

And was returned. Chen smiled at him. "A gift, yes. That I am here with you."

He held out his cup and the younger one filled it. They looked east and down. With their sons and farm workers they had cleared the brambles and bushes on this slope and planted mulberry and chestnut trees, on the advice of farmers who owned the nearby land. Neither brother was knowledgeable in country matters, both were willing to learn. There were people to be fed.

After a silence, the older one said:

> *Last night I drank too much by East Slope.*
> *I came home late, under stars.*
> *Leaning on a stick, I listened to the stream.*
> *They still trouble me—the longings of body and heart.*
> *When may I forget the busyness of the world?*
> *The sorrows of Kitai? The night was almost gone.*
> *The wind had died away. Only ripples in the stream.*
> *Perhaps I'll leave here in a small boat alone*
> *And sail until I find the sea and then go on.*

His younger brother drank, refilled both cups, was silent. Eventually, he said, "That is new."

"A few days ago, yes."

Chao said, "You have come back. Don't go away."

Chen flashed his well-known smile. "Ah. You are suggesting I am truly back? That this is still me?"

The younger one didn't return the smile. "I am," he said. "I am suggesting that."

Then, because there was no real way to avoid it much longer, he told his brother the other news that had just come, along the roads, across the rivers, this time from the court.

He was the one being asked to go away. It was an honour, a redemption from banishment. But it was also north, far past the capital, beyond the Long Wall, which had once been their border and wasn't any more, and there was danger up there, always.

A bird sang in the tree above them, another answered from down the slope. The morning was windy and bright. White clouds moving overhead, blue sky, yellow sun.

ᘖ

Through two years now of irregular but ongoing invitations to attend upon him at court or in his garden, the emperor of Kitai has never indicated a wish to take Shan to his couch or bed.

It is a relief, but because she tries to be honest with herself, she has also sometimes wondered why he shows no inclination in this way. Her mirror does not assist: a tall woman, good features, still young. Slim, in the current fashion, where women of good family are not to be "showy."

Of course not all the women in the Genyue are of good family. It is common for a gathering of, say, scholars and poets invited to the imperial garden to be interrupted by an arrival from the women's quarters of the palace in an escorted litter.

The emperor will then withdraw into a pavilion with the young woman thus transported. Curtains will be drawn for the encounter, though sounds do carry.

Those engagements are conducted in the presence, inside the curtains, of the registrar of Imperial Congress, an unsmiling man. There are usually two other women inside who—Shan understands—disrobe both participants and, on occasion, assist the august emperor in the task of bringing his companion to her climax of passion ... while, of course, denying such release to himself.

It is stipulated thus in the texts and doctrines of the Arcane Path. Only by undertaking congress in this way will a man achieve the enhancement to his life force that such encounters can provide.

Shan has sometimes tried—and always failed—to imagine herself in an act of lovemaking with three spectators standing by, one with a brush and paper, observing narrowly then scrupulously recording details of time and result.

Result. In a certain mood she can laugh at the thought, but these moods are harder to come by of late.

She has read two of the Arcane Path books of intimate instruction. *Secret Methods of the Dark Girl* is the best known. Her father has it in his library. She has, a little desperately, attempted to employ some of the guidance therein in bed with her husband. Qi Wai has professed amusement at her efforts.

He is withdrawing from her. It began, she thinks, around the time the emperor started favouring her—favouring *them*, in truth, though she knows it is a delicate matter to say this to Wai. She wonders if his mother or father has suggested that his prestige as a man is undermined by the attention paid his wife.

But the truth is that because of this imperial favour she and her husband live in one of the largest houses in the imperial clan compound. Her father now has a home with them, a small house on the far side of their large courtyard. They even have a warehouse nearby, with a permanent guard, to hold their growing collection, Qi Wai's pride, his life's joy.

Though Shan had begun to speculate, perhaps a year ago, that his joy might also lie elsewhere now.

But what can she *do*? Pretend she isn't happy that their elegant, cultured emperor values her songs, her *ci*, sung by one of his entertainers, or simply read the way he would read a poem? Is all this improper for a woman, in Qi Wai's eyes (and others')? Is that it?

Husbands can withdraw from their wives. Indeed, it is often the case that they are never close to begin with. But this—this *reason* for a change would be painful for Shan. She misses their journeys together, sharing discoveries. With her husband she has been able to travel. He has always been an eccentric man, but they did share passions, and now he declines to share, in all ways.

Her father, at least (and always), offers only approval and delight at her triumphs. She feels pleasure and a daughter's virtue, that she's able to give him a place to live in comfort. Her memory of the time he was so nearly exiled comes at night sometimes, along with the image of an assassin in her room.

She can usually talk to her father. She doesn't about these thoughts, however. Nor to anyone else. The women in the compound seem to have collectively decided that Shan is unladylike, deeply improper. That writing songs or poetry is unbefitting—an attempt to evade or escape her proper status and role.

There is envy here as much as anything, her father has pointed out, and envy is—as the Cho Master wrote long ago—always and ever a part of the human condition.

But it is powerful, and can isolate you. She doesn't want to tell her father these feelings. He will grieve—and blame himself. Some things, Shan has come to understand, you carry alone, and hers are small burdens, not on a scale that ought to matter.

She has wondered if Wai is of the belief that she is being bedded by the emperor. Would that explain his change?

It isn't their being childless, though a husband can send a wife back to her family for this. She has always known Wai has no interest in children. Within the imperial clan the impulse to protect one's old age with a younger generation of filial caregivers simply doesn't arise. The members of the clan are supported by the court as long as they live and through their funeral rites—which means supported by the people of Kitai, out of taxes and tariffs.

Shan knows the enormous, growing clan she's married into is hugely expensive and that they do *nothing*, by long-standing decree, for the empire. No kin of the emperor's line is allowed anywhere close to power or influence. There are too many stories of insurrection and conspiracy from the past. They are provided for, kept together, and watched: trivial, glittering ornaments. To aspire to more is to become dangerous.

She feels helpless when stories of drought or hardship in the countryside reach Hanjin. What can she do about it? She can write songs, but songs don't change the world, especially not a woman's. Perhaps their not having children—more members of the clan to be supported—counts as a good thing, though she's aware in the night sometimes of their absence, among other kinds of longing.

As it happens, she is fairly certain, though she cannot prove it (or say it), that she is capable of conceiving. The physician she'd quietly consulted thought so, and noted, cautiously, that sometimes the "complexity" in such matters could lie with the man diffusing his essence in various ways.

Shan isn't sure where Qi Wai's "essence" is going. She does know that their once-shared passion for the collection, the journeys taken together, purchasing and cataloguing done side by side, the pleasure of discovering then assessing calligraphy or pottery or bronze from long ago ... they don't do that any more, not together, not side by side.

A WOMAN IS COMING to sing for the emperor of Kitai.

A number of his principal advisers have assembled in a pavilion in his garden, waiting for him to arrive. They will listen to the singer with varying degrees of attention and impatience, though with faces schooled to simulate extreme concentration, because that will be the emperor's expression. Shan has seen this many times now.

It is well known how he values music, poetry, painting, calligraphy, the role of beauty in shaping the serene heart of his dynasty. His Genyue has been designed to mirror the empire, offer that harmony. A few of those here share these feelings; the rest have learned to present the illusion that they do.

It feels today as if summer might be ending. The paulownia leaves will fall soon, wild geese have been seen flying south. A season of restlessness, sadness, always some fear as winter comes. People die in winter. Not here so much, but elsewhere through Kitai.

From conversations overheard, Shan has understood that something significant took place this summer among the barbarians beyond what remains of the Wall. They have just learned of it, it seems. Decisions are to be made.

Waiting for the emperor, but largely ignored (one woman among important men), she hears a steppe name she knows, of course—Xiaolu—and others she does not. The Altai is one of these. She understands this is another barbarian tribe. An attack. A rebellion?

There are evidently divisions among those here to meet with the emperor and shape Kitai's response. Some seem to want to use this new tribe to put pressure on the Xiaolu; others urge caution, saying not enough is known. Shan can hear the striving in male voices.

The old prime minister, Hang Dejin, has been sitting quietly, keeping his thoughts to himself—or saving his strength. Perhaps he is simply waiting for the music. He does not look well, Shan thinks. His son, Hang Hsien, is behind him, and the imperial heir, Chizu, is nearby.

There are those here who think the emperor ought to step aside for this son, be released to think only about his art and his garden. Chizu says nothing, of course. Shan has never heard him speak. Some of the younger princes, appearing in the clan compound for feasts (or private encounters), are more bold, but the heir, in Kitai, needs to be cautious.

She is thinking of words to describe all these tense, duelling voices in a *ci* when the emperor arrives. Hang Dejin is helped to his feet to offer his greeting. He has long been excused the three salutations. Shan performs them with the court, forehead to earth, greeting the lord of Kitai, of the Five Directions, ruling under heaven with the blessing of the gods. The soldiers who escorted each of the guests here remain at a distance, Shan's guard among them.

The singer is also here now. She emerges from her sedan chair, with assistance. She is dressed in green-and-gold *liao* silk, cut lower than court fashion allows, and with wider sleeves. Her scent as she passes is rich, disturbing. She is small, astonishingly beautiful.

Shan, the only other woman present, is in dark blue to her ankles, high to her neck, slim-fitted, narrow sleeves, no adornments save her mother's ring and one her husband gave her years ago. She wears no scent. In this, she does not rebel against the constraints upon well-bred women, how restrained they are expected to appear when in public.

She has thought about fighting this, but there are so many marks against her name that to add another just for the sake of doing so feels wearying. Besides that, her link to the emperor is too hugely important to risk his displeasure carelessly. For one thing, with the prime minister so evidently failing in health ... who and what will follow? She has her father's security to think of, even her husband's. Her position here, undefined as it is, is some assurance for all of them in an unsure court these autumn days.

Her newest song is to be sung now, for the first time, and that is a different kind of test. She had frightened herself writing it, but not enough to hold it back. *I may not be such a clever person after all,* she'd thought, walking here with the guard (another new one, they change often) sent to escort her.

They are gathered not far from the colossal rock-mountain that has already been moved once to be more aesthetically harmonious, align more precisely with auspices and the emperor's desire.

According to a report sent some time ago, but never presented to Wenzong, one hundred and twelve men had died bringing that rock here, hundreds more were injured, some cripplingly. Animals also died, pulling it on rollers or carrying heavy equipment, their carcasses left where they fell. Fields were trampled, gouged deep, crops ruined. The bridges of twelve cities were destroyed along the Grand Canal to allow the barge bearing the rock to pass through them and bring it to Hanjin.

The singer, seated now on a stone bench, changes her position gracefully, tunes her *pipa*, looks politely at Shan and smiles, a small salute. She is breathtaking.

The music is very old. The words are by Lin Shan, the woman receiving such favour from the emperor, only child of amusing, inconsequential Court Gentleman Lin Kuo (who wanders freely in the Genyue, writing about it, with permission). She is married to the equally eccentric Qi Wai of the imperial clan. They know all about her. It is important to know about people invited to court, to the garden.

It is the general view that there is no good reason to be found, either in lineage or marriage, for her to be summoned here so often, receive such largesse from the Dragon Throne. Writing *ci* that please the emperor, wielding a competent writing brush ... are *these* avenues to access now? For a woman?

Possibly so, though there is no evidence yet that this one has aspirations, and the father is harmless. The husband is away much of the time, collecting old writings, bells, bowls, suchlike. He has an entire storehouse of these things.

He has also, word is, become smitten by a very young girl. Has apparently purchased her from her pleasure house and set her up in a house in Yenling. Not unusual, and no wonder, really, with the wife so unnatural. There are no children. If the emperor had not so manifestly favoured her, odds are Qi Wai would have put her aside by now. Such is the talk.

It has also been established—because such things matter—that the emperor has not bedded her. She can be considered comely, this Lin Shan, though hardly proper in her deportment, at ease among so many men, and she is too tall for Twelfth Dynasty taste.

The singer, by contrast, in green and gold, with her exquisitely shaped eyebrows and her scent ...

SHAN CANNOT LOOK for long at the other woman without glancing away. The singer is gifted (of course she is, to be here) with both her instrument and her voice, and her beauty dazzles. But every time Shan looks she sees the woman's feet, bound in the newest fashion for pleasure girls.

The mincing, hobbled gait with which the singer had made her way from her litter to the pavilion, assisted up the three steps by a man at each elbow, feels like an assault to Shan, seeing it.

And it may not remain confined to the pleasure districts, this ... innovation in beauty. She has heard women talking in the clan compound about this, most dismissing it with disdain as proper only to courtesans, but others suggesting it might become a way for daughters to gain attention, using their bound feet as an expression of their commitment to being beautiful—and properly submissive.

She has spoken of her revulsion to her husband, who was unusually silent, and then to her father.

Lin Kuo, with a third cup of saffron wine (she'd also had three cups, that night), had said, "Daughter, if the men of our time forget how to ride and hunt, and are carried by bearers wherever they go, even to the house next door, how do they ensure women are even more diminished? This. This is what happens now."

Her father, universally seen as ingratiating and bland, has never grown the fingernail of a little finger as a symbol of contempt for martial skills and arts. True, he cannot draw a large bow, but he knows how it is done (and has taught his daughter how, defying tradition again), and the two of them can—and do—often go on foot about Hanjin, or ride into the countryside. Shan has vivid memories of quick-stepping to keep up with him, as a child.

The woman playing here, singing Shan's own dangerous words set to "Butterflies and Flowers," will not be able to step down from this pavilion when she is done. Not without leaning, all helpless, scented fragility, upon a man.

She is singing now, poised and alluring, curved over the instrument, her voice offering the much-loved tune, with the words of Shan's song ... for that is what a *ci* is, new words to old music. From where she stands, Shan watches the emperor. It is always wise to watch the emperor.

> *Tears slide down my face to fall*
> *On the silk of my gown.*
> *I sing over and again*
> *Sima Zian's song of parting from a friend.*
> *"West of Iron Gate Pass ..."*
> *They say mountains can go on forever,*
> *And mountains keep you from us now.*
> *Alone in the house I hear the sound*
> *Of rain falling in the courtyard.*
> *Partings disturb the heart.*
> *I cannot remember*
> *If we drank wine in farewell*
> *From cups deep or shallow.*
> *It is so long ago that you left.*
> *Ask the wild geese to carry your words*
> *North again to us.*
> *Hanjin is not so far as the spirit realm,*
> *Lying out in the dark sea on another island.*

It is dangerously direct, this song. Much more than a song can safely be, especially about this man, and with that last line.

She is aware that she might have been foolish, and that others may suffer with her. She can't entirely understand the impulses that lead her this way. They have to do with facing her fears, she knows that.

The singer ends with the last notes from her *pipa*, then looks around, smiling brightly upon all of them. Shan wonders if she's understood what she was singing. Probably not, she thinks, then wonders if she's being ungracious. There is a quick, chilly murmuring as soon as the singer stops. Then an abrupt silence, as those making disapproving sounds realize that the emperor is smiling. (It is always wise to watch the emperor.)

He is doing so not at the singer, but at the other woman, the one who'd written those reckless words. The courtiers feel trapped suddenly. Shan sees it: they are caught in their too-quick disapproval. That won't make them like her any more, but they wouldn't have, anyhow. She might as well have worn perfume, she thinks, inconsequentially.

Amid the slide and rustle of autumn leaves in the garden, the emperor of Kitai looks at her. He says, his clear, quiet voice, "Clever, Lady Lin, not to finish the line from Master Sima."

He is, in many ways, an extraordinary man. She lowers her eyes. "Thank you, gracious lord, for noticing. It would not fit the music, and I judged that everyone knows the words."

"Good poetry is like that," he says. "We do not forget it."

"Yes, my lord," she says. Her heart is beating fast.

"Or the poets," Wenzong adds gravely. His smile has deepened, however. "We don't forget them, either. He has not been on an island for a long time, Lady Lin. Unless I am misled"—a glance to where two of his principal councillors stand and the oldest sits, with permission—"Master Lu has land and a house. He has been permitted to write again. Indeed, I have some of his recent poems."

She risks it. "As have I, exalted lord. They are what put me in mind of him, and so I wrote a song. He is ... is he not still exiled from the shining forth of your countenance?"

She is quoting another long-ago poem with the phrase, one that he will also know. She frames it as a question. She has been coming to him for some time now. She has learned a few needful things.

There is another stir, anticipating an imperial rebuke, ready to seize upon it. Some of them would like the chance, Shan realizes, to tear her apart. They are hunting dogs. A pack, snarling at each other, attacking outsiders who seek to enter, to draw closer to the shining forth.

She sees one man open his mouth. To be the first.

The emperor laughs aloud, gently.

"I don't think Lu Chen wants to be here, Lady Lin, however bright my countenance might be. Picture him happy on his farm, writing poems, even trying out your own *ci* form, which he does do. He is better there than at my court. I am better with him there, writing. Kitai is better. We need not return to the old days in this."

The seated prime minister, Hang Dejin, lifts his head, a seamed, sunken face, and smiles thinly. Memories, Shan thinks, of old battles. The prime minister is not an enemy now, she thinks, though it is possible she is wrong.

The emperor has been gentler than she deserves. She should leave it. She needs to bow, right now, to this man who can have her killed or exiled (and her father). Who, instead, speaks kindly to her, among these hunting dogs.

Instead, she says, "He has spent his whole life serving Kitai, serene lord. He writes about that desire in the new poems. He also wrote about it long ago, as prefect in Shantong, when he fought famine there. Is this a man to withdraw from the world?"

A flicker of disapproval in Wenzong's face. The Shantong famine, twenty-five years ago, had been a difficult affair. Many had denied it was coming, denied its severity when it did arrive. Some still think it was exaggerated by Lu Chen, as part of the faction wars, to discredit opponents in power.

There are limits to imperial patience, and she is a woman speaking too boldly about matters deemed beyond her. She lowers her head again. Were she a different person, perhaps she'd be clothed differently, entreating his kindness in other ways. Perhaps she'd even have her feet bound, she thinks bitterly, to elicit solicitude and care from all of them.

"Sometimes," says the emperor of Kitai, thoughtfully, "it is otherwise. Sometimes the world needs to withdraw from the man."

He rises, a very tall man. It is a dismissal, for most of them.

She and the singer and a dozen others, including the heir, she sees, leave the pavilion and proceed, escorted, towards different gates along the swept-clean, curving paths of this garden that is a treasure of the world.

There are matters of state the emperor must (briefly, distastefully) address.

Her song, written with her most careful brush strokes, lies on the writing table inside the pavilion, beside a painting of a plum tree branch in autumn that the emperor has done himself. *A better artist than an emperor,* Shan heard someone say once, very drunk.

She still doesn't know if submitting her *ci* has been a mistake. It probably has.

Escorted by a guard, Shan walks towards the gate nearest the clan compound. She has always insisted upon walking, though all the others leaving now have stepped into two-carrier chairs to be borne where they need to go. She is aware that this is seen as an affectation on her part, not remotely proper. Her father walks, however, so she does.

She wonders, briefly, what the guard beside her thinks about these matters here. If he has any views they are probably about the indignity of her being on foot.

The land rises ahead of them, built up into forested hills, the trees brought from far away. The path winds between these, as through a valley, towards the distant gate. She hears birdsong: a nightingale, even on a cool autumn afternoon. Far from home, she thinks. There is a grove of bamboo, then one of sandalwood trees from the south. Their scent is wonderful.

The path bends to reveal another boulder on the right side, taller than Shan, as wide as it is tall, pitted and scarred as if by eternity or the gods. They walk past. She has stopped to gaze at it sometimes, but not today, she has too much to think about. Her guard glances at her. He wears a Hanjin city guard uniform, this one. They change. She doesn't keep track. Fruit trees are ahead now, and flowers past their season. The wind is from the north, the hills above are thick with trees, leaves changing colour on some of them. It is a bright day.

She is thinking about the poet, a memory of a corridor in Xi Wengao's house, late night, Peony Festival, years and years ago. She'd been so young, excited to be among great men with her father, the promise of what life might offer.

In the darkness of that corridor he had turned to look back when she called after him. She had wanted him to come to her. First time she'd ever wanted a man that way. He'd stood a moment, then turned and walked away, honourably.

She is thinking about desire, and youth, and a rumour she has heard this morning about her husband, when the guard lays a hand on her arm, which is shocking, really.

"Stop!" he says. Not a request.

The hand on her arm tightens, then Shan is pushed downwards, hard, to her knees. The guard steps in front of her, unslinging a round shield from his back. Then he, too, kneels, screening her with his body. It is all happening very fast. He is looking upwards, she cannot see past him down the path.

He swears aloud, crudely, lifts the shield.

And an arrow thuds into it.

Shan cries aloud in shock, the guard cries out, much more loudly. "*Guards!*" he roars. "*Here!* An assassin!"

There are guards all over the Genyue, of course, the emperor is here. Several come running from behind them and from the direction of the southern gate. Her own guard remains where he is, protecting her with his shield, his body. Shan sees the shaft and feathers of the arrow, embedded in his shield.

"What? Why?" she says. "Why would—?"

"*There!*" her guard shouts, pointing up and to their right, into the built-up hills above the path. The trees there are pines, green. They will be green all winter. A shelter for anyone who wishes to hide in them.

The other men react at speed. These are the imperial guardsmen. Those serving here will be the best the empire has, protecting the emperor.

Shan sees them move off, running, fanning out as they climb the hill to their right. There are paths among the trees, these groves are groomed and tended.

Her own guard remains in front of her. Two others now stand behind, more protection. Others are running to the pavilion where the emperor is with his advisers, deciding matters of importance.

There is shouting, the sound of agitated men. Shan feels the hard racing of her heart.

And something else. She is looking up at the hills. She says nothing, obediently motionless, on her knees between tense, watchful men. Others run past, shouting excitedly. She has some thinking to do, she realizes.

From the corner of her eye, past the body of her guard, she had caught a glimpse of that arrow's flight, glinting in sunlight as it descended from trees. It had not come from the right side of the path.

CHAPTER XII

For the prime minister of Kitai, perhaps the worst part of a long and challenging day—and now night—was the awareness of what his son was feeling, in the chill of autumn with the moon in the window now.

He couldn't see Hsien's face clearly, of course—that infirmity was part of why he was withdrawing from the court—but he knew his son, and he knew what he'd just done, himself. And though Hsien would be schooling his face with care (he always did that), there was a new feeling in this room where they had laboured together all these years.

It had to be almost impossibly difficult to have spent a life assisting one's father, dutiful and unobtrusive (though indispensable), with a tacit understanding of what one's own future was to be—and then learn, in the course of a day of shocks and swift changes, that that future did not, after all, involve becoming prime minister after the father stepped aside, laden with honours and heading home.

And what was almost worse, to learn who was now to be recalled, despite everything, to take the position Hsien had been training for (and waiting for) all these years.

He was weary (he was almost always weary now), but he'd taken care to explain clearly, for he knew he was inflicting grief, and even shame. He wasn't a man inclined towards love, didn't entirely understand it, but his eldest son had been a comfort to him, an extension of his hand, even of his eyes, lately, and he wasn't happy causing pain here. Besides which, a man's most proper ambitions were always about family, and his son had children, there was a Hang family lineage.

The direct succession to office they'd both envisaged (though never spoken about) was impossible after the conference in the palace this afternoon: their gathering having moved from the garden after an assassin had appeared near the southern gate.

Surely Hsien could see it? His father stood firmly against allying with these new barbarians, the Altai. If the emperor chose, nonetheless, to explore such an alliance, and Hang Dejin used that imperial decision as his excuse to finally step aside, how could the prime minister's son, the extension of his arm, take the highest office?

Beyond that, Dejin said (for a second time), sipping tea at night, his view of the Altai alliance was a real one, not shaped by court intrigue.

The first reports of a steppe rebellion had suggested to some that this northeastern tribe might be the tool to push the Xiaolu out of the Fourteen Prefectures. Those same reports conveyed an entirely different message to an old prime minister.

The peace on the border, despite forays and incursions, had lasted two hundred years. That was a long time. A *long* time, Dejin repeated, unnecessarily. His son knew these things.

The Xiaolu were a known factor. Understandable, predictable. Their desires could be addressed. They wanted trade and order, were building an empire of their own in the steppe lands. Conflict with Kitai would damage them at least as much as it would their "elder brothers." And Kitan money (gift or tribute) funded their bureaucracy, their city-building, and riders to control the other tribes.

Trade was what kept both empires intact. That and the absence of war. It had been the key to policy for Hang Dejin. Privately— though it was not a thing he could ever say—the prime minister was entirely willing to let those Fourteen Prefectures remain lost.

Let them be the subject of songs and drunken laments and boasting. His goal had been peace, along with the centralizing of power. If his family had grown extremely wealthy in the process, that was also good, of course.

The sad, sloppy war against the Kislik had been the initiative of others, playing upon the emperor's desire to honour his father. The prime minister had made that clear, over and again, as the campaign failed dismally (and savagely), dwindling towards a treaty that left the border almost exactly where it had been before so many people died and so much money was wasted.

Kai Zhen had been exiled for that war, among other failings. That, of course, was what made it so hard for his son to accept that it was that same Kai Zhen being invited back to assume the prime minister's office.

It had been meant to go to Hsien, and when Zhen had been exiled the path had seemed very straight. Of course, in Kitai it was known that paths had to bend and curve, or turn at angles, to prevent evil spirits from following them.

The prime minister sipped again. The tea was good, he knew, properly prepared, but he didn't *taste* things any more. Another loss to the years. Good wine was wasted on him, as well, except in memory: the recollection of taste. Did you truly taste anything later in life, have any experiences at all, except through the memory of other times, sometimes long ago?

Lu Chen, the poet, lifelong foe, would have views on this. An unexpected thought. Chen's exile now was just across the Great River. His brother had been summoned to be the emissary to these Altai. That, too, had been someone else's idea, but Dejin approved: Lu Chao was astringent, precise, not likely to offer an opinion to curry favour. If he didn't approve of the alliance he would say so.

The rivalry, enmity, the bitter faction wars? Well, they were old men now. Could that be made to matter? Perhaps he and the poet might exchange letters, poems. Discuss the rush and burden of their time. With the wars at court so long past, maybe it was possible.

He saw a shape against lantern light. Hsien came to fill his cup with tea off the brazier. The wind blew outside. Autumn. They had two fires lit.

Dejin said, "When this new campaign fails, if it happens at all, when the emperor sees we were right, Kai Zhen will be gone again. *That* will be your time."

"Yes, Father," said his son, with a restraint that was painful to hear. He had often wondered if he'd made his boy too deferential. A prime minister needed controlled passion, coldness, even anger to deal with those around him—who would have these traits. There were *wars* around the Dragon Throne. He remembered his battles with Xi Wengao, the Lu brothers. Lives and families had been ruined for a decade before he'd won.

Was his son fierce enough, was he *hard* enough to have battled through those times and come out triumphant? He didn't know.

He knew Kai Zhen was. The man had a curious weakness concerning his long-time ally, the eunuch Wu Tong, and he was vulnerable to women of a certain kind, but at court he would be merciless.

Zhen would see this alliance through with the Altai. He would do it because the emperor seemed to have decided again that it was his duty to his father to regain the lost prefectures, and that this insurrection in the north was a pathway to that.

It would mean breaking the treaty with the Xiaolu, sending their army against a far more formidable foe than the Kislik had been (and they hadn't defeated the Kislik). It would involve coordinating attacks with barbarians they knew nothing about, then hoping ancestors and fortune and the will of heaven came together to achieve a proper result.

Hang Dejin did not see that happening. He saw danger. In fact, though he did not say this even to his son, he feared disaster. So not only could Hsien not follow him into office now, with his own position staked out against this plan, he didn't *want* Hsien carrying the responsibility for what might come.

He himself would be with their ancestors soon enough, crossing to the other side, but duty to family did not end with one's life. That was what the Cho Master taught.

That was why, for example, he had taken measures, working through the newly appointed, quite clever chief magistrate of Hanjin, to place Kai Zhen under constraints, even before he received the summons to return. It was possible, it was necessary, to anticipate events. That was how you *shaped* them.

Even now, after decades in power—fighting for it, losing it, regaining, awake late on many nights like this, various moons in various windows—he could still feel a pleasure almost sensual in the deftness of intrigue, moving pieces on a game board, seeing, even nearly blind, so much further than everyone else.

છ્જ

Everyone else had been happy. Wang Fuyin, settling in to his position as chief magistrate in Hanjin, had received a note from the prime minister expressing "satisfaction" with his efforts.

Given that the message had come late this afternoon—after the arrow attack—there was no uncertainty about what was meant.

Fuyin had told them as much, and had poured an exceptional

wine. During the course of their time with the magistrate, Daiyan had begun learning to judge wine, among other things.

Even Ziji, normally cautious, had been cheerful in the aftermath of what they'd done. Earlier, in the garden, he'd broken the bow in two, tossed the pieces into the stream above the waterfall, at two different places along the rushing water. He had also broken and discarded his second arrow. They'd allowed themselves two; if he'd missed twice there would have been no time for a third. Ziji was, even more uncharacteristically, visibly pleased with the result of his arrow's flight, loosed at exactly the right moment—when Daiyan and the woman were ten steps past the big rock.

Daiyan might be the best archer, whether as an outlaw or now as leader of the magistrate's guard, but Ziji had been with him long enough and worked hard enough to be a clear second.

His arrow had arced a very long way to hit the shield Daiyan had thrust in front of the woman they were supposed to be trying to kill.

The rest of the day had also gone as planned.

Until a second message came just before sundown. Which was why Daiyan was not entirely at ease as he and Ziji made their way through the city in response to a request that amounted to a summons. Not to the palace—that honour was tomorrow's—but to the compound beside it where the imperial clan resided.

The woman's father had asked him to visit this evening. So that he might express his gratitude, he'd written.

Problem was, Daiyan wasn't certain it was the father's initiative. He couldn't have explained this to the others. It was an intuition, vague, unsettling. They wouldn't have understood. The other two hadn't been walking with and then kneeling in front of the woman, meeting a startlingly calm gaze as shouting and running had begun in the Genyue.

Daiyan had been the one to look away. There had been something too observant in that glance. It was unsettling him still as he and

Ziji walked, cloaked against the chill, through the bright, crowded evening streets of Hanjin.

It was always bright in the capital, and the streets were always crowded. Vendors and performers, night markets, men or women calling from outside restaurants and pleasure houses. A throng of people among the sounds and smells, out to amuse themselves, push away the night, make money. There were pickpockets. There were games of chance at busy corners, scribes writing letters, fortune tellers promising to speak with dead ancestors or advise on decisions to be made. A small man from the deep south had a tropical bird on his shoulder. The bird would say a line of poetry for a copper coin. The moon was up, nearing full.

Daiyan judged that half the men he saw were drunk, or headed there. Hanjin at night was not a quiet place. It had taken getting used to, when they'd arrived. He still wouldn't say he was easy here. The capital was a way station but necessary. Where he needed to be.

He knew that in the old capital of Xinan, far larger than this one was, the city and ward gates had been locked at sundown and people remained, with rare exceptions, in their wards until the dawn drums. Hanjin was different. You could go anywhere all day and night, you could go in and out. The city gates were never shut.

He wasn't sure if it was better this way or not. There was freedom for an ordinary man to be abroad after dark, but that meant less control, less discipline. A harder city in which to deal with crime, for example.

Although that last would not be his concern much longer, if tomorrow's promise held.

He was still attached to the chief magistrate's guards, but Fuyin had been as good as his word: Daiyan had been made a sub-commander, then *the* commander, stepping smoothly up in rank. If he was promoted again now, after this morning's heroism, and brought over into the army proper, he'd be entering as a commander of five thousand, possibly more.

It *was* possible. He needed it to be so. Events were suddenly moving fast. If a war was being devised for next year, and it might be, he had to have a rank that made it possible for him to *do* something about the army.

They would not succeed against the Xiaolu if they proceeded the way they had against the Kislik. The eunuch—Wu Tong—who had commanded there was still alive, blame shifted neatly onto others. He might even be coming back here since Kai Zhen was now set to return. Wu Tong had been the one, with Zhen, to begin the Flowers and Rocks Network. They were bound together by that.

The magistrate was allied with the old prime minister in today's affair. Fuyin was being permitted to know some things.

For mostly unguessable reasons, Hang Dejin seemed ready to allow his disgraced deputy back into power, to the very highest rank, as he stepped away. But, it seemed, he also wanted Kai Zhen placed on notice, given a warning that he'd be watched. Today's events had set both of these things in motion—the return *and* the warning—or so it seemed.

"Are we being used by him?" Daiyan had asked the magistrate this afternoon.

"Of course we are!" Fuyin had laughed. "He knows more than the rest of us together."

"Then why is he leaving?" Daiyan had persisted.

Wang Fuyin had been silent a moment.

"He grew old," he finally said.

Walking the streets, Daiyan was still thinking about this. What the prime minister was trying to do might run against Daiyan's own desire. What Ren Daiyan wanted, for example, if this were all to happen, was to kill Wu Tong when he arrived at court: the man had shaped the disaster of Erighaya *and* the Flowers and Rocks. Both were marked against his name.

It would do nothing to bring back the dead, but it might ease unburied ghosts, and the wounded hearts of those who survived them.

The man who had swung a bamboo weapon in a bamboo grove was no longer young. He had been hardened, even more than he knew, by years in the marsh. He was bleakly determined to help Kitai avoid another defeat, and to regain the Fourteen. And serenely convinced that he was the person to do it.

There are some men (and women) like that.

This part of his nature had not changed. In the well-built, neatly bearded man striding through Hanjin, his father and mother would have recognized the determination and urgency they'd always seen in their younger son.

If one was allowed hindsight, Ren Daiyan was never likely to have become a *yamen* clerk by the Great River gorges, near the rising lands that led in turn towards the mountains at the border of Kitai, where the Queen Mother of the West was said to dwell in glory on a summit near the stars.

ZIJI WAS ALSO having difficulties.

Everything this morning had gone as planned. Their coordination had been precise. It was, he'd said to Daiyan and the magistrate over one of the wines Fuyin was so proud of, too easy. They should not have been able to do what they'd done quite so smoothly. They might be very skilled, but even so ...

Given such complete success, it was puzzling how strangely Daiyan had been behaving since receiving a perfectly proper invitation to the home of the man whose daughter they had saved.

"He wants to thank you," Ziji had said. "What is wrong with that?"

"It isn't his home," was all Daiyan said.

He'd been quiet as they dressed, and grim-faced as they went through the streets. It wasn't like him. One of Daiyan's skills lay in making others feel confident, better than they were. Ziji had seen him doing it for years. He didn't feel that way now, walking beside his friend ... though he did like the city at night.

Ziji had expected to be overawed by Hanjin. The magistrate had warned them when they'd come north from Jingxian. And the first days and weeks, trying to grasp that more than a million people lived within these walls or just outside them had been hard.

But to his surprise, Ziji had discovered that he enjoyed the capital, the anonymity that came with the size of the city. A man could take a walk and a few steps down some street or lane no one would know who he was.

There was a lake to the west, man-made, just beyond the New Zheng Gate; they called it the Reservoir of Lustre. There were pavilions all around it, some for the emperor and court but some for ordinary people, too, and it was open day or night (all night!), and there was music and wine. You could take a boat out on the water, be served drinks and food from another boat, hear singing, and the sound of flutes.

There was a park south of this. The Garden of the Chalcedony Grove they called that one. It was enormous, wild in places, exquisitely groomed in others. *Like the world*, Ziji thought, walking there early one morning, surprising himself.

Hanjin offered an odd kind of freedom. You didn't stand out in any way among so many strangers. No one you knew would be there to laugh if you played a game of chance on a street corner and lost some money. He didn't like losing money any more than the next man, but the games were amusing and the men who ran them were invariably sly and funny.

There were thieves on the streets. Ziji's training made them easy to spot. But he was a well-built man, and he carried a sword; he wasn't concerned. He didn't wear his uniform on these walks of his. The ones who ran the games would have folded their tables and disappeared if he'd come up to them dressed that way.

He had the feeling they could be posted here for years and he'd still be finding new things: sellers of knives, birdcages, fans, flowers. There were wine bars, tea shops, theatres, public gardens, alleys to explore in privacy, alone. Someone had said there were two hundred and thirty different kinds of rice dishes here.

He'd spent his youth in a village where everyone knew everyone else's business, or tried to, then years in one barracks or another, then he'd been among the men of the marsh. Life in Hanjin was so different it came to Ziji as a kind of intoxication.

Still, underneath everything lay loyalty to Ren Daiyan. An awareness, near the centre of himself, that his role in life was to do what he could to assist the other man because Daiyan's role in life felt ... well, it felt as if it mattered, and through that, Zhao Ziji's existence in the world might come to matter too.

Ren Daiyan made you feel that way. Usually it was an under-the-surface thing. Daiyan lived like the rest of them, could take a drink or three—or seven—same as anyone, and he certainly liked the singing girls.

He wondered what Daiyan was like with courtesans. They had never shared two women and a room, though some of the others liked doing that. Daiyan was private that way, and Ziji supposed he was, too.

But his friend didn't tend to keep his mood, or the reasons for it, quite as dark as he was doing this evening under the moon, which was almost hidden by lantern light and smoke. You couldn't see the stars very well in the streets of Hanjin.

In silence they walked towards the palace but turned east just before it, to the clan compound. They identified themselves at the nearest of the gates. They were uniformed tonight, of course. The guard was respectful, but careful. One of the imperial clan women had been attacked this morning in the emperor's garden, they were on notice.

MOST OF US live with fear, Court Gentleman Lin Kuo was thinking as he waited with his daughter for their guest. *His* guest. With her husband away, Shan could not possibly invite a guardsman to their home. He had sent the invitation.

What we fear can change, but it is always there.

For a long time he had been trying to understand how his daughter, his only surviving child, had managed to be otherwise. It came from her mother, or her ancestors, but not from him, or he didn't think so. He wasn't a brave man.

Unless you could somehow propose that educating a daughter as he had constituted courage—and he didn't see it that way. He had come to regard it as an act of selfishness. He'd wanted a child who could share aspects of the world that moved and engaged him, and though the child that remained to him happened to be a girl, he simply hadn't allowed that to alter this desire.

No, Lin Kuo held to his belief: apprehension and the longing to mitigate it was what drove most men and women. People feared the future and based that on the past, or false tales of it.

Strangers in your village were bad because a traveller had once robbed your wife's cousin while passing through. A crane had been seen flying south the night your grandfather died; cranes became an omen in your family. A pretty wife was a risk because someone's pretty wife had betrayed him with a soldier. And soldiers? *All* of them, especially high-ranking officers, were feared ... because of what had happened hundreds of years ago.

Shan had had lamps lit in their reception room. The fire was built up, the windows shuttered against the autumn chill and wind.

In these years of the Twelfth, Lin Kuo often thought (though he had never written it down, he wasn't a brave man) that they had built ideas of the world and its proper ordering upon the ruins of long-ago chaos.

They had shaped a vision of court and civil service holding mastery over the military—accepting a weakened army because of that. A price paid for controlling their commanders. The Kitan army was vast, it was punishingly expensive—and it had no leaders halfway worthy of the name.

A commander who could create loyalty and inspire soldiers to victories ... such a man could do what had been done all those years ago: bring an empire crashing down in fire and blood and desperate starvation.

Such was the fear, Lin Kuo thought. And perhaps it was because of this that Kitai wasn't what it once had been. On the other hand—and there *was* another way to see this—they lived today in peace. The recent war had been their own decision, a folly of the emperor's, spurred by ambitious civil servants. Peace was theirs if they wanted it.

Their emperor was unpredictable. Lost to painting and his garden and arcane rituals of the Path, then suddenly emerging with speeches about ancestors and the need to pay fealty to their memory.

His understanding tonight was that they might be once more devising schemes in the palace, weighing a new alliance, aiming dreams north again.

Lin Kuo stood in a handsome room decorated with antiquities his son-in-law had collected. He was waiting with his daughter for a visitor on an autumn evening in the capital. He was uneasy about this encounter. He didn't understand the invitation.

He looked at Shan. An arrow had been loosed to kill her today. Why should a young woman be the target—twice, now!—of someone wanting her dead? How did the world encompass such a thing?

She sat in her favourite chair, composed, straight-backed, dressed in blue silk with silver birds along the border of her robe, a cup of wine at her elbow.

He thought of her mother, dead too long, lost to both of them. Their look was very different, his two women. Shan was taller, taking after his own family. Her walk was stronger. His doing, that, years of striding unfashionably through the city together, even outside the walls. Her eyebrows were finer, her eyes more wide-set, if memory could be trusted after so many years. Her body was more angular, her fingers longer.

Her voice was different from what her mother's had been, more bold. His doing, again. He had unleashed these things in her, allowed them licence to emerge. But they had been in Shan, within her. He hadn't created them. He did believe that.

What the women he'd loved did share, Lin Kuo thought, was the quiet certainty he saw in his daughter now. When his wife had believed she was right about something the world could be beset by flood and earthquake, torrential rains or killing drought, a tail-star falling in the sky, and she would not change her mind.

Shan was like that.

It made him uneasy. How could mortal men or women feel such certainty in the world? About the world? He didn't know what his daughter was doing, she hadn't told him, but someone had tried to kill her today.

She'd ascended so high into the emperor's dragon world that the height itself frightened her father. You could fall from heights. People did. A quieter life was surely better. It left you free. He'd lived in that belief.

She had told him that word in the compound this afternoon was that the prime minister was stepping aside, going home to retirement.

Kai Zhen was being brought back.

It was Kai Zhen who had ordered him exiled to Lingzhou.

A servant entered, quick, small steps, hands clasped, eyes downcast, to report that two men had come to call, what should be done?

You couldn't always live long enough, Lin Kuo was thinking, standing near his daughter, his wine still untouched, to outrun what you feared. Indeed, it was possible to live too long, so that terror had time to catch up with you on the path through light and shadow.

HE IS DRESSED DIFFERENTLY, of course. Formal officer's uniform, not a working guard's outfit. A dark cloak against the chill, one sword. The other man, a fellow officer, she has never seen. They bow twice to her father, once to her.

The man who was guarding her today—his name is Ren Daiyan—is to be honoured tomorrow morning by the emperor. For quick thinking and proper action, saving the life of an imperial favourite, preventing a desecration of the Genyue's harmonies.

The second thing more important than the first. She could find this amusing, but she needs to know more now, to deal with the fear she's hiding.

She lets her father speak. She is watching this Ren Daiyan. He is of above average height, light on his feet, still young. You couldn't call him a handsome man, but his eyes are arresting: observant, intense. He looks at her briefly, then concentrates on Lin Kuo.

"You are welcome, officers," her father says. He is anxious, she knows it, she can't help him with that yet. "Will you honour us by sitting to take wine?"

"We are on duty, still," says Ren Daiyan. His voice is courteous, educated. He had been shouting orders, conveying rapid information to other soldiers this morning. The tone had been very different. "All soldiers and guards in Hanjin are considered to be on duty tonight," he adds.

"Because of me?" Shan asks, keeping her voice light, letting it sound overawed, trying out that tone.

"And other matters, my lady," he says, politely.

The second man, heavier, broad-shouldered, has remained a step behind him. That one looks uneasy, Shan decides, but she must not read too much into it. He would be anxious just being summoned after dark to a large home in the clan compound. He might be worried about holding a wine cup the wrong way. She sips her own wine. Her hand is steady.

"What other matters?" she asks, giving up on the awed voice. It isn't the approach she needs, and she isn't good at it, in any case.

They are going to realize, soon enough, that this evening's invitation was from her, not her father, improper as that may be. They might as well learn it now.

"We have not been informed," says Ren Daiyan.

"Really?" Shan says, raising her eyebrows. "Might it be the prime minister's declared intention to resign?"

She is watching closely, and so sees how he registers this change in tone, absorbs it—and shifts his attention to her. It takes no time at all. He is a ... forceful presence, she decides, for want of a readier phrase. His hands are relaxed, she sees. Not a man who fidgets or betrays himself.

The other one, whose name they do not yet know, looks even more alarmed. *Just wait*, Shan thinks. But she's too tightly wound to enjoy this; there is danger here.

Ren Daiyan says, "We have not heard anything of that, Lady Lin. It is beyond us. We are only guards, officers attached to the chief magis—"

"Really?" Shan says, again, interrupting this time. Women don't do that, of course. Nor do women say, as she now does, "And will the chief magistrate be aware there was no real attempt on my life today?"

Silence. She is aware of her father, his astonishment.

"My lady," says Ren Daiyan. "What are you saying?"

She smiles. "I haven't, yet."

"Most honourable lady, I fear I ... I do not ..."

She lets his voice dwindle away. Allows a pause in her reception room, among the artifacts of antiquity. A poet employs pauses more than a songwriter does, but she knows they are there to be used.

She says, "Is your companion the man who loosed the arrow this morning? That would make sense, that he would be the one you'd bring."

"I do not understand," says Ren Daiyan. His voice is impressively calm.

She says, "Guard Officer Ren, I saw the arrow flying. I saw how you blocked it and then turned your shield to the right. I saw you point right, not left when others came running. You sent them the wrong way. Tell me," she asks, sweetly, turning to the second man, "did you have enough time to get away without trouble? Discard the bow? You'd have had to do that, of course."

Third silence. Voices can be heard from outside, faintly. Silence has many different shadings and tones, she thinks. Can be such varied things, far beyond mere absence of sound.

The second man spreads his hands, almost helplessly, a mute denial. Ren Daiyan is staring at her now. She is aware of being *seen* this time, assessed. She looks straight back at him.

She says, "I have sent two letters under seal. One to the Imperial Censorate, and one to a man my father and I trust, by courier, this evening. If harm befalls us they will be opened. Otherwise they remain sealed. The letters are quite detailed as to the events of this morning." She sips her wine. "I thought I should tell you that. Are you sure you won't take wine?"

What follows is not what she expected. She can't say what she'd thought would be his response, but it wasn't laughter she'd been ready for.

"Oh, well done, my lady!" says Ren Daiyan after some moments, regaining his composure. He grins, the smile changes his features. "I had heard stories about you, I admit it, but none of them were even near to truth."

"Daiyan!" the other man mutters, awkwardly trying to be discreet—as if every word spoken or whispered cannot be heard in a quiet room.

"We will gladly take wine," says Ren Daiyan. "It will be an honour."

Shan manages a smile of her own, though she has been unsettled by his amusement. She stands to pour for them, as is proper. The second guardsman looks, she thinks, as if he's in water some distance out in a lake, searching for the shore.

Ren Daiyan accepts a cup. "Tell me, honourable sir," he says, turning to her father, "where did you find these Fifth Dynasty bells? They are among the best I have seen."

Shan carefully pays attention to the wine, pouring for the other man. She puts the beaker back on the brazier.

"My son-in-law and my daughter are the collectors," her father says. He will not be feeling calm at all, but he won't let her down.

"We found these two near the burial grounds by Xinan," she says. She walks to the other man and hands him a cup. She smiles at him, turns to Daiyan. "I'd not have expected a guardsman to know Fifth Dynasty bronze."

"And you'd be right in that," he says. He walks over and examines a temple bell more closely. It is the prize object of all things in this room. Her husband's joy. "Whose hand is the inscription? I know the lines, of course."

Of course?

"Duan Ting's calligraphy, we believe," she says. This exchange has become astonishing. "He was an adviser to the last emperor of the Fifth."

It is still considered bad luck to name that last emperor.

"And the words are Lu Lung's, am I right?"

"You are," she says.

He turns, grinning widely. "My teacher would be proud."

Shan says, resolutely, "Would he be proud of your deception today?"

She wants more wine, herself, but fears to take her cup, lest her hand be seen to tremble now.

"I believe he would," says Ren Daiyan. He has an odd expression on his face as he says it.

"Daiyan!" the other man rasps again. "What are you—?"

Ren Daiyan lifts a hand. It is almost gentle, a soothing gesture.

He says, looking from Shan to her father, still beside the bronze bell, "It was judged that a curb might be needed for Kai Zhen, coming back to power. You two were the reason, in part, he was exiled. It seemed to make sense as a stratagem. You can see that?"

Shan takes a deep breath, then she does walk to her chair and reach for the cup. If her hand's unsteady, so be it. She stands by the table. There is a very fine bowl on it, Third Dynasty. And a ritual axe, a tiger on the handle, also from the Third.

"I think I understand. The prime minister ... he is part of this, then?"

She probably should not be asking that, she thinks. It may be better not to know.

But Ren Daiyan is nodding. "Of course he is. Are we fools? To do this ourselves? In the Genyue?"

She manages a shrug. "Fools? I wouldn't have been able to answer, before tonight."

"And now?" he asks, and she sees amusement in those eyes again. He is so far from what she'd expected it makes her feel strange.

"I doubt the chief magistrate is foolish. And you won't be," she says. "What are you, then?"

Shan will remember that moment all her life. Her father will, too, as it happens, and so will Zhao Ziji.

"I am the man who will take back the Fourteen Prefectures," says Ren Daiyan.

His is the shaped silence this time. Shan finds she has nothing to say. No words come. The sensation lasts. Words can leave you. She puts her cup down, carefully.

"Shan," her father says, "this has nothing to do with us. It is not ours to pursue, surely?"

She shakes her head stubbornly. "But it is, because I have some conditions."

"Gracious lady?" says the second soldier, also looking shaken.

Ren Daiyan is gazing at her from across the room, beside the bell. His expression is curious. She would like to understand it but she doesn't.

"This morning was a lie," she says.

"A deception that *helps* you!" Again it is the second soldier. Daiyan is waiting. Looking at her.

"Or implicates us in a conspiracy," she says. "Me and my father, both of us."

"That is unlikely," says Ren Daiyan, finally speaking.

"Not the most reassuring word," she says.

He smiles again.

It angers her, suddenly, that amusement. "An arrow was loosed in a place where the emperor was present!"

"It was," he agrees. "But how are you helped by betraying us?"

"Betraying?"

He looks at her. Then murmurs, "You'd prefer a more reassuring word?"

And, astonishingly, Shan hears her father's laughter.

Daiyan looks at Lin Kuo. "Our interests are not the same here, honourable sir, but we judged that they march together. You do need protection from Kai Zhen. He is a man known for a long memory. Your daughter's exalted status might help, but it might also not be enough."

"And your interests?" her father asks, bravely. "Marching reassuringly with ours?"

Daiyan smiles. His face really does change greatly when he does that, Shan thinks again, irrelevantly.

"I would have been unlikely to achieve the rank I require, without something unexpected."

"Like this morning?" she asks.

"Like this morning," he agrees.

"And the prime minister? His interests?"

For the first time he looks rueful. "I would not presume to guess all that Prime Minister Hang is devising. Neither does the chief magistrate, my lady. The old one goes deeper than any of us."

"But if you were forced to guess? By a woman who has sent letters unmasking you?"

The other soldier is sweating beneath his hat, she sees. She feels little sympathy.

Ren Daiyan reaches out and touches the bell, a caress. She watches him think. He says, "You do know, if there is any unmasking, it will include the prime minister, my lady. It is unlikely he'll be pleased."

She is what she is, has already considered this.

Shan feels an impulse, unexpected in the extreme, and yields to it. She says, "I lied about the letter to the Censorate. The other one I did send ... I will write again and ask him to destroy the first one."

He doesn't look triumphant. He says, quietly, "Thank you for that trust."

"You were honest with me. Or so it seems."

He smiles. "I'm merely a guardsman. Not accustomed to intrigue."

"And I am so accustomed?"

"It does appear so, gracious lady."

She is trying to decide whether to be angry. He adds, "Your question about the prime minister? I can guess two things. I am sure there are more. The emperor will now be reminded of Kai Zhen's earlier attempt on your life. Minister Kai will need to be cautious—regarding you, but also in other ways. The prime minister, departing, has sent him a warning."

"I see that. And the second thing?"

"We believe the prime minister does not approve of this new alliance in the steppe. I think he is content to have matters remain as they are in the north. If he leaves now, whatever follows is not his doing."

"Ah. So you set yourselves against him," Shan says, thinking hard.

"We would not do that," Ren Daiyan says. "I am not so reckless. Or I hope I am not. But I will try to make any war a successful one this time."

"But you do want war," Shan pursues. Her heart is beating fast, she isn't sure why. She gazes at him, trying to read his face.

Yet another silence. Another *sound* to silence.

He says, "Yes, I do want it. We will not take back our rivers and mountains without fighting. And I ... I was born into the world to win them back."

The hesitation, Shan thinks, isn't uncertainty. It is something else.

LATER, AFTER THEIR GUESTS have gone, she lies in bed watching the moon, not even close to sleep. She is reliving the conversation from the moment the two men walked into her reception room.

She is thinking about how a man still young, only a guard commander for the magistrate, not carrying any army rank at all, had said those last quiet words—and they hadn't sounded vainglorious, or absurd.

They'd sounded, she thinks (being a poet, after all), like a Fifth Dynasty temple bell ringing far off, somewhere unseen, hidden beyond a bamboo grove, a stream, green hills.

છ૭

If one walked or was borne west through the courtyards of the imperial clan compound, and then allowed through a guarded door at the very end, one would enter the central corridor of a new building in the palace complex.

In this handsome structure could be found, in rooms on either side of the hallway, the imperial calligraphers: those whose training and discipline allowed them to produce notices, commendations, proclamations for steles, as if in the emperor's own hand.

In the evening these rooms were empty unless something extreme and urgent was underway. One could go down the silent corridor, past three more pairs of guards, and come out through larger, double doors into a courtyard of the palace grounds.

At night, as now, it would be quiet. The open space was torchlit so the crooked paths were visible for the occasional civil servant working late, crossing from one wing to another, and so that intruders were easily detected by the considerable number of guards.

On the far side of this open space one room was so brightly lit that night it seemed to be on fire. Fire was an endless fear in the capital, in all cities. On the upturned roof gables of every building in the palace complex there were an odd number of ornamental decorations. Odd numbers symbolized *water*, even ones *fire*. You took what measures were possible.

In that one large room fifty lanterns were burning, with all the windows open lest the heat overwhelm. The brilliance was dazzling. In that luminous chamber the nearly blind prime minister of Kitai was sitting at his writing table, crafting a late-night letter to his emperor, his last official document.

Brush, ink, ink stone, paper. The hand as steady as he could make it for this farewell. What would follow in Kitai, at court, would not be his task or burden, for better or for worse.

He had laboured a long time here. Had done some good, he knew—and some evil. If an emperor was to be free to devote himself to paintings and a garden and the pursuit of immortality, others had to make hard and harsh decisions.

Sometimes they would be correct in these, sometimes they would not be. But it was time now, past time, to withdraw. Some here would celebrate, some would mourn, some would curse his name until he died, and after. Sometimes bodies were uprooted from graves or tombs. Revenge could follow you past the doors of death.

He wondered, as those who have known great power sometimes do, what history would make of him and his works. Thinking so, about being judged, he lowered his brush to the ink, to the paper.

He wrote slowly, and with pride. He had been a scholar before the progression of civil servant, minister, prime minister.

When he was finished, he let himself sink back with a sigh onto a cushion. His back was a difficulty, among many. Brush down, he allowed his mind to turn and drift, to imagine his home in the countryside west of Yenling, the quiet at Little Gold Hill. The seasons as they changed, leaves appearing, leaves falling.

Around him in the room, at a signal from his son, servants began putting out and carrying away lanterns ... letting the fierce brightness fade. The prime minister of Kitai smiled to himself at the thought: too easy an image for a poem, given that he was leaving.

You wanted to do better than that.

Eventually there were only a handful of lamps left, and the two fires on a chilly night. The servants were gone, his son remained. His son always remained.

He listened to the wind outside, in the night.

"Take it across now," he said, gesturing to the letter he had written. "He will not be asleep."

"You are certain of this, Father?" his son asked quietly, respectfully. He'd known Hsien would ask.

"I am always certain," said Hang Dejin. "I have had to be."

ख

There are skills shared between outlaws and soldiers. One of these is the ability to fall asleep. A brief rest on horseback or under a hedge, a quick slumber in a barracks. There would be times when it was not possible. One needed to be able to sleep whenever it was allowed.

Daiyan was aware that morning would find him at court for the first time, and he'd need to be alert, vigilant, extremely careful.

He knew he should be sleeping and he knew it was impossible. Too much roiling through his mind, expected, unexpected. So he was walking the streets again, alone this time, and thinking of his father.

A quiet life in the west, Szechen province, Honglin prefecture, Shengdu Village. Beyond barricading mountains, close to the Great River gorges. An obscure, honourable, dignified existence. Pursued in accordance with Cho Master principles, though with a quiet evading of those aspects of interpretation that had seemed to Ren Yuan to be unduly harsh—on women, children, human frailty.

Every morning, except on stipulated holidays, he had presented himself at the *yamen* and set about his tasks for whichever sub-prefect or magistrate or sheriff was there giving commands, behaving in a manner arrogant or courteous, thoughtful or foolish or greedy. It didn't matter to Ren Yuan, one's duty was to Kitai, and to one's family.

It had been a very long time since his son had seen him. But Daiyan knew with certainty that if his father was alive and healthy, he was doing this as he always had. He'd be at the *yamen* this morning.

He would have received a letter from home, he thought, if things were otherwise. They knew where he was now. He'd written when Wang Fuyin had been promoted to Hanjin and taken them with him, as planned. Commander of the guard of the chief magistrate of Hanjin; a father and mother could take real pride in that. It was rising very high.

And this morning he would be presented at court.

His father's pleasure would be so great (but so quiet) to know that a son of his would actually appear before the Celestial Emperor to perform the obeisances.

By the teachings of the Master, Daiyan knew, this was his truest task in life: to bring his father and mother the pride, and security, that came from a child doing well, acting honourably.

He'd failed in that for a long time. An outlaw of the marsh did not allow pride. Even now, he asked himself, if his father were to learn that Daiyan's appearance before the emperor was the consequence of a deception, would he still be proud?

Walking without awareness of destination, wrapped again in his cloak, Daiyan heard the warning cries of night soil gatherers ahead of him, and was briefly disoriented: they were forbidden to work until extremely late, near dawn. Then he realized it *was* extremely late. Hanjin, in the cold hours before the sun, was still crowded. It was astonishing how many people found reason to be abroad. The moon had long since set and the stars had changed, wheeling west.

He realized he was hungry. He bought a warm meat pie from an all night vendor, ate it as he walked. It was dog meat, which he normally disliked, but another thing you learned as a soldier (or an outlaw): you took food and drink as it came to you, because it might not always come.

The soldiers retreating from Erighaya had mostly died of starvation and thirst, not in battle. It was long ago now, the Kislik war, that retreat, but it obsessed him still. In certain moods— alone, awake at night—he couldn't pull his mind from the images it brought.

He had wanted to fight there once. To do heroic deeds.

He bought himself a cup of tea and drank it, standing by the cart and brazier with others. Some shifted away from him: an armed guardsman. Not all people abroad at this hour were in the street for reasons they would wish investigated.

He handed back the cup, moved on. His thoughts were everywhere tonight, it seemed, and nowhere useful at all.

He had been absurdly happy, a child passing a test at school, to recognize that Fifth Dynasty bell in her reception room. Why had that mattered? What did it signify to a man aiming for military rank and a northern war that he knew the poet whose words were on a bronze that a woman (and her husband) had found?

Yes, Tuan Lung would have been pleased his pupil knew this, but Lung himself wasn't even a teacher now. He was working up and down the Great River. Doing some good, perhaps, but also deceiving some people out of money they needed, at times.

The world didn't allow you clean, clear judgments very often, it seemed to Daiyan. He envied those who thought otherwise, who lived otherwise.

A woman called to him from a doorway. He wasn't in the pleasure district, but there were women like this at night all through Hanjin. She moved into the lantern light and he saw that she was actually pretty. She sang a fragment of an old song: *Alone on my balcony, and the north wind takes my tears ...*

In another mood, perhaps. Not tonight.

He heard a shout and a terse reply, then the sound of clashing weapons. He considered going over that way. In this mood, it might help to draw a sword. But if one man killed another in the dark, well, that happened every single night, and he had—didn't he?—a larger goal, a greater purpose.

He was still astonished at himself for the directness with which he'd spoken of that to the woman and her father. What must they have thought of him? The arrogance, the deluded folly.

But there came a point, perhaps, when you needed to make clear, or clearer, what you intended with your life, or you might never do it. You could be in shadows forever, Daiyan thought. Perhaps at court that was a way to power, but he was a soldier. Or he would be one later this day.

The north wind takes my tears ...

There were several million Kitan living in the north, ruled by the Xiaolu, farming for them, paying taxes, subjugated. *Under the savage yoke.*

He didn't like that last, well-worn phrase. Tuan Lung had taught them how lazy poets tried to elicit a reader's response with words designed to tug at the heart.

Truth was, most likely the Kitan farmers and villagers in the Fourteen Prefectures didn't much care who governed them. They'd have to pay taxes either way. Be subject to the yellow dust off the steppe in summer, and snow and bitter cold when winter came. Drought afflicted them whichever empire claimed their farms.

If the Golden River flooded, no emperor was likely to save their land or lives. If a daughter disgraced herself or a son died of fever, or hunting wolves, did it matter who ruled over you?

Even so, Ren Daiyan thought. Even so, Kitai was so much less than it had been, so much smaller. And you didn't, or you shouldn't, turn your back on history. That farmer whose thoughts he was imagining could be wrong. No steppe emperor would store grain against flood or drought for his Kitan farmers, but emperors in Xinan had done so since the Third Dynasty. There were granaries in the west right now.

The emperor of Kitai ruled with the sufferance of the gods under heaven, and the sanctity of his reign did turn on his compassion for his people. The man on the Dragon Throne could be led astray by bad advisers. He could be weak, foolish, self-indulgent, he could fail. But he could also be helped and guided back to glory.

The sounds of the street fight receded as he walked on. You couldn't address everything the world presented you to heal or amend. He was a soldier, not a poet. He was going to try. To amend. Maybe that was the difference between the two, though he was probably wrong in that. Too easy a thought. And soldiers could break the world.

She'd had a deadly hold over them, that woman, Lin Shan, because she knew about the arrow.

He couldn't believe a woman in fear for her life had been able to comprehend what was happening in the garden. The one thing they hadn't accounted for ...

He could have tried to dissemble, deny. He'd been aware of the dismay on Ziji's features when Daiyan admitted she was right.

But she knew. She *knew*. Her gaze had been one of those looks that goes into you. Not many people were like that, not in his experience, and never a woman. Challenges in a look, yes, from a drunken outlaw or soldier, even a sober one once or twice, gauging his chances in a fight.

Those he'd known and dealt with. He was strong and clever, quick, knew how to kill a man.

He probably should have gone to where that street fight was. Or maybe go back and claim that woman, the unexpectedly pretty one under the lantern. Sometimes your thoughts could be a trap, and you needed to quiet them somehow. Wine, a brawl, a woman, music.

Maybe all of those, he thought, which made him smile in the dark. He walked between the lanterns of food stalls open late and the lights lining the canal, meant to prevent drunken men from falling in and drowning. You could put up lights, but you couldn't always save men from themselves.

He felt a change in the wind. Dawn coming. He'd be going to his emperor without having slept. It was time to go back to the barracks. He'd need to clean himself up, and change again. Fuyin had arranged proper clothing for Daiyan today, being presented at court. He turned to double back, and almost bumped into someone walking too close behind. He knew that trick.

It took recklessness to try to snip or lift the purse of a guardsman. He grinned at the man's horrified expression. He let him scurry away. There were, Daiyan thought, many different ways of being brave. And as many of being foolish beyond words.

She had released them from the hold she'd had. But with the old man, the prime minister, a part of what they'd done, she'd been in a difficult position. Denounce them, and under the torture that would follow one of them would probably name Hang Dejin, and her own security against the *new* prime minister would disappear. And her father's. Daiyan had watched her, eyes on her eyes, as she worked it through.

At the end, in that room among bells and bowls, porcelains and a black ceramic horse, old scrolls on tables, and one enormous urn from a thousand years ago, she'd nodded.

"I see it," Lin Shan had said. "Our fate is tied to yours. In this, at least."

Daiyan had bowed. To her first, this time, and then to the father, who reminded him of his own.

It was possible, he thought now, to be living your slowly unfolding life, or thinking you were doing that, and come to a moment when so much changed you realized that it was really just starting. Right then.

Everything to this point, this night, felt to him to have become a prelude, like notes played on a *pipa* to tune it, ensure it was ready for the song yet to come.

He stopped walking and looked around. And realized that he was back in front of the clan compound, standing before one of the gates. They would let him in, he could identify himself, he was in his uniform.

He stood there a long time, then turned to walk back to the barracks in a rising wind.

IN BED SHAN HEARS the wind beginning to blow towards dawn. She gets up to go to the window and look out. There is no reason for her to do this. It is cold, but she lingers. The moon is long since gone. Stars and ragged, moving clouds.

There are, Shan thinks, too many poems about women at windows, their tumbling, cloud-like hair, their scent and jewellery, the jade stairs leading up to them, and their sorrow, waiting for someone who does not come.

She looks out upon the world they have been given in the time they are allowed.

PART THREE

CHAPTER XIII

It was all difficult, and in so many different ways.

Kai Zhen, once deputy prime minister of Kitai, was not a man who had ever sought out the harmonics of the countryside. He was a different sort of man.

He'd experienced this life, of course—this wasn't his first exile. The tedium of the last time had driven him to do all he could to end it, and the result had been a very great change in his life.

Exiled south many years ago, he'd first encountered Wu Tong, and he and the clever eunuch had devised a strategy to claim the attention (and trust) of the emperor.

With word reaching them of Wenzong's intention to create a garden in Hanjin to mirror the empire, align it with celestial forces, they'd begun sending rare plants and trees and arrestingly pitted rocks for the Genyue, along with Kai Zhen's poems and essays. Never on political subjects, of course. He was still in exile, and he wasn't a fool.

The Flowers and Rocks Network was born of this, and had become what it was—which included being the avenue, wide and graciously shaded, for Kai Zhen's return to court, bringing the eunuch with him.

He owed what he had become to rocks, sandalwood trees, birds, and gibbons, he sometimes said. He hated gibbons.

He hated the isolation here. A sense of being hopelessly cut off from everything that mattered, the feeling that time was running, passing, disappearing.

When you were exiled, a majority of the people with any claim to significance wanted nothing to do with you. They didn't even reply to letters sent—and most of them were people who owed him greatly. When you fell in Kitai, you could fall a long way.

Among other things, once out of power he'd lost the river of income that came with high office. All of his homes, except this one, had been forfeited.

He wasn't poor, of course. This estate was good-sized, successfully farmed by his people. But neither was it the case that he could ignore matters of domestic finance.

He had surrendered two of his concubines. Luxuries he could no longer justify. They were pretty girls, talented. He'd sold them to men attached to the *yamen* in Shantong. Neither woman had been entirely sincere, to his mind, in her protestations of grief when the news was conveyed to them.

Not that he could blame them too greatly, if he made an effort to see things clearly. Life here on the Kai family's ancestral estate was dull, not especially comfortable, and being a lesser woman in a household dominated by his second wife was ... well, harmonious was not a word one would apply.

There were times when he wondered about this marriage, the speed with which he'd entered into it. But Tan Ming had an uncanny ability to sense when he might be musing along these lines, and even more unsettling skills at doing such things as altered his reflections.

He'd thought Yu-lan had understood the nature of his needs. Ming was even more inventive and discerning in that regard. He had remarried quickly, there was no question, but it was also true that he'd felt an extreme need to swiftly distance himself from what his first wife had done.

Her body had been burned. Attempted murder in the clan compound. The assassin, her assassin, had confessed. Wives, he thought, had an unfortunate tendency to undertake actions of their own, even in a dynasty where women were raised to know that this was not proper.

He'd come to this conclusion long before two letters arrived in autumn rain one afternoon, changing his life again.

The first was from the emperor (though not in his own hand). It summoned him back to Hanjin, to court. More, much more: it invited him to return as prime minister of Kitai.

The gods were good, the heavens benevolent! The old man had *finally* elected to withdraw. And for some reason (which would need to be worked out) he was not putting forward his pallid son as successor.

Reading the words again, Zhen's heart began hammering as though it would burst the wall of his chest. He felt dizzy. He controlled himself, in the presence of the couriers. Not wise, to allow someone to see weakness before he took office! He sent them away with a lordly gesture, to be given rooms, baths, food, a girl, *two* girls each. Serving women would do for couriers, and he still had those.

Then he sat down, alone in his workroom. There were lamps lit, though only two, lamp oil was expensive. There was a fire going, it had turned cold in the past week. He sat at his desk and opened the second letter.

He read this one through twice, as well. Whatever Hang Dejin wrote required to be considered with extreme care. There were words beneath the words, brush strokes unseen but signifying more than what one read on the silk paper. The hand was the son's, not the father's. The father, may his soul rot in blackness forever when he died, was nearly blind, after all.

Blackness now, blackness waiting, Kai Zhen hoped.

There was much to assess, including a fairly clear indication of why the old spider was departing, and why the son was not to follow him. But it was the last lines, especially the very last sentence, that chilled Kai Zhen.

He actually shivered, both times he read the words. It was as if a bony finger had reached down through all the *li* that lay between, past hills and valleys, slow and rushing rivers, orchards and rice fields, silk farms, cities and villages and outlaw-plagued marshes, to touch his heart.

Control your woman, Hang Dejin wrote. End of letter.

A finger like a knife, Kai Zhen thought. Those last words followed a terse description of a violent incident in the Genyue, the attempted killing of an imperial favourite.

All the gods help me, Kai Zhen thought, at his desk, by the lamp there. At a moment when celebration should have been bursting within him like New Year's fireworks, he was cold—yet sweating with fear.

He cursed the old man for a long time, careless of who might hear him. The foulest words he knew, the most vile and savage imprecations. Then he took something from the desk and went looking for his wife.

They sat together in the smaller of the two reception rooms. After a time he asked her to fetch her flute, to play for him. She always did what he asked of her, she was flawless in that way.

While she was out of the room, and after the serving woman had been sent to bring food for the two of them, Kai Zhen poisoned his wife's wine.

She couldn't be strangled or stabbed. Even in a place this remote, there was too much risk of someone—anyone—revealing that the mistress had died violently. That, in itself, could become another weapon for the old man who was stepping aside, but not truly stepping aside.

No, Tan Ming would die in her sleep tonight, if precedents for this powder held true. They would mourn and bury her with a pearl in her mouth, to keep her spirit in.

But he was cursed, he was utterly cursed if he'd allow her to live to be another sword at his throat, held by Hang Dejin. He needed to be more ruthless than the blind one, and he could be.

There was violence in his new wife, he had reason to know it. But there was no possibility that she had devised an attempt on the life of that woman in the Genyue. Not from here, not timed so elegantly to coincide with his summons back to power.

But the history of his family with that family—that fatuous court gentleman and his unnatural daughter—was widely known. If he were inclined to attach blame to himself (he wasn't, really), it was true that he'd signed the order of exile for Lin Kuo to Lingzhou Isle. A mistake, though who could have known?

He'd miss Tan Ming, he thought, sitting by the fire, waiting for her to return and drink the wine that would end her life tonight. He missed his first wife, still.

He would never marry again, he decided, sipping his own autumn wine. Wives, lissome and subtle as they might be, were a vulnerability.

ↁↂ

An emissary to the barbarians, Lu Chao has told his nephew, must imagine himself a woman.

He is to pursue the same closeness of observation, discreetly looking and listening, to apprehend the essential nature of the men they encounter.

This is the way women live, at court and elsewhere, he'd explained to Lu Mah on the ship that carried them north along the coast. Women sought a space in the world this way.

He has used this conceit in the past. He has been north in this capacity before, meeting twice with the emperor of the Xiaolu, bearing birthday gifts the first time, negotiating (fruitlessly) for the return of the Fourteen Prefectures, or a portion of them, on the second occasion. Slow travel overland, with very large retinues, for proper dignity.

This is a different journey. By sea, only a handful with him, and done in secrecy.

An emissary must not act in the normal manner of men, Chao believes. The court, the empire, are to glean knowledge and understanding from his journey beyond borders. He is not to allow any bold or reckless thing he does or says to impact upon events.

He is to watch. Count horses and horsemen, observe the presence or absence of hunger or resentment, note those men around the barbarian leader who look away when certain words are spoken. Talk to these later, if he can. Learn who might have the leader's ear, and who is unhappy because of that.

He asks (courteous) questions, remembers answers, or writes them down—encoded. There have been incidents in the past when writings were seized, embarrassingly.

He cheerfully eats (he has warned his nephew) appalling food, and drinks the fermented mare's milk the barbarians love overmuch. He makes himself and Lu Mah begin doing so on the ship, to prepare. His nephew is seasick, and the *kumiss* is not a help. If Lu Chao had been a less kindly man, he might have laughed. He does record it, with amusement, in a letter to his brother, Mah's father.

But drinking is important on the steppe. Respect attaches or fails to attach depending on how one handles a great deal of it. In this regard, he has told his green-hued nephew, they are to show manhood.

Also with the women they'll be given. Mah is to understand that these will not be like the scented beauties from pleasure districts. The two of them will smile when offers are made, he admonishes, then perform with vigour when the women arrive in their yurts at night. Mah is to consider it a part of their task.

They will not talk to these women, though it is not a real risk, as few of them will speak Kitan. One or another might, however, it is always possible, so careless speech to each other in their presence is also not to happen.

There are, Lu Chao says, many things to learn, and many ways that missions can go wrong. Emissaries have been killed, though not for some time. The Xiaolu have an emperor, capital cities, aspire to being civilized.

But they aren't going to the Xiaolu.

THE FIRST TASK is to assess how respectfully they are being treated. That turns, in part, on the distance inland they must travel with the escorts waiting for them when the ship finally makes landfall well north of the Wall.

Is the kaghan of this new tribe, the Altai, meeting them after an equally long journey, or are they going farther towards him?

If they'd been sent to the Xiaolu emperor, it would have been appropriate for him to greet them at one of his capital cities, but this is not an emperor they are meeting. This is a rebellious tribal leader, and they are extending—*possibly*—the support of the Kitan empire to him. He needs to come towards them.

As they ride from the sea through a hilly landscape, not yet the unsettling emptiness of the steppe, Chao asks casual questions of the interpreter the Altai party has brought. Answers are unsatisfactory.

The Altai ancestral lands are north of the Black River, towards the Koreini Peninsula, the man answers. Chao knows that. But their kaghan and his riders are not there now, of course, the interpreter says.

"Where are they?" Chao asks politely.

Vague gestures to the west are offered. There has been fighting, he is told.

He knows this, too. This is a rebellion, after all. That is the reason for his presence here. Representing his emperor. Offering an assessment, negotiating. Should they support this rebellion? What will the Altai offer in exchange?

The Fourteen, of course, are the prize.

Lu Chao is hesitant about his mission. He's kept that to himself (of course), but his thinking is not intricate. If this emerging tribe is strong enough to destabilize the steppe, then it is strong enough to disturb a secure border relationship for Kitai. But if this is simply another restless, transient tribal rising, what is the point of supporting it and antagonizing the Xiaolu?

This is all, in a word, unpredictable. Are the Altai simply unhappy with Xiaolu assertions of power, but ready to be submissive to Kitai if helped to triumph, or are they wild, like wolves?

The Kitan hate wolves. They cannot be tamed.

"Where is the fighting?" Chao asks, looking this time at the party leader, hating that he needs an interpreter. Only one of the small, bare-chested, bowlegged men sent to meet them speaks Kitan, or admits he does. They all ride brilliantly.

Eastern Capital, he is told.

Their party leader is an exceptionally ugly man, not young.

"They are attacking the Xiaolu's Eastern Capital?" Chao asks, keeping surprise from his voice. That is very fast, if it is true.

The interpreter translates for the leader, waits for an answer, permits himself a smile.

"We have taken it," he says. "We are dealing with it now, and recruiting new riders there."

Dealing with it. Chao can imagine. He has noted that smile. He keeps his own expression bland, though he is startled.

"Your kaghan is all the way there?" he says. "How will he come this far to meet us?"

He is listening carefully. A slight hesitation in the exchange between interpreter and leader. A sharp question and answer. Lu Chao makes himself, hearing this, become very calm.

"You will meet with our war-leader," says the interpreter. "It is Wan'yen who comes."

"The kaghan does not come?" Lu Chao is thinking fast. The interpreter is not smiling as he translates.

"The kaghan is fighting. I said this."

"You said the kaghan's brave riders have already taken the Eastern Capital."

His words are translated.

The leader shakes his head, an obstinate movement. The interpreter shakes his head.

"The war-leader is coming," he repeats.

Sometimes it happened on missions such as this that you needed to do something that placed you—and your party—at risk of death.

You prayed then, and hoped to be remembered by your family. There would be no grave or proper burial. Not here.

Lu Chao, a modestly capable rider, no more than that, succeeds in reining in his dark-brown horse. He lifts a hand and calls out, in his own language, to the six men here with him so far from home. They all come to a halt.

"We are going back," he says to them. "To the ship."

He looks past the interpreter, his expression cold, his eyes on the leader of the Altai party. "I require you to escort us back," he says. "With our gifts. The august emperor of Kitai will demand this of me. His emissaries do not meet with lesser figures. You have cost us time and effort. The emperor will not be pleased with the Altai."

The interpreter translates. Chao is watching the leader, his hard, expressionless eyes. The man looks at him. Their gazes lock.

The Altai leader laughs, but not with real amusement. He barks some words. The interpreter hesitates, then says, "He say Wan'yen is not lesser man. He is war-leader. He say you are only seven men.

You can be killed and your goods claimed. You will keep riding, he say."

Lu Chao stares at the Altai leader. There is a wind blowing from the west, the man's hair is whipped by it. There are woods to the north. Not yet the steppe he remembers.

"All men die," he says, slowly, clearly. "We can only go to our gods with honour, serving our lords as best we can." He turns to his men, including the nephew he loves and honours. "Let us go. Back to the ship."

Their ship will be waiting. It will wait as long as it must. Until they return or word comes that they are dead.

Lu Chao manages to turn his horse. It is a good horse, he knows enough to know that. It is difficult to start back east, the sun high, wind blowing, aware that he can be killed from behind, right now, this moment. Death is here. He moves without haste, not looking back. A prickling sensation.

He would like to see his wife again, his sons. His brother. He would like to see his brother again.

Life does not always give you what you want.

Hoofbeats, coming fast. The leader of the Altai is beside him, grabbing Chao's horse's reins. He forces the animal to a halt. He does it easily.

Chao turns to him. With an instinct he cannot explain (how do you explain an instinct?) he snaps, "You speak Kitan, I know this. Or you would not be here. So hear me. You can kill us, take these gifts. You can force us to go with you. Either way you destroy forever any hope your kaghan has of Kitan support. You make an enemy of the emperor of Kitai and an army of a million soldiers. Is this your task? Is it your wish?"

He is watching, as closely as he can. The way a woman watches. He sees anger, black as a forest, in the man's cold eyes, but also—it is there!—he sees uncertainty, and Lu Chao knows, sometimes you do know, that he has won.

And sometimes you don't know, or you are simply wrong.

The Altai leader says, no pretense of not knowing Kitan, "Pick a man to die. One will be shot, and then each one, until you are left. Then you will come west with us."

He has ignored his own guidance, Lu Chao is thinking: about being careful. An angry man is one thing, an angry man who is uncertain and afraid is unpredictable. Every woman at the court, every woman in her own household, could probably have told him that.

He looks at the Altai rider, but does not meet the man's eyes now—that was a mistake, too obvious a challenge. Death may be among them, but it need not be summoned.

He says, quietly, keeping this to the two of them, "And what do you think happens when I am forced to go west? What will I do? What will I say when I return home with my party murdered? What will I advise my emperor about the Altai?"

The man says nothing. He licks his lips. His horse skitters sideways. Chao decides that is significant. No steppe horse would move like that unless the rider was unsettled.

Chao adds, "I do not care which man you shoot, or if you kill me. Every one of us knew his death might come when we began this journey. But what will you tell your kaghan? That you killed the entire Kitan party? What will he do to you?"

Still, no reply. The horse is calm again. Chao is looking at the man's hair, avoiding his eyes: the shaved forehead and top, the long growth at the sides, whipped by wind. He had told the others about this, that they might be ready for the strangeness.

He speaks a third time. *Silence after this*, he tells himself. After this he must start east again. They may be killed in the next moments. He would like to sit with his brother again and drink summer wine.

He says, "It is your choice. But I do not think every man in your party likes you, and some will be ambitious. The tale they tell may not be the one you want told, if we die. We are riding to our ship. Do what you choose."

He lifts a hand, preparing to call to his party.

"Wait," says the Altai leader, low and fierce.

Lu Chao lowers his hand.

Blue sky, white clouds racing east, wind down here as well, in the grass. They are too far from the forest to hear the sound of it in leaves.

The Altai clears his throat. "There is no disrespect. The war-leader commands beside the kaghan. Perhaps more than him now. He is younger. They act together. We ... we went farther and faster than we thought. The kaghan would have come to you if the Eastern Capital had not surrendered so quickly."

His Kitan is better than the translator's. He says, "The kaghan had to stay, to bring the Xiaolu warriors into our riders, joining us. That is Yan'po's skill. Wan'yen and his brother lead in battle. That is their skill. Battle is finished, so Wan'yen can ride to you."

Chao looks past him, out over the grass. They have heard words to this effect in Hanjin, in the memoranda prepared for him when he accepted this embassy. That these Altai are really led by two brothers, not the old kaghan. They know little more. It is why he is here. To know more.

And he sees a way now to move forward. Not to be killed in this windy, faraway place. He nods twice.

"Thank you," he says, makes it as gracious as he can, as civilized, a lord accepting something offered. He is the voice of the emperor of Kitai. He says, "We can wait here for the war-leader."

He sees the other man take a breath, and realizes how afraid this one had been. He'd have had to shoot if Chao had turned and started back east. No choice, his fellows watching, having heard what he'd said.

You needed to be so careful about what you said.

"This is wrong place to wait," the Altai says. "No food, no *kumiss*, no good yurts. No women!" He forces a smile.

Chao smiles in return. "Where are these things?" he asks.

"Best are six days. We have stopping places ready for you each night. Six days is a good place by a river, you meet with Wan'yen, war-leader. Discuss. He is riding fast to be there."

Chao's mental map is quite good. Six days from the coast is reasonable. The other man is coming farther.

"We will ride four days," he says. "Send a man ahead to arrange for the best food and women to be there. I will wait for your war-leader in yurts four days from this place."

The Altai leader hesitates a moment, then nods. "This will be done," he says. He smiles again. "Jeni women there for you. Most beautiful of all."

"And *kumiss*?" says Lu Chao, an offering.

"Always *kumiss*," says the Altai. "*Kumiss* tonight, for you and me!"

Chao nods again. He turns his horse under the high sky he remembers. They begin to ride on. The grass is very tall, there are wildflowers and bees. Small animals startle as they pass. He sees larger, antlered ones in the distance, in great numbers. Hawks hover and wheel, and later a solitary swan tracks their path towards the sun as it goes down.

THE WAR-LEADER Wan'yen says nothing at all about where they are meeting. It is as if the extra riding for him is beneath consideration, a waste of words to discuss, of thought to assess.

The man speaks no Kitan, they use an interpreter, the same one as before. From the outset, from first glimpse before first words, Chao's uneasiness about this mission has only deepened. The man is too hard, too assured. This is not a supplicant for aid in freeing his tribe from the Xiaolu's yoke, lying heavily on the steppe. He is impatient, confident, intelligent. Chao is aware of being assessed, every bit as much as he is judging what he can of the Altai leader.

He has only his nephew with him in the yurt. Wan'yen sits

opposite with the translator. A woman, one of the Jeni (their women are more appealing than he'd expected), serves *kumiss* as cups are emptied. Chao drinks slowly, ignoring the speed with which the other man drains his own.

This is a negotiation not a dinner party. He is permitted to display restraint. It feels proper to do so.

In the event, it doesn't seem to matter. Wan'yen's proposal is immediate, direct, and he does not waver from it. *Impatient*, Chao thinks again.

The Kitan are offered four of the Fourteen Prefectures. Not the most important ones, north of Hanjin, but over west, above what remains of Xinan—and only if Kitai takes the Xiaolu Southern Capital and hands it to the Altai. That is the first thing. The second is going northwest from there to take the Central Capital together. If these things are done, four prefectures will be returned to Kitai.

All silk and silver sent in spring and autumn will continue to be sent—to the Altai.

The Altai kaghan, Yan'po, will be named emperor of the Altai when the Central Capital falls. He will not be called nephew to the Kitan emperor. He will be younger brother to an older brother.

Lu Chao has not expected this man to be aware of diplomatic symbols. He is making mental adjustments rapidly.

If this is agreeable, the interpreter translates, we will communicate by sea and arrange for our riders to meet your army outside the Southern Capital next spring.

Is it agreeable?

The war-leader drinks. His eyes are impossible to read, past what he allows to be obvious ... which is complete and unwavering confidence. How does a horseman from where this man was born have so much of that? What does it say about his tribe?

Carefully, Lu Chao says, in his most grave voice, "It is not agreeable. Tell this to your kaghan, or address it now yourself. We do not go roaming over the grass to help one tribe defeat another. For a thousand years and more Kitai has seen tribes rise and fall in the steppe lands. We have remained."

He pauses to let the interpreter catch up.

Wan'yen laughs. He *laughs*.

He drinks again, wipes his mouth. He speaks, visibly amused. The interpreter translates: "What are your dynasties, your kingdoms and rebellions, if not tribes rising and falling? Where is the difference?"

The question is a disgrace, it is ignorant. Chao suddenly wants to speak a poem. Sima Zian, Han Chung, his own brother, *himself*, and say *that* is the difference, you *kumiss*-sodden barbarian. He wants to assert porcelain from Shantong, peonies in Yenling, the parks and gardens of Hanjin, *music*. He wants to be home.

He draws a breath, keeping his features expressionless. He says, slowly, "Perhaps, one day, you will come as a guest to us, and you will learn the answer to your question."

The interpreter translates, and Chao thinks he sees something in the war-leader's face. The man drinks again. He shrugs, speaks one word.

"Perhaps," the interpreter says.

Lu Chao is thinking quickly. He says, "Have you authority to amend your terms? Or must you ride to your kaghan? I will not wait so long. If you need to go back, another man will meet you, perhaps at summer's end."

He waits, lets the translator finish. He says, "But for aid from our armies, for gifts to your tribe when it declares itself an empire, for our guidance in that difficult change, we require the Fourteen Prefectures."

He pauses, throws a bone, though it may be more than he can offer: "And we can indeed discuss what status and kinship your emperor has in Kitai. Emperor Wenzong is known for his generosity."

The eyes of the war-leader meet his. If he were truly acting as a woman would, Lu Chao thinks, he would look away now. But there are moments when his analogy is not precise. He *is* Kitai, sitting here, he is an empire of more than a thousand years and must not be outfaced by a steppe rider with nothing behind him but grass and herds through all that time.

Sometimes you had to change roles in the midst of an encounter.

The war-leader stood up quickly. Lu Chao remained where he was, cross-legged, his cup beside him, his nephew silent just behind. Chao allowed himself a smile, eyebrows lifted. Wan'yen spoke, first hint of discomfiture in his voice. Chao waited.

The translator said, "War-leader will speak with kaghan and his brother. It cannot be that we give back so much land. You lost it long ago. Time does not turn back. It is not the way the sky god made the world. Maybe five. Maybe six of fourteen. The brothers will speak with the kaghan. We send riders to you before end of summer."

"Riders? Past the Southern Capital?"

Wan'yen shook his head, amused again, when the question was translated.

"War-leader says it is easy for Altai to pass by Xiaolu guards and come to you. He says plain north of Hanjin is wide open for riders."

A message in that, Lu Chao thought.

He stood up. There was power in being the one seated, but not in tilting one's neck to see the other man. "The plain is open going north, as well," he murmured. "Curious, how that is, isn't it?"

A moment, the translation, then the war-leader laughed. He grinned. He spoke. The translator said, "Esteemed Wan'yen says emissary is good, amusing man. He will eat and drink with you tonight, ride to kaghan tomorrow. He also says, Altai will destroy Xiaolu, with Kitai or not with Kitai. It is foretold and will happen."

Lu Chao bowed. He was the empire and the empire was nothing if not civilized. His nephew did the same. They went out of the yurt into the morning vastness of the grasslands, stretching in all directions, disturbingly, as if unending.

LATER THEY DRINK AND EAT. At night he makes love to a Jeni woman. When she has gone at his request he lies awake, thinking as clearly as he can after too much *kumiss*.

He will have time to consider all of this on the ride east, on the ship going south, before he is ushered into his emperor's presence on the Dragon Throne in Hanjin.

He already knows what he will say.

He has spent his life saying what he believes to be true. He's been exiled for it, three times, has come near to being executed more than once.

That can happen, even in a civilized empire.

CHAPTER XIV

The second man in Kitai to learn details of what happened on the steppe was the army's most newly appointed commander of five thousand, Ren Daiyan.

It was not an accident. He had taken himself north and west not long after his transfer to the military, was gleaning what he could above the trading city of Shuquian, having quietly crossed the Golden River into Xiaolu lands.

It was disturbing and strange, being in one of the Fourteen Prefectures, the rivers and mountains of longing.

Shuquian, not far from the river, not far from the Wall, had been an important city from the Second Dynasty onwards. The families that had founded and dominated Kitai once had all been from the north.

It was much reduced, marked a limit of the empire now. The river was the border with the Xiaolu here. One of the lost prefectures lay on the other side, irrigated by the river, ruled by the barbarians.

It wasn't especially difficult to slip across the river, and almost all people living in barbarian lands here were Kitan farmers. Governed from the steppe, paying taxes north, but Kitan. So Daiyan could blend in, once he braided his hair in the style forced on the Kitan living here.

He was alone. Ziji remained unhappily in Shuquian, on Daiyan's orders, providing a story for him and his whereabouts. Commander Ren was exploring around the city, as far as anyone else knew.

What he was really doing was breaching the treaty: a military man in Xiaolu lands was subject to death if found and diplomats' accusations relayed to Hanjin. But he *was* a soldier now, an officer, and if their army was going to war next year against the Xiaolu, information would matter.

Men went quietly back and forth here all the time. If either or both governments raised tariffs or asserted new monopolies, it simply increased the benefits—and the likelihood—of smuggling. Risks became worth taking. One of the realities of living near the border was taking tea or salt or medicines illegally north, crossing the river on a moonless night to an arranged assignation, bringing back amber or furs or simply silver. Silver was always good.

You could be imprisoned and beaten or executed as a smuggler if caught coming back to this side, too, although that last fate probably didn't apply to a military commander—if he could prove his identity in time.

Tonight, he was hiding in a small barn, headed back south after a week north of the river. He was slathered in a foul-smelling unguent, face and hands and ankles, against the biting insects of a northern summer. He'd been told by the man who'd sold the unguent to him that it was sovereign against the night-biters.

The seller had lied, Daiyan had decided.

The man deserved a foul and vicious ending, ideally bitten to death by mosquitoes. Daiyan kept using the unguent, having nothing better to try. He swore a great deal, but under his breath.

The two water buffalo in the barn knew he was here, and the

three goats. The farmer didn't. There was no dog or he'd have had to kill it, probably.

The barn was very hot on a summer night, and it smelled. But he had heard tigers in the darkness, and he wasn't going to sleep on open ground tonight.

Ren Daiyan feared two things that he knew of, or admitted to himself. One, from childhood, was being buried alive. He could never have been a tomb-robber, and it had nothing to do with ghosts, or magic wards placed within.

The other fear was tigers, though he hadn't had it as a boy. People from Szechen learned how to be cautious. There were deaths, people and livestock, but usually that had to do with someone being careless. Only after he'd left home, living in the open for years, had he engaged with tigers.

He'd killed two with his bow, in and around the marsh. One more with a sword when the creature had surprised him and was too close too quickly for an arrow. He could not remember being so terrified, before or since that evening. The world-swallowing sound of its roaring as it leaped in a half-moon twilight was with him now, years after.

He had been acclaimed for that sword-thrust into the open jaws of the tiger. He had a scar on his chest from that encounter. Had he not twisted away as he thrust, he'd have been dead. The kill had become legendary among the outlaws by the time Daiyan left. He allowed that to happen, but knew the truth—how fortunate he'd been. How nearly his life had come to an end that night, wasted, trivial.

The Kitan, as a rule, hated wolves more than anything else. Daiyan would take a starving winter wolf pack over a tiger any time at all. Accordingly, he was in a hot, stinking barn tonight, instead of finding what air he could on some elevation under the moon.

He wanted a drink. He didn't have anything. Had finished his flask of *kumiss*. The barn was sloppily built, cracks in the boards and roof. It would leak terribly in rain. The moon was bright through the roof cracks, which made it harder to sleep. Would also make it a little tricky crossing the river tomorrow night, but he knew where to do that now: smugglers left boats hidden on each bank. He wasn't worried.

He slapped at something drilling his forehead like a woodworker's tool. His hand came away bloody, the colour made strange by moonlight. He thought of his bed in the chief magistrate's *yamen* in Hanjin, of the good wines Wang Fuyin offered, the food to be found in the streets of the capital.

He twisted his thoughts away. There was more to pull at him in memories of Hanjin beyond a soft bed or street food. There were channels down which he would not allow himself to go.

He'd left the capital shortly after the ceremony at which he'd knelt before his emperor and received imperial recognition: the gift of a city home with servants, silver, and the rank he now held in the army of Kitai.

It had been a turbulent, uneasy morning in the palace: Prime Minister Hang Dejin had resigned the night before. Daiyan's ceremony had been brief. He'd spent the whole of it imagining his father and mother watching, even just learning of it. He could almost hear the loud beating of their hearts, see their faces. You bore children to bring you pride, with luck, and perhaps security in your age.

He had money now, would send them assistance, as was proper. He could help others, too. He could even marry. He'd thought briefly about that, of having a son. But then he'd taken steps to have himself posted west—to Yenling, then on to Xinan.

He was a soldier. He'd achieved that, finally. He was a ranking officer, and he knew why he was alive in the world under heaven. All else was distraction.

Ziji came west with him, of course, and one of the other men who'd left the marsh with them. The others chose to stay with the magistrate. He couldn't fault them for that. Their lives were their own, and Hanjin was a better place to be, serving in Wang Fuyin's guard a smoother life than the army and following Daiyan in his journey.

It was Ziji, and the man who'd joined them, who were foolish, if you looked at it with any intelligence. He thought about Hanjin and what lay there—who lay there. He'd grown skilful at forcing his mind away, and he did so now.

Moonlight shifted as the moon rose, finding angles to slide into the broken-down barn, silver the straw and the animals.

There were so many poems about the moon, he thought. The great Sima Zian was said to have drowned in a stream, trying to embrace the reflection of the moon like a lover, after a lifetime of writing about it.

Daiyan doubted it was true. When someone became famous, legends gathered around him. It happened even on a small scale. He had heard once, sitting unnoticed at an inn, that the outlaw Ren Daiyan was a tiger hunter, had killed two dozen, most of them with a knife.

The world liked its stories.

He thought of the tales he'd heard this week, roaming among villages here, posing as a would-be smuggler looking to trade for amber later this summer in exchange for powdered tiger blood.

Tiger blood was a cure, in Kitai and up here, for just about everything. It was subject to a strict government monopoly and very, very expensive, since killing tigers for their blood was not a sensible way to feed oneself.

He'd heard a great many tales over drinks with potential trade partners. One story he had been told, several times, wasn't pleasing, or reassuring.

The northeastern tribe rebelling—they were called the Altai—had, if people in border villages could be believed, already taken the Xiaolu's Eastern Capital.

There was considerable unrest, even down here. Well, there would be, if the news was true. It was unnervingly fast. The Xiaolu garrisons assigned to keep peace among their useful Kitan farmers were bristling and uneasy. They might be summoned north to fight, Daiyan thought in the night barn, slapping at things biting him.

That could create opportunities. Not that he had rank or assignment to do anything about it yet. His difficulty was straightforward and unavoidable: if a war came next summer, as was rumoured everywhere now, with Kitai exploiting events on the steppe, it was going to arrive too soon for him to do the things he knew needed to be done.

He would have to rise too quickly in an army that moved slowly. Even being here, gathering information ... why was he the only officer in Kitai who seemed to see the need for that, and willing to risk the consequences?

He did know the answer. It wasn't difficult. It was the same answer that explained Erighaya, or the loss of the Fourteen in the first place, the failure to regain them.

Kitai feared its army even more than it relied upon it.

You couldn't build—or defend—an empire, enmeshed in that duality. And he couldn't appear too hasty or ambitious himself, or he'd make enemies in the army *and* at court.

He decided to see how long he could last without slapping at anything. He heard the steady swishing of the water buffaloes' tails and their low, unhappy sounds. They were being bitten alive, he knew. At least they had tails.

The tidings about the Eastern Capital baffled him. Like the other Xiaolu cities, it was walled, fortified, garrisoned. The only way he could make sense of this—a small northeastern tribe, no matter how fierce, taking a major city—was by assuming other tribes had joined them *and* that the soldiers in the city had chosen to surrender, even go over to the rebels.

He didn't know if that was true, but it was all he could come up with. There were conflicting stories about where the Xiaolu emperor was right now. He was gathering his forces, he had fled to the west, he was in a drunken stupor, he was dead.

He'd have liked to talk to a soldier, had thought of capturing one and interrogating him somewhere they'd not be interrupted, but that carried so much danger, beyond the risks inherent in his being here, that he'd put the idea aside.

Besides, it was unlikely that a soldier posted this far from events would know more than rumours, and Daiyan already had those.

He slapped, swore. Hadn't lasted long, had he?

He heard a sound outside. He became very still.

Not a roar or snarl. The barn's animals would have let him know if a tiger was approaching. No, this was the other thing a man needed to fear at night, in a place where he wasn't supposed to be.

He rose silently. Slipped out of a slanting beam of moonlight. Unsheathed his short sword, the only weapon he had, besides a knife. You couldn't wander in Xiaolu lands, posing as a smuggler, and carry a bow and quiver.

There was too much light in here. There was no door in the back of the barn, but he'd loosened a loose board further when he'd first come in. He could squeeze out that way. He went forward, put an eye to a crack in the wall.

It was horses he'd heard. Now he saw torches. Four, maybe five riders, and if those approaching were even remotely capable, one or two might be watching the rear of the barn already. Although, since he'd heard them, they might not be so capable.

Still, if there were men back there, squeezing through the board would leave him exposed in moonlight. Not how he wanted to be taken, or die.

He wondered, idly, who had reported him. It wasn't an important question. These were dangerous times. A stranger, not one of the usual smugglers, arriving in a village, asking even casual questions over *kumiss* in a drinking place ... that might be worth a word to the garrison, curry favour there against harder times possibly to come.

He did spare a moment for bitterness about Kitans informing on another Kitan, but only the moment: they lived here, this was the reality of their lives, and it wasn't as if the emperor in Hanjin had done anything to reclaim them, for all the poems and songs. Not this emperor, not his father, not his father's father, all the way back to the treaty that had handed these people over like bargaining pieces to barbarians.

They didn't owe Daiyan anything. If he was captured or killed, someone might be rewarded, someone's children might eat this winter, and live.

THERE WERE FOUR RIDERS. Ren Daiyan himself never said there were more than that. He never told anyone but Ziji the details, in fact—he wasn't supposed to have been north of the river at all. But the farmer in whose barn he'd planned to spend a night avoiding tigers was Kitan, of course. The farmer hadn't reported him. He happened to be one of those who longed for rescue and redemption by his own emperor, though his family had lived here for generations and he'd never known anything but the Xiaolu and couldn't say they'd been savagely harsh, either.

The farmer had heard soldiers from the garrison riding across his field at night, had seen the torches they carried. He'd come out, quietly, to watch what was happening on his land. His hair was unbraided. He didn't care if they saw him like that by his gate, you were allowed to be that way in your home, when you slept.

He saw what took place by his barn. He talked about it afterwards. Indeed, he talked about it all his life, and the story spread, in the light of other events that followed.

The most widely told version was that twelve soldiers from the garrison had come to take or kill one man, but the one man was Ren

Daiyan, still only a commander of five thousand, just appointed earlier that spring.

THEY KNEW HE WAS HERE, obviously.

So there were three ways to do this. He could wait, sword ready, just inside the doors, kill the first man through, then burst out past him or over him, and take one or, ideally, two others before they had time to react.

There might be five, with one at the back, but he didn't think so. They'd want to stay together. No one would want to be alone on the other side, and barns here didn't have rear doors.

Or he could get out before they were ready, avoid being trapped in here. They had torches. It was possible they might try to burn him out. Xiaolu horsemen wouldn't be concerned about setting fire to a Kitan farmer's barn.

He didn't want to be trapped in a burning barn. Odds were they would only do it if they had to force him out, they'd want him alive to interrogate. He'd have done it that way, but he didn't know a great deal about the Xiaolu—not yet. And interrogation generally killed you, anyhow.

He was calm but also angry. You were supposed to be spiritual at times such as this—edge of death, the doors you might be crossing through. He'd had a few such moments. Anger helped more.

It was too soon to die. Too much to be done. He chose the third option. He went quickly to the back, the loosened board. He pushed his small pack out, listened for a reaction. Nothing. He pried the board away, twisted sideways, sword arm first, and worked through. A splinter caught his arm, ripped, drawing blood.

A wound. It was possible to find that funny.

He was out, in moonlight. Half moon, west by now, not brilliant, but too much. He moved quickly. Left the pack where it was, looped wide from the barn, opposite direction from the house. He dropped to his knees when he cleared the shelter of the barn walls, crawled, belly-flat, at speed (a skill you learned), a good distance.

He could keep going. They might not find him.

But they probably would. He was on foot; they had horses, and would send for others, and dogs. They'd know someone had been inside the moment they opened the door. He was too far from the river and the border to just run, and there would be guards there, too, of course, who would be alerted by a rider getting ahead of him. He needed a horse.

He also, being honest, didn't feel like running from four Xiaolu horsemen.

This was his first-ever encounter with them. Maybe his last, but tonight might be, in a real sense, the opening moments of something he had been preparing for since a bamboo wood outside Shengdu. Or since entering another forest near his village, dead men behind him, becoming an outlaw, teaching himself ways to kill.

Two of the riders had dismounted, holding torches, were approaching the barn. Two, predictably, remained on their horses, a short distance away, holding their bows, covering the other two. Men did things in combat that could be anticipated. Sometimes these were clever, more often they were just ... the usual way.

Daiyan stayed low, crawling. He came up, ghost-silent, an agent of death, behind the nearest horseman. The man was in darkness, the torches were held by those on foot. The horse was well trained, perhaps more so than the rider, posted among farms of docile Kitan subjects.

The man died silently: an upward rush, a leap, a knife to the throat, slicing. The horse, as Daiyan had guessed it would, shifted only slightly, made no sound as its rider died. Daiyan slid back down, holding the soldier, lowering him silently into burnt summer grass.

The two on foot had reached the doors. They were trying to sort out how to hold torches and swords and open the barn. Finally, they jammed the torches into the ground and unhooked the door bolt together. They tried to be quiet about it, but the metal groaned and rasped. By the time it was free the second man on horseback was also dead, also without a sound.

Daiyan took the rider's bow and quiver, and mounted his horse. He had made a point of handling steppe bows, to learn them. They were smaller, for use in the saddle, and the arrows were smaller too. You could adjust. It was only a matter of practice. Most things were. He killed the first of the men on foot by the barn doors. It was easy, the torches were burning there.

The second man turned. Daiyan saw shock and horror in his face. A young face. He shot that one in the eye. An arrow to the face was a message of sorts.

He wondered if anyone had been watching. The farmer might have heard riders approaching. He decided it didn't matter. He wasn't going to kill the farmer. He collected another horse, used the long lead the Xiaolu always had to hook it to the one he was riding. He was going to go fast now, two horses were better. He rode around the barn and reclaimed his pack from near the loosened board. Came in front again, quickly, but not hurrying—there was a difference—and collected a second quiver. He extinguished the torches. He started south. It was good to be holding a bow again, he thought.

It was also good to have made a beginning here. It did feel as if that was what had happened.

It had all been a matter of moments. He ripped the sliver of wood from his arm. He slapped at an insect. He rode for the river under the moon so many poets had loved.

ZIJI WASN'T SUPPOSED to be here, a long day's ride above Shuquian. He also knew it was the right decision, whatever Daiyan might say.

The smuggler patrols were more active in summer because smugglers were. He couldn't do anything about the north bank, but he had rank enough to have his own men patrol a stretch of the river on their side—the best place, they'd been told, to try to cross the water.

You could go just about straight north-south here as you crossed. The river was sluggish at this point, shallower in summer, thick with the loess soil that gave it its colour and name. The banks were steep to east and west but easier here where the river widened and slowed. Farther east, silt floods were an endless danger, no matter how many dikes and barriers Kitai had built on both sides (in the days when they controlled both sides) over centuries.

A good swimmer might be able to get across here, though there were said to be creatures in the murky water that could kill you. Horses could swim it carrying riders, and had in times of war. But the small pole-pushed boats or ox-hide-covered rafts dragged by horses (or by camels in the west, he'd heard) were the best way.

The river was the border here. To east or west it wasn't. East, towards Yenling and then the capital, it curved south, almost to Hanjin, belonged to Kitai on both banks, with the border halfway to the Wall. To the west, where the river began, its course was disputed with the Kislik.

Although that was another kind of lie, Ziji thought. It was lost, not disputed. Given by treaty to the Kislik again, along with access to the far-off lands that the Silk Roads once had offered. He wondered what Jade Gate Fortress looked like now. It had been the gateway for treasures of the world, once.

Idle thoughts on a summer night. His second night up here. The excuse had been easy enough: he was training men, and watching for smugglers was a relatively safe way to do it. Their deception was that Commander Ren Daiyan was with them, was leading them. Instead of being the reason Ziji was here, waiting and uneasy by moonlight. Daiyan wasn't late yet, but if he didn't come tonight he would be.

They had a good company, if undermanned, not quite the designated five thousand. Most of their soldiers were at two barracks, one near Xinan's ruined walls, the other halfway to Shuquian. The ones they'd brought north were a select group and he trusted them. Daiyan was good at judging men and binding them to him, and Ziji knew that he was, too. There was no point, one of his own officers long ago had said, in not knowing what you were *good* at, if you were terrible at most things. The man had meant it to be cutting, amusing, but Ziji had heard it differently. He'd made it a code of his own with men he commanded, in the marsh, in the magistrate's guard, here.

He watched the shallows of the riverbank, moving his small horse east, then doubling back. The horse was not young, or especially good. They never had enough good horses. Another thing they'd lost when they lost domination of the steppe. Once this part of the river had been the scene, every spring, of a massive horse fair, when the steppe people—allowed cautiously down through the Wall—paid *them* tribute.

Now they bought horses, in the limited numbers the Xiaolu allowed, or from what remained of Tagur in the west. Kitai had never had enough proper grazing land, and now it had hardly any.

Ziji wasn't an expert rider. Few of them were. There weren't enough horses, not enough chances to become better, even in the army. When they fought barbarians it couldn't be a cavalry war, they were slaughtered in those. They won, when they won, with foot soldiers in massive numbers, on terrain that made it hard for horses, and with an edge in weaponry.

If they remembered to bring them.

There was a half moon tonight, but he saw nothing in the river. Smugglers tended, for obvious reasons, to prefer moonless nights. It had been impressed upon all soldiers that the government monopolies and tariffs paid for *them*: food, shelter, clothing, weapons. *Smuggling hurts the army* was the repeated message.

Most soldiers didn't believe it, Ziji had come to realize. He didn't believe it himself, entirely, though obviously the emperor had to pay for his soldiers somehow.

Still, it could be hard to see how their swords and barracks wine and food were connected to the arrest of a few men brave enough to cross the river and deal with animals in the dark and Xiaolu guards on the other side. Odds were that anyone coming across this way would be Kitan. They had a treaty agreement to stop smugglers, but Ziji didn't think any soldier's heart was in it.

They were more likely to be listening for animals, especially those men patrolling on foot. Tigers rarely attacked a horseman.

Ziji had thought about setting an officer's example, doing foot patrol himself, but he was here for a reason, and might need to cover ground fast, or as fast as the wheezy creature he was riding could. The little horse was sweet-natured, he'd give it that, but the two of them would be hard put to win a race against a determined donkey.

He heard hoofbeats, behind him to the south. There were no reinforcements scheduled tonight. Ziji turned. He was puzzled, not alarmed.

"Reporting for river patrol, Commander Zhao!" A high-pitched voice, peasant's diction and tone.

Ziji swore. "Fuck yourself, Daiyan! How'd you get behind us?"

"Are you joking? Fat bullocks could swim the river and get behind you," Daiyan replied in his own voice. "I thought you might follow me north."

"Discipline me for disobeying an order."

"It wasn't quite an order. I didn't want to have to discipline you when you disobeyed. How many?"

"Brought twenty-five to Shuquian, ten here last night and tonight." Daiyan was riding a good horse, with a second on a lead behind it. "Steal those?"

Daiyan laughed. "I won them in a drinking contest."

Ziji ignored that. "And their riders?"

Daiyan hesitated. "Tell you later."

Which told him. "You learn anything?"

"Some. Later. Ziji, there's likely to be trouble. We don't want to be around."

"You mean those two horses don't?"

"I do mean that. But also our soldiers."

"Part of the 'more later'?"

Daiyan grinned in the silvered night. He was still wet. Had swum the river on his horse, it appeared. "Yes. What do I need to know? How did you explain being here to the commander in Shuquian?"

Ziji shrugged. "You're a good commander, wanted us to understand the border. It was all right."

"You're becoming a better liar."

"The 'good commander' part, you mean?"

Daiyan laughed. "Anything else?"

Ziji was happy and irritated at the same time. That happened a fair bit with Daiyan. It seemed to him sometimes that he was like a father with the other man. The feeling you might have when a missing child turned up safely—relieved and angry at the same time.

He said, "One idiot is roaming around, west of us. He'll need to be moved if you say trouble's coming."

"Roaming? What do you mean?"

Ziji realized he wasn't unhappy telling this. A small yielding to irritation. "Remember the woman whose life you saved in the Genyue, more or less?"

"Of course I do," Daiyan said. His voice changed. "She and her husband were in Xinan when I left. You mean they—"

"She's still there, at the aristocrat's inn. But he's here, looking for bronzes at some old temple in the valley. He has bullock carts, servants with shovels. For his collection. Remember?"

"Qi Wai is here? Tonight?"

"I just said that."

Daiyan's turn to swear. "He'll need to be brought into Shuquian in the morning, along with everyone else who has no obvious business up here. If someone's stolen horses and ... done whatever else north of the river, the Xiaolu will feel entitled to cross and demand we help search for them. I don't want this becoming a border incident."

"I see. And where will those stolen horses be?"

"A long way south by sunrise. Unseen, I really hope."

"I'll ride with you."

Daiyan shook his head. "You stay, since you were so keen to follow me up here. Have our men spread word that people need to get inside the city. Tell the regular soldiers you heard something. Get them to help. But find Qi Wai yourself. He's imperial clan, he can be an incident all by himself if this goes badly. Make sure he knows your rank ... and that you were in his house. He's probably going to be stubborn, from what I've heard. He's passionate about that collection."

He turned to go. Looked back over his shoulder. "You'll get this other horse when you catch up with me at our barracks. I brought it for you."

"You're going straight there?"

"Straight there."

It was a perfectly good course of action. Those don't always unfold as intended.

CHAPTER XV

"Absolutely not! There is an enormous ceremonial vessel down there, Fourth Dynasty, superb condition from what we can see, inscribed, magnificent, extremely rare. I am not leaving until it is out of the earth and in my cart."

A stubborn, determined streak had often served Qi Wai of the imperial clan well. Most men didn't like to push back when you pushed. He knew he was regarded as eccentric and was content with that. It could be useful. It helped that he had stature, by way of his family, and also by way of his wife, lately, though that aspect of things was somewhat complex.

The soldier confronting Wai from horseback was a man of strong build, not especially young. He was a deputy commander of five thousand, evidently, which was a respectable rank. One that entitled him to converse with Qi Wai, but certainly not to give orders to a member of the imperial clan.

The man had addressed him with acceptable deference. It appeared he had actually been inside their house in Hanjin:

accompanying the one who'd saved Shan's life in the Genyue last autumn. This was very unexpected.

Not that it mattered, in terms of what he intended to do. He hadn't come all this way to get up and go on some soldier's orders.

He wasn't sure what this officer was even doing here, northwest of Shuquian, on the weedy, overgrown grounds of a long-abandoned Cho temple. On the other hand, it wasn't really of interest to him. No civilized man concerned himself with the comings and goings of soldiers.

And he had a ceremonial vessel to dig out from where his experience and intuition had—correctly!—told him something might be found. And if there was one magnificent bronze there were almost certainly going to be other artifacts. He wanted engraved ceremonial cups. He was lacking in those, especially from the Fourth and further back. A dream, always, was to unearth a chest with preserved scrolls. He'd done that once. The memory could trigger a man's hopes of doing so again. A kind of desire.

He glared up at the officer sitting astride what—even to Qi Wai's unpractised eye—seemed a remarkably broken-down horse. The man looked back at him with an expression that could only be described, startlingly, as amused.

"I will not give you orders, of course," the soldier said gravely.

"Of course, indeed!" snapped Qi Wai of the imperial clan.

"But I will do so to your labourers."

There was a pause as Wai considered that.

"If you stay here, you stay alone, sir. And I must commandeer the cart and get it into the city. We have our instructions. The Xiaolu are going to be crossing the river today, it's just about certain, and they will be unhappy. We are to leave nothing of value for them. And I trust you enough, my lord, to believe the objects in this cart have value."

"Of course they do! Great value!"

Qi Wai began, uneasily, to feel as if the encounter wasn't going quite the way he needed it to.

"As you say." The officer nodded calmly.

He turned and spoke commands over his shoulder to the five men accompanying him. In turn, they moved towards the hole in the ground where Wai's men were digging (not very diligently just now) around the partially excavated bronze.

"What are they doing?" Wai demanded, summoning all the authority he could.

"Telling your men that Xiaolu riders are likely to be here before the end of today. The same thing I am telling you, my lord."

"We have a peace treaty with them!" Qi Wai snapped.

"We do, indeed. We may have breached it last night. A smuggler from our side. Stolen horses. It is possible there were casualties on the north side of the river. We do not want casualties on this side. We especially don't want one of them to be a member of the imperial clan."

"They would not dare!"

"Forgive me, but they would. Perhaps a Xiaolu diplomat would be properly aware of your lordship's importance, but an angry soldier is less likely to be cautious."

"Then you and your men will stay and defend me! I ... I order you to do so!"

The officer's expression was no longer amused. "Sir, it would give me great pleasure to kill Xiaolu in your defence, but I have instructions otherwise, and I know of no way that you can override those. I am sorry, my lord. As I said, I must bring your men. If you stay, you stay alone. If it makes you feel better, your death will probably cost me my own life, for leaving you here."

He trotted the old horse gingerly over towards Wai's hired labourers. These, Wai saw, were already climbing with unseemly haste out of the hole around the massive bronze.

"Stay where you are!" he shouted. They looked at him, but didn't stop climbing out.

"I will have you all beaten!"

The officer looked back at him. His expression this time was displeasing—you would have to call it contemptuous.

"No call for that, sir," he said. "They are doing this under military orders."

"What is your name, you accursed fool?"

"Zhao Ziji, sir. Serving under Commander Ren Daiyan at the Xinan barracks. You may find me there, sir, if you wish. And you can certainly file a complaint with a magistrate up here or in Xinan."

He turned away again. His men were organizing Wai's labourers. They were taking the cart with the artifacts that had already been unearthed.

Wai watched as they started across the trampled ground towards the dirt road that would intersect the larger one leading to Shuquian's walls.

He became unpleasantly aware of two things. A solitary bird was singing in a tree behind him, and he was about to be equally alone in the ruins of the temple.

He watched the receding party. He looked around. The river was out of sight, but not far away. The bird continued to sing with an irritating persistence. The group of men was proceeding steadily, with the cart.

Xiaolu riders, that soldier had said.

"I need a horse, then!" he shouted. "Give me a horse!"

They stopped. The officer looked back.

They put him in the cart. He bounced and jostled painfully all the way to Shuquian, which they reached late in the day. He held one of the ceramic bowls in his lap, cradled in both hands. They were going too fast, it was almost certain to break if he didn't protect it.

Behind them, it was later learned, thirty Xiaolu horsemen forded the Golden River that same day and ranged through the countryside, looking for two of their own horses and the man who'd taken them.

They were careful at first to damage only property, not seriously injure anyone. But then one farmer was rather too insistent in resisting their desire to look inside his barn. A Xiaolu rider, not understanding the shouted words but seeing a scythe waving in the farmer's hands, decided this was sufficient to justify his desire to kill someone.

One of the four dead soldiers two nights ago had been his brother. The rider was reprimanded by his leader. The two horses weren't in the barn. For want of anything better to do, they set fire to it.

⁤ℭ⁤ℴ

Shan has been in Xinan only once before, and not for nearly so long as this. It is the strangest place she's ever known.

The contrasts are inescapable: between past and present, glory and ruin, pride and ... whatever came when pride went away.

There had been two million people here at the city's peak; there are less than a tenth of that now. But the walls and gates, where they still stand, enclose the same vast spaces as before. The central north-south avenue, the imperial way, is humbling, it is overwhelming. You feel, she thinks, as if those who built this, who lived here, were more than you could ever dream of being.

The untended parks and gardens are enormous. Much as she hates being carried in a litter, it is impossible to deal with Xinan otherwise. The imperial way alone is more than five hundred paces across. She finds it difficult to believe what she is seeing, what it says about the past.

Chan Du wrote a poem about Long Lake Park at the southeastern edge of the city, about court ladies in silken finery (kingfisher feathers in their hair) arriving on horseback to watch a polo match. How the air was changed and brightened by their presence and their laughter.

The charred and looted palace is full of echoes and ghosts. It seems to Shan, carried there one morning, that she can smell burning, hundreds of years after. She walks (insists on walking) in the walled palace park through which the emperor had fled on the eve of the rebellion in the Ninth, when everything came crashing down.

As well as her litter-bearers, she's had two men guarding her, at the appalled insistence of the city's chief magistrate, a fastidious, anxious man. A good thing, that morning in the palace: wild dogs appeared, and backed away only when one of them was killed.

She hadn't intended to be in Xinan at all. She'd insisted on coming with Wai on the usual summer journey west. He hadn't wanted her to. She'd had a secret thought that she might try to glimpse his concubine in Yenling, the one he wouldn't bring into their home the way a decent man should.

But when they'd arrived in Yenling Shan had felt a revulsion against her own thoughts. It was too humiliating—not just the presence of an allegedly very young girl here, but the distorting image of herself, spying on her. Was this what she'd become?

She would not allow it to be so. So when Wai suggested she stay there while he continued west and then north to Shuquian, she'd said she'd go as far as Xinan. He hadn't refused. Probably happy to have her out of Yenling, she thought.

She didn't go north with him. Once, it would have simply been what they did together. They'd have gone about the countryside, searching. They'd have spoken to village elders and temple clerics, dug up or purchased artifacts, made drawings and notes of the things they couldn't move or buy, for their collection.

The collection, she thinks, isn't *theirs* any longer. She loves the bronzes, porcelain, scrolls, steles they have, but she isn't passionate about claiming these any more. Not as she had been once.

Life can change people, Shan thinks. She makes a face at the banality of the thought. She is sipping tea, late afternoon, at a tea house just outside the principal western gate of the city. This is where, in the days when Xinan was the centre of the world, friends would break willow twigs at parting, in the hope they'd meet again.

The guards and her litter-bearers are waiting outside. She wonders what the four men think of her. She decides that she doesn't care. As usual, that isn't entirely true.

Once, the collection was another way in which she—and her marriage—were different from the way the world tried to make you be. That's gone now, she thinks. She is losing a battle to the world, the weight of it.

She writes a song one morning, before it grows too hot to concentrate. Sets it to the music of "Late Night on a Balcony." There had been a time when she'd hated that song, all the songs and poems like that one, about abandoned courtesans, their disordered silk and scented cheeks, but the words to the tune are her own now, and different.

When she is finished she puts down her brush and looks at her inked characters, what is said and half said on the paper. Suddenly she feels afraid, not knowing from where this came, who the woman in this song really is—or the woman at the desk, writing and then reading the words:

> *Yesterday, I sat by the city gate*
> *And looked away west as far as I could.*
> *No one coming along the imperial road,*
> *Only ghosts and the summer wind.*
> *I am not perfect like Wen Jian was,*
> *Jade pins aslant in her hair,*
> *For whose love an emperor drifted from his throne.*

Walking in gardens among weeds
Where chrysanthemums once grew,
I feel the gaze of those who think this is immodest,
As improper as Cho Masters find peonies.
Today, by a dry fountain in a courtyard,
I ask for endless cups of tea.
I would like to drink saffron wine, cup after cup,
Listening to wind chimes in the trees.
No, I will not refuse to drink with you.
This flower will not be like any other.

მ×ნ

Late one afternoon, the ship carrying Lu Chao, honourable emissary of the emperor of Kitai, back from his encounter with the Altai tribe of the steppe was caught in a storm.

They had only a little warning, but the mariners were capable, if terrified. The pleated sail was folded and lashed to the deck. The passengers, including their most illustrious one, had ropes tied to their waists to keep them from being swept overboard. Of course, if the vessel broke up or overturned this would achieve nothing.

The sky went from blue to streaked purple to black. Thunder boomed. The ship was tossed and then spun completely around by the wind and waves. All those aboard believed their time had come to cross over to the greater dark. Those who die at sea cannot have proper burial. Their spirits never rest.

Chao fought his way, crawling and staggering, to where his nephew clung to one of the wooden wheel-blocks on the deck. His own rope was just long enough to let him do this. He dropped down beside Mah. They looked at each other, faces streaming with rain and salt sea water. It was too loud in the storm to speak. They were together, though. If this was the end, they would cross together. He loved his brother's son as he loved his own.

Below deck, in a metal casket with a heavy lock, were his memoranda and recommendations from his meeting with the war-leader of the Altai. If the ship went down, they would never be known.

Farther east, and south, beyond the storm—in a place where there were never storms—lay the island of the gods, Peng-lai. A haven for the souls of those whose lives had been truly virtuous. Lu Chao did not imagine his spirit going there. His nephew's might, he thought, rain whipping his face. His nephew had gone to Lingzhou, to care for his father. There was a lifetime's worth of virtue in having done that. Lu Chao could pray it might be rewarded. He did that, soaked through, clinging. Lightning filled the whole of the western sky for a vivid moment, then the land was lost in blackness and waves. He gripped the wood as tightly as he could.

THEY DID NOT DROWN or die, not one man on board. The ship endured, the storm finally passed as evening came. It was very strange: afternoon blackness giving way to an evening brightness. Then it grew dark again. Lu Chao saw the star of the Weaver Maid as the clouds passed over them and away, thunder fading and gone, the last flashes of lightning.

They pulled up the pleated sail. They carried on, in sight of the shoreline as mariners did whenever they could.

He lived to return to Hanjin and the court. He presented his report and offered his views to the emperor and the honourable Prime Minister Kai Zhen, also returned from exile, installed in office by then.

After Lu Chao concluded, he was thanked, graciously, for his efforts, and given a proper reward on behalf of the empire. He was not asked to do anything further in this matter, nor offered a position at court, or in any prefecture.

Chao went home, therefore, travelling into autumn with his nephew to the farm by East Slope, to his brother and his family. He was home by the Ninth of Ninth, the Chrysanthemum Festival.

The thoughts he'd shared before the Dragon Throne had been unequivocal, and urgently expressed.

Small events can be important in the unfolding, like a pleated sail, of the world. The survival of an emissary, say, or his drowning on a ship in a sudden summer thunderstorm.

But sometimes such moments do not signify in the sweep and flow of events, though obviously they will matter greatly to those who might have thought their lives were ending in rain and wind, and for those who love them dearly and would have grieved for their loss.

A different storm, but with lightning and thunder as well, and a torrent of rain, caught Ren Daiyan near Xinan. He took refuge at the edge of a wood. You didn't go under trees in the open (he'd seen men killed by lightning) but a forest was all right, kept you relatively dry, and this storm didn't look as if it would last.

He wasn't in a hurry. He was off the main road already, though couldn't have clearly explained why he was headed towards Ma-wai. Perhaps just because he'd never seen it, the fabled hot springs and the structures built around them, what would be left of those.

He was alone. He'd collected six of his soldiers back at Shuquian and ridden with them until this morning, when he'd sent them on to their barracks outside Xinan. Soldiers had been protection on the journey south, and they'd also masked him. A man alone riding a very good horse with another tied behind, in the days after the Xiaolu had almost certainly recorded a protest at the *yamen* in Shuquian about murder and horse theft, was not a good idea.

He didn't know what else the Xiaolu had done. There might

have been violence. Probably had been. He'd been moving fast, outpacing any news. He'd hear it later at the barracks. Better to be there and settled in before tidings—and questions—emerged.

He didn't *regret* killing the first four barbarians of his life, but he wouldn't proclaim it the most prudent thing he'd ever done. Made it harder, for one thing, to report the tidings he'd heard about the fall of the Eastern Capital.

That mattered, if it was true, might change things. It needed to be assessed. The goal, after all, wasn't to destroy the Xiaolu, or the Altai, or any other tribe. *Someone* had to rule the steppe. No, the goal was the Fourteen, and they needed to sort through how to achieve that.

He didn't have answers. He didn't know enough. It was disturbing, how fast a Xiaolu city appeared to have fallen to a small tribe from the northeast, if the rumour was true.

Under trees, he listened to the hammer of the rain. He kept his hand near his sword—he was in a wood he didn't know. His horse was quiet, which reassured somewhat. The other horse he'd sent on, ridden by one of his soldiers. That one would be Ziji's when his deputy commander came back south. Daiyan wouldn't deny the pleasure of riding horses this good. They made you realize what you'd been missing. Could make you want to be a cavalry officer, he thought.

The rain was steady, though the thunder had moved on. The wind made a sound in the leaves and the leaves dripped all around him. There was a smell of forest, earth and decay. There were flowers by the edge, where light could fall.

They had passed the turnoff to the imperial tombs yesterday, seeing them to the east, high mounds off the main road, overgrown paths leading to them. Five dynasties had laid their emperors to rest in mausoleums that vied with each other for preeminence. Their emperors, and one empress.

Daiyan could remember his teacher speaking of her. Empress Hao was vilified in all official writings. You were supposed to spit if you named her. Teacher Tuan had laughed when one of the students had done that in the classroom.

"Tell me," Tuan Lung had asked, mildly, "how does an empress carry the burden of a rebellion one hundred and twenty years after she dies?"

"She destroyed celestial harmony," the spitting student had said. That was doctrine, they'd been reading it.

"And seven emperors between her and the rebellion couldn't shift it back?"

Daiyan had never thought about that, not as a young man. You didn't challenge what you read, you memorized it.

"No," Teacher Tuan had continued. "Empress Hao didn't bring down her dynasty. Don't let anyone make you think she did. If it is an examination question, write what they want to hear. Just don't believe it."

Tuan Lung had been a bitter man, but he'd given them things to think about. Daiyan wondered what his teacher would have been like had he passed the *jinshi* examinations and risen in rank.

Well, he wouldn't have been travelling up and down the middle reaches of the Great River, with a donkey and a different boy each year. It was summer now. Tuan Lung would be along the river, doing what he did.

It was possible for people to enter your life, play a role, and then be gone. Although if you could sit on a horse in a wood under dripping leaves years after and think about them, about things they'd said, were they really lost?

There were disciples of the Cho Master who could probably offer learned answers to that. For Daiyan, if a man, or a woman, had been in your life but you never saw them again, they were gone. A memory of someone wasn't the man. Or woman.

Rain and solitude could do things to your thinking. He shifted the horse forward a little, leaning over its neck, peering at the sky. The clouds were lightening. This would be over soon. He decided he'd wait a few more moments. He felt curiously hesitant, in no hurry to go forward.

He didn't mind being alone. There wasn't a lot of quiet in the army, not for a commander of five thousand men. Maybe that was why he was lingering now, branching off the road, heading for the pavilions of Ma-wai. The barracks held a lot of men. Xinan had people, as well. Not nearly so many as once, but—

Daiyan's head whipped left. The sword was drawn instinctively. But there was no threat, the horse was undisturbed, though it lifted its head at his own quick motion. He'd seen a flash of colour, a darting brightness, but close to the ground, too low to be a tiger, and it was gone. Tigers didn't like rain, he reminded himself—at least that was the country wisdom in Szechen.

That pulled forward a better thought. With normal courier time, his parents would probably know by now what had happened to their younger son, his rank, his reception at court. Bowing before the emperor. And they'd have received the money he'd sent.

You had larger goals and smaller ones in life. He let himself imagine his father reading his letter about the emperor. He let that thought draw him from the trees and back onto the path to Ma-wai.

THE BREEZE WAS in his face and the clouds were moving swiftly east. After a little while the sky was blue under a bright sun and it began to grow warm, though the storm had broken the worst of the heat. His hat and clothing dried as he went.

He came to Ma-wai late in the day. There was no one here. There was no reason for anyone to be here. Whatever treasures this place had once held—and they were the subject of legend—would long ago have been stolen or destroyed.

So who would come to a ruined imperial playground haunted

by so many ghosts? He feared tigers and being buried alive, not ghosts.

He rode in through an archway across the road. It was strange, even doing that. The arch still stood but the wall on either side had crumbled. You could step over it, ride through wide gaps. Stones would have been carted away to shore up farmhouses or make pasture walls. Long ago.

Once through the arch, the path was wide, bending at intervals, the way they always did. There were trees on both sides, willows, paulownias, chestnuts. He saw a bamboo grove to the right, peaches and flowering plum on the other side. The grass and earth were overgrown, untended, wet from the rain. The buildings and pavilions lay ahead, with the lake beyond, flashing blue, ruffled in the breeze. It was quiet. His horse's clopping hooves on the path, and birdsong.

This had been a retreat for court and aristocrats for a long time, as far back as the Fifth Dynasty, when Xinan had first become the capital. The hot springs here had been an imperial refuge in all seasons. Music and luxury, exquisite women, sumptuous feasts, healing waters rising from underground into the bathing pools. It had reached a peak of elaborate decadence in the Ninth, as so many things had. Wen Jian, the emperor's Beloved Companion, had ruled here and died not far away, still young.

It seemed to Daiyan that his people had known true glory and great power in the Third Dynasty and in the Ninth. Before the Third and after the Ninth and between the two of them had been violent internal wars, chaos, famine, and hardship. Although the two times of splendour had also ended in war, hadn't they? (Tuan Lung's voice again. Did you always hear your teacher's voice?)

And now? Their own time? It depended, he thought, on what happened next. Didn't it always depend on that?

He dismounted in the shade of an oak tree, forced a spike into the ground with his boot, then looped the horse's lead through the eye and tied it so the animal could graze.

He walked towards the nearest building, long, very large, low to the ground, wings going north-south. It was open, the doors were missing. The steps up were marble. He wondered briefly why no one had broken these and carted them away.

The corridor he entered was empty of decoration or artifact. No sign of burning. It was just ... abandoned. There would have been silk screens for the long row of windows once; now the afternoon breeze came in, stirring dust on the floor.

Daiyan opened doors at random. None of them were locked, many were gone. He walked into a dining hall. There was a platform couch against one wall. The legs were sandalwood. Someone ought to have taken those, he thought.

He passed the branching corridors, kept going, though aimlessly. He had no purpose here. He opened the last door at the far end of the hallway. A bedchamber, very large. At this western end the wind was stronger, blowing off the lake. The bed frame remained, four strong, carved posts. Daiyan saw two once-hidden doors in the panelled wall. They were broken, hanging awry, leading to some inner corridor.

This had been a palace for play, by night as well as by day.

He didn't bother looking into the hidden passageway. Whatever had once been here wasn't any more. He imagined music, lantern light gleaming off gold and jade, women dancing to music.

He turned back and took the southern hallway this time. It led him, eventually, outside. He looked left and saw his horse, far away, under the tree. He followed another uneven path and entered a large, round, enclosed pavilion.

One of the springs was here. He wondered why he was surprised. It wasn't as if looters could carry away hot springs. He supposed he'd thought it might have been blocked up.

There was a medicinal smell, sulphur and something else. He walked over and knelt and dipped a hand. The water was very hot. He smelled his fingers. Yes, sulphur. There were two broken marble benches around the perimeter of the room. There would have been many of those once. He saw a dais on the far side. For musicians, he guessed. They would play dutifully while naked men and women of the court took the healing waters, or lay with each other beside them. He could picture that, too. Probably the musicians had been behind a screen.

On the walls he saw frescoes, their colours faded. The light was good since the windows here had no coverings either. He walked over and looked. Men riding horses, playing polo. One of them was an emperor, you could tell from what he wore. Another panel showed a single horse with its handler. If the man was not a dwarf, this stallion was so large it made Daiyan's steppe horse look like a child's pony. He read the characters written beside the horse: *Great Crimson*. That was a famous name. The Emperor Taizu's Heavenly Horse from the farthest west.

Ren Daiyan looked more closely, being the new rider of a good horse. He doubted it had really been crimson. Reddish, maybe. It was a magnificent animal, looking alive on the wall after centuries. The painter had been very skilled.

The next panel showed more riders: a woman followed by two others, all richly clothed. The first of them was exquisite. She had gems in her hairpins, at her ears, about her throat. Wen Jian herself, it had to be. Behind the women were hills, and Daiyan realized they were the hills north of Ma-wai. North of here.

He looked at the pool again. He thought—for the second time—that he heard music. Could a place hold the memory of the sounds it had known?

He walked outside, filled with an unexpected sadness. He went towards the lake. It was bright in the sunlight, blue and white with waves in the wind. There were no boats, though he saw piers where they would have been moored. The lake was larger than he'd expected. To the southwest, he knew, it was skirted by a road that ran right down to the imperial road. A postal station inn along that shoreline had seen a great tragedy. He wondered if the inn was still standing, in use, or if it had been abandoned, burned, torn down as unlucky when the rebellion in the Ninth had finally ended.

He saw a small island, treed, overgrown. He remembered reading that there had been pavilions of alabaster and rosewood here where musicians made music, flute and *pipa* and drum, as boats carried the court lazily across the lake, back and forth, back and forth, while candles floated on evening waters.

He caught a scent of perfume from behind him. He ought not to have been able to do that. The wind was in his face.

He would never know for certain what made him *not* turn. Maybe it was that—the direction of the wind, but catching that scent. Something unnatural. He ought to have turned, he ought to have drawn his sword.

He shivered, a hard spasm. Then he remained very still, staring out over the water, but unseeing now, waiting. The hairs on the back of his neck rose up. He heard a footfall on the path. No sound of lost music any more. He didn't know what it was, this perfume, but there was a woman here.

He was afraid.

She said, "I let you see me in the wood. I gave you a chance to turn, go among people. You came here instead, alone. That was a choosing. I like when a man does that."

Her voice was low, slow, impossibly seductive. His mouth went dry. Desire swept over him, a wave surge far greater than anything in the wind-whipped waters. He couldn't speak.

Daiji, he was thinking. Fox-woman.

It was Ziji who feared all foxes, the tales of the *daiji,* who could change shape into a woman's form and destroy a man.

"I know your name," she whispered, a breath.

Her voice was a caress. It reached into him, around him, like sure fingers finding his manhood. And in it he heard, he was sure he heard, a threading of desire. Her own desire.

He did not turn. They could not compel you, that was the tale. They could lure you, draw you. You went to them, shaped by longing. How could a man say no to this? To them? They were immortal, or nearly so. They broke you with lovemaking in a woman's shape, endless, world-ending, leaving you a worn, wan husk of what you had been, returning to your village, city, farm, to find a hundred years or more had passed and everyone you knew was dead and the world changed.

He heard another step. She was right behind him. Her breath on his neck now, warm as an invitation at summer twilight. He was trembling. He stared desperately out at the water, at the isle.

She touched him. He closed his eyes. One finger, tracing a line down his back. She brought it up to his neck, and then slowly down again.

Daiyan forced his eyes open. He continued facing west, the water, the setting summer sun, but he was nearly sightless. He was fiercely aroused, erect—a channel for need. He was going to turn to her. How did you not? He was lost. He was about to be lost.

Her scent was all around him. He didn't know what it was. He could almost taste it, her. Her touch excited him beyond any previous understanding of desire. It shaped something near madness, a hunger. They were alone here, by the lake waters of Ma-wai, where music and lovemaking had held sway for so long.

He said, fighting hard for words, "*Daiji*, goddess, I have tasks in the world. In ... in this time."

She laughed, low in her throat.

The sound of it unknit his strength. His legs were weak. He thought, *I may fall down.* She touched his hair, beneath the black, pinned cap he wore. She was here, right behind him, and he realized the scent was *her,* not perfume. He would turn, he would gather her so ferociously and—

"Every man has tasks," she said. "I have seen so many of you. I may even have seen you before. I am eight hundred and fifty years old. I have been in the far south and west. I have been by river waters and by mountains. Some men embrace their duties, some flee from them. It is not a thing that matters to me."

"Goddess, I do not want to flee from mine."

He felt her breath again on his neck. She said, as if musing, "I could allow you to return to those, after. I can do that."

He closed his eyes again. They were not to be trusted, *daiji*. They did not share the world of men, only intersected it at times, like roads meeting in a darkness.

"Goddess, I am afraid."

"I am not a goddess, foolish man," she murmured, laughing again.

"To me you are," Daiyan managed to say.

"Am I? How do you know?" she whispered. He felt her touch him again. "You haven't kissed my mouth. Haven't looked into my eyes to see my need. Seen my body, what I am wearing for you, Ren Daiyan. Tasted what I will give you."

She would be wearing red. *Daiji* always did. Her fingernails would be red, her mouth would be ...

He wasn't able not to turn and take her to himself, for however long—years, decades, perhaps forever—she decreed it should be.

My own need.

It would end for him here. Weak with yearning, raw with it, he yet cursed his own folly. He ought to have carried on with his soldiers. He'd been among others, guarded by them. He ought to have understood that flash of colour in the wood in the rain. It had been orange. Like a tiger, yes, but also like a fox.

Xinan was so near, only down the road, half a day's ride on a good horse. The courts had gone back and forth so easily. And yet the city—the world—seemed unimaginably far away. Left behind when he'd left the road.

That could happen. That was why you didn't leave the road.

He realized there weren't any birds singing now. Had they

stopped in the moment the *daiji* appeared, when he'd caught her scent behind him, on the wrong side of the wind? Birds would fear a fox, and sense the uncanny when it came.

He was alone. In this place and in the world. No anchor to anywhere, to anyone, only a sense of duty, his foolish, vainglorious feeling of destiny since childhood. And what could that do or be against her, against this surge inside, when she was what she was and had come for him, here, today, beside these waters?

He ought to have gone to Xinan. To the vast, shattered ruin of the old capital where there were still people to be among, noise, confusion, chaos, protection, where even now, today ...

He took a breath.

Where even now ...

And so it was he found his anchor, amid the fever and force of the spirit world, amid such fierce desire, the waves that were upon him and inside him. Duty was not, it seemed, enough. You needed something more, however improbable—or unacceptable. You took your anchor to the mortal world where you found it, if you did.

He said, "*Daiji*, you may kill me. My life was in your hands from the wood in the thunderstorm, it seems."

"In my hands," she said, laughing again. "I like that." He thought of a fox, hearing that sound, untamed, wild.

He pushed on, fighting the ferocity of need. She would be beautiful beyond words or imagining. She could *make* herself so, if the tales were true. She was here, the tales *were* true.

He said, "I will not plead for my life, but for the needs of Kitai, what I want to do for it. I don't think ... I don't know if that means anything to you."

"It doesn't," she said almost gently. "*The needs of Kitai?* How could it? But why would I kill you, Ren Daiyan? Fear a tiger, need me. I want your mouth and your touch, I want all that is you for as long as we wish, while the sun and stars and the moon circle and circle us."

Circle and circle.

To what world, and when, would he return?

Anchor. Find it again. An image, lamplight in an evening room. Something from the mortal world. To hold to. To hold him. He remained very still. He realized he could do this, he wasn't trembling any more.

He said, "You should kill me. Because I will not come to you willingly, *daiji*, not away from what I was born to do."

Amusement again in the low voice. "Why would I care if it is willingly, Ren Daiyan? Because I am here, you were born to come to me."

He shook his head. "I will not believe that to be true."

She laughed yet again, a different note. "It excites me that you resist. My body is telling us so. Turn and see. I am showing it. When you are inside me, when all we know in the world is that, it will be sweeter, deeper."

"No," he said again. "I cannot be lost. I need to be in the world right now. Will you ... can you have pity, *daiji*?"

"No," she said simply. "It is not what I am."

He understood. She wasn't human, and pity was. He took a breath and he turned around, after all.

You faced the darkness when it came to you, or the light. You found your courage and your strength. He did not close his eyes.

He did stop breathing for a moment. The late sunlight was upon her. Heart-shaped face, pale skin, utterly smooth, long neck, wide, black eyes, long hair to her waist, blue-black, unbound. Her lips were, yes, red. Her fingernails were long and red. Her dress was red as he had known it would be. It was gauzy silk, moved by the wind, shaping to her body, showing it to him as she had said, and yes, she was aroused, he could see. She looked very young. She was not.

She smiled. Her teeth were small and white. She said, "No pity, but I will know your needs more surely than anyone ever has. Trust me in this, Ren Daiyan."

Anchor turning to shield, or to spar of wood, bobbing on river rapids or amid the huge, dark tumult of the sea (which he had never seen).

He said, clinging to that spar, desperately mortal, "My needs I have told you. Kill me if you must, but I will remain who I am as I die. I am sworn to one thing."

"And that is?" Her voice changed again; you could hear something not-human in it. She wore golden sandals, jewelled, open-toed. The wind swirled silk against her legs, gathered it at her thighs.

She was a river or the sea, he could end here.

He said, "To never forget our rivers and mountains lost. To bring them back."

One thing in his life, he'd just said. Almost true. It had been entirely true when he walked down to this shore. But now there was another thing, from the springtime, remembered. Spar in a storm.

The *daiji*, more beautiful than the heart could hold, smiled. "Bring them back? And a hundred years from now? Two hundred years? It matters where a border lies?"

Bit by bit, he was becoming aware he could stand here, before her. He said, slowly, "*Daiji*, I can only live in my own time. I cannot speak for those who come after, or what the world will be. We are not made that way."

She did not move. The wind moved, lifted her hair. He could not measure time here, with her. He was nearly lost in the red of her lips, the white teeth, the hard swell of her body, offering itself to him under silk, promising him, for as near to forever as the world allowed.

Nearly lost, but holding. She wore nothing under silk. Her eyes were so large. He could take a single step and kiss them shut. He could brush her lips with his. She would ...

As in a dream he heard her say, "This is not pity. I do not know what that is. I am curious, though. And can be patient. You may see me again or you may not. Go, Ren Daiyan, before I decide otherwise. You are being foolish, may leave this place for a cold, bitter life, but I will let you taste it."

He seemed to be trembling again, after all.

"Do you ... do you know the future, *daiji*?"

She shook her head. Her hair in the wind. Her earrings made a music with the motion. "I am not a goddess," she said. "Go."

Halfway to his horse, walking along the path, not looking back, with the lake and the *daiji* and the wind behind him, he felt a sudden, searing pain, white as a sword from the sun. He cried out, felt himself falling, unable to stop.

"A gift," he heard her calling down the path. "Remember me." Then he lost all awareness of the world.

CHAPTER XVI

She is still trying to decide what she most feels about Xinan: anxiety or heartbreak. There is something lost about the city. Ordinary life seems insignificant when people appear in sparse, scattered numbers—like islands, each one—on an avenue as wide as the imperial way. The scale of it mocks them, she thinks.

The Gate of Glory by the western wall, where she's gone several times now to drink tea under willow trees, is a magnificent reproach. There is too much irony in the name, in the ruin of the tower that once crowned the gates.

There have been efforts made by emperors to resettle Xinan over the years, she knows, urging people to move back, offering incentives. They have borne little fruit, and bitter. Few, it appears, want to live among so many ghosts. It was never the wisest choice for a capital in the first place, so far from the Grand Canal, a challenge to feed in times of drought. Xinan became what it was because the earliest emperors came from this region. This was the heartland. Many of them are buried nearby, in the great tombs.

It would be entirely possible, Shan thinks, to begin to hate the Ninth Dynasty if you spent time here. There is something oppressive, humiliating about how glorious it once was.

Who would want to live traversing the two colossal, almost-empty market spaces, each larger than many good-sized towns? The vendors and occasional entertainers and beggars seem adrift in the vastness. Scale and distance make you feel insignificant, your cherished life a pale, bitter thing, as if you were already another ghost.

Not her usual way of thinking. She is aware of feeling restless, on edge. It is hot, there have been thunderstorms all week. Her songs betray her mood. She throws most of them away. She has been thinking about leaving, going back to Yenling, or home to Hanjin, although the capital in summer is even hotter than this. She can leave a message here for Wai, he'll follow when he comes back south. She isn't certain why she lingers.

The inn where she's staying is good. The innkeeper has a bad leg, uses a stick to move about. His wife is sweet-natured, attentive to Shan, soft and pretty. Her husband looks at her with affection whenever they are in the same room. Interestingly, she looks at him the same way. They don't act or speak as if being in Xinan makes them feel diminished. Perhaps their expectations of the world haven't led them that way. Perhaps, Shan thinks, they have each other.

She has gone several times to a temple of the Path in the southeastern quadrant, seventy-first ward once, though that means nothing now with the ward gates gone and Xinan an open city, as they all are these days. No one is locked into a ward at night in the Twelfth Dynasty. Maybe they are better than the Ninth in this way, though when she reads of what women were allowed to do and be back then the thought frays at the edges.

She has made a generous donation to the temple and been granted access to their documents, scrolls going back four hundred years, at least, in no order at all, never sorted through. Tossed in chests, on shelves, piled on the floor in one room. Mice and insects have gotten to some of them. She combs through these scrolls without energy or enthusiasm, listless as a bored servant brushing her mistress's hair on a hot afternoon.

They are records of gifts to the temple, offered or requested prayers, itemized shipments of supplies: *Four kegs of Salmon River saffron wine,* and the price paid.

She does find a journal, from the years of the great rebellion when the city was looted and burned: an unnamed steward's chronicle of his efforts to keep a distinguished house safe in the back and forth of rebels and court. It describes the summer when the Tagurans had used a time of chaos to strike far into Kitai, looting Xinan—what was left of it—before retreating to their mountain plateau.

It is a taste of the past, a voice from across a chasm. She offers another gift and buys this one for the collection. It would have excited her once, doing so. She'd have waited eagerly for Wai to come back so she could show it to him, then they would take turns reading it to each other over tea or wine. Perhaps decide to find out more about this steward, what happened to him and that house. How the scroll came to be in the temple. There are so many stories, she thinks, and most of them end up lost.

SHE WRITES A LETTER to Lu Chen, makes the finding of the journal a part of it. The poet is alive and safe, his exile reduced to a family property near the Great River. She had sent him a song in spring, the one she wrote about him—sung by the girl with bound feet, in the Genyue, on the afternoon an arrow flew down from above.

That had been a complex day and evening, she thinks.

Lu Chen writes back now, to whatever she sends him. He honours her, doing so. He admires her *ci,* he says. He writes his own, sends them to her. She still tells him he is abusing the form, trying to erode the simpler themes of the song form, turning it into an extension of formal verse. She'd said that to him as a girl, the first day they met, in Xi Wengao's garden. It frightens her, how long ago that is.

It is clear the poet enjoys when she engages with him like this. He teases her with sly verses, inviting laughter. Shan wants him to challenge her. He keeps doing what he's doing—offering courtesy, wit, attention.

He has invited her—with her husband—to visit East Slope. She would like to be there now, Shan thinks in the vastness of Xinan. She imagines harmony, civility, discourse under shade trees, laughter.

Master Lu's brother and son are in the far north, or perhaps already back in Hanjin. Lu Chao had been named imperial emissary to some tribe in revolt against the Xiaolu. That uprising is being assessed, she knows, as an opportunity. Lu Chao, summoned from exile, had been an unusual choice for the mission—unless they wanted him dead, she remembers thinking.

There are easier ways to kill a man. Her father had explained it to her: Prime Minister Hang Dejin, since retired to an estate near Yenling, almost certainly had not wanted to send the army north. By dispatching Lu Chao, famously independent, he'd addressed his concern. If Chao urged a treaty and military action with this tribe, it would be an honest view from an experienced man. If he came home arguing against an alliance, it could not possibly be said to be a coerced or dishonest position.

The new prime minister, Kai Zhen, had arrived back at court and immediately begun talking of the glorious opportunity presented to them. It would take a brave man to speak against the prime minister, her father wrote Shan.

The Lu brothers are nothing if not courageous. That much is obvious, has been for a long time. From Lu Chen's letters, it seems sometimes as if the poet has decided that, having survived Lingzhou, there is nothing more in life he needs to fear.

She'd memorized—and promptly burned—the last poem he

sent before she left home to come here, a reply to her song from the imperial garden. She doubts hers was the only copy of the verse, however. Burning it protects her but not him.

> *When a child is born*
> *The family prays it will be intelligent.*
> *Intelligence having ruined my life,*
> *I only hope the baby will grow up*
> *Ignorant and foolish.*
> *Then he'll be successful all his days*
> *And be recalled to court as prime minister!*

Shan remembers blood rushing to her face as she read the words. She can flush recalling them now. A kind of awe. Who dared write this way? Even as she'd laughed in breathless astonishment, she'd looked around to be sure she was alone. The paper had felt hot in her hands, the characters of the poem were flames. She'd sent them to the fireplace, turned them to ash.

SHE'D DECIDED TO GO to Long Lake Park this morning but the innkeeper's wife had urged her to wait—another storm was coming, she said. The morning sky had been clear, but Shan wasn't feeling assertive or emphatic about anything, and she'd agreed to stay close to the inn.

She's written to the poet, then her father. Just before midday the storm strikes. The sky grows so wild and black she can't even write in her room. She stands near the window and watches the lightning, listens to thunder boom and crack over Xinan.

After it passes she moves out onto the wet balcony. Already she can feel a sweet coolness to the air. It won't last, but the rain has settled the summer dust and Shan hears birdsong. There is rainwater in the stopped-up fountain in the courtyard below. The leaves of the pear trees glisten.

She tells one of her girls to summon the litter-bearers and her guards and she heads for Long Lake Park. It is midsummer, the days are long, she will be back before dark, even in a city so vast.

She smiles at the innkeeper's wife when she goes downstairs. "Thank you for the warning," she says. The woman looks pleased, glances down and away. Shan misses her father suddenly. Maybe she will go home after all.

I want a child, she thinks, out of nowhere like the storm, startling herself. *I want a child.*

Long Lake Park is in the farthest southeastern sector of the city, by the wall. It had been the people's park, unlike the imperial one behind the palace, where the feral dogs had frightened her.

This sector is also the highest in Xinan. From here the city is laid out before you, neat in its symmetry, appalling in its ruin. You can see as far as the palace in the north and the Gate of Glory to the west, with its broken tower.

There is another tower here, an important Cho sanctuary once, ten storeys high. It still stands but isn't safe, her guards tell her— the stairways are crumbling and the floors above the third level are uncertain. There are marks of fire on the outside walls, she sees. It is probably going to fall soon, the taller of the two guards tells her. He's the one who looks at her for longer than he should when he speaks.

She thinks about climbing it, at least partway, but there is a line between independence and foolishness. If she is injured, the four men with her will suffer for it.

There are paths through the park, overgrown with weeds and coarse grass and wildflowers. It is possible to imagine what this place was like, however: sunlight, bright boats on the water, horsemen and horsewomen, a polo game, music, the green grass groomed, and the flower beds. Fruit trees and locust trees and willows near the water. Chan Du, most moving of all poets, had been here one day, had written a famous poem:

... the lady with jade pins in cloud-coiled hair,
Wearing the scent only she is permitted.
She rides past the drifted snow of willow catkins
And flowers bend towards her.

Wen Jian, of course, had died young. One of the Four Great Beauties, the last of them. She wasn't someone to envy. More a matter of thinking about what happened to women who shone too brightly. *When the music was still playing, grief came upon us ...*

And *that* was a dark thought. Shan gives her men permission to take her home. They have been waiting for that, she knows. The sun is west and they've a long way to carry her.

She is in bed early and surprises herself by falling asleep. She wakes in the night, though, she often does when travelling. It is very late. The inn is quiet. There are few guests this summer. She hears the sound of the water clock. She wraps her robe around herself and goes out on the balcony, looking at the eastern sky. The last quarter moon is up, hanging in the branches of a tall tree in the courtyard, half hidden by leaves. It is very beautiful. She watches it so long it frees itself and climbs above the leaves among the stars.

ᴔ

Daiyan didn't know how long he'd been lying on the path. He felt a strangeness to the air, and to the feel of his own body. He sat up, then stood, carefully. Started walking. No pain, but something had altered. *To remember me*, she'd said, the *daiji*. He didn't know what that meant, but how would he have been likely to forget her? The memory could arouse him again.

If he turned back? If he stood by the water (the wind calmer now) would she come to him again, hair drifting free? Poems sometimes described lovemaking as "clouds and rain." He thought about that.

Not a useful line of reflection. He came to his horse. He

untethered it, mounted, left Ma-wai under the same archway through which he'd entered.

He kicked the horse to a gallop. There was a need to be alert. It was late in the day, and the road could be dangerous, especially after darkfall, for a lone man riding. Bandits, animals, his horse could stumble and fall, break a leg. You could lose a road at night. Dangers, he thought, of ordinary life in the ordinary world. The moon was waning, would offer little brightness, and not until later.

He rode. He still felt strange, shifting his shoulders as if something prickled, or as if he was being watched, from the woods, from the fields.

He could so easily have been lost back there. To strange music, the spirit world, to beauty, desire, time. It seemed to Daiyan that if he closed his eyes he would see her, catch the scent that had come to him from the wrong side of the wind. Clouds and rain. The glory of her mouth, silk blown against and around her thighs. *I know your name*, she had said. *Taste what I will give you.*

He shook his head, urged his horse onward, riding down the raised centre of the road (reserved for the court or imperial couriers, once) at a speed that suggested he was fleeing something.

Or racing to something else. There would be lights ahead, even in fire-scarred, ghost-haunted Xinan. The presence of people abroad. Or in the loud barracks outside the walls where his men would be. Or an inn. Yes, that. A place where he could drink a great deal of wine and think about the image that had come into his mind, that he had clung to inwardly, as he turned to look at the *daiji*, into those eyes, at her hair free of hairpins in the breeze.

He was reckless with the horse, riding too fast as darkness fell on the empty road. It seemed to him, in a way that made no sense, that he could not possibly fall from a horse on this road and die, or be killed by thieves lying in wait. Not tonight, after what he had just encountered. The world could not unfold that way, he thought.

It could, of course. He was wrong. Danger is not protection from danger. Tigers can follow fox-women, lightning follow lightning. But he did survive that ride as the sun went down and ushered the stars into the summer dark. His horse's hooves drummed that ancient road and the Xiaolu stallion did not lose the way or stumble. Daiyan heard an owl hunting once as he went, from the woods to his left, and the sharp, cut-off cry of whatever it was that starlight's cold killer had been pursuing.

Not him. Not tonight, at least.

The moon was just rising when he saw the lights of Xinan ahead of him and came up to one of the northern gates, beside the empty palace's burnt walls.

Once, the city gates would have been locked at sunset, no entry without an imperial pass until the dawn drums sounded. You were beaten if you tried to get in after curfew—over the walls, swimming along the canals. Here, in this much-changed time, cities remained open, men came in and out after dark, moved freely, spent money, let noise and lanterns and music carry them through the night hours if they chose.

Just outside the wall, Daiyan reined up to think. He patted his horse's neck. The animal was brave and strong and had moved at speed for a long time. It was possible to love a horse, he realized.

On impulse, or perhaps not, he removed the over-tunic that marked him as a soldier and revealed his rank. Soldiers entering cities needed to identify themselves. In the way of thinking for a long time, *they* were a danger. He decided he wasn't going to carry on all the way around the wall and west to the barracks. He folded the tunic into his saddlebag and entered Xinan between torches at the gate. He nodded to the bored guards there. They weren't guarding against anything much. Not here, not any more.

The palace loomed on his left, empty, dark. His own emperor slept, or lay awake, in another city a long way east.

He knew Xinan a little by now. They'd been in the barracks for some time before he'd had that idea of going north into Xiaolu lands alone. It had seemed a useful plan. It wasn't unfolding that way, necessarily.

He'd never ridden through Xinan by night, however. There were people about, but nothing like in Hanjin, or even Jingxian after dark. Those he saw seemed scattered, like pieces on a game board at the end of a game. He found himself on the wide immensity of the imperial way. He'd felt empowered, excited, *expanded* by the size of it the first morning he'd been here, earlier this summer. He'd seen it as a symbol of what Kitai had been—and could be again. The past wasn't a burden, it was a challenge. They could be worthy of it. His life, he had thought, was all about achieving that.

Shortly after arriving he'd sent his entire company into the city at intervals, had the leaders walk or ride them in formation down this avenue. He'd spoken to them at the barracks afterwards. He had told his soldiers that their task, their shared ambition, was to become worthy of that roadway from the palace to the southern gate. He'd spoken strongly, he'd *felt* strong.

It was different at night, under stars and a just-risen moon, alone, his horse's hooves echoing. The imperial way was nearly empty, there was nothing here but vastness. Men would be in wine shops, at small night markets, food stalls, singing girl houses. Or asleep in their beds.

He turned off the imperial way, and turned again, and then again. He came to his destination, without having fully acknowledged to himself this was where he'd been going all along.

He gave the horse to a sleepy stableboy, ordered it rubbed down, given water and food. He offered a handful of coins for the labour. He didn't count them out, saw the boy's startled surprise, watched him lead the horse away.

He stood a moment in the dark street before the inn's locked door. The boy led the horse into a stable yard, the hoofbeats receding. There was no one abroad. Daiyan turned away from the inn's door without knocking. He walked a little distance from the stable. He climbed the stone wall and dropped down silently into a courtyard.

It was a good inn, the best in the city. There was a fountain, not flowing any more, though rainwater had collected from the storm, he saw. There were trees around the edges of the courtyard and beside the fountain. He couldn't have explained what he was doing here, entering this way, over the wall like a thief.

He walked to the fountain. He looked up and saw the moon, which had cleared the horizon and the wall. He turned to look back at the inn, three storeys tall, in the summer night.

She was standing on her balcony, wrapped in a robe, and she was looking down at him.

Spar by the lake at Ma-wai. Held in his mind as he turned to face a *daiji*. Real now, in the night. Here. An image holding a man to the world, keeping him from being lost. He was afraid again. A different kind of fear. There were different kinds.

He moved slowly forward to stand below her. He lifted his open hands out from his sides. He said, quietly, directing his voice, the way you learned to do when you commanded others, "I mean no harm, my lady. We have ... met each other before."

"I know who you are, Commander Ren," she said.

It was dark where he was, down in the courtyard, only a waning moon behind him. He wasn't wearing his military tunic.

"How?" he asked. Her hair was loose on her shoulders.

She said nothing to that, only stood there, looking down. He heard wind chimes in the branches of one tree behind him.

He said, "Forgive me."

The chimes, wind in leaves.

She said, "We will wake someone. You may come up."

IT IS AS IF SHE'S EXHAUSTED all her courage with those words. It is one thing to challenge the world, but she's just invited a man into her bedchamber at night.

She leaves the balcony, re-enters the room. There is always a small brazier left burning for her, a wine vessel and candles beside it. She lights a candle at the brazier and crosses the room to use that to light the lamp on the desk they have provided for her. It is understood that she wakes in the night and writes sometimes.

Her hands are shaking, she sees. It is difficult, in fact, to deal with the candle and the lamp. Her heart is beating very fast.

She is lighting the second lamp, beside her bed, when she hears a sound from the balcony and he climbs over the railing there. She blows out the candle, sets it down, turns to look at him. She places her hands inside her sleeves, folded before her. They are still trembling.

The bed linens, she sees, are in disarray. Of course they are. She can feel that her cheeks are flushed. She moves away from the bed, towards her desk.

He stops just inside the room. The night is behind him, and the moon in the window. He bows, twice. "Forgive me," he says again.

"I invited you, Commander Ren." It would be easier, she thinks, if her hands would only be still.

He inclines his head. He seems calm, self-possessed. She remembers that about him.

"I am able to report to you, Lady Lin, that your honourable husband will be kept safe in the north."

"I was unaware he was in danger," she says. Which is true.

"I have outraced tidings. There has been trouble across the river. Someone killed Xiaolu soldiers, took horses. I had my soldiers move people into Shuquian in the event there was a response. I sent my best officer to your husband."

"The one I met?" she asks. "The one who loosed an arrow at me?"

Her hands are all right now, mostly.

He seems uneasy for the first time. She doesn't know if that is good. She doesn't know why she's asked him up. Or, she doesn't want to think about it, more accurately.

He says, "Yes, my lady. Deputy Commander Zhao."

She nods. "My husband can be difficult when someone tries to take him from his work for the collection."

A first, faint smile. She remembers him with their bronze bells, how he'd known about them.

He says, "Deputy Commander Zhao can be difficult at all times, my lady."

She feels herself smiling, doesn't want it seen for some reason. "A battle of sorts, then?"

"I am quite sure we will have protected your honourable husband, my lady."

She nods her head again, tries to make it brisk. "I am being ungracious to a guest. I have wine. Will you let me warm a drink for you?"

He looks awkward again. "My lady, I have ridden all day and until just now tonight. I am embarrassed. My clothing, my boots."

Some things can be addressed, if one is able to think clearly.

"Do not give this a thought. You have brought me reassuring word. I am grateful. There is a basin of water on that table by the wall. I will pour the wine and then sit at my desk to leave you privacy. You may take a tunic of my husband's from the chest when you have washed."

"I dare not presume so much."

She laughs quietly. "If your men saved his life, I think you may."

She turns, not waiting for him to reply. She is pleased to see that her fingers are steady when she picks up the wine and seats it on the stand over the brazier. She readies two cups, keeping her back to the room.

She hears him moving, a grunt, the sound of boots removed. Then other sounds, water splashing softly. She is thinking about what he has told her—a way of not thinking about anything else.

She says, still facing away from him, "Commander, why were your men even up by Shuquian?"

A pause, she can picture him hesitating over the basin. He says, his voice careful, "Routine patrolling along the river. We need to understand the conditions there."

"Do you? Are they not other commanders' prefectures up north?"

For the second time, amusement in his tone. "Do you study the military divisions of Kitai as well as shaping poetry, Lady Lin?"

"Not in any detail," she murmurs.

The wine isn't ready yet. A dipped finger (which one isn't suppose to do) tells her as much. She crosses to her desk, head averted. She sits beside the lamp there. There is a silence. Then, whatever this encounter has been, it becomes something else.

He says, "I am sorry. I spoke untruthfully. The trouble north of the river was caused by me. I crossed the border, disguised, to see what I could discover. Zhao Ziji brought others of our company north, out of concern. I killed four Xiaolu horsemen. Took two horses."

She spins around. She had said she would not. *Why did you do that?* she wants to say, but also, *Why are you telling me this?*

But words aren't there for her. He is bent over the basin, bare to the waist, his back to her. She sees what she sees. She brings both hands to her mouth.

In Hanjin, in her home, the night of the day he'd blocked an arrow in the Genyue with his shield, she and her father had heard him say, *I was born into the world to win them back.*

Now she sees his upper body. His naked back. She tries to imagine a man doing this. She cannot.

Through her fingers, she whispers, "When ... when did you have that done to you?"

He turns quickly. Sees her looking at him.

"My lady! You said—!" He stops. He takes a step back, away from her, stands against the wall beside the balcony, as if trying to find a place to defend himself. From her?

"Have what done?" he asks, his voice altered. "What do you see?"

Her eyes widen. "You don't know?"

"Lady Lin. Please. *What do you see?*"

She brings her hands down. Slowly, carefully, she tells him.

Sees him close his eyes, leaning against the wall. He stays like that.

"You really didn't know?" she repeats.

He shakes his head. He opens his eyes, looks at her, she makes herself hold his gaze. He takes a step from the wall, standing very straight now, facing her. He holds a square of fabric in one hand, he had been washing himself. There are droplets of water on his face and torso.

He draws a breath. He says, "My lady, I did not just come to report about your husband. Not so late at night."

Instinctively, she folds her hands in her sleeves again, then changes her mind and lets them fall to her sides. She waits. Her heartbeat, again.

He says, very quietly, "I met a *daiji* this afternoon by the lake at Ma-wai."

The words drop into the stillness of the room like pebbles into a pool. Shan looks at him. She is aware she is holding her breath.

He says, "She did this to me, when I went away from her."

She makes herself breathe. She is biting her lip. A bad habit. She says, carefully, "You lay with a fox-woman today and you are—"

"No. I did not. I was ... I was able to look at her and then walk away."

"I ... didn't think men could do that. If the tales ... if they are true."

He looks, she is thinking, like a man who truly has gone into the spirit world. It never occurs to her not to believe him. She thinks about that, later. His eyes and his voice, and what she's seen on his back.

"I didn't think so either," Ren Daiyan says. He sets the cloth down by the basin, so he stands empty-handed before her, shirtless, and he says, "I did so by thinking of you."

Then, after another moment, he adds, "I am sorry, my lady. I have shamed myself. I will go now. Please turn your back again while I dress."

She finds she cannot speak. It seems brighter in the room, though, and not from moonlight or the lamps.

WHAT DO YOU SEE? he'd asked, and she'd told him, standing on the far side of the room in a green robe, beside the lamp on her writing desk.

Never forget our rivers and mountains lost.

Those were the characters. The *daiji* had fixed his own words, his lifelong heart's desire, onto his body. He was tattooed like a western barbarian, a compelled soldier, a criminal branded with his crime.

But this was different. This was from the spirit world. He understood now why he'd felt that searing blade of pain as he'd walked away from the lake. He had passed out, lost the world. He'd rejected the *daiji*, as she thought, for his task in the world, and she'd given what she'd called a gift—to remember her by. Remember the lost prefectures, or remember a lost world of delight—that could have taken him away from this toil.

The *daiji* hadn't known (he believed) about the spar in his mind. The woman standing here now.

He heard himself telling Lin Shan, after all, about Ma-wai, how he'd been able to turn and face a fox-woman and still hold to the world, to his own time, to mortal life, because of her, because of the mortal woman in this room.

He hadn't meant to say it. He didn't think he'd meant to say it, coming here. He hadn't meant to come here. He didn't think he'd meant to come here.

He hadn't thought she'd be on the balcony.

Could a man be any more confused? He didn't know, today, tonight, what he thought. About anything. How was the world intended to unfold? Was it fine silk unwound in a merchant's shop? Or a stained hemp cloth opened to reveal the dagger that ended a life?

He said the only thing he could think to say, having confessed what he hadn't known he would confess.

"I will go now. Please turn your back again while I dress."

He would put on his sweat-stained tunic, his boots, climb down again (he was good at that, he was skilled at all such things), reclaim his tired horse, and make his way to the barracks. Where he should have gone in the first place.

The woman's hands were by her sides. He had seen that they'd been shaking, before. He was observant, he'd always been observant. Her courage, and trust in him, had been very great. The hands weren't trembling now, he saw, and she didn't turn her back on him.

Her voice was gentle. She said, "The characters. The calligraphy. The ... the *daiji* did this in the emperor's hand, Ren Daiyan. Slender Gold. You are marked as no one has ever been."

"You believe me?" he asked.

It mattered a great deal, he realized. He scarcely believed himself, his own story. Fox-woman's scent, wind blowing the other way. Red silk in that wind. He heard wind chimes behind him now, outside.

"I think I must. I have seen your back. They are flawless, the characters. How should we imagine we understand all things under heaven?"

He was silent, looking at her.

"You are very composed," she said. "If that just happened today." She finally turned, but only to go to the brazier. She lifted the wine vessel and poured out two cups.

I need to go, he thought. She turned back to him, cups in hand.

"Composed? No. I am ... not myself. I would not be intruding here otherwise. I am sorry, my lady."

"You can stop saying that," she said. "I am ... honoured that in some way I helped keep you among us, Commander Ren." She crossed the room, extended a cup. He took it. She was too close.

He said, "Qi Wai will be safe. I am very sure."

She smiled at that. "You said. I believed you." She sipped from her wine. He put his down untouched, beside the basin. "Will you turn around?" she said. "I would see those characters again."

He turned around. What else was he going to do? She put her cup beside his. A moment later he felt her finger on the first character on his back, right side, at the top. *Never forget.*

Slender Gold, the emperor's brush. He was not himself tonight. He was looking at the moon, above the courtyard wall and trees. Self-control was something in which he had always taken pride. His goals were held before him. Life steered by them, as by a star. He had walked away from a *daiji* today. He was still here, in this world. Because of her.

He cleared his throat. "My lady, this is difficult. I am not entirely able to ..."

She was following the second character down, then back up, then to the third, as if making the brush strokes. The *mountains*, the *rivers*.

"Not able to do what?" she asked, and she was closer than the fox-woman had been. He heard strain in her voice. He closed his eyes, facing the moon.

"To show ... proper respect, if you do this," he said.

"Good," said Lin Shan, and finished tracing the last character, low on his back: *lost.*

He turned and took her in his arms.

TWO THINGS SHAN remembers later, from the time after he brought her to the bed, from when they were together there. One is astonished, breathless laughter rising in her, the release of it.

"What is amusing?" he'd asked, and she told him how she'd just then been trying to remember a passage from *The Dark Girl and the Emperor*, one of the old texts of lovemaking, a trick women could do.

He laughs (a relief, that he does) and tells her, "You need not, Shan. This is not a pleasure house."

And so, "No pleasure?" she'd asked, making her voice go upwards in false indignation. He'd laughed again, then lowered his mouth to her breasts, one and then the other, answering her that way.

The second thing, later, when he is above her, inside her. He pauses, leaving her suspended in a never-known place between need and something near to pain, and he says, "You must know I am yours, all my days."

"That is good," she says, her body open to him, to his gaze.

He says, after a moment, "You understand I am a soldier."

She nods her head.

"And that there may be war."

Again, she nods. In that moment her hands are on his back, needing him even closer, deeper in, urgently—and the fingers of her left hand find the character for *Never forget*.

She does not know, then, or now, in morning light, after he has gone, what this all means, what it *can* mean, if anything at all, but she knows it isn't contained by what had been her life before she'd stood on the balcony and seen him by the fountain.

She isn't thinking clearly, Shan decides, but she feels the world and her body as new today, even amid the ruins of Xinan.

MID-AFTERNOON A MESSAGE comes from him—a strong, clear hand—thanking her for wine. She laughs, reading it.

That night he is in the courtyard again, and then her room, her arms, hungry for her, astonishingly so. After lovemaking, he talks—like a man who has never had a chance to do that. She learns of Shengdu and his parents, about bamboo swords and the teacher who left in a time of drought.

She hears of how he'd left the world he knew, still a boy, after killing seven men, becoming an outlaw himself. And then the day he'd left that behind. He tells her—as he had in Hanjin—how his whole life has felt to be pointing him, like a spear, to battles in the north. Regaining their lost glory. He says he feels as if he has been marked for this all his days, and cannot explain it.

But her hand is on his back again (she is drawn, almost helplessly, to tracing the characters there) and she knows this about him, by now.

He asks her (no one ever has) to talk about her life. She says, "The next time, perhaps? What I want to do now doesn't involve talking."

"Are we back with the Dark Girl?" he asks, laughing a little, but she hears the change in his voice, knows he is aroused, and it pleases her, and startles her, that she can do this to him with a few words spoken.

"She never went away," Shan says.

THE MOON RISES, leaves the window again. The man leaves her again, as he must. Another note comes late in the morning, to where she sits at her writing desk. She is very tired. She knows why.

The letter tells her he has been summoned to Hanjin and the court, must leave that same morning. "I mean everything I have said to you," he writes.

He had been able to walk away from a *daiji* only because of her, he had said. And, *I am yours, all my days.*

Lin Shan, the clever one, too tall and thin, overly educated for a woman—a discredit, it is widely said, to her sex—has never thought of herself this way. As someone to whom such words could be spoken. It is a gift, she thinks. The world holds something it has never held before.

༄

In fact, the summons turned out to be a lie. It was not from the court.

Daiyan would not learn that for some days. Responding to it, he rode east that morning, alone again, because he needed to be alone with his thoughts.

Ziji caught up to him, however, on his own new Xiaolu horse, having returned to the barracks the evening before and following east immediately—and that was all right. Ziji being with him was all right.

He thought about hiding the *daiji's* marks from him, knowing Ziji had always feared fox-women, something in his youth, but there was no point—they would be seen eventually.

So he showed his friend on the first night, readying for sleep in an imperial inn, and he told him the truth of what had happened at Ma-wai. Most of the truth.

Ziji was as disturbed as he'd expected him to be. As anyone would be?

"You just walked away from her? Because you ..."

Because of the spar. But that, Lin Shan, was his own. Needed to be private. He said, "You are looking at the reason. The characters on my back. She marked me with what I said to her."

"She just let you go? You were able to do that?"

He sat down on his bed, visibly shaken.

"She called it a gift. It doesn't feel like one. Maybe it is."

"The calligraphy is ..."

"The emperor's. I know."

"How do you know? Who told you?"

A mistake. "A few at the barracks saw it," he said. "Then I used a bronze to look. I am not going to hide this. It may even help, in some way."

"Backwards, the characters in a mirror."

"Yes, but you can tell Slender Gold, even reversed."

"She let you go?" Ziji said again, wonderingly. And then, "I don't like this at all."

"I know you don't," said Daiyan. "I didn't want it, you know."

"Are you sure?" said Ziji. An odd question. Then he turned on his side on his bed and fell asleep, or seemed to do so.

THEY WERE WAYLAID some days later, a little west of Yenling. It was done brazenly, right on the imperial road, in summer's bright daylight.

Just before the men appeared and surrounded them, Daiyan had been thinking of his father. He'd been picturing him at his desk in the *yamen*, imagined as younger than he would be now. He was as he'd been all those years ago when his son left home. He'd been thinking about that, his father, while riding a Xiaolu horse on a road far away, wondering if he'd ever see him again.

CHAPTER XVII

Dun Yanlu had been chief of the personal guard of former prime minister Hang Dejin for almost twenty years. A prime minister had access, of course, to all the guardsmen of Hanjin, and could claim soldiers in the imperial army, as well. But he was permitted one hundred guards of his own, in uniforms that indicated that allegiance, and Yanlu had commanded these for a long time.

He still did so, though their number, by regulation, was now twenty, since Minister Hang had withdrawn into retirement near Yenling.

The favoured eldest son, Hang Hsien, had been the one to tell the guards they were free to leave and would be paid off handsomely (this proved to be true) for their service, depending on how long they had been with the prime minister.

In the event, the majority of them chose to seek positions elsewhere in the capital, though none ended up in the guard of the new prime minister. There was far too much suspicion between the two men for that to happen. Even Dun Yanlu, who would never have called himself the sharpest of thinkers, knew that much.

His own strengths were loyalty and steadiness. He respected the son but he loved the father. He cursed the way of fate that had brought blindness upon the old man, forcing him from the court where he was still needed, to this distant estate.

Fourteen guardsmen had elected to join Yanlu in coming to Little Gold Hill. He'd recruited four others, evaluating competence carefully, though it had to be admitted that really capable men were unlikely to choose serving a retired minister in the countryside. The pay was excellent, but boredom was a factor, lack of opportunity another. They weren't even in Yenling itself, no access to the evening pleasures of the empire's second city: the estate was most of a day's ride west.

In fact, the son, Hsien, had suggested to Yanlu recently that it might be time for him to think of marrying, starting a family. He had their permission, would always be welcome at Little Gold Hill, whatever came.

Yanlu knew what that meant. It meant *after my father dies*.

It was a generous thing to say. Hang Hsien was a good man. It wasn't really fair for Yanlu to blame him for their isolated life here. But if Hsien had been a stronger, more compelling man, wouldn't he be prime minister himself now? Instead of the one who was led around on a donkey's lead by degenerate wives and a eunuch.

There was no love lost for Kai Zhen among the men at Little Gold Hill. Not that it mattered. They were all retired now. Their lives had already begun to follow the routine and the rounds of the countryside. The guardsmen were farm workers as much as anything else. The estate was prosperous and there was always work to be done. In addition, they were on alert for the villages around, to deal with outlaws, fires, animals, even murders, if the magistrate from Yenling sent word asking them to. The magistrate did ask, once he understood that the former prime minister was happy to have his guards play this role. It placed the man in their debt, even Yanlu could understand that, but he didn't see how it would matter.

A quiet life, after Hanjin and the palace. It was likely, Yanlu decided, that his days of pride at being near to important men and moments were over. You drank from whatever cup you were offered. A man had a limited span to live, and a more limited time to amount to anything. He wasn't young any more. They were allowing him to marry, had assured him of a place.

There were worse ways to grow old, he thought, imagining a young body warming his on winter nights, bringing him ale or sweetened wine in the heat of summer. There were girls on the estate who were easy to look at. One had a ripe, promising figure. Yanlu had no family name, no false pride, it made things easier.

Then one afternoon a messenger arrived on a horse pushed hard, and not long after Dun Yanlu was summoned to the writing pavilion in the garden. It was summer, midday, hot. Hsien was with his father, no one else. The messenger had been sent to the main house for a meal and a rest.

Yanlu was given his instructions in the old man's measured tones: tomorrow he was to waylay two men riding east along the imperial road and bring them to the estate.

Descriptions were precise, even to horses (very good ones), clothing, and weapons carried—the men had been observed as they came east. Hang Dejin still employed couriers loyal to him, with access to the fastest horses at posting inns along the way.

The two men, he was informed, were to be treated with respect, not harmed. They were to be disarmed and brought to the farm with extreme discretion. They were dangerous, Yanlu was advised.

He selected five men, two of them archers, though he was old-fashioned and didn't really trust bowmen. He dressed, the next morning, with pride, happy to be in action again, to be serving. He felt no need to understand what was happening. He wasn't one of those men who was always guessing at the purposes of his betters.

One of the girls he liked smiled at him from where she was feeding the chickens as the six guards rode out. He still looked good on horseback, in uniform, Dun Yanlu decided, squaring his shoulders. It was early morning, not yet hot.

IT WENT VERY EASILY. Yanlu was prepared to say as much if asked by the father or the son back at Little Gold Hill.

Other than a single look exchanged between them, followed by a brief hand gesture from the younger man, the two soldiers had proved to be no trouble at all. Not surprising, given that six armed men had emerged from both sides of the road in a deserted spot and surrounded them.

Yanlu had spoken courteously, but he'd left no ambiguity as to their intentions. The two men were going to be relieved of their weapons and taken off the road right there.

Their destination? It would be revealed. Their weapons? Would be returned, depending on how they conducted themselves. (He was guessing at that.) They sat their horses coolly, unsmiling, but did not resist as two of Yanlu's men went forward and took swords and bows from them. The archers, on opposite sides of the roadway, kept their arrows trained on the soldiers throughout.

Yanlu did see that curious expression flicker between the two men, although he wasn't skilled at reading such looks. It was likely to have been apprehension. Frightened men behaved in a variety of ways. You didn't have to be a sage or a scholar to know that, just to have commanded men for a time.

BACK AT LITTLE GOLD HILL, bowing the two soldiers into the former prime minister's presence, a successful day began to change, in ways that were not pleasing.

"Thank you for coming, commander, deputy commander," the old man said gravely. "It is kind of you." Yanlu saw both soldiers bow twice, properly.

"You are very welcome, sir," said the younger one. It seemed he was the commander, not the older, bigger man.

"You were also good to spare my guards." Hang Dejin's expression was difficult to read, but Yanlu's ears pricked up. *What was he saying?*

"Little point wasting six lives." The answer was brisk. "You had their leader wear your livery, after all."

"I didn't, in truth. I was certain he would, though, once given the task of bringing you here."

There was a silence, then startling, unexpected anger from that younger soldier. "What? You *know* we'd have killed them if he hadn't worn that uniform. And you let him ..."

"I was quite certain he would. As I just indicated. Will you take wine, Commander Ren?"

"Not yet, thank you. I am unhappy. You played with lives today."

"I have few diversions in retirement," Hang Dejin murmured.

"My lord!" Dun Yanlu had heard enough. "This arrogant soldier is failing to respect you. I ask permission to discipline him."

"Denied. Commander Ren, will you help train my guard commander? He is a good man, one I trust and value."

Train? Yanlu felt himself flushing, despite the praise.

"I am not inclined to do so, just now," said the younger soldier. The older one, careful and watchful, had not said a word.

"Indulge an old, blind man," said Hang Dejin.

"And you will explain why we are here?"

"Of course."

The younger soldier turned to Yanlu. "Very well. You had the archers too close to the road and directly across from each other. Never do that." His voice was matter-of-fact. "When we dismounted, my horse was behind me, the other was moved ahead by Commander Zhao. If we had let our reins go, and dropped and rolled towards each of your bowmen, there is a good chance one or both might have shot the other. The archer on the north side was visibly nervous, likely to let fly without thought if either of us moved on him. Ziji?"

"Both archers had improper grips, thumbs wrongly positioned, they were not going to loose arrows accurately. It is a common error, easily corrected. The other four of you still had your swords sheathed when we dismounted. Courteous, but careless. You were also too close to us. We'd have taken the archers first, as Commander Ren has said. I can generally deal with two civic guardsmen with little difficulty, and Commander Ren, who is particularly an archer, would have had the choice of using the bow of whichever man he killed to shoot the other two swordsmen if they didn't rush him— or drawing his own sword if they did."

Ren Daiyan added, "Your youngest guard, the small man, west side—his sword belt is too high. He needs to wear a shorter sword or become an archer. The blade drags the ground unless he pushes it up, and that means he can't unsheathe it properly."

"I know," muttered Yanlu, unhappily. "I have told him."

"He wants the long sword for the look of it. It is understandable. But it doesn't work for him."

"I know," said Dun Yanlu again.

"You were all dead men as soon as you came up on the roadway," said Ren Daiyan. Yanlu understood who this was now, the man had a reputation. "It would not have taken us long, I'm afraid. There are ways of surrounding and forcing the surrender of armed, capable men. If we have time, we will be honoured to share thoughts with you."

He could have said *teach you*, Yanlu realized. He hadn't.

Ren Daiyan turned back to the former prime minister. "My lord, you were reckless with six lives, and you say you value this man."

"I also said I was certain he'd wear the uniform."

"'Quite certain' was the phrase. Yes, I heard. And you were as certain that I would see it and react to it?"

"I was."

Ren Daiyan shook his head.

"Is he shaking his head?" the old man asked his son.

"He is," said Hsien, amused.

A moment later, for the first time, the man named Ren Daiyan also smiled. He shook his head again.

"Are you enjoying your retirement, my lord?" he asked.

The blind man laughed. Yanlu didn't understand. He didn't expect to. He was thinking about his archers, directly opposite each other, north and south of the road. And Kou Chin *would* change swords from today, or be dismissed.

Ren Daiyan waited for the old man's laughter to subside. "Now, please, my lord. Why have you interrupted our journey to the palace? You will know we have been summoned."

"But you haven't been," said Minister Hang.

Yanlu took a sudden, extreme pleasure in seeing the expression on Ren Daiyan's face.

"I summoned you," said Hang Dejin, "not the court. Why would a newly made commander of only five thousand be invited to that meeting? Once more, will you take wine?"

"Yes," said Ren Daiyan this time, and the word was a kind of surrender, after all.

ZIJI WATCHED DAIYAN take hold of his anger and master it. It unsettled him that his friend could actually be *angry* at the man who had essentially ruled Kitai for so long.

How did one have that kind of response? Anger? In the presence of this man? Directed at him? How did someone from a village in the west, newly an army officer, still young by almost every measure, have the temerity to be this way?

There were answers. Perhaps the most important was tattooed on Daiyan's back. Some men knew, early, where they stood in the world. Or where they believed they were meant to stand.

For himself, he stayed watchful, his usual manner in an encounter like this. Although that was a foolish way to put it. What encounter had ever been like this?

They'd been lured here by deception, it was clear, as the younger Hang continued to speak, explaining. The last of a relay of messenger birds sent winging to their barracks near Xinan had come from this farm, not from the court.

It was a crime punishable by execution for anyone not formally authorized to use the messenger birds. The birds were part of a jealously guarded system. That fear of punishment, did not, it seemed, affect the former prime minister.

Yes, there was to be a gathering in the palace as soon as the emissary sent to the barbarians returned. Lu Chao had landed on the coast, was making his way to court. Hang Dejin knew this, even on his farm. He was making efforts to keep abreast of such matters. And he wanted Ren Daiyan to be there.

They were waiting to be told why.

The old man said, "Did you not stop to wonder, Commander Ren, why the court would request your presence? Would it be for ... experienced counsel?"

"Of course I thought about it. I decided they'd learned of my journey across the river. Maybe by way of birds from Shuquian. There was enough time for birds to go both ways. So I thought I was being invited to offer a second report from Xiaolu lands. Or perhaps a third or fourth. I don't know."

This time it was the blind man and his son who looked startled.

Of course. They hadn't known of his journey.

Daiyan smiled at the son, at ease again, or seeming so. Ziji had decided by now that the old man wasn't completely blind. He might prefer to be thought so, any advantage he could find.

Daiyan went on, not waiting for questions. "My lords, if you didn't know I went north, how did you intend to have me admitted to that council? I assume that is what you want? Otherwise this is a great deal of effort to share wine with two soldiers."

Too much irony, Ziji thought. Daiyan was still young. You could forget, then be reminded.

Question for question, from the old man: "What did you discover there? What do I need to know?"

It was interesting, that Hang Dejin would put the question that way, on a remote estate far from power. But then, if you thought about it, perhaps he wasn't so far.

And Daiyan was answering. "My lord, the rumour is that the Eastern Capital has already fallen to the Altai. No one is certain where the Xiaolu emperor is."

Something else they hadn't known, obviously.

"You believe this? That the city has fallen?" It was Hsien this time.

"It seems unlikely, so swiftly. But the story was widespread, and there is great uneasiness."

"That would be so whether the rumour is true or not." The son again, a quiet, precise voice.

Daiyan nodded. "I agree, my lord."

After a moment, the old man spoke, as if musing aloud. "You seem a useful sort of man, Ren Daiyan. You have initiative. I wish I had been able to make use of you years ago."

Daiyan smiled briefly. "I was an outlaw in the marsh, my lord. I believe you know this. Not much aid to the prime minister of Kitai. Besides, I am a very great admirer of Lu Chen."

"As am I. Our best poet."

"Even on Lingzhou Isle?" There was a challenge in the words.

"He seems to have written some fine things there," said the old man in a bland tone. "I did order him released."

"Only when Kai Zhen fell. And after how long?"

"Ah, well. The wheels of the empire are sometimes slow to turn, regrettably."

"In the army, superiors take responsibility for errors by subordinates."

"Not always. As you know. It is a part," said the old man, "of why you are here." Hang Dejin turned in Ziji's direction, eyes vacant, a milky whiteness. "Tell me, Deputy Commander Zhao, your thoughts on your commander's mission across the river."

He was changing the subject, but also doing something else. Ziji cleared his throat. These moments did come: people trying to take his measure. He could seek refuge in a soldier's mumbling discretion. He didn't feel like doing that.

"I thought it foolish, and I told him so. He was nearly caught. He killed soldiers, stole two horses, caused a border disturbance. A member of the imperial clan was up there, he could have died. That would have forced a response. There is little to learn from a frontier garrison. Not so as to rely on, at any rate."

"You allow him to speak this way of you?"

Hsien was looking at Daiyan. The captain of the guards, the one who had led the ambush, had an expression that suggested the same question was in his mind.

"He is my friend," Daiyan said.

The old man was nodding his head. "Friends are good. I have had few I trusted. My son now, only."

And so, of course, Daiyan had to open his mouth and say, "Then why is he not prime minister?"

Ziji winced, tried to hide it. *Oh, Daiyan,* he thought.

Hsien's expression went from startled to angry. The old man's remained bland, nothing more than thoughtfulness to be seen.

"Easy enough," he said. "Because he will better serve Kitai as the *next* prime minister, if we go to war now and it ends badly."

So much for discretion, Ziji thought. He was trying to understand why Daiyan and the old man were being so direct with each other. He couldn't. He couldn't sort it out.

"If it goes wrong, someone must be blamed?" Daiyan said.

"If it goes wrong, someone *should* be blamed," said the old man. He had wine at his elbow. He reached for it carefully and sipped. "You know the Cho Master's words: the sage is not found ahead of the people leading them to the future, he comes along after, picking up treasures that have been lost or left behind."

"We still need leaders," said Daiyan.

"We do. Not always the same as a sage."

"No. But we still need them." Daiyan hesitated, and Ziji suddenly knew what was coming. "My lord, I have always ... from very young I have known I was to play a role in fighting for our rivers and mountains."

"The Fourteen?"

"Yes, my lord."

The old man smiled kindly. "Many boys dream such things."

Daiyan shook his head. "No. I was, and I am, *certain* of it, my lord. I believe I am marked for this."

Here it is, thought Ziji.

"Marked?" said Hang Hsien.

"My lords, I ask permission to remove my tunic before you. There is a reason."

Two pairs of raised eyebrows, then the old man nodded.

So Daiyan showed them the tattoo on his back, the writing placed there in the emperor's hand, and told them how it had come to be. The son described the characters to the father. His voice was awed.

Daiyan put on his tunic again. In the silence, the first voice was Hang Hsien's.

"Where do you come by such certainty? All your life, you said?"

It was an urgent question, Ziji thought. Perhaps because Hsien lacked that sureness?

He saw his friend trying for an answer. Daiyan said, "I do not know. I should not be like this, if that is what you are asking. Is it possible ... can a man be born into the world to be something, for something?"

"Yes," said the old man. "But even if he is, it doesn't always happen. Too much can intervene. The world does what it does. Our dreams, our certainties, crash into each other."

"Like swords?" Daiyan said.

The old man shrugged. "Like swords, like ambitions at court."

"Which brings us back to this meeting in the palace?" Daiyan said.

"It can," said Hang Dejin. He smiled.

"I asked you before. How did you intend for us to be admitted to that room? And why? If it pleases you, my lord."

So the old man finally told them about the tree.

Did so while they drank apple wine and ate from small plates of food on a summer afternoon in his garden. Again, as with the arrow in the Genyue, it seemed their interests were not identical but could be made to march together. And the old man, moving pieces on a game board, might even now be the one who saw farther than anyone else.

Ziji, listening, found himself thinking back to the marsh, to days when their ambitions extended to no more than finding food, surviving cold nights, ambushing a party of merchants, maybe a Flowers and Rocks company.

He remembered the day—swift image of another summer— when he himself had been tricked by Daiyan while carrying a birthday gift meant for Kai Zhen, who had been deputy prime minister then. Life could circle and loop, he thought, in ways that might even persuade you there was a pattern to it.

They had been carrying nightingales in jewelled cages. Ziji had insisted on opening the cage doors himself, setting the birds free. A long time ago. He had joined his destiny to Daiyan's that day.

He'd never regretted it. He didn't live or think that way. You made your choices, they gave you a path to walk, closed others off. But he did feel, more than ever now, that arrows were being loosed and they were arcing very high.

☙❧

Shan has arranged with the gate guards at the northern wall to send word to the inn when her husband enters Xinan. She wants to greet him, she has explained.

It is true, and for more than one reason.

When a messenger does come riding, she is in the courtyard of the inn beside the fountain under shade, late morning. The fountain is flowing again. Shan has given money, a gift to the innkeeper and his wife, to unblock it. They had always feared it would be a major task, require digging up the courtyard and perhaps under their wall to the street, but in fact it is a blockage in the pipes just below, easily addressed. The music of water, the play of it under sunlight, is in the courtyard again.

She goes to dress and adorn herself. Qi Wai has several slow, heavy wagons, the messenger reports, so there is time. She arranges for the man to be paid.

When she's ready, she has herself carried to the imperial way, to wait by the entrance to their ward. There were heavy gates here once, she can see where they'd been set into the walls.

In the sedan chair, through a lifted-back curtain, she finally sees carts coming south along the imperial way. Small children are running beside them. Her husband is at the head of this party, riding a horse. Wai isn't a bad rider for a man who never had any practice young, and given how such skills are despised by the court and civil service. He has forced himself to become adequate on horseback during the travels undertaken for his collection. Their collection.

Shan steps from her chair and stands in the road, dressed in green-and-blue silk, hair coiled and pinned. She wears silver bracelets and hairpins, has her mother's lapis earrings in her ears, a perfume sachet about her neck. She sees Wai smile as he approaches.

He pulls up, proud on his horse. She says, "I would have come out to greet you as far as Cho-fu-Sa, as in the poem, but it is entirely the wrong way."

"We'd have missed each other." He chuckles.

"Welcome back, husband," she says, casting her eyes down. "You bring new discoveries."

"A great many!" Wai says, as she looks up. He really is happy, she sees. "Shan, I found a warrior figure kept back from the first emperor's tomb for some reason. The workshop was there!"

This is enormous news. "Will they let us keep it?"

"Maybe not, but I will still be the one who found it for the emperor. And now we know what they look like. Because of our digging up north."

"You will show me, I hope."

"I always do," he says. This was true once, not so readily of late, but he is in such a pleased state right now.

"Let me escort you to the inn," she murmurs. "I have ordered a bath prepared, and a change of clothing set out. After you eat and drink, perhaps you will be kind enough ..."

"I hope you will dine with me," he says.

She smiles.

She gives him three cups of strong wine when they reach the inn. For the first time since the ritual New Year's coupling, they make love in his chamber after he bathes, before the meal awaiting them downstairs. It is important, of course, but she enjoys it, and sees signs that he does, as well.

What have I become? she thinks. The paths life offers, where they take you, what you find along the way, as you go.

After, also before they eat, he takes her out to the guarded stable yard and shows her what he's found, shifting packing straw in the carts, opening strongboxes. Scrolls, a stone plinth in fragments to be reassembled, tripod wine holders, a bronze drinking vessel with two owls, back to back, on the lid. Stones with imperial inscriptions and memorials, ceremonial bowls in very good condition, one from the Second Dynasty, he thinks. A ritual axe from even further back, with a tiger on it if you look closely. He shows it to her, traces the outline.

And there is the warrior. Terracotta, half a man's size, beautifully rendered, wearing arms and armour. Almost perfectly preserved— only one hand broken away where it would have rested on the hilt of a sheathed sword. Shan looks at it in wonder. She sees her husband's pride. She understands it.

Historians have recorded that guardian figures were buried with the first emperor, thousands of them, but not one has ever been seen, and the tomb is hidden underground. Now they have one, and Wai will take it to the court.

She brings him her own discovery from the tower here, the unnamed steward's record of a distinguished house in the terrible years of the Ninth's rebellion. Qi Wai praises her, adds it to the other treasures. They will catalogue it all at home, he says.

She bows and smiles. Looks again at the small warrior he's brought back, thinking of how long time can be. Later, in her own room, her own bed, listening to the fountain again, she finds herself weeping.

It is soundless, but the tears won't stop. He is too far away already, and marked by a *daiji* with the words of his fate.

Sometimes you could choose a road and it might lead to a laneway and then a quiet place where you could make a home. But Ren Daiyan's path is not like that, and she can see it, acknowledge it in the dark.

His life's dream did not lead to a countryside where birds might wake you in the morning and you could walk under leaves to a pond, perhaps see lotus petals floating on the water, goldfish swimming below. He is not, Shan realizes during a long night in Xinan, a safe man to love, his *life* could not be safe. And so she weeps. Hears the fountain outside.

This flower will not be like any other, she had written here. But it isn't entirely true. Isn't she just another woman above a courtyard under moonlight, her heart too far away, and in the wrong place?

Several days later, on the road back east, approaching Yenling, her time of month comes, quite normally.

CHAPTER XVIII

Lu Mah, the son of the great poet, who had accompanied his father to Lingzhou Isle, had a night cough and recurring fevers that never left him after his time on the isle.

It was possible to see him as deserving great rewards in life for filial devotion on the largest scale, although some believed a man's destiny was like the random fall of tiles in a celestial game played with mortal lives.

Whatever the truth of that, Mah would never forget that time beyond the world. He dreamed of it, woke in the nights from those dreams. He had expected to die, or to bury his father there. His father always said his life was a gift of the girl who had left Lingzhou with them and died south of the mountains. Mah remembered her very well. He thought he'd been in love with her, for gentleness in a terrible place. They lit candles for her.

If asked for the most vivid day in his life, he'd have said that it was the great conference at the court, when he and his uncle returned from the steppe and were summoned to report.

It was the first time—and was to be the only time—he ever stood thus, in the presence of the august Emperor Wenzong, guardian of all his people under heaven.

A great many distinguished men assembled that morning, elaborately dressed, the mighty of Kitai, taut as drawn bowstrings. Lu Mah would have found himself trembling with fear, but his uncle's presence was a rock, and standing beside him as they waited he drew strength from that.

Lu Chao, tall and lean, betrayed nothing with his expression or posture in the moments before he was summoned to speak. He had done this before, Mah reminded himself. His uncle knew this court.

Prime Minister Kai Zhen was addressing the emperor. He was an enemy of their family from a long time back. They were not to show any sign of that, Lu Mah knew.

As the prime minister spoke, Mah's uncle looked straight ahead and, in a practised manner, lips barely moving, told his nephew the names of those gathered that morning. He didn't know them all. He, too, had been exiled for many years.

Even the reception hall intimidated Mah, though his uncle had warned him about this. Lu Mah had never been in a chamber remotely like it. Marble columns in six rows, sheathed in bands of green jade, disappearing into shadow at the far end beyond the throne. There were ivory sconces and alabaster pillars for candles and lamps. The ceiling was so high, and there was more jade there, in swirling patterns.

The emperor, wearing the blue soft crown of ceremony, sat on the Dragon Throne, on a dais in the centre, three steps up. The throne was wide, intricately carved, magnificent, a symbol in itself, brought forth for occasions of significance. This was one of those. They were to learn—to decide—whether Kitai was going to war.

The prime minister appeared to be finishing his remarks. He was congratulating the emperor on being alert to all opportunities on behalf of his people and his noble ancestors.

Near him, another tall man—the eunuch Wu Tong, whom Mah's father and uncle despised—stood quietly, hands folded in sleeves, a picture of grave, agreeable serenity. Beside the throne, a little behind, was a man of about Mah's own age, the imperial heir, Chizu. Mah's uncle had said he was clever, and spent his life hiding it.

There was a feeling, a vibration in the air like an almost-heard *pipa* string. Despite his uncle's presence, he felt afraid, after all. They had enemies here, and what his uncle was about to say ...

Then it seemed to be time to say it. The prime minister turned towards them, offering a smile that had nothing in it of welcome or warmth to go with the ritual words of appreciation.

Lu Chao bowed, still expressionless, and stepped forward as he was named, leaving Mah alone, no one beside him. He felt an urgent need to cough, his nervous cough, and fought it. His eyes went around the room. His gaze met those of a uniformed military officer, about his own age as well, among those standing to the left. The officer was looking at him. He nodded at Mah, and smiled. A real smile.

His uncle hadn't named this one. He was standing with the chief magistrate of Hanjin, whose name Lu Chao had offered: Wang Fuyin. Mah's uncle had said he was ambitious, and shrewd, of undetermined allegiance.

Everyone here seemed to be ambitious and shrewd. Lu Mah had long ago decided that this was not a life for him: sorting through, let alone shaping, moments such as this.

He missed East Slope. He had done so from the morning they'd left. He wasn't his father, he wasn't his uncle, had no desire to be. He was content to honour and love them both, serve them with devotion, serve the gods and his ancestors. It was his hope that this would be acceptable as the course of a man's life.

Kai Zhen, who had a beautiful voice, said, "Illustrious emissary, your emperor awaits your words."

The emperor, Mah realized, had not yet spoken. He was also tall, slim-shouldered, elegant—like his writing, Mah thought. Wenzong had a restless gaze. An impatient man? Were you allowed to think that way about the emperor of Kitai? The emperor's eyes were on Mah's uncle now.

Kai Zhen added, "Be not hesitant to speak, honour the empire and your office."

Lu Chao bowed again. He said, "The revered and exalted emperor will know, of course, that ours is not a hesitant family." There was a collective intake of breath. Mah bit his lip, lowered his eyes.

The emperor of Kitai laughed aloud.

"We do know that!" he said, in a light but very clear voice. "We also know this journey was a difficult one, going and coming, among primitive people. Your efforts will not go unrewarded, Master Lu."

"My reward is any service I can do Kitai, illustrious lord." His uncle hesitated. Mah decided it was a pause for effect. Chao said, "Even if my words might displease some in this chamber."

Another silence. Not surprising.

"They are duly-considered words?" the emperor asked.

"It would shame my family if they were otherwise, my lord."

"Then tell us."

His uncle's voice was not as rich as Kai Zhen's, Mah thought, but it was assured, and the room was quiet for him. His father, speaking, also had that effect on people, on a room, Mah thought, and allowed himself pride.

Lu Chao, also belted in red (emissaries were deemed of highest rank during their service), was saying, directly to the emperor of Kitai, exactly what they'd agreed he would.

He reported first, calmly, that it was the Altai war-leader who had met with him. "It was not their kaghan, but I judged that this was the more important man, the one driving their rebellion, more so than the aged leader of the tribe. This man's name is Wan'yen."

"Not the kaghan? Was this an insult to Kitai? To the emperor?" The prime minister's question was quick, edged. Mah's uncle had told him he would ask this.

"I judged it not to be, as I just said. Wan'yen is the man we need to assess. He had ridden fast and very far to meet us at a place I designated. He came all the way from the Xiaolu's Eastern Capital."

The first crisis would come with this, his uncle had told Mah.

"They were negotiating with the Xiaolu there?" It was the emperor himself.

"No, exalted lord. Wan'yen of the Altai told me that the Eastern Capital had already fallen to them, in no time at all. In the first months after their rising. The Xiaolu emperor's whereabouts were unknown. He was, as we say here, in the wild."

"*That is impossible!*" The voice was a new one: the eunuch Wu Tong. An interjection that was either startled or pretending to be. "You have been tricked or misled!"

"A Kitan emissary? Tricked by a barbarian tribesman? You think so, Master Wu?" Lu Chao's voice was cold. There was surely a title he should have given Wu Tong. He hadn't done so. "And if he did, what would that say about these Altai?"

"What would it say about our emissary?" Wu Tong replied, as coldly.

It hadn't taken long, Lu Mah thought, for ice to enter the room.

In the nervous shuffling that followed, someone stepped forward on the opposite side of the chamber. You had to be brave to do that, Mah thought. He saw that it was the chief magistrate, Wang Fuyin. He was plump, not tall, neatly bearded, in a very-well-fitted robe of office. He extended two hands, palms meeting, for permission to speak. Mah's uncle, who had the right to do so at that moment, inclined his head towards him.

"Please," he said.

"We can offer the illustrious emperor confirmation of what his emissary has just told us," said the chief magistrate.

"And who might 'we' be?" asked the prime minister. Mah didn't hear any affection extended to the magistrate, either.

"The former captain of my own guard, now a military commander. His name is Ren Daiyan, a man known to the emperor as a hero. He is with us this morning and can report, with his majesty's gracious permission."

"Why a hero?" asked the emperor.

"He saved a life in the Genyue this spring, gracious lord. A favoured writer, the Lady Lin Shan? You honoured him for it with the rank he holds."

Wenzong's brow knit briefly, then he smiled. The emperor had a benevolent smile, Lu Mah thought. You could be warmed by it as by the sun.

"We do remember! You have our permission to speak, Commander Ren," said the emperor. The smile faded. Was he remembering an intrusion in his beloved garden, or unsettled by conflict emerging here? Mah had no idea. He really didn't want to be in this room.

The young man who'd been looking at him a moment ago stepped forward, without apparent anxiety. He wore a military uniform and boots, not a court robe and slippers. Mah didn't know the different insignia well enough to identify his rank, but he was young, couldn't possibly be high enough to properly be addressing this company.

Rather him than me, Lu Mah thought. Watching, waiting, he had a fleeting, wistful image of the stream east of their farm, as it would be now, on a morning in summer, light filtering through trees.

WHEN YOU LIVED and travelled and fought beside a man for years, you learned to recognize tension in him, however thin the edge might be, however invisible to others.

Zhao Ziji, at the edge of the room among the magistrate's guard, watched Daiyan step forward. In the deliberateness of his friend's movements he read an awareness of how high the stakes of this game now were.

He was afraid, himself. His role and that of the other three men with the magistrate was purely symbolic. They were escorts, a symbol of rank. Wang Fuyin was extending him a courtesy, giving him his old uniform for the day, allowing him to be present.

The fact that Ziji had a thin, hiltless blade strapped to the back of his calf was enough to have him executed if it was found. They weren't checking boots, that wasn't what frightened him. The knife was only there in the event something went wrong on a grand scale and he and Daiyan ended up in a jail cell. Blades helped there. He had experience with that, not with this. Here he'd look a fool, wrestling his boot off to claim a tiny knife. He felt better with a weapon, though, even a useless one.

He hadn't nurtured any powerful impulse to be in this room. That wasn't the way his mind and desires worked. Yes, he could now tell his children, if he ever had children, that he'd been in the throne room of Hanjin before the Emperor Wenzong. Had heard the emperor speak. Maybe it would help get him a wife one day, though he wasn't sure he wanted a woman for whom his merely standing at the edge of this room beside a marble pillar would matter that much.

Foolish, foolish line of thought! No, he was here because he was aware that Daiyan was grateful for the support of friends. So he was watching, and so was the magistrate, as Daiyan prepared—for a second time—to set in motion something devised by an old, nearly blind man.

Ambitions and dreams put you at a drinking table with unexpected companions. Cups were filled and refilled, making you drunk with the illusion of changing the world.

He watched Daiyan bow three times, a soldier's obeisance, not a courtier's: respectful, unpolished. He wasn't pretending to be something he was not. It wouldn't work here.

Ziji heard his friend speak then, his voice even and direct. "Great lord, I can report that what your illustrious emissary heard in the northeast is being said farther west in barracks and villages above Shuquian. The tale is indeed that the Eastern Capital has fallen to the Altai."

Ziji turned his gaze to the prime minister and the eunuch beside him. Daiyan couldn't do that. Ziji could, from back here. Daiyan's words were a direct refutation of Wu Tong's. The prime minister was too poised to reveal any response. Not at this distance, and not to someone who didn't know him. The eunuch's mouth was thin, however, a line like another knife, Ziji thought.

The emperor of Kitai spoke then, directly to Ren Daiyan, born the second son of a minor *yamen* clerk in the west. He said, "How do you know this, Commander Ren?"

DAIYAN TOOK A STEADYING breath. He needed to be calmer. But you could grow dizzy if you took even a moment to grasp that you were being directly addressed by the bearer of the mandate of heaven, wearing the ceremonial crown, in his throne room. He couldn't dwell upon that, or think of his father.

He said, "I was there myself, great lord. Having been posted west with my company, I felt it proper to learn as much as I could about the Golden River border."

"You went across the river yourself?"

"I did, my lord."

"Into Xiaolu lands?"

"Yes, my lord."

"With how many men?"

"Alone, my lord. I posed as someone looking to smuggle salt."

"That would be illegal," the emperor said.

"Yes, illustrious lord."

Wenzong nodded thoughtfully, as if something of importance had been confirmed. It occurred to Daiyan how, secluded in the palace, the emperor was so vulnerable to information being kept from him. He hadn't even known about Erighaya. A reason why this morning mattered so much.

He was careful not to let his gaze slide to where the prime minister stood. It was Kai Zhen's first wife who had tried to have Shan killed. But the bitter complexity of life and politics meant that he and the prime minister might want the same thing this morning.

"And you believe the stories you heard, about their Eastern Capital ... you believe these were true?" The emperor's brow was furrowed.

"I was unable to decide, my lord. Until this morning. I did not know what the distinguished emissary would say. Now ... yes, my lord. Your servant believes it to be true. It comes to us from the Altai and from the Xiaolu."

"*Wait.*" It was Kai Zhen. Which meant Daiyan had to look at him. He turned, schooling his features. "If you had no idea what the emissary was going to report, why are you even here?"

The old man had told him this would happen. The old man had just about written this out as an evening theatre performance. Except that they were where they were.

Daiyan said, "My lord, I informed the chief magistrate, as a trusted friend, what I'd learned north of the river. He told me the imperial envoy was returning to Hanjin. He urged me to seek leave to come here, offered a place in his company, in the event my information might matter. I hope I did not transgress."

The timing, if anyone checked carefully, would be a problem— for information to have gone east and back west that fast without using the forbidden birds. But the old man had been quite sure (he was always quite sure) this would not be checked. Not in time, at any rate.

"No transgression," said the emperor of Kitai. He straightened his tall form on the wide throne. "Commander Ren, we are pleased to have brave men such as you serving us. We will give expression to that pleasure later."

Daiyan bowed again, three times, meaning every one. He stepped back beside the magistrate. Fighting was easier, he thought. Tigers were easier.

The magistrate bowed to the emissary, yielding back his right to speak. Lu Chao resumed. "This is indeed helpful, my lord. It confirms me in the view I wish to share."

First defining moment, Daiyan thought. And again the old man, like a spider in his web, had told them what he'd thought would follow.

Lu Chao said, "Illustrious lord, I believe the Altai are a danger to us, not allies. The Xiaolu are a known presence. They are not newly ambitious, their emperor is weak, and word is that his sons are equally so, and divided."

"They hold our land!" snapped the prime minister. "We can get it back! The Fourteen Prefectures!"

"I am deeply aware of what they hold," said Lu Chao. His voice was extremely calm. "I doubt any man in this room is unaware of it."

"We can use this chance to get them back!" The eunuch this time. It was as if they were in a canyon, Daiyan thought, and he was an echo of Kai Zhen.

"I believe this is the matter under discussion. It is why I was sent north, is it not?"

"You were sent north to assist Kitai and the emperor." Kai Zhen again.

"And I have returned to do this as best I can. I ask humbly: Do you wish to hear me, prime minister?"

Daiyan, watching closely, was of the opinion that the prime minister would rather not, in truth, but Kai Zhen could hardly say that. What made things worse was that Daiyan knew himself allied in this with a man he hated. How did the world create such unions?

The tall emissary, younger brother to the poet, said, facing the throne again, "If the Eastern Capital has fallen already it means the Xiaolu empire is rotting away, my lord. Cities like that can be taken at speed only if the gates are opened in surrender. That means the attacking force has been swelled by other tribes, and the Xiaolu are turning on their own."

"If this is happening, our own course is clear!"

Kai Zhen was obviously determined to break the other man's persuasiveness. On his farm, Hang Dejin had guessed that this, too, would happen. He'd said that Lu Chao could deal with it. What he did not know, he'd said, was what the emperor would do. Wenzong, even after years of being studied, could be unpredictable.

Lu Chao said, "I do not believe it is clear at all, my lord emperor. If we intervene on behalf of the Altai, as the prime minister suggests—"

"He has said no such thing!" exclaimed Wu Tong. The eunuch's voice was a little too loud.

"Of course he has," said the emissary gravely. "Are we children? Is the emperor a child? *Our course is clear?* What course would that be?"

No answer. The man was good at this, Daiyan thought. And again the strangeness of his own position was brought home to him.

Prime Minister Kai Zhen of Kitai wanted a northern war. So did Ren Daiyan, middle-ranking military commander, son of Ren Yuan, a clerk. One could laugh, or decide to get very drunk.

In the silence, it was the emperor who spoke. He sounded tired. There had been years and years of this, in his father's days, through his own long reign. "Master Lu, offer your counsel. You are the one who has spoken with these new barbarians."

Again a formal bow. "Gracious lord. Let the peoples of the steppe fight each other again. Our task, our wisest course, is to be watchful, defend our borders, present a firm and guarded front to both the Altai and the Xiaolu."

Wenzong's mouth was also thin now. This was not what he'd

wanted to hear. The emperor had come to this room, Daiyan realized, thinking about conquest. Reconquest. He said, "You do not believe we can induce the Altai to give us back the Fourteen, in exchange for our aid?"

"They do not need our aid, serene lord. I will tell you what they offered. I proposed, as instructed, that for our assistance they return the Fourteen Prefectures."

"Exactly so," said Kai Zhen. He said it quietly, but everyone heard.

Lu Chao didn't look at him. He said, "Wan'yen, their war-leader, smiled at me. I believe he laughed."

"The barbarian!" exclaimed Wu Tong.

"Yes," said the emissary. "*Exactly so.*" His voice was a precise mimicking of the prime minister's a moment ago.

After a pause, Lu Chao went on. "He offered four prefectures, in the west, north of Xinan, not the lands above us here. In exchange we are to take the Xiaolu Southern Capital ourselves, then join them with our armies in attacking the Xiaolu's Central Capital. We are to hand over to the Altai the Southern Capital, and to continue sending all current gifts, but to the Altai, once their kaghan is installed as emperor. And he is to be named *brother* to the emperor of Kitai. Not *nephew*. Not *son*."

There was a silence. Silence could be loud, Daiyan thought. In it, Lu Chao finished, as if ending a poem, "This is what Wan'yen of the Altai said to the emissary of Kitai."

Daiyan's heart was thudding. It felt as if a battering ram were hammering at the bronze doors of the room, so shocked was the response of those assembled.

Into this rigidity, Lu Chao added, almost casually, "I told him this was unacceptable to the celestial emperor. That we required all Fourteen Prefectures to be returned if we were to care which tribe ruled the steppe. He said, perhaps five or six, *if* we took the Southern Capital and joined them fighting north."

"The man has been stripped of his reason by the gods," Kai Zhen said loudly. "He is marked for terrible ruin." But his tone had altered, you could hear it. The arrogance of what they'd heard ...

"He is a barbarian," Lu Chao agreed. "But they feel no danger, no threat from the Xiaolu, and the other eastern tribes have already yielded to them. I will say it one more time: I do not believe they need us to take the steppe. I believe we need to make them fear our power and so must hold it in reserve."

"Could we help the Xiaolu against them instead?" It was a grey-bearded man from behind Kai Zhen.

"I considered this, my lord, all the way home. But how do we begin such a conversation? Do we ally with an empire that is falling? I wondered if this rebellion might simply be a desire for freedom in the east. If so, it would have been sensible to assist, and claim back some of our lands. It is not so. They are chasing an empire. My lord emperor, celestial lord, we need to be wary. There is a great deal to be lost."

"And *gained*!" cried the prime minister, his confident tone restored. "They are inviting us to take the Southern Capital! We take it, and we *hold* it, and then we negotiate for more after they've worn themselves out against the other cities!"

Now Lu Chao did turn to him. "And who takes the Southern Capital for us? What force of ours? After what happened in the west against the Kislik, for years?"

Daiyan fought the impulse to step forward. A ludicrous impulse, but it was why he was here. *Wait, if this happens*, the old man had said.

"The emperor's loyal armies will, of course," said Kai Zhen.

"And who leads them?"

"Wu Tong is our most experienced general." Behind him the eunuch's expression and demeanor were grave and calm again.

"Because of years of losing in Kislik lands?"

"No one wins every battle," the prime minister said primly.

"Truly. And the emperor isn't informed of every defeat."

An open attack. Erighaya. The disaster there, which Wu Tong had led, having been given command by Kai Zhen.

Another nervous ripple in the room, men shuffling, adjusting clothing, looking downwards. The words were reckless to the point of personal danger. But at the same time they did remind the emperor of something that mattered. Kai Zhen had been exiled over events in that war.

Almost time, Daiyan thought.

He looked back over his shoulder at Ziji, beside a pillar at the edge of the room. His friend was staring at him. Ziji looked frightened. This was not their kind of battlefield. There was enmity here, nakedly on display, going back decades through the faction wars. Kitai was on the brink of a decision that could reshape the empire, and battles from long ago were still being fought in this room.

"Serene lord, forgive me for speaking, but of course I can take the Xiaolu's Southern Capital with our brave soldiers." Wu Tong's voice was smooth, sailing above the choppy waters of confrontation.

Lu Chao stared at him. "Will you remember to bring siege engines?"

Daiyan saw the emissary's nephew, the poet's son, close his eyes at that. Then the young man opened them again and squared his shoulders. He moved a little—towards his uncle, not away. That took courage, Daiyan thought. And love, perhaps.

He had thought the throne room was tense before. He understood now that he understood nothing, truly. He was here as an instrument, agreeing to be such because it matched (he believed) his own desire. *And because you are a fool*, Ziji had said to him the one night they'd spent at Little Gold Hill.

He might be. Weren't the young allowed to be reckless? But he knew his answer: reckless with their own destiny, yes, not with the lives of others.

The next voice was the emperor's. "Prime minister, you believe we can take this city and hold it? You believe General Wu Tong is the best leader of our armies?"

Directly addressed, Kai Zhen stepped forward in front of the emissary. Head high, voice and appearance sleek as *liao* silk, he said, "Great lord, I do, and I do. I believe this is the appointed time for you to honour your beloved father and grandfather and regain our rivers and mountains."

"And Wu Tong?" Repeating it. A direct question.

It is time, Daiyan thought.

"He is loyal to the throne and to the imperial civil service, celestial lord. He carries no taint of military ambition."

Not, *He is a brilliant leader of men*. No. *He is loyal and has no ambitions as a soldier*. The old, old fear, going back centuries to the Ninth Dynasty and its great and terrible rebellion. So many millions dead. A chasm in the history of Kitai. What commanders might do if given too much power, if too much loved by their soldiers, if not kept utterly under control.

I could die today, Daiyan thought. He thought of a woman, moonlit, in Xinan, seen from beside a fountain.

He stepped forward. As near to the throne as the prime minister of Kitai. As advised (spider spinning his web), he dropped, touched his forehead to the floor three times, then straightened.

Do not speak, Hang Dejin had told him, preparing this moment. Kneel and wait. If he has honoured your first remarks about going north of the river alone, he will turn to you. *Wait for that*.

He waited. The emperor turned to him.

Wenzong's eyes were colder than before. He said, "What is it, Commander Ren?" He'd remembered the name.

Daiyan said, "Your servant fears to speak, my lord."

"Clearly you do not, or you would not be where you are. You have done loyal service. Speak to us, unafraid."

Quietly, he said, "My lord, it is about the prime minister's companion and general, Wu Tong."

"What vast presumption is this?" cried Kai Zhen.

The emperor lifted a hand. "The man has been honourable and brave. Go on. We are listening."

Daiyan drew a breath. No artifice in this pause. He was terrified. He said, from his knees, in front of the three steps of the dais and the Dragon Throne, "Exalted lord, celestial emperor, it is about a tree."

CHAPTER XIX

It was possible, if you had lived long enough, and knew the people and the ceremonies extremely well, to anticipate and shape events at court, even from a distance.

It was also—the old man had to admit this, if only to himself—a sharp, vivid pleasure to do so. His battles had never been fought with swords, but they had been fought, and usually won.

Hang Dejin was outside again, in his garden at Little Gold Hill, late morning. He preferred being outdoors now, when it was possible: sunlight gave things shape and definition. Shadows took the world away. He looked over to where his son was working on papers, most likely to do with the farm. Hsien was attentive in that way.

His own mind was far off, in the palace, the throne room. Word had come yesterday at evening, by one of his illicit messenger birds, that the emissary was to be received this morning.

So the old man was sitting on a cushioned chair, drinking Szechen tea, listening to birdsong, surrounded by the scent of flowers, and picturing a room he knew very well.

The teachings of the Master urged that men were to be guided by loyalty to family. Also by service to the empire, seen as an extension of family honour. If so, he could say that what he was doing now was for his descendants, down through the future of the family, however far it might go.

If pressed to speak pragmatically, he'd have offered the opinion that, as currently constituted, the Kitan army was best used as a large, massed deterrent along their northern border, manning forts and cities while building up defences through autumn and winter against what might happen next spring.

Using barbarians to control barbarians, that was the ancient doctrine of Kitai concerning the steppe. Let them slaughter each other. Help them do so. Kitai had intervened at times, to promote one leader over another, one tribe against a second and third. In those days, those years, their own army had been a force that signified.

For many reasons, and some could be laid at his own doorstep, Hang Dejin did not think this was true today. The Kislik war—his own war—had shown as much.

When you subjugated army commanders to bureaucrats at court (people like himself), you ensured a measure of stability within your own borders. But you also raised hard, cold concerns about military pride and competence when you sent that army, with the generals they had, to fight for Kitai. And so ...

And so, if Kai Zhen pushed hard for war this morning, and a failed war might undo Kai Zhen, the old man in this distant garden was content. It served his purposes.

He'd needed to tie any war to the prime minister. Then—with a young man's tattooed back startlingly revealed here—he'd thought of a sudden, splendid way to link any possible *success* to himself. To make the pattern work either way. It was clever. It was more than that.

There might be dark reverberations to war, like thunder too close on a summer day, shaking cups and bowls on a banquet table, but his judgment was that any fighting would end up much like the

Kislik campaign: losses, gains, stasis in the field, soldiers dying, and farmers, anger at increased taxation ... and a treaty deriving from weariness on both sides.

And then a new prime minister to succeed the one blamed for all these things. He had looked at it, over and again, in the still-clear eye of his mind.

He glanced towards his son. In this light he could make him out, the shape of a man beside him in the pavilion. Hsien had his brush in hand, was writing a letter or a note. A good man, his oldest son, attentive, capable, calm. Possibly, just possibly, hard enough to do the things that needed to be done in high office. Although that you never knew for certain until the testing came. He hadn't known it of himself. Before being tested you were just a shape; the office gave you substance.

If he'd judged the pace of the meeting in the palace rightly, the young soldier he liked well enough (and would be sorry to see killed) would be speaking soon or was speaking now. And then he would remove his tunic in the throne room before the emperor, just as he had here at Little Gold Hill, when Hsien had described to his father, voice trembling, what characters were inscribed upon the man's back, and in whose hand.

Whatever plans you shaped, in office or out, you needed to be ready to adapt to new possibilities that came.

There might be deaths and chaos. He judged these would be controllable, though he was aware that he might not live long enough to know. That was why you had sons, wasn't it? Why you did what you did for them.

He knew that mortal judgment was endlessly fallible. Too many things could not be guided or anticipated. Fire and flood. Famine. Childlessness. Early death. A sudden fever in a wintry night. He sometimes imagined them all, men and women, children, everyone in the world, sailing down the Sky River in the hugeness of the dark, surrounded by all the stars.

Some tried to steer the ship. He had tried. But only the gods could do that, in the end.

☙

Standing near his uncle again, having thought (foolishly) that he might defend him physically, if it came to that, Lu Mah listened as the soldier told them about a tree.

It was a *huai,* a scholar-tree, one of the longest-lived of all. According to legend, associated with ghosts and spirits. Apparently, one of these was, right now, even as they gathered here, being carried along the Wai River to the Great Canal and from there would come up to Hanjin, having been uprooted from an estate near the Wai.

It was being brought, this most recent treasure of the Flowers and Rocks Network, to grace the Genyue. It was said to be majestic, magnificent. It was, the soldier said, three hundred and fifty years old.

"The Flowers and Rocks activities are the responsibility of Wu Tong, I believe," added the soldier, whose name was Ren Daiyan. He was standing again, at the emperor's impatient gesture. If he was afraid, Mah thought, he wasn't showing it.

"They are," said Wu Tong comfortably. "And this tree is indeed magnificent. I have monitored all reports from the beginning. It may be the finest example in the empire, my lord. It belongs in the Genyue."

"Indeed," said the emperor. "You have served us loyally in matters of our garden."

"Not so," said Ren Daiyan, firmly. "Not in this, exalted lord. This is a betrayal of you and the Genyue and of Kitai."

Mah looked quickly at his uncle and saw the same shock he felt. Perhaps more: his uncle would know precisely how reckless these words were. Mah could only guess, and know he could never have spoken them. The words could not have formed in his mouth.

"This is an accusation? In court?" It was the prime minister. His voice was brittle with fury.

"It is."

No salutation, Mah realized. Was this man trying to destroy himself?

The prime minister seemed happy to do it for him. "August and serene lord, I request permission to have this soldier removed and beaten with the heavy rod." Kai Zhen's fury was obviously real. His features had flushed.

"Not yet," said the emperor of Kitai, though he paused before he said it. "But Commander Ren, you are being uncivilized, and I must assume that you know it, even if you are new to our court."

"I am being truthful and loyal, gracious lord. In your service, and Kitai's. My information comes not from myself, but from the former prime minister. The honourable Hang Dejin told me I had to speak to the emperor of this, before it was too late."

Lu Mah swallowed, his mouth dry. He understood almost nothing here, but terror still claimed him. The old man was in this, too! He pushed his hands into his sleeves to hide their trembling. He wanted to be at East Slope more than he could say.

"*He* sent you here?" Emperor Wenzong's eyes widened. A hand went to his narrow beard.

"I was coming here, exalted lord. He stopped me on the way, received me at Little Gold Hill, and told me something he thought you needed to know."

Kai Zhen was still and watchful now, Mah saw. He looked like a hooded snake. Mah had seen those on Lingzhou, uncoiling before they killed.

"And what is it that we need to know?" the emperor said. Also watchful now.

Ren Daiyan said, "That the Genyue's sanctity, its role as a mirror of Kitai, as the harmony at the centre of our harmony ... all this will be shattered if that tree is planted."

"Why, Commander Ren?"

It was Mah's uncle, surprisingly. Standing not far from the soldier.

Ren Daiyan turned and looked at him. He bowed, as he had not to the eunuch or the prime minister. "Because, my lord emissary, it was uprooted, without ritual or respect, from a distinguished family's graveyard, where it shaded illustrious graves. An act of desecration and impiety by a man who cares nothing for right behaviour, even if it weakens and endangers his emperor."

Lu Mah was horrified. If this was true it marked a profound transgression. A *huai* tree was half tree, half ghost to start with! And taken from a family burial ground? It was a crime against ancestors, spirits, the gods. They might have, they probably *had* shifted the graves, if the tree was that old! Whoever this family was, to bring such a tree, haunted by angry spirits, to the emperor's own garden? The mind could reel and stagger!

"What graveyard?" asked Wenzong. He was frightening to look at now. The Genyue was sacred to him, everyone knew.

Ren Daiyan said, "The Shen family, my lord. I know the glorious emperor will know them. We all do. General Shen Gao made his family's name as Left Side Commander of the Pacified West, leading our armies there with honour. He lay under this tree, my lord. One son, also buried there, served as principal adviser to a prime minister, another guided and served the next emperor, is famed for his poetry and for—"

"For his horses," said the emperor of Kitai. His voice was dangerously soft. "This is Shen Tai?"

Ren Daiyan bowed his head. "It is, my lord. His grave, too, lay under this tree, sheltered by it. And his wife's, his sons'. Many grandsons and their wives and children were also buried there. There is also an inscribed memorial to his sister, who is not there only because—"

"Because she was entombed with Emperor Shinzu, north of Xinan."

"Yes, illustrious lord."

"It is *this* tree, from that ground, that is being brought here? To be placed in the Genyue?"

Lu Mah saw the soldier bow his head again in silent affirmation.

The emperor drew a breath. It could be seen, even by someone ignorant (and Lu Mah knew he was), that he was in a white, savage rage. Emperors, he thought, didn't need to hide their feelings. Wenzong turned to his prime minister—and to the man beside him.

"Minister Wu Tong, you will explain."

Equanimity and poise had limits, it seemed. "Great, great lord," the man stammered, "of course I did not know this was so! Of course I—"

"You have just told us you reviewed all reports, Minister Wu."

Another silence. A feeling of doom embedded in it.

"Even so ... even so! I did not know where it ... how it was ...of *course* I shall have those responsible dealt with. In the harshest ways, serene lord! The tree will be returned and ..."

Serene was not the word Lu Mah would have chosen.

Ren Daiyan, young as he was, lacking rank though he did, turned and faced the eunuch.

"You blamed others for Erighaya, too," he said.

And when no one replied, he added, very clearly, "In an army, properly led, commanders accept responsibility for failure when the emperor's needs are not met and his people die."

During their long journey north by sea, then inland to meet the Altai, and then back home, Mah and his uncle had had a great deal of time to talk. Lu Chao enjoyed conversation and had a lifetime of wisdom to share.

He'd told his nephew that a career in the civil service could offer a feeling of duty fulfilled: to Kitai and one's lineage, in the best tradition of the Cho Master.

In Hanjin it could also, he'd said, be dramatic and exciting, as men circled the throne in the quest for access and power. It could also be terrible and destructive, he'd added.

Watching the emperor turn a stony gaze to his prime minister, Lu Mah decided this was one of the terrible moments. He knew—everyone knew—that Kai Zhen and Wu Tong had risen towards power together.

Until, right now, the cost of that became too high.

He hadn't thought it was possible he could ever feel pity for Kai Zhen. But the man's face in that moment, as he looked at Wu Tong and then turned slowly towards the palace guards, was the image of someone in pain. Surely you were uncivilized and cruel yourself—a barbarian—if you didn't respond to that, Lu Mah thought. Or, perhaps that inner response was what made him unsuited to this room, this world.

"Take Minister Wu, guards." The prime minister's voice was strained. "Hold him in custody, at the emperor's pleasure."

Pleasure wasn't the right word either, Mah thought. He lowered his eyes and kept them down.

৩৩

They were in the chief magistrate's home in the southern part of the city. Daiyan didn't wait for their host to pour wine. He crossed to the brazier and drank off three cups, one after another. The wine was very hot, Fuyin liked it that way. It almost burned his tongue.

"He had no choice," the magistrate kept saying. "The prime minister. No choice."

Fuyin was still shaken by what had happened in the throne room. They all were. Ziji had taken a chair. He'd almost fallen into it.

"It didn't even matter," Daiyan said to the magistrate. "What he ordered was changed."

"He knew it would be, I think."

Daiyan poured two more cups, took one to each of the other

men. These were companions, trusted, they were alone. And he still felt afraid. Ziji held his cup distractedly, without drinking. Daiyan took his hand and brought the wine towards his friend's mouth. "Drink," he said. "Call it an order."

"From a general of fifty thousand?"

Daiyan grimaced. He was that now, which was part of the fear—a sense the world was moving very quickly.

"To his commander of twenty-five thousand, yes." He watched Ziji drink, then turned to the magistrate. "What do you mean 'he knew'? He ordered Wu Tong taken to prison—"

"And the emperor ordered him executed, as soon as the facts of the tree are confirmed. This, added to Erighaya? He can't survive. There is no way to save his life. Unless your information ... ?"

"If my information is untrue, I'm dead, and I suppose you are, too. For speaking up for me. Drink your wine."

"It isn't, is it? Untrue?"

Daiyan managed a shrug. "The old man has no reason to want me killed. I was unhappy about just about everything this morning, including removing my tunic and watching the emperor of Kitai step down to look at my back, but I'll wager the story of the Shen tree is a true one."

"Wager your life?" Fuyin said, forcing a crooked smile. He couldn't manage more, Daiyan saw.

"Already have."

The smile went away.

"They'll have their confirmation by tomorrow night or the next day," Ziji said.

Daiyan nodded. "And Wu Tong dies. What happens to the prime minister?"

The magistrate sipped his wine. "My own wager? Nothing. The emperor knows he wasn't controlling the Flowers and Rocks any more. And Wenzong needs him. He wants this Altai alliance." Wang Fuyin looked at him. "So do you."

Daiyan sighed. "I want to take our lands back. I don't care what tribe we ally with. I'm only a soldier."

"A general now. No *only* about that."

"But posted in the wrong direction."

Ziji stirred. "You really thought they'd give you the attack on the Southern Capital? Right away? Oh, surely not, Dai."

No one else used his childhood name. Daiyan shook his head. "No, of course I didn't. But I'm afraid—"

"You're afraid whatever old man they appoint will be as bad as Wu Tong," Fuyin said. "And do you know what? He *might* be! We may be humiliated up there, show our weakness. Then what?"

Daiyan crossed the room and poured more wine. He carried the flask and refilled cups for the other two. Back at the brazier he set the flask down, moved some coals with the tongs so it wouldn't overheat. He turned to the others.

"Then we have real trouble next summer. And will have to hope the prime minister is very good at negotiations. In the meantime, Ziji and I are going to try to make one army as good a force as Kitai has seen in a long time."

"Will they accept you? The other generals?" It was a serious question.

Daiyan laughed, but heard bitterness in the sound. "Of course they will. I'll just show them what's written on my back."

That is my own calligraphy! the emperor of Kitai had exclaimed. There had been wonder in his voice, and pride. *Even the spirit world knows my hand!* he'd said.

The magistrate shook his head. "All because of a tree," he said. "Why did the Shen family even permit it? Surely ..."

"It wasn't them. The old man says they sold the estate generations ago. Moved south. Those who own the land now were offered a great deal of money for the tree, and the graves weren't their graves."

"Even so!" said Fuyin. "It is *such* a crime that—"

"Money, and a strong message that they had better accept it," Daiyan said. "We know how the Flowers and Rocks works."

The magistrate nodded. "I know you do. And the emperor would have been so pleased to have it, if no one had told him."

"Too many years of him not being told things," said Ziji grimly.

Fuyin said, "We forced him to act this morning."

"The old man did," said Daiyan.

Fuyin sipped his wine. He was silent a few moments, and then, "Do you know, I believe I have just made a decision."

Daiyan grinned sourly. "You will attack the Southern Capital yourself?"

No smile. It was a bad joke.

"Unlikely. No, I am going to resign my position. Withdraw south to Shantong where my family is. I think this is about to become a difficult court, and I ... I have books to write."

"You just decided this?" Ziji asked. His expression was odd.

"Between one sip and the next." Fuyin sat up straight.

The other two exchanged a glance. "Your wife won't be pleased," Daiyan said, thoughtfully.

Fuyin winced. Finished his cup. "I will deal with my wife," he said, with more bravado than confidence, Daiyan judged.

But he understood the magistrate. After this morning he couldn't see a man of virtue wanting any part of the court. Which left it to the men without virtue.

And himself? A general, promoted so fast, too fast. A huge reward this morning, and the salary of his new rank, which meant more money to send home, money to *build* a home one day. But his thoughts seemed to be going down a different path as he filled his cup again. He intended to be drunk this evening.

You could chase a dream all your life. What happened when you caught it? He wanted to ask Shan that, hear what she said, hear her voice. She was probably with her husband, travelling this way.

ℰℐℴ

Two days later, at twilight, they slit the throat of the eunuch Wu Tong. He had created the Flowers and Rocks Network for the emperor's garden, and had commanded Kitai's armies in several fields of battle, including the northwest, where he'd made some errors of judgment and showed what could be called a lack of leadership.

It is possible to say that no man should be judged by another for how he acts when in immediate fear of dying. It is also possible to say that those who aspire to office and power must accept the burdens that come with those, including such judgments.

The body was burned and the ashes scattered in water, as was normal practice in such matters.

The scholar-tree of the Shen family was taken back to the estate above the Wai River, with some difficulty, as it was travelling upstream now. The best gardeners of that prefecture were assigned to oversee its restoration, and men came to repair damage done to the gravestones and the graves. Prayers were offered and contributions made at nearby chapels of both the Cho Master and the Path, and in the imperial palace itself. The tree was replanted with care and tended attentively.

It did not flourish. Not long afterwards, it died. Sometimes things uprooted cannot be restored, even in the same ground.

ℰℐℴ

Approaching Yenling, Qi Wai tells his wife about the girl.

Shan hasn't asked, hasn't really wanted to know. Perhaps once, but not now, since Xinan. But she can't very well tell Wai *not* to speak to her.

And so it is, at a posting inn west of the city, that she learns over dinner one of the ways she's been wrong about her husband.

The girl is seven years old. He had taken her from a house in the best entertainment quarter of Hanjin. She'd had her feet bound earlier on the day he saw her, though not yet with the bones broken, in preparation for a life offering the newest fashion in feminine beauty.

Wai had been there with friends that night, listening to music, drinking saffron wine, eating fish cakes. He is the sort of man who adds such details in a story. Through a curtain he'd seen the child shuffling down a corridor, heard her weeping.

He purchased her the next morning. Had her taken to Yenling, to a house his family owns. They had the permission of the imperial clan administration to have a place there, because of his own travels. He is paying for her care and upbringing. Her feet are undamaged. Her name is Lizhen.

Shan finds herself weeping at the table. "Why Yenling? Why not our home? Why not *tell* me? This is ... this is an honourable thing you have done!"

Her husband looks down at the table. He says, uncomfortably, "She is a sweet child, frightened of the world. She ... Shan, she is not capable of living or being educated as you have. It is too hard, unless someone is as strong as you are."

As strong as she is.

She is still crying, which damages his argument, she thinks. But he's right about the one thing ...it *is* hard.

"You thought, if you brought her home, I would insist that she ..."

She wipes at her eyes. Sees her husband nod. She says, trying to speak carefully, "I had heard rumours of a girl, and the binding. I thought you had a bound-foot concubine."

His face shows horror. "I would never do that! She is seven years old, Shan!"

"I didn't know." But Shan is still what she is. She says, "And if she were fifteen, not seven?"

Wai shakes his head firmly. "Never. This fashion may be coming, but it is not for me."

"I'm glad," she says. "Will you ... will you take me to see her?"

He nods. Then hesitates. "You thought I had a concubine in Yenling?"

Wai is a clever man. Awkward, eccentric, but his intelligence is real.

"Yes. I'm sorry. Of course you could have one at home any time you want. I didn't think you wanted one. You never spoke of it."

"I don't want a concubine."

He seems about to say more, but does not. She doesn't push him. She has learned enough for one evening.

Two nights later, in the house in Yenling, she lies in bed alone in the chamber assigned to her, having met the child—who is exquisite, and desperately shy—and she listens to the sound of lovemaking from the next room.

He is telling her this way, though the hints had been there from when they first entered the small courtyard here this afternoon.

She hears Qi Wai's quiet voice through the wall, and then another, deeper than his—the tall steward of this house. His name is Kou Yao. He has long fingers and large eyes.

Many things have become clearer, in the dark.

ON THE ROAD EAST the next morning, escorted, she is clear-eyed and clear-headed. Her husband has remained for a few days in Yenling. He will follow with his new finds from the northwest soon.

She is trying to decide whether his behaviour the night before had been cowardly or courteous.

Cowardly, because he hadn't the courage to speak to her and explain. Or courteous, because a man didn't need to explain anything to his wife at all, and because he'd allowed her to be private and alone when she came to understand what might be the pattern of their lives, going forward. She decides that his conduct can be said to be both.

The child will remain in Yenling. The chaos and rivalries of the clan compound mean it is not a home for an extremely shy girl, taken (everyone would know it, little is hidden) from a pleasure house.

Shan's conversation with Wai early this morning had taken place with no one else present. She hadn't been especially submissive. He wouldn't have expected it from her.

"I understand a great deal now, and I thank you. But there is something I must say."

"Please," her husband had said. He'd flushed, but met her eyes.

"There is a child in this house. You are responsible for her education and upbringing. Wai, you will have to be discreet. Even if it means locating your ... the steward somewhere else."

"His name is Kou Yao," he'd said. But eventually he nodded. "I understand." He'd tilted his head sideways, a gesture he has. "Thank you."

"Thank you," she'd said, in turn.

THEN, FINALLY, she is home. She sees her father, embraces him. There is a letter for her. Their steward brings it to her chamber.

Daiyan has written. He is gone. He has been greatly promoted in rank, after events at court. He is going to meet his new army. *His* army. Fifty thousand men. Wu Tong the eunuch is dead. It appears that Kitai will be going to war in the spring, which is the season of war. Everyone knows that.

He writes, she reads. "*I needed you, to be with you, hear your thoughts, the night all this happened. I am becoming aware that this will always be so, and not possible. But it eases me, to know you are in the world. My apologies for the hasty brush strokes here.*"

She shakes her head. They are really very good, his brush strokes. But she is seeing them through tears. War is coming. In the north.

On his back, placed there, *burned* there, by a creature from the spirit world, are words in the emperor's hand. She had been the first person to see them. A room in Xinan, above a courtyard and a fountain.

There is such a strangeness to the world, Shan thinks. More than anyone could ever record or understand. She dries her eyes and goes down to see her father, whom she loves, and who loves her with no ambiguity or uncertainty at all.

☙

Through autumn and winter, plans are made. Couriers leave Hanjin on a steady basis; others return in wind and rain. Not long before the New Year the first snow falls. The Genyue is silent and beautiful.

One army in the northwest is drilled and sharpened like a blade. The newest high-ranking general in Kitai isn't much liked by his peers, having risen too swiftly for anyone's comfort, but it is seen that his soldiers don't share this feeling.

It is also noted, over time, that the men he is training become remarkably disciplined. Commander Ren Daiyan leads forty thousand of them south, assigned to deal with a bandit uprising that has become a full rebellion on both sides of the Wai River. There are many reasons for unrest. The Flowers and Rocks Network has continued to operate. Forests have been destroyed to provide timber for new palace buildings. Taxes were raised again at harvest time.

Of course they were. A war is coming. Everyone knows.

It is reported that Commander Ren himself takes the field against the rebels with a sword and a bow. A bow, of all things! His men battle in and through woods and marshlands. Some of the other high-ranking commanders, hearing of this, make jests: about how Ren Daiyan is well suited for marsh warfare, given his origins.

His engaging in combat himself is regarded as undignified and disturbing by the other leaders of the Kitan army, a bad precedent.

The bandit rebellion is suppressed, quite rapidly. There are stories, probably exaggerated, about strategies used against them in the difficult, trackless ground.

The rebel leaders are executed, but only the leaders, it is reported. It seems that about ten thousand of the rebel fighters have been accepted by the new general into his army. This is also disturbing. They come north with him to the lands above Yenling.

They are too late to participate in the spring offensive against the Xiaolu Southern Capital.

That rebellion by the Wai River—and the need to send an army to deal with it—will come to be seen as profoundly significant by those looking back on the events of that time.

Four Altai riders, led by the war-leader's brother, arrive in Hanjin early in winter, slipping through Xiaolu patrols, apparently with ease.

They are treated respectfully enough, given that they are primitive barbarians. They have no concept of court procedure or manners and are reportedly harsh with the women sent to them. Prime Minister Kai Zhen's intention is to take the Southern Capital of the Xiaolu, as these Altai wish—but not to give it over to them, as they also wish. Not for only four or five of the lost Fourteen.

No, Kitai is not to be dealt with in that way. Not by steppe riders, and not by ignorant northeastern tribesmen, most particularly. There are limits to generosity.

The war-leader's brother—his name is Bai'ji—is not presented to the emperor. It is absurd to even think such a thing could happen. The Altai party meets Kai Zhen once, in circumstances and with a ceremony meant to overawe them. They are ushered past hundreds of courtiers into the prime minister's presence.

Not evidently overawed, the war-leader's brother asks through his interpreter why the walls of the city on the northeastern side, by the imperial garden, have been permitted to fall into disrepair.

The prime minister declines to answer. He quotes the Cho Master. He offers modest gifts of silk and porcelain.

After the Altai have started back north, the prime minister has the man responsible for maintaining the walls decapitated, along with his principal subordinates. Their heads are spiked above a gate. The walls are ordered to be repaired.

The mood in the city is, unsurprisingly, tense. Excitement and apprehension. There is some relief when the rebellion in the south is reported to have been suppressed. The Wai River is uncomfortably close to the capital, and the rebel forces had grown large.

The prime minister accepts the emperor's congratulations for this victory. He is rewarded with a painting of an oriole and plum blossoms rendered by the emperor's own exquisite brush.

There is winter snow, not unusual in Hanjin. Children play in it, laughing. The emperor's beloved songbirds of the Genyue are gathered by men and boys trained to do this, and are moved to a large, heated building—newly built, expensive—where they may fly free among trees and bushes until the cold season ends.

The emperor performs the New Year's rites with sumptuous ceremony. The new music for the rituals is played for the first time, using intervals cleverly derived from the measured length of the fingers of the emperor's left hand. There are fireworks, as always. Hanjin celebrates all night for three nights.

It snows again before the Lantern Festival. Red lanterns against white snow, red dragons in the dragon dance, and a full moon rising over all of Kitai, over all the world under heaven while fireworks flash again.

On the day of the Cold Food Festival the dead are mourned and graves swept clean. The emperor has already left the city in a long procession to visit the tomb of his father. He kneels there in highly visible homage. The war that is coming is being described as an act of filial devotion. It is known that the last emperor, Wenzong's father, had always mourned the rivers and mountains lost.

Spring comes.

When the world changes greatly this can occur because of a single dramatic event, or because many small elements, each inconsequential in itself, fit together—like the pieces of a wooden puzzle box, of the sort sold in any village marketplace for a few copper coins.

PART FOUR

CHAPTER XX

He felt the wind when it rose. He'd been waiting for it. Dawn was close, which meant battle was.

It was one thing, Zhao Ziji was thinking, to defeat poorly organized and badly armed rebels in marshlands he and Daiyan understood. It was another to hold a line against massed Altai horsemen. The Altai were not allies against the Xiaolu any more but invaders.

Spring and summer had gone catastrophically wrong.

They were in open country—bad for them, ideal for the steppe riders. They'd had to fall back from the Golden River because their forces farther west, near Shuquian and charged with defending it, had been overrun with terrifying ease, even with the river as a defence.

That meant that if Daiyan had stayed up there, using the river as a barrier, his army would have been encircled and destroyed. The Altai could then have ridden to Yenling, which would have been open, undefended.

Daiyan had sworn bitterly (which was pretty much what Ziji had

403

done) when a messenger had come racing from the west with the news of Shuquian—then he'd ordered his sixty thousand to pull back.

How did commanders with over seventy-five thousand men, facing far fewer than that among the barbarians, and with the river ahead of them that the horsemen had to cross ... how did they lose that ground so quickly?

Ziji did have an idea. Two, in fact. One was that the generals in command were stunningly incompetent. One of them had been expecting to retire this summer, not to prepare himself and his men to fight an invasion. He'd been building, it was said, a handsome property south of the Wai.

The other reason had to do with terror. Raw fear in the face of the dreaded steppe riders, the tendency of frightened men with open space behind them to break their line and run for that open space.

Ziji didn't want to think about Shuquian, what might be happening there now. The Altai were savage in taken cities and towns. That was how they created fear. Fear was a weapon.

And here they were, halfway back from the river towards Yenling, trying to guard it, blunt the thrust of this part of the invading force. To the east, in the plain above the capital ... well, they had no way of knowing for certain, but given their commanders there, knowledge, when it came, was unlikely to reassure.

Cursing the gods and nine heavens was no help. Cursing the emperor and his advisers was treason, and equally useless. They were where they were. Historians, Ziji thought, could debate how it had come to this. There would undoubtedly be conflicting views, sharp words exchanged over cups of tea. He wanted to kill someone. He would have a chance soon. He might die here.

Grey in the east, and a hint of more than that, stars gone there. Ziji peered forward, squinting to see. The Altai would wait for light, they could ride faster.

Daiyan had done what he could. They had low hills to either

side rising into higher ones behind, and on those elevations he'd placed his best archers, defended by men with their new two-handed swords, the ones he'd devised himself last summer. They worked, once you learned how to use them. You attacked the horses, chopping at their front legs, crouching low. If a rider's horse went down, the rider was likely dead.

Daiyan had been saying this, and making his officers repeat it, right down to leaders of fifty men, drilling and drilling. This morning was real, however. It was one thing to practise in a barracks, or hold the bank of a wide river, knowing the enemy would have to cross through a rain of arrows. It was another to be in the open, waiting for horsemen to appear with the first light.

Daiyan had the left side and Ziji the right. They were all on foot, their horses well back with the handlers. There was no point, none at all, trying to match cavalry with steppe riders.

Their archers were just behind them. From the time of his promotion, Daiyan had begun recruiting and training bowmen. Archers were disdained, within an army that was itself disdained. Daiyan called it folly. There was more than enough folly to go around, Ziji thought.

He looked east again. A pale light now. A few clouds on the horizon, quite beautiful. Then the sun. He heard hoofbeats, like the ending of the world.

ℭℌ

The prime minister of Kitai knew himself to be shrewd, experienced, not in any way a fool. He'd shaped a triumphant career in the intricate civil service of Kitai, and had arrived at the very summit. That said a great deal about a man.

Accordingly, awake in his bed in the middle of a night in Hanjin, he struggled to retrace the steps that had led them to this point. People were fleeing the city, large numbers of them, abandoning their homes, taking only what they could carry or load on carts. The gates were still open. They might have to be closed soon, and people knew it.

Others, mostly *jinshi* students so far, were speaking openly, recklessly, in turbulent streets, of killing him and the other principal advisers of the emperor. *Killing* them!

The emperor was terrified. Wenzong never left his suite of rooms. He didn't even walk in his garden these days, although it had been a wet autumn, and cold, to be sure.

How had it come to this? You made a decision that seemed wise, on reflection, after consultation. (Consultation protected you.) Then another decision was suggested, even compelled, by the first. And then a third was guided by that second, like a dancer's steps by music. Perhaps you then made demands in late summer that carried a risk, but one that could be managed, you judged, and which fit like a gold-link belt with the emperor's desires regarding the lost prefectures.

When his emperor expressed desires, a prime minister had to address them, didn't he?

So you initiated diplomatic action, advanced stern conditions in pursuit of those desires. Surely that had been proper? Especially when you considered the long glory of Kitai against crude, untutored tribesmen from the northeast.

It was possible, just, that a milder tone, more limited claims of territory, might have been wiser. But really, who wasn't wiser after the event?

So you ended up where you were now, awake and cold and afraid in an autumn night. He wondered how late it was, or how early. When morning would come.

He missed his wives. He missed Wu Tong, though for different reasons, naturally. Actually, the prime minister realized, sitting up in bed but keeping the blanket over him in a cold room, for some of the same reasons.

There were women in his household who could address his physical needs (more or less). But his wives and his long-time ally had all been very good at listening to his thinking aloud, then bringing their own cleverness to what they heard.

One wife had killed herself. He had killed the second. Wu Tong had been executed—for uprooting a tree. An action that would never have been known if an old blind man had let it remain hidden. There was always an old man somewhere. There was always someone.

Too easy to feel sorry for himself tonight, thought the prime minister of Kitai. Darkness and solitude, the bleak time before dawn. Here he was, doing the best he could to satisfy his emperor and empire, but doing it alone, without confidants, and helplessly awake on a moonless night with the Altai coming. Coming down upon them like a plague. Past the ruined Long Wall, across the rivers, through the grasslands and the harvest fields. Horsemen of night.

The Kitan armies over by Shuquian had broken and fled. Already! They had learned that this morning, an ice-cold message on wings. The army defending Yenling—under that commander he didn't like—was at grave risk of being encircled. The prime minister had no idea how the commander would deal with that, or if he even could. The prime minister wasn't a military man, he'd never pretended to be.

And their army north of here, defending the capital and the emperor and more than a million people, was the same force that had failed in spring to take the isolated Southern Capital of a leaderless, crumbling Xiaolu empire. That failure had set all of this in motion. A boulder tumbling down a hill, he thought, gaining speed.

He still didn't understand how they had failed there. They'd had ninety thousand men! Couldn't any of them *fight* any more?

And right after that failure, the Altai, with a smaller army, had ridden south in early summer, appearing before the gates of the Southern Capital at sunrise one morning. So it was reported.

Their arrival had so terrified the inhabitants that the city had been opened to them before the sun went down. Not even a fight! This, after the Xiaolu had ridden out, *twice*, and defeated Kitan forces with an ease (by report) that was humiliating.

It was their hopeless commanders, Kai Zhen thought bitterly, in darkness. He thought there was a hint of light in the east, through his window. (It was only dawn, he thought, not hope.) What had happened to the army of Kitai?

He was aware, but tried not to dwell upon, how many elements came together in that question. It was too late for irony. He was too cold. He was afraid.

Wu Tong would have known what to do up north, he thought. Although that was probably an exercise in deceiving himself. His old ally had been capable of dealing with upheavals within Kitai, routing peasant rebels, executing them in large numbers to send necessary messages through the countryside. But he had never achieved a real triumph against barbarians. There was Erighaya and, truthfully, there was everything leading up to Erighaya.

And tonight, out there under the stars, the soldiers of three commanders who had (of course) survived the rout of their armies— racing at the front of the retreat from the Southern Capital—were all that stood between the capital and disaster. Wan'yen, war-leader of the Altai, leading the eastern part of his forces himself, might be about to descend upon the imperial city of Kitai. What, thought Kai Zhen suddenly, would historians make of him?

If they were fortunate here, if they were profoundly fortunate, the barbarians would demand only treasure: silver, silk, jade, gold, jewellery, certainly Kitans to bring north as slaves. Depending on how much they wanted, taxes and extortion could probably deal with it. Given enough time, they could rebuild.

But if the Altai were coming for more ... if this was going to go beyond a teach-a-lesson raid for Kitan arrogance in demanding so much land, then *ruin* wasn't the word for what lay ahead of them.

He looked to the window. Greyness. Pale light. Morning.

ତ୍ୟ

He wasn't supposed to be in the front line of a battle. Daiyan knew it. Not since the Third Dynasty had commanders led their men in the field, and back then it had been ... well, it had been the great heroes, hadn't it? The men of legend.

He didn't see himself as one of those. He saw himself as trying to stay alive right now, and hold this field. Kill as many of the horsemen—and their horses—as he could. He heard himself swearing as he hacked and dodged amid the screaming of men and horses. The smell was bad with entrails spilling.

The Altai were upon them, above them on their horses. But they weren't breaking *through* them. Daiyan wanted to look over, see how Ziji's right side was holding, judge how his archers were doing from the elevations on both sides, but there was no time to step back. A horse loomed, lathered in sweat, teeth bared. Daiyan dodged right, dropped to one knee and hacked at its near front leg. He felt the curved blade bite, heard a new scream over screaming. The animal buckled; the rider, who had been leaning left to slash at Daiyan, went over the horse's neck.

The man landed on his head. Daiyan saw his neck snap, though there was too much noise for him to hear the sound. That one didn't need killing, though. He'd seen enough broken necks.

He chopped at the horse's throat and it died. You needed to do that. He stood up quickly. A lull in front of him. A space. He wiped at blood on his face, looked left and right, breathing hard. His gloves were slippery. The ground was slippery. Intestines and blood.

The archers in back had to be careful, with the front ranks of the two armies intermingled in hacking gore. The bowmen were supposed to aim towards the back of the Altai forces, at the horsemen stopped—for now—by the Kitan foot soldiers standing their ground.

It was too hard to see anything clearly from down here among his men and the enemy and the downed, thrashing horses. You could be killed or maimed by a fallen horse. That's why you dispatched them.

You needed luck in battle, he thought, as much as anything else. Almost as much. Men could shape their own fortunes, fates, lives, if only in narrow ways. A battle might be one of those. Perhaps a war. Their swords were an example, the ones he'd designed last year. They *worked*. Were you allowed, amid the reek of ripped-open bodies, to take pride in that?

You held the lengthened grip in both hands. You crouched to the right, putting yourself in a difficult position for a rider trying to strike downwards on his wrong side, and you chopped at the horse. If a rider fell, you killed him, and then you killed the horse so its legs would be still. It was ugly, it was savage. There was a kind of pain in Daiyan, a sense of waste and loss, killing animals so beautiful. But they were carrying the riders of the steppe, and those riders were trying to destroy Kitai.

You did what you needed to do when that was so. He thought of his mother suddenly, safely far away, then he thought of Shan, who wasn't safe at all.

He wiped at his face again. He'd been cut on the forehead, he didn't know when. There was blood in his eyes, he had to keep wiping it away. He could imagine how he looked. Good, he thought. Let him appear a savage today.

A moving shadow overhead. He looked up. Arrows, another black, sky-blocking wave of them arcing north. His archers from behind, and those posted to either side, aiming properly, trained properly. A year of that and more. That was how you changed a war from being a matter of fortune and the gods.

The riders had bows, too, but they loosed at close range in a fight like this, not with vast curtains of arrows. The barbarian triumphs were on horseback, they didn't think about setting foot-archers behind an army. (How would they keep up?) They raced over grasslands, the best horsemen in the world, and—just about always—foot soldiers and bowmen and any feeble opposing cavalry broke before them, or they died.

It might happen here. Daiyan had no way of judging the ebb and buckle of this as the sun rose on his right. They hadn't retreated yet, he knew that much. He was standing where he'd begun, men to either side of him. There was still a space in front. He plunged his sword in the earth beside him and drew his bow. Childhood weapon. Outlaw weapon.

He started shooting, arrow after arrow. Release, notch, release, at speed. He was known for this, he had a gift. Altai riders fell where he aimed. He went for their faces. That frightened men. An arrow in the eye, in the mouth, out the back of the head.

Two riders saw him, turned their mounts to charge. He killed them both. He was still cursing without stopping, his voice loud and raw. He was still wiping at blood running down to his right eye. The men beside him were using their bows, too, now. He'd drilled them in this. A year and more. You *trained* an army.

He'd thought they'd be the ones invading. He'd thought they'd be in Xiaolu lands this summer. Fighting north of the river. The long, bright dream.

Instead they were desperately defending Yenling with no clear idea what was happening to the west, where their other army had crumbled, and with no news of the capital either. Wasted thoughts. Nothing he could do about any of that. Right now you fought to drive them back, to break them. To kill as many as you could. What followed would follow.

Two truths of being where he was: your men saw you beside them, heard you scream in fury, watched you with sword and bow. Followed your lead. Soldiers fought more bravely when a commander was with them, not poised to flee from some ridge well back. But from down here that same leader couldn't see what was happening, make judgments and adjustments.

He'd posted four officers he trusted on the two ridges. They had drummers and flag signals with them to send commands. Trusted men weren't invariably strategists, but how skilled would he have been himself? This was his first battle. You didn't count fights against peasant rebels.

You didn't count bamboo swords wielded against imaginary foes in a wood by your village on mornings long ago.

IT WAS ZIJI WHO REALIZED that the Altai were breaking. Hu Yen, from the slope to the right, with the drums and flags, was ordering a slow advance. He was cautious to a fault, was Yen, and they'd discussed how a retreat could be a feint.

Weary as he'd ever been, but uninjured, Ziji started moving forward, waving and shouting to his men. They went past downed horses and riders. He killed anything that moved.

On his left he saw Daiyan doing the same, leading his own men on. Daiyan was bleeding from his head. It would need tending to. Not now. Not if he could stand and hold a sword or bow.

Arrows were being loosed from behind and on both sides, in long, carrying, killing arcs. The Altai had turned right around, he saw now—they were trying to get away from that deadly rain. They were retreating, they really were. Those who had advanced farthest were stumbling amid the dead and downed of their army and the fallen of Kitai. The trampled ground was ugly and wet. The arrows kept coming. They blotted the sky, a moving darkness each time they were loosed, then light again. Ziji was surprised to see how high the sun had climbed.

Ahead of him, the Altai were fleeing across the wide expanse of the battlefield. This had never happened to them, Ziji thought. Not against the other eastern tribes, not against the Xiaolu, not in Kitai.

You were permitted to exult, but only briefly. This was one battle, and others had been lost, and would be.

And this one wasn't over yet.

DAIYAN WAS READY to move into the open space before him but he waited for the signal. Then they heard it from the drums. Hu Yen on the right and scarred Ting Pao on the left both knew what was to come next. They had spoken of it as recently as last night, they had prepared it.

The drums were steady, carrying their message. He saw the Altai in flight before them, picking their way past and over bodies. They couldn't be chased at speed, not riders fleeing foot soldiers. But they could be ambushed.

The drumbeat changed. He'd been waiting for it.

From the hills on both sides of the open ground where they'd arranged this battle, new arrows began to rain down, and then— from each side—more foot soldiers emerged, and his own ten thousand cavalry, held in reserve, burst from the screening hills where they'd waited all morning as the Altai surged past to meet the main body of their army.

He'd set up two possibilities with his officers on the slopes. If their men showed signs of breaking under the riders' assault, the drums were to signal their horsemen from hiding and the hidden archers would fire at will towards the middle of the Altai horde. With fortune, and skill, this might break the advance of the enemy, turn enough of them to let the ground troops stand.

But if the soldiers of Kitai held, if they wreaked havoc with swords and arrows, if they did what they were here to do and the Altai turned back, their wave broken ... then Daiyan's horsemen and the second wave of archers were to attack the retreat. Their riders would smash into the enemy, forcing a halt, letting Daiyan and Ziji's advancing soldiers catch up. They would take the barbarians on three sides.

The bowmen and foot soldiers in reserve were rebels from the south. He'd offered amnesty to any man who joined his army, and a soldier's wage to anyone who could use a bow. "Turn your anger against real enemies," he'd told them in a marshy field by the Wai River. "Let anger drive us north again."

He saw the Altai reining up as they encountered fresh Kitan horsemen thundering from both sides. He saw them struggling to decide which way to turn in swiftly narrowing space. He saw them begin to drop as arrows began to fall. He caught up to the nearest ones. They were enclosed, uncertain. He set aside his bow, his sword was rising and falling, hacking and chopping, he was deep in blood.

COMMANDER REN DAIYAN'S army killed so many of the invaders that day, on a plain north of Yenling, that the earth in that place could not be farmed or grazed for generations. It was called an accursed place, or a sacred one, depending on who you were. There were ghosts.

That autumn morning and afternoon saw victory on a scale unknown for a long time in Kitai. It was on their own soil, against intruders, not pushing their northern borders back to where they once had been, but everyone knew—poets, farmers, generals, historians—that men fought more valiantly defending their land and families.

That day's fighting would be sung in Kitai. It would be chronicled, become part of one man's legend. But it wouldn't shape or define the events of that year or the ones that followed. That happens sometimes.

To the west, Xinan, once the bright glory of the world, fell undefended to the Altai force sweeping down upon it. The army sent to stop them by the Golden River had melted away like snow on slopes when spring comes with plum blossoms.

Xinan had fallen before. It had been sacked before. It would not be historically accurate to say this was the worst, but it was very bad.

In the east, above the imperial city, a different Kitan army would face the Altai and their war-leader, Wan'yen. The results would be predictable. The road to Hanjin lay open, afterwards.

ଏଓ

Shan's husband and her father, who are supposed to shape and guide her passage through the world using the teachings of the Cho Master and his disciples, are both determined to stay in Hanjin. Neither will leave, though for different reasons.

She is angry and bewildered. Is it one's duty to accept the folly of others and die—or be seized for slavery? Is that their acceptable fate? Do neither her father nor her husband realize that a court gentleman and a member of the imperial clan will be immediate targets of the Altai when they come?

They'd learned the results of the battle north of them. Word is all over the city. It is impossible to keep such tidings confined. Not in Hanjin.

There is widespread panic. Panic, Shan thinks, is an appropriate response. Would it be more philosophic to be indifferent? To expect heavenly intervention? A tail-star bringing death to the invaders?

Is it wiser, perhaps, to stand under cypress trees and discuss the best way to balance duty to state and family?

She is angry as much as frightened. There had been nothing necessary about this calamity. It has been caused by arrogance and incompetence. She does not want to stay. If their leaders have undertaken to destroy them through vanity and cowardice, that doesn't mean every man—or woman—needs to placidly accept it.

Although, in truth, there is nothing placid about the city now. A great many men, most of them students, have been gathering in front of the palace each morning, and staying past darkfall. They are shouting for the heads of the imperial advisers. Soldiers keep them from the gates, but the crowd has not dispersed.

A stream of people—massive crowds—are reported to be spilling out of Hanjin in all directions at all hours. From her balcony Shan can see some of this, over the compound wall. They are mostly heading south, of course, though some (with money) are going towards the sea, hoping to find a boat to take them away, also south.

Others are apparently going west towards Yenling, where one army (she knows whose army) has made a triumphant stand for Kitai, for civilization, destroying an Altai force.

So the second city of the empire is still defended, and rumour is that part of that army is headed this way. They are mostly on foot, however, and the Altai coming south are horsemen. She wonders if Daiyan is riding. He must be, she thinks. She wonders what will happen when he comes.

There is no clear word yet from Xinan, farther west. There is an expectation in the city, a dread, really, that the tidings will be bad.

They still have fighting men, the imperial guards, the magistrates' guards, soldiers posted to the capital, and they have their massive walls, but the field armies of Kitai are unlikely to be here before the horsemen come.

Why, then, would one stay? Her father had answered simply, the evening before, sipping tea, looking up at her, where she stood confronting him.

"They won't stop here, Shan. Some will sweep around us, and people fleeing are likely to be killed or taken. And the ones that are not, hiding in forests or fields, are probably going to starve with winter coming. This has happened before. How will so many descending on the countryside or into villages and towns be fed?"

"How will they be fed *here*," she'd demanded, "if we are besieged?"

"Not easily," he'd admitted.

Already some servants sent out to the markets have not returned. They are fleeing, of course. There are reports of food being stolen at night. Sometimes even by the guards, someone has said.

Her father added, "Here, at least, the court is in a position to negotiate from behind our walls. We have granaries and well water. It depends what the northerners want. I don't think they like sieges."

"Do you know that or are you just saying it?"

He'd smiled. The smile she'd known all her life. He'd looked tired, though. "I think I read it somewhere," he said.

Northerners. Her father didn't call them barbarians. He'd stopped doing that some time this year. She isn't sure why.

This morning, a windy autumn day, she's come outside to find her husband. Wai is in their courtyard, among the plinths and bronzes he's brought back from all over Kitai. Years of love and labour. He is warmly dressed. She is not.

"Why are we staying?" she demands.

Wai is also drinking tea, from a fine, dark-blue porcelain cup. He wears gloves. He answers her, an unexpected response.

It seems he has attained a new awareness of the honour and importance of the imperial clan. So he declares. He is courteous (he is always courteous). His father, he informs her, has expressed the view that at times such as this, one turns to rituals and tradition, trusts the emperor, who holds the mandate of heaven, trusts his advisers.

"Trust Kai Zhen?" Shan exclaims, not all that courteously. She can't help herself. "Who was going to exile my father to Lingzhou? Whose wife tried to have me killed?"

"Personal quarrels must surely be set aside at times like this," her husband murmurs. He sips his tea. "All of Kitai is in danger, Shan. Although my father believes," he adds, "that we will be able to offer enough in tribute to appease the barbarians. After that, after they carry it away, we can address issues of responsibility at court. That is what he says."

She is still angry. "What about Yenling? The girl, Lizhen? The steward?"

He meets her gaze. "The steward's name is Kou Yao," he says.

Shan nods. "Yes. So, what about Kou Yao? Are they also waiting for whatever comes?"

He gestures, aiming for the casual. "I decided to send them south, to my mother's property. It made sense."

It made sense. She stares at him. Awareness comes, illumination. "Do you know what I think?" she asks.

Qi Wai manages a small smile. "You'll tell me, I hope."

"I think you are unwilling to leave the collection. *That* is why you are staying. Why we are. You don't want to lose it. If leaving is right for them, it should be for us!"

His eyes flick towards his newest treasure, the tomb warrior from near Shuquian. It is so old. It is the history of Kitai, one measure of it.

He shrugs, again trying to seem at ease. "I certainly wouldn't trust anyone else to take care of it," he says.

Shan feels sorrow suddenly, not anger any more. Strange, how quickly rage can go. Overwhelm you, then disappear. It is windy, clouds swift above them, the trees rustling. Geese are flying south, she's seen them every day.

She says, quietly, "Wai, you understand that even if your father is right, if this becomes some enormous tribute to the barbarians, they will take the collection. All of it."

He blinks several times. He looks away. He looks very young. She realizes that his nights are filled with such images, a torment.

"I wouldn't let them do that," her husband says.

LATER THAT SAME DAY, towards sundown, Lin Shan, daughter of Lin Kuo, wife of Qi Wai, is summoned to the palace. She has not been there since summer.

The emperor is not in his garden. It is cold, a hard evening wind blowing. Shan has changed into her best blue-and-green robe, with her mother's earrings again. It fits her well, high to the neck, duly modest. She wears a fur-trimmed cloak over it. The men who come to bring her have indicated that she is to proceed with them immediately, but they always say that. She takes the time to change and attend to her hair. It is pinned, of course (she's a married woman), but not in anything like court fashion.

She isn't one of the women summoned to be beautiful.

She is taken by the guards down the long corridor that links the compound with the palace. The wind is sharp as they cross a courtyard, and then another. She has her hands in her sleeves. She is shivering. She is thinking about songs. He will want one. It is why he summons her.

She has no idea what the emperor's mood or mind are now. Does the Son of Heaven know the same fears as ordinary people? The people she hears shouting outside the compound, the ones she knows are funnelling out of the city right now, through the hard chill of this twilight?

Wenzong is in a room she's not seen before. It is heartbreakingly beautiful. Subtle, not overbearing. Beautifully carved sandalwood chairs and tables, a wide couch of rosewood with green-and-gold silk cushions, the scent of the rosewood hovering.

There are flowers in white-and-red porcelain vases on tables (fresh flowers, even in cold autumn). The tables are ivory and alabaster, green and white. There is a jade dragon. Lamps are lit and three fires for warmth and more light. There are scrolls and books on shelves and a writing table with the four tools of the craft. The writing paper, she sees, is palest, creamy silk. There are six servants and six guards. Food is on a long table against one wall. There is tea, and wine is being warmed. This might be, Shan thinks, the most beautiful room in the world. She feels sorrow.

Smaller than his formal reception chambers, this is the chamber—it is obvious—Wenzong uses for his quiet pleasures. His paintings adorn the walls. Orioles, bamboo in leaf, a flowering peach, the blossoms so delicately rendered you can imagine them quivering if a breeze came into the room. Every painting has a poem written on the silk, Wenzong's own calligraphy. The emperor of Kitai is a master of these things.

His city, his empire, are being invaded by hard men on horses, bringing bows and swords, anger and hunger, scenting weakness. Men for whom this room, its history, its *meaning* are next to nothing, or entirely nothing.

What might superbly painted springtime blossoms of a peach tree mean to them? Or the old poem by Chan Du beside the image, in a hand so elegant the words might as well be gold or jade?

What is lost if this is lost? Shan thinks. She feels that she might cry if she isn't very careful.

The emperor wears a simple red-and-yellow robe with an over-robe and a soft black cap pinned on his head. He sits on a wide chair, not a throne. There are circles under his eyes. He is not yet fifty years of age.

Two sons are with him here. The heir, Chizu, and one of the others, she isn't sure which. There are so many princes and princesses, children of different mothers.

Chizu looks angry. The younger brother looks afraid.

The emperor is quiet, thoughtful. Shan looks for the prime minister, Kai Zhen. She considers him her enemy—though she is too trivial for him to know that, or care. He is not here. It is not a room of state.

The emperor of Kitai watches her as she performs the obeisance. She sits up, hands on her knees. There are dragons and phoenixes worked in jade on the marble floor and there are small jade pieces on the small round tables near the emperor's chair. He holds a yellow porcelain cup. He sips tea from it. Sets it down. He says, "Lady Lin, there is a *pipa* here. Will you offer a song? Music warms a cold night." An old saying.

"Gracious lord, there are so many better singers. Would you not have one of them ... ?"

"Your voice is pleasing to us, and your words are. We are not of a mind to summon performers tonight."

Then what am I? Shan thinks. But she understands. She is a poet, a songwriter, not a trained singer or dancer, and the words are what he wants, not crafted performance by someone exquisite.

She has sometimes wondered what it might be like to be exquisite.

Which words? It is always a decision. What words for a cold autumn evening, with their army scattered and the Altai coming down and Hanjin in frightened chaos?

She feels the burden, feels herself inadequate.

The emperor looks at her. He rests an elbow on one high arm of his chair. He is a tall, handsome, slender man—like his calligraphy. He says, "You are not being asked to capture the times, Lady Lin. Only to offer a song."

She bows again, her head to the marble floor. It is too easy, sometimes, to forget how intelligent he is.

A servant brings her the *pipa*. It is decorated with a painting of two cranes flying. A log settles on one fire, sending up sparks. The younger prince looks quickly that way, as if startled. She recognizes him then. This is the one the people call Prince Jen, a name of affection, a hero from long ago. His name is Zhizeng. Eighth or ninth son, she forgets. He doesn't look especially heroic, Shan thinks.

Not being asked to capture the times.

Who could do that? she thinks, but does not say. She says, "Serene lord, accept a humble offering. This is a *ci* I have written to the tune of 'Silk-Washing Stream.'"

"You do like that tune," the emperor of Kitai says. He is smiling a little.

"We all do, my lord." She tunes the *pipa*, clears her throat:

I stand upon my balcony,
Looking down on ancient bronzes
Beside the courtyard fountain.
The evening wind rises.
Geese fly overhead, going south.
Leaves fall into the fountain,
One and then another.
Far away, mountains gather clouds.
Somewhere it is raining.
Here it grows dark under the river of stars,
Then the moon rises over houses and walls.
Shadows of trees lie along the ground.
I cannot keep the leaves from falling.

There is silence when she is done. Both princes are staring at her.
This is so strange, she thinks.

"Another, if you will be so gracious," says the emperor of Kitai. "Not about autumn. Not falling leaves. Not about us."

Shan blinks. Has she erred? Again? She busies her fingers on the instrument, trying to think. She is not wise enough to know what he needs. How could she understand her emperor?

She says, "This is set to 'Perfumed Garden,' which we also all love, my lord." She sings, though it requires a voice with more range than hers, then she offers a third song, about peonies.

"That was very well done," says the emperor, after another space of quietness. He looks at her a long time. "Please convey our greeting to Court Gentleman Lin Kuo," he says. "We will let you return home now. Music has layers of sadness, it seems. For you as well as for us."

Shan says, "My lord. I am sorry. I am—"

Wenzong shakes his head. "No. Who sings of dancing, or laughing cups of wine, in the autumn this has become? You have done nothing wrong, Lady Lin. We thank you."

A servant comes over and takes the *pipa*. Shan is escorted back the way she's come. It is even colder in the courtyards as they pass through. The moon is rising ahead of them, as in her song.

Her father is waiting at home, worry written on his face, relief when she walks in.

Later that same night word reaches the imperial clan compound that the emperor of Kitai has abdicated the throne, in sorrow and shame.

He has named his son Chizu as emperor, in the hope that the Altai will accept this as a gesture of contrition for arrogance displayed in dealings with them.

I cannot keep the leaves from falling, Shan thinks.

LATER STILL, the moon west by then, there is a footfall on her balcony. The door swings outward, sound of wind and leaves, and Daiyan is there.

Shan sits up in bed, her heart beating hard. How is it she has almost expected him? How does that happen?

"I fear I am making a habit of this," he says, closing the balcony door quietly, stopping halfway into the room.

"Not enough of one," she says. "You are welcome beyond words. You heard the news? The emperor?"

He nods.

"Will you hold me?" she asks.

"For as long as I am allowed," he says.

‹›

Many days later a letter came to East Slope. They paid the courier, offered him a meal and a bed. He was going on to Shantong in the morning with other letters for other officials.

This one was addressed to the younger brother, not the poet. Lu Chao was no longer an exile after his service as envoy, and though he had declined a position at court, he had been rewarded handsomely and had friends there again. It was permitted to befriend him.

The letter informed him first that future communication would become precarious or impossible, and his correspondent apologized for that. The Altai were expected very soon. Hanjin would be surrounded, besieged. What would follow was not known. Countless numbers had fled the capital, were roaming the countryside looking for haven. Xinan had been taken. Reports were grim. Yenling had not yet fallen.

Then the letter told about the emperors. The one who had stepped aside, the one on the throne now. His son.

Lu Chao went looking for his brother.

Chen was in his writing room, a fire lit. He looked up from his desk, saw his younger brother's expression. He read the letter. He began to weep. Chao was unsure why he was not doing so himself. He looked out the window. Trees, some stripped of leaves, some evergreen. Their gate and wall. Sun, clouds. Ordinary sun, ordinary clouds.

Later, they gathered wives and children, servants, and shared what they had learned. Lu Mah, who had changed since the journey north, who was more confident and more questioning, asked, "Father, uncle, who is responsible for this?"

The brothers looked at each other. His father, dry-eyed now but uncharacteristically subdued, said, "It goes back too far. We might as well blame the river of stars, or heaven."

"Not the prime minister?" Lu Mah asked.

A short silence.

"If you like," his father said, still quietly.

"Not the emperor?"

An anxious murmur from his stepmother and some of his cousins.

"If you like," his uncle said.

CHAPTER XXI

Wan'yen, war-leader of the Altai, struggled at times with the disturbing thought that his younger brother was a better man than he was. Or a harder one, which was much the same thing in their world.

Wan'yen and their kaghan, Yan'po, were both still trying to find air to breathe in the rapidity of change through the past year and more—since the night they had taken the Jeni camp and begun their move out into the world.

His brother had no such difficulty.

Until Bai'ji had persuaded him to see things otherwise, the kaghan had resisted the idea of naming himself an emperor. He'd been unhappy with abandoning tribal traditions. A court, councillors, walled rooms, walled cities? Taxation, and Kitan servants from the taken prefectures to administer granaries and building works, as they had done for the Xiaolu? It did not please Yan'po.

Wan'yen understood this feeling. It was not the way of the grasslands. And though there was hardship to remember if you thought back to their homelands by the Black River, and the bitterness of existence there, it had been hardship they understood and their fathers and grandfathers had known it too.

It made men stronger, that life. They took pride in things that deserved pride. There was nothing appealing, to his mind, about a house, however large, inside walls, however high. And Wan'yen had little taste for the luxuries that came if you were an emperor, or his war-leader.

Women, yes, but he had never lacked for the company of women. You won them in the tribe with your prowess, or outside it with your sword. Not lying on cushions, drinking *kumiss* (or the dreadful Kitan rice wine) and having them brought to you by others.

Wan'yen liked warfare. He liked riding across the steppe at speed, then seeing the terror in others' eyes when the Altai suddenly appeared against a long horizon. *That* was how a man claimed a woman—and his own pride. He liked nights under stars, listening to the wind and the wolves. He had a gift for the work of blade and horse and bow, and leading other men into such work.

He didn't particularly want to live in what had been the Xiaolu's Central Capital now that it was theirs, and neither did the kaghan.

On the other hand, if Wan'yen listened to his brother's private words, the kaghan—the *emperor* now—would concern them for only a little longer.

Yan'po had aged since their sweep out of the east had begun. He was angry, bewildered, not a triumphant leader. He was a figure of the past, Bai'ji said to his brother—exactly as the Xiaolu emperor had been before the Altai leaders had sat cross-legged on the grass and watched fire ants turn him, screaming, into a skull.

They wouldn't do that to their kaghan, of course, Bai'ji had said. There were quieter ways of sending a man from this side of the doors of death, letting him begin his passage through the spirit world where everything was inverted and the Lord of the Sky awaited the souls of men.

At that point in the conversation, Wan'yen had asserted himself. He'd had to do it firmly, since Bai'ji was stubborn in his views. The kaghan, the emperor, was not to be harmed in any way, Wan'yen made clear. Whatever the sky decreed as his fate would come to pass without intervention. Did his brother understand? Did Bai'ji accept this?

Bai'ji eventually did, or said so. There was now a different thought in the older brother's mind, however. If the younger was a harder man, and perhaps saw himself as a better one, why stop with Yan'po, with removing only the old man as an obstacle to his own ascent? Why not carry that same design as far as a brother less likely to die naturally any time soon? Bai'ji seemed to have no difficulty with cities and walls and an empire. He appeared to enjoy having captured women brought to him.

Wan'yen's own thoughts were simple. In most ways the steppe was a simple place. A leader was as strong as his largesse. If riders were rewarded in ways that mattered to them, the leader was secure. You could say he was loved, but that would be foolishness. You didn't live long if you thought your horsemen carried affection for you that would last when they were hungry, or felt insufficiently assuaged with the spoils of conquest.

So he had started south, in the wake of the absurd, arrogant Kitan demand for all their surrendered northern lands, even after their abject military failure against the Xiaolu. They were going to teach Kitai a very expensive lesson—carry back north more treasure than any steppe army ever had.

Wasn't that ambition enough? A triumph to be sung around campfires? *More than any riders had ever claimed. From the Kitan capital itself!*

No. It was not enough, it appeared, for his brother. From where Bai'ji sat his horse, on Wan'yen's left side, where he always was, it was only a beginning.

"We demand a tribute that will destroy them," Bai'ji had said on their way to Hanjin. A Kitan army was broken behind them, tens of thousands killed, the rest in flight, all directions.

"Yes," Wan'yen had said.

"They humiliate themselves to gather it for us. They kill each other in Hanjin to seize silver and gold to bring into our camp."

"I agree."

"And then we say it is not enough."

"What does that mean?"

His brother had shaken his head, with the smile Wan'yen had never liked. Bai'ji was smaller, Wan'yen had always been able to beat him in a fight when they were young. But his brother's eyes were cold, and he had that smile.

"Don't you see? We require a sum that is beyond them."

"And they can't do it, but we take everything they gather. Yes. I agree."

"No," said his brother, too bluntly. "No! We take all of that when they bring it to us, and then we say it does not meet what they agreed to give. And then we take Hanjin, brother. Make it ours. As a start."

"A start?" Wan'yen had asked.

This conversation had been yesterday evening, last ride of the day before making camp. A cold night coming, but they'd known colder in the north.

"Kitai is ours, my brother, once their emperor and all his heirs are captive. We hold the capital, we hold Yenling. Xinan is empty, it doesn't matter. We can burn it or leave it for the wolves. Brother, we *rule* Kitai, through men we choose. Their farmers pay *us* their taxes, they bring *us* their grain. We choose among their women, brother. Their officials serve us the same way they have served this fool emperor—or they starve like animals in winter."

"You want to stay here? Not go home?"

His brother had smiled again. Bai'ji was a handsome man.

"There is a sea to the south," he'd said. "We have heard of it, yes?

I think you and I should ride our horses into the shallows of that sea, brother. And lay claim to everything between the Black River and those waters."

"Why?" Wan'yen had asked. His brother had turned away, almost quickly enough to hide the expression on his face.

༄

People began dying in the city when winter came. The first ones were buried properly, their families observing rites. But when the numbers began to grow large, Ren Daiyan, sorrowing, ordered that the dead be collected and burned by soldiers, with all respect possible.

Food was in short supply but not at starvation levels yet, in part because so many had fled the city, but the very young and the elderly were vulnerable to the cold when firewood gave out. The Altai controlled the capital's Great Canal port, of course. They had the city surrounded. There was no way of supplying Hanjin.

Daiyan had made it in just before the gates were closed against the arrival of the steppe riders. He remembered the morning they had awakened to see horsemen outside the walls in a winter dawn. They had come in the night, to be here, filling the plain, when Hanjin awakened.

There was horror in that, and a driving, besetting anger, but also a feeling of overwhelming strangeness. He thought of the *daiji* at Ma-wai. Barbarians here felt nearly as unnatural, as if this, too, came from a world that was not their own. On clear nights he looked up at the stars and wondered.

He was one of the three commanders charged with the defence of Hanjin. Daiyan was the one who suggested opening the inward gates of the Genyue when it turned bitterly cold, allowing ordinary people into the glory of the emperor's garden—to chop down trees and break up the wooden structures there. He had proposed it, and approval had come from the palace that same day. There was a different emperor ruling now. Not the one who'd built that garden.

He had thought he might feel some satisfaction dismantling the extravagance of the Flowers and Rocks Network. He didn't. He couldn't find that feeling in himself, watching men and women, wrapped in whatever clothing they could find, take awkward axes to trees that had been lovingly placed in a garden meant to mirror the world.

They would burn, carefully rationed, in fireplaces throughout Hanjin. There was no mirror any more.

After a short time the Genyue was a wasteland. Groves annihilated to stumps, great cypresses, oak stands, cedars, birches, the orchards ...

The animals had been killed some time ago to feed the court. They'd eaten nightingales.

Walking in the nakedness of the Genyue, alone towards sundown on a knife-sharp day, snow beginning to fall from a blank sky, Daiyan had another idea. You could be sorrowful, thinking about the end of beauty (however it had been achieved), but you still had a task, and the city was besieged.

He rode back to his barracks through muffled streets and summoned their senior engineers, the men who built and armed their catapults, and he had them set men to smashing mountains and rocks in the garden. Some of these had been brought up from the bottom of lakes, killing men in the process, destroying bridges and buildings along the canal to get them here for the emperor's delight.

Two days later the first heavy projectiles began flying from the heights of the Genyue, to crash at sunrise among the tents and horse pens of the Altai north of them. They wreaked damage on a dramatic scale, causing shouts of alarm from men and screams from dying horses.

One pen was smashed open, Daiyan saw, watching from on the wall (he was exposed, but he did that deliberately, to be seen by both sides). The horses broke free, causing chaos as they bolted wildly through the Altai camp. A fire started.

It was satisfying to watch, but it wasn't about to break a siege, however unhappy the riders might be out there. It was colder where they came from, and they had no children or aged among them to begin the dying.

It was a short-term blow, no more than that. A boost to morale, unsettling the enemy. One more clever idea for Commander Ren Daiyan. They hated him by name now, the Altai. They knew who had destroyed their army above Yenling.

They still hadn't taken Yenling. Ziji and most of Daiyan's army were defending it. He had raced here along the imperial road with half of his cavalry but there weren't nearly enough of them. Not to break out and engage in the open. And not to defend the city if it came to that.

He half expected his own execution or surrender to be one of the Altai demands. He had thoughts about what was really happening here.

He'd said none of this to anyone. Not even Shan, though he had a sense sometimes that she knew. She had knowing eyes, and the endgame here would certainly involve the women.

He wasn't even supposed to be launching attacks with the catapults. Terms had been negotiated, after all. The Altai had promised to withdraw if Hanjin bought its way out of shame.

The numbers could break your heart. They could break an empire. Two million units of gold. Ten million of silver. Twenty million strings of cash, or the equivalent in jade and gems. Two million bolts of silk. Ten thousand oxen. Twenty thousand horses—because of course they wanted all Daiyan's horses. *Now*. From the city.

It was simply impossible. They could stretch some way towards it if city and palace emptied out entirely, but they could never raise this much. Everyone knew it, on both sides.

So Daiyan waited, and surely the court was waiting, for the next heavy footfall from outside the walls: the demand that was coming.

Heartbreak, and a rage that threatened to choke him.

And an awareness that they had brought this upon themselves. Demanding the return of all Fourteen Prefectures when they hadn't taken the one isolated city tasked to them.

The nine heavens and the gods knew Daiyan wanted that land back, but you needed to win your rivers and mountains, you didn't send a messenger to a triumphant steppe army—when your own had done nothing—and *demand* concessions. Were they so truly lost in folly?

He knew the answer. The answer was horsemen outside the walls and people dying inside. Smoke everywhere, fires for the dead, charred bones, no graves. A punishment, the riders were calling it, a lesson taught. It made him clench his jaw whenever he slowed enough to think about it. He wasn't sleeping at night. Watchers on the walls would see Ren Daiyan come among them in the darkness, hear his voice asking if all was well.

A lesson? To Kitai, from horsemen who scarcely had *writing*, who had been nothing even two years ago, a tribe barely known by name, in a wilderness halfway to the Koreini Peninsula.

There was madness in such thoughts. The world could change too swiftly for men to address. Daiyan wasn't a philosopher, he didn't take a historian's long view. He wanted to shape his *own* time with a bow and sword.

Hanjin was cold and hungry and terrified. They were abusing their own people in the search for valuables.

Soldiers had been ordered to go from house to house making sure no one held back silver, jade, gems, coins, the least amount of gold. Women's earrings and hairpins were seized from their inner quarters. Bracelets and necklaces. Hiding places were discovered. Most people were bad at hiding things.

Servants had been offered a reward if they informed on their masters. Daiyan wanted to kill the bureaucrat who had come up with that idea. He knew, by now, something of how officials thought: the informing servants would be stripped of their rewards in the next wave of seizures.

He was angry all the time, tangled in pain. Hurling rocks at the Altai from the city walls didn't do anything to help. He needed to master this feeling. People were depending on him. There had to be survivors in Hanjin, and elsewhere. There had to be a next stage, a new page that could be written. Cities fell, empires didn't have to. There could be—there *would* be—better words for historians to write and read in the scroll of this time.

The abdicated emperor was now called the father-emperor. Wenzong kept to rooms in a wing of the palace. No one had seen him for some time. No one knew what he'd thought of the order to destroy his garden. Perhaps he approved? If the garden had mirrored the world and the world was chaos, falling like a star fell ... ?

It was Chizu who now ruled, who had authorized the seizure of wealth all through the city. Who had negotiated—through Prime Minister Kai—terms for buying peace.

One of Daiyan's officers had suggested, only half in jest, that they use the throne for firewood in their barracks. In the square before the palace the students were still marching back and forth, in snow or slanting rain, demanding the heads of the "Five Felons": Kai Zhen and his principal ministers. That might happen, Daiyan thought, but not yet. He understood this, too, now. He was learning. Men's lives might be part of the negotiations. Women's, too.

You hated the terms the court had accepted, and you could anticipate what was coming next. But if you were a soldier, a military commander, what would you say to your emperor and his advisers if you strode into the throne room?

Let us fight them, Kitai will triumph!

Only one army, his own, had held against the horsemen. The others had been crushed like grain under the stones of a mill, then scattered like husks in wind.

The army had failed, not just the men at court with their little fingernails. Once, men might have sat in a wine shop and debated how this had come to be. Was there anything more pointless, when you were in the midst of the calamity, with more to come?

ఎం

He comes to her when he can, over the wall at night, through the courtyard, and up to her balcony. It is as if they are in a song or a poem, but this is not a place for singing.

She can see he is not sleeping well, if at all. After they make love, he does seem able to rest sometimes, his features sliding back towards youthfulness when his eyes close beside her.

She lies awake and looks at him, or sometimes traces, in fear and wonder, the *daiji*'s markings on his back. The words of his destiny—or the spirit world's amusement or revenge?

He had resisted a fox-woman, stayed among them here, in this time, because of her. Because of Lin Shan, daughter of Court Gentleman Lin Kuo, who has been accused many times of being a disgrace to her sex, to the decreed and accepted principles of their time.

She is loved. It is the strangest of all sensations in the world.

He told her, tonight, before collapsing into sleep, that in the morning he will enter the palace to say something that may end his time as a commander of their forces here. Or end his life. He has asked her to ensure he is awake before sunrise so he can be gone from her chamber unseen.

He is trying to protect her reputation, her privacy, her existence.

"I would do it better, of course, by staying away," he'd said some nights ago, on this bed, after she'd told him she knew that was what he was doing.

"I need you here," she'd replied.

She wonders if her husband and father realize the thing she has deduced by now.

The soldiers collecting the treasure of Hanjin have reached the clan compound. They have set up in the largest square, and people are expected to bring their silver, gold, gems, jade, coins. The collectors have begun going from house to house, searching for what might have been kept back. Hanjin is being sacked by its own people.

Shan has already taken them her jewellery and silver, wedding gifts from the Qi family, and her own more recent gifts from the emperor (the old emperor). Qi Wai has carried out their strongboxes of cash, and her father took them his own.

Only her lapis earrings, not valuable but a link to her mother, has she kept back. She's placed them on the altar in their front room. Perhaps when the house is searched, items on an altar will be respected, especially if they aren't worth much.

But the thing she's grasped is that they have *not* been searched.

It is widely known that Qi Wai and his unusual wife have a collection of precious objects. Wai has been in agony, expecting the soldiers and civil officers, the dismantling of the collection. He has spoken wildly of arming the servants, wielding a sword.

But no one has come.

Shan had walked out some days ago, wrapped against a cutting wind, to the storage warehouse they'd been granted by the emperor who admired her songs and her calligraphy.

Snow had been falling, slantwise, stinging. It was getting near to the New Year's celebrations. No plans were being made. There would be no fireworks this year.

The lock on the warehouse door was intact. There was a symbol on the wall above and beside it. The character for "fox." She stayed for a time, thinking, then the cold had forced her to move on. Arriving home, she looked up and saw the same symbol to the right of their front door, small, high up. You needed to be looking for it.

No one has touched their collection; no one has entered the house.

She looks at the man sleeping beside her. They hadn't made love tonight. He was so weary he'd stumbled and almost fallen entering from the balcony. He'd declined when she offered wine. She'd taken off his boots and sword, removed his tunic, made him lie down on her bed, slipped in beside him.

There is always desire when she sees Daiyan, she's had to learn to deal with that new thing in herself. But there is a deeper truth. She loves, as well as being loved.

He had fallen asleep almost immediately. He has not moved. Shan watches the rise and fall of his breathing. She wants to guard him.

She wakes him, instead, as promised, watches him dress and go out into the starry dark. It is cold in her room. There is no firewood any more, it is being used to burn the dead.

⚬

The prime minister of Kitai finds himself wishing he were a braver man. Physical courage, however, has never been a part of his training, or what he's needed to prosper.

The skills a man has needed to rise in Kitai these days are very different. The ability to memorize the classics for the examinations, to write of them intelligently (and with an elegant brush). To cultivate the right mentors and allies. To understand the lines of power at court. To seize an opportunity when it presents itself.

There had been courage needed during the faction wars. You were aware that if an emperor chose the wrong party you would be exiled by triumphant enemies, and impoverished, or worse.

He also knows that his recurring vision—of walking out through one of the gates and into the Altai camp, surrendering himself— would achieve nothing at all.

The barbarians aren't about to abandon a siege simply because the man who sent arrogant demands appears among them to be killed or displayed in mockery back north. And besides (he also thinks) his demands last summer were only made because the emperor wanted them to be. He can almost persuade himself of that.

It is certainly what they have told the Altai: that the old emperor has resigned in shame, has admitted his folly. His son, the serene and illustrious Emperor Chizu, has a different understanding of the way of things. He wishes to acknowledge the dignity and importance of the great Altai people and their esteemed emperor, Yan'po. Also, of course, Emperor Yan'po's honoured commanders, the brothers Wan'yen and Bai'ji.

The new emperor of Kitai has confided, in another letter written by the prime minister, that he would never have made such intemperate demands regarding lands Kitai had lost long ago.

Emperor Chizu desires to make redress for his father's errors and to live in celestial harmony with the new lords of the vast north. Kai Zhen had rather admired the elegance of his own last turn of phrase there.

But only briefly. It is a lingering foolishness to think in this way. As if a turn of phrase matters. As if barbarians can grasp it, or care.

And the same vanity applies to any idea of heroically sacrificing himself. There will be nothing heroic about what is coming to Hanjin. It is likely, however, that his death will be demanded. If not by the Altai, then by those still standing outside the palace gates.

This morning they are to receive the most current report on the treasure being gathered. It is hardly necessary. There won't be enough. They are unlikely to reach even a quarter of the terms they have agreed to meet.

Before the recording officials are ushered in, however, a different name is announced, and a man the prime minister hates comes into the throne room.

The room is still warmed by fires, perhaps the only adequately heated space in the city. Kai Zhen watches this man remove a cloak and hand it to a guard. The guard bows respectfully.

Ren Daiyan is armed, the prime minister sees. That sword he claims to have invented (something to do with horses), and a bow and quiver. He is famed for his archery. *Can a skilled archer shoot himself?* the prime minister wonders, acidly.

He is too tired to summon any real anger. The commander looks tired as well. Not as young as when Kai Zhen first saw him, in this room in springtime—when Ren Daiyan brought the message that killed Wu Tong. The tree. That foolish, unnecessary tree.

He'd made a point of learning some things about the man after that encounter. An inconsequential family, an outlaw for years in the marshes near the Great River. Illustrious background! Once, that history might have been a weapon to use against him. Not any more. They were recruiting outlaws now. Swords and bows.

Ren Daiyan stops in the proper place and performs his first bows to the new emperor.

Once, coming anywhere near this room while armed would have caused his arrest and probable execution. Now, it is a reflection of Commander Ren's duties and rank, and what has come upon them this winter. He is the only man the Altai are reported to fear, since that battle north of Yenling.

Because of that, this man, Kai Zhen thinks, watching the commander approach and perform the obeisances, is probably also as good as dead. The tribes of the grasslands are said to have inventive ways of killing those they most hate. The thought does not improve his own state of mind.

DAIYAN REMEMBERED the throne room. It had changed, however. Most of the artifacts were gone. Even the paintings had been taken from the walls—though those surely weren't being seized for the barbarian treasure.

Then he understood: they'd been the father-emperor's own artwork. His son was removing them. The throne was what it had been, and the painted screens behind it: rocky landscapes, river gorges, birds flying, tiny fishing boats at the very bottom. On the Dragon Throne sat Emperor Chizu, about the same age as Daiyan. Chizu was smooth-chinned, round-faced under his black cap.

An array of advisers and younger princes stood behind him. The prime minister was nearest the emperor, on his left side. Daiyan waited to be recognized.

The emperor remained watchfully silent. It was Kai Zhen who spoke. "You have matters to share with the court, Commander Ren?"

A smooth voice, as ever, but the man was visibly under strain. Daiyan said, carefully, "I do, Minister Kai." He faced the throne. "Thank you for receiving me, most serene Lord of the Five Directions."

It occurred to him that they were using titles of supreme grandeur as wards or talismans against the shrinking truth.

Chizu still did not speak. Daiyan realized he had never heard him say a word. The emperor nodded, though, graciously enough. Daiyan took a breath.

"Serene lord, I have come from the warehouses where the wealth of Hanjin is being gathered." He paused. The fires crackled. The warmth was seductive after the harsh cold everywhere else.

He said the first thing he had come to say: "It is the counsel of your military commanders, my lord, that we stop collecting it now. We abuse our people no more. We send what we have to the barbarians and that is all."

"They will not accept it." The emperor's voice was light, quick, precise.

"They will not, my lord. Your servant humbly agrees. But there is nothing we can do that will meet the terms imposed. They will not accept *any* treasure we send out as being sufficient. And in the meantime we are destroying the will and courage of our people."

"We need the gold, commander. We have accepted terms."

"Terms we know cannot be met, gracious lord. We will ravage our city, turn household against household, servants against masters, execute people for hidden bracelets, and the horsemen will *still* come when it is done. And, gracious lord, we know what else they will demand. We all know."

"Say it," said the emperor of Kitai. Which was unfair, except that an emperor didn't have to be fair.

And so Daiyan did. One of the things that had been destroying his nights. He lifted his voice, making sure it was steady. "The barbarians will assign a value to our people. To artisans of all kinds. They will claim them as slaves, chain them, and march them north. Many will die on the way. If they take enough, they can lose a few. Like their horses." Bitterness, the need to be careful.

"Every man," said Emperor Chizu, "owes a duty to the state. No one alive is free of burdens."

Daiyan looked at him a moment, then lowered his eyes. He said, "My lord, they will also attach values to our women. As slaves, to be taken away. So much for a serving girl, so much for a courtesan." He stopped, made himself go on. "So much for a well-bred woman, for one of the imperial clan, for a woman of the court. Wives and daughters. A great deal for a princess. Your sisters. There will be a very high value for those."

The only sound was the fires.

"A woman," said the emperor of Kitai eventually, his voice still calm, "also has a duty to the state. We have ... our ancestors sent women north before, princesses to be wed."

"By the thousands, my lord? Enslaved?" His voice had risen.

"Have a care, Commander Ren!" said the prime minister. "Remember where you are."

"I know exactly where I am!" Daiyan snapped. "I am in the throne room of the empire of Kitai which is the centre of the world."

Chizu was gazing at him. He was a smaller man than his father, sat slumped in the great chair as if weighted down. "The centre of the world," he repeated. "And so instead of these things you describe, commander, you would have us do what?"

He knew what he wanted to say. He had come here knowing.

"I would have us fight, illustrious lord."

There was a murmuring, mostly fearful.

He said, "Great emperor, Hanjin is not all of Kitai. What happens here will shape what happens throughout the empire in the time to come. If we are defiant, we kindle a spark. A memory of courage. The barbarians are far from home, they don't like siege warfare. And they will soon hear of trouble behind them to the north, with their armies here, not on the grasslands holding what they have only just taken from the Xiaolu."

"And how do you know this?" It was the prime minister, his voice harsh.

"Any good soldier knows it," said Daiyan. He was half lying, trying to make himself believe it was true. "Power in the steppe must be defended or it will be taken away. The Altai can easily lose what the Xiaolu lost! The other tribes will not love them, only fear them—and only if they are present. There will be fighting behind them. Depend on it."

Silence. He pushed on. "And our own people ... if we offer an honourable example they, too, will resist. There are past a hundred million of our people, great lord! This is not just about our own lives, our own time, great lord." He lowered his head. He was close to tears. It was the exhaustion, he told himself.

"And so what is it you want? We send what treasure we have now and say that is all, go home?" The emperor's face was intent, sharp.

Daiyan lifted his head. "My lord, your commanders propose something else. We send the treasure, yes. But we tell them more is being gathered. We keep them here, waiting. Hanjin is cold and hungry, but most of us can survive, if we ration carefully. We keep the Altai out there in winter as long as we can, without fighting."

"And then?"

"And then we do fight, my lord. Half of my army can come this way from Yenling. Men can get through to them with messages. The messenger birds can fly past arrows if they are released at night. I know my officers in the west. They have been working to gather the forces broken above Xinan. We still hold Yenling, my lord! We can send a good-sized army this way and those of us here can break out from our gates when that army comes. We can—"

"No," said the emperor of Kitai, and then again, "No," and it was remarkable how much finality a voice could hold when it spoke from a throne.

CHAPTER XXII

Two guards escorted Daiyan from the throne room of Kitai. Beyond the double doors they walked along hallways and through antechambers empty except for other guards, and then they came to the great doors that were opened to let them out into winter.

He stood at the top of the wide stairs and looked down on the palace grounds. It was a bright morning, the sun shining on a dusting of snow. There was an enormous square in front of him, buildings on three sides. The palace had been designed for splendour, power, majesty, to overawe.

Four guards marched over from their right. The original pair saluted and turned back. Daiyan wasn't impressed with the salutes, but these weren't his men.

The new ones led him on. He was still bitter. He didn't speak, neither did they. They went down the stairs, past stone dragons at the bottom, crossed the square in a cutting wind under a blue sky. The snow drifted across the ground. There were curved bridges over artificial streams. The water was frozen, he saw. He remembered winters in the marsh, a long time ago.

They led him up the stairs into the next building instead of along the crooked pathway around it. To be out of the wind, he thought. He was wrong.

Just inside, one of his escorts stopped.

"Your presence is requested," he said, and gestured.

There was a door slightly ajar. No one else was here. It was a ceremonial building, for rituals of the Sacred Path. All the clerics—the ones who hadn't fled—were probably gathered in one room allowed a fire, Daiyan thought. There would have been precious objects in here. They'd been taken away, gathered for the Altai.

It occurred to him to decline, but there was no reason to do that. He had no idea who wanted to meet him here. After what had just happened, it didn't seem to matter. Their course was set, like stars.

He walked across to the partially open door. He entered the room. It was an interior chamber, quite dark, with no lamps lit. He closed the door behind him.

He turned around, his eyes adjusting, and then, quickly, he bowed—three times, then three times again—and he remained on his knees on the dusty floor.

"That is not necessary any longer," said the father-emperor of Kitai. "Stand, please, Commander Ren. We ... I wish to speak with you."

They were entirely alone. Daiyan worked to control his breathing. His heart was pounding, even though this was the man whose inattention to matters of the world had—as much as anything else—brought them to this shivering, starving state, with invaders at their gates.

But you didn't *think* of an emperor that way.

Wenzong was seated on a chair in the middle of the almost empty room. Two long, bare tables along the walls. Nothing hanging, nothing covering the floor. He was wrapped in furs and wore a hat with flaps that covered his ears. There was no fire.

Small things: Daiyan would remember after how wrong it had

felt, that he was alone in a room with the man who had been the Son of Heaven and that the room was so sparsely furnished, all treasures taken away, and no fire lit in winter's cold.

Wenzong looked as he had both times Daiyan had been in his presence: once, to be promoted for saving the life of the emperor's favourite writer of songs, and then bringing word of a tree uprooted from a distinguished family's graveyard. A man had died because of that.

On closer inspection in the half-light gloom, that impression of sameness was a lie, shaped by reverence more than anything. Wenzong looked as weary and worn-down as ... well, as all of them did.

I ought to hate him, he thought. He didn't. He couldn't.

"I am greatly honoured, exalted lord," he said.

Wenzong twitched his head. "No reason to be, any more," he said. "My status means nothing. I mean nothing. Stand, please."

Daiyan stood. He cleared his throat. He said, "You withdrew to help your people. That means something."

"After failing utterly to protect them? No. I should not be alive, I carry too much shame."

Daiyan lowered his head. He had no idea what to say.

"I have offered to surrender. To take the prime minister with me into the barbarian camp. Let them carry us north as an indication of contrition, acceptance of responsibility."

Daiyan looked up. "They would not go away, my lord. Not before taking all we have."

"I know," said the man who had built the Genyue, who had authorized the Flowers and Rocks. Who had probably had no idea how it supplied his beloved garden. Who *should* have known.

Daiyan said, "I tried to tell this to Emperor Chizu. If the barbarians are set on taking everything in Hanjin, there is no reason for us to be their servants in doing so. Make them fight us for what they want."

"And leave a memory for Kitai. I heard you. It is why I am here."

"You were in the throne room, my lord?"

"Behind the screen. An old device. There have even been times when a trusted empress hid back there to advise, afterwards."

"The emperor seeks your advice?"

Wenzong smiled thinly. "No. But there are some still loyal to me, and I have ways of being in that room when it seems necessary."

"I am sorry," said Daiyan, though he wasn't sure why.

Wenzong stood. A very tall man, half a head above Daiyan, thin as an artist's brush. "I came to say that I agree with you. It is better, if we are to fall, that we do so with pride. To let the story run down the years. It is not just about our own lives. That was well said, Commander Ren."

Daiyan lowered his head again.

"Commander," said the father-emperor, "you must leave Hanjin. If I could order you to do so, I would. I believe you are the one who can best lead resistance, and that will not happen if you are killed here, or taken away as a prize."

"It is always more than one man, my lord."

"Always. But a man can make a difference." Wenzong hesitated. "By his virtue, or lack of it."

"And a commander who flees a city under siege, my lord? A city he is charged to defend? If he assembles an army to fight, against the will of his emperor? You heard what was said. The treasure we have gathered is to be sent through the gates this week. One of your sons, Prince Zhizeng, goes as hostage against delivery of the rest."

"He didn't want to," said Wenzong softly. "He was chosen for the wrong reason. Those two of my sons have never liked each other."

Daiyan looked at him. This face with the narrow beard was the face of Kitai's sorrow, he thought.

Wenzong said, "There will be no entirely correct answers, Commander Ren. We are mortals, trapped on one side of the river of stars, with the Weaver Maid on the other, divided from us. And how shall we hope to cross to her?"

What was there to say to that?

"What will calligraphy considered fine as gold mean in years to come?" Wenzong asked.

Again Daiyan had no answer. This was deeper than he could go.

"I didn't think you would leave," said Wenzong finally. "But I thought I should tell you my wishes, nonetheless. You are dismissed, commander. Conduct yourself with honour. You have our gratitude, whatever follows."

He walked to a door on the far side of the room. There are always other doors in palaces, Daiyan thought. He was close to tears. The door was opened from the other side when Wenzong tapped once upon it. He turned back a last time. Slender Gold they had named his calligraphy; he might have been the finest painter of his time.

"The ruins will declare that the garden was beautiful," he said, and went out. Daiyan never saw him again.

ᘛᘚ

Three days later, not long after sunrise, the ruin of Hanjin began.

Carts pulled by bullocks or by horses began rumbling through the principal northern gate. It took a long time. The Kitan leading the carts were sent back in for more as soon as they'd taken treasure out. Altai riders took over.

There were men on the walls and at the gate who counted the numbers and later compared tallies—to preserve details for a record they hoped would survive. And there were others who did use these numbers in histories of that time.

There is a value to precision, when it is possible. There is, equally, a problem with illusions of exactitude. Despite claims otherwise, no one knew, for example, exactly how many died in the various sackings and burnings of Xinan, either during the rebellion in the

Ninth Dynasty when it had been the glory of the world, or before that, in the Seventh, or at the hands of the Altai that same autumn.

Similarly, there were records made and preserved of the colossal treasure sent out in those carts, but it was acknowledged that the values were inflated, to make it appear that Hanjin was coming closer to the agreed-upon sums.

The barbarians, although they had men who understood finances and calculations (mostly Kitan clerks, from the occupied prefectures), did not bother checking. Not with the fixed intention they had of taking everything.

The day the carts rolled out happened to be mild, sunny, with a breeze from the west. The records indicate as much. There was probably birdsong.

Prince Zhizeng, ninth son of the father-emperor, brother to the reigning one, accompanied the treasure. He rode a good horse, though not one of the best—why give it to the barbarians yet?

He rode unfashionably well. He was in his early twenties, almost as tall as his father, though plump, round-faced. His nickname was Prince Jen, after a celebrated figure from the early days, though he wasn't handsome or brilliant. A poet had written a verse about him a few years ago, making that association, and the poet was well known, the verse memorable. Such things can shape a reputation, quite apart from any link to truth. Writers have the power to do that.

He was very much afraid as he passed through the city gate and came among the barbarians, and he wasn't entirely successful in hiding this. He was a hostage against delivery of the rest of their agreed-upon sum, and there was no indication how they were going to do that. There had been talk of assigning value to men and women, and offering them to make up the (very considerable) difference.

But even if that happened, why would the Altai give back young Prince Jen?

He was inwardly cursing his brother—and his father, unfilial as that might be. He was certain he would never return to Hanjin. The only question left was whether he died here in some horrifying way, or they carried him north and his days ended far from home.

He was unarmed, of course, as were the six men escorting him. Not nearly enough for a prince's dignity, but it was what the steppe riders had allowed. The Altai might disdain to examine the rumbling carts as they took possession of them, but the prince's escorts were closely observed for weapons on the wide roadway outside the gate. Not that they feared these hapless Kitan handing over all their wealth, but they had their orders, and the two brothers who led them ... well, those two they did fear.

Ren Daiyan, in the dark-green tunic and brown over-tunic of the prince's livery, did have a thin knife inside one boot: the concealed blade Ziji had devised for them years ago.

Only a handful of people knew he was out here, disguised. Prince Jen (silly name) wasn't one of them. Daiyan had two reasons for being here. One he had barely acknowledged to himself. The other was that he wanted to see the brothers leading this force. There was no particular military sense to that, but it mattered to him to have faces to attach to the names ravaging Kitai.

It had occurred to him that if he killed the war-leader and his brother today, the Altai might fracture into dissension, a battle among warriors to succeed the old kaghan, now called an emperor. The leaders here might gallop back north, stake out their claims, attack each other.

Most likely not. Most likely they'd be even more savage when they took the city. For the man who took command here, control of Hanjin's unimaginable wealth, returning with its leaders and women, would surely be a winning roll of dice in any conflict on the steppe.

Besides which, he had no way of killing them. He wasn't even sure he'd learn who they were, these brothers poised to take the city.

They were going to take it. Hanjin was being *handed* to them. He had tried to speak up for resistance, and Emperor Chizu's face had gone bleak.

"No," he had said, and Daiyan had had the feeling he himself was being carefully noted in that moment, and not happily. Did it even matter any more?

Some in the palace claimed to believe the Altai would go home once they had enough slaves: the next step of these hideous negotiations. Daiyan flinched away from even imagining it. What was a princess of Kitai worth as a concubine? As a slave to wash a horseman's feet, be claimed for his pallet, exalting him among the riders? What sum could possibly be proposed?

And how much for a woman from the imperial clan? If she was young? Could write songs? If her calligraphy was better than any man's? The bitterness in his throat gave him an understanding of what taking poison might be like.

In the far distance, he knew the river would be shining in the light. The Golden River curved a long way south here, nearing the sea. There had been elm trees lining the road all the way to the riverbank. They'd been cut down by the Altai for firewood.

Their yurts and horse pens filled the plain. They stretched as far as he could see, and there were almost as many to the west and south. They had judged there were about eighty thousand of the horsemen here, mostly on this northern side. He had conjured battle plans in sleepless nights. If Ziji could bring an army quietly from the west they could coordinate an attack against the smaller contingent of the Altai on that side, do it swiftly, savagely, at night when the riders didn't like to fight. Ziji could fall upon their rear as Daiyan burst through the southern and western gates with his cavalry and the soldiers of the city. Those soldiers weren't the best men, they weren't his own, but surely they would battle for Kitai if properly led?

They could use fireworks to light the sky, frighten the enemy, let them mark their foes—for one of the dangers in night battles was attacking your own forces in the wild dark.

He could put archers on the ramparts, sending arrows down on the riders here as they tried to sweep around to help the others. He didn't have enough good archers but he had some.

They would be outnumbered, his soldiers—they'd have to be, to leave Yenling defended properly—but they could fight bravely and die if they were destined for that, and leave a legacy of honour. They could try to ensure there *would* be a future for Kitai. That this invasion, this cold, hard sorrow, would be but an episode, a dark chapter among many over centuries, but not an ending.

If he'd been allowed. You could only do so much, if you were not the Son of Heaven. In fact, he thought, you could only do so much if you were.

He rode behind the prince, head lowered, but eyes alert. He had his other, barely acknowledged reason for being here. He needed to pay attention, and hope for luck. Surely some small good fortune might be vouchsafed them here by the Queen Mother of the West, from her mountain peak beside the stars?

The Altai lining the roadway were mostly smaller than the Xiaolu he'd seen in summer. They wore their hair with the front and crown shaved, long on the sides and down the back. They wore no headgear. Some had no tunics or vests, proudly bare-chested in winter to prove their hardiness. They carried short bows and short swords. Most were on horseback, though there was no need for that just now. These men, he thought, must feel themselves to be in an unfamiliar world when not on a horse in open country. It was a reason he'd believed they could fight them, in the close engagement of a siege breakout at night.

He'd never, in sober truth, believed that he could defeat them, even with Ziji bringing forces up. There were too many riders, they were too experienced, he'd have only some of his own army.

He'd been through this in his mind too many times. There was nothing left to think about. He was escorting a young prince to what was certainly his death, one way or another. The prince knew it. You could read it in his face. Daiyan wished he could say *Don't let them see it*, but he couldn't. Bitterness. The dregs of bad wine.

The Altai lining the roadway and back from it, watching the procession, were laughing, grinning, pointing to the riches on the carts. The sun was up. Gold glittered in the wagons, the flash of gemstones, silver. Sunlight on surrender.

The noisy, laden carts were being led towards the back of the encampment, nearer the river. Adjusting his hat against the brightness, Daiyan saw a cluster of men to the left, waiting, or so it seemed.

A rider detached from that cluster. He trotted a grey horse over, came up to the prince. Zhizeng flinched as the man drew near. Daiyan saw the Altai rider grin. The man feigned a blow. Zhizeng, to his credit, did not move this time. Daiyan couldn't see his eyes, but the prince's head was high now, after the one lapse. *Good for him*, he thought. The rider stopped smiling. He seized the horse's reins from Zhizeng and led him over to the group by the road.

Daiyan looked at the other escorts. They'd stopped, apprehension in their faces. They would be over there, in that group, he thought: the two brothers. He needed to hear what was said.

"Come," he commanded, though he had no authority here.

Sometimes authority came because you claimed it. He twitched his reins, moved off the road. The other five followed him. He stopped a judged distance away from the group to which Prince Zhizeng had been led as if he were a child on a pony. Daiyan could see them clearly but he posed no obvious threat, unarmed, head submissively lowered, another of these weak, frightened Kitan handing away an empire, uncertain where to be just now, outside their walls.

He watched. Someone lifted a hand and pointed. He saw where the man pointed and he marked it in his mind. Small gifts. He gave thanks. It was what he'd come out for, besides killing two men, which he couldn't do.

A rider trotted his horse over to him and the other escorts, gesturing violently towards the city gate. They were being ordered to go back. Other Altai came, made it clear with their signalling. There was no chance to resist. There was no point.

He turned back with the other five. They went past carts still rumbling out. They would be rolling through the gate for most of the day. A short day, he thought, then midwinter twilight. Probably snow later. It was almost the New Year, time of festivity.

He looked back once. Saw Zhizeng, Prince Jen, among the Altai, alone. They had made him dismount, had taken his horse. It wasn't his any more. The prince was standing among mounted enemies. His head was still high, his back and shoulders straight. No sign of fearfulness or submission, Daiyan saw.

People could surprise you. Could make you proud unexpectedly, move you to grief.

೦ഌ

With the first warnings that arrived, of the Altai coming down in great force towards Yenling, Hang Dejin had sent his son away, along with almost all the attendants and labourers and the women at Little Gold Hill.

There was difficulty with Hsien. He had been determined to remain with his father, or to bring him with them. The old man was fairly certain that his own son was aware of the courage shown by Lu Chen's son, accompanying his father to Lingzhou. People honoured that filial devotion. Given that Hang Dejin and Lu Chen had been fierce political opponents, it would have been difficult for Hsien *not* to be thinking about another son and father.

Of course he might be unfair in this surmise. His own son had been unfailingly loyal all along, ever present, anticipating needs, skilful and adroit in all tasks. There was some difference between being steadfast in the palace, in high office with great rewards, and going to exile in a deadly, distant place, but loyalty was still loyalty in a son. Hsien had almost surely expected to be prime minister after his father, but had just as surely understood (or said that he did) why this had not been, in his father's view, the right time. That view had been proven calamitously correct.

Sometimes you might prefer to be wrong, the old man thought.

There were only three servants left to him, plus a man to deal with the animals, and two in the kitchen. Seven souls on a working farm of several buildings. It was winter now, and cold. They had completed their usual preparations before the others went away. With only the seven of them they had more food and drink than they needed.

They had been safe from the Altai, thus far. The horsemen had Yenling encircled, but not securely, and not without casualties. The Kitan commander there, Zhao Ziji was his name (he had been here, with the other one), was extremely capable, it seemed. He (and the other one, Ren Daiyan) had inflicted a ferocious defeat on the Altai north of the city, destroying a large part of the steppe riders' army—and the idea of Altai invincibility. The horsemen investing Yenling now had come through Teng Pass from Xinan in the west.

The stories from Xinan were bad.

He was old, had read widely in history, had *lived*, it sometimes seemed, through a great deal of history. He knew of many times when cities had been taken by savage foes. The thing you realized, with a long enough view, was that darkness could pass, changes could come and bring light back. Sometimes, not always.

He had made it clear to his son as autumn drew to a close: he would end his own life with his own hand—after proper prayers honouring his ancestors—rather than leave this farm and flee through winter, slowing all the others down, likely succumbing on the way to their southern estates.

"There comes a time," he'd told Hsien, "when a man needs to stop. I am stopping here. If the barbarians withdraw and the farm remains, come back to me. I do not intend to die but I am at ease if it happens."

"I am not," his son had said.

He had turned out to be a surprisingly emotional boy. He was a man of past forty years. It appeared he loved his father, beyond simply honouring him. Philosophers said that honouring a parent was mandatory. But it didn't always happen. Declaring something to be imperative didn't make it so. Philosophers overlooked that. Sometimes prime ministers did.

"Do you know," he'd said to his son (their last conversation), "the barbarians have a set of beliefs about the afterworld."

Hsien had been silent, waiting. His son was just a blurred shape in a room by then. He kept his rooms well lit or he'd have been entirely locked in darkness.

He said, "It seems they believe that in the afterworld everything is backwards. Colours become their opposites. Black creatures are white, light ones dark. The rising of sun and moon are at the opposite end of the sky. The river of stars runs the other way. And so, my son, perhaps in the afterworld, when I cross over, I will see you clearly again. And be young."

He had permitted Hsien to embrace him before he went away, leading the others south to where the rest of the family was. It had been awkward, the son stooping, trying for self-control, the seated father lifting his head vaguely for a kiss. He did give his blessing. It was deserved, had been earned, even if not among snakes on Lingzhou Isle. And the old man still had hopes (diminished, it was true, by present events) for the future of their line.

That had been autumn, after harvest. The Altai had ridden from Xinan, later in the season. As winter came they came, he thought; cold enemies in cold days. He had no one to dictate poems to now. He ought to have kept back one man who knew how to hold a brush, grind ink, write words dictated to him. Mistakes had been made.

Little Gold Hill was set well back among rising and falling countryside, hidden in a valley, not easily found from the imperial road, which ran like a ribbon of civilization from Hanjin, past Yenling, past Xinan, towards the lost places of the west. The lands of the Silk Roads. Names like bronze bells ringing.

He had wanted to see those places once. Long ago. Now he sat in darkness on a farm in winter. He had food and wine and firewood. He couldn't read, there was no one to sing to him. He had thoughts, and memories. He heard owls hunting at night.

One of those remaining was a young guardsman. He sent this one back and forth to try to ascertain what was happening beyond the valley's winter stillness. He urged caution. There was no pressing need for him to know what was taking place in the world, there was nothing he could do, but habits of a lifetime were not easily set aside when one grew old.

This was how he learned that some of the Kitan army in Yenling had smashed through the horsemen surrounding the city and had gone off east.

They would be looking to find other Kitan soldiers, the old man thought. To create danger and disturbances for the barbarians, so far from their grassland home. To make them want to leave. He wasn't trained or versed in the craft of warfare, but some things an intelligent man could work out, with time to think.

He sent the guardsman around to nearby farms. Some of them, more exposed, more easily found from off the road, had been burned. People were dead, his guard reported, emotionally. He had seen things ...

"I need you to find me someone who knows how to write properly," Hang Dejin said. "I feel as if my hand has been cut off."

The guardsman went out the next morning, looking for an educated man among the snowy hills west of Yenling. Not an easy task.

THE ALTAI RIDER-GROUP LEADER, foraging again with his twenty men, was angry and unhappy. All of the horsemen were, in truth. His riders didn't particularly fear him (an added source of displeasure) but any Kitan they found had cause to do so.

This siege of Yenling had gone on too long, without any of the rewards that had accompanied the easy taking of that other city to the west. Commanders needed to ensure their horsemen received a due share of pleasures and treasures, especially if they were keeping the riders far from home in winter.

It wasn't the cold—it was colder where they came from, the wind howling, driving from the north across vastness.

No, the problem here was the distance from everything they knew, the alien, enclosing quality of these rising and falling, farmed and irrigated, marked-off fields. Forests everywhere. Ditches and canals and hedgerows and lines of trees: all hard to ride across. The sky was too close here. Did the Lord of the Sky even come this far south? A disturbing thought. Some of the horsemen had wondered if you would cross properly to the afterworld if you died down here in Kitai.

Add hunger and the boredom of a siege. Men fought each other in their camps over nothing. Add that the commander in Yenling, one of those who'd defeated them (a shocking event), was unnaturally skilled at sorties and ambushes. The Altai were losing men as well as patience here. Note all of this, and for good measure add that his superior officers had made it clear they were displeased with the results of his forays west.

Any wonder he'd hacked the arms from the first two farmers they'd encountered this time out? Done it himself. Blood in the snow. Screams before they were silent. But that meant they couldn't use their interpreter to question those two about farms and food in these twisty, evil hills and valleys (he hated hills and valleys).

His second-in-command had muttered a query when he'd used his sword on a third captured peasant, but he'd needed to do something to get rid of the sour, stale feeling of inactivity. Blood did help. *Kumiss* wasn't enough and they didn't have enough *kumiss* any more.

Killing men sent a message, he told himself. Fear was useful. Although there weren't many Kitan who needed that message any more. They hadn't found even one woman, for example, in weeks of riding out. Some of his foraging party forced Kitan men for their pleasure, but the captain found that undignified.

He grunted, but with a degree of approval, when one of those he'd sent north of the road came back to report they'd spotted a man on horseback, tracks in snow, moving cautiously.

They tracked him to a small farm, marked where it was, and continued following him when he left. It was easy to follow a man in country such as this, with tracks in snow.

They marked the two other farms this Kitan visited. They left them alone for now, followed the solitary figure back, later in the day, to a larger, hidden farm in a valley well north of the road, shielded on two sides by woods. They'd have continued to miss it, the group leader thought, looking happily down on hearth smoke. There were many buildings. There might be women.

There weren't, although there was a satisfying amount of food in granaries and storehouses and there were cows and chickens and a dozen pigs. Three horses. Only a handful of men, the rest had fled. People were always fleeing. They found the guard they'd tracked, five servants, and then an old, blind man in a room blazing with light.

The old man was sitting in a handsome chair and the room was filled with the sorts of treasures the Kitan valued. The Altai captain thought these were items of immense triviality, except for the precious metals and gems, of course. Still, orders had come that they were to collect and ship home to the Eastern Capital anything found. He'd be well served by this discovery, and ought to be able to keep back a few things for himself. The day had become a good one, after all.

The old man spoke a few words in his own tongue. His voice was unexpectedly forceful, arrogantly so, the captain felt. Their interpreter replied, the old man spoke again.

"What is he saying?" the captain rasped.

The Kitan interpreter, properly subservient, said, "He asked if I was the scribe he had sent for. I told him not so. He asked if you were Altai with me. I said yes, I am interpreter. He asked my family name and I told him. He says ... that he can smell you. He calls me a traitor, and instructs me to say he despises you as barbarians."

As the interpreter spoke, the old man calmly drank from a wine cup at his elbow, reaching out carefully with his hand to find it.

The Altai captain listened to it all, gave a bark of laughter. "Does he say such things? Shall he live?"

The old man asked a question, head turned towards the interpreter's voice. The interpreter spoke to him.

"He says?"

"I tell him your words. He says Kitai will live whether he does so or not and that he has lived long enough if barbarians are in his home."

That was enough defiance, the captain thought. Words like that could undermine his standing. He drew his sword. A little late, in the event. The old man's head stiffened. It flexed backwards then came forward heavily, all the way down, as if his spine had been severed.

The wine, of course. The old man had been prepared.

He looked at one of his riders. The man strode forward and confirmed what was obvious. After a long, angry moment, feeling deprived and insulted, the captain turned to the interpreter. He urgently wanted to kill him, for the words that had left his mouth, but the worm was necessary still. He could be cut apart later, when they left to go home.

He assigned men to begin gathering food supplies on whatever carts were here, and arranging to herd the animals back to camp. He permitted them to do whatever they wanted with the servants.

It was still a good day, he told himself, but the encounter had left him unhappy. It was as if the old man had escaped him, crossing into death. They cut his hands off and left him there, in his chair, unburied, unburned. Let him rot, let animals feed on him.

That didn't happen. After the riders left in the morning, having spent the night at Little Gold Hill, men slipped down from the hills and came to the farm. The Altai would be returning, of course, possibly even today, with carts to carry away plunder from the estate. Working quickly, the Kitan gathered as much as they could of food and valuables. They burned, in haste but with honour, the slain servants and the two guardsmen.

The body of the former prime minister was carried away from Little Gold Hill, his last home. They retrieved his severed hands and wrapped them in cloth.

In a valley not far away, Hang Dejin was buried, properly, with great respect, though without the ceremony a better, brighter time might have allowed. Snow was falling. The winter ground was hard. But he had been a great man, a leader of Kitai for many years, and there was no stinting in the labour. The gravesite was marked with certain signs that might allow him to be found, should that brighter time ever come.

There was no immediate way to send word to his family in the south, but they did find out, eventually, the manner of his passing.

The interpreter, an educated man, survived, fleeing some months later across fields and into the woods from the Altai camp, enduring in the forest because the weather was warming by then and because the steppe riders moved on from Yenling. Because of this, because he lived, and wrote down his recollections of that day, men came to know what Hang Dejin's last words had been—or the words attributed to him.

There were peonies in Yenling when spring came, even in that year. Flowers grow, whether or not men and women are able to celebrate them, wear them in their hair.

CHAPTER XXIII

Court Gentleman Lin Kuo died that winter, not long before the New Year.

He wasn't particularly old, but had suffered from a breathing difficulty for a number of years, and he caught a chill and fever in the bitter cold, with the shortage of firewood. He succumbed not long after taking to his bed. It could be called mercifully swift. A physician had been summoned, and actually attended—unusual in that time, but this was still the imperial clan compound. He'd tried two different decoctions, and essayed moxibustion on the court gentleman's chest, but was unable to avert the end. There were so many deaths in a bleak time. What could be said about one more? What words to close a life?

He'd been somewhat respected, somewhat a figure of amusement. A gentle man, stepping carefully, inconsequential in almost all ways that might be said to matter. Intelligent, obviously. He had passed the examinations on only his second effort, which was noteworthy, but had done nothing with his *jinshi* status, never agitated for or held a position at court or in the provinces. Had seemed content with his stipend as a graduate. Not a man of ambition.

He'd enjoyed good wine and food, thoughtful company. Spoke wittily, but in a soft voice, and many times his comments went unheard in a loud gathering. He didn't seem to mind. He laughed when others said clever things. He recorded these in journals or letters. He read widely. He wrote to many people. He kept friendships on both sides of the faction wars that dominated his youth and continued into his later years. He showed courage in this, but did so quietly. It might be said that his declining to pursue a court position was a declining to take sides.

His one encounter with the greater sweep of events came later in life. He was sentenced to exile on the orders of the deputy prime minister, all the way to Lingzhou Isle, which would undoubtedly have killed a man with breathing difficulties. The sentence had been reversed by the emperor himself, in circumstances of drama and consequence.

He'd been a notably tall man, Lin Kuo, slightly stooped as if apologizing for that. His formal calligraphy was clear, very straight along a page, not memorable. His running hand, which few ever saw, was different: intense, energetic.

Gardens were a passion, and he travelled widely to observe and record (with permission) the properties of members of the court and various country estates of those who had withdrawn from Hanjin. He crafted an essay about Emperor Wenzong's beloved Genyue. His writing style in these little pieces was perhaps too much enthused or flattering, and this caused some later historians to dismiss his essay on the imperial garden. They judged that no earthly garden, even an emperor's, could ever have been as Lin Kuo described the Genyue before it was destroyed. His was, in fact, the only detailed record of it that endured.

There is an element of the random, the accidental in what

survives. It isn't always a matter of fame or prominence. There were poets of the Third and Fifth Dynasties, and even among the giants of the Ninth, of whom little was left but the praise of their peers, and their names. The same was true of painters, calligraphers. Their work endured, often, only in copies made of originals, if it did so at all. There are poems about paintings, but the paintings are lost.

Lin Kuo's little book on the Genyue survived because he sent copies, with modest personal inscriptions, to some distinguished figures in the provinces, some of them south of the Great River— which was where copies were later found.

He married once, not long after passing the examinations, and never remarried when his wife died, or even took a concubine, which was unusual. It was said, by those who had bothered to take note of it, that theirs had been a love match. He had one daughter.

Nonetheless, if there is a value to a quiet life, there may be said to have been value to Lin Kuo's. Not every man or woman sailing down the river will be a figure of force or significance. Some are merely in the boat with all of us.

An emperor had written long ago that in the presence of a good man he was given—as in a bronze mirror—a reflection of how to live a virtuous life.

Lin Kuo himself would have said that his legacy was his daughter. Or no. He'd have believed that, but never voiced the thought, for fear of putting a burden of such weight upon her shoulders, which would be an improper thing to do to anyone, let alone a child so dearly loved from the beginning of her days to the end of his.

∞

They are eating maggot-infested rice in the clan compound now, and the well is guarded all the time, each family limited to three small containers a day.

They collect their rice and water each morning. Cooking the

rice is a difficulty. They are all dismantling interior walls and floors in upper rooms for firewood. Houses are dangerous, people have fallen and died.

Shan has taken one of her husband's old hats and stitched hers inside it, for warmth. She looks, she thinks, like a market performer, making children and farmers laugh for coins dropped in a box.

The markets are empty. There is nothing to sell. People mostly keep indoors, out of the wind. Those abroad in Hanjin are often looking for access to the houses or shops of the dead—for wood, for scraps of food. For anything. They have eaten all the cats and dogs. The city guards and the soldiers, Daiyan's soldiers, are patrolling. They have instructions to kill those found looting. They have done so. Order, or the illusion of order.

She goes herself each morning to the main square of the compound to get their food. She takes two of the four women who have remained. The others had all fled before the gates were locked. They line up, bundled against the cold. She finds that she hardly feels it. Grief is a deeper cold.

Qi Wai has been properly sympathetic; he'd honoured her father. Her husband is a haunted man these days. She hears him go out at night sometimes. She knows where he goes.

He is terrified that the strange safeguarding of their warehouse will be rescinded and the collection taken away. She knows who has ordered this, he does not. It bars him from sleep or rest, this fear. He can't understand why the collection remains undisturbed though almost all else of value in the city has been gathered—and sent out in wagons through the northern gate a week before.

So he guards the warehouse. In the cold dark alone, or by daylight after the weak sun rises. He is exhausted, haggard, his beard unkempt. One morning, catching him before he goes out, as she returns with their rice, the servants carrying the water, Shan makes him sit down and she trims his beard, acting as a servant might.

Or a slave to a conquering horseman. She dreams, when she does sleep, of grassland in all directions, emptiness.

Negotiations have begun as to the valuation of men and women to be given over to the Altai. They want craftsmen, it seems, and men with skill in numbers. They want women. She tries to imagine the recording of these assessments, out by the yurts. Younger women are valued more, so are aristocrats. She is the daughter of a court gentleman. She is of the imperial clan. She is still young. She dreams of the steppe, wakes in the cold nights.

The New Year is almost upon them.

Her father is dead. She lights his candle each morning, leaves a (small) dish of cooked rice on the altar at evening, and each afternoon she writes out a line of poetry, or words from the Cho Master, folds the paper carefully, and leaves that on the altar, too.

She has heard that some animals burrow deep and curl themselves tightly around their own heart to sleep through the winter, barely alive.

She feels that way. She doesn't expect springtime will be an awakening. She remembers the teachings concerning when it is judged virtuous for a woman to take her own life rather than accept some levels or degrees of shame.

She discovers that she is too angry to do that. She wants to kill someone else, not herself. She wants to live to help undo what this has become, or see it undone by others, since she is only a woman and has no sword.

She learns one morning, as word reaches the compound, that Prime Minister Kai Zhen has been strangled in the night by order of the emperor. The new emperor.

This is also the fate of four other principal advisers, it seems. The "Five Felons" the students had named them, shouting and protesting in front of the palace. The Altai had wanted the prime minister alive, it is said. There has been, it seems, a kind of compromise: his body has been sent out to them, to do with as they wish. There is shame here, too.

The students who had been demanding these deaths have now dispersed. She no longer hears them from over the compound wall. She wonders if they feel satisfaction. Shan had expected to feel some kind of pleasure at this news, a vengeance achieved for her father, justice done.

She does not, wrapped around her heart in the cold. She thinks of that crumbling, dangerous tower in Xinan, near the garden where the court and the people of the city had gathered in springtime long ago, ladies riding with feathers in their hair, poets watching them.

Late afternoon of the day before New Year's eve, a message comes from Daiyan.

In his own hand it instructs her to be with Qi Wai outside the Never-Ending Riches Tea House by the western city gate at sundown tomorrow. They are to dress as warmly as they can and carry nothing. The last character is stressed. They are to be ready for a journey. She is to burn this letter.

She stares at the characters a long time. She burns the letter. She goes to find her husband. He is not in his rooms. She puts on her layers of clothing and her undignified hat and finds him in front of their warehouse on the far side of the compound. It is a grey afternoon, not as cold as some have been. There will be snow before night, she thinks, looking at the sky.

Wai is pacing back and forth before the locked doors of the storage building. There is no one else in the square. She sees an old sword propped against the wall and she sees the mark above the door that has protected it to this point. Nothing will protect it if the Altai enter the city.

She bows. She says, "Greetings, husband. We have been offered help in escaping tomorrow night. One of the commanders, the one who saved me in the Genyue. We need to make ourselves ready."

His eyes have become strange, quick, darting, on her then past her, as if fearing attackers rushing across the square or into it from either side. It is as if this siege—all the dying, awareness of what might come next, negotiations for human lives—all of it has undone him. He is not alone in this, Shan thinks. She's nothing near what she'd have called her own self. No one is, surely. How could you be?

He says, "I cannot leave, Shan. There is no one to guard it."

She feels pity, reaching in through the cold of her heart. "Wai, you cannot guard it. You know this. You must know it."

"I do not know such a thing! It would only be street thieves. My father says—"

"Your father said the horsemen would go away. They are not going away. It is not street thieves, Wai. Our court officials are outside the walls setting a price on members of the imperial clan. On me, on you. On your father and mother, Wai. On everyone they think worth anything."

"Worth? What am I worth?" he cries, anguished. "To them?"

"Not as much as me," she says, and regrets it, seeing his face.

He takes a breath. His head bobs up and down. "Yes. You must go," her husband says. "I know this. They want our women. You must not stay if there is any chance to get out. How? How is this man to do this?"

"I don't know," she says, because she doesn't. "Husband, you must come too. We are being given a chance, past when we had any right to hope for one. We ... you can build another collection. You know you can."

He shakes his head. "My life is inside this storehouse."

Simple words, and she knows them to be true. She is not his life, no one is. Bronze bells and tripods are, stone plinths, court seals, fragments of bowls and vases, a sculpted figure for an emperor's tomb ... a record of what Kitai has been.

"Then you must start again," she says. "If we survive. You *need* to build it up again, so that others might know."

"I cannot," Qi Wai says. "Shan, wife, I cannot. You go. I will follow south if I survive this. If ... if I do not and you do live, to honour me please look after Lizhen if you can. And ... see that Kou Yao is all right."

She looks at him. Feels the first soft flakes of snow beginning to fall. She looks up. Snow on her cheeks. She feels no anger. Only sorrow.

"Wai—" she begins.

"Go," he says. "This is my proper place. Whatever the gods decree will happen." He spreads his feet as if to steady himself.

She lowers her head. "It is wrong for a wife to leave her husband in this way," she says.

He laughs suddenly. A sound from long ago when they'd been young, newly wed, travelling together, cataloguing what they found, holding objects up to sunlight or lamps lit after dark.

"As your husband I command you," he says.

She looks up, sees that he is smiling, that he knows the words have nothing to do with them, what they have been in their time.

Flakes of snow are on his hat and cloak, and on her own. It is growing dark. No one is abroad. Why would anyone be abroad? Tomorrow is the eve of the New Year, a time of celebration, red lanterns and dragons, fireworks. Not this year.

She bows to him twice. He bows to her.

She turns and leaves, crossing the empty square, muffled in falling snow, going up another darkening street towards home, in the winter of Hanjin's fall.

ର୍ଷ

At sundown the next day, New Year's eve, traditional beginning of two weeks of festivity, the northern gates of Hanjin were opened, as they had been for several evenings now, to allow their negotiators to come back in.

It was to be a quiet night, no music, no fireworks. There would be prayers, rituals, invocations at cold temples. In the palace, the young emperor would beseech good fortune for the coming days and a renewal of his mandate from heaven. None of the customary celebrations were planned.

None took place. The gates were never closed that night.

The first Altai riders came in with the returning negotiators, in force and at speed. They killed the gate guards, then others flooded in, spreading through the city like a river bursting its banks, and the fall of Hanjin began that night.

It seemed that someone in authority among the yurts had decided that this game, this back and forth of sums attached to courtiers and court ladies and hat-makers and musicians, had grown tiresome.

There were riders to be assuaged, far from home and so long away, and the steppe celebrated the same New Year as Kitai, under the same new moon and stars, or under a grey-black sky and falling snow.

捴

Daiyan was aware it was a deadly undertaking, and his desire to live was intense enough to make him afraid. He was trying not to let Shan see that. He knew she was observant. It was in her way of being.

He hated tunnels, being underground, always had. But it wasn't their avenue of escape that was disturbing him, it was what came after, for him. The part he hadn't told anyone about.

He was waiting for a signal in the dark of New Year's night. He was remembering (the way the mind worked) fireworks when he was a boy. The wonder and joy, light bursting in the sky then falling in showers of green and red and silver.

They were out of sight near the principal western gate. Beyond it lay the Garden of the Chalcedony Grove, with its man-made lake where pageants and boat competitions had been performed for emperors in their splendour.

Stars slipped in and out of clouds as he watched, and then were finally gone as a heavier bank of clouds rolled in from the north. It began to snow again. He turned to the woman he loved and might lose tonight. He said, "The snow is good for us. For this."

There were two men with them. His best officer in the city and another, chosen for a different skill. He'd had to choose. The other soldiers were likely to die here. Men he knew well, some of them. Leadership in war was a dark thing.

Up by the northern gates, the Altai were coming in. Daiyan had gone over the wall alone two nights ago, before the rising of a waning moon. He had captured an Altai guard at his patrol post. They'd become careless out there, over time, contemptuous.

He'd taken the man to an interpreter and had done what needed to be done to get information before he killed him. In any case, the defenders of Hanjin had been able to see what was happening from inside the walls: horses being readied, movement in the camps. You didn't mobilize eighty thousand men and their horses without someone being able to understand.

He ought to have been there by the northern gates. He ought to have ordered them shut, even if that meant barring their own people outside. Or he could have tried to stop the negotiators from going out this morning. He didn't have that authority, and it wouldn't have mattered. He knew the Altai had been weakening the city walls all this time. He knew his forces couldn't hold those breaches. If the riders had wanted to enter Hanjin, they could have entered any time—or they could enter now. There came a point when you couldn't stop what was coming.

Sounds carried, muffled by the heavy night. Shouts, some screams. Looking back, he saw fire. He closed his eyes and then opened them. What he was doing he needed to do. He could die fighting at the northern gate or he could try to do something that might make a difference. It ached in him like a wound, though, not to be there right now. It could be frightening sometimes, the desire to kill.

Beside him, Shan said, "Snow is good? Really? Is anything good tonight?"

She was hearing the sounds, too. He couldn't think of a reply that wouldn't say too much. He didn't want her to know what he intended to do. He heard an owl from outside the wall. It wasn't an owl. It was time.

The tunnels had been built more than two hundred years ago. Two of them, going out to south and west. They were almost unknown, closer to legend than anything else. It had been Wang Fuyin, the magistrate, his friend (where was his friend tonight in the south?), who had searched them out in the archives, records on brittle scrolls. And then they'd found them.

Daiyan and Ziji had explored both tunnels in the springtime, sharing this with no one. He had dealt with his old fear, you had to do that all the time in life. They'd needed to pick locks to get in through doors beneath old buildings, but they'd been outlaws a long time and knew how to do that. Then through those doors and under the weight of the earth, carrying torches. Old beams and posts, skittering sounds, the lifelong fear of being crushed alive.

Flickering darkness, uneven footing. Both tunnels went a long way past the city walls. Ziji had counted paces. Daiyan remembered those crouching walks, the anxious awareness that the exits might have been blocked up after so long, wondering what would happen if the torches went out.

They'd emerged from the western one by pushing up together, hard, on a heavy wooden door, spilling earth. They had found themselves in a bamboo wood under a spring moon. They'd closed the door in the ground, covered it again carefully, walked back to Hanjin and through the city gate. The gates had still been open then, the world coming in and out, the nights a brightness equal to the days. Or so poets wrote, exaggerating. Women and food vendors had been calling to them, someone was breathing fire, someone had a gibbon trained to dance.

The southern tunnel's exit had proved to be more exposed—still distant, perhaps useful, but in the open. The magistrate had guessed there'd been woods that way, back when the tunnels were made.

Now he led Shan up the steps and then inside the abandoned structure next to the tea house. It had been a singing girl house once. A valuable property, so near a major gate. They had already broken the lock on the front door. It was dark inside; one torch became three, each of the men carried one. They went towards the back and down a flight of stairs, carefully.

"The step is broken here," he said, and Shan put a hand on his arm and stepped down two at once. At the bottom they walked along a corridor, turned when it turned, and came to the doorway he and Ziji had found—not long after they'd first come to the capital, to Hanjin, the centre of the world.

"It is a long way," he told her, and the other two, who would not know this tunnel either, "It comes up well beyond the walls and the Chalcedony Grove. We will have to stoop at times, so watch your heads, but the air is all right. I have done this before."

"Who built this? When? How did you find it?" Shan asked, and he realized that he loved that she was asking, wanting to know.

"I'll tell you as we walk," he said. "Ming Dun, bar the door on this side when we get in." Dun was the man he knew was very good.

He talked as they went. Sometimes men (or a woman) needed to hear a leader's voice. There were different ways to lead, more ways to fail, he thought.

He remembered Ziji counting, that first time. First times were the hardest for something like this. Now, he knew there was an ending to the tunnel. What he didn't know was what they'd find when they came up.

The owl call was some reassurance, but this was a night of chaos and violence, the ending of a world, and it was foolish to wish for certainty. He knew the Altai were above them, and there were fires in the city.

He held her elbow for a time, then the tunnel narrowed and they had to go single file. He went first, still talking, Shan behind him, then the two soldiers.

He was fleeing the sack of Hanjin, and he was one of the men who'd been given command here. He fought shame as best he could but it was difficult. If he'd been younger, he might have sworn oaths of vengeance and redress. He remembered vows before the family altar in Shengdu, when he'd been certain he was alone. Rivers and mountains, an oath to reclaim the lost. A boy talking to his ancestors, making sure his older brother didn't hear.

An oath was nothing, the doing was all. And you could fail. Men failed more often than otherwise, he thought.

They had invited him to the palace some nights ago, to be the man who killed Kai Zhen.

He had declined. When it came time, he'd discovered that such an act was not in him, not in this way. If the emperor of Kitai chose to execute his prime minister for evil counsel given to his father (pursuing the father's desires) that was the emperor's right, and duty. There were men paid to serve as executioners, using a sword, strangling, other means.

He hadn't grieved for the prime minister. Not that. He'd wondered who would follow Kai Zhen, and then he'd realized, bitterly, that it might not matter.

He said, "I suppose two hundred years ago they were remembering rebellions. They wanted ways to get out."

"There are others like this?" Shan asked. Her voice was even.

"One that we found. But it comes up exposed."

"And this one?"

"You'll see. Not much farther. I promise."

"I'm all right," she said.

They walked in silence.

He cleared his throat. "Qi Wai would not come?"

"He would not come. He's defending the collection. He found a sword."

"He can't do that. You know it."

"He knows it, too." She paused. "He said it was his life."

"I see," he said, although he really didn't.

She said, "Some losses we might not wish to live beyond."

He thought about that. "Our lives ..." he began, then stopped.

"Go on," said Shan.

Their steps in a tunnel, torchlight on walls and beams. It was a certainty men had died building this. He wondered if she could hear the scurrying of rats under their voices. Probably, he decided.

He drew a breath. "Our lives aren't only ours."

She was silent behind him as they walked, then said, "Daiyan, what are you planning to do tonight?"

She astonished him. She had, from that first evening in her home, among the bronzes and the porcelain.

You know I love you, he wanted to say, but was too mindful of her reputation, with two men behind them. And if he said it, she'd be even more certain he had something dangerous in mind.

The path started to slant upwards.

"We are here," he said, not answering her question, knowing she'd be aware of that.

WHOEVER BUILT THIS TUNNEL, Shan thinks, had a planning sort of mind. There is a stone bench here at the end, to stand on, and even brackets in the reinforced earth walls for torches to rest in, to allow the men carrying them to put hands and shoulders to the door to the world above.

She likes when she sees evidence of forethought. It reassures. It declares that not everything men or women do need be careless, uncertain, ill-judged. Perhaps tonight, this winter, this New Year's eve, she needs to find, or claim, indications of order and intelligence.

She feels alert, and fearful. Daiyan intends something beyond escape, but she doesn't know—can't know—what it is. She has been sleeping in a way, closing herself off, since her father died. As if to shut her eyes and deny what is happening, the way a small child does. She remembers doing that. If you can't see someone—or some shuffling spirit creature in the dark—they can't find you.

Daiyan taps twice above his head, standing on the bench. He pushes upwards with both hands, hard, but the door shifts more easily than he's expected. She hears him swear, feels, with that, a clutch of apprehension.

Then a voice. "I know you aren't very strong. Thought we might help."

"If you brought a horse for me, as promised, I will have it trample you first," says Daiyan. "Help us up."

A horse for me.

Shan says nothing. He helps her onto the bench. Hands reach down and pull her up from the tunnel into—she sees, as they set her on her feet—a forest grove.

Bamboo trees. It is hard to see clearly, they have lit no torches. No moon, of course, it is New Year's eve. Heavy sky in any case. It is snowing. It is unexpectedly quiet, they are indeed a long way past the walls. They are out from a city under attack.

Daiyan had tried to save Qi Wai, too. Wai had refused. They'd bowed to each other and she'd walked away. She has an image of him, right now, this moment, as she stands in a night grove, snow on branches above: her husband before their warehouse, gripping an old sword awkwardly, watching fires. Waiting for barbarians.

"My lady," says a voice she thinks she should know. A figure bows to her.

"I'm sorry," she says. "I cannot see who you are."

"Commander Zhao, my lady. We have met, in your home, and I escorted your husband from Shuquian in summer."

"Yes," she says. And then adds, "You shot an arrow at me. Are you going to do it again?"

He coughs. Someone laughs softly—Daiyan, coming up behind her.

"You will want to be careful, friend. She has claws when she needs them."

"Then I will do all I can to make her a friend," says the man named Zhao Ziji. "There seem to be no tigers, by the way. You need not be frightened."

She thinks he's speaking to her, but he isn't. Daiyan laughs again. "Remind me why I missed having you with me?"

"Because everything goes wrong when I'm not?"

It is meant as a jest, she realizes, but Daiyan doesn't laugh this time. "That's true enough," is all he says. "Tell me what we have."

"Twenty men here. Too close for more. Three thousand cavalry west about thirty *li*, concealed, though the Altai aren't patrolling. I left orders they are to remain hidden but to kill any horsemen that find them."

"What's happening at the walls?"

"They were going in through the north gates, then some of them reached this side from inside, and the south. All the gates are open. They are in. You can see." His voice is quiet.

"See the city?"

Daiyan walks past his friend and the other men—Shan can see their shapes now. He moves to the edge of the grove. She follows. She stands beside him and looks at Hanjin as it burns. A glow against the sky. Fire and snow.

Fire and snow, she thinks. And hates herself a little in that moment, because the phrase is already lodged in her head, and she even knows which old song's tune she can work with to make something new about the calamity of this night.

What is she, that her mind can turn this way in the midst of terror and flight and people dying? The snow keeps falling. She says, "My father's spirit will be happy he did not live to see this."

Daiyan says nothing. He turns to Zhao Ziji. "Three horses? Good ones?"

"Yes," the other man says. "Do I have any hope of persuading you this is folly?"

"No," says Daiyan.

He turns to Shan. He doesn't touch her. "I am coming back, if the gods allow it. If they do not, Ziji is the one you trust, and Ming Dun, who was with us in the tunnel. They will take you south of the Wai, or across the Great River, if it comes to that."

"What are you going to do?" she asks, and she is able to keep her voice calm. Her hands are trembling. It is cold out here, she tells herself. She is wearing her foolish double-hat.

He tells her. He does tell her. Then he goes, still not touching her, riding out of the shelter of the grove with one man, into night and falling snow.

CHAPTER XXIV

Some things were kept simple on the steppe, had been for hundreds of years, all tribes.

As one of those who'd endured that terrible, unexpected defeat north of Yenling (he'd survived by fleeing, how else would he have lived?), Pu'la of the Altai understood why he and others from that humiliated army were on guard duty in the camp tonight, rather than being allowed to share in finally sacking the city.

His leader was a decent man, and knew Pu'la's father. Pu'la's father was important, close to the war-leader and the kaghan—or emperor, as they were told to call him now.

Their leader had promised to send back riders with Kitan women later tonight, for the guards left behind. Thoughtful of him, and prudent. One didn't want to anger horsemen, and Pu'la and the other three posted with him here were blood-born Altai, not conquered tribesmen recruited for this assault. Belonging meant everything on the grasslands. Your tribe was your home.

Even so, anticipating diversion later and drinking *kumiss* now, it was difficult to stand outside a yurt and see, not far away at all, what his people were doing to the arrogant Kitan and their city. See it, and not be a part of it.

There were said to be an amazing number of singing-girl houses in Hanjin. Surely there'd be women to bring out? Pu'la was young. He wanted a girl right now more than he wanted gold.

He watched the fires. Another had started, towards the west, near the city wall on that side. He counted a dozen good-sized fires. Hanjin was going to be a pyre. The Kitan would rebuild it for their new masters. That was how these things went, Pu'la had been told.

It was a glorious beginning to a new year, reversing generations of humiliating deference. Even after the Kitan court began sending tribute north they'd called it a gift, insisted the Xiaolu emperor name himself a son, or at best a nephew, of Kitai's.

Well, everyone knew what had happened to the emperor of the Xiaolu. Bai'ji, the war-leader's brother (Pu'la's hero), drank *kumiss* from his skull.

And the Kitan emperor wasn't going to be lord of anything after tonight. The intention, Pu'la knew, was to take him and every one of his sons and daughters north. Bai'ji had vowed to bed the empress of Kitai with her husband forced to watch. That was a man, Pu'la thought. He drank from his flask.

He didn't expect a perfumed princess to be brought out for them tonight, he wasn't foolish. But you could still imagine things in darkness, couldn't you? Smooth skin, scent.

He'd never admit it to anyone, but he had been ready to go home after that battle west of here, when a part of the Kitan army had proved not to be so helpless, after all. He'd been sure he was going to die. But it was only that one army, all the others here had broken before the riders, they had fled much as ... well, much as Pu'la had fled, though you didn't have to let that memory spoil tonight.

He didn't like being left here, but it was long established that the division of spoils included camp guards at full share. Someone had to guard the horses and treasure and prisoners.

And back here he wasn't going to meet anyone wielding one of those two-handed swords, not the way he might have, racing through some city lane lit by flames. There were still soldiers in Hanjin. Better to be here in the open, Pu'la thought. It was always better in the open. And he was, after all, performing an important task among the yurts.

He died on that last thought, not the one about fearing a sword. That had come a moment before, while the man who ended his short span of days (Pu'la of the Altai was seventeen years old, his father's only son) had been levelling a bow.

It was a similar death—on guard at night, an arrow—to that of another young rider two summers before. O-Yan of the Jeni, fourteen years of age, had been killed by an arrow loosed by Pu'la's own skilled and deadly father on the night the Altai attacked the Jeni camp, beginning their assertion of themselves upon the world.

There might have been a lesson, a meaning, in this, or not. Most likely not, for who was there to learn of it, and what would the teaching be?

ᴓ

Kang Junwen was to live an unusually long life, most of it south of the Great River, most of it in good health.

He became, in his later years, a follower of the Sacred Path, grateful for his gift of days. He did regard his existence as a gift, not something earned or merited, though he'd been courageous many times in his youth and honoured his ancestors always. He had many stories, but the one he told most often, because it involved Ren Daiyan, was of the night Hanjin fell—what the two of them had done under the falling snow and clouds that hid the stars.

After emerging from the tunnel that led out of the burning city, he and the commander—just them, leading a third horse—had ridden from the grove where their soldiers had been waiting.

Before departing, Commander Ren had removed his tunic and over-tunic, leaving himself only a fur vest. The commander unbound his hair, like a barbarian's. Junwen had done the same, clothing and hair. He'd looked—couldn't help himself—to see if he could spot the words of the tattoo the commander was said to have on his back, but it was dark, and the vest would have hidden it anyhow.

He didn't know what they were about to do, or try to do. He didn't permit himself to feel the cold. When a man is young, he can decide such things.

He didn't want to die, but he fully expected to be with the spirits of his father and older brothers before the sun rose. He wasn't going to let himself be captured and enslaved.

He was a Kitan from one of the lost prefectures, had lived under the barbarians all his life, subject to them. He and his family had been farmers, paying harsh taxes to the Xiaolu who ruled them, regarded as something between servants and slaves.

Then one night in a summer years ago his father and two older brothers had been caught and executed—an example being made—for smuggling tea and salt. Junwen, not yet a man, had been made to watch, along with everyone in their village. His mother had collapsed to the ground beside him when her husband and children died. The Xiaolu hadn't bothered beating her, had only laughed. One of them spat on her as he rode away.

Lives can flow into and out of a moment.

His mother died within the year. Junwen and his sister and her husband kept their farm going, barely. Then taxes were raised.

He fled south in the turmoil that followed the Altai rebellion in the east. He joined the Kitan army north of Hanjin. He was old enough by then, was given a sword and boots, no training. A small man, but wiry, from the occupied lands. Spoke with an accent. People underestimated him.

Junwen had been among those in the army sent to attack the Xiaolu's Southern Capital—and so among those who'd failed to take it, crushingly defeated. He'd been part of the retreat, sheathed in his rage, and then he'd been in the army sent north to hold back the Altai when they came down in force.

He had fled again, with the survivors of that disaster. Most had scattered, seeking to get as far away as they could. Junwen had gone straight to Hanjin. His shame had been very great. He was not a coward, and he hated the steppe riders—as a Kitan and for his family. A boy had been made to watch his father and brothers killed, and had heard the riders laughing.

During the siege of the city he'd identified the one commander who seemed to be a leader of the old sort, as from the days of glory when Kitai had subjugated the steppe, forcing tribute and humility. He'd managed to get himself attached to the company of Ren Daiyan, and then to speak directly with the commander, make him understand that Kang Junwen, son of Kang Hsao-po, was ready to do anything necessary, or possible, against the barbarians.

He'd explained that he spoke the language of the steppe because of where he'd grown up. A Xiaolu accent, their quick, slurred vowels. He understood everything said to him, and would be understood.

So it was that he came to find himself leaving the city down a long tunnel on the New Year's eve when the Altai burst through the gates of the city. And then—now—he was wearing only a vest in the winter night, his hair falling free, riding towards the enemy camp.

To their right the city was on fire. They could hear the hooves of Altai horses and the harsh, wild shouts of triumphant men as riders swept around the walls and continued to burst through the western and southern gates.

Surely this night, Kang Junwen thought, was a calamity that would never be forgotten. A black moment in the telling of the world.

Commander Ren was silent as they rode. They were trotting the horses, not galloping—the ground was uneven, visibility poor. They came to a cluster of oak trees, too few to be named a grove. The commander gestured and they dismounted. They tied the horses and left them there. They walked now, carefully, peering through snow and night, listening.

It was Junwen who saw the campfires. He touched the commander and pointed. Ren Daiyan nodded his head. He put his mouth to Junwen's ear.

"There will be guards. You have to carry me. I am wounded, my horse fell, I fell, you are bringing me back. Can you carry me?"

Junwen simply nodded. He could do whatever this man asked him to do.

"Can you make them believe we are riders?"

"Yes," Junwen whispered. "I am not afraid."

That last was a lie. He was afraid, but it wasn't about to stop him.

Commander Ren Daiyan squeezed Junwen's shoulder. He said, barely a whisper, "You are a good man. Get us through the outer guards and keep walking until they can't see you any more. We will do this, the two of us."

The two of us. Kang Junwen didn't know what *this* was, but it didn't matter. He'd been called a good man by the commander, he was bringing honour to his lost family. His heart was full. It pushed away fear.

He lifted Ren Daiyan over his shoulder as if he were carrying a weight of harvested grain on their farm. He was careful of the commander's bow and sword, and of his own sword (he wasn't a bowman).

He staggered with his first steps, then steadied.

After fifty paces or so, nearing the campfires, he made a decision. He didn't wait for the guards to challenge him. He shouted, in the language of the steppe, his Xiaolu accent, "Are you there? Light us through! A man is wounded."

"No lights here, fool!" The reply was blunt but not suspicious. Why and how should any of the helpless, vanquished Kitan be coming this way? The guard was Xiaolu by his voice, no trouble with Junwen's speech.

"Where are the shamans? Their yurts?" Junwen gasped, as if exhausted. He saw the shapes of guards ahead, holding the short bows of the steppe. He approached.

"Straight back of here. They have a swan banner. You'll see it. How is it out there?" The voice was envious, not quite sober, a man missing the blood-joy of conquest.

"Didn't fucking *get* there," Junwen snapped. "Got told to bring him back. I'm fine, but both our horses went down."

"The fuckers still have those swords?" a second guard asked. This one was Altai.

"Never saw. But the ground's bad."

"Get him inside, then. Swan banner. Bad luck for him."

"Bad luck for me," said Kang Junwen, as he carried his commander and the memory of his father into the enemy camp, frightened and defiant, grieving and proud.

HIS LIFE HAD BEGUN when he first did this, Daiyan thought. He moved around to the back of the prisoner's yurt, away from the fire, and killed the last guard with an arrow in the throat (you shot men there to eliminate the chance of a dying cry).

He was thinking of the road to Guan Family Village. He'd been fifteen. He remembered, on a winter night in a barbarian camp, how he had felt, walking into the forest, leaving everything behind. It had been as if he were outside of his own body, watching himself go.

It was dangerous to be so distracted, to be living in this moment and in the past. Hanjin winter and Szechen springtime. The mind, he thought, silently returning to where he'd had Junwen wait, could be strange. A scent or an image could take you back years.

A fox darted across the snowy ground.

He was sure it was a fox, even in the darkness with only the one watch fire burning in front of the yurt. His heart began hammering. He couldn't help it. It didn't stop running, the fox, it only ... let itself be seen. His tattooed words felt as if they were burning on his back.

He made himself ignore this. All of it. The past. The message, if it was a message. The spirit world was always nearby. Sometimes you saw it, became aware of it, but it was always there.

He touched the other man on the arm. Junwen didn't jump or startle. Only turned, ready. A good man, Daiyan had decided. Had said as much to him. This one truly hated the horsemen. Daiyan didn't know why that was so, he hadn't asked, but it didn't matter. Probably something in his family. Hatred could be useful. You could be driven by it.

Daiyan turned, the other man followed. Snow was still falling, lying thinly on the ground. There were sounds around them, but not many and not too near. Few of the riders had remained behind. Guards on the perimeter, at this yurt, there would be more at the back of the camp where the treasure had been gathered.

Who would want to be left behind? Tonight was a fierce, red culmination. They'd been here a long time, tethered in one place.

It was going to be savage in the city. People would die badly, and other things would happen, too. You could be driven hard by hatred, Daiyan thought again. You still needed to be precise. He was here for a reason. Kitai needed to go on past this night.

It was very dark behind the yurt. A dead man was lying in the snow. Trained by years in the marsh, Daiyan pulled his arrow from the rider's throat. You never left arrows if you could avoid it. He saw Junwen dragging the body from in front away from the fire there, to the back. A good thought. He pulled the arrow from that one too. He went up to the yurt.

There was a chance another guard was inside. Daiyan drew his sword and slashed hard, a ripping, two-handed stroke through heavy cloth. Then he was in, twisting through the opening, ready to kill again.

One low brazier, a very little light. Enough, after the blackness outside. Only one man here. He stood up quickly from a pallet on the ground. He looked startled, but not—a good thing—afraid. There was no fire in the yurt, no warmth. Two small bowls beside the dull glow of the brazier, the crude pallet, a bucket for night soil. Nothing else. It was wrong, it was entirely wrong.

Daiyan dropped to his knees. He was breathing hard. An excess of emotion. He lowered his head. Junwen came in through the tear behind him, sword in hand. The soldier froze for a moment—he hadn't known what they were here to do—then he, too, knelt, let go of his blade, and pressed hands and forehead to the ground.

"My lord prince," said Ren Daiyan. "We have come for you. Forgive me, but we must go quickly, and it will be difficult."

"There is nothing to forgive," said Prince Zhizeng of Kitai, only son of the father-emperor—only direct successor to the Dragon Throne—not trapped inside Hanjin.

His hair was already unbound, he'd been lying down to sleep. He suffered them to help him remove his tunic, to make him look like them, like a steppe rider in the night. After a hesitation, he pulled on his own boots. Daiyan felt an impulse to help, but did not. He handed the prince a knife. He had only the one sword.

Then he took the scroll he'd carried here and he laid it on the pallet, where it would be found.

"What is that?" said the prince.

"I want them to read it," was all he said.

He looked to the back of the yurt. Junwen had gone out that way, now he reappeared, carrying the body of one of the guards. He dropped the man inside, went out again. He did the same with the other three, moving quickly, quietly. Another good thought. The longer those deaths went undetected ...

When Junwen was done he straightened, waiting. The prince went over and kicked the nearest guard in the head with a booted foot. *He is entitled*, Daiyan thought.

They went out the back. No stir, no alarm in the vast, dark camp. A few fires burning, far apart. Distant, drunken voices, a song. Soft snow from heavy clouds. The sounds from Hanjin came through this shrouding as if from farther away than they were, as if already in the past, already history, no less terrible for that.

THE CHO MASTER had instructed from his grove that duty to the state and the family were absolute. The teachings of the Sacred Path were somewhat different. They emphasized balance in all things, and this included a man's words and the stories he told.

So Kang Junwen, even in his later years, when someone was usually forgiven for or even expected to stretch the silk of youthful stories, never did so when he spoke of that night in the Altai camp and what followed.

It seemed his telling resonated more strongly with listeners because it was offered quietly, not dramatized. He was a southern rice farmer and a former soldier, not a market performer, and he was telling a true tale from a dark time. He would simply relate, briefly, how Commander Ren Daiyan had put four arrows in four throats from the darkness by the prince's yurt, how not one of the guards made a sound, and none of them heard another one die.

There were, he came to reflect, other ways that one might have thought to tell a story. He could have spoken more about himself, but he never did. He knew what his listeners had come to hear, and his own glory, honour, pride emerged as a reflection of Ren Daiyan's because he'd been there. His own face, young that night, as if seen in a moonlit pool. He did think of it that way, awkwardly or not.

He was also aware that memory could mislead you, or be lost. He vividly remembered the day he was married, for example, but everything blurred in and around the time his wife had died, and that was much, much later.

THEY LEFT THE YURT where the prince was being held. The commander led them towards the farthest edge of the camp, beyond where the guards who had let them through would be. Ren Daiyan whispered briefly to each of them. Junwen had always assumed it was the same thing, but he couldn't *know* that, that sort of thing made stories difficult, or opened them up to being changed.

In his ear the whisper was, simply, "Walk as if we belong here and have somewhere to go."

They moved briskly but didn't run. They saw men by a fire, drinking from a flask passed back and forth. Junwen wasn't sure what they were doing back there, not on guard, not obviously wounded. That group ignored three men passing in the night, if they even saw them.

Towards the southern boundary of the camp, near where guards would be, Daiyan made them halt beside an empty yurt with no fire in front of it. He spoke quietly to each of them again. There were harsh sounds south of them, from the city; they rose and fell but never stopped. Kang Junwen would never forget those noises. He remembered wanting to kill someone.

The commander did the killing.

The guards out this way (had Ren Daiyan seen this, expected it?) were widely spaced, not clustered together as those where they'd entered had been. He used his bow again.

He fired from quite close to each one. As the first guard slumped, Junwen stepped quickly to stand where the fallen man had stood— so that the next guard over to their right, if he looked this way, would see a figure still on duty. Moments later, that next guard over, just visible in darkness, also died. Prince Zhizeng stepped into his place.

Ren Daiyan had disappeared, farther west, to where the next man in line would be. Junwen had no doubt as to that one's fate. He stayed where he was, facing south, outwards, as if vigilantly on guard.

And it was while doing so, standing thus, that he heard someone approach from behind, and an Altai voice call, "My fucking turn then, piss on it all. Yours for *kumiss* and a fire."

Kang Junwen turned smoothly, as if to greet someone, and he drew his sword and plunged it deeply—into a man already falling dead, of an arrow.

"Well done," murmured the commander, coming up, bow in hand, crouching, not to be seen.

Junwen said, "There will be two others coming."

"There were," said Ren Daiyan. "It is all right. We can go."

"We can prop this one up."

"If you know how, you do it," the commander said, and Junwen thought he heard the faintest breath of amusement. "I don't."

"Watch me," said Kang Junwen quietly. He took the second dead man's body and positioned it facing south, then he manoeuvred the first one sitting upright, leaning against that one's back. It looked, from a distance, as if a guard was sitting down, or crouching, but present. He pulled the two arrows, for Ren Daiyan.

"Until they topple," he said. "Maybe they won't."

Not something he ever knew. He did know that no alarm was raised as they slipped over to where the prince was standing stiffly, staring out, as if at his post, and then the three of them moved—running, finally—out of the camp and into the night.

IT HAD ALWAYS PLEASED Daiyan to identify someone he thought might be a real soldier and be right about it.

This one, Junwen, was new, had done well getting them into the camp, while in there. There was burning to their left, but where they were running it was black. He stayed beside the prince, a hand out in case he stumbled. He worried briefly whether he'd be able to guide them straight back to the oak trees where the horses were, but then he saw a torch and realized someone was there ahead of them.

"Wait!" he snapped. And then, to Junwen, "If I don't come back, lead the prince around to the west and then to the woods where the others are. Report to Commander Zhao. Kitai will be depending on you."

He didn't wait for an acknowledgement. He slipped his bow from his back and fitted an arrow as he ran, an effortless movement, the way some men might brush a hand through their hair. He bent low, moving fast, silent as a spirit. He was afraid, though. If there were numbers here, if they'd seen and seized the horses ...

Only three, and just arrived. The riders had dismounted, were collecting the tethered horses, talking among themselves. Not alarmed, by the sound of it. They might be drunk, might even think they were playing a joke on other riders. They would not be expecting Kitan soldiers from a burning city.

He had done this so many times. It was not a *good* thing, if you were aimed (like an arrow) towards a virtuous life, but it was almost possible, after many years, to forget you were ending lives.

You told yourself it was necessary when you were first starting. Some didn't think about it at all. Some he'd known took joy in killing. He tried to remember when he'd stopped worrying about the ghosts of those he killed.

He loosed, slotted another arrow, released, and then a third—the torch one of them held made it easy. He shot that one last, of course.

It wasn't as silent as back in the Altai camp. These three were close together; the torch-bearer saw the other two fall. He cried out in surprise, and one of the horses reared up.

Someone made a sound to Daiyan's right.

Four men, not three. As likely as anything this one had just gone off to relieve himself, or perhaps he was being a good soldier and checking the area where they'd found something unusual.

The sound became his death. Daiyan dropped his bow. The startled grunt he'd heard sent him running through blackness to where an Altai stood on snow-covered, uneven ground.

This one he killed with a sword. The two-handed blades were no good for thrusts. He swept it in a scything motion as if cutting summer grain in a different life. Another ghost to his name when he came to cross to the afterworld.

He had things to do before that happened. Hanjin was being overrun. He thought of the women there. Of ordinary men, children who would never grow out of childhood now. He wasn't going to spare a moment to think of the mother or father of this man lying at his feet.

He dried the sword on the ground. He reclaimed his bow, went back to get the two men with him. They took all seven horses. He also took a dead rider's sword and sword belt and gave them to the prince. Junwen silently retrieved Daiyan's arrows and handed them over.

The snow stopped falling as they came back to the bamboo wood. Approaching, Daiyan hooted like a marsh owl, and Ziji let them live.

They went back to the grove by the tunnel's entrance. They dismounted there. Daiyan looked around. Darkness, shapes of men. If Kitai was to survive, Hanjin be avenged and regained, it would begin in this wood.

He said, "It is done. We need to move south fast, and have our cavalry meet us on the way because we will be pursued. We need food and drink and proper clothing for Prince Zhizeng, who is with us now."

And, as he'd expected, as was entirely proper, hearing the name every man knelt down, and the woman he loved.

ଚ୪ଚ

He could hear horses and shouts and running feet and screaming. His stomach was roiling and twisting, as if he'd swallowed snakes. There were fires, licking the frames of houses up to swallowtail roofs, though not in this square yet, where Qi Wai stood on guard in front of their warehouse.

The square was empty except for him. He knew that wouldn't last. He held a sword. At some point that began to feel foolish, and then a little later (he hadn't put it down) it didn't. He had no idea how to use it, but it was, if nothing else, an honourable way to die.

He'd been stationing himself here against looters in the streets. His own people. Even against them, he knew he wasn't intimidating, but his thought had been that they might prefer to look somewhere else, where no one at all was on guard, rather than run any kind of risk.

The barbarians thundering through the city would not think that way when they came, and they would come, even if this was a dark, obscure corner of the clan compound. The horsemen would be navigating the city, Wai thought, towards the palace grounds or the entertainment districts first. They would get here, though. Tonight, in the morning, soon. He looked up at the snow. It was soft, even beautiful.

He thought of his mother and father. His father had said, with his easy, enviable confidence, that the barbarians had come only for silver and silk. That they'd withdraw when payment had been made. "After that," he'd said, "we will take the silver back by trading with them at the border, as we've done for years." The appropriate people would be punished, the new emperor would name new advisers, all would go on.

His father might be dead by now on the other side of the compound, and his mother. Thinking of the Altai and the stories of their conquests, Wai hoped she was dead. A twisting thought.

His mother was a cold, severe woman, but he'd respected her, and she'd honoured his own path, his choices, the ones she'd known about.

She'd chosen a wife for him who had been, for years, as much a companion as anything else. He still couldn't say how and when things had changed. Sometimes a man needed something else in a wife, in life.

His thoughts of Kou Yao, his steward, his lover: those were not complicated. He wanted him south and safe with the child. As safe as the times allowed men and children to be. He'd done what he could about that. As for Shan—his wife might be out of the city by now.

He hoped so. She'd come to ask him to join her, wearing her amusing, ridiculous hat. He had declined. They had bowed to each other. There came a point, and he had arrived there, when you couldn't separate yourself from what you'd done all your life, what you'd loved.

What he'd loved and done lay, much of it, behind him in the warehouse. He wasn't about to claim he was being virtuous or brave, standing here awkwardly holding a sword, but he was being true to himself before the world and the gods. Maybe that would come to matter, in some way?

He heard a crash, then a roaring sound, and he startled, afraid. He looked left: a red-orange thrust of fire into the sky, screams from that direction. A house had fallen, beyond the wall of the compound. He tightened his grip on the old sword, waiting in an empty courtyard.

Behind him, behind the locked door, were objects of grace and power, from the Third, the Fifth, the short-lived Sixth. Ritual tripods and bells, one of them massive, brought to Hanjin from the Wai River with great effort. There was jade on lacquered tables, protected in caskets—all colours, green and white and pale, pale yellow. One carving he loved was nearly black. There were figurines and ornaments and vases. Huge wine vessels. Jewellery. There were vases and bowls and cups and ewers, some so old they had been in the world longer than Kitai. There were scrolls—government regulations, edicts, personal journals, poets' letters, poems, essays, even an order of execution. In the high-ceilinged warehouse were plinths with inscriptions he (and his wife) had transcribed over the years.

These things, and the ones kept at home until this winter, these were the grace and labour of his days. They were what he was. *I have been*, Qi Wai thought suddenly, *a small man carrying a small torch, looking back, and further back*. He had tried to light the road along which they had all come. It was not, he thought, a bad way to have lived.

He really had no idea how to use this sword, beyond gripping the hilt and swinging it, one way and then the other, the way small children sometimes did with sticks of bamboo, imagining themselves heroes of the old days. Then their real education began and they learned that in this Twelfth Dynasty such dreams were not suitable, and later they began to grow the little fingernail long on their left hand.

When the first of the riders came into the square they did so without torches and the fires were distant enough that Qi Wai was able to remain unseen in the darkness by the warehouse. He actually wounded the first man to approach the locked door, swinging the blade with all his force. He was startled when the sword bit into the man's side, the *impact* of it, the crudeness. He had no time to feel more than that. The next man's sword ripped into his belly and tore upwards viciously. Qi Wai wore nothing resembling armour, only layers of clothing against the cold. That thrust took his life, sent him through the doors of death into the long night.

The warehouse doors were smashed open behind his body, some looting was done, but it was very dark and eventually most of what was in there, carefully inventoried through the years by Qi Wai, son of Qi Lao, and his wife, the poet Lin Shan, was carried away north to the steppe, along with so much else, and so many people, in a terrible procession.

There are many ways to live a life. His had not been celebrated at all, but he'd offered a real contribution to the state, the empire, which was more than most of the imperial clan ever had. He had been eccentric but not dishonourable. Nor was his manner of dying lacking in honour, when Hanjin fell to the Altai. He had no proper burial. None of them did from that night. There were many ghosts there, too.

PART FIVE

CHAPTER XXV

Just as with the spirit on Lingzhou Isle, Lu Chen had been the only one at East Slope ever to see the ghost there.

The poet had believed from the first that this girl had claimed or intercepted his own death, as they'd waited for spring to free the mountains of snow and let them come home from exile.

He saw this one rarely, usually on the roof of the main house, twice by the stream at the eastern edge of their property as he rose to walk home at dusk from his favourite bench under a tree. And once in his writing room, on the New Year's eve Hanjin fell.

His candles and lamps had flickered, all at once. One of the candles went out. He looked up. He saw her across the room beside the thin smoke of the extinguished flame. Just for a moment, looking at him, then she flickered as well and was gone. He sensed, in that gaze, that there was a message in her presence this time, and then he had an immediate certainty about what it was she'd come to tell him.

They were aware of what was happening in the north. They knew Xinan had fallen and that Yenling and Hanjin were besieged.

Friends, the ones who hadn't yet fled this way, sent letters, warnings, laments.

Spirits could be swifter. Most spirits were not benevolent. He knew (he absolutely knew) that this one was.

It seemed to have grown dark outside, he saw. He'd had his attention on his paper and brush. He didn't write anything more in that winter twilight. He went looking for his brother.

They were welcoming the new year. Of course they were. He was late, his son had been about to come get him. They celebrated quietly at East Slope, not as one did in the cities or even the villages.

In Hanjin itself the emperor would normally lead a great procession to the Temple of Benevolent Auspices and the rituals of renewal would be performed, accompanied by the musicians of the court. After the emperor returned to the palace, fireworks and parades illuminated by round, red-paper lanterns would begin. Street performers and men with huge dragon masks would be everywhere. People would fill the streets all night to greet the year with joy.

The poet stood in the doorway of his own reception room. He had no news from any earthly source. Only this inward sense from the spirit world. It would be wrong, he decided, unjust, to mar the household's mood with that.

He managed a smile of apology for being late. He knew he'd be forgiven, they were used to it. He was a man who could lose a day to words. He looked at his wife, at his family and his brother's and their gathered servants and farm workers, many of them loyal through years of hardship. They were safe here, he thought. Surely they were.

His heart, as he smiled at those he loved, as a year ended and a year began, was heavy as a stone at the bottom of a lake.

❧

That same night, from a wood near Hanjin, a small party started south with a prince of Kitai in their midst.

Clouds remained all night and it would begin to snow again in the morning. Ziji queried splitting the party, southeast and southwest, to divide pursuit. Daiyan decided otherwise. It would split their own force, too, and they'd be outnumbered by too much, whatever size party was sent after them. Better to keep together.

They had no doubt they'd be pursued. They were moving as fast as they could. Prince Zhizeng was not yet a problem, though he was likely to tire later. He was frightened—more obviously so now, Daiyan thought, than he'd seemed in the yurt. It was as if he'd accepted his fate back there, had not allowed himself to imagine freedom, and now that he could ...

Men were so varied, he thought. Men and women. How could anyone claim to understand another person? Who could read a soul? He moved up at times from rear guard to ride beside Shan. They'd given her the gentlest horse they had, but this pace would be hard on her. He did know she'd ridden horses all her life, with her father, with her husband, searching for the past throughout Kitai.

Her only words, whenever he came up, were, "I am all right. Do whatever must be done." Each time, like the refrain of a song.

He halted twice and food and drink were shared. Zhizeng first, offered by a kneeling soldier. But the prince was the one, both times, who urged them back into their saddles. His gaze, as they ate or as they rode, kept going over his shoulder, north into night, as if fearing the sudden appearance of riders, like demons.

It was possible they'd be caught tonight. However hard they rode, they would never be as swift as the steppe horsemen. Ziji had picked his two best riders to go west, with orders for their waiting cavalry. Those two would not stop.

Daiyan walked over to the prince at their second halt.

"My lord," he said formally, "I request permission to share our intentions, for your approval." This was a man born to rank and luxury but not to power. He'd have to begin learning that last.

"Go on, commander."

"I expect pursuit. With good fortune, not until morning."

"And without good fortune?"

"They'll be on their way now, tracking us."

"Then shouldn't we be riding?"

"Yes, lord. But horses and men must rest. We cannot ride a whole night straight through."

"The Altai can."

"Perhaps. But I don't believe you can."

A silence. Perhaps not the best way to have put that.

"Go on," the prince said again.

"We have cavalry to the west, from the army that holds Yenling. They were kept a distance away, to remain unseen. Riders have been sent to bring them this way. Half will try to intercept any pursuit. The others will meet us by a village we've chosen between here and the Wai."

"How many men?"

"Fifteen hundred in each party."

"That ... that is a good number," said the prince. "And they will escort us across the Great River?"

Daiyan's turn to be silent. He swallowed. "Our intention, my lord, was to head for Jingxian, summon our southern armies to meet us there. If we are to make a stand, drive the barbarians back when the weather—"

"No," said Prince Zhizeng of Kitai.

He said it loudly. Nearby conversations stopped. Daiyan heard the horses as they snorted and shuffled. They were at the edge of a poplar grove, sheltered from the wind.

The prince said, "No, Commander Ren. Those are not our desires, nor our commands. You are to escort us across the Great

River. We wish to be safely removed from the barbarians. We will go to Shantong on the sea. We will command our army to defend the Great River's southern bank, and summon officials from all prefectures to attend upon us at Shantong."

It was never entirely quiet in a night. Especially among a company of men. The sounds of horses, soldiers, trees in wind. But it felt quiet now. As if the stars were listening, Daiyan thought.

"My lord," he said slowly, searching for the right words, "the Altai are far from their homeland. They will have trouble already back in the Xiaolu lands, and holding our prefectures behind them. Our people will not easily submit. The people are courageous! They need only a sign, a signal from us—from you—that Kitai has a leader, a prince."

"They will have no leader in us, no prince, no emperor, if we are taken."

It had taken no time, Daiyan thought, for Zhizeng to assume the imperial *we*. His brother, his father, the rest of his family ... there was no way to know if they were alive right now. Perhaps the assumption of power came more easily than he'd thought.

He tried again. "The barbarians will hate fighting in the south! We have land—rice fields, marshes, forests, hills—their horsemen cannot easily manage. And we know how to fight there. We will defeat them. And then move back north. Kitai depends on you, my lord."

"Then, Commander Ren, Kitai depends on you to keep us safe, doesn't it? Shouldn't we be riding?"

You did whatever you did, whatever you could, Daiyan was thinking, and there came moments when the world would not unfold to your desires and designs—unless, perhaps, you forced it to. There was suddenly too much to think about.

"Yes, my lord," he said. He turned to give the order to mount up.

"One more thing," said Prince Zhizeng.

Daiyan turned back, waiting in the dark.

"We are grateful for what you did tonight. Our escape. It was well done, commander. We will expect you as a good soldier, as a *loyal* soldier of Kitai, to continue this. The larger decisions, whatever they are to be, are made by the court. That is not to change, Commander Ren."

There were also moments when certain things could be said— or not. He could say they were fleeing in a winter night from a burning city because decisions by the court ...

He was a *yamen* clerk's second son. This man was, as best any of them knew, the only prince of Kitai not dead or in captivity tonight.

"Yes, my lord," was what he said.

He gave orders, as commanded, and they rode.

He stayed mostly beside Shan for that part of the night. He was aware of her looking at him, as if sensing his disquiet. Finally, she said, "There is only so much one man can do. We cannot steer the world, where it goes."

He didn't know how she knew to say that. Perhaps some people *could* understand the thoughts of others? He didn't answer, but he didn't leave her side.

Eventually, he said, quietly, "You shine for me like the brightest star of summer."

He heard her catch her breath.

"Oh, dear. That one? I am so much not a goddess, not the Weaver Maid."

"For me you are," he said. "And I don't know if I will be allowed to steer across the stars to you."

He dropped back, to take up his proper position at rear guard, guarding her, guarding them all. They didn't stop again until the first hint of morning appeared on their left.

❧

The Altai camp on the night of the fall of Hanjin, and into the afternoon and evening of the next day, was a place of drunken chaos. What else but savagery, historians later wrote, would one expect from barbarians?

Women were indeed brought out from the city, along with terrified boys and men, and even some of the palace eunuchs, for sport. There was also a great deal of wine rolling out on wagons.

The horsemen didn't like Kitan wine, but it could get a man drunk, and the conquest of the imperial city was reason for drinking. Celebrations could turn violent, but men at war needed their release, any good commander knew that.

The dead guards at the southwestern perimeter were not discovered until late in the morning. The tidings didn't make their way to any functioning leader for some time. They were puzzling deaths, but no obvious action seemed to be demanded in the midst of triumph.

Those posted near the dead watchmen had evidently abandoned their stations in the night. The city was taken, women and drink were coming out. What sort of man would stay on duty or report to his post at such a time?

It wasn't until evening, with snow falling again, that someone remembered that their Kitan captive would need food.

It occurred to one of the higher-ranking leaders that it might offer good entertainment to make the prince watch them play with some of the women. None of the leaders in the camp, including the two brothers commanding them, were entirely sober. They'd had the rest of the imperial family rounded up by then— men and women, the young emperor and the older one. It had been easy.

The dowager empress of Kitai and the younger one had, unfortunately, killed themselves in the palace before the riders reached the women's quarters, making a liar of Bai'ji, who had sworn to have the young one while her husband watched. His brother, the war-leader, had pointed out that her body was available, eliciting much laughter, though not from Bai'ji.

The three riders sent to the prisoner's yurt, also laughing with anticipation, discovered that he was gone.

There was a rip in the back of the yurt, made by a sword. There were four dead guards inside. There was a note on the prisoner's pallet.

It is untrue to say a man can be shocked into immediate sobriety, but the three men did move with speed—and apprehension—back to the place where their leaders were drinking. One of them carried the note. It remained rolled into a scroll, unopened. He held it carefully, as if it were poisoned. It might indeed be poisonous for him. Bearing bad tidings to a drunken leader was not a sound plan if one wished for a long life among the Altai.

There was tumult when they reported their news. Wan'yen, the war-leader, not as drunk as most of those around him, stood up and came forward. He was given the scroll. He opened it. He could not, of course, read Kitan. It was some time, a tense, dangerous interval, before a translator was found.

This man read the note by torchlight and then stood silent.

"Go on," said Wan'yen. The war-leader's voice was frightening. His brother had also risen to his feet by then. Bai'ji held his famous skull-cup, filled with Kitan wine.

"It is just defiance, great leader," said the translator.

"Go on," repeated Wan'yen.

Hearing that tone, the three men sent for the prince each felt deeply relieved that he could not read or speak Kitan.

The man who could do so, a Xiaolu tribesman, cleared his throat. It could be seen that his hands were shaking.

He read, a voice so low one had to strain to hear, "Your days and nights are short now. The sun will soon see your bones. There is no rest or home for you here. We can be among you any time we wish. Just as your army above Yenling found no mercy you will find none. You have taken the first steps towards your own destruction."

No one spoke for a time.

"Who wrote this?" Wan'yen was standing very straight.

The translator cleared his throat again. "It is signed by Commander Ren Daiyan. He is the one who—"

Bai'ji killed him with a sword from behind, the blade going through the man's body and out his belly. The red tip of the blade came, some noted, close to touching his own brother, standing in front of the interpreter.

"We know who that dung-face is! He didn't need to tell us." Bai'ji drained his cup. He pulled his sword free with some effort. "Dung-face!" he said again, loudly.

"Perhaps," said his brother, who was holding no wine. "But he killed four of your own men picked to guard a hostage. I recall you requesting that detail. For the pleasure, you said."

"Don't remember," said Bai'ji, with a wide gesture. "You like making things up."

"No. I dislike our camp being entered and important prisoners being freed. You know what that man means."

"He means nothing, brother. The city is ours!"

"He is a prince of the direct line. He matters! You were the one who wanted to take all of Kitai, to ride a horse into the southern sea!"

Bai'ji spat into the fire. "Can still do that. But first, kill those useless guards who let him escape."

An uneasy murmur. Wan'yen's mouth twisted. "You are too drunk to even listen. They *are* dead, brother. Put down your wine!"

"Hold my wine as long as I want. We have to kill Ren ... Ren Dung-face."

"I agree. And recapture the prince. They'll have a day's start."

"Nothing! They can't ride, the Kitan."

"Agreed again, brother. Take five hundred men. Leave now."

"Me?"

"I did say that."

"Now? I want to ... I want *five* palace women in my yurt!"

"They may be there but you will not be. Little brother, go! This is a command. Those were your men guarding him. You will kill Ren Daiyan and kill or recapture the prince."

"Now?" Bai'ji repeated.

His brother made no reply, only stared at him.

Bai'ji's was the glance that faltered. "All right! I will!" He reached out the hand with the cup and someone took it from him. "See?" he said. "I put down the wine! I obey your commands!"

"Take our best trackers, it will be harder in the dark."

"Then we will go in the morning. I want *five*—"

"No. Now. I do not want that prince surviving. He is too important. The Sky God guard you in an alien land, brother. You wanted to go south. This is your first chance."

The brothers faced each other over the dead body of the interpreter. There was blood on the snow. The younger still held his sword.

"Doesn't have to be me," Bai'ji said softly, in a voice that seemed to exclude everyone but his brother.

"Yes, it does," the war-leader said, equally quietly.

There was a moment, there sometimes is, when a great deal hung suspended as the snow fell, torchlit. It was possible that the younger brother might have killed the older, or tried. The older one was aware of this, and was ready, balanced, a hand casually close to his own sword hilt, although he was most nearly sober, and so grieving at what might come next, where the night had gone.

If this had happened, if there had been a killing either way, it might have changed what followed in the world. Or not. It is never possible to know with certainty. We cannot go back and do something differently to see the result.

Bai'ji sheathed his sword.

Five hundred horsemen, with fifteen hundred very good horses, left camp not long after, riding south, the burning city quickly behind them, darkness sweeping in. They were led by the younger of their two leaders, his presence a marker of how urgent this mission was judged to be.

The three men who had carried the tidings of the prisoner's escape ended up walking away from that fire alive. A decision or an oversight, it was unclear which. They never knew, themselves.

☙

Two thousand, one hundred, and fifty-seven carts laden with treasure left Hanjin for the north.

Seven convoys of captives went with them or after them, some fifteen thousand people, including the entire imperial family of Kitai (except for one prince, the ninth son) and almost all of the extended imperial clan. Some of the latter had died in the clan quarter. Some had actually swung swords, trying to defend their homes or women. They were supposed to be captured, but a horseman could only endure so much indignity from a Kitan.

There was some anxiety among those guarding the convoys, as they stretched out, about being attacked on the way north.

Most of the Altai force remained south, and the guards were significantly outnumbered by their captives. There were also large numbers of Kitan soldiers and outlaws roaming the northern prefectures, almost all the way up to the former Xiaolu Southern Capital.

The guards kept their captives moving quickly, most of them on foot, and there wasn't a great deal of food. Men and women were beaten if they lagged, and they had to collect their own firewood and carry it as they moved. Large numbers died on the way north and were left unburied where they fell.

These deaths did not include either the former emperor or the recently proclaimed one, his son. These two had been mockingly renamed by the Altai war-leader in a ceremony outside the city walls before the first convoy started north.

The Emperor Wenzong—tall, gaunt, grey-haired, grey-bearded— was given the title Lord of Muddled Virtue. Much amusement ensued. His son, to even greater hilarity, was proclaimed Doubly Muddled Virtue. They wore placards around their necks with these names in two languages, with additional characters declaring them deluded leaders of slave rebels.

Both men would survive the journey, most of it side by side in an ox cart. They were taken first to the Southern Capital, then the Eastern, and then, for greatest security, all the way to a city in the far north of what had been the Xiaolu empire and was now that of the Altai. Their survival ended up being important, though not in ways anyone anticipated in those early days.

Prime Minister Hang Dejin, the man most likely to have thought all this through, was dead at Little Gold Hill.

Emperor Wenzong had been celebrated for his art and a lifelong appreciation of beauty. He wrote poems endlessly on the way north. A number of these were preserved because some of those in the terrible convoys did escape, though none of the imperial family, closely watched, did so.

On rough paper obtained for him, Wenzong wrote:

> *After all this time the great enterprise stops.*
> *I was a fool not to heed wise advice,*
> *Listening instead to those urging madness.*
> *Humbly I now travel ten thousand* li,
> *A captive among my people.*
> *I eat cold rice from cracked bowls*
> *And sleep on hard ground.*
> *My hair is thin upon my head.*

To think how in the palace of Hanjin
I was saddened and demanded music
When jade halls grew cool in autumn.

ဆာ

Enterprises do not necessarily stop, even after disasters, or simply because a humiliated leader, guilt-stricken about his own mistakes, believes it so.

Daiyan had two men trailing behind as they raced towards the Wai River as fast as the presence of the prince and a woman allowed. It was a week's hard ride, more if the weather turned worse. He had not yet explained Shan to Prince Zhizeng, nor had the prince asked. It was, he had come to understand, an aspect of being imperial: you didn't even notice certain things.

The trailing men came racing up on the fourth afternoon. A party of Altai were closing. Would be upon them by evening, or in the night.

"How many?" Ziji asked quietly.

"Not easy to tell," one rider said. "We couldn't let them get too near us." He was exhausted. It was snowing again. "Five hundred, at a guess."

Ziji swore, but under his breath. Neither of the reinforcement cavalry companies from the west had yet arrived. The one sent to cut off the Altai had—obviously—not done so, and the others were to meet them at the Wai, many days south yet.

It was a difficult, defining moment. It was seen by those watching anxiously that Commander Ren Daiyan smiled. That would be remembered.

"Sometimes it feels as if you can see patterns in life," he said to his oldest friend. "I know this country. So do you. We've been here."

"He said five hundred, Daiyan," Ziji said, keeping his voice low.

Daiyan's smile only deepened. Shan, leaning against her horse not far away (her legs were weak and her back ached), felt the strangest sensation, seeing it.

"I did hear that," Daiyan said to Ziji. He raised his voice, to be heard. "Let's go. I know where we lose them. And I need two men to head west to find our reinforcements. They won't be far."

That last he didn't know with certainty, but sometimes you led men by pretending the sureness they needed to see in you, because they would be watching, wanting to hope.

HE WAS SOBER, had been by the end of the first night of this cold chase, he'd even left his wine cup deliberately behind. Bai'ji was also angry—a fury directed back at his brother, the war-leader. That he'd address when they returned.

It disturbed him, a little, how close he'd been to killing Wan'yen in the midst of their camp. He wasn't unsettled by the idea of killing, but because that would have been the wrong way, exposing himself. He wasn't the only ambitious man in the tribe.

He'd decided some time ago that his brother was too weak, too narrow, too *limited* to properly succeed their aging kaghan—who was even more limited, in truth. Wan'yen couldn't grasp the larger possibilities. He'd mocked Bai'ji about riding to the southern sea. The two of them riding, he'd said, like a good younger brother.

Didn't it *excite* Wan'yen? That thought? Doing something no horseman of the steppe had ever done, had ever even thought to do?

Obviously not. What excited his older brother was humiliating Bai'ji, sending him off on this chase of a small party (they'd realized they were pursuing about twenty Kitan), which could easily have been assigned a lesser rider, leaving Bai'ji to his deserved pleasures.

Instead, he was galloping through this unpleasantly hilly, broken-up country, around clusters of winter trees and across choppy farmland with ditches and canals, leading unhappy men. The fugitives were going faster than expected, but not as fast— never as fast—as steppe riders with three horses each could go.

There had been arrows loosed at them from hidden places at twilight and in the grey before sunrise. Some of his men had died, or been wounded. Twice the riders at the front were tripped up at night by ropes between trees lining a road they followed. There was chaos each time, men and horses breaking limbs. That meant death for the horses, and usually for the riders, out here.

He'd sent men to hunt down the archers, or those who laid these traps, but no one was found. It was close, dense country here. Farmers' fields, then forests. The sky too near under a moon or wintry sun, when either of them showed.

They were close now. From the tracks (off the road, heading southwest) Bai'ji judged they might overtake the fleeing party by darkfall. His brother owed him.

Owed him a death, in fact. But not to be done in rage, or among others, where he might be seen to be in the wrong as a younger sibling owing loyalty. There were ways of accomplishing this that would leave a clear path, under the Sky God's heaven, for a man who understood what was possible now. Kitai was huge, wealthy. It was ripe as summer fruit.

He could bring this fleeing prince back, or kill him. Wan'yen had said he didn't care. Bai'ji saw no reason to slow themselves on the way back. The prince was dead tonight.

He also needed to kill the other man, Ren Daiyan. His brother was afraid the prince could become a symbol. Bai'ji knew better. It was the warrior who was more likely to become that—the man who'd destroyed an Altai army, who had entered a guarded camp and escaped with a prisoner, leaving a mocking note to be read aloud.

That one was dangerous. He had only twenty men here, however. A horseman, a leader of the Altai—or their emperor—could always use two drinking cups, Bai'ji thought.

THAT NIGHT NORTH of the Wai the cloud cover finally broke and a waxing moon shone among hard and brilliant stars. What followed became the matter of legend.

Marshlands change year to year, season to season. Trackways through them alter, high ground will subside or be covered by rising water, an islet of firm footing will disappear, or emerge. It was important not to be overconfident, especially in the dark. What did not change was that marshes, everywhere, are very bad for horsemen.

These were not the marshes south of the Great River that he and Ziji knew like they knew the homes in which they'd each grown up. But years in such terrain gave you instincts and awareness that extended to other watery places. And they *had* been here, when they put down the rebellion in the season they were sent this way by Kai Zhen. He'd been prevented by that from going to battle the Xiaolu at their Southern Capital—which was never taken, or not by Kitai.

He'd recruited ten thousand rebels here and south of here, for these marshes extended almost all the way to the Wai. Three of those men were with him now. For them, this land was home in the deepest, most powerful way: a refuge in the midst of danger. A place to lure enemies, and destroy them.

He'd said he knew how to lose the pursuing riders. It became more than that. Which is why the histories—and the legends— came to include this story, this night, that watching moon.

There are many difficulties pursuing a fleeing enemy into unexpected marshes in the dark. One is that if a retreat becomes necessary, either a genuine flight or a strategic withdrawal until morning, it is not easy for a large company of riders (each with a pair of horses strung to the one he rode) to turn around and find a way out.

Turning around is difficult, even for the best riders in the world, in wet, sucking bog, or surprisingly deep water, a landscape alien to their grassland lives. Horses will panic, lose their footing, and fall in the thick, clinging mud. Creatures in the swampy water will hungrily find their legs and bite, and *that* will make horses scream in pain and terror, rear up, topple each other—and their riders.

And if rapid, deadly arrows are being loosed at them from higher, hidden ground, even by only twenty men (every man Ziji had brought knew how to use a bow), then carnage will result, dying men and horses, since blood and thrashing hooves and loud noises in a night swamp will bring other hungry creatures, some of them large.

Some of them human. There are always outlaws in marshes.

It took the nearest of these little time to grasp what was happening here. Horseflesh is sustaining meat for a man in winter, and many of them had children and wives with them. There were rocks and heavy sticks, knives, old, rusting swords, scythes, even a few bows. Men who knew where they were treading could approach the riders carefully, unseen, and dispatch a wounded man or beast.

Legends tend not to linger upon the ugliness of such unholy nights. Or the appearance of a killing swamp in morning under a winter sun. Legends dwell upon courage, redemption, glory, revenge. Honour. Not wet leeches on the eyeless face of a dead boy from the grasslands whose hands and feet are already gone.

None of Daiyan's party knew which man was the leader of the Altai company sent after them, none would have recognized the war-leader's younger brother if they'd seen him. He was unrecognizable by morning, in any case. The later stories that told of single combat between him and Ren Daiyan on raised ground were only that: stories told.

A handful of Altai did escape, those towards the back of their party. Daiyan didn't order them pursued. They'd carry word of what could happen to steppe riders south of Hanjin—or they'd be killed on the way back. Or killed by their own leaders when they returned, for having failed.

He didn't greatly care. He made certain the prince was all right, and Shan, and his own men. They had no casualties. None. He confirmed that arrows were being reclaimed. He looked for the outlaws who had joined them in the dark, but they'd melted back into the marshlands and he couldn't blame them for that. They would return when Daiyan and his men had gone. He had his soldiers chase down as many healthy horses as they could.

They lit torches. He became aware that there was something new, a kind of awe, in the way his men were looking at him—and a different expression in the eyes of Prince Zhizeng.

He thought of speaking to the prince again, using the night's triumph to again urge that they make a stand at Jingxian, rally the armies, drive the horsemen back, regain Hanjin—and then the north.

His judgment told him that this was the wrong time. In that, as it happened, he was correct. Princes can draw very different conclusions than one might expect, even from the moments and men (and battles) that save their lives, leading them nearer to a throne they want. Zhizeng had expected to die from the time they'd learned the pursuit was closing in. He had lived with terror from the moment they'd entered the marsh at night.

In the darkness before sunrise they lit fires for warmth and posted guards against tigers, which they heard but never saw. Ziji made no jests about them, not that night.

They did not fear pursuit any more. They would proceed with speed from here on, but not urgency. They could rest and breathe and sleep.

Daiyan spent the last part of the night with Shan on elevated ground. She fell asleep against his shoulder as he leaned against a twisted, mossy tree. He realized he didn't care any more if they were seen. He needed her there. He didn't expect many opportunities going forward.

Before falling asleep, she said, "Be careful with the prince," which was his own thought.

He slept a little, fitfully, woke before the sun. Stayed where he was, because she was still sleeping. Heard winter birds as the sky began to brighten and the shape of the world came back.

ᘒᘓ

Hanjin was theirs, but Wan'yen still preferred to spend nights in his yurt. He had never liked walls, wasn't sure how he'd adapt to them, or if he wanted to.

The shaman came to him at sunrise, elk-fur vest, bells and drums at his waist, painted eyes, twin scars on his shoulder blades.

"I had a dream," he said.

Wan'yen didn't like his shaman, but liking them wasn't what mattered. He was tired, half asleep. He cleared his throat and spat onto the ground beside the fire. It was warmer this morning. The snow had melted. It would come again.

"What must I know?" he asked.

"Your brother died last night." No warning at all. The words cold. He was like that, the shaman. "Most of his party died with him. There was water," he added.

Wan'yen had not expected the feeling that overtook him. He'd been near to killing Bai'ji beside this fire, several nights ago.

"Water? He drowned?" His mouth was dry.

"An arrow," the shaman said.

"You know this with certainty?"

The shaman didn't even bother answering. The painted eyes fixed his a moment, then looked away towards the morning sky where an eagle could be seen.

Wan'yen was careful to show no emotion. Shamans could not be trusted. They walked in a different world. Between worlds.

He was fully awake now. He was calculating numbers in his head. He was good with numbers. He was good at making decisions.

He summoned his leaders to the yurt and they came. Some were drunk, had been since the city fell. He named the ones to be left in command here and gave his orders concerning Hanjin. The walls were to be rebuilt, this was their city now. He named those who would lead the treasure carts and captives north. Those men were happy. They were going home.

He took thirty thousand riders and went south. He sent messengers west to the army still besieging Yenling. Twenty thousand of them were ordered to do the same thing he was doing. He might arrange to join the two armies. He'd decide later. You didn't fight campaigns in winter, everyone knew it, but sometimes circumstances forced you to go against old wisdom.

An escaped prince could rally and rouse Kitai. That was why he'd needed the man recaptured. Now it became a different kind of war they were fighting, he and this Ren Daiyan. He found himself remembering a night in the northeast, when he'd been humiliated, made to dance between fires.

Wan'yen didn't like being made to dance.

These soft southern people, before they even shaped a thought of fighting back, claiming pride, seizing hope, needed to learn exactly what they were facing. How red and wide a swath of death the horsemen from above the Black River could shape, even in winter.

He would call it avenging his brother, his riders would like that, understand it. In truth, he was breaking Kitai. So savagely no man would think to lift a sword, a stick, a bow, would dare raise his *head* in a village or on a farm when a steppe horseman rode by.

He wasn't chasing the prince, he had no idea where he'd be going, and Kitai was very large. His brother had wanted them to ride together to the southern sea. His brother had been ambitious and a fool and was dead.

Late on their second night riding south, perhaps because he'd had too much to drink before retiring, he found he could not sleep. He was remembering Bai'ji, growing up together, first wolves, first battles. He went from his yurt and looked up at the stars. He felt himself wrapped in sorrow and memory. The feeling passed. It never came again.

ഛ

"Should we be moving everyone south?" Lu Chao asked his brother the poet, later that same winter.

It was too cold to be outdoors, even on a sunny day. They sat on either side of a built-up fire in the older brother's writing room, drinking tea.

"Where?" Chen asked. "Where would you have us go?"

"I don't know," the younger brother admitted.

"We have people to feed. This is finally a working farm because of my sage and dedicated labours."

Lu Chao permitted himself a sibling's snort of amusement.

The older brother smiled. After a moment, he added, "The river will protect us. They won't get across."

Chao looked at him. "You are certain of that? Or you are trying to make yourself believe it?"

The poet laughed. "I am cursed with a clever brother. It is unfair." He drank his tea. "I am certain of nothing," he said. "But this is a long way for the Altai to come, and surely someone will organize to defend the Great River, if not the Wai."

"Surely," the younger brother said wryly. Then added, in the same ironic tone, "Our valiant armies?"

Chen made an equally wry face. He said, "I am too old to move again, brother. Let that be my answer."

"You aren't old," Chao said.

"*My hair is too thin to hold a pin*," the older one quoted.

There was a footfall in the corridor. Mah stood in the doorway.

"My son," said Chen. "Join us. We are discussing how youthful we feel. I intend to do my exercises. Shall we be outlaws and attack a mountain temple for hidden gold?"

Mah shook his head. "You'd better come," he said.

IT WAS A SMALL PARTY approaching, but not so small that they couldn't overrun East Slope and kill them all. There was no hidden gold here, but there was food, there were animals, and enough of value to lure danger in this time of chaos. People were on the move everywhere, dispossessed, hungry, mostly coming south, with the barbarians in the north.

Lu Mah and the steward had already assembled the farmhands and household men. Each of them held a heavy stick or a weapon. They were arrayed near the gate. The numbers, the poet thought, were approximately equal. Those approaching were on horseback and had real weapons, however.

He looked back towards the door of the main house where his wife stood: his second wife. A woman he admired more than he loved. She was that sort of person. He didn't think she'd minded. A different sort of relationship, later in a life. He admired her now, seeing her alert, attentive, not visibly afraid.

Looking within himself, he found sorrow but not fear. There were experiences he still wanted from life, from days under heaven, but he'd expected to die long ago. Everything after Lingzhou felt like a gift.

His thoughts were with the younger ones, whose gifts ought to lie in front of them and might not. If this was a raid they had no chance.

"I know the leader," Chao said suddenly. Chen turned to him, eyes wide. "And also, I think ..."

He trailed off. Chen stared at his brother. "What?" he said, perhaps a little sharply.

"Third man, grey horse."

Chen looked, the young man was unknown to him. The armed riders had reached their gate.

The leader dismounted. He bowed. He said, "I believe we are in the presence of the Lu brothers at East Slope. May I be permitted to express my very great honour?"

Not an attack. Not death coming along the road.

Chen, older brother, bowed in return. "We are honoured by your salutation. I am embarrassed not to know you. Permit us to welcome you to East Slope. May I ask who you might be?"

The welcome first, then the question.

"Of course," said the man who'd spoken. "Honourable Lu Chao will not remember me, but I had the honour to observe him at the court when he returned from the steppe."

"But I do remember," said Chao. "You are Commander Ren Daiyan, and you should have been the man we sent to take the Southern Capital."

Chen blinked, then looked more closely at this visitor. Heavily armed: sword, knife, bow, arrows in a quiver. Youthful-looking, though not someone you'd be likely to call *young*. He had a lean face and hard eyes, a soldier's eyes, though they altered with Chao's words, became ironic, intelligent. Not hard, on further reflection.

"Soldiers serve where they are sent," he said mildly. "I am not important. But we are escorting someone who is." He gestured to the man on the grey horse.

It was Chao who reacted first.

"My lord prince!" he exclaimed. "I thought that I ... Oh, heaven be thanked!"

He knelt and placed his forehead and his palms on the cold ground of the yard. Chen, hearing that word *prince*, did the same, and behind them the others followed. But he had no idea ...

Another soldier swung easily down from his horse and assisted the one Chao had named a prince to dismount.

"Prince Zhizeng," said Ren Daiyan with helpful clarity, "appears to be the only member of the imperial family not taken in the fall of Hanjin."

"It has fallen, then?"

A ghost had told him. This was the first living man to say the words.

"New Year's eve. We escaped that night."

Lu Chen slowly rose to his feet. *Zhizeng?* The poet was racking his memory. What number son? Twelve? Nine? Who kept track if you weren't at court where these things mattered as much as food and poison did? He was a son, though, an imperial son. And alive.

"My lord prince!" he exclaimed, as his brother had. "We are humbled beyond words. How are you among us?"

"The intercession of the gods," said Prince Zhizeng piously.

There would have been men involved, too, Chen guessed. Probably these men. He looked at Ren Daiyan. "What may we offer you? Here is shelter, and hearts loyal to Kitai."

"Good," said the prince, answering. "We will be grateful for these things."

Chen looked over at Mah, who stood up now and moved to open their gate. He didn't look back but he knew his wife and his brother's wife, all the women of the house, would be flying, as if into battle, to make East Slope as ready as it could ever be for what had arrived.

Ren Daiyan was smiling slightly. It changed his features. Chen smiled back. He had found, through the years, that people responded to that.

"How did you find us?" he asked.

The commander said, "We were guided by a member of our company who appears to have relied on descriptions you sent in writing."

"I sent? In writing?"

He felt baffled again. It was not displeasing, to have life startle you sometimes. He thought suddenly of a theme for a poem: how it was not good for a man to feel his existence would hold no more surprises.

"I remembered," said another of the riders, moving a horse forward, "that you told me East Slope was just east of Mai-lin Stream, very near the Great River, and not far from the real site of Red Cliff—and the false one you wrote about in a poem we discussed in the garden of Master Xi Wengao, in peony season."

He stared. Then he clapped his hands in delight. He looked at her and his smile came from his heart. He thought: How could any man be so foolish as to imagine life would serve him only the expected? It wasn't a good idea for a poem, it was an *easy* thought, not worth the grinding of ink.

"You are very welcome, Lady Lin, you and our prince, and the commander, every one of you. Please enter, grace us with your presence. There is wine and food and whatever comforts we may offer. We will hear your tale whenever you wish to tell it."

"Forgive me, Father. Please?" It was Mah, who still held his grandfather's ceremonial sword. He looked at the commander. "Are you being pursued? Is there danger we need to defend you against?"

That was graciously put, his father thought.

Ren Daiyan smiled at Mah. He seemed to be a man with access to that. "Thank you," he said. "I remember you, as well. You were with Lu Chao that day in court. No," he said. "We are not being pursued. Pursuit was dealt with, north of the Wai."

He looked over at the prince, who had already stepped through the open gate and was approaching the main house.

"We will intrude upon you only briefly," Ren Daiyan added. "Some of us will escort the prince to Shantong, which is his desire. He will be safe from the Altai there."

"And others of you?" Chen asked. He'd caught something in that tone.

"Others will be going back north, and we will lay down our lives if need be, fighting the Altai there."

Instinctively, Lu Chen glanced back. The prince had stopped walking, had turned around. He was looking at Ren Daiyan. Chao had turned as well, same instinct? The brothers exchanged a glance.

"If it is possible to bathe," said Lin Shan, ending a stillness, "I will offer six songs of praise before sundown."

"I would like to have them," said Chen.

They had the farmhands deal with the horses. The poet led their guests inside to where fires had been quickly lit and food was being prepared. He gave the prince his own chair, nearest the front room hearth. They offered wine, and then a meal. They listened to stories told. They told, in turn, what they knew, which wasn't very much.

They had songs from Lin Shan after night fell. She sang of the victory at Red Cliff, not far away from here, but long ago.

It was proposed and accepted that she stay here with the Lu brothers and their families, a guest honoured for herself, and in the name of her deceased, honourable father and that of her husband, who was also very likely dead, it seemed, or taken north with others of the imperial clan.

The prince had repeated his intentions: he was going to Shantong, nestled between the coast and West Lake. Wealthy, beautiful, steep streets from the harbour, goods bought and sold from ships coming and going all year long, from the Koreini Peninsula, from the southern sea, from beyond that.

Chen knew it well; he'd been prefect there when young, when their faction held power. West Lake claimed a part of his heart forever. He'd built the long, low bridge across the far side, for people walking by the serene stillness of the lake. They'd named it for him when he left. Lu Chen's Bridge at West Lake. He could go back. Serve at a new court, if asked. He'd looked at the prince at their table. He was unlikely to be asked. Perhaps his brother would be?

Hanjin had fallen. Kitai needed a court and an emperor.

Shantong was probably the best place, yes. And Zhizeng was in the direct line of succession. It made sense.

From his bed he heard the wind chimes in the paulownia in the garden, a quiet music. He'd always liked wind chimes. The moon was bright, just past full. Sima Zian had been the poet of the moon. Chen had joked, when younger, that it was unfair: if any of them wrote of moons since Master Sima's day, they were only imitating the Banished Immortal.

Another phrase for a poem came to him. Latterly, he would make himself get up, even in the cold, light a lamp, grind ink, water it, and write characters down, for fear his memory might surrender offered words before sunrise.

This phrase, he knew, would not leave him.

He whispered it to himself. *"From Hanjin to Shantong is the path of our sorrow."*

He said it again. He listened to the wind chimes and the wind. The moon moved away. He lay awake. He was aware, being observant, and a lover of women all his life, that Ren Daiyan and Lady Lin Shan would likely be together now, in the commander's chamber or hers.

He wished them what joy they could find—in these times, in this night of shelter at East Slope. Then he slept.

CHAPTER XXVI

By the beginning of spring, after a winter of savagery, the twin armies of the Altai had joined into one marauding force, taken on reinforcements, and moved across the Wai to the banks of the Great River.

Spring was the normal time for war. The riders' purpose changed. This was now an invasion force. The ease with which they'd succeeded through winter had altered intentions: they were driving to Shantong and the court of the escaped prince, the just-crowned young emperor there.

It was evident, because they didn't trouble to hide it, where they were going. They sent a demand for surrender. Their messenger was killed. The Altai war-leader ordered three villages north of the river razed, every inhabitant killed and left where he or she lay. They didn't get every single one, although they tried. Some of the men escaped (some took their wives and children) and sought to find their way south or into the woods or swamps. Some joined the rabble that called itself the army of Kitai.

As it happened, the horsemen gathered their forces on the

526

Great River not far from the battle site of Red Cliff, where an invading army had massed almost a thousand years before. Their current location was near enough for the ensuing confrontation to eventually become known as the Second Battle of Red Cliff.

The line between history and storytelling isn't always easy to draw.

The Altai were not a marine people, but by now they had large numbers of Kitan labourers to serve them, mostly under duress but some not coerced. There are always those who judge the direction of the wind. Kitan fishermen and craftsmen were set to work building the small-boat flotilla the army needed to cross the river in springtime spate.

In the first battle at Red Cliff, long ago, foot soldiers and archers had waited on opposite banks, and boat had confronted boat in the wide river, until a celebrated, heaven-granted change in the wind (a change shaped by magic, some said) let empty ships on fire be run north into the invading fleet.

It was different this time.

The Altai in their small boats scudding back and forth in the dark did establish a landing on the southern bank as a misty morning dawned. Rain fell lightly, the ground was tricky on the bank, but there was only a shallow climb up, in a place chosen carefully.

The first steppe riders established their landfall. They made their way up from the riverbank, they took up positions to defend it, bows and short-curved swords in drizzling rain.

They had slaughtered and burned their way farther south than any tribesmen ever had. They were grim and triumphant, the hardest fighting force in the world.

What they did not know, preparing to control a chosen landing place for the horses now swimming across, was that they'd been permitted to land.

Normally, defenders used a river as a barrier to keep an enemy on the far side. In a very few celebrated battles, a general had placed his own army with a river at their backs, to eliminate any chance of retreat, compel courage.

This time, the man leading the gathered forces of Kitai in this part of the world had elected to do things differently.

WAITING IN THE WET, weedy land above the river, Zhao Ziji was afraid. They had heard the Altai splashing ashore, then the sounds of them clambering up the bank. Daiyan wanted a good number of them on land—and cut off. Ziji had always been more cautious, going back to the days when their plans involved no more than attacking a taxation officer's guards. Perhaps it was because he was older—though he didn't really think that was it.

Some men seemed to be born prepared to assess a risk and then take it. But they could still make mistakes, any man could, and this one might be too large to recover from, Ziji thought.

He looked at the eastern sky through the slantwise rain. The Altai always tried to time things for sunrise. They knew that about them. It was important. The wind was from the west, which meant the current was even faster. If all was unfolding as it was meant to, they'd soon hear—

Shouts and distant screaming from the river reached him in that moment. Ziji smiled thinly. Fear slipped away, replaced by something colder. He remained motionless, hidden. His men beside and behind him did the same. His own instincts for timing in battle happened to be very precise. He whispered an order to those nearest: *Hold, not yet.* Heard it being relayed quietly. He had their very best men with him here.

With the growing sounds from the river—which would be the panicked noises of horses and the men guiding them in the water— the Altai below them on this bank began to shift and stir. They'd be uneasy now, some would be turning around. This was supposed to have been a secret crossing, to the west of where they'd massed their main force to be readily seen building boats.

The invaders had brought half their horses this way, well back from the river, unseen, to a spot even farther upstream from here—where they could swim across not fighting the current, letting it bring them to this chosen place where there was a good landing ground and a shallow slope.

The boats being built at the main camp east—those were real, but they were also a clever dissembling, meant to seduce the Kitan into massing there. They were to be used *after* this secret landing. What the Kitan army was not supposed to know was that the Altai had all those other boats and a large force hidden to the west, and these were the ones who'd come down to the river now, to cross it in the dark.

The plan was clever. Wan'yen was a war-leader who deserved his rank, it was agreed among the horsemen. Only his brother might have been as brilliant and bold.

Once ashore, this western force would mount up and compel most of the Kitan army to move hastily upriver to face them—allowing the other part of the steppe force to cross from where they were.

Kitai didn't have enough good soldiers to fight them at two different places. And once the riders were on that side of the river ...

THE RAIN DIDN'T BOTHER Daiyan, he hardly noticed it. He'd lived so much of his life in the open, all seasons, all weather.

Over the years, he had also discovered, to his surprise, that he liked being on water. He'd never yet seen the sea, but rivers and boats felt unexpectedly natural for him. "I'd have made a good fisherman," he'd told Ziji once, drunk, and his friend had laughed.

But he'd meant it. Paths offered and taken could lead the same man to very different lives. He might have been a scholar taking the *jinshi* examinations if there hadn't been a drought one year when he was young. And what if he hadn't been chosen one day when Magistrate Wang Fuyin needed another guard for a journey? Or, even, if you were letting your mind drift, if seven outlaws hadn't been where they were that afternoon?

There were so many ways for a life to have been different, moment by moment, year after year. So many paths that did not lead you to this boat, this night.

On the other hand, he thought, rain dripping from his leather helmet, on any of those he'd not have met Shan.

An image had come to him on their one night at East Slope, in her chamber. He'd told it to her. It had to do with the seals emperors used to send out with commanders long ago. The seals would be broken in half. One half would go with the army; the other remained guarded at court. If new instructions had to be sent, the messenger would carry the emperor's half of the seal, so the commander would know that the orders came from the throne and not from someone trying to deceive him. They'd fit the two halves together and know the words were true.

"You are like that for me," he'd told her.

She'd been sitting up in the bed, hands around her knees, listening. It was dark, but he knew her by then and knew she wasn't smiling. And indeed, she said, "I'm not sure I like all of that."

"Which part?" His hand was on her ankle. He found it difficult not to touch her, even after lovemaking. They'd had so little time, ever, and he was leaving before morning, before the prince awoke—because the prince was going to order him to come to Shantong and guard him there, and Daiyan was not going to do it. He couldn't refuse a command, so he had to be gone before it came.

He was going north. There was an army to gather.

Shan said, "The part about the commander at war. Those two halves of a seal fitting together don't speak of love."

He thought about it. "Trust, then?" he asked. "At least that?"

She took his hand in hers, lacing fingers. "You are too clever to be a soldier." Then she shook her head. "Don't say it. I know. We need our soldiers to be clever. I do know."

"Thank you," he murmured. "You can do all of the conversation. Make it easier for me."

That time she laughed.

He said, "Shan, I am a leader of whatever we have left, and there are those who want to destroy us. We can't always choose the times into which we are born."

"We can't ever choose those," she corrected. "You should sleep, if you are leaving in the dark."

"If I sleep," he remembered saying, "I lose time with you."

"No you don't," she said.

She sang him to rest, an old song, her voice low, almost a whisper, her hand in his hair.

He'd awakened before dawn. She was beside him, still awake, looking at him. He'd dressed and left, on a road that had led him north and west, a shadow in winter, moving quickly, gathering men and sending them south, tracking the barbarians. He'd ended up back at the Great River now, near East Slope again, and it seemed to be springtime.

"There they are!" said Kang Junwen, beside him in the boat. Junwen had been with him when they'd rescued the prince and had never left him since.

Daiyan peered into rain. A moment later he heard sounds, then he saw the smaller Altai boats and the horses labouring in the water. They'd be swimming a long way in a swift, cold current, but these were the best horses in the world, excepting the legendary ones from the west that no one living had ever seen.

He didn't like killing horses, and he needed as many as he could get. That was one part of this risky, elaborate plan: to strip the Altai of their horses, providing mounts for the Kitan cavalry he wanted.

So Daiyan and his force, in larger boats with forty men each—a fleet of these assembled and brought downriver from the west— were as precise as they could be with that vast herd in the river. The horses were being guided by some men riding them (brave men);

others of the Altai were in among them in the boats they'd made and carried to the water in the night.

They began by wounding horses to cause panic. Then they concentrated on the boats as they came among them. Ramming them, setting fire to them with arrows. There was a legendary association of fire with war and victory here. He didn't mind adding to that.

They were a devastating surprise, utterly unexpected, and the steppe riders knew nothing of watercraft. Daiyan began shouting, his men in their boats did the same. They wanted the sounds of fighting and fear to reach the southern bank. They could hear Altai screaming as they were plunged from broken boats into the water. Their small craft were shattered in collisions or they caught fire and men leaped from them. Die in water, die in flames.

They should not be here. They had made a mistake coming here. Few horsemen of the steppe ever learned to swim.

It was morning now, still raining, but he could see what he was doing. He fired steadily, arrow after arrow. The captain of his boat was a river pilot, most of them were. Men who plied their trade bringing goods up and down the Great River, or across it, many of them sons of sons of sons doing the same thing for generations.

This was their land, their home, their river. Their *rivers and mountains*. The steppe riders had been unspeakably brutal as they'd swept through the lands above and below the Wai. They had left a trail—and a tale—of ugly death. They had intended that, wanted to terrify Kitai into a crouched, huddled submission, make it fear to fight back, to bond behind a new, young emperor.

It was, in purely military terms, a good idea. It wasn't going to work, Commander Ren Daiyan had decided. They couldn't choose the times in which they lived, but they could face their days and nights with courage. And cleverness mattered, too. Shan had said it for him, their last night.

He'd had spies in the Altai force, among those conscripted to build their boats. They'd kept their heads down, those men, cutting trees, hammering, and kept their ears open, listening.

He'd had scouts ranging widely, marsh outlaws many of them, trained by a lifetime of hiding (as he had been), skilled in stealth. He had known about the boats being built west of the Altai main camp. He had known their size, their numbers. He knew where the horsemen intended to make a landing on the south bank of the river—because it was the only easy slope up from that shoreline for fifty *li*.

Ziji and the best men they had were waiting for them there. Men who'd won the battle north of Yenling.

The barbarians were deadly on horseback, no one rode like them, had horses like theirs. But sweeping to their battles in a thunder of hooves, they were not, Daiyan had decided, as subtle as the Kitan. As subtle as *he* was.

You won wars, you defended your people, with what you could, with all you could. That included gathering men and boats even farther upriver, and killing any horsemen who ventured so far on raiding sweeps. They had done that. They had done it with a hard joy. No one was tortured or mutilated (they were not barbarians) but none of those riders went back east along the river, or home to their grasslands.

Then word had come: the small boats were being carried to the bank. It would be tonight, the first landings timed for sunrise.

He knew Ziji would be receiving these same tidings, and he knew Ziji understood his task. It didn't mean he could *do* it, or that Daiyan could, here on the water, but you kept those doubts to yourself. None of your men needed to see or hear them in you. An army won when it thought it could win. Or, perhaps, when men thought about what would happen if they did not.

Here they stop, Daiyan had told his soldiers and watermen upriver. *Here is where the tide starts back.*

The sun had been setting red into a long bank of clouds. The rain had not yet come. They'd untied their own craft and cast off. He'd shouted his words as loudly as he could, heard them picked up and echoed from boat to boat, carrying to those out of range of his voice.

The Commander, they called him by then. No one thought of him as young that spring. They thought he was the man who might save Kitai.

Boys younger than he had been when he left his village, their features stiffened into masks by horror, farmers and labourers, bandits, workers from the salt and iron mines, men from the south and his own far west, bitter northerners fleeing charred cities and villages—all came to find Ren Daiyan.

The horsemen knew about the broken army of Kitai. They'd smashed most of those forces last summer and autumn. They did not know, or cause themselves to learn, how many there were in the new army taking shape in the rice lands of the south, or about the river craft assembling west of where their own two-pronged crossing was to happen.

They paid a great price for this, on the river and beside it, as a rain-swept morning dawned.

YOU LEARNED TO WAIT, Ziji thought. It was not a skill that could be extracted from military texts or barracks conversations. You needed to be in battles, commanding, holding back your anxious, eager (frightened) men until the moment that spoke to you and said, *Now. Now we go.*

He heard that voice in his head above the riverbank and he unleashed the best archers and foot soldiers Kitai had. The soldiers with their horse-killing swords and the archers trained in, among other things, how to protect arrows and bowstrings and kill with them in rain.

On this bank the Altai were mostly on foot, only a few of the horses had yet made it across. The screaming from the river was loud now, panic-stricken, and the light was growing brighter, allowing his archers to pick out targets from where they were positioned up a farther slope, in bushes and low trees, defended by men in front of them.

The archers were the first attack, rapid volleys cutting down the Altai as some of them tried to rush the slope and others turned helplessly back towards the water where their companions were dying in boats.

Ziji could imagine their terror, their rage: they were trapped and dying on water, far from their grasslands, in this wet, congested land. And it went against all expectations—after the effortless campaign that had drawn them south in the sure and firm belief Kitai was theirs.

"Forward now!" Ziji roared. He heard it taken up by his captains along the line. His battle rage was up, driven by memories of the north, knowledge of what these barbarians had done. He had seen an elderly woman in front of an isolated farmhouse, lying on the path to her own door. Her hands and feet had been cut off, were lying beside her, and her belly had been ripped open. The horsemen had wanted to overwhelm and terrify. He and Daiyan had discussed it, explained it to others. They understood this, fear as a tactic of war. That didn't take away a need to kill, it drove that desire forward, like a tidal bore.

The fight changed. Once he and the ground troops moved, their archers had to stop—they became a rear guard now, picking off Altai who broke through, either to rush them or flee south, since there was no escape into the water.

They couldn't swim, and Daiyan's men were here now, timing the current for dawn, crashing into the Altai boats, setting fire to them, killing with arrows—and being slain, some of them, for the barbarians would always fight.

It had been, in truth, a clever plan for crossing the river. Clever, that is, as far as steppe riders were concerned, whose warfare was about fear and the shock of thunder. But the glorious empire of Kitai had known more than a thousand years of warfare and rebellion—and *writing* about both of those, and this Twelfth Dynasty still had some leaders here on the bank, and on the river.

With a full heart and a hard rage, Zhao Ziji came from his place of concealment and he led his men crashing down into the Altai on the riverbank, the ones sent first, to secure a landing place.

It was never secured. They fought bravely, the barbarians. You could never deny them courage. But this dawn ambush in rain was so sudden and unexpected and *fierce*. It wasn't supposed to have been like this at all. Even brave men could see their own death coming, and be undone.

Ziji's men smashed into them like a felled tree rolling down a slope. His were natural foot soldiers, fighting against men who were at home (only at home) on horseback. And the river and the wet slope meant there was nowhere for them to go.

On the water, some of the Altai boats slipped through to the shoreline, men were struggling to get out and join this fight. His archers, Ziji was unsurprised to see, were already responding. Arrows flew over the heads of those fighting up here, killing those trying to clamber from the boats. Horses were dying, too, though he saw some thrashing ashore. He didn't like killing horses, but this was war, it would be savage. What else would it be?

He blocked a blow with his small shield, angling it to have the sword glance and slide, controlling the impact. He swung his blade sideways and low, feeling it bite into the thigh of the man he was facing. The sword hit bone. The Altai's face contorted, his mouth gaped, he went down into the mud. Ziji kicked him hard in the head with a booted foot, moved on towards the river in the rain.

TO THE EAST, on the north bank, Wan'yen, war-leader of the Altai, was drinking earlier, and more, than he customarily did on campaign. He was using the skull-cup his brother had made. He told people he did this to remember his brother.

He had been awake and outside his damp yurt, waiting for a signal, when morning dawned with cold rain. He knew tidings would take time to come from the west, but he hadn't slept well, and was on edge and angry, ready for battle. This was almost as bad as a siege. You built boats. And waited.

The river was far too wide to see across even in sunshine, and in this morning mist you'd have to get very close on the water to discern anything at all on the southern bank.

He hated the river. Hated it by now as if it were a living thing, an enemy in itself, an ally of his foes. Compared to this, the Golden River in the north, though lethal when it flooded, was nothing to cross. This one he thought of as some monster. The Kitan pictured it that way, he knew. There were river gods, and water spirits in the form of dragons. Or of women who would come to lure and drown you. He needed to conquer this river by crossing it.

He sent for a messenger and ordered four boats out. They were to get as close to the other side as they dared, then watch and listen. He understood that it would be difficult, wearying, for the boatmen to keep their craft in one place, fighting the current and the wind. Was he supposed to care?

He needed to know the moment word reached the Kitan army that the Altai had made landfall to the west. The opposing force would begin moving then. Panicking armies weren't quiet. They'd hear the sounds in those boats on the water, maybe even see movement through this intolerable greyness as the Kitan rushed off, most of them, to face the riders who'd crossed.

At which point his own force would move. They'd master this river, thrusting farther into Kitai than any foe had ever gone. It aroused him, thinking of it.

This wasn't even a proper empire any more. That prince they'd held captive might call himself an emperor, but what did that mean? For one thing, his father and brother were alive! The Lords of Muddled Virtue and Doubly Muddled Virtue. They still amused him, the names he'd given those two before shipping them north in a cart like the plunder they were.

By evening today he expected to be across this river and riding for Shantong, where that prince was hiding, probably pissing his bed.

He went down to the water for a time, looking into nothingness, the heavy, dark current. Rain lashed him. He decided this was foolish, it was going to take at least the morning, probably longer, for word of a dawn landing to come to the Kitan, then across to him. He went back to his yurt. He ate. He drank from his brother's cup. Men came and went, cautiously. They offered him a girl. He declined. He wondered if it would stop raining. He went out again, came back in.

No word came, and no word came. And then they learned.

YUN'CHI OF THE ALTAI had no immediate desire to kill anyone. Not in those first terrible moments of mud, chaos, and blood on the south side of the river as the light grew, showing dead and dying companions all around him. His desire was for escape. Anything else—everything else—could wait.

He was a steppe rider. He felt half a man without a horse. He couldn't even think of fleeing on foot, and there was no way to get back across this accursed river.

Sword out, but twisting away from the slippery, savage, losing battle, he ran west, then back towards the water. And there, by the grace of the Lord of the Sky, he found a horse on the bank. Tied-high reins, no saddle. He confirmed it was unhurt and he swung up.

A Kitan soldier came at him in the rain, sword out. He was running a jagged course, to be a harder target. Yun'chi shot him from horseback. His people were the terror of the steppe, of the world.

He fled, kicking the horse away from the fight, then up the treacherous slope from this sodden place. There was screaming. The ground was terrible, the horse exhausted from the river. Yun'chi was as frightened as he'd ever been. They had been told this would be a simple landfall, a glorious deception. They had only to endure the water and come ashore.

Instead, they had been ambushed on the bank and on the water, and he found himself alone in alien country on the wrong side of the river.

He reached a muddy track and decided to head east, towards where the main body of their own army would be (on the other side!). He was incapable of any clear thought as to how to get back across.

He saw that his hands were unsteady, holding the reins. A humiliation! He was no unblooded youth, his *son* was with him in their invading force. Yun'chi had been part of the rising from its beginning. Not a man of status in the tribe, but a true Altai nonetheless. They had cut through the other tribes like a blade through summer grass. And even more easily down to Hanjin and then south, destroying, to this river.

They'd been weary, yes, after so long a campaign, but there'd been so much wealth won here, and Wan'yen and Bai'ji were generous with their riders.

Bai'ji was dead. Slain pursuing an escaped prisoner. There seemed to be a Kitan general who was equal to the brothers. They never spoke his name, a superstition.

Yun'chi, urging a stumbling horse towards the sun, wondered if it was that Kitan commander who'd done this to them here.

Bai'ji, he thought, would have said he was being a coward, for leaving his fellow riders. Fuck Bai'ji, he thought savagely. Fuck Bai'ji, dead months ago.

He had no good idea what to do. His first thought: find a fisherman, force him to cross north, sword at throat. He was a steppe rider, a figure of terror here, but he was alone, and terror, he was discovering, could slide the other way.

He was also wet and tired, and realized he was hungry. They had been in the boats most of the night. He had been sick on the river. He wasn't the only one. Men were not intended to be on rivers so wide, especially not in rain at night, in a swift current.

It was better on a horse, though this one was close to breaking down beneath him. He slowed it to a walk, had no choice. He saw no one on the road for a long time. Word of the Altai force along the river would have driven people away.

Late in the morning he overtook a solitary bullock cart. He killed the driver, left him in his seat, sprawled in death. The cart was empty, though, and the driver had no food, not even a flask of wine. He was old.

Yun'chi began to worry about outlaws in the woods he passed. He was alone, after all. He kept himself as alert as he could, although between exhaustion and fear it was difficult.

Just past midday the rain stopped. The clouds began to break up and he saw the sun. It was still cool. The wind was behind him. He heard birds singing. It felt as if they were mocking him. He wondered if his son was dead.

Some time later he saw smoke rising from a farmhouse chimney. They had been raiding isolated farms all winter long, taking whatever they wanted, including pleasure, leaving ashes and bodies. Through his tiredness, a nudge of anger rose within Yun'chi. Whoever was living here, away from the river, would not get him north, but there would be food in there, and smoke meant warmth—and vengeance could be taken.

He could feed the horse. Maybe find a saddle. He spoke to it, told it they were going only a little farther now. He called it *my heart*, which was what he'd called every horse he'd ridden since he was a boy.

ZIJI LOOKED CLOSELY at Daiyan as he came ashore. He seemed unhurt. He himself had a cut on his left arm, no memory of when he'd received it.

They set their men to rounding up horses and dragging boats on shore. They would need to cross back north, or head downstream— depending on what tidings came from the east.

The ambush had worked as if the Queen Mother of the West, peering down from her pavilions, had decided Kitai deserved something this morning as a small redress for all that had happened.

"Other bank?" he asked. "Their riders who didn't embark?"

"We should have word soon," Daiyan said.

There were dead men all around them in the mud, and the wounded were crying. They had soldiers dealing with their own and killing the enemy where they lay. They were not taking prisoners. A small group of guards stayed by the two of them, making sure none of the riders could suddenly rise from feigning death and strike down the man leading them here, leading them on from here.

Daiyan would say *the two men*, but it wasn't true.

Over on the north bank, near where the Altai had launched their boats, Daiyan had positioned another contingent of soldiers. They had crossed the river north two weeks ago, hiding, waiting.

If all went well, those soldiers would have fallen upon the remaining Altai *after* the majority of the riders were in boats and away and the horses were swimming. They should have been able to pound the enemy between the high ground and the water.

As they had done here. In their battle above Yenling last autumn they had wreaked havoc with two-handed swords and concealed archers. This morning's victory was, as best Ziji could tell, an even more comprehensive triumph. They'd taken so many horses it was a wonder. He looked up. The rain was a drizzle now, the clouds moving. They'd see the sun soon.

The next important moment, Daiyan had said, would be when Wan'yen of the Altai was informed of this defeat—what he did with his army downstream on the far bank. He might decide, in fury, to push across. He had his boats, they'd been building them for weeks.

Daiyan—Commander Ren—had said he had dreamed at night, and prayed, that the Altai war-leader would do that: try to cross the Great River and land in the face of massed archers and foot soldiers, with Daiyan and Ziji and the boats coming downstream with their men.

Ziji knew they had a capable man commanding opposite the Altai. He would know how to kill riders in boats, approaching in daylight.

He became aware that Daiyan's expression had changed.

"What is it?"

"Thought of something. Will any of them have been able to flee, escape around you?"

"I'm sure some did. But they'll be alone, or in very small numbers, cut off from ..."

He stopped. He felt cold.

"Dai, I'll go myself," he said.

"No. I will. Get me a horse!" Daiyan snapped to one of their guards. The man looked startled, then ran.

Ziji shook his head. "You can't! You need to be here to command. You may be crossing the river, or going downstream. We don't know!"

"No, I have to—"

"Dai!" said Ziji. "I'm going. Right now. As quickly as I can ride. I promise you!"

Daiyan stared at him, his mouth a thin line. He took a breath. *"Please,"* he said, then repeated it.

Ziji assembled a dozen men, found horses. They started east, riding fast, but it was late in the morning by then.

CHAPTER XXVII

Shan had awakened thinking of her husband. She'd been crying, emerging from a strange, slow dream: she and Wai in a vast tomb, alive, among terracotta soldiers guarding a long-dead emperor. Wai looking and looking and looking at the wonders around them, then turning to her, and his face ...

Word had come a few weeks ago in response to a query from Lu Chao, who had sources still in the ruined north. Hanjin was no longer burning, was being rebuilt—Kitan labour, of course. The conquerors were allowing burials, insisting on them now. They wanted life resuming, taxes and tribute paid. The clerics were doing what they could to name and number the dead.

The bodies of Qi Wai and his parents had been identified. The letter did not say more than that, which was probably just as well, given some of the stories being told.

With permission, she's added a candle for her husband beside the one for her parents, to the altar at East Slope. It seems to be her home now, this farm. An undeserved gift, she thinks.

The poet had been with her when she'd done her first rituals at the altar. He'd offered his own prayer, then stayed quietly, leaning on his stick, to honour her dead. There had been one candle, set a little apart from the others, that she'd seen him lighting last. She didn't ask.

She had felt, that end-of-winter morning, a sense of wonder that she was alive, that Lu Chen was alive, that they were standing here. She had placed her mother's earrings on the altar, again glancing at him for permission.

If the mornings are at all pleasant now, she likes to take a long walk around the grounds after eating. Meals at East Slope are odd, there are many people here, but only the farm workers eat a morning meal together. Sometimes Lu Mah joins them, sometimes the steward does. Then Mah goes to his workroom and attends to the records of the farm, managing it. Everyone seems to have their own rhythm here, only occasionally intersecting. She's never been in a household like this.

Some nights the poet doesn't come home. No one seems concerned. Usually, she's learned, he'll be sleeping in the temple in the village across the stream. He likes to talk with the clerics there. He brings them wine.

His brother writes and reads letters all day long, urgently seeking information. He sends memoranda to the new court. Lu Chao is still a court official in his soul, wishing to serve what remains of Kitai. He hasn't been summoned by Emperor Zhizeng and his new prime minister. Shan thinks he is torn between duty and a longing to remain here in whatever peace can be found.

How did you find peace in a time like this? Was it even a proper desire? Desire, even the word, makes her think of Daiyan.

It is raining this morning. In bed she listens to it, and the wind. The dream of Qi Wai fades. She feels guilt, sorrow, though more of the second thing. He had left her, truly, long before the end. She has come to understand that. But memories of a time when they shared much more than a husband and wife normally would ... these memories deserve sorrow.

She has with her the last catalogue they'd assembled of the collection. She thinks one day she might do something with it, write an introduction, tell their story.

If she lives. If Kitai survives. The Altai are encamped at the river downstream, on the other bank. It is spring. They are building boats, Lu Chao has learned. They mean to cross.

She had written her own letter west in winter. A sense of duty moving her brush. She sent it with soldiers going that way. The courier service is disrupted. People are on the move all over, the ones not dying. There are reports of bandits everywhere, soldiers turned outlaws, starvation.

She's had an answer back, however, a reply that found her here. Everyone knows East Slope. Everyone knows Lu Chen the poet lives here. He is, she thinks, a beacon fire for what Kitai has been.

Can one man be the soul of an empire? Isn't the emperor supposed to be that? She doesn't know this young emperor at all, remembers seeing him only once or twice in the Genyue. No words had been exchanged between them on their flight south.

The mandate of heaven falls where it falls—and can be withdrawn. But the poet here, Shan thinks, his words, courage, humour, tenderness, and anger—he might be what people want the time before the fall to be remembered for, whatever comes next.

The steward, Kou Yao, Wai's last lover (his only one?), has written that he and the child are safely with Qi Wai's mother's family, well to the south. They'd arrived with a letter and the document confirming that Lizhen had been adopted as Wai's daughter. Family honour will require she be sheltered there, Shan knows, brought up as a girl from a good family should be. If they survive. They are a long way off. Surely they will?

She has thought, some mornings when she wakes, that she should have the child brought to her, she is her mother, formally. But it is a foolish, dangerous thought. Wai hadn't even wanted her to know of the girl's existence, afraid she might lure the child into her own path.

She wouldn't have. She knows too well how hard this is. But she has decided she must honour Wai's choice. She will wish only good things to the child he saved, but she has no home to bring her to. She's a guest here. A welcome one, honoured, accepted even by the brothers' wives who rule the women's quarters, but this is not her own home.

She hasn't started thinking about that yet. Where could one go, in any case? Nowhere now, with armies on the river. One stayed here, looking out the window at a rainy morning, and thought of a father and a husband, dead, and of a man dearly, astonishingly loved, fighting for Kitai. Was he on the river, too?

He was, as it happened.

She is restless. Feels trapped by the steady rain. Tries, at her desk, to shape words for a song about the way war broke through to the smallest parts of a life, but it feels overwrought, forced. She doesn't see herself as large enough to write about this war, Hanjin's fall, the scale of suffering.

The great Chan Du, long ago, had written:

> *... I cannot find rest*
> *Because I am powerless*
> *To amend a broken world.*

Terrifying, that any man could carry such a weight within himself. She'd never imagine she—or anyone!—could have such power. Amending the world? That was for gods.

She's kept awake by longing some nights and by sorrow on others (sometimes the same night), but hers is not the task of remaking the world. Unless—she thinks on that rainy morning at East Slope—it is to alter the ways a woman might move through it, and she believes she's failing in that.

Lu Chen has written that the measuring of a life can only begin after it is over. She wonders, abruptly, how Daiyan's will be measured. For a soldier, she imagines, it depends on whether he wins on his battlefields.

The rain stops eventually. She hears water dripping from the eaves and the leaves. She sips her tea. Through the window she sees the brothers walking over the wet grass to the path leading to the stream.

They have a favourite bench, under a very old tree. Chao is carrying the wine flask and cups. His brother leans on his stick, but moves briskly. Both wear hats and outer garments. It is not warm and there is a wind, but the sun seems as if it wants to appear. Shan smiles, seeing them talking animatedly already, thinking yet again of the gift she's been granted, being here.

Later, she puts on warm clothing and the doubled hat everyone teases her about and she goes from the women's quarters towards the western orchard. She'll leave the brothers their privacy, take her own walk, watch the clouds breaking up. The peach blossoms have not yet begun, but the first buds are appearing, she's been watching for them.

It is cold, even when the sun does break through. It is hidden again, returns, shadows chase the land. The wind threatens to pull her hat from her head. Shan holds it with one hand, imagines how she must look to anyone watching. Such an elegant lady of the court! An imperial favourite, familiar with the paths and gazebos of the Genyue.

Those are gone.

In the orchard at East Slope she looks up and sees green buds dreaming of being flowers. They have already had plum blossoms, a first sign of winter's end, along with orioles and willow floss, and now (soon) there will be peach blossoms. Could you accept a simple lesson of renewal, she thinks, when so many people had died?

Something catches her eye. She turns. She sees, astonished, a fox at the end of the orchard, edge of the meadow, bright orange, motionless, watching—not her, the other way.

Shan turns her head then, among the trees, and sees an Altai rider dismount from his horse. She watches him draw a sword and slip over the fence west of the gate and the path to the main house.

Everything seems to become extremely slow, though her mind is racing and her heart hammering. The farmhands will be west and north, working the fields. She can slip from the trees and run that way for help, but all the women are in the house, and the children. The brothers have gone the other way, towards the stream, and what could they do?

She sees the man, his hair loose down his back, move towards the main house, the nearest one. She thinks it is empty. She needs it to be empty. But he will go on through, and the women's quarters are the next building he'll reach.

Shan decides what has to happen now. It is the only thing she can even think to try, in a broken world. People are dying everywhere. No one can expect to be safe. She thinks of her father. She wonders where Daiyan is.

She screams, as loudly and as frantically as she can. Once, and then a second time.

Then she is running from the orchard into the open, away from the main house and the women's quarters, towards the meadow at the back and the blue-and-green-painted gazebo there. Letting herself be heard and seen.

One look back and yes, he is following. She is well ahead, chasing the only idea she's had. A vain, foolish thought, an indication of how ill-adapted women are to moments such as this.

But moments such as this are not supposed to be part of the world, she thinks. Barbarians at East Slope? Anger is in her then, usefully. This man and his people have been killing children. They burned and savaged Hanjin. They killed her husband. Through hunger and cold they killed her father. Who'd taught her, all her life, not by the imposed rules of the world, but according to what he saw in her, and with love.

There are two bows in the gazebo.

Lu Chen and his son had taken to practising with weapons on Lingzhou Isle. They had done so at first light, as exercise and amusement. They'd kept on doing it here, to the amusement of all the others. She has watched them pretend to fight with swords, swearing dire imprecations at each other, sometimes rhyming, like figures in a puppet show.

There is a straw wall set up behind the gazebo, a square blue target on it. They would practise archery there. When one of them hit the target, those in the house would hear mock shouts of triumph and valour.

She reaches the gazebo. She draws breath and screams her warning one more time. Warning, and lure. She wants him following her, to give the others a chance to scatter. The men will be too far away to hear, unless someone is coming back to fetch their afternoon food and wine? A life could end or continue, turning on something like that.

She darts up the three steps and inside, one more glance back. He isn't running. He knows he has her trapped back here. He has a bow, he could shoot her. He hasn't taken it, still holds the sword. He should be afraid, Shan thinks desperately. Her screams ought to make him know he's been seen, has lost his surprise. He doesn't look fearful. She knows why he doesn't want her dead yet.

She seizes the smaller bow, the poet's, she grabs for arrows. Her hands are shaking. She hasn't done this since she was a girl. She and her father, like Mah and his father here.

She steps out from the gazebo, facing a steppe horseman. He stops for a moment when he sees the bow. She hears him laugh. He starts walking again, not hurrying at all. He says something. Of course she doesn't understand.

She tries to remember how to do this. She drops three arrows at her feet, keeps one, nocks it to the string. She's too slow, her hands are shaking so much. A deep breath. Her father had read in a text on archery that this was what you did to steady yourself. Mornings in their garden, him explaining why it was wrong for Kitai that no one well-bred did this any more. No mention of her being only a woman. Except a tale told once, as if casually, about Wen Jian, an emperor's beloved long ago, and her sisters, hunting with the court.

She raises the bow. Deep breath, slow exhale. The rider is approaching, not hurrying, not even trying to forestall her. He laughs again. She releases.

The arrow flies hopelessly off to the left. She always used to let fly left. Her father had been unable to find a text that explained this, had only urged her to make herself expect it, anticipate, adjust.

She stoops quickly, takes another arrow. If he speeds up only a little, she'll never—

There comes a cry from the meadow behind the Altai warrior. He turns quickly, for it is a man's voice this time. Beyond him, striding boldly over the grass, almost running, Shan sees Lu Mah, the poet's son, with a sword in his hand.

The intruder laughs again. And why not? Why should he fear a plump Kitan in a bunched-up green robe, clearly awkward with his blade, so obviously not a soldier?

Mah shouts something, not just a cry this time. The Altai snarls in reply, and steps forward, balanced, to face Mah. He will kill the man first, of course. They are alone here, the three of them.

Shan nocks her second arrow and begins to run towards them over the wet, bright meadow grass. The sun is shining. The wind continues. She needs to remember the wind, control her breathing, her hands, her drift to the left when she looses an arrow.

She knows what else she needs to do, beyond all of that.

Mah shouts again, defiantly. He and his father had wielded weapons on the isle. Perhaps he'd learned well, perhaps they'd had a teacher, another exile? Perhaps he can—

Blades clash. A grinding of metal. Disengagement. Mah cuts. He is blocked, too easily. The Altai makes some sort of twisting motion, shifts his feet. Mah's sword flies from his hand, away into the grass. As quickly as that.

No pause, no exulting. With a soldier's efficiency, with an indifferent ease that breaks Shan's heart, running towards them, the man sweeps his blade flat and it takes Lu Mah, who had gone to Lingzhou Isle with his father and refused to leave him—takes him in the side under a lifted arm, cutting too deep for life.

The Altai jerks the blade free and thrusts it into Mah's chest, through the dark-green robe, and blood is suddenly everywhere, so much of it, and Mah is wavering, still on his feet for one terrible moment, and then not, a moment more terrible.

The Altai turns then. Battle-trained. Red sword.

And Shan has come *right* up to him, for this is the thing she'd needed to do, beyond all calculations and memories of lessons long ago. She needed to be this close. And her hands are briefly steady, her breathing steady, her anger a cold, bright star as she looses her second arrow from barely an arm's length away, so close she can smell the Altai rider, and she aims for his face.

His mouth is open to laugh, or shout. Or perhaps, perhaps to scream? The arrow flies into his mouth, through teeth and throat and the back of his head and his sword falls and he falls, beside the poet's son, beside Lu Mah, on the grass there, in the sunlight, in the spring.

TIME BECOMES STRANGE. Shan is uncertain how and when certain things happen. She is aware that someone is holding her upright beside Mah's fallen body and that of the Altai she's killed (she has just killed a man). She understands that it is the poet's wife, and that Qing Zemin is weeping, but Shan doesn't remember seeing her come out, or the other women here.

She sees some of the children at a distance, outside the women's quarters. They have been kept away, obviously. She thinks, *That is good, they should not see this.* But perhaps they should, perhaps they need to know this is the world.

She can't stop shaking. Her throat is so dry. She doesn't seem to be crying. She closes her eyes. Qing Zemin smells of her perfume (she always does). Her hand is strong and tight across Shan's waist. She is murmuring softly, not even words, the way one might soothe a child or a frightened animal.

But this is her stepson, Shan thinks, and she knows—because she's seen—how much loved Mah has been in this house, by all of them. How much he's been needed.

I need to be comforting her, she thinks.

She has to stop shaking first. She is afraid her legs will give out if she isn't held up.

At some point, someone says, "Look," and she does look and sees the two brothers coming across the grass from the edge of the property, past the plum trees, and something begins crying in her heart.

The women make way for them, a pathway to a body. The younger brother, the uncle, has a hand on the poet's arm to steady him, but it is Chao who is weeping.

Mah's father sets aside his walking stick and kneels in the wet grass by his son. He takes Mah's hand and holds it between his own. He looks at his son's face. Shan sees his robe and over-tunic being stained by water and by blood. He keeps looking at Mah's features. They aren't distorted or afraid, Shan thinks. He seems to have crossed over with a calm heart. His sword lies a little distance away, very bright on the grass.

"This is extremely sorrowful," Lu Chen says finally. And with those words Shan's own tears come.

"I'm so sorry!" she cries. "It is my fault!"

The poet looks up. "Surely no. You killed the barbarian, did you not? It is wonderfully brave."

"But I missed! I sent my first arrow awry. To the left. The way I *always* ..." She trails off. Her throat is choked.

"You killed an Altai warrior, Lady Lin. You saved us all."

"No," Shan cries. "Look at him! I didn't!"

"I am looking," his father says. "But it is not your error in any way. I am ... I am guessing Mah rushed out to give you a chance to run away and you did not. Did he call out?"

"Yes," Shan manages. "Yes, he did. He was ... the man was coming for me at the gazebo."

The poet nods. Beside him, above him, his brother's face looks lined and old and tears are on his cheeks.

Lu Chen is still holding his dead son's hand. "Did he ... Lady Lin, did Mah say anything? If you would be good enough to tell me ..."

Shan is nodding, almost convulsively. Lady Qing still holds her. "I didn't understand," Shan says.

The poet looks up at her. His eyes are wide and deep. He says, "He challenged him?"

She does not know how he knows.

She nods again. "He ... he said, 'Evil district overlord, we are storming your fortress now!'"

"Oh, sweet child," Lu Chao, the uncle, says.

But Mah wasn't a child, Shan thinks, suddenly confused. And, *Surely he doesn't mean me?* But then she hears a new sound and looks away from the tall man to the two on the grass, one dead, one holding the dead one's hand, and she sees a father begin to weep for his son.

TIME IS RUNNING AGAIN, it is passing overhead, going through them, carrying them away with it, though no one leaves the meadow. It is all strange. Broken. Shan doesn't know how long they've been here now. Sun and cloud, warmer and then cold again as shadows slide and the wind remains.

It is Lu Chao beside her now. He is very tall. He holds her. She can lean against him. She is still trembling. She wonders if she will ever stop. The poet is still on his knees on the grass. Shan thinks: someone should take him inside, bring him dry clothing by a fire. But she also thinks, has a stone-hard aching sense, that Mah's father knows that when he releases his son's hand it will be forever.

Other sounds. They look that way, towards the front of the property, and fear comes again, blade-sharp. Men are here, a number of them. *Are we dead now?* Shan thinks, cannot help herself.

Then she recognizes the one at the front of this new group, hurrying on foot towards them across the meadow, and she looks for another man and doesn't see him.

Zhao Ziji drops to his knees beside Mah, across from where the dead man's father holds his hand. Ziji presses his face to the wet, cold earth three times. He says, "I will not forgive myself."

The poet looks at him. "Why so? How is this your doing at all?"

"We should have known some of them might escape, come this way!"

Ziji, whom Shan had begun to know a little and admire a great deal on their journey south, is in great distress.

"Have they crossed the river, then?" It is Lu Chao, beside her, his voice holding to calm, but with an edge in it. "Are they coming?"

"No, no," Ziji says. He stands. Shan sees he has a wound. His men are behind him, their horses by the fence. "They are dying and dead," Zhao Ziji says. "We destroyed an Altai force west of here. Towards Red Cliff. On the riverbank and on the river, trying to cross in secret."

"Destroyed them?" Chao says.

"Yes, my lord. Commander Ren learned their plan, which they had thought was hidden. We ambushed them on the water and cut down their advance guard on this shore. Others of our men attacked those remaining on the northern bank. We have claimed all the horses that swam the river. My lords, it is a very great victory."

Lu Chen looks at him. "So this one here ... ?"

"Was fleeing for his life. Trapped on the wrong side of the river."

"He must have been very afraid," the poet says.

Shan has no idea how he can even frame such a thought.

"There will be others?" Chao says.

"Undoubtedly, my lord. We will search them out. But ... it is impossible to track every man who flees a battlefield."

"Of course," says the poet. "Of course it is, Commander Zhao." His voice is gentle. He is holding his dead son's hand. "Well done, commander. Well done, all of you."

Ziji looks at the Altai rider's body. "How was he killed?"

"The Lady Lin Shan killed him with an arrow," says Lu Chao.

"What?" Ziji turns to her in disbelief.

Shan needs to speak, has to clear her throat first. She says, "My father ... my father taught me. A little. When I was young."

"You put an arrow in an Altai warrior?"

She nods her head. At least she isn't shaking any more. She still feels lightheaded, as if she might fall.

"Oh, my lady, Daiyan will never forgive me," Ziji says. "I will never forgive myself."

Shan shakes her head. It is remarkably difficult to speak. She says, "No. It wasn't you." And then, "Is Ren Daiyan all right?"

Ziji is still staring at her. He looks over at the dead Altai and back to Shan. He shakes his head in wonder. "He was going to ride here himself. I told him I would do it. He needed to stay, my lady. We don't know what they will do at their main camp when they learn of their defeat. It is very important. If they decide to cross, Daiyan has to take the boats downstream."

"Is that bad?"

Ziji draws a breath. "Lady Lin, if the Altai try to cross now we will destroy them."

"Let us hope they try, then," says Lu Chao gravely.

Ziji is still looking at her. Awkwardly, he says, "I am speaking truth. He was going to ride here alone as soon as we realized some of them might have fled."

"There are many other farms, villages. East Slope is only one," Shan says. She really needs better control of her voice.

"Yes," says Ziji. "Of course there are. But ..."

He leaves it at that, and so they all do.

FIVE OF HIS COMPANY remain when Ziji goes back west. Shan can see he is torn, he has an expressive, revealing face: he wants to stay to honour the dead man, see him buried, assuage his own needless guilt, but he's a commander away from his battle and every movement shows his urgent need to know what is happening. They are taking the body of the horseman away with them, and the horse. Horses, she knows by now, are extremely important.

Lu Chao tries to protest about the men left here with them, says the soldiers must surely be needed elsewhere. Ziji insists that East Slope will be doing them a kindness, housing and feeding these men while they patrol the countryside for Altai stragglers.

It is, Shan knows, largely a contrivance on his part, if a clever one. He's a clever man, Daiyan's friend. These five are staying to defend this farm. And her. She is in no state of mind to work through how she feels about that. She does know the protection is a comfort as twilight comes. She keeps revisiting that first sighting of the Altai from the orchard. She remembers there was a fox, letting itself be seen, looking that way. She has no idea what to make of that. She isn't thinking clearly. She killed a man today. She is a woman who has killed.

Mah's body is in the reception room in the main house. Incense on a brazier, one tall white candle burning. His stepmother and his aunt have tended to him. They'll have washed him and clothed him—as she remembers doing for her father, though he'd been denied burial during the siege. She thinks of Mah, running towards her and the Altai.

His father has remained in that room throughout, sitting by one wall, watching in silence. The silence of respect, for a young man, unmarried, without children, is proper. The father's presence in the room, his tears before, his visible grief, are formally a breach of correct behaviour. But who is going to deny him this? Really? Who would do so?

It appears that the last words Mah shouted, the ones Shan heard but did not understand, were what father and son used to cry during their exercises on Lingzhou, making a game of it, finding laughter together in a terrible place.

Shan has roused herself to go out and bid farewell to Ziji. He'll be riding through darkness. Chao, manners flawless, even now, is with him by the gate.

"I will send word," Ziji is saying as she comes up. "We'll have a good idea by morning, I think."

"You and your men honoured Kitai today," Chao says. "And perhaps you have saved us all south of the river."

"Not all," says Ziji.

"War is bad things happening. How can we be so arrogant as to believe we control all that will unfold?"

"We can try to plan," Ziji says.

"We can try," Chao says, and in the fading light Shan sees his gentle smile and it hurts her heart.

"Wait, please," she says suddenly, and is hurrying back up the walk and into the main house. The door has been draped with a white sheet to signify a death. There is a small bell beside it, on the left side.

She goes to the altar and takes something and goes back out. The sky is clear. The wind has died down, is only a mild susurration in the trees by the path. She sees the evening star.

She comes up to Ziji beside his horse. "Give this to him," she says. "Tell him it was my mother's. The other is on the altar here, in memory of my parents. Let him have this from me."

He looks at the lapis earring, then at her, then briefly at Lu Chao, standing there.

He says, "Of course." And then, after another pause, clearing his throat, he adds, "Lady Lin, he is a soldier. None of us can—"

"I know this," she says briskly. She is afraid she's going to cry again. "Guard yourself, commander. We need you very much."

"Thank you," he says, and mounts up, and he and his men ride along the road between trees towards the first star of the evening and whatever darkness or light the future holds hidden, as in a box without a key, for all of them.

ℚ⋈ⓐ

Wan'yen of the Altai did not order any messengers killed, but only because there was no first messenger bearing tidings of disaster. Some of their riders did come racing east, fleeing, but word had preceded them.

The Altai learned of their catastrophe from words wrapped around an arrow loosed from the river. Wan'yen sent boats out to pursue the archer who had dared come so close, but he didn't expect to find anyone. It was maddening.

He had the note read to him and his rage became something like a fire in summer grass—the sort that nothing can stop until it burns itself out. The message was sent in the name of Commander Ren Daiyan of Kitai, and directed to "the barbarian leader." No name, although of course they knew his name!

It detailed exactly what Wan'yen's plan for this morning had been, where his force had been sent to cross the river—and how it had been destroyed on both banks and on the water. He was thanked for his generous gift of horses.

It was too detailed. Wan'yen was unable to doubt what the

message was telling him. This man, this Ren Daiyan ... he needed that one dead, or he might die of the choking vastness of his fury.

He ordered his army to the boats.

They were going to cross right here, now, even towards day's end. He thought: the enemy will not expect us to come so late. It will catch them unawares!

They would make landfall against frightened Kitan soldiers on the other bank—and hack their limbs from their bodies and eat their hearts. This Commander Ren would not be in that opposing host, he'd been upriver, and Wan'yen's best riders were here with him (always). His fury would become theirs.

The camp sprang into motion on his command, word of the defeat running (like that grassland fire) through it. Their boats were here. These they'd been building by the river, to be seen: the secret ones had been upstream. He didn't know how they'd been found, he didn't even know what force Ren Daiyan had used. The Kitan army, what there was of it, was *here,* opposite him. Had farmers and outlaws beaten warriors of the steppe today?

The horses. The Kitan said they had his horses. It felt like a wound. A blow to the chest, where the heart was.

He stepped up onto the observation platform they had built by the river. He looked out over his host assembled here, the best of the grasslands, an army never even nearly defeated from the time he and his brother had led their tribe out of the northeast, that first attack against the Jeni. He was pleased to remember that. They had begun with a night ambush, the strength of surprise. He would speak of that now, remind them all.

He placed his hands on his hips, a gesture he was known for, legs apart, balanced, to control the world. He looked out at his army, his riders.

Small things can tilt and turn the world. A change in the wind had decided the first battle of Red Cliff. The illness of a kaghan or the death of a named successor (one man, only one man) had altered the destiny of the steppe many times. A stray arrow in a battle might take a leader. A proud man might be ordered to dance around a fire. So many random moments. Even a simple thought might come ...

It was a memory of the grasslands in spring: that night by the Black River and the Jeni camp. It came clearly to Wan'yen where he stood facing his army. He could almost smell the night air in another spring, hear the whisper of the grass in the clean wind under stars.

He turned around and looked at this wide, deep, malevolent river. He thought about swamplands and wet rice fields, hedges and terraced slopes and thick woods and this sky. This sky. Even when clear it was too close. This was not the Lord of the Sky's realm, not the heaven they knew.

And it occurred to him, as his heart began to change and his thoughts caught up with it, that if Ren Daiyan had been able to take the Altai's western force on the river as they crossed, he could be out there on the water now, and the Great River was wide, and his men could not swim, or fight properly in boats.

Some writers later, describing the events of that night and day, wrote that Wan'yen of the Altai had seen a spirit-dragon of the river and become afraid. Writers do that sort of thing. They like dragons in their tales.

The war-leader looked back at his army, battle-ready men prepared to cross and destroy. He looked again at the wind-ruffled current of the river and he could not see the far bank. He looked west, upstream, and there was nothing there. But in the eye of his mind Wan'yen, as shrewd a leader as his people had had in a long time, was seeing boats and boats and boats, waiting out of sight for word that his men were on the water. Being upstream made a difference, just as high ground did in battle. If they were there, they could do the same thing they'd done at dawn.

They were there. Something told him they were. Ren Daiyan was waiting for him, out of sight.

He drew a breath. His brother, he thought, would have been chewing his cheeks in fury. He would have already been in a boat waiting for Wan'yen's order, forcing the order. He'd have cast off already! His brother had chased Ren Daiyan into a marsh, and died there.

Such small things sometimes. Memory, recollection of a scent, of stars, the sound of wind in grass. Feeling suddenly too distant from a homeland. Not afraid, never afraid, but too far away beside a dark river.

He changed his mind.

He turned to his riders and announced they were heading back to Hanjin. They would summon reinforcements and deal with this river another year, he said.

He could hear—he could *feel*, as a good leader should be able to do—the relief that swept through his army. He felt it in himself, with a secret shame. There would be deaths ahead for that shame, he vowed then. There were a great many Kitan between them and the imperial city that was theirs now.

And just then, in that instant, a thought came to him, another small moment. They so often are, or begin that way: the ideas that ripple and ripple through the world.

Before they left they burned their boats, that the Kitan might not have any joy of the labours here. Then they killed the captives who had built the boats, the ones who did not manage to flee in the evening darkness. There was a message to leave behind, and warfare is, after all, about such messages.

They started north in the morning.

Many lives were saved by this decision beside the river. Many lives were lost. A storyteller, guessing at or finding certainty within, can offer the thoughts of a war-leader as he ordered a retreat after ordering an advance. Honourable historians record events as best they can and, often challenging each other, suggest the consequences. There is a difference.

That army that reached the Great River marked the farthest the Altai would ever come into Kitai. That day on the river was important. Some days are.

SOME DEATHS MIGHT not appear important. Their ripples seem limited, as if in a rain pond, reaching only a family, a farm, village, temple. The imagined pond being small, hidden, a few lotus petals briefly disturbed, bobbing, settling again.

But sometimes a too-early death stops a life from flowering late. The plum tree blossoms at the beginning of spring, the peach is later in the season. There are lives that begin slowly, for many reasons. Lu Mah, the great poet's son, had never been permitted to take the examinations, coming of age during his father's and uncle's early exiles, then insisting on accompanying his father into his last exile, the one that had been expected to kill him.

We cannot know with anything like certainty how someone might have grown. We reflect, surmise, grieve. Not every hero or leader shows promise young, some come late into glory. Sometimes a brilliant father and uncle might show a path, but their accomplishments might also stand *in* the path for a long time.

Lu Mah was kind and honourable, respectful, brave beyond words, had increasing wisdom and a loving heart. He was diligent, his humour sly, his learning acquired by listening. His generosity, if initially known only to those nearest to him (the pond, the lotus flowers bobbing), was large and defining. He had gone south with his father. He'd gone north with his uncle. He wasn't a poet, not everyone is.

He died too young in a war in which too many died.

We cannot know, being trapped in time, how events might have been altered if the dead had not died. We cannot know tomorrow, let alone a distant future. A shaman might claim to see ahead in mist but most of them (most of them) cannot truly do this: they go into the spirit world to find answers for today. *Why is this person*

*sick? Where will we find water for the herds? What spirit is angry with
our tribe?*

But sometimes storytellers want to inhabit certainty. They
assume more than mortals ought. A tale-spinner by a hearth fire
or gathering a crowd in a market square or putting brush to paper
in a quiet room, deep into his story, the lives he's chronicling, will
deceive himself into believing he has the otherworldly knowledge
of a fox spirit, a river spirit, a ghost, a god.

He will say or write such things as, "The boy killed in the Altai
attack on the Jeni encampment was likely to have become a great
leader of his people, one who could have changed the north."

Or, "Lu Mah, the poet's son, was one whose personal desire
would have kept him living quietly, but his sense of duty and his
great and growing wisdom would have drawn him to the court. He
was lost to Kitai, and that made a difference."

However boldly someone says this, or writes it, it remains a
thought, a wish, desire, longing spun of sorrow. We cannot know.

We can say Mah's was a death too soon, as with O-Yan of the Jeni,
their kaghan's little brother, slain in the first attack of a grassland
rising. And we can think about ripples and currents, and wonder
at the strangeness of patterns found—or made. A first death in the
north and the death farthest south in the Altai invasion, in the years
of the Twelfth Dynasty when the maps were redrawn.

But then, maps are always being redrawn. The Long Wall had
once been the forbidding, fiercely guarded border of a great empire.
We look back and we look ahead, but we live in the time we are
allowed.

THEY BURIED LU MAH in the family cemetery on an elevated part
of the property at East Slope, for it was known that high ground
was best for the spirits of the dead. The graves there were shaded
by cypress trees and by a sweet-pear, because of the old, old poem:

The sweet-pear tree—
Never cut a twig of it.
Never hew it down.
Under it, Shao lies at rest.

That ground overlooked the stream to the east, and, on a clear day up there among the dead, one could sometimes see the line of the Great River to the north.

Following tradition at the burial, an ancient fear of the spirit world, all family members but one dutifully turned their backs as the farm workers lowered Lu Mah's body into his grave.

It was seen, however, that his father did not turn away, but stood watching his son go down into the earth. He later said he did not fear Mah's ghost at all. And a storyteller might say: Why should he have done so? Why should he ever fear his son's spirit in any way until the end of his own days?

CHAPTER XXVIII

The new prime minister of Kitai, serving the new emperor in his new imperial city of Shantong by the sea, often wondered if they were all being governed and guided by a dead man. His father, specifically.

Hang Hsien sometimes imagined that even the ways in which his approach to the court differed from his father's might have been a deliberate shaping. The old man had been subtle enough for that: to make his son sufficiently independent to think he was forming his own views, but to have those views be infused with the father's will, and his lifetime of experience.

Hsien did know, because it had been explicitly laid out for him, that the appointment of Kai Zhen as prime minister in the time before the Calamity of Hanjin had been a stratagem in itself.

The old blind man had sensed a catastrophe coming, and didn't want his son to follow him and face the consequences. Hsien had been sent away south before the Altai reached Yenling and Little Gold Hill. Before his father died there.

Hsien hadn't wanted to go, had protested. But being south, right

565

here in Shantong when the prince arrived, he had been positioned with precision. A piece on a game board.

He'd been invited to court, before it really was a court, and asked to assume the office he now held. To undertake a new reign with the august and exalted Emperor Zhizeng—who had been called Prince Jen by the people, after a hero from a distant time.

People were easily deceived. Everyone liked legends. Hsien didn't think this emperor was heroic, although he wondered if any prime minister ever thought that about an emperor he served. On the other hand, he didn't imagine himself a hero, either. Wouldn't he have stayed (and died) at Little Gold Hill with his father if he were?

Still, he would do what he could, he *was* doing what he could, to stitch the torn fabric of an empire together. There were difficulties, you could say. Huge swaths of land had been savaged in the north, with famine widespread. The Altai had raided all the way to the Great River before being turned back in a wondrous, unexpected triumph.

There were bandits everywhere, often soldiers of their own armies who had turned outlaw and predator rather than fight the horsemen. Hungry men, displaced from farms and burnt-out villages, with their families starving, could be wolves to each other. It was recorded in chronicles of earlier dark times—and they were living through it now.

They had no tax base of any stability, no ready sources of revenue. Hsien was deeply concerned about taxation and revenues, he always had been. You could call it a passion. Even the government monopolies—tea, salt, medicines—needed to be built up again. Kitai was all about trade, and how did you restore trade in times like this?

They had lost control of the north, but the barbarians didn't have control there either, dealing with unrest and anger and starving people roaming the countryside. That was no help to Hang Hsien in trying to finance an empire and shape an imperial policy here. It was *hard*, what he was trying to do.

He also had challenges he didn't think any other imperial adviser had faced. He certainly couldn't find records to parallel his dilemma. Nor could he talk to anyone about it. This particular circumstance was, as best he could tell, unique. It didn't make him feel fortunate, being unique.

But the truth was, his emperor, exalted Zhizeng, was ruling here, governing what men were already calling the Southern Twelfth Dynasty, sitting on a newly fashioned Dragon Throne, *and his father and brother were alive.*

Was he truly an emperor, if so? Or only a regent, a guardian of this new throne, bound in duty to family and heaven's mandate to ransom his brother and father in any way he could, at any cost? And if he did that (or his prime minister found a way to do it) what happened to him? And would that prime minister be appreciated for his achievement? Or executed?

It was known by everyone who mattered that Zhizeng and his brother Chizu had shared very little love—to put it delicately, as a principal adviser ought, even in his private thoughts.

Hsien often talked with his father in those thoughts. Often he found answers to questions by imagining the brisk, remembered tones, but not to this.

Zhizeng clearly liked being emperor of Kitai. Had no evident desire to cease being so. A younger son, overlooked, ignored, regarded in the end as disposable—he'd been sent out to the Altai as a hostage, hadn't he?

He spoke from his throne of endless grief concerning the sad fates in exile of his father and brother—and the rest of his family, of course. He led prayers and rituals with exemplary piety. Kitai, he declared to his court, had wandered too far from right conduct. He wondered aloud in the throne room in Shantong, in tones of sorrow, if his beloved father and brother were even alive.

His prime minister, very well trained, understood this. All of it. He understood more, given private conversations of an oblique but unmistakable nature.

"In my heart," the emperor might say to him when they were alone in a chamber or on an evening terrace overlooking West Lake, "in my heart I fear they are dead, Minister Hang. How could a civilized society expect otherwise from barbarians? They were taken so far! Beyond our reach. Do you know what the barbarians named them?"

"I do, illustrious lord," Hsien would say, each time. Everyone knew.

"Lord of Muddled Virtue! Doubly Muddled Virtue!" the emperor would exclaim (each time), with an odd intensity, as if tasting, Hsien thought, the texture of the terrible names.

And, invariably, at some point in these conversations, Emperor Zhizeng would say, "Prime minister, we need to be *very* careful with our army in the north. Armies and their commanders are dangerous."

"Indeed, serene lord," Hang Hsien would say.

Their army and commander were, as it happened, winning battles.

They had swept so far on captured Altai horses they were said to be approaching Hanjin itself, by the last report they'd had. That last letter from Commander Ren Daiyan, leading their forces above the River Wai, had invited Emperor Zhizeng—saluting him with all proper respect—to begin planning to move his court back to Hanjin as soon as it was retaken.

Amazingly, they expected to do that before autumn ended. Ren Daiyan wrote this, sending word by messenger birds in a long southern relay of flight. They would then move on, he added, to the barbarians' Southern Capital, the one Kitai had failed to take before, setting in motion the calamity that followed.

Commander Ren thought they might have four of the lost Fourteen Prefectures regained before the New Year's celebrations. He closed with expressions of devotion to Kitai and the throne.

Hanjin? Before autumn ended! It was midsummer now. The

nights would soon be growing longer. Hsien closed his eyes and imagined a strong and vengeful Kitan army moving by day, by night. It was a pleasing image. A man could feel pride.

On the other hand, Emperor Zhizeng, however respectfully saluted, was going to be profoundly disinclined to move his court. He wasn't about to place himself any nearer to the Altai who had held him captive and then pursued him when he'd escaped. They'd even caught up to him, leading to a terrifying fight in a night swamp. That sort of experience could define a man.

Hsien could almost hear his father's voice saying this.

The prime minister, in a judicious exercise of a senior adviser's role, had not yet shown the emperor this most recent letter from his commander in the field.

Hsien had other concerns, almost certainly linked to these tidings. An Altai emissary was on his way here by ship along the coast, which was *very* unusual for them. The ship had put in to port twice, flying a white flag. The emissary would believe he was outstripping any report of his coming. He wasn't, of course. The riders still didn't know about the birds. It was, Hang Hsien thought, yet another reason they were barbarians, however deadly they might be when thundering across a countryside, burning helpless villages.

However savagely they behaved with old, blind men.

The prime minister of Kitai felt that his troubles were about to deepen in complexity. Their army was heading for Hanjin? Expecting to retake it? Ren Daiyan intended to go north from there?

It was extraordinary. Impressive. It was a problem. His father, he thought, would have known how to deal with this, negotiate the rapids of a rushing river, steer between rocks.

Those rocks became sharper, deadlier, when the Altai emissary and his translator arrived and requested a private audience with the emperor and his prime minister. This was granted. No one else was in the room except imperial guards out of hearing distance.

Certain things were said in that chamber, not discreetly. Barbarians were not discreet. Proposals were conveyed to the emperor of Kitai from Wan'yen, war-leader of the Altai.

The emissary was dismissed without reply but with adequate courtesy. The emperor and his principal adviser walked from the reception room onto a late-summer terrace. The emperor looked out.

He said, "It is very beautiful in Shantong. West Lake, the hills, the sea. We very much like the palace we are building here. It is suitable. We should do what we need to do."

Only that. It was enough. Rocks sharp as swords.

ᘒᘓ

There is no sense of danger at East Slope any more as summer ends, only sorrow and time passing. The poet has been so careful to keep his grief as private as he can, not to impose it on the rest of them. They all see it, nonetheless. How can they not? It seems to Shan that Lu Chen is moving more slowly now, but she is aware it could be her own feelings making her think that way.

He still walks most days with his brother to their bench above the stream, still writes in his writing room, spends some nights with the holy men on the other side of the stream. She can hear the temple bell when the wind is from the east.

Ziji's soldiers had stayed for many weeks as spring became summer. They and others on patrol found and killed a number of Altai trapped on this side of the river, most of them without horses.

The ordinary people of Kitai hereabouts—not bandits, but farmers, villagers, clerics, silk weavers, even a spirit master and his boy—had joined in the hunt. The children of this district were happy to act as spies and scouts. It became a kind of game. Find the barbarians.

Some children died. Some farmers and their families were killed. In midsummer a dozen Altai tried to force their way across the river, coercing the ferryman at a crossing place. They were anticipated, the river was being watched there. The barbarians were cut down by fifty men. That time it was bandits who did so. The ferryman died, and two of his sons.

They have been hearing stories from the north, where the Altai had run wild. Tales of horror from where Kitai began, in the flood plain of the Golden River. They had been a northern people, the Kitan. She wonders if that is about to change now.

She is restless in summer nights. She sees fireflies, smells night flowers, watches the phases of the moon. She writes to Daiyan, not knowing (she never knows) if letters can reach wherever he is, across rivers and a broken land:

> The scent of red lotus has faded.
> I look for a letter in the clouds.
> Soon wild geese will be flying north,
> They will form a character overhead: return.
> The window of my room fills with the moon.
>
> Blossoms drift in the pond.
> The stream flows north to the river.
> My body aches in this quiet place,
> Wanting to be where you are.
> My eyes close on moonlight,
> But my heart flares like a fire.

☙

It is impossible for them to besiege Hanjin.

Even with all those who fled before the Altai came last year, and all those who died, there were still more than half a million people in the city, along with thirty thousand steppe horsemen holding it.

Daiyan's army was almost twice that size. He had archers, foot soldiers, and horses now, their own cavalry, after the victory by the river.

The Altai could try to break out. They would fail.

But the horrors of another siege running into winter, starvation upon starvation, would fall on their own people. The barbarians would claim all the food in Hanjin, then turn to cannibalism before they killed their horses. He forced himself to acknowledge this. It had happened before.

So he was unable to establish a siege, reverse what had happened here last year. Fortunately, they didn't have to.

There were risks, and they'd have only the one chance, most likely. He needed to think it through, choose the right night, have people ready inside, got word to them. But it could be done: they could enter the city the same way they'd come out on New Year's eve. There were two tunnels, and they could use both of them.

He needed the right men to go with him under the walls, silently up stairs from cellar rooms. And then burst into night streets to kill the guards at the southern and western gates and open those gates—and the redeeming army of Kitai would flood in, and the people of Hanjin would rise up to greet them, join them, and the Altai would be trapped in a space where their horses could not help them, and they would die.

He intended to let a handful go back north to carry word, create terror on the grasslands, in the cities there.

Then he would follow, swift as vengeance sometimes needed to be, and with so many of the riders dead the Southern Capital of this new empire of the steppe would fall—and a part of the Lost Fourteen would be theirs again, at last.

It was a dream, unfurling like a banner in wind. He was lonely amidst an army, and he was tired all the time, but this was what he'd been born into the world to do.

They are waiting for the new moon. Three nights from now. It might be an excess of caution but any soldier would tell you it was easier to slip into a night lane when the guards had no light by which to see their death coming. They had journeyed so far and were very close. He wouldn't let this fail by being impatient at the end.

And Wan'yen, the war-leader, was inside the city. You didn't wilfully add risk when you knew a capable man was on the other side. You didn't fear an enemy, but you needed to respect what he could do.

There were tales of victorious Kitan generals having captured barbarian leaders brought before them, bound, stripped naked, so they might do the killing themselves, or watch it done while drinking wine.

Daiyan didn't care about that. He wouldn't exalt a horseman that way. The war-leader could die by the arrow or blade of whichever Kitan soldier found him. They might not even know who he was when he was slain. That happened, especially at night. But the Altai would know. The riders would lose force and hope if he fell.

That was as far as Daiyan gave thought to the man. This was about the empire, not his own conflict with some horseman from the fringe of the steppe.

They needed to be reminded of what Kitai had been, what it was to be again now. They needed to be made afraid or they would come back.

And that last, he knew (he did know), was the darkness down this road they were on. He made himself look away from the thought, turn back to the walls of Hanjin. Plan next steps, make sure they were executed properly. He was only a soldier. The officials advising the emperor would shape what came after, it had almost always been that way.

Early the next morning a white flag was seen above the western gate. Two of the Altai came out. One of them spoke Kitan. They were direct. They tended to be. They offered to surrender the city and withdraw north if hostages were given to ensure that the Kitan army would not attack when they reached the Golden River and prepared to cross. Once across the river they could outrun any pursuit.

Daiyan looked at Ziji, standing beside him. Ziji was gazing back at him, a wry look on his face. They had thought this would happen. The riders had no desire to be trapped through a winter. They hadn't expected Daiyan to follow so far, so fast. They hadn't thought any of this would happen, from the disaster on the Great River onwards. They wanted to go home. And regroup to come back.

Daiyan needed these horsemen dead and burnt in pyres, not riding safely north to return. Kitai needed that to be so. That required a slaughter here. You didn't command in war if you wanted the world to be delicate as plum blossoms.

"What hostages are you proposing?" Ziji asked. His voice could sound frightening when he wanted it to.

The horseman who spoke their language looked at the other, more senior, and translated. The senior one looked straight at Daiyan and spoke. The other translated again.

"We need only your commander. He will be released as soon as we have crossed the river."

"I see. And to ensure that?" Ziji asked. His voice was winter-cold, but this proposal was not a surprise.

"We leave our war-leader," said the Altai. "Then they are exchanged. It is proper."

"It isn't," said Zhao Ziji. "But we will consider what you have said. You may return at sunset for our reply. Go now."

The tones of a man leading an army with the advantage here.

The horsemen turned and rode back into Hanjin through the western gate. The one that Daiyan intended to open for his army in two nights.

They watched them go. Ziji said, quietly, "I still believe they would kill you and let him die."

"Perhaps. It might be a good exchange for us. With both brothers dead, I'm not sure the Altai—"

"Stop it!" Ziji snapped. "No more. You are wrong. They have a dozen war-leaders to replace those two. We do not."

Daiyan shrugged. He didn't agree, but neither did he particularly want to die by the Golden River to test this belief. He had reasons to live, for Kitai, for himself.

Shan had sent him a poem in a letter by courier from Jingxian. *My heart flares like a fire.*

At sunset the two riders came back. Ziji told them they needed another night to consider the proposal. He asked if anyone else could serve as a hostage to the river. He explained that Commander Ren was dearly beloved of Emperor Zhizeng and assigning him such a role could not be done without risking the wrath of the emperor. The Altai, he said, would surely understand. After all, august Zhizeng had been a hostage himself, freed by Ren Daiyan.

He'd allowed himself a smile, saying this.

The Altai went back. Ziji's intention was to keep this discussion going, delaying until the new moon. He raised the idea of launching the attack tomorrow night. The thin sliver of a moon would not affect anything, he said. Daiyan shook his head.

"They dislike the dark of moon. You know they do. Two nights from now we end this part of this war."

"And then?" Ziji asked.

Daiyan shrugged again. They were standing outside his tent, the sun setting red in an autumn sky. "Depending on how many men we lose, and we will lose men, we go north right away or wait for spring and reinforcements. But we are doing this."

It was shortly after that, Ziji would recall, that they saw a small party riding towards them from the south, lit by that low sun, coming along the wide road to and from what had been the imperial city of the Twelfth Dynasty. The first star had not yet appeared.

He remembered watching them approach, his last moment of a certain understanding of the world.

IT WAS FUYIN, Daiyan saw. Their friend, once chief magistrate here, now governor of Jingxian. They had ridden past his city, stopped for a night on their way north. Jingxian, as he'd expected, had not been attacked in the winter. The Altai had raided villages, towns, farms, but had no stomach for another siege. After the horsemen had withdrawn north in spring, Wang Fuyin had been summoned from retirement to re-enter the city where he'd been magistrate years ago. Honourable men answered when their emperor called.

Daiyan raised a hand in greeting. Fuyin lifted his and smiled.

You learned to know a man. It was not an easy smile. The governor reined up in front of them. His escort remained some distance away, watched closely by Daiyan's guards.

"You ride better than when we first met," Daiyan said.

"I've lost weight, I've had practice." Fuyin gestured at the walls. "You've come a long way very fast."

"We are going to take it," Daiyan said. "You can be here to see."

"You've come a long way yourself," Ziji said. He wasn't smiling. "What has happened?"

A small hesitation. "Shall we ride a little distance?" Fuyin said. "The three of us."

Daiyan led the way in the direction of the grove where the tunnel from the west gate came up. He didn't go that far. He didn't want attention drawn to that wood. He stopped on a rise of land under a pine tree. The sun was low, the light made the landscape vivid and intense. To the east, the walls of Hanjin gleamed. A light breeze, a hint in it of the cold to come.

"What has happened?" Ziji said again.

They were alone. Daiyan's guards had followed, but kept their distance in a wide ring around them. Their commander mattered too much to be unguarded in the open.

Fuyin's hair had gone greyer in the time since he'd left the capital, and he had indeed lost weight. It showed in his face, creases in his neck, there were lines under his eyes. He dismounted stiffly. He'd have been in the saddle a long way. And that meant something, of course, that the governor himself, their friend, had come.

Fuyin said, "May I ask a question first?"

Daiyan nodded. He dismounted as well, and Ziji did. "Of course."

"You really expect to take the city?"

"In two nights," Daiyan said. "They have offered to withdraw but I don't intend to let thirty thousand riders go north. We have them trapped."

"Many deaths," Wang Fuyin said.

"Yes," Daiyan agreed.

"I mean of our own people."

"I know you mean that."

Fuyin nodded. "And if you were to let them retreat?"

"Thirty thousand riders, along with the numbers they recruit, will be back next spring."

Again, Fuyin nodded. He looked away, towards the shining of the walls in the distance.

"Say it," Daiyan murmured. "They sent you because it is a hard thing to say."

Fuyin turned back to him. "Our lives would have been so different, wouldn't they, had I not sent for you to guard me that day?"

"Life is like that," said Daiyan. "Say it, friend. I know you are only a messenger. This is from the court?"

"From the court," Fuyin said quietly. "They sent word to me by messenger bird, that I was to find you as fast as I could ride."

"And you did."

Fuyin nodded. He drew a breath, spoke formally. "The glorious

Emperor Zhizeng greets his military commander Ren Daiyan and commands him to withdraw his force from Hanjin and bring it south of the Wai River immediately. You yourself are instructed to report to Shantong to explain to your emperor why you have taken our armies this far without orders."

The breeze blew. A bird sang somewhere west of them.

"Why you? Just to say this?" It was Ziji. It was obvious how shaken he was.

The same distress could be seen in Fuyin's face. "They were afraid you might not do it. I was to urge you, prevail upon you."

"They really feared that?" Daiyan asked. Of the three, he seemed least disturbed, or showed it least. "And you? What did you think?"

Fuyin looked at him a long time. "I am a bad servant of my emperor. I spent the whole of the ride here trying to decide what I wanted you to do."

"Have I a choice?" Daiyan asked softly.

His friends looked at him. Neither answered.

It was a moment, on that open ground towards sunset, that could be described in many different ways. The river of stars, in the legends of Kitai, lies between mortal men and their dreams. There were no stars visible in the sky yet that autumn day, but a poet might have placed them there.

Daiyan said it again. "Have I a choice?"

The bird west of them, continuing. The wind in the solitary pine.

Ziji said, "You have sixty thousand men who love you."

"Yes," said Wang Fuyin. "You do."

Daiyan looked at him. He said, "Is there a treaty already made? Have you been told?"

Fuyin looked away. Said quietly, "The Wai River as border. We acknowledge their superior status. Our emperor is younger brother to theirs. We pay tribute, silk and silver, there are trading markets at four places along the border."

"And the silver comes back in trade." Daiyan's voice was barely audible.

"Yes. In the old way. They want silk and tea and salt and medicines. Even porcelain now."

"We have a great deal of all of those."

"And food. We have rice to sell, with the new crop system in the south."

"We do," Daiyan agreed. "The Wai River? We give them everything down to there?"

Fuyin nodded. "For peace."

"The emperor understands they have been retreating since we smashed them in spring? The Altai are proposing to *surrender* here if we only allow them to go home."

Fuyin's face was grim. "Think it through, Daiyan. Be more than a soldier. What happens if they offer to surrender? What could we demand in exchange?"

Only the bird for a long time, then another joining it, north of them.

"Ah," said Ren Daiyan finally. "Of course. I see it. I have been a fool, then?"

"No," said Fuyin. "No, you haven't!"

"Tell me!" said Ziji. And added, "Please?"

"His father and brother," said Daiyan. "That is what this is."

HE WALKED OFF ALONE, west. The other two let him do that. Daiyan's guards were visibly anxious but Ziji gestured for them to stay where they were. The sun was low now and Ziji, looking for it, found the evening star. Twilight soon. He turned to Fuyin.

"What would have happened had you come three days from now? If we were already inside?"

Wang Fuyin shook his head. "I don't know, my friend."

"This isn't a small thing. Your coming now."

"No."

"Is there something you haven't told us?"

Fuyin shook his head again. "There may be things they didn't tell me."

"Could we pretend you haven't arrived yet? That you were delayed and ..." He trailed off.

Fuyin's smile was wistful. "Not unless you kill the men who escorted me."

"I could do that."

"No, you couldn't," said Wang Fuyin.

Ziji looked away. "Very well. If the Altai surrender and sue for peace, the emperor has to demand his father and brother back as a term. I see it. So let him do that!"

"Imagine he did. What would happen?"

"I don't know. I'm just a soldier. Tell me."

"Chizu would kill him as soon as he came home."

"What?"

"A younger brother who had sat the throne? The famous Prince Jen, who saved the empire, rescued his hapless brother, forced the barbarian surrender? Of course he would be killed!"

Ziji opened his mouth, then closed it without speaking.

Fuyin said, "Our friend has a decision to make. We are living through one of the oldest stories of Kitai."

"What do you mean? The imperial family?"

"No. Army and court. If he refuses to withdraw he is in open rebellion as of today. All of you are. Our fear of our own soldiers made real."

Ziji looked at him. "And if he accepts, we surrender half of Kitai."

"That is what this is," said Fuyin. "There is probably more I don't know. Be glad we are not Daiyan."

HE FOUND HIMSELF THINKING about his father again. It was strange, or perhaps it wasn't, how many of the roads you were on could lead you home in your thoughts.

He hadn't heard from Shengdu, from his father, in almost two years. Not surprising, given the times and the distance. He'd written. Told them where he was, what he was doing, knowing it would be terribly outdated when read.

In the last letter to reach him his father had written that they were all well and that he was greatly honoured to still retain his position as a clerk in the *yamen* under a new sub-prefect.

He was the senior clerk, Daiyan knew, and the *yamen* would fall into disarray without him, but his father would never write that. He'd probably never allow himself to think it.

He must be greatly changed now. An old man? A year had aged Fuyin, what would the tumble of years have done to his father? His mother? He had a sudden memory of how she used to put a hand on his head then give his hair a tug, impatiently, loving him.

He had been a boy when he rode out. Going farther from home than he ever had in his life. On a horse! All the way to Guan Family Village, where someone had been murdered! He could conjure up the excitement he'd felt, the fear of shaming himself, his family. His father.

You lived your life, in the teachings of the Master, to never shame your parents. Ren Yuan had lived that way, with an unforced sense of responsibility.

He'd hoped his clever younger son might be a scholar, bringing so much pride to all of them in that. He'd paid money that wasn't readily available to a teacher that young Daiyan might have a chance to pursue a destiny that—who could know?—might lead him to the examinations. Perhaps one day to stand in the distant presence of the emperor. A father could go happily to join his ancestors if he knew he'd made that possible for his son.

Daiyan looked up. He'd been here for some time, lost in thought, staring blankly at the grass and some late wildflowers. The sun was on the very edge of the horizon, preparing to descend and bring the dark. The star of the Queen Mother of the West was above it, bright, always bright, as she stood on the terrace of her home and looked out, shining, on the world.

West was his home, too. West was his father.

He was what he had been raised to be. Your path in life (through marshes, over hills, across so many rivers) might have you do things that did not make you proud. But you knew—he knew—what he was, what Ren Yuan needed him to be, to the last of his days.

Fuyin had said that he didn't know everything about the treaty just made. Daiyan thought he could guess at another part of it. It surprised him sometimes, how much he could see. Perhaps he was, after all, not just a soldier with a bow and sword. He remembered the old prime minister at Little Gold Hill, a spark that had passed between them. Recognition? Could a blind man recognize you?

That one could, he thought.

You needed to be cold as Hang Dejin had been, hard, sure of yourself. You needed to *want* power and, perhaps more than anything else, believe no one but you could properly wield it. You could be a good man or not, live with honour or not, but you needed to want so very much to stand beside the throne.

Or sit upon it.

Every dynasty, every single one, had been founded by a soldier, even this Twelfth, which feared its army so much and had fallen.

It could come back, of course. They could fight the riders and win. He believed he could do that, he *knew* he could do that.

Or they could try to shape a peace lasting long enough to let children be born who knew nothing of war, whose *fathers* knew nothing of war, who never went to bed at night fearing hoofbeats hammering the dark, and then fire.

He stood there, looking west. The sun went down. There were other stars now. He wondered if he'd ever see his father again.

He walked back to the other two and he told Ziji to order their army to make ready to start south in the morning. They had received orders from the emperor. Honour and duty bound them to obey.

A CLEAR NIGHT, AUTUMN. The river of stars overhead, both blurred and bright, dividing heaven in two. Whatever might happen on earth among men and women—living and dying, glory and gladness, sorrow and sorrow's end—the stars did not change. Unless one counted the occasional tail-star that appeared, sometimes very bright for a little while, and then dimming, and then gone.

CHAPTER XXIX

It is turning colder, there have been frosts at night. The leaves are gone from the paulownias beside the path and from the elm and oak trees. Some of the leaves are brightly coloured in the meadow, blowing across. The children have pushed them into piles and they play in them, leaping and laughing. Shan has a fire in her room in the mornings to cut the chill when she rises from under the duck-and-drake quilt.

There is still no rhythm or order to mealtimes at East Slope, but she makes an effort to have morning tea with Lu Chen if he's spent the night at home and not across the stream.

She goes from the women's quarters to the main house on awakening, performs her invocations at the altar, then waits in the library, listening for signs of him, and she walks into the dining room at the same time he does. She knows he isn't deceived by these accidental encounters; she also knows he's pleased to see her.

She can divert and engage him a little. They argue about the *ci* form: her belief he's denying its nature, trying to make it more like formal verse. He points out this is the first thing she ever said to him. As if she needs reminding, she says.

This morning she asks about the Kingdom of Chu, briefly rising in the west before the emergence of their own dynasty—one of many small, warring kingdoms absorbed into the Twelfth. In the library here she's read historians blaming the last king of Chu (and his advisers, of course) for allowing poets and musicians too much influence at court, making it dissolute and doomed to fall. There is a song from Chu she loves ... *When the music was still playing grief came upon us.* She wants to know what Lu Chen thinks of all this.

He sips his tea, is beginning an answer when one of the older farm workers, Long Pei, appears in the doorway. Protocols at East Slope are relaxed, but this is unusual.

It seems there is a man up among their graves this morning. Pei does not know who it is. No, he has not accosted or questioned the intruder. He has come straight here.

The man carries a sword.

She knows it has to be Daiyan, and it is. There is no way she should be so certain of this, no way he can be here (alone!) when he's commanding their forces in the north. Rumour from the court has been about a possible truce and treaty, no details yet.

The poet goes up the slope beside her under leafless trees. She walks at his pace, forcing herself to slow down. A bright, clear morning with a breeze. An arrow of wild geese overhead. Several household men follow them, carrying whatever weapons they have found. Pei did say a sword, and Shan has said nothing, though her heart is pounding.

She sees him standing by Lu Mah's grave under the cypress tree. He turns as they approach. He bows to the poet, then to her. They both do the same.

"I crossed the river at night. I feared I might wake the household, coming so early, so I thought I would pay my respects here first."

"We are an early-rising house," says Lu Chen. "You are most welcome, Commander Ren. Will you honour us by entering East Slope? There is food, and morning tea, or wine if you prefer."

Daiyan looks tired. He looks different. He says, "I am sorry about your son. I still feel it was my—"

"You are not permitted to feel that," the poet interrupts firmly. Then adds, "It is his father saying this."

There is a silence. The men behind them are no longer tense, seeing who this is.

"Daiyan, why are you here?" Shan asks. She has been looking at his eyes. "What has happened?" She is an impatient person, always has been. Some things change as you grow older, some do not.

He tells them, standing in the East Slope graveyard in the morning's light. A complexity of hope and fear rises in Shan. His words seem to confirm the rumours there will be peace now. It is almost beyond belief, but Daiyan's eyes say there is more.

"Everything down to the Wai?" the poet asks quietly.

Daiyan nods. "So we were told."

"That is a great many people we are surrendering."

"Yes."

"And you would have ... ?"

Anguish in his face, as if he cannot hold it back. But what he says is, formally, "I would only do what my emperor and his councillors order me to do."

The poet looks at him for a long time. "You were outside Hanjin? When they ordered you back?"

"I was."

Lu Chen's expression is compassionate now, more than anything. "Come," he says finally. "Please join us, commander. Are you able to stay a while before going to Shantong?"

"I believe I can," Daiyan says. "I would like to stay. Thank you. I am very tired."

There is still something else. Shan can feel it. Something he isn't saying.

IT IS UNLIKELY, she finds herself thinking that evening, that there is a room with more intelligence in it throughout Kitai (what seems to be left of it) than any room at East Slope when both brothers are present. It is an extravagant thought, a conceit, but she's allowed some of those, isn't she?

It is Chao who says, over wine after the meal, "There was an emissary to the court at summer's end, came by sea."

"We know this," says his older brother.

"But now we also know," says Chao, "what he will have said in private, to shape this truce."

"Ah. Yes, we do," says the poet. "Someone among the Altai is clever."

"I don't," says Shan. "I don't know what we know. Tell me?"

East Slope, she has often thought, would have been her father's haven, too. She can *see* his alert, curious face turning from one speaker to another, immersed in the joy of lucid conversation.

Chao looks around. Only the four of them in the room now, the other women have withdrawn, and his own sons. The women of East Slope have accepted that Shan is a special case. Mah would have been here.

Chao says, "Lady Lin, they hold the father-emperor and the son who succeeded him. So, if they release them both ... ?"

He takes up his cup, drinks, leaves time for Shan to work this out. Candles flicker on the table.

It takes her a moment. Why would the Altai release hostages? Why would that be clever? Weren't the imperial prisoners a weapon? A way to threaten Kitai and the new emperor? Wasn't Emperor Zhizeng bound to do all he could to ...

"Oh," she says. And then, "Who is properly emperor if Chizu comes back? Is that it?"

These are words that can have someone killed, speaking them or even hearing them.

Lu Chao nods. "Indeed, it is," he murmurs. "And we know the answer to that question. So does Zhizeng."

Daiyan is silent but she can see he's grasped all this. Probably from the beginning, then thinking it through on the long way south from Hanjin. He hasn't travelled alone, of course. Only crossed the river himself by ferry in the night to come here. His escort had arrived later in the day. Ziji is not with him. He is commanding the army, which is—as ordered by the emperor—now on this side of the Wai.

Everything north of it is being surrendered. Or betrayed?

She thinks she understands the look in Daiyan's face now. He had been, it seems, about to take Hanjin. He'd said they were prepared to go north after, carry the war to the Altai.

More fighting, more deaths of soldiers, and of people caught between soldiers. But he'd wanted to shatter the horsemen, the threat of them, let Kitai be again what once it had been. Be more than it had been in their time.

HE COMES TO HER LATER, discreetly, although by now there is no shame, or secrecy required. Not at East Slope.

He is weary and weighted. Their lovemaking is tender and slow. It is as if he's traversing her body, making a map of it for himself. A way to get back? A dark thought. Shan pushes it away.

He is above her just then. She tightens her fingers in his hair and kisses him as deeply as she can, draws him into her body, into everything she is.

After, lying beside her, a hand on her belly, he says, "I could see you in pearls and kingfisher feathers."

"Daiyan, stop it. I am no goddess."

He smiles. He says, "This house is surely the best place in the world for you."

It frightens her, his tone. She says, "It is, except for any place in the world where you are."

He turns his head, looks at her from very close. She's left a lamp lit, to see him by. He says, "I don't deserve such a thought. I'm only ..."

"Stop it," she says again. "Have you ever seen how your friends and your soldiers look at you? How Chen looks at you? *Lu Chen*, Daiyan!"

He is quiet for a time. Shifts position to lay his head on her breast. "He is too generous. I don't know what any of them are seeing in me."

She tugs his hair then, hard. "Stop it," she says a third time. "Daiyan, they are seeing virtue like a lantern, and Kitai's honour. And there isn't enough of either in the world."

He doesn't reply this time. She moves a little and wraps her arms around him. "Sorry if I hurt you," she says, meaning his hair. "I know you are delicate as silk."

He laughs a little.

"My mother used to do that," he says. Then, quiet as a breath, "I was close, when Fuyin brought me the order to retreat. I was very close, Shan."

"To what?" she asks.

He tells her.

"Not so much honour in a commander rebelling against the throne, is there?" he says. She hears the bitterness. And then, "I still could, Shan. I could get up right now and ride to the Wai, claim my army and lead it south. To the court. Another military leader's uprising in Kitai! Wouldn't that be a lantern of virtue?"

She finds she cannot speak.

He says, "And it is so *wrong*, that we let the horsemen go, that we are surrendering so much. Yes, for peace, yes. But not shaped this way—for this reason!"

Her heart is pounding. There is fear in the room now, in her, and she finally understands (she thinks) what she's been seeing in his face since morning.

She isn't quite there yet, however.

I BELIEVE I CAN. I would like to stay, he'd said, up by the graves. He was wrong, it seemed.

Twenty men were waiting outside the gate and fence, when he woke in the chilly morning and left the room, leaving Shan asleep. Walking out to them alone, past the frost-silvered grass and flower beds, he recognized their livery, then he recognized one of them.

Daiyan came up to the gate. The one he knew, their leader, bowed on the other side. He said, "Commander Ren, we have been sent to escort you to Shantong. My hope is that this is acceptable to you. Prime Minister Hang Hsien sends his respects."

"How did you know I would be here?"

"We were told you would likely come here."

A little amusing, a little unsettling. Daiyan saw Junwen and two others, armed, hurrying over, a little too briskly. He lifted a hand to slow them.

"I know you," he said to the guard leader. "You served Hang Dejin at Little Gold Hill."

"I did."

"It is a sorrow, how he died."

The man lifted his head. "It is."

"You serve his son now? At court?"

"I am honoured to do so."

"He is fortunate. I gather your presence means I am not to be allowed to linger here at all?"

An awkward hesitation. It was, Daiyan thought, an unfair question. "Never mind," he said. "I will say my farewells and join you. I take it my men can ride with us?"

"Of course," said the guard.

Daiyan suddenly had the name. "Thank you, Guard Officer Dun," he said.

The man flushed. "You are good to remember, commander," he said. The man hesitated again. He opened his mouth, then closed it.

"Go ahead," Daiyan said.

Dun Yanlu flushed. Then said, "Is it true? You were outside Hanjin?"

"We were."

"And could have taken it?"

Daiyan hesitated. "I should not speak of these matters."

Dun Yanlu, an older man, a little stocky, grey in his beard, nodded. Then, as if impelled, "But ... *could* you have? Taken the city? Killed them there?"

There was discretion, and there was something else. What people needed to know about their empire, their army, themselves. It did have to do with virtue, pride. *A lantern*, Shan had said.

"Of course we would have," he said quietly. "The city was ours. They were trapped and dead."

Dun Yanlu swore then, softly but at length and with some eloquence. "Forgive me," he added.

"No need," said Daiyan.

STANDING BY THE GATE between the brothers, she watches him ride away. An escort sent all the way from Shantong is a mark of honour, surely? It doesn't feel that way.

Lu Chao has said he is going to follow south. Many things are happening, are being decided. Matters of great importance. An honourable man has a duty to bring what talent he has to the service of the state, and Chao is, after all, the last emissary sent to the Altai. He has spoken with the war-leader himself! He will go, play whatever role he is allowed.

There is, of course, no place for a woman in any of this.

She lives between worlds, suspended. And Daiyan was right last night: there is nowhere in Kitai better for her, more a home, than East Slope.

She watches him go away. *Any place in the world where you are.*

It has been an agitated morning. Daiyan's men, the Lu family, the escort waiting. Chao's grandchildren were excited by so many guardsmen at East Slope. There has been no chance to be alone.

Watching by the gate she realizes, aching, that she'd said nothing to him when they mounted up. She waits. He looks back, riding. She says everything she needs to say with her eyes. Or as close to everything as she can.

The road bends south and down to find the bridge across the stream, and the riders are gone from sight.

☙❧

The honourable Wang Fuyin is one of those who will be granted a long life by the gods, and good health to the end (and who can fairly ask for more than that?). He is greatly respected for his achievements, both in serving the state and in his writings on the proper conduct of magistrates during criminal investigations.

Fuyin would always say that among all the moments in his life, the autumn day Commander Ren Daiyan appeared before the emperor in Shantong might have been the one carved most vividly into memory, the way words can be carved into stone. Of course words in stone, if they are not destroyed, outlast the carver, and memories do die.

Protocols in Shantong were less rigid than they had been in Hanjin, and vastly less so than in earlier dynasties, when a man summoned might wait a year before being received. It was a smaller court and a less opulent palace. Revenue was an issue, and so was security.

The emperor spoke of security a great deal.

Fuyin had made what could only be considered a reckless

decision. He had left Jingxian—his own city now, his place of responsibility—in the hands of his deputy governor. He had found a ship on the coast to carry him to Shantong, immediately after watching the army begin its withdrawal from the walls of Hanjin.

He was acutely aware of how close Kitai had been to open rebellion.

The problem for him was that he still didn't know how he felt about that. About Ren Daiyan's decision to accept the order he himself had carried north.

Ambivalence was treasonous, of course, but thoughts would not kill you if no one knew your mind. If no one who mattered could see your face, read your eyes.

It would have been infinitely more prudent to go straight back to Jingxian and stay there. Jingxian was well south of the border proposed. It was safely in the new Kitai, Southern Twelfth Dynasty. First year of the reign of the illustrious Emperor Zhizeng.

He was not a bold man, Wang Fuyin, by his own assessment. He'd left Hanjin before the siege began, anticipating what might come.

Yes, he'd worked with Daiyan and the old prime minister in a scheme aimed at Kai Zhen, but throwing in your lot with a master such as Hang Dejin had seemed a prudent, not a reckless thing to do, and this had proven to be so.

This act, on the other hand, hastening south by ship to be at a nervous court, unsummoned, in the midst of its shaping a treaty with vast implications, then choosing to be present when he was known to be a friend of the commander summoned to defend his actions ... this counted as recklessness, by any measure one could propose.

That boy he'd impulsively ordered to be one of his guards long ago had become a man who elicited behaviour such as this, such ... well, loyalty, in fact.

His wife, busily furnishing the governor's mansion in Jingxian to her evolving satisfaction, would not be happy if she knew any of this, so he hadn't told her. That was easy enough. Nothing else was.

GENERAL SHENWEI HUANG had commanded the Kitan forces defending the approach to Xinan in the west. He had not been leading the army sent to take the Xiaolu Southern Capital, and then defend the imperial city when the barbarians came down.

That was why he was still alive, still in a position to command. The west had been less important, his failure had attracted less attention—and less consequence.

The commanders above Hanjin had been executed by now, most of them.

Shenwei Huang had made it south from his own disastrous battlefield, hurrying past Xinan (which was doomed to fall) and across the Wai River.

He had found a fair-sized barracks attached to a town called Chunyu near the Great River, established that he outranked the officers, and made these soldiers, smoothly enough, his own small force. There'd been no one to gainsay him. If any one thing mattered in an army, it was rank.

His new troops patrolled against outlaws until winter, when the Altai began their campaign of vengeance. Commander Shenwei elected to abandon Chunyu and lead his men across the Great River into the region near the marshes.

His soldiers were not generally unhappy about this, even if some did desert to stay in or near the town. The Altai had better than fifty thousand riders. They were doing terrible things, and it wasn't as if Shenwei Huang's small force was going to stop them, was it?

In the event, their town and barracks proved to be far enough south and west not to have been endangered, but, really, what would have been the point of taking chances?

A little later, in spring, after the Altai had been stunningly defeated in the east, Commander Shenwei made his way to

Shantong—it had become clear the new court would be there. He sent his soldiers back across the river to their barracks. They had served their purpose.

He presented a cautious presence in the early days at the new capital, for fear that someone who mattered might know too many details of his actions in the north, or just dislike him (there were a few of those). But, he swiftly realized, the chaos of the court's arrival, crowning a new emperor, assembling the rudiments of a functioning bureaucracy, meant there might be room for a man clever in certain ways—if not, perhaps, especially skilled on a battlefield.

Commander Ren Daiyan had slaughtered a large number of the Altai on the Great River. The barbarians were retreating north. Ren Daiyan, a man not entirely normal, in Shenwei Huang's view, was following them.

Word began to emerge in Shantong that a peace treaty was being negotiated. Whatever the terms might be, Shenwei Huang realized that he was unlikely to have to fight the Altai any more.

He felt reasonably confident of being able to deal with bandits and rogue troops on their side of any new border—if he was given enough men, of course. Extreme numerical superiority was the great secret of warfare as far as he was concerned. And timing was the key to success at any court.

Accordingly, when it was made known that Ren Daiyan had been summoned back from his wild (and evidently unauthorized) adventure in the north and was almost certain to lose his command—well, what man of ambition would not see a chance hanging in front of him, like fruit on a low branch?

Huang was able to procure an audience with the emperor and his prime minister. It cost him some money, but that sort of thing always did.

He wasn't sure how he felt about the new prime minister. Hang Hsien was the son of the most alarming of the previous ones, so he bore watching, that much was clear.

Shenwei Huang had judged his young emperor to be both anxious and direct, and he tried to address each of these things. His message was simple: the unpredictable Ren Daiyan was an obvious concern, but no affair of his. Huang had no doubt the court could deal with the man. Commanders could not, in Kitai, be unpredictable.

Commander Ren's army was another matter. His army was very large, and likely to be dangerously loyal to him and to his deputy commanders, his friends. Commander Shenwei humbly proposed that he be sent to take control of that force, which would be along the Wai by now—if they'd followed orders. Following orders, he added, was what he'd done all his life in the service of the empire, even when faced with overwhelming forces opposing him.

He proposed to divide that army into four smaller ones (he'd given this thought). A single force that large was dangerous, he said. He would post three army groups along the Wai, east, central, west, and change their commanders regularly. The fourth would be assigned to deal with outlaws wherever they might be found, or provincial governors with unseemly ambitions in this challenging time when Kitai needed every man to be loyal to a fault.

The emperor listened, the prime minister listened. They suggested he remain in Shantong while they considered his proposal "in the light of larger affairs."

He was summoned back two days later, to the throne room this time. Important advisers were present. Standing before the new Dragon Throne, Shenwei Huang was elevated three full degrees in rank and named Left Side Commander of the Pacified Border.

He was ordered to travel immediately, with trusted officers, to take command from whomever Ren Daiyan (not Commander Ren, Huang noted) had left in control of that army. He was to proceed, once there, as he'd suggested to the emperor. His ideas were regarded as sound, his loyalty commended as an example.

Shenwei Huang was deeply gratified but not unduly surprised.

Turbulent times meant opportunities. History taught as much to any man with eyes to see.

HAD HE BEEN PRIVY to the exchange between emperor and prime minister that took place after he'd left that first, private audience, a shadow might have fallen upon his pleasure.

"If that ridiculous man," said the emperor of Kitai, "had any more wind in him, kites could fly when he spoke."

The prime minister laughed aloud, startled. The emperor smiled briefly. Hang Hsien would later regard that moment as the one where he first began to think the nervous, intense young man he was serving had perception and understanding. That they might achieve some things together, sustain a dynasty, and Kitai.

It was agreed between them that Shenwei Huang would be promoted and extolled and sent to command—and divide—the army of Ren Daiyan. His ambition was laughably transparent and his incompetence as a soldier was known to both men in the room. But neither of these things, for the present, was seen as a *threat*, and that was critical just now. It was a precarious time.

The man could always be dismissed, stripped of any new rank, when need came. Such things were easily done, the prime minister told the emperor.

"Sometimes we might be required to do more," the emperor said thoughtfully.

The two of them had had a very different encounter in this same room with the emissary sent from the Altai in summer. Terms had been proposed, some in writing, some not.

Negotiating a peace was a delicate affair. You demanded, and had demands made of you. You rejected and accepted, gave and were granted, depending on your need, and your power.

LEFT SIDE COMMANDER Shenwei Huang left the city seven days later. He crossed the Great River with fifty men and a hundred horses, heading for the Wai and command of a battle-hardened army of nearly sixty thousand.

He never reached it.

In the extreme disruption and violence of a terrible year, when so many had fled the Altai, displaced from their homes, sheltering in woods or swampland or roaming the countryside, there were even more outlaws than was customary in Kitai.

Some of the bands that had formed were very large. Indeed, this was the task Huang had proposed for a quarter of the army on the Wai: to clean out the more dangerous outlaws, starting with those in the southeast, alarmingly close to the emperor.

His escort of fifty included twelve senior officers, carefully chosen for the unlikelihood any of them would conspire against him—or be likely to achieve anything if they did.

The soldiers, his personal guards, were perfectly capable. But the outlaws that attacked their party outnumbered them significantly and fought with surprising skill. Shenwei Huang was experienced in exaggerating the numbers of his foes when he'd had to report a lost battle, but in this instance there really were two hundred men who ambushed them at a point between the Great River and the Wai, loosing deadly arrows from the woods while springing forth to block the road before them and behind.

They were not, however, outlaws.

∞

Ren Daiyan was led before his emperor the same day he arrived in Shantong.

Not even a chance to change his clothing, rest, take a meal. He was dusty from the road, barely had time to wash his face. He still wore riding boots. His sword and bow were taken at the palace doors.

The throne room was crowded, with a buzz and hum of anticipation. This afternoon's encounter, it was generally agreed, was likely to be both entertaining and important. It might even represent a defining moment in this new empire of the Southern Twelfth.

The prime minister of Kitai was uneasy for many reasons. He wasn't sure how he felt about the crowd here, the number of witnesses who might spread various reports. His usual method of resolving such dilemmas—what would his father have done?—afforded no immediate solution. He had proposed making this encounter a private one. The emperor had refused.

He did wish that the governor of Jingxian had not taken it upon himself to be here. Wang Fuyin had arrived in Shantong before the commander. He had every right to be present, as a distinguished member of the new bureaucracy. He was also a friend of Ren Daiyan's.

There was a worrisome phrase in use, from a new song by Lu Chen. It was being sung in marketplaces and pleasure houses: *From Hanjin to Shantong is the path of our sorrow.*

That was bad. He needed to do something about it. You could ban songs, phrases, poems, punish those caught singing or speaking them. It wasn't generally a good idea, especially not if the writer was as celebrated as this one was. Better, really, to make the words *untrue.*

He needed time for that. And help. There was a chance to make this succeed, he did believe that was true. A peace that endured, trade bringing more back than they sent north, the double-crop rice fields feeding Kitai from Szechen to the sea. A new Kitai could become something that flourished and endured.

He needed a chance. He needed a good emperor, one not defined by his fears. He looked at his emperor, the one he had. He looked down a crowded room at the man walking slowly towards the throne, like a soldier come from a battlefield.

His father had liked this Ren Daiyan, had said as much at Little Gold Hill.

The commander looked tired, which was to be expected, given how far he'd come and their decision to give him no time to rest, prepare, consult with anyone. At the same time, there was a hint of amusement on the man's face when he glanced at Hang Hsien, as if he understood these strategies.

His bows to his emperor were precise, unstinting. Three full obeisances, three times. When he rose to Zhizeng's gesture he turned and bowed twice to Hsien. He was smiling.

Hsien wished the man hadn't smiled. He wished he didn't feel so uneasy. He doubted his father had ever felt this way in a throne room. Well, perhaps at the very beginning?

His father, blind and frail and alone, had ended his life when his home had been invaded by Altai riders. This man, Ren Daiyan, had been intending to destroy the last invaders in Kitai and retake the capital.

There was, Hang Hsien thought, no way to be easy here.

FUYIN HAD POSITIONED himself in the second row of officials, most of the way towards the throne. Governor of a large city, formerly chief magistrate of Hanjin, he was entitled to be this close, even had a right to the first row, which he'd chosen not to take. He wanted to see what was happening, but not be too visible. He worried about his expressions, what he might reveal if he wasn't cautious. Although if he were truly cautious he wouldn't be here at all, would he?

"We are pleased to see you prompt to our summons, Commander Ren," said the emperor of Kitai. His voice was too thin for real majesty, but it was clear and precise.

"Kitai's servant is grateful to be received, exalted lord. And honoured to serve the empire in any way I can."

He should probably have said *the emperor* or *the throne,* Fuyin thought. He wiped perspiration from his forehead. The man on his left looked at him curiously. The prime minister, he saw, was standing right next to the throne. In the old court prime ministers had positioned themselves more to one side. Protocols had changed, were changing.

The Wai River was to be the northern border of Kitai. This city was now their capital. This was their emperor.

Their emperor said, "Does that service include recklessly endangering the largest part of our army? Leaving this court utterly exposed?"

It is here, Fuyin thought. There was to be no subtle emergence of the point today. And the emperor was doing this himself. Fuyin wiped his face again, with a silk cloth, ignoring the man on his left.

He saw Daiyan react—saw the moment when his friend realized how direct today would be, *what* this summons was. He saw him take a breath, the way one does before shouldering a burden, accepting it. Daiyan lifted his head. He looked at the prime minister for a moment, then back to the emperor. He smiled. *Stop that,* Fuyin wanted to cry. *You are dealing with a frightened man!* And then, very suddenly, with no warning at all, a thought came to him.

As it happened, the same idea in the same moment occurred to the prime minister of Kitai, watching as intently: that Ren Daiyan, before his emperor and the court, might be addressing others beyond this room, or even their own time.

Long after, Wang Fuyin would say, truthfully, that he'd had this thought and had feared it, as one feared an angry ghost on a moonless country lane.

Daiyan said, voice pitched to carry, "Serene lord, all that your servant has done has been with a mind to safeguard Kitai. And its emperor."

"Is it so? Racing, without orders, *towards* the Altai forces?"

"Towards the rescue of the emperor's suffering people, my lord."

The prime minister stirred, seemed about to speak, but it was Daiyan who went on. "I had a battle-tested army, and we had destroyed half the barbarian force, as the emperor knows. As they knew. They were in retreat, and smaller than us."

"They were smaller when they shattered our armies above Xinan and Hanjin!"

"But not above Yenling, gracious lord. As I believe the emperor will be generous enough to remember."

Who in the room—or on the throne—would not remember? The emperor looked suddenly to his left, to his prime minister, as if for help. Fuyin still had that odd sense that Daiyan was saying words he had not intended when he'd walked in. That something had changed for him with the emperor's first question.

Hang Hsien cleared his throat. He said, "The Altai were *inside* the city, Commander Ren." He used the title, Fuyin noted. "Winter was approaching, any siege you undertook would have caused our own people inside the walls ..."

He stopped, because Ren Daiyan was vigorously shaking his head, another transgression. He was a soldier, a *soldier*, doing this to the prime minister of Kitai!

He said, gravely enough, "My lord prime minister, I thank you for your thoughts. For considering such matters. I agree. We could not have subjected Hanjin to a siege. We were not about to do so."

"You'd have flown over the walls?" The emperor, his voice a little too harsh.

"Gone under them, my lord." Daiyan paused. "The same way I came out last winter when I saved the illustrious emperor from the Altai camp." He waited again. "And then guided him safely here, destroying his pursuers."

Such a dangerous game, Fuyin was thinking. But Daiyan had to do this, didn't he? Remind them all, in this very public way, of the things he'd done for Kitai. For Zhizeng.

It was the prime minister who answered. "Kitai and the glorious Emperor Zhizeng are aware of the services you have rendered in the past. It is not a response to current error to cite previous deeds."

"Perhaps not," said Daiyan, quietly, "but might they not be a response to allegations of disloyalty?"

A murmuring. *Oh, Daiyan, please*, Wang Fuyin thought. *Have care.*

The prime minister said, "No such allegations have been made, Commander Ren."

"Thank you," said Ren Daiyan. "May I ask then what I am doing here? Instead of killing barbarians who rode through Kitai murdering our people? I should be serving my emperor by freeing us from their oppression!" For the first time an edge in his voice.

Hang Hsien said, "It is the task of the emperor and his advisers to determine what course Kitai is to take, Commander Ren. It is not for a soldier."

And here it was, Fuyin thought. The old battle and the old fears. This endless clash, this chasm ... the sorrow of the land.

Time's river flowed east, never to return, the sages taught. But there were so many ruins along the banks. Commanders rebelling, millions dead, dynasties falling. Armies as weapons against the state, the court, the emperor under heaven. Military leaders seizing the mandate of heaven for themselves. Chaos and savagery, wilderness inside walls. The heart crying for what the eye saw.

"Of course it is for the court to make such decisions," said Daiyan, quietly. "But must the emperor's loyal commanders not do *their* tasks properly in the field? When invaders come upon us?" Passion again in his voice. "We had beaten half of their army, they were weary of warfare, and I knew how to get into Hanjin! We were about to destroy the last barbarian force in our land. Tell me, my lord emperor, how would it have been disloyal for me to do that for you? My life is sworn to the service of Kitai. August lord, my body is marked with characters that say as much."

Absolute silence. A feeling in Fuyin's heart of something larger than he could hold inside. He wasn't breathing, sensed that others around him weren't doing so either. And he still felt, terribly, that

Daiyan had made some decision, had *understood* something. He wasn't only speaking to them any more. Through them, perhaps, that they might remember, and tell.

But the young man on the throne was not weak or uncertain about his own needs and desires, his own understanding, even in the face of something like this. This, too, needed to be known, and Governor Wang Fuyin and the court in Shantong learned it then.

"No," said the emperor of Kitai. "No. Loyalty is humility. If you had been wrong, if they had reinforcements come, if your plan to enter the city failed, if you were defeated in that battle, we were naked here. No soldier of Kitai can take that much upon himself! And there were things you did not know, did not wait to know. We had agreed to a peace, a border, trade. No more slaughter of our beloved people, who are—always—the endless duty of an emperor."

Fuyin swallowed hard. This one, too, he thought. This one had passion as well. He, too—

Daiyan said, "And in that peace, what of your serene lordship's beloved people in Hanjin? In Yenling? Xinan? In poor, abandoned Shuquian in the north? In every town and village above the Wai? Every farm? Are they not your endless duty, too, my lord emperor? Are they not Kitai?"

"Not any more," said the emperor, his voice clear and absolute.

It seemed to Wang Fuyin that the room vibrated then, as if in the aftermath of the sounding of some great bell.

He saw the emperor look calmly around, then back at the man in front of him. Zhizeng said, "We had decided so. We had decided Kitai needs peace more than anything. And there are prices to be paid, exchanges made, in any treaty. We have been forced, by errors before our time, to do as much."

He gestured, one hand, a dismissal.

Men came forward. Ren Daiyan was led away. He had entered

the throne room by himself. He left escorted—surrounded—by six guards.

He was taken from there to the prison of Shantong, a structure beside the palace, on the hill above the city, built down into the earth. There were no other prisoners held there at that time. It was for Ren Daiyan alone.

FROM HIS CELL, if he stood on a bench, there was a view through iron bars of West Lake in all its beauty below. Sometimes music could be heard, sometimes a woman's voice singing, drifting up from red lantern boats on the water, even in autumn, if a night was mild under stars.

As time passed, bringing colder nights, there were no more pleasure boats on the lake after dark. The sound one heard, listening from up the hill, was pine trees in the wind as winter came.

CHAPTER XXX

The first magistrate appointed to prepare the formal charges of treason against Commander Ren Daiyan withdrew from his office after a brief interval, surrendering the great honour of that assignment with abject and extreme regret—citing duties to his family in the southwest compelling an extended absence from court.

The second judicial official selected by Prime Minister Hang Hsien also lasted only a few weeks. In this case, it appeared, challenging concerns regarding his own health required him to undertake a period of rest and the ingestion of certain arcane remedies.

The third magistrate, established to be in impeccable health and with family located in the capital, had not yet completed his investigations.

He did concede, in a private encounter with the prime minister, that there might be *some* difficulty in presenting a conclusive case for treasonous behaviour. He also, cautiously, made mention of widespread public admiration for the imprisoned man. There were reports of songs and poetry, tea room and entertainment district talk (loose, idle talk, he hastened to add) concerning the commander's heroism and loyalty and his well-known victories. There was even a poem—men were saying it had been written by Ren Daiyan himself (which was surely nonsense, the magistrate was again quick to say)—about avenging the Calamity of Hanjin.

It appeared to be widely known that Commander Ren's forces had been preparing to retake the imperial capital—the *former* capital, he amended—with a stratagem when they'd been ordered to withdraw.

No, the magistrate had no notion how all this information was being disseminated. Did the illustrious prime minister know, perhaps? There was no reply. He hadn't expected one.

Would it be at all possible, the magistrate inquired casually, as if merely musing aloud over tea, to simply have Ren Daiyan dismissed from rank and command with honour, perhaps as one who had done more than Kitai could fairly demand of any man? Let him slip into obscurity somewhere? Didn't he come from the west? Couldn't he ...?

The prime minister of Kitai thought, privately, that this was a perfectly good idea. He'd had the same thought more than once, often late at night. He was, however, only a servant of his emperor, who held a different view, and there were other elements at work in this affair, important ones.

Aloud, he said only that there were dimensions to the matter that he could not, the magistrate understood, discuss.

The magistrate understood entirely, absolutely.

He was urged, in calm, forceful language, to proceed with making the case for treason. He was to remind himself that his emperor was trusting him and that the future for a man could be either bright or dark. He was also advised, gently, that it would not be acceptable if he were to become ill, or discover concerns that might take him from his task.

As it happened, the prime minister had read the poem in question. One of his spies in the city had brought him a copy, affixed, apparently, to a wall in one of the mercantile streets. There could be times, Prime Minister Hang Hsien thought, when the new printing devices might cause more trouble than any benefits they offered.

He had heard Ren Daiyan speak, more than once now. He didn't, for a moment, doubt that the lines could be his. He had them in memory already:

> *The rain stops as I stand on the wide plain.*
> *I look at the clearing sky and let loose a warrior's cry.*
> *My battlefields have covered eight thousand* li.
> *We must not sit idle or we will grow old with regret.*
> *The shame of Hanjin lingers.*
> *When will the sorrow of the emperor's people end?*
> *Let us ride our horses and carry our bows*
> *To shed the blood of barbarians.*
> *Let us restore Kitai's glory of old,*
> *Recover our rivers and mountains,*
> *Then offer loyal tribute to the glorious emperor.*

Earlier that autumn, even before the first appointed magistrate had decided he was needed elsewhere, a message had arrived for the prime minister from the River Wai.

It ought, properly, to have been sent directly to the emperor, under the new rules instituted by Zhizeng, but the sender might be excused for not knowing how court protocols had changed.

Commander Zhao Ziji, entrusted on a temporary basis with command of the (very) large Kitan army currently positioned on the south bank of the Wai, presented his humble and respectful compliments to the prime minister of Kitai and regretfully begged to advise him that certain military personnel, evidently sent north from Shantong, had encountered one of the many bands of outlaws between the Great River and the Wai.

It was Commander Zhao's lamentable duty to report that these honourable soldiers—some fifty or so—appeared to have all been slain, though Commander Zhao could not confirm this, since some might have escaped, and he himself had received no communication from the court as to who these soldiers were and what their number had been.

One of them, in a commanding officer's uniform (what was left, after the bandits had stripped much of it away), he himself recognized from the western campaign against the barbarians: a particularly incompetent and cowardly man named Shenwei Huang. Perhaps he was being sent to the border for discipline by his peers, after his failures in the past? Commander Zhao sought guidance.

He added that he had immediately sent cavalry to search out the bandit killers, but the countryside was wild, as the prime minister undoubtedly knew, and had been badly disrupted by the Altai horde that had swept through in winter and during their retreat in spring. He had doubts they would ever identify the perpetrators of this appalling deed.

He closed by expressing the fervent wish that the prime minister would soon see fit to return Commander Ren Daiyan to the army, so that his far greater skill and wisdom could be brought to bear on calming a difficult situation along the new border. The last thing they needed, he wrote, was trouble here, including the possibility that bandits might cross the Wai and raid on the Altai side, breaching any treaty!

The prime minister of Kitai wasn't normally prone to the affliction of headaches, but had he felt one beginning behind his eyes, reading this.

He hadn't the least doubt what had happened. He had many doubts as to how to proceed. He realized he needed to know more about this Zhao Ziji. Was the man ambitious? He didn't think so, remembering him at Little Gold Hill, but men did change, and that army's commander was imprisoned here, which could cause such changes.

If Commander Zhao and a force of sixty thousand on the Wai decided that they were displeased with current judicial processes, what might they do?

On the other hand, he had an emperor whose desires were clear (if never spoken aloud), and they *did* have a treaty now, with terms and conditions (not all written down), and the barbarian army had indeed survived to get home from Hanjin. They would surely be engaged in recruiting new riders even now.

Meanwhile, trade had already begun at designated places along the Wai. The government was trading, collecting tariffs. Normal life was beginning—just beginning—to resume. There was money coming in, finally. The Altai needed rice, they needed medicine, they wanted tea and salt. Surely the barbarians understood all this? Surely the treaty made as much sense to them? If so, his plan, the emperor's plan, had a chance to succeed. But there were so many things he needed to do right to make it happen.

Dreams of his father did not help.

THE CONSIDERABLY BESET prime minister avoided one particular meeting for a long time that autumn, then decided he was being cowardly. He received the honourable Lu Chao—a man he respected even more than he did the older brother, the poet.

The Lu brothers had been opponents of his father. Both had been exiled during the faction wars of the previous generation, and Hsien's father, in turn, had been banished in the (fortunately brief) time they were in power. But it was Hang Dejin who had brought Lu Chen home from Lingzhou Isle and begun the downfall of Kai Zhen.

The man currently imprisoned in a cell beside this palace had been a part of that. It was, he imagined, about this man that Lu Chao wished to speak. It wasn't a difficult guess: there had been letters from East Slope.

There were times when Hsien thought that living quietly on some estate—like Little Gold Hill, perhaps, but here in the south—would make for a better life than the one he was living now.

He was usually able to dismiss such selfish ideas. It would be unfilial to withdraw, and disloyal to Kitai.

He received Lu Chao in a room he used for such purposes. A servant poured chrysanthemum tea into porcelain cups of a distinctive red hue, then withdrew to stand by the door.

Hsien had alerted the emperor about this meeting; he was instructed to report after it was over. The emperor remained, that autumn, what he had been from the beginning here: attentive, direct, afraid.

Lu Chao praised the elegance of the teacups and the simplicity of the room. He congratulated Hsien on his assumption of office, and offered the view that the emperor was fortunate in his principal adviser.

Hsien expressed his gratitude for these words, his regret concerning the death of Chao's nephew, and asked after Lu Chen's health.

Chao bowed his thanks and said his brother was in health but quiet of late. He spoke, in turn, of his sorrow to have learned of Hang Dejin's death, the unkindness of such an ending after a distinguished life.

"There are many sorrows in this time of ours," Hsien agreed. He gestured to two chairs and they sat beside each other with a small table between.

Lu Chao said, "War brings grief. So does surrender."

"Is peace a surrender?"

"Not always," said the tall man. "Sometimes it is a gift. Shall we say, with the sages, that it depends on the terms given and taken?"

"I think so," said Hsien. His father would probably have asked a sly question of Lu Chao, pressed him for definitions that revealed his own views. Probably Chao would have seen that, and deflected the question back.

He said, surprising himself, "This is the emperor's treaty, honourable sir. I am making of it the best I can."

Lu Chao looked at him, a grave, thoughtful man. The older brother, the poet, was the impetuous, reckless, brilliant one. Or had been, perhaps, before his son was killed.

Chao said, "I see. Would there be, perhaps, unrecorded terms to this treaty that are ... of particular importance to the emperor?"

He was delicate, fair, discreet.

Hsien said, suddenly, "I would be grateful to have you here in Shantong to advise the emperor with me."

Chao smiled. "Thank you. I am honoured by your words. Your father would not have agreed."

"My father is gone, to my sorrow and Kitai's. Much has changed."

Another thoughtful look. "Indeed. Two emperors are imprisoned, hostages, in the farthest north."

"It is," said Hsien carefully, "the daily sorrow of Emperor Zhizeng."

"Of course it is," said Lu Chao. And repeated, "Of course it is."

They understood each other. It was possible to do that, with the right man, without forcing words into dangerous existence. It was sometimes *necessary* to do that, Hang Hsien thought.

He said, "I am not speaking idly, sir. Will you consider coming to court to shape a new Kitai?"

Lu Chao inclined his long neck in a bow from his chair. He sipped from his tea appreciatively. He said, "I could not do so while Commander Ren Daiyan, to whom we all owe so much, is imprisoned, or if he is punished for loyalty."

It was, thought Hsien, probably what he deserved. It felt very much like a blow. From quiet, tacit, shared understanding, to this.

His hand was steady as he sipped his own tea. He had been well trained. But it was difficult to speak for a moment.

In the silence, Chao spoke again. "You need not answer me, but it is my thought—and my brother agrees—that this matter might have been one of those terms of the peace that can never be written down or spoken aloud."

Hsien was remembering another meeting in this palace, in a larger, more richly decorated room: the Altai emissary, himself, the emperor of Kitai.

He looked at the man beside him. Thinning hair, greying beard, simple cap, unassuming clothes. He felt too young, too inexperienced for this, though he knew he really wasn't. A changed world could need younger men, and it wasn't unfair to say the older generation had destroyed the dynasty.

Without speaking, but forcing himself to meet the other's eyes, he nodded. He owed this man that much, he felt.

Lu Chao said, "It is a sorrow."

And Hsien, after a moment, said, "It is a sorrow."

☙

Yan'po, who had been the kaghan of the Altai tribe for a long time and then, somewhat against his nature, an emperor, lord of the steppe, had died in his Central Capital at the end of summer.

He was wrapped in a red cloth and placed outside the city walls on the grass at twilight for the wolves, as was the custom of his people. He was not young, Yan'po, and his death hadn't been unexpected. He had never entirely mastered the change from tribal kaghan to emperor of many tribes. In some ways, he'd just been carried along, swept into the world, by his war-leaders.

Word of his passing did not reach the Kitan court, or even the Altai Southern Capital, for some time. There were those who wished to delay the report to their own advantage, perhaps hoping to succeed Yan'po.

If so, they were forestalled in this desire. They died, unpleasantly.

At the time of Yan'po's death, Wan'yen, the war-leader, had been trapped with an army of thirty thousand, the best soldiers of the grassland, inside the recently conquered Kitan city of Hanjin. His tribesmen in the north did not know this either. Information travelled with great difficulty in that time.

Eventually, as it was later explained on the steppe, Wan'yen's terrifying reputation, and that of his riders, caused the encircling Kitan army to turn, like the dogs they were, and flee south. Wan'yen could have pursued the cowards again, but instead he returned in triumph to the steppe, and there he received tidings of Yan'po's passing to the Lord of the Sky.

Wan'yen accepted the homage of those sharing this news. He drank *kumiss* with his tribal leaders. Informed that there were foolish pretenders in the Central Capital, he immediately started north and west—with half of his army. The rest of his soldiers remained in the Southern Capital, against the unlikely event that the Kitan decided to come north, If so, they would need chastisement like the coward-dogs they were.

The new emperor of the steppe was crowned at the beginning of winter—a new crown was made for the occasion by captured artisans, with jewels taken in the sack of Hanjin.

Emperor Wan'yen swore, in rites led by bell-and-drum shamans, to accept and fulfill his duties to all the tribes of the grassland and the Lord of the Sky.

He did not live long enough to do this in any significant way. He died the next summer, still young, still vigorous.

He did not die in battle, which would have been honourable, or of old age as an elder of his people. A deadly spider bite had forced the sawing off of his right leg and the green poison followed, as it often does. In his last agony Emperor Wan'yen was heard to loudly shout his brother's name over and over, and to cry wild words to do with dancing and a fire.

His reign had lasted five months. It was followed by a violent struggle for succession.

The peace between the newest steppe empire and Kitai, however, would last more than two hundred years along the border of the Wai, with almost unbroken trade, diplomats exchanged, even gifts between ever-changing emperors on their birthdays, as the rivers flowed, and the years.

ൟ

Fear and fury define her, even amid the quiet of East Slope, and the autumn and winter nights are sleepless. She is tired and close to tears in the cold mornings.

It isn't a question of being only a woman. None of the men has been able to achieve anything. She is thinking of Ziji, of Wang Fuyin, of the Lu brothers. Chao has even been to Shantong, spoken with the prime minister.

Daiyan is in a prison assigned to him alone. Such an honour, she thinks bitterly. She feels helpless and enraged.

When her father was ordered to Lingzhou she'd pushed herself to actions deemed unfitting for a woman. She wrote to the court. She remembers how many times she revised that letter so the characters might be perfect.

And she saved her father's life. She also remembers waiting in the dark for the assassin they'd had warning might come. She can recall, relive, the anger driving her as she struck the man herself. *She* had been his target. Her body, her life. No judicial officer would strike those first blows for her.

If it was not proper conduct for a woman, she would live with that, although she is not happy remembering how satisfying the assassin's cries of pain had been. There are places in the self, Shan thinks, where it might sometimes be better not to look.

But now, each day dawns with him still imprisoned. How do you live a life when someone at the heart's core of your existence is where Daiyan is now?

Everyone is kind to her but she doesn't want kindness! She wants to be able to change what is happening, change the world, this part of it. Perhaps—after all—she is more like the long-dead poet than she'd realized. Perhaps, like Chan Du, she, too, wants to amend a broken world?

But only one small break, where a man lies at night behind bars in Shantong. She wants to break those bars. She wants him here.

Lu Chao, returning weeks ago, had had little comfort to offer. The magistrates being assigned were unhappy with their task, he said. Two had withdrawn. There was, if one valued justice at all, no way to find or fashion treason in anything Daiyan had done. He'd defeated an enemy and followed a fleeing army to destroy it.

How was that treasonous? What orders had he defied on the way north? There were no orders given! And when they came, when the terrible command to retreat had come, Ren Daiyan had retreated, and presented himself to his emperor.

Shan does the one thing she can think to do, even if it marks betraying a confidence. Sometimes you needed to do that.

Daiyan had shown her a poem on his last night at East Slope. He'd said—as he had said before—"I am not a poet. This is for you only, Shan."

She read it, twice. She'd said, "You keep saying that, and this makes a liar of you. I would like to show it to Lu Chen and—"

"No!" he'd said, clearly anguished by the very thought. "Not to him. Or anyone! I would feel humiliated. Who am I to write words that he is forced to read?"

She remembers tugging at his unbound hair, hard.

"My mother used to do that," he'd said. He'd told her that once before.

"You probably deserved it!" she replied.

"No," he murmured. "I think she only ever did it out of love."

She kissed him on the lips, and shortly after he'd fallen asleep in weariness.

Now she betrays him. Shows the poem to both Lu brothers. And then there is more. They send it to Fuyin in Jingxian. He knows a man who runs a printing press, one of the newest kind. His own books on the duties of magistrates have been printed there.

Copies of Daiyan's poem are made, secretly. Some are posted on walls in Jingxian at night. Some are sent elsewhere. They begin appearing in Shantong.

Soon there are many more than they have printed themselves, and the whole world seems to know that the words, the heroic, honourable words, were written by Commander Ren Daiyan, who lies a prisoner of the new emperor and his prime minister.

> *Let us restore Kitai's glory of old,*
> *Recover our rivers and mountains,*
> *Then offer loyal tribute to the glorious emperor.*

Such an obvious traitor, men say mockingly, over wine, over tea, walking in the streets.

Mockery can be, the poet says at East Slope, a weapon at a time like this. His brother, who has been in Shantong, cautions both of them: "They have negotiated their peace. If Daiyan's fate is entangled in that ..."

If it is, Shan understands, then poetry is no weapon. There are none to hand. No bows and arrows in the gazebo in the winter of the garden.

On the morning of the New Year's eve celebration she walks with the poet to the stream and across the bridge to the temple of the Path. The bell is ringing as they approach. She has heard it often from the house, when the wind is from the east, carrying the sound. Lu Chen has never brought her here before. Women are not usually welcome at temples. He is saying something, bringing her to the clerics here, his friends.

They are shy and gracious. She drinks a glass of wine with them, and they all salute the coming year and offer prayers for the dead and for the future of Kitai.

A year ago today, Shan thinks, she had been in Hanjin, knowing disaster was coming, preparing to escape, with Daiyan. She had gone to find her husband, outside the warehouse that held their collection.

He'd refused to come. She had urged him to do so. She had truly wanted him to come. They had bowed to each other, then she'd walked away in twilight amid the snow. She has her cup refilled with just a little more wine and she drinks to Wai's memory, to his name.

Returning to East Slope the poet refuses to let her take his arm in support, though she tries to mask the gesture as her own need. They pause on the bridge, looking down to see if there are fish. Sometimes the men of East Slope or the clerics fish from this bridge, he says. Sometimes they are fortunate.

Nothing to be seen today. It is a cold, dry afternoon, pale winter sunlight. The water runs clear. She imagines how cold it would be to touch, to taste. There is almost a thought for a song in this. She feels a kind of traitor for even having images come into her mind. She knows Lu Chen would upbraid her for that self-reproach. She knows he would be right.

Approaching the farm they pass through the gate and there, standing on the walk, looking at the main house between bare trees, with the pines set farther back, Shan sees two ghosts on the roof in the late-day light.

A man and a woman, very close to each other, though not touching. They are smoke and shadow, as if they could drift away if the wind grew stronger. They seem to be looking down at them, at her.

Shan makes a small, involuntary sound. The poet turns to her. He follows her gaze. He smiles.

"I don't see them this time. Are there two?"

She only nods, staring up at the roof.

"That is Mah," his father says. "And the girl from Lingzhou."

"I have never seen spirits," she whispers. "I am afraid."

"They mean us no harm," the poet says gently. "How could they mean us harm?"

"I know that," she says. Her hands are shaking. "But I am afraid."

This time he does take her arm as they walk into the house.

HOUSES DO HAVE GHOSTS, and they change—the houses do, over time, who lives in them, and the spirits also change. East Slope was no different in this regard, although the home of the Lu brothers remained a refuge for a long time for many different people, a place like a light shining softly in the night through trees.

In due course, Commander Zhao Ziji came to leave his position in the emperor's army. He withdrew from all public life and service. He made his way to East Slope and he was welcomed, and he lived there all the rest of his days.

Early on he took a wife. Her name was Shao Bian, from a town called Chunyu, farther west, on the other side of the Great River, across from the marshes he had known for so long.

She had strange red hair, Shao Bian—ancestors from beyond the borders and deserts, it was said. Ziji also brought to East Slope her aged father, once a teacher, but rendered infirm by a hard life as a watchman in the mines after a son became an outlaw. That son was dead, as far as anyone could discover.

For his wife's younger brother, whose name was Pan, Ziji arranged an education and then training as an officer in the cavalry of Kitai.

His wife was said to be extremely clever, as well as unusual in her beauty. She was taught calligraphy and other learned skills by the poet Lin Shan, in the time when she, too, still lived at East Slope.

In her turn, Zhao Ziji's wife, with his approval, had their own daughter taught those same skills. Their daughter married a *jinshi* graduate, bringing honour to their family. Their sons became soldiers, both of them, and then withdrew from military service, with high rank and honourably, after many years.

Zhao Ziji was buried when his time came in the graveyard on the high ground above the farm, within sight of the stream, and the river on clear days. He lay under a cypress tree near the brothers Lu Chen and Lu Chao, who were close by each other, as was judged only proper, for they had been together all their days, whenever it was allowed.

There also with all of them was the poet's son, Lu Mah, whose name had already become a byword for loyalty and a son's love.

Above the poet's grave his own words were written:

> *Bury me high up on the green hill*
> *And in night rain grieve for me alone.*
> *Let us be brothers in lives and lives to come*
> *Mending then the bonds that this world breaks.*

In the year of her husband's passing Zhao Ziji's wife and his sons were offered a gift from the second emperor of the Southern Twelfth Dynasty, and they accepted this. They were granted a good-sized estate not far away, in exchange for East Slope.

From that time on East Slope became a place of homage and pilgrimage, people coming from far away, bringing flowers and sorrow. The estate was maintained by Kitai, by succeeding courts, to honour the Lu brothers lying there, and the poet's beloved son, and it endured as such for years upon years while the rivers flowed.

After both brothers were gone, the two ghosts, a young man and a young woman, were no longer seen by anyone. Not up on the main house roof at twilight, nor in the meadow or the fruit tree orchards, nor above the farm in the cypress trees or the sweet-pear tree of the graveyard. It was said that they had gone to wherever it is they go, wherever we go, when we cross over and find rest.

☙

Daiyan still stood up on the bench sometimes to look out through the bars in the high, small window. He didn't know if this was foolish, and it didn't matter if it was, to him. He had done his share of foolish things. But he felt a need at times to see out and down, to the lake, the city. He couldn't quite see the sea from here, but some nights he could hear it.

Not tonight. It was New Year's eve, and Shantong was loud and joyous below the palace hill. That was proper, he thought. Life continued, a year closed, a year began, men and women needed to acknowledge they had lived through that turning.

He was recalling other New Year's eves, not only the one a year ago in Hanjin. You couldn't linger in just one time, one memory. He remembered fireworks at home, sub-prefects through the years supervising guardsmen setting them off in the *yamen* square. He remembered being small enough to be afraid of the brilliant colours bursting in the night, standing close to his mother, reassured only when he saw his father smiling at green and red and silver in the moonless sky.

He remembered his father's smile astonishingly well. Some things, Daiyan thought, endure as long as we do. The rivers flow endlessly east, their currents carry everyone, but in some way we are still in the distant west, and some of us are at home.

There were magnificent fireworks here, in patterns that could make a watcher feel like a child again. He saw a red peony bloom in the sky and he laughed at the artistry. He wondered at how a man standing where he was could laugh at anything. What did it mean or say, that he could be made happy, even briefly, by craftsmen playing with light and fire outside these bars?

The cracks of the fireworks were steady now and came from many places. There were some here on the palace grounds, others down by West Lake, from boats on the water. The night was loud and bright. People knew there was a peace now. Life not death, perhaps, in the year ahead? But what man could truly know that?

Given two more nights in autumn, with a new moon like tonight's, he would have taken Hanjin back.

The sounds outside were loud, but he had lived this long as an outlaw, then a soldier, in part because his hearing was very good, so he did hear the footfall in the corridor behind him. He was down off the bench and waiting when the door was unlocked and opened.

The prime minister of Kitai walked in alone.

Without speaking, Hang Hsien set down a tray with a brazier on the small table in the middle of the room. He had carried it himself. A flask of wine rested on the tray, being warmed. There were two dark-red cups.

The prime minister bowed to Daiyan, who did the same to him. The door, Daiyan saw, had been left ajar. He thought about that.

Sounds outside. The crack and snap, then lights bursting.

"I apologize," he said, "for the cold, my lord. I have no fire, I fear."

"I think they believe it might be unsafe," the prime minister said.

"Likely so," Daiyan agreed.

"The food has been acceptable?"

"Yes, thank you. Better than soldiers often eat. And they send clean clothing, and a barber, to shave me, as you see. He has not slit my throat, either."

"As I see."

"Will you sit, my lord?"

"Thank you, commander."

Hang Hsien took the stool. Daiyan shifted the bench so they were opposite each other at his table.

"I brought wine," the prime minister said.

"Thank you. Is it poisoned?"

"I will drink with you," Hang Hsien said, undisturbed.

Daiyan shrugged. He said, "Why are you here? Why am I here?"

The room was not well lit. One lamp only. It was difficult to read the other man's face. Hang Dejin's son would be skilled at hiding his thoughts. He would have learned how to do that.

The prime minister poured two cups before answering. He left them on the table. He said, very calmly, "You are here because the Altai demanded your death as part of the price of peace."

And so it was spoken, finally.

He had known, in a way, all along. It was different, though, knowing something in your thoughts, and then hearing it confirmed, made real, planted in the world like a tree.

"And the emperor accepted this?"

Hsien was no coward. He met Daiyan's gaze. He said, "He did. In exchange he demanded of the barbarians that his father and brother be kept in the north forever, whatever formal demands he might make for their release."

Daiyan closed his eyes. A loud crack came from behind him, outside, in the world.

"Why are you telling me these things?"

"Because you have been an honourable servant of Kitai," said Hang Hsien. "And because I know it."

Daiyan laughed, a little breathlessly.

"I am aware," added Hsien, "that this might sound strange, given where we are."

"It does," Daiyan agreed. "You aren't afraid to be alone with me?"

"That you will do me harm? Try to escape?" The prime minister shook his head. "If you had wanted to, you could have had your army here by now, threatening us with rebellion unless you were freed."

Your army. "How would I have sent a message?"

"Not difficult. I am quite certain you instructed them to stay where they were. They may not have wanted to, but your soldiers will follow your orders."

Daiyan looked at him by the light of the one lamp. "The emperor is fortunate," he said, "in his prime minister."

Hsien shrugged. "My hope is that Kitai is."

Daiyan was still staring across the table. "Was it difficult, being your father's son?"

An unexpected question, he saw.

"Trained to think in this way?"

Daiyan nodded.

"Perhaps. It is just the nature of the task. The way a soldier needs to be ready to go into battle, I suppose."

Daiyan nodded again. He said, softly, "What you've just said suggests you don't expect me to be able to tell anyone what I have heard."

A silence. The prime minister sipped from his wine cup. He said, in an easy voice, as if conversing of the weather or the price of winter rice, "My father had us both gradually rendered immune to the more common poisons, in doses that would kill another man."

Daiyan looked at him. He nodded. "I knew that."

Hsien's turn to stare. "You did? How ... ?"

"Wang Fuyin. He is even cleverer than you know. It would be wise to make use of him as much as you can. You should bring him here." He made no movement towards his wine. "You want me to make this easier for you?"

A longer silence. Then Hang Hsien said, "Commander, they broke into my father's room and his life ended there. They violated his body and left him for beasts. They didn't know people would come to bury him. It is not how he should have ended his days. So please understand that none of this will ever be easy for me."

After a moment he added, looking past Daiyan at the bars, "No soldiers are with me, the guards outside have been dismissed to join the celebration, and both doors are open—this one and the one to the outside."

And now Daiyan was startled. Men could do that to you (women, too) however much you thought you were prepared, however much you thought you knew the world.

"Why?" he asked.

Hang Hsien looked across the table at him. He was still a young man, Daiyan thought. His father had died blind and alone. Hsien said, "I had a thought when you stood here before the emperor."

Daiyan waited.

"I believe you decided that day that it might be necessary for you to die."

"Why would I do that?" He felt uneasy, exposed.

"Because you concluded, Ren Daiyan, that Kitai needed an example of a commander whose loyalty led him all the way to his death rather than resist the state."

And this, too, he had never thought to hear spoken aloud, by anyone. He hadn't even framed it in his mind (or heart) so clearly. It was very difficult, hearing it now, brought into the world with words.

"I would have to be a very arrogant man."

Hsien shook his head. "Perhaps. Or simply aware of why we fell, why we were so unprepared, so easily defeated. Tell me," he asked, "was it difficult to accept that order to come back?"

Oddly, it had now become difficult to draw breath. He felt as if his mind was too open to this man.

He said, "I told the emperor. We had a way in. We would have opened the gates from inside and flooded through. Hanjin is no place for horsemen. They were dead men in there."

"And you still came back. Knowing that?"

Another crack of sound from outside. His back was to the window but he saw the other man's glance go there, and the room was briefly brightened by a light behind him.

"I vowed loyalty to Kitai and the Dragon Throne. What kind of loyalty would it have been if I—"

"If you became another message for another four hundred years that army commanders could never be trusted not to covet power? And seize it with their soldiers."

After a moment Daiyan nodded. "Yes, partly that. And also ... duty? Just duty."

The prime minister looked at him.

Daiyan turned away. He said, "I am not an emperor. Of course I'm not. I had no desire to be. If I refused those commands it was rebellion." He looked at the other man, placed his scarred hands flat on the table.

"And so you returned, knowing your own life was—"

"No. Not that. I am not so much a hero. I did not know what you have just told me. No one knew those terms of the peace."

"I think you did," said Hang Hsien gravely. "I think that in some way you knew, and came back regardless. To make some kind of shining of a soldier's loyalty."

Daiyan shook his head. "Believe me," he said, "I have no wish to die."

"I do believe you. But I also believe you feel a ... heavy duty. Your own word. I said it already: you are an honourable servant of Kitai."

"So you bring me poison?" He ought to have laughed, or smiled at least, but he didn't seem able to.

"And I leave two doors open behind me."

"You might explain that, as a courtesy."

Hsien did smile. "You are even more formal than I am."

"My father taught me."

"So did mine."

They looked at each other. Hsien said, "If you were to leave here tonight and go somewhere, change your name, live unknown, hidden from men and the records of history, it would please me to know I did not cause your death, Ren Daiyan."

He blinked, astonished. His heart was beating faster.

"Unknown? How so?"

Hang Hsien's expression was intense. It could be seen even by the one flickering light. "Change your hair, grow a beard. Become a cleric of the Path, wear their robes. Grow tea in Szechen. I don't even want to know."

"I am dead for everyone I know?"

"For everyone. It would be as if you'd left our world. Our time. If you are faithful to me in this."

"And if I am somehow found? If some soldier recognizes my voice? Or an outlaw I once knew? If someone ever sees my back? If word spreads and men come rallying to me? If someone announces that Ren Daiyan is alive in the south while you are taxing heavily, claiming a new monopoly for the state, doing something people hate?"

Hsien's turn to briefly close his eyes. He said, "We are always doing something people hate. I am willing to accept that risk, I suppose."

"Why? It is foolish! Your father—"

"My father? He would have had you tortured into a confession by now. For these words of mine here he would have denounced me to the emperor and watched while I was executed."

"The emperor. You would tell the emperor ... what?"

"That you were killed here tonight and your body burned so it could never be buried and honoured."

"Burned as a traitor to Kitai?"

Hsien shook his head. "I have been running through magistrates. No man wants to make that finding, Ren Daiyan."

"There will always be someone who can be bought."

"Always. But you are too important. I'd need someone known to be honourable. This is the very beginning of a dynasty. These things are important."

"But if I disappear, in the eyes of the world you will have murdered an honourable commander of Kitai's armies?"

"A heroic one. Yes. I imagine the emperor will grieve in public, be angry, and lay blame—"

"On his prime minister?"

"More likely on treacherous guards here."

"Because he needs you?"

"Yes. He does."

"You'd have to find some treacherous guards to execute."

"Not difficult, commander. That is likely to happen the other way, too."

"If I die in this room?"

The prime minister nodded. "Someone always needs to be held responsible." After another moment he stood up, and so Daiyan did. Hsien looked down at the table, the wine cups. He said, "It is painless, I am told. And quicker if you drink two glasses."

He turned, not waiting for a reply. At the door he removed his furred and hooded outer garment and dropped it on the cot.

He hesitated, then turned back a last time. "This, also, is something I believe. It would have been blood and war and famine and fire if we fought them. For generations. This peace, this surrender of so much, is hard as death, but it is not children and old men dying. Our lives are not only ours."

He walked from the cell.

HE SEEMED TO BE ALONE. He wasn't certain how much time had passed. He was sitting on the bench, back to the window, elbows on the table. His hands had been covering his eyes. He felt dazed, dizzied, the sensation one had after a blow to the head. He'd had his share of those—from his brother at home, in the marsh years, in battle. He pushed his hair from his eyes and looked around. The door was still open, there were two cups of wine on his table and a flask on the brazier, which had burned out. There was a fur-lined garment on the bed.

The fireworks seemed to have stopped. *It must be very late*, he thought. He rubbed his eyes. He went to the window with the bench and stood on it and looked down. There were still sounds from the city below but West Lake was dark now under the stars.

He stepped down. He shivered. Then he realized he must be truly shaken, deeply disturbed—because there seemed to be a light in the room and it wasn't from his lamp. He thought of ghosts, the dead.

Fox-spirits were said to be able to carry their own light, cast a glow if they wanted to, lure night travellers that way. So could some ghosts, theirs were said to be silver-white like moonlight. There was no moon tonight. New Year's, new moon. He thought of the *daiji* at Ma-wai. Had he gone with her perhaps he'd have survived, after all, to return to another time, not this one, not these wine cups on the table.

There were, he suddenly remembered, tales that for some, when the tall doors opened for them, they could see the light of the other world, the one to which they were going, before they crossed.

Doors. The cell door was open, and the one down the corridor, Hang Hsien had said. There was a hooded garment here to hide him. He knew how to leave a city. Every outlaw worth anything at all knew how to do that.

He looked at the two wine cups. Quicker with both, Hsien had said. *Our lives are not only ours*, he had said.

Not a bad man. A good one, you had to think. He had known some good men. He thought about his friends, about wind in your face on a galloping horse, about waiting for dawn and battle, the beating of your heart then. The taste of good wine. Even bad wine sometimes. Bamboo woods, the sun through leaves, a bamboo sword. His mother's hand in his hair.

Could a man live if he left everything of himself behind? And if trying to do that, he was found after all? What happened then? Was everything undone? Made a lie? But couldn't a man trained as an outlaw hide himself in a land as large as Kitai still was, even with so much lost? He thought about Kitai. He had a swift, vast image of the empire in his mind, as if he were flying above it, like a god, among stars, seeing it far below, the rivers and mountains lost, and maybe found again one day.

He thought about Shan then, someone found, the astonishing, undeserved truth of her, and love. He could hear her voice, even here, now. Sometimes a sweetness in the world.

He thought of his father, finally. In the far, far west, at home. Where all the rivers started. He had not seen him for so long. Dreams could lead a man away from home. Honour and duty, pride and love, he thought about them. You tried to do the right thing with your days, he thought. He lifted the nearest cup.

☙❧

The body of Ren Daiyan was never found. This would have been to preclude the possibility of a shrine, veneration, something that might have undermined the court and its intentions in this matter.

But the absence of a body can also lead to legends, tales, for we have our needs and desires concerning heroes. And so there *were* shrines and altars, eventually, all over Kitai, with statues of the commander—some on horseback, some standing with a sword. Often, outside these temples there would also be a statue of a kneeling, shackled, head-bowed figure: Hang Hsien, the evil prime minister who had murdered the hero (sending poison or an assassin's blade) against the will and desire of the illustrious Emperor Zhizeng, founder and saviour of the Southern Twelfth Dynasty.

For generation upon generation, those visiting one of these shrines, coming to honour Commander Ren or seek his spirit's intervention in their own troubles, would spit upon the kneeling figure of Hang Hsien.

History is not always kind or just.

AT THE HEART of the legends about Ren Daiyan was the story that the commander had had an encounter with a *daiji*, and he had resisted her out of duty and devotion to the empire, and she had branded him with the words of his loyalty to Kitai.

It was accordingly believed afterwards by some that she might have spirited him away from his cell, from his death, and he could be living in another time, or even in *their* time. Others, skeptical, would point out that there was no story ever told of a fox-woman intervening to help a mortal man. That wasn't what they did. And to this, the reply would be made: Was there ever a mortal marked as Ren Daiyan had been?

It was known, also, that the much-loved poet Lin Shan had left the estate at East Slope where she lived, not long after Lu Chen and his brother died, going off in a cart with only one companion. This was not unusual in itself, she had been their guest, the brothers' presence had sustained her, and she had undoubtedly brought a brightness to both of their lives.

But it was also rumoured that she went away, when she did, to the far west, all the way to Szechen, where she had no family at all, and this was judged to be puzzling. Unless, the argument was made triumphantly, one remembered that she had been very closely linked to Ren Daiyan, and he *was* from the west.

The details of her life slipped from the knowledge of the world. That did happen for those living quietly, but still ... it made a person think, didn't it? Her poems and songs remained, were collected, widely printed, widely sung, were loved and they endured, a different kind of immortality.

Lin Shan, of course, is the one who wrote the song "River of Stars" that mothers sang to send their babies off to sleep, that children learned in school and men sang behind the water buffalo and the plough, that courtesans offered to a *pipa*'s music in rooms behind red lanterns, that women sang to themselves on balconies above fountains, or lovers to each other in the darkness of a garden, vowing that the sad fate in the song would never be theirs.

There were also tales about a son. We have our longings.

The village of Shengdu in the west, past the river gorges and the gibbons, also became a shrine, a place of journeying, for that is where Ren Daiyan, loyal to the last, had been born. There one could find his father's tended grave, and his mother's.

Rivers and mountains can be lost, regained, lost once more. Mostly, they endure.

We are not gods. We make mistakes. We do not live very long.

Sometimes someone grinds ink, mixes it with water, arranges paper, takes up a brush to record our time, our days, and we are given another life in those words.

ACKNOWLEDGEMENTS

River of Stars is a work shaped by themes, characters, and events associated with China's Northern Song Dynasty before and after the fall of Kaifeng. It is an increasingly well-chronicled period, although causes and elements are—predictably—a matter of dispute.

I have, as often in my fiction, compressed the timeline. Although several of the characters are inspired by real men and women, the personal interactions in the novel are inventions. I have written and spoken extensively as to why I find this melding of history and fantasy to be both ethically and creatively liberating.

Among other things, I am significantly more at home shaping thoughts and desires for Lin Shan and Ren Daiyan, or developing the characters of my two Lu brothers, than I would be imposing needs and reflections (and relationships) on their inspirations: Li Qingzhao, the best-known female poet in China's history, General Yue Fei, or the magnificent Su Shi and his gifted younger brother. Not to mention other figures at the court (including Emperor

Huizong himself) in the time leading up to and through the dynasty's fall.

There is a standard disclaimer to the effect that academics whose writings or personal communications have been of assistance to an author are not to be held responsible for what is done in a work of fiction. I have used this, but find it slightly disconcerting. Who would ever hold scholars accountable for what a novelist does in using their work?

Nonetheless, I do anchor myself in reading widely and by asking many questions. I am indebted to a number of people, and especially to those whose patience with private queries, and support for what I was doing has been considerable.

Anna M. Shields, author of *Crafting a Collection*, was generous, not only with her knowledge of both culture and history, but also in going back and forth on theories that emerged from my reading of others. I am grateful to acknowledge also assistance given by Ari Daniel Levine, whose expertise very much includes the period and events considered in *River of Stars,* and who sent me a number of monographs by other scholars.

In China, Bai Wenge shared a great deal of information. My old friend Andy Patton, deeply engaged with Song culture himself, was an ongoing source of support and challenging discussion.

As for the texts, I'll begin with poetry, which I come to through translation. Of course so much is lost. At the same time, the creativity and passion offered by many translators of the great Song poets is inspirational.

The poems in the novel are largely variations—sometimes cleaving near to an actual work, sometimes veering away. There is, as one example, a poem allegedly written by Yue Fei, the source for my Ren Daiyan. It is almost certainly a later creation, part of the legend-building process (which is a theme of the novel), but I have used it as the basis of the verse I give to Daiyan late in the book.

I have read the work of too many translators to cite them all without seeming overzealous, but I'll be indulged, I hope, if I mention my admiration for Stephen Owen and Burton Watson, two of the giants of the field. The intelligence and craft of their work aided me greatly.

Su Shi's life and writing (including his exile to the far south) have been usefully examined by Lin Yutang. The remarkable Li Qingzhao's work was brought over into English by Kenneth Rexroth and Ling Chung (using the poet's name-form Li Ch'ing Chao), and more recently, with a very personal approach, by Wei Djao.

For the history of the Song Dynasty the best concise overview, to my mind, is Dieter Kuhn's *The Age of Confucian Rule: The Song Transformation of China*. Beyond that lies the massive *Cambridge History of China,* volume 5, part 1. That volume was, for my purposes, anchored by Ari Daniel Levine's two chapters on events leading up to the fall of Kaifeng and the calamity itself. The dynasty's move to the south, in its early stages, is chronicled in a chapter by Tao Jing-Shen.

F. W. Mote's *Imperial China 900–1800* has an almost book-length section on the Song, and he's especially good on the steppe people and their own challenges and inner pressures. Morris Rossabi edited a volume entitled *China Among Equals*, which seeks to place the Song in a larger context, beyond merely dealing with "barbarians at the gate." The great French historian Jacques Gernet wrote a small, engaging book called *Daily Life in China on the Eve of the Mongol Invasion*. I permitted myself to extrapolate backwards in making use of some of his details.

I was aided by Stephen West's and James Hargett's articles on the imperial garden (Genyue), by Suzanne Cahill's on sex and the supernatural, and by Peter J. Golas on rural life in the Song.

I was much engaged by the work of Patricia Buckley Ebrey. Her *The Inner Quarters*, on the lives of women in the Song, is fascinating, including a hypothesis on the origins of foot-binding.

With Maggie Bickford, Ebrey edited a collection of essays on the reign of the emperor who loved his garden so much, whose calligraphy and painting were wonders of the age, and who ruled over a dynasty's fall: *Emperor Huizong and Late Northern Song China.* The contributors assembled are not far from being a who's who of major scholars in the field.

One of them, John W. Chaffee, has written on the change in access to power (through the examination system) in *The Thorny Gates of Learning in Sung China,* and also on the imperial clan and its ambiguous, expensive status in *Branches of Heaven.* Two distinguished figures wrote books I found illuminating and exciting: Ronald C. Egan's *Word, Image, and Deed in the Life of Su Shi* examines that astonishing writer and man; Egan's *The Problem of Beauty* is a look at the aesthetic thought and ideals of the dynasty. *"This Culture of Ours"* by Peter K. Bol is a major work on the intellectual and cultural transition from the Tang Dynasty (the inspiration for *Under Heaven*) through several hundred years to the Song ... and that shift is an underlying aspect of this novel.

Brian E. McKnight's *The Washing Away of Wrongs* (wonderful title!) is an annotated-and-introduced translation of a Song Dynasty magistrate's treatise on forensic medicine, and his *Village and Bureaucracy in Southern Sung China* (the spelling of the dynasty's name varies in English) was also helpful.

On the divisions, rivalries, and procedures of ritual masters, village mediums, and Daoist priests in dealing with malevolent spirits (and on the supernatural in general), Edward L. Davis's *Society and the Supernatural in Song China* offered details and reflections.

John E. Wills, Jr., has written a lovely book entitled *Mountain of Fame: Portraits in Chinese History,* with chapter-length profiles of Yue Fei and Su Shi—under yet another name variant, Su Dongpo. (I respectfully decline to take responsibility for differing name versions in English!) Those familiar with the wonderful fourteenth-century *Outlaws of the Marsh* (often called *Water Margin* in English, and there are other variants of the title) will recognize, with a smile, I hope, an ambush technique involving a ladle, wine, and poison.

There were many more books. I fear to write an essay here instead of acknowledgements. I will add that research and correspondence with those professionally engaged with the period I am researching has always been a pleasure, and this was particularly so for *River of Stars*.

I continue to be surrounded by talented people committed to the novels I write. My agents are friends: Linda McKnight, John Silbersack, Jonny Geller, Jerry Kalajian. So, too, are my long-time editors Nicole Winstanley and Susan Allison, and this author is aware of how lucky he is in all of these people. Catherine Marjoribanks was again indispensable as copy editor, and Martin Springett provided an equally indispensable map.

In an increasingly interconnected world, my online presence has been mediated by Deborah Meghnagi Bailey, who created www .brightweavings.com, and by Elizabeth Swainston, Alec Lynch, and Ilana Teitelbaum, who have sustained and extended it.

Finally, and as always, I am made more than I would otherwise be by some people at the heart of my life: Sybil Kay, Rex Kay (my first reader), and Laura, Sam, and Matthew, for whom, and from whom, all of this emerges.

Photo by Beth Gwinn

Guy Gavriel Kay is the international bestselling author of twelve novels. He has been awarded the International Goliardos Prize for his work in the literature of the fantastic, is a two-time winner of the Aurora Award, and won the World Fantasy Award for *Ysabel* in 2008. His works have been translated into more than twenty-five languages.